The Companions of
the Silence

The Companions of the Silence

by
Paul Féval

translated, annotated and introduced by
Brian Stableford

afterword by
Jean-Marc Lofficier

A Black Coat Press Book

ISBN 978-1-61227-706-6. First Printing. February 2018. Published by Black Coat Press, an imprint of Hollywood Comics.com, LLC, P.O. Box 17270, Encino, CA 91416. All rights reserved. Except for review purposes, no part of this book may be reproduced or transmitted in any form or by any means, electronic or mechanical, including photocopying, recording, or by any information storage and retrieval system, without permission in writing from the publisher. The stories and characters depicted in this novel are entirely fictional. Printed in the United States of America.

TABLE OF CONTENTS

Introduction

Les Compagnons du Silence by Paul Féval, here translated as *The Companions of the Silence*, was initially published as a serial in the weekly periodical *Le Journal Pour Tous* between 6 June and 19 September 1857 before being reprinted in book form by A. Cadot in nine volumes in the same year. Its serialization overlapped with that of the author's most famous historical novel, *Le Bossu*, which appeared in *Le Siècle* between 7 May and 15 August 1857, and also those of the exceedingly long *Madame Gil Blas*, which ran in *La Presse* from 22 July 1856 to 16 September 1857 before being reprinted in a 22-volume edition, and *Les Errants de nuit*, which ran in *Le Pays* from 26 June to 3 October 1857. For more than two months in the summer of 1857, therefore, Féval must have been writing all four serials simultaneously.

Although Féval's commercial success continued for a further twenty years, and his career limped on for another ten years thereafter until his death in 1887, he was at his peak in the decade begun with that summer of 1857 when he was working on four novels simultaneously, at least two of which can be reckoned among his best. Previously, his career had proceeded in fits and starts. Born in Rennes in 1816 he initially set out to follow in the footsteps of his father, who was a lawyer, and qualified as an advocate before deciding in 1838 to go to Paris and attempt to make a living as a writer. He published his first significant work of fiction in 1841, and published a number of short stories thereafter, mostly based on the history and folklore of his Breton homeland, but it was not until the boom in feuilleton fiction began in the mid-1840s that his endeavors really began to pay off.

Having published a couple of atypical serials, Féval was commissioned to produce a pastiche of Eugène Sue's enormously popular *Les Mystères de Paris* (1842-3; tr. as *The Mysteries of Paris*), *Les Mystères de Londres* (1843-4), to which the pseudonym Francis Trolopp was attached (Frances Trollope, the mother of the more famous Anthony, was then a very popular English novelist). Féval could not take the work entirely seriously but the tongue-in-cheek approach he adopted added a dash of humor that worked to the serial's advantage and became one of the hallmarks of Feval's work. Although Sue was necessarily a major influence on the work, Féval also recycled elements from his own *Le Loup Blanc* (1843), which is basically a transfiguration of the English legend of Robin Hood. That too was to prove crucial in shaping the future direction of his work, in which he recycled his materials—including that particular formula—time and time again.

Everything went well for Féval for the next four years, but just when he was getting into his stride, the economic disruption associated with the revolutions of 1848 made the marketplace much more difficult, and the recovery was slow. Féval fared better in the wake of the 1851 *coup d'état* that gave rise a year later to the Second Empire; although he had been an ardent affiliate of the Romantic Movement he was not, like Victor Hugo and Alexandre Dumas, a Republican—indeed, he was a ultra-Royalist, having given his allegiance to the Bourbons in 1830 rather than Louis Philippe—so he was in no danger of exile when Louis-Napoléon came to power, but for the next ten years he still had to live with the severe censorship introduced by the new regime.

Féval coped with that restriction better than many of his fellows, already being something of a specialist in the historical fiction that became a leading genre in the 1850s precisely because writing about the present day became such a ticklish business, and he immediately returned to prolific production once the marketplace could handle the requisite volume of material. Unfortunately, the effort began to affect his health, and in 1854 he suffered what would nowadays be called a "nervous breakdown." He was soon cured, after having been treated by a homeopathic physician, although the fact that he fell in love with and married the doctor's daughter probably had more to do with his recovery than the medicaments he was prescribed. At any rate, two years thereafter he was not only fighting fit again but filled with a new zest, which he poured into the four serials that ran simultaneously during the summer months of 1857. That verve shows very obviously in both *Le Bossu* and *Les Compagnons du Silence*—although it appears to have been *Madame Gil Bla*s that he hoped at the time would make his fortune and secure his reputation—and he probably never managed to find quite as much impetus again, even though his marriage continued to be happy and fulfilling, eventually producing eight children.

When he began it, Féval probably planned *Les Compagnons du Silence* as a potboiler, and he did not hesitate to recycle, yet again, the basic plot of the legend of Robin Hood, which he had not only used in *Le Loup blanc* (1843) but more recently and more substantially in *Bel Demonio* (book version as *Beau Démon*; 1850). *Les Compagnons du Silence* is very obviously a follow up to the latter novel, even recycling the central character's nickname among the several aliases employed by the hero. In much the same way that *Bel Demonio* had further complicated the plot of *Le Loup Blanc*, however, and turned up the melodramatic pitch considerably, Féval felt compelled, in recycling the plot again, to add a further degree of complication and at least to try to ramp up the melodrama to an intensity that he had not previously attained.

In the event, that process of melodramatic inflation did contrive to reach a new extreme; indeed, the peak of development that Féval attained in *Les Compagnons du Silence* was so splendidly theatrical that future exercises in a similar vein had no option but to take a step back and find new directions of development, with the result that the novel also forms an important bridge between the author's earlier tales of heroic banditry and the pioneering exercises in crime fiction that began with *Jean Diable* (1862; tr. as *John Devil*) and continued with the famous series featuring the criminal organization of *Les Habits Noirs* (7 volumes 1863-75; tr. as *The Blackcoats*).

Les Compagnons du Silence contains several references, albeit oblique ones, to some of the key works of fiction that inspires and pioneered the fugitive subgenre of Romantic bandit fiction. The footnotes to the relevant remarks give further details, but the most significant factor to note in that context is that *Les Compagnons du Silence*, although not the absolute final word of the genre, was certainly redolent with its death-knell, and illustrates some of the reasons for that fatal decline. Primarily, it showcases the moral difficulties associated with representing as a hero someone who is, in effect, a career criminal and a multiple murderer. Although evil circumstance has cast him in that role, Beldemonio, alias Il Porporato and various other names, even though he makes a habit of trying to right the evils wrought by the law that has proscribed him, leaves his author with an awkward diplomatic problem in trying to decide exactly how to reward him. The prevailing morality of the day, at least as it applied to popular serial fiction, put severe restrictions on the extent and nature of the triumph that he could be permitted to achieve.

There are, of course, ways around that sort of obstacle, and Féval was very good at finding them, but the boundaries were nevertheless in force; he seems to have been forced by editorial intervention on several occasions—very obviously in *Jean Diable*, for instance—to change direction sharply in his serials in order to flatter, or at least not to offend, the prudishness of the most censorious sector of the audience. *Les Compagnons du Silence* appears to have been planned from the start with the restrictions in mind, and thus retains a greater coherency than some of the author's other works, even though it still has the abrupt and clipped ending typical of feuilleton serials, which were necessarily designed to keep readers hooked by constant suspense built up and maintained in the mid-section of the story, and often became cursory when the long-anticipated climax actually arrived.

The principal adaptation used by authors employing morally equivocal heroes, logically enough, had always been to provide them with adversaries who are far more evil than they are. The melodrama of Il Porporato's story, in consequence, is supplied by the villain who is not only scheming to bring him down but everybody that he loves or might love, and it is in the remarkable characterization of the villain in question that Féval found a new, and arguably unsurpassable, extreme. That is the novel's true strength, and it is the astonishing complexity of the villain's evil machinations, coupled with the extremely difficult situation from which he is operating, the supply the novel with its exceedingly taut narrative tension and its unusually complex plot.

The great majority of Féval's novels were initially published as feuilletons in daily newspapers, but *Les Compagnons du Silence* obtained several advantages from being published in weekly parts, each of which was considerably longer that the 1400-1700 words typical of a newspaper feuilleton slot. That schedule gave him more time between episodes to think about and plan what was to come, and although the story is certainly not free from belated improvisations and hastily-contrived coincidences, especially in the immediate run-up to the hasty climax, the continuity and coherence of *Les Compagnons du Silence* is considerably better than the vast majority of feuilleton novels, and the intricacy with which the trap set for Il Porporato is contrived and executed is quite spectacular.

Féval did, of course, go on try to cap what he had done in the novel, and he experimented with various modifications of the thriller formula in order to do that, *Jean Diable* and the Habits Noirs series certainly brought his endeavors closer to the modern formulae that he helped to pioneer, and thus have a gloss of apparent sophistication when seen through the lens of hindsight, but that progress also involved a kind of weakening. The charismatic arch-villain of the Habits Noirs series, the Colonel, is a watered-down version of the arch-villain of *Les Compagnons du Silence*, just as the criminal organization of the Habits Noirs is shadow of the splendid secret society of the Silence. In the same way, the heroes of Féval's later melodramatic thrillers are often more sympathetic and more plausible than Il Porporato, but they certainly cannot compete with him for Romantic flamboyance.

Although Il Porporato's crew of sidekicks is more conventional, and may seem—again seen through the lens of hindsight—to be merely stereotypical, they too have a definite charm that was unusual in their day, Fiamma adding a usefully perverted complication to the hero's tortured love life. The manner in which that narrative package is employed makes the novel a significant precursor of modern superhero fiction, in which garishly costumed administrators of justice are frequently backed up by a supportive cast of eccentric experts, and routinely have to grapple with problems in their love life corollary to their double life.

If—as its reputation and long-term sales record clearly suggest—*Le Bossu* is a better novel than *Les Compagnons du Silence*, that success results from, the fact that it simply avoided the problems that Féval tackled so robustly in *Les Compagnons du Silence*. The central character of *Le Bossu* is allowed to keep his heroic credentials intact and uncompromised, thus entitling him to a conventional "happy ending," and is story is essentially linear, proceeding step by step, while the multi-stranded plot of *Les Compagnons du Silence*, which packs the bulk of its development into a period of twenty-four hours, is considerably more labyrinthine.

If the novel is flawed in those two respects, it is because the excess of the ambition made a complete success impossible, at least in 1857—but it was that same over-reaching ambition that took the novel into previously-untrodden narrative territory, and made it such an important stepping-stone, not merely for Féval but also for other writers of feuilleton fiction who, seen as a collective, made an enormous contribution to the development of modern popular fiction.

Les Compagnons du Silence is, however, by no means only of historical interest; it remains very readable, perhaps more so than some of the author's more celebrated works—although Féval rarely fell short on that score—and it certainly is not lacking in the essential quality of panache.

This translation was made from a copy of the 1998 Phébus edition of *Les Compagnons du Silence*, which seems to be incomplete, lacking one episode whose absence is footnoted. The translation posed several problems, particularly the issue of treating the names and titles of characters, almost all of which are rendered in the French form rather than the Italian in the original, although the Italian versions are sometimes employed. As the text specifically makes the point that Julian and Céleste always use the French forms of their names rather than the baptismal forms, it would obviously have been inappropriate to substitute the Italian ones, except when the text does so. The characters that Féval routinely calls Lorédan and Angélie probably did not call one another that—and Féval dutifully substitutes Loredano on some occasions when Italians are referring to the character in question in dialogue—but I thought it best to use the versions given in the original. Given that European aristocrats of the time, especially those living under a Bourbon king, were at least as likely to employ the French forms of their titles as any others, I have mostly followed the author's lead in that regard too—for instance, employing Comte rather than Conte and Comtesse rather than Contessa or Contessina, except in the few instances where the original text does so. With respect to place names, the author usually uses French forms rather than Italian ones, but does not do so invariably, and sometimes switches between the two, arbitrarily in some instances. In general, I have smoothed out the text in that regard by preferring the Italian forms, just as I have unified the spelling of names that are rendered differently at different points in the story.

Brian Stableford

THE COMPANIONS OF SILENCE

PROLOGUE: THE SEVEN IRON RINGS

I. The Martorello

There was once a terrestrial paradise. Pythagoras, the son of those fortunate lands, called them the garden of the world. It was Magnia Graecia, bathed by three seas: Daunia, where Horace was born; Lucania, where Hannibal dealt a terrible blow to Roman power at the Battle of Cannes; and also Apulia and Campania, where the same Hannibal went to sleep delightfully on his bed of roses and laurels. From Parthenope to Sybaris, from Sumo, the fatherland of Ovid, to Drepana, at the very tip of Sicily, favorable Ceres spared humans the labor of the fields. Flowers and fruits grew without cultivation. Nowadays, it is known as the Kingdom of Naples and the Two Sicilies. By searching hard, Hannibal would find the wherewithal to reconstitute the delights of Capua; but Ceres, dethroned, no longer protects the idleness of those peoples.

There has been something akin to a great chastisement. The luxurious bark that covered the earth of Calabria has been violently ripped; a wind of ruination has blown, leaving adorable oases here and there in the desolate countryside, as if to intensify the regret of the disinherited sons of the fortunate for the splendors of the lost Eden. Thus, when the scourge of war has passed over an illustrious city, a few columns remain standing, escaping the stupid club of the Cyclops, and those debris of bronze or marble suffice for thought to reconstruct the glorious past.

It is said that on one winter evening in the year 1783, the earth began to render profound and unusual sounds; a veil of blood covered the sky and the serene seas that bathed the gulfs of southern Italy experienced a long frisson. The earth trembled thirteen times between sunset and sunrise. In the black night, Etna and Vesuvius blazed like two sinister beacons confronting one another across space. The next day, the Tyrrhenian Sea, the Ionian Sea and the Adriatic were covered in debris. You might have thought that an immense whirlwind departing from the plateaux of Abruzzo had passed over Italy, uprooting cities and forests. Calabria, the region of Otranto, the Basilicata, and the principal cities were disrupted from top to bottom. Thinking that he had had a hideous dream, the city-dweller searched for his native city and no longer found it. The villager tried in vain to recognize the field that he had sown the day before. Centenarian forests were felled and flattened like frail stems of wheat over which a hurricane had passed. Strange vapors gushed from the disemboweled earth; rivers had changed their beds; entire towns had disappeared, of which nothing remains but the name.

Those idle peoples are easily cowed. After that, on both sides of the Apennines, there was a lugubrious discouragement. The laborer lay down on the edge of his ravaged field. Priests came to preach the crusade of toil. Momentarily, the Italians were seen to be gripped by a laborious fever—which is a miracle—but the plow had hardly traced new furrows, and quarried stone had scarcely marked out a few feet of the enclosure of a reconstituted house, when the mountain uttered its cry of distress for a second time. The level of the sea, unusually, suddenly rose by twenty-four feet and covered plains that had never felt the sea breeze.

There was a prince who governed the town of Scylla, opposite Charybdis on the Sicilian coast. He left his palace and boarded his ships with his entire court. But in the same way that the voyager, if ancient poetry can be believed, once could not flee through that redoubtable pass the death that came from the right and the left alike, as avoided Scylla sent its victims to Charybdis, the earth and the sea, two enemies, united that day against condemned humanity. The palace was destroyed, the fleet was smashed; the prince perished with fifteen hundred of his subjects.

And since that day, although the Mediterranean has returned to the profundities of its bed, the land of Italy, epileptic and dilapidated, has had periodic grand mal seizures. Three thousand shocks were felt in the four years that followed, which represents more than two quakes per twenty-four hours. Bottomless lakes formed in places where there had been towns. Not far from Oppido, a round hole can be seen that seems to have been produced by a prodigious cannonball launched from the sky. Around the rim of the gulf, the earth is split in a star-shape, like a window that a bullet has traversed.

The Apennine range is strong. It resisted for a long time, but in the end, the strata slipped in large areas and, suddenly stripping the flesh from the colossus, exposed the somber granite of its bones. After four years, that poor beautiful land, exhausted and vanquished, fell asleep; it will sleep for a long time. Half a century gone by has not enabled the gigantic scars of those wounds to disappear.

The southern part of the Bay of Sant'Eufemia, situated in second ulterior Calabria facing the Aeolian isles, forms a beautiful semi-circular beach, the curve of which, seen from the open sea, recalls exactly the idea of the antique amphitheater. There are a few fishermen's huts there, as gray as the rock that shelters them. In the morning, from the dark blue of the sea, one can see the lateen sails of half a dozen boats standing out. The long antenna sustains the triangular sail, and you might think from a distance that it was the elongated wing-span of some great sea bird. Sometimes, the steamer that provides the ferry service between Naples and Palermo goes past, leaving its long plume of smoke behind.

From the beach, where the golden sand is mixed with a brown dust that resembles pulverized lava, one perceives, when the sky is clear, a dark patch in the middle of the Tyrrhenian Sea. That is Stromboli, the southernmost of the Liparian islands, where the famous brigand Fra Diavolo hid, it is said, for nearly a year. From the southern coast the view is limited by Capo Vaticano. To the north, there are the heights of Pizzo, where Murat as executed in October 1815. The landscape is beautiful, but it speaks of solitude and sadness. One experiences there something of the sentiment that grips the heart while passing through ruins. And yet there are no ruins. The circular stretch of sand rounds out its immense curve.

Here and there, a young woman with a bold stride descends the path that rises to firm ground with a pitcher on her shoulder. The weary song of fishermen extending their nets on the beach arrives, and sometimes, in a calm, a felucca lowering its sails in order to ship its oars, sends the rhythmic song of the Sicilian oarsmen to the shore. In the evening, if the breeze is fresh, a slender tartan suddenly bounds forward on the curt waves and attacks the coast with crazy temerity. Night falls. In the distance, in the direction of Capo Vaticano, where the customs officers are, rifle-shots are heard. The tartan returns to Lipari. The contraband is ashore.

Toward the center of the curve, the Brentola, which has its source above Monteleone, opens on to the sands and goes to scatter its course in thousands of slender threads of water. It was on the Brentola that the *cavalieri ferrai*—the blacksmith cavaliers—of the Martorello once labored before the restoration of 1815.

There are no ruins visible along that shore, but there are memories. The Martorello is a rather wide valley that arrives obliquely at the beach through a narrow gorge, where the Brentola cuts through the little chain of rocks. From the shore one does not perceive the Martorello unless one is placed exactly in front of that gap.

A customs post built in blocks of stone stands on the cliff that is within it. The other corner is covered with vegetal earth. A few dwarf fig trees, myrtles and wild lemon trees form a small clump surmounted by the large trunks of two green oaks. That copse is known along the coast and forms a reference point for mariners.

A cart track, collapsed in many places, passes between the left bank of the Brentola and the crag on which the customs post is situated. It turns abruptly, like the river itself, and plunges into the valley in the midst of virgin terrains where, in the background, rice is sown, and, at the summit of the folds, odorous mustard. Five hundred paces from the defile, where several traces of a barrage can be found, the two piles of a wooden bridge whose apron has disappeared and a few items of debris are bogged down in a marsh of sorts.

The river has made this place its own, finishing off and dissimulating the ravages that the work of man has made. Swollen by the barrage, it has taken possession of the location where the most beautiful forge in Calabria, and perhaps in Italy, once stood. That marsh is exactly where the buildings were that were destroyed and razed to the grounds in the epoch of the disasters of 1815.

Nearly a hundred families were dispersed and transported, some to Sicily to the Val di Demo, the others to the principalities. The family dwellings, constructed in wood for the most part, were burned.

There are no ruins to testify to that destruction either, for the stone foundations of those humble dwellings were buried a long time ago in the brambles and the long grass. The new population, composed of mountain men from the northeastern slopes of the Apennines, knows almost nothing about the history of the former inhabitants of the region. The environs of the forge, invaded by the waters, have been deserted. What was called the village, a group of between fifteen and twenty huts, was situated much further to the south, beyond the road that leads from Monteleone to Messina. There was only a single building there in 1822, made of wood and marble debris, occupied by an old woman nearly a hundred years old.

It is said in the regions that spirits haunt the ruins hidden under the grass. Even though old Berta had lost all her children years ago, and lived alone in her poor cabin, songs had been heard coming from her door, when it stood ajar. And often, a light ran along the river in the middle of the night, while a hoarse voice called out a name that no one was able to make out. What is certain is that the waters, always coming nearer and nearer, had soaked that land, which was cracked, as if chapped, by volcanic shocks, over a wide area.

That new marsh, the fermentations of which operated at great depths, brooded malaria in spite of the proximity of the coast. The malaria, whose hearth was probably in the very ruins of the forge, extended into the distance and desolated the entire region. On Sunday, when the bells of the convent of the Corpo-Santo announced the morning mass, there was a procession of phantoms climbing the hill.

A Neapolitan mile from the marshes of Martorello, at the very back of the valley, which runs almost parallel to the shore, behind the shelter of the cliff, one finds the post road going from Monteleone to the little port of Tropea, and then to Nicotera and Palmi. Tropea is a steamboat station between Naples and Sicily. At the place where the road crosses the Brentola over a small stone bridge stands a square house, solidly built, which appears to be at least fifty years old. An inscription painted in legible characters above the main door announces to travelers that they are in the presence of the Osteria—which is to say, the inn—del Corpo-Santo. A few paces from the inn, the road, the valley and the river make an abrupt turn in order to take a direction perpendicular to the shore.

The river, the valley and he road turn in that fashion in order to skirt a rather steep rocky slope, as the summit of which stands the majestic convent of the Corpo-Santo, which has given its name to the humble osteria.

On 15 October 1822,[1] Battista Giubbetti, a coach-driver[2] of Monteleone, returning from the little port of Palmi, was carrying four passengers in his brand new carrozza, three in the interior and one in the cabriolet, serving as a seat. His vehicle was hitched to two good Abruzzo horses, freshly shod and well plumed with woolen tufts: a fine rig whose outfit had been arranged on departure from Monteleone by Battista's young wife. In young households everything is spick and span while the gaieties of the honeymoon are still felt.

Battista was a jovial fellow, slightly pale and very thin—typical of the region—but well-proportioned and wearing his effeminately curly hair proudly. He was pressing on, even more eager to arrive than the travelers. Inside, there was a man of about forty, of unhealthy appearance, and wearing a black silk bonnet on his bald head. He occupied the rear seat on his own, as per the express terms of his contract with Battista Giubbetti.

On the front bench, and adolescent and a young woman were sitting backwards. The adolescent was wearing the semi-clerical costume that enables the students of seminaries to be recognized in all countries. The girl was wearing a short gray dress and a French straw hat. That was not an opulent costume, but the young woman did not seem to care about that. In spite of the mischievousness of her gaze and the finesse of her charming smile, she seemed even more reserved than her companion. She was a young nun in embryo, as the other as a candidate for the priesthood. Both are abundant in the kingdom of Naples.

She was pretty, and also beautiful. We could almost say that she was more beautiful than pretty, but for the infantile and unexpected friendliness of the charming smile that continually pierced her decent and austere mask. That mask was a product of education; nature made her smile. And there was something truly original about the struggle engaged, on the terrain of that delightful face, between natural petulance and taught reserve.

The design of her face was both delicate and bold. Her forehead, intelligent to the highest degree, was crowned with black hair whose richness was dissimulated rather than shown off, lost beneath a little cotton bonnet with no ornamen-

---

[1] The text I am translating has 1823, but that is also the year cited for the next section of the text, set some months later, and 1822 is consonant with the significant fact of seven years having elapsed since Mario Monteleone's death in 1815.

[2] The term that I have translated as "coach-driver," *veturin*, has no precise English equivalent. Battista is not an ordinary cab-driver but someone more akin to a modern bus-driver, whose vehicle runs to an approximate schedule, making regular stops but also dropping passengers and picking them up anywhere along the route.

tation. Without that bonnet, the poor straw hat would have been almost elegant. Her gaze was thoughtful but became grave at will. A high collar gave to the dress the same impression that the jealous bonnet inflicted on the hat. And yet, without that severe accoutrement, it would have been easy to divine the fine suppleness of a figure already formed, which would have caused the shiniest pleats of satin to creak. That fact, which indicated simultaneously kindness, infantile grace, and a certain adventurous and bold spirit, brightened with a smile so affectionate when she looked at her brother that the most indifferent individuals would have sensed interest born within them, almost affection.

The seminarian with the long blond hair, awaiting a tonsure, had to be her brother. There was a resemblance between the two children that was unmistakable. The gravity of the young man was simply more sincere and more naïve. To judge by appearances, the brother was eighteen years old and the sister sixteen. Speaking in whispers, they sometimes employed Italian and sometimes French, and in either case their language was of an equal purity. Reciprocally, however, they only pronounced their names in French. The brother was named Julian, the sister Céleste.

The man with two places at the back also had a French name. When the coachman had boarded his passengers at the moment of departure he had initially called for Monsieur David. Monsieur David had maintained silence since the beginning of the journey. He had scarcely given the young couple sitting facing him a morose and distracted glance. Only, Céleste having pronounced the word "brigand," Monsieur David had shrugged his shoulders with an immense affectation of disdain.

People traveling in Calabria often pronounce the word "brigand." Skeptics do as the man in a black silk bonnet did: they shrug their shoulders. Monsieur David had particular reasons for shrugging his shoulders like that when people talked about brigands. He had a bilious and pensive face: the head of a Genevan, slightly narrow but trenchant and decisive. One could not say that he had an evil physiognomy; in our utilitarian century the word "evil" has arrived at no longer having any meaning; it is necessary to replace it by more precise expressions. There was, therefore, in Monsieur David's cold and sad gaze a profound fatigue that could easily be translated by the word *misanthropic*. There was bitterness and severity in the lines of his mouth. His brow was receding, but had height; the abrupt curve of his hooked nose was provocative. In sum, the general aspect of the face indicated reflection, reserve, austerity and egotism.

There remains one person for us to depict: the coachman's companion, the one sitting on the cabriolet alongside Battista Giubbetti. In the coach-driver's book he had given his name as the Chevalier d'Athol. He had arrived in Sicily by ferry and had only booked his seat as far at the convent del Corpo-Santo. He was a handsome fellow with an alert and sovereignly valiant manner. Meditation did not stifle him, at least in appearance. His gaze, clear and insouciant, was scanning the landscape, while his slender fingers, as pale and pretty as the fingers of a Comtesse, rolled a thin cigarette. He was very young; one would only have credited him with twenty-two or twenty-three years, but for the silky black moustache that shadowed his upper lip. Half-lying as he was in the cabriolet, one could not judge his height, but you would have divined that he was tall, and the very nonchalance of his pose implied a marvelous flexibility.

It seemed that everything would be easy for that handsome idle lion, except perhaps the stiff and knotty awkwardness of our fashionable gentlemen. It is necessary not swear to anything, though; awkwardness is within the range of all adroit individuals, and intelligent men have the fortunate faculty of being idiots when the occasion warrants it. Perhaps, if necessary, the Chevalier d'Athol could have weighed down the supple grace of his torso and posed as a springless mannequin on a English sidewalk, every bit as grotesque as a stuffed sportsman. His costume indicated a habitual traveler.

Although tourists are not exactly abundant in these parts, they do come every year. Fifty Englishmen take care to carry away in their pockets a few clods of earth from the gulf of Oppido.

Our traveler, whose mouth allowed to pass a musical and sonorous speech, could not be an Englishman; and yet Battista, the honest man, called him "Milord." Such is the result of the fever for travel that the cutlers of Birmingham have had for fifty years. Whoever strolls around in Greece or Italy passes for the indigenes as a manufacturer of razors, and immediately receives the title of Milord. Furthermore, the name of Athol is illustrious on the other side of the channel; it belonged to a former sovereign of the Isle of Man. It is inscribed, with a ducal title, in the peerage of the realm. It is a great name borne by great lords. Let us say right away, however, that our Chevalier d'Athol had no right of succession to the peerage. He had the bold sap of his youth and fate.

The road that climbs from Tropea to Monteleone goes down into the plain first and then doubles back, repelled by the base of Mont Mimo, in such a fashion that it goes along the coast briefly before arriving at Capo Vaticano.

"Look at that, Milord," said Battista, at the moment when a bend in the road unmasked the Tyrrhenian Sea. "What a view! In the background, you can easily perceive Sicily, the former Trinacria... or Sucania, capital Syracuse, in the time of the Romans...Presently Palermo; products: excellent wines, fruits, wheat, oil, silk, wool. Cotton, sugar, manna, honey, wax...pure and healthy air, fish-rich sea, celebrated for its volcano, which is named Etna, which rises to three thousand and some meters above sea level. There are mines of gold, silver, copper, lead and iron...quarries of porphyry, marble, jasper, agate and emeralds. It produces alum, vitriol and sulfur...but Your Excellency is coming from there," Battista interrupted himself, belatedly.

All coach-drivers are to some extent cicerones; they seize with a certain pleasure the opportunity to reel off their patter.

"To the left, with your permission, Milord," Battista went on, "are the Liparian islands, of which the principal..."

"What is there now in the Martorello?" the young voyager asked, abruptly.

Battista almost dropped the reins. He looked at the traveler covertly. "His Excellency has been to the area before?" he asked.

"I asked you, my friend," repeated the Chevalier d'Athol, "what there is now in the Martorello?"

"Well," the coachman replied, "in the Martorello, Milord…there's nothing, so far as I know."

"What has become of *the Six*?"

"*The Six*?" Battista repeated with an innocent expression. At the same time he administered a master stroke of the whip to his animals.

The Chevalier d'Athol began to whistle a tune by Fioravanti[3] very softly:

Amici, alliegre andiamo alla pena!

A pretty Neapolitan tune, Milord!" murmured the coachman, whose agitation was visible.

"What has become of *the Six*?" repeated the traveler.

"*Ohime!*" muttered Battista. "There's no shortage of people who known music."

"Give me your hand," ordered the Chevalier d'Athol, "if you know charcoal and iron."

Tremulously, Battista extended his hand.

"All right, all right," he said, feeling the double cross that the stranger traced in his palm. "I've heard mention of that from an agent of King Ferdinand, who was looking for it in the direction of Monteleone…"

The Chevalier d'Athol smiled and said: "You're a prudent fellow, my friend. Then letting go of Battista's hand and looking him in the face, he pronounced distinctly: "There is something stronger than iron."

"It is faith," replied the coachman, without hesitation.

"There is something blacker than charcoal," added the young traveler.

"It is the conscience of a traitor."

"You're a companion?"

"You're a master! By the grace of God! I have a wife and child on the way, but by Saint John my patron, precursor of Christ, if it's necessary to go, I'll go!"

"What has become of the Six?" asked Athol for the third time.

"Excellency," replied Battista, "if you're a master, how can you not know that?"

"Speak," said the young traveler, "in the name of charcoal and iron!"

"There were seven," murmured the coachman.

"I know where the tomb of the seventh is," pronounced the Chevalier d'Athol, in a melancholy fashion.

---

[3] Valentino Fioravanti (1764-1837) was a famous composer of comic operas, who was particularly popular in Naples. The line quoted translates approximately as "Friends, let's head for trouble gladly."

II. Mario Monteleone

Battista removed his hat respectfully, and made the sign of the cross. "The seventh was a saint," he said. Then he resumed, in a somber manner: "When Mario Monteleone, thrice a Comte, twice a Baron and master of the blacksmith knights, was murdered, the six gentlemen were proscribed...I'm repeating what I was told, Excellency. They came one night: it was the fifteenth of October 1815.[4] They had the doors of the convent del Corpo-Santo opened out there, above the Martorello, and declared a vendetta against the murderer of Mario Monteleone."

"The name of that murderer?" Athol asked.

As the coachman hesitated and went paler, Athol added: "Won't you dare to pronounce it?"

"It's four weeks ago today," Battista replied, lowering his voice, "that the Marquis de Francavilla died."

"How did he die?"

"From the thrust of a Calabrian dagger through the heart."

"And the Marquis de Francavilla was the governor of the Pizzo during the executions?"

"Yes, signor...and at the moment of his decease, steward of the second ulterior Calabria."

In the Estates of the King of Naples, the steward is the chief of the provincial administration. His powers are far more extensive than those of our prefects.

"Francavilla was guilty," said the Chevalier d'Athol, as if talking to himself, "but it wasn't him who killed the saint Monteleone. Have the Six not gone higher?"

"Higher?" repeated the coachman. "No... Giacomo Doria died in his bed...his two children have his heritage."

"Comte Giacomo was suspected, then?" asked Athol, sharply.

"I'm repeating hearsay," said Battista, for the second time. "It was the Dorias who got Monteleone's property. And Comte Giacomo was in the region when the misfortune happened."

The young traveler was pensive.

"And lower?" he said, suddenly.

"Lower?" repeated Battista, again.

"Has the vengeance of the Six been lower down?"

---

[4] The text I am translating has 1816, but that is contradicted by the account given later in the chapter, and it is unlikely that Battista would have made a mistake with regard to such an important date.

"Ah! You see, signor, I can only talk about what's said...there's the colonel."

"Trentacapelli?"

"Exactly. Trentacapelli was found, a long time ago, on the Cosenza road, with his face in a puddle...and the blade of a Calabrian knife sticking out of his back."

"It was the knife of a companion?"

"It was the knife of the Silence."

In the interior, the man in the silk bonnet had closed his eyes. He seemed to be asleep.

"It's quite true, little sister," said Julian, who was holding Céleste's hands in his. "I'm destined to be a minister of resignation and charity; I only ought to have pacific thoughts. Well, I sense myself gripped involuntarily and drawn by stories of warrior battles, and even the other battles that are fought in society, with a drawing room for a dueling ground and passion for a weapon. I'm sometimes afraid..."

"Nothing is forcing you to receive orders. Julian, my dear brother," the young woman replied.

"Nothing? What about my vocation?"

"If you regret society...," Céleste began.

He interrupted her with a movement of anger. "Oh, you're very fortunate! You don't regret anything!"

Céleste stifled a sigh. She replied, however, while her eyes hid their brightness behind half-closed lids: "I don't know anything, my brother."

"Nor do I," said Julian, naively.

"What can you regret, then?"

The seminarian took on an expression of self-importance. "How can I explain what's happening within me?" he exclaimed. "Can't you understand? I'm suffering!"

Céleste lifted up her brother's hands and pressed them to her lips. The carriage arrived at the summit of Capo Vaticano, and all of the vast landscape, calm and bleak, of the bay of Sant'Eufemia, unfurled before our travelers.

Now that Julian was no longer speaking, Céleste felt remorse for having interrupted him. Between people who love one another, superiority is almost always a slavery. One cannot ignore that superiority; it penetrates by way of love. Céleste pressed Julian's hand between her own.

"Look, brother," she said. "Here's the famous gulf about which you've been talking to me since the beginning of the journey. Recount me two or three chapters of *Victoires et Conquêtes*."[5]

This is a chapter of defeats and reverses, my sister," Julian replied. "His story is here in my head, much better engraved than if I'd read it somewhere. It's an eye-witness that reported it to me, the good Manuele."

"Our dear Manuele is in it?" exclaimed the young woman. "Oh, I beg you, Julian, tell me the story; it will be as if we were talking about our excellent father."

At that moment, Monsieur David's eyes opened imperceptibly. He darted a rapid and trenchant glance at the children who were facing him; then he let his eyelids drop again. Save for that entirely physical movement of the eyelids and the sudden brightness that shone momentarily in his pupils, the physiognomy had not changed at all.

"Do you think that Manuele is really our relative, Céleste?" asked Julian, suddenly.

"I'd be desolate if he weren't," the young woman replied, sharply.

She waited with a sort of anxiety, thinking that her brother was about to add something on that subject, but Julian broke off the conversation.

"Yes, yes," he resumed. "Manuele often told me about it. There's a Comte de Monteleone in it who resembles the heroes of Greece and ancient Rome. It's not because of King Murat that I have Manuele's story so present in my memory, it's because of Mario Monteleone."

"I'm listening," said Céleste, striking a attentive attitude and crossing her beautiful white hands over her knees.

Julian, however, seemed to be dreaming, and did not say anything.

"Well?" said the young woman, reproachfully.

"I was thinking," said Julian, darting a glance at Monsieur David to see whether he was still asleep, "about our present and our future, Céleste. Our past is brief and we know nothing about it except that we owe the light of day to a French family, exiled and proscribed. Revolutions are the same everywhere; they throw poor condemned orphans here and there into foreign lands. I was thinking about the orphan children of that Mario Monteleone."

"He had children?" Céleste interjected.

"Three children, all three of whom were stolen, by an inexplicable fatality, and whom he never saw again; three children for whom he wore mourning successively, and for whom he searched for a long time, a very long time, in France, in Germany, everywhere…and always in vain. Three children who were their poor mother's heart, especially the younger two, to such an extent that after

---

[5] The reference is to the 26-volume *Victoires, conquêtes, désastres, revers et guerres civiles des Français de 1792 à 1815*, attributed to "a Society of Military Men and Men of Letters," published in Paris between 1817 and 1825,

23

their abduction, Mario Monteleone was alone with a dead woman in a deserted house. His wife had lost her mind."

Céleste was listening. Her eyes were full of tears.

"Our mother died in Sicily," she murmured. "Manuele told me that."

Julian passed his hand over his brow, and his face, becoming paler, took on an expression of discouragement.

"I don't know...no, I don't know, Céleste, where this profound sadness comes from that, at times, makes me disgusted with life. It seems to me that a great misfortune is upon us and around us, a misfortune that began with us and will only end with us. I've made many efforts to divine it; I haven't been able to do it. But there's one precise and ineffaceable point in my memory. That's the day when we saw our good Manuele for the first time. We were in that farm in the vale of Mazzaro, where we were being brought up by charity. I saw him running toward us with his arms open...and we, timid and suspicious, fled at the sight of that stranger."

"He told us that we were his children that day," murmured Céleste.

"He told us that we were going to be rich and happy. We followed him into that cheerful house not far from Catania. Every day he wrote letters, and I remember that he said to me once: "If I weren't your father, Julian, would you love me just the same?"

"He said that to you?" said Céleste, curious.

"Yes...and he talked to me about my mother, who was coming from far away to search for me, doubtless from France. Suddenly, he went away. When he came back, he was much changed."

"I remember that!" Céleste exclaimed. "He was ill..."

"And in his bed, when we approached, he looked at us with eyes full of tears."

"I remember that," Céleste repeated.

"I was already grown," Julian went on. "It was the end of autumn, seven years ago.[6] As soon as he could get up again, he took us to Girgenti to buy mourning clothes."

"He told us that his brother was dead," Céleste put in. "I had a black dress..."

"Was it really his brother who was dead?" murmured Julian.

"Why would he have lied to us?" the young woman replied.

Their hands had come together again. They looked at one another. Julian was the first to look away.

"Céleste," he said, "I believe I shall die young." Then he added: "I pray to God that he takes you before me, Céleste, so that you won't be alone down here!"

---

[6] The text I am translating has six years, which is obviously wrong.

"You're good," murmured the young woman, whose eyes became moist. "All your heart is in those words."

"Manuele is sad," Julian went on, not even trying to struggle against the current of his melancholy. "He quit us with death in his heart. I don't know why, on receiving his last letter, in which he sent us ten ducats and asked us to meet him in this unknown place, the idea of his poverty seized me for the first time. We've never lacked anything, my sister, but where does Manuele get the money he gives us?"

Céleste raised her large eyes toward him. "I've asked myself that question very often," she pronounced, in a low voice.

"Before me!" said Julian, surprised. "You don't tell me everything you're thinking, then, Céleste?"

"Everything that can make you happy, Julian," the young woman replied, "I tell you."

At that moment, whether intentionally or involuntarily, Monsieur David stretched himself on his banquette and reopened his eyelids slightly.

"Listen, little sister," said Julian, immediately abandoning that subject of intimate conversation, "it's necessary for us to take things higher... Mario, of the princes of Benevento, Comte de Monteleone, Palazzi and Viserte, Baron of Civita-Gala and Vittole, was the cousin of King Ferdinand and the greatest lord in Calabria. Orphaned of his father and mother, he had been raised at the court with the heir of the Dorias and Francis, Royal Prince of Naples, Ferdinand's only son.[7]

"The King loved the three adolescents with an almost equal tenderness, and if he sometimes gave one of them a greater share of his caresses, it was Mario Monteleone. The King said: 'My son Francis de Bourbon and Giacomo Doria are gentlemen; the Monteleone boy is a prince.'

"The King's affection must have been very great, for he did not cease to love Mario Monteleone when, drawn by the ideas of liberty that gripped all gen-

---

[7] In fact, Ferdinand I of the Two Sicilies (also known as Ferdinand IV of Naples) had eight sons, Francesco or Francis being his second, although Francesco did succeeded him. The present story subsequently adds a second son, younger than Francis. Ferdinand was deposed twice during his long reign, first when the his kingdom was briefly replaced by the Parthenopean Republic in 1799, after Ferdinand—a Bourbon—had declared war on post-Revolutionary France, and then again by Napoléon in 1806, who first put his brother Joseph, and then his brother-in-law Joachim Murat, on the throne of Naples, although Ferdinand continued to reign in Sicily. Ferdinand was restored as King of Naples for a second time in May 1815; Murat, after fleeing to Corsica, attempted to regain control in October of that year by fomenting a rebellion in Calabria, but the plan came badly unstuck, and he was captured, imprisoned in the Castello di Pizzo, and swiftly executed.

erous hearts at the end of the last century, he sided with the reformers. Giacomo Doria followed him. Even Prince Francis, seduced by Monteleone's eloquence, lent a hand to the movement, it is said, and was ambitious for the title of liberator of Italy. But Mario Monteleone did not want foreign rule, and when the French general Championnet came to lay siege to Naples in 1799, he mingled, arms bare and with red belt around his body, with the battalions of fishermen and lazzaroni who defended Naples with so much heroism.

"King Ferdinand shook that hand still black with gunpowder. He embraced Mario for a long time and called him his son. Then he asked him: 'Nephew, what do you want?'

"'Sire,' replied Mario Monteleone, 'I want the liberty of Italy.'

"King Ferdinand I, the same one who governs us today and whose reign has already lasted fifty-four years, promised reforms. Mario Monteleone waited; then, tired of waiting, he said a final adieu to Ferdinand de Bourbon, quit the court for ever and retired to his estates.

"That was toward the beginning of this century. At first Monteleone lived in solitude. He only had one friend, Giacomo Doria, his former companion in arms and pleasures. When Giacomo Doria returned to Naples, Monteleone remained alone with a young relative raised by charity in his family and who took the place of a sister. Her name was Barbe de Monteleone. Mario loved her for her generous and submissive spirit, her select education and her piety. Perhaps Barbe loved Mario in another manner.

"I seem to be able to see that woman, of whom Manuele made me the portrait more than once. She had a beautiful face, but an accident she had had in childhood had deformed her figure. Her unequal shoulders and her shortened and twisted torso imprinted a seal of deformity on her entire person. In order to dissimulate it she wore loose garments in severe colors, similar to those of nuns. She was a few years younger than her relative and protector.

"When Mario married the beautiful Maria des Amalfi in 1801, Barbe gave the young bride a welcome full of grace and affection, but she was seen to grow thin and pale. She was gripped by a malady of languor. It was thought that she was going to die. The Comte de Monteleone's secretary, a German, had a savant physician from his homeland come. Barbe was saved, but her face always retained a mask of livid pallor.

"Maria des Amalfi, the Comte's new wife, was from a great family but had no fortune. The Comte had no need of one. What would a dowry have added to his immense domains? She had the beauty of an angel. Her heart was as angelic as her beauty. She brought the Comte her charming youth, her gentle soul full of amour, her cultivated mind and her noble heart, able to sympathize with all misfortunes.

"A short time after Barbe's cure. God wanted to bring the joy of the Monteleones to a peak. Maria gave him a son. What hopes there were around that dear crib! And what amour! Barbe, more carried away than the young mother herself, could not get enough of his caresses. She disputed the newborn with the nurse, always wanting him in her arms. It was a calm and pleasant spectacle that the great hall of the manor offered in the long winter evenings. The noble face of Monteleone seemed to reflect all the friendly smiles that expanded around the cradle in which his hopes were concentrated. But suddenly, a veil of mourning covered those family delights and tender hopes.

"One morning, the tearful nurse brought the empty crib. Barbe tore her hair out. Her dolor was even more poignant, in a way, than the grief of the father and the mother. After the first moment of amazement, they asked what hand could have delivered that terrible and cowardly blow. What was the response? The nurse had her mother in the vicinity, and old woman named Berta.[8] All Berta could say was that a troop of zingari had camped in the valley. That Berta belonged to Barbe. Like Barbe, she adored the child and the mother.

"Couriers departed in all directions. Barbe awaited their return at the highest window in the manor. As soon as she perceived them in the distance she ran to meet them. But no one had seen any Bohemians or children. The last hope died. A bleak sadness filled the manor, previously so joyful. That lasted for a year.

"But Monteleone had resources in his heart against the anticipation of death that is discouragement. He looked around, and saw that there were miseries to relieve, wounds to scar, and good to do. That day, he woke up. There was the Monteleone estate, a whole country, ruined by earthquakes, by the epidemics that always follow cataclysms and by the inveterate idleness of the inhabitants.

"Monteleone said to himself: 'That is my task. God will see my efforts and take pity on me.' He also said: 'I shall make men of these wretches. For the first time in a hundred years, a population of toilers will be seen in Calabria.'

"The great Comte Doria, his former brother in arms and pleasures, had once shared his ideas of liberty. Monteleone wanted to have him as an associate, and make him part of his generous designs. The Doria estates were confined within his and were in a similar state. But Doria no longer remembered the aspirations of his youth, and when Mario had confided his designs to him, he only laughed at them 'The Dorias have only ever made use of one tool,' he replied, 'and that is the sword.'

"'Cousin,' said Mario, 'we Monteleones are as well-reputed a family as you. If you don't want to help me, I'll act alone.' And he set to work.

"During his reign—for he was a king in that part of ulterior Calabria— olive trees were seen to grow and flourish, vines climbed as high as elms, golden maize undulated in the breeze on the once-desolate hills. The beech gave manna,

---

[8] The author subsequently changes his mind about the relationship between Berta and the nurse, making the young Mario's nurse her granddaughter, but I have left the text as given here and elsewhere because that change was obviously a late improvisation.

and sown rice threw an opulent mantle of verdure over the marshes. That was not enough. The nurse of the world has two teats: agriculture and industry. And as the stupid pride of the Calabrians opposed his design, he took a hammer in his hand one day and began to strike iron on the anvil. That caused a great noise. Throughout the Kingdom of Naples everyone was talking about Mario Monteleone, *il Benefattore*, as they called him. Young courtiers laughed whole-heartedly, thinking about his forge hammer, but the people blessed him.

"King Ferdinand heard mention of his forges, the principal one of which was at Martorello, a few miles from here, and the King said, laughing: 'Once in my life, I want to see my Calabrians working.'

"But what attracted him above all was his former ward, whom he called ingrate, and whom he accused of having abandoned him. He left Naples with the intention of bringing him back at any price. That was in 1805.

"Mario, Comte de Monteleone, received Ferdinand de Bourbon in a leather apron, with a hammer in his hand.

"When the King had seen his Calabrians working, he changed his opinion, embraced Monteleone, and said to him: 'Stay here. You have resuscitated a kingdom for me.' He gave him the Great Cross of the Order of Saint Ferdinand, and solemnly authorized the Association of Gentlemen Blacksmiths—the *Cavalieri ferrai*—of which Monteleone was the grandmaster. Six men of confidence that he had, mostly his friends and relatives, composed that organization of gentleman blacksmiths. It was abolished a few years later by the same King Ferdinand.[9]

"The forges of the Martorello were founded; a town had surged from the earth, a town that is now dead. For a few years, Tropea was a commercial port. English ships brought oil and took away iron. The wood came from the Sila, the great forest in the Apennines east of Cosenza, from which a thousand oaks, beeches and chestnuts could be taken every year until the end of the world without exhausting it. The revolution was complete, the peaceful revolution. The country was alive. Strangely enough, the race grew visibly taller. Physical beauty, expelled by poverty, returned to this Magna Graecia, which had been its fatherland so long ago.

"During the events of 1808, Mario Monteleone and his adherents resisted French influence as best they could. Mario even made a voyage to Sicily in order to offer Ferdinand de Bourbon, his master and his friend, the aid of his sword. The King said: 'I was expecting you.' Mario kissed his hand, with tears in his eyes. The gentleman reawakened in him.

---

[9] There is some confusion here; Féval seems to think that Ferdinand was not deposed for a second time in the Kingdom of Naples until 1808, the year when Murat became king, but he was actually deposed in 1806, Joseph Bonaparte being given the throne in the interim. On the other hand, Féval does realise that Ferdinand was in Sicily in 1808.

"It was during that voyage to Sicily that lightning struck the house of Monteleone for a second time. God had taken pity on his servant. Happiness had returned to the family. Time had not sufficed to scar the wound that was bleeding in the hearts of the Comte and the Comtesse, weeping for their first-born. But the union of those beautiful souls had been blessed twice more. Maria des Amalfi, still young and charming in the full bloom of her beauty, had brought two more children into the world, a son and a daughter.

"You're going to believe that you're in the middle of a romantic story, my poor Céleste," Julian interjected at this point, "But it's Manuele who told me this, who is not a poet! I'm not adding anything to his oft-repeated words.

"The good Mario Monteleone had the heart necessary to savor passionately the holy joys of the family. He was so happy, that man, that he wanted to concentrate his happiness, assemble all his delights into a bundle and build a temple to his felicity. In the middle of that valley, whose prosperity was his work, a marble pavilion was built. In the ground floor room, whose walls were refreshed by its position, which was a little below the ground, the nuptial bed and the two cribs were placed. The nuptial bed was between those two white couchettes, where two amours were asleep. It was there that he retired with Maria des Amalfi, more beautiful by virtue of her tenderness of a happy mother; it was there that he tasted, in this world, all the delights of paradise.

"Do I need to tell you that the first misfortune had altered the prudence of the father and the mother? Have I any need to tell you what scrupulous precautions surrounded those two cradles? The children grew older. If Monteleone passed for the Providence of the land, Maria des Amalfi was its angel. The amour of an entire people mounted good guard.

"When Monteleone came back from Sicily, no one came to meet him on the road where he was searching for the eyes of Maria, his wife, and his two cherubs. No one! When he crossed the threshold of his house, a bleak silence greeted his entrance. 'My wife!' he cried. 'My children! Where are my children and my wife?'

"No response. Finally, one of the six gentlemen blacksmiths, the German who had been his secretary, said to him: 'Master, gather all your courage. God has struck you. You no longer have children and your wife is dying.'

"Monteleone went into the marble room. He went to sit down at his wife's bedside. She did not recognize him. In her delirium, she talked about his children. She saw them and she kissed them, and those chimerical kisses put death into the heart of the unhappy father.

"This is what had happened. The valley of the Martorello is only separated from the shore by a narrow hill or cliff, at the summit of which lived the old woman named Berta, the mother of the maidservant who took care of the children. A few days before Mario Monteleone's return, the maidservant went to see her old mother, and took the two children in the little carriage in which she was accustomed to pull them. That evening, she came back crying and weeping.

Masked men had come into Berta's cottage; they had stolen the two children, and from the top of the hill the maidservant had seen the kidnappers rowing forcefully toward a Barbary felucca at anchor in the waters of Stromboli.

"Monteleone could not interrogate the maidservant; she had drowned herself in the waters of the Brentola. Barbe, struck as violently as the mother herself, could only moan and weep. Monteleone had the marble pavilion walled up, where the nuptial bed and the two cribs remained. It was like the tomb of his happiness.

"Maria des Amalfi could not render her soul to God. She recovered, but the clement God took pity on her and did not return her reason. Her madness was to believe herself dead.

"One evening, *the Six* met in Mario Monteleone's house, and the German said: 'Master, those who are devoted to you have reflected for you. Hazard does not strike in exactly the same place twice. It required, in order to carry out two such coups, the hand of a traitor. Who does harm, except the person who is interested in doing harm? Now that you no longer have children, Giacomo Doria becomes your legitimate heir...'"

"What!" cried Céleste, interrupting her brother's story. "Could it be?"

Julian resumed: "This is what Monteleone replied to that insinuation: 'Giacomo Doria is my cousin. Barbe, my relative, had already talked to me as you have done; I reprimanded her severely. May God preserve for Giacomo the two children that he has! I forbid anyone who loves me to attempt anything against the house of my cousin Doria!'"

"He was a saint," murmured Céleste.

"Yes," said Julian, "he was a saint...and God treated him as such, since he made him a martyr.

"Monteleone was proscribed by the new government and saw all his titles confiscated. However, King Joachim allowed the forges of the Martorello to subsist, which he placed under the surveillance of a steward or special prefect; there were neither exactions nor any violence. The Six, as the gentlemen blacksmiths were called in the absence of their master, who was the seventh, continued their work, but really organized a secret society. That society, which is said still to exist in spite of the proscriptions pronounced against it, took on considerable proportions and contributed greatly to the revolution of 1815.

"Strangely enough, Monteleone, exiled in Sicily, had the same fate as King Murat on the throne of Naples. Two attempts were made to assassinate him. It was during a sojourn that he made with his relative Barbe and one of the Six, his right arm, his man of confidence, the German I have already mentioned several times. Barbe and the German accused the Dorias. Monteleone did not believe it. He had found Giacomo Doria again in Sicily, Giacomo was the happy father of two children, a son and a daughter. The son was already of age.

"When the fall of Murat and the restoration of Ferdinand put an end to the exile, Monteleone, Doria and his son Lorédan crossed the strait in the same boat and sat side by side in the same carriage. At the beginning of October 1815, Mario Monteleone was returned in triumph to the midst of the population of Calabrians who were his family.

"It was thirteen days later that Joachim Murat, proscribed in his turn, attempted a disembarkation in the Kingdom of Naples. But fortune was no longer with him. He saw his hopes vanish in an instant. In a matter of hours he found himself without an army and followers, wandering in the land that had been his kingdom. In the last twilight of dusk, the King, who was alone with Franceschetti and a faithful Frenchman, tried to read a placard suspended from a pole, thinking that it would tell him the name of the place where he was. The placard was a notice signed by Marquis Francavilla, governor of Pizzo. It promised a reward of twenty-five thousand ducats to anyone who delivered the head of the brigand Joachim Murat, so-called King of Naples.

"That made him smile: 'That's very little,' he said

"However, he had no alternative but to reembark. Murat's two companions interrogated the horizon. As far as their eyes could see, there was no trace of any ship. The ship-owner, a Maltese named Olivier Barbara, had received his payment; fearing the consequences of the bold enterprise, he had set sail a few hours before. The King, the general and the Frenchman were then on the shore, at the foot of that cliff that you can see over there, little sister, on which stands the coastguard's watchtower. Behind the hill, a valley opens through which the little river Brentola runs. Our fugitives thought that they were much further to the north.

"After having wandered along the shore for some time, still looking for their ship, which they could not find, they arrived, exhausted by hunger and fatigue, on the road where we are. A large house stood a thousand paces from the shore, on the edge of the valley, which they now took in the reverse direction. The house was full of noise and light, there was a feast therein. They knocked, and the door was opened; they were granted hospitality.

"In the dining room there were a dozen men at table around the master, somber and sad in the midst of the celebration. A place remained empty next to the master. It was the Monteleone house, where his return was being celebrated. The empty place belonged to Maria des Amalfi, his mad wife. The guests were, firstly the Six, then a few gentlemen of the Bourbon party, including Giacomo Doria and his son Lorédan. Monteleone had ordered that his new guests be introduced.

"Franceschetti advanced as far as the door, He only needed one glance to recognize the noble and masculine head of the master. 'God help us!' he whispered, moving closer to Murat. 'We're in the power of Mario Monteleone!'

"The latter asked: 'Why are my guests not coming in?'

"Already there was whispering around the table. The noise of the fusillade that had taken place that afternoon had carried as far as the Martorello. Joachim appealed to Mario Monteleone by his name. 'Don't go!' people cried from all sides.

"The master had risen to his feet. Everyone did the same and wanted to follow him. 'Stay!' he said to them. And he responded alone to the appeal of the stranger. There were valets in the entrance hall.

"The stranger said to the master: 'I can only name myself to you.'

"The master sent the valets away. Murat and Monteleone had never seen one another before that day. Murat looked at Monteleone before speaking. 'What do you want with me?' Monteleone asked

"'Shelter,' replied the King. 'I'm exhausted by fatigue. And bread and wine; I'm hungry.'

"'Those are things that one does not refuse anyone, signor,' said the master.

"'I'm proscribed,' said Murat.

"'So was I, yesterday,' said Monteleone.

"'I have done you harm...perhaps unjustly.'

"'May God forgive you, signor. Myself, I shall do you good.'

"'Without asking my name?'

"'Without asking your name.'

"The blood rose again to the stranger's pallid cheeks, who threw back the cloak wrapped around his face, took a step forward and said: 'I will tell it to you, Mario Monteleone. I am Joachim Napoléon, King of Naples.'

"The master bowed profoundly, and remained bareheaded thereafter. 'Sire,' he said, 'I thank Your Majesty for honoring my house with your visit.' He picked up a torch and went out first through a lateral door. Murat followed him silently.

"They went up to the first floor of the house. 'Sire,' said Mario Monteleone, offering the King a seat. "May God wish that Italy never has a master harder than you. What you have done against me is a matter for your conscience. I am, it is true, a faithful servant of Ferdinand de Bourbon, but you are my guest. Under my roof, I swear to you, you will eat in peace and sleep tranquil.'

"He went out, and soon returned bringing food and wine. 'As regards myself,' he said, 'I trust my friends and my servants. With regard to Your Majesty, I only trust myself.'

"The King sat down at the table and ate avidly. Monteleone served him, with his head bare.

"After the meal, Monteleone guided the King by the hand to his own bedroom. He said to him: 'In order for your enemies to reach you, Your Majesty, they will have to pass over my dead body.' And he lay down on a mattress, fully dressed, across the King's door.

"But treason was watching. At three o'clock in the morning, the door of the house was broken down. Five hundred men-at-arms and more than a hundred infantrymen were there. The usual warnings were not issued. Five officers went to the King's room after having put guards on all the exits.

"At the first impact, Monteleone fell to his knees, pierced by three wounds. He did not let go of his sword, Franceschetti and the Frenchman, awakened with a start, discharged their pistols in the corridor at the moment when Murat appeared at the door of his bedroom. None of the five officers had the sad honor of putting their hands on the King of Naples. The soldiers found their five corpses lying around the unconscious Monteleone, but, swords in hand, Murat, Franceschetti and the Frenchman had succeeded in escaping through the widow. They were only captured on the sea shore after a desperate resistance.

"You know the rest, little sister, at least in regard to Murat. Murat was judged, condemned and executed within two days. Monteleone was similarly condemned for having taken up arms against his legitimate sovereign. But no one in the country believed in the execution of Monteleone, the father of the Calabrians, the benefactor and the saint, the man who had suffered for his fidelity to Ferdinand, the friend and relative of the Bourbons, the son of the princes of Benevento.

"Twenty thousand voices—an enormous number in this region—shouted all night outside the Castello di Pizzo to demand the liberty of Monteleone. The Marquis of Francavilla had it announced to the people that a courier had departed for Salerno, where Ferdinand was temporarily in residence, to implore the royal clemency. They waited, but while they waited, they were not idle. The gentleman blacksmiths were there. A violent action was organized in case Monteleone was marched to the scaffold. There were ten times as many conspirators around the Pizzo than there were soldiers in the garrison. Even if the town were blown up, it was necessary for Monteleone to be free.

"They waited for two days and two nights. On the morning of the third day a royal courier appeared at the far end of the road, galloping and waving a white flag. There was only one cry: 'Mercy! Mercy!'

"The King had, in fact, granted mercy.

"The companions of the iron, drunk with joy, raced to the castle. Every one of them was happier than if he had saved his wife or his child. They had prepared a stretcher ornamented with foliage and flowers in order to carry their father in triumph to the Martorello. But it was a cadaver that was deposited on the triumphal stretcher. Monteleone was dead in his cell. Some people said that the previous night, a man wearing a mask over his face had been introduced into the prison.

"Those who said that added that Monteleone had been strangled with the aid of a belt. But how can one believe the fables that come and go among the people? There had been a murder, that was the truth. The responsibility for the murder could only fall on the King's men.

"The reprisals were not immediate. That immense crowd, mute and stupefied, gathered around the stretcher and accompanied the dead man to the

Martorello. On the way, the populations of the region joined the procession. The funeral was held at the convent del Corpo-Santo, of the order of Saint Bruno, the old towers of which loom up there on the mountain. The entire country was there, and the entire country was able to notice the absence of Maria des Amalfi, Comtesse de Monteleone, the master's widow. Maria had disappeared.

"While climbing the mountain of the Corpo-Santo, the six knights of iron had placed themselves ahead of the stretcher. They were not seen during the funeral service. But in that immense church, ten times too small for the crowd that pressed all the way from the altar to the very rampart of the convent, there was a stir after the *Agnus Dei*. Six masked men had come to kneel at the holy table.

"The priest—a strange thing that impressed the audience profoundly—gave them communion without them uncovering their faces. When they got up from the holy table, they marched toward the stretcher where Monteleone's body was still in its open coffin. They extended their hands over the cadaver, as if they were pronouncing a silent oath within themselves. On the middle finger of each of their hands there was an iron ring. The six rings were similar.

"The body was lifted up. Those who were able to enter the crypt saw an open grave, and above it a gibbet with a block and tackle. The open coffin was attached to the ropes in order to be lowered into the earth; the six masked men did not move, but at the moment when the coffin swung over the gaping hole they extended their hands.

"The rope, which had begun to slide, stopped. And while the six hands with the iron rings remained extended in the attitude on the oath, a voice that emerged from no one knew where pronounced these words: 'We give seven years of our life to the vengeance of our master. The holy earth will not cover our master until his murderer has paid the debt of blood. That is promised under oath in the presence of the crucified Jesus.'

"The six masked heads inclined. The terrified crowd flowed away while the great organs of the church played the lugubrious song of the *Dies irae*.

"The next day, the palace of the Duc de l'Infantado and the house of Francavilla were the prey of flames. A week later, one would have searched in vain in the Martorello for any trace of the flourishing town that had risen up around the forges. The forges were destroyed because they had become the heritage of Giacomo Doria. Giacomo Doria and his son Lorédan were suspected of having organized the infernal plot. But Manuele did not accuse them. Manuele affirmed, on the contrary, that Giacomo Doria, and above all Ferdinand de Bourbon, made every effort to discover the traitor and avenge the murder. He added that if ever a Monteleone presented himself at the court, he would be the first in the kingdom. Manuel must know...

"Now, this is what is said: 'The companions of iron swore a vendetta and went into the mountains. The six knights, relatives or friends of Monteleone, had taken up the carbine; they were bandits.

"it is also said that every year, on the same day as today, the fifteenth of October, the bells of Corpo-Santo ring the funeral knell, and that the somber nave fills up with mysterious worshipers. It's the anniversary service of Mario Monteleone, who is not yet avenged..."

Julian fell silent. The carriage reached, with difficulty, the extreme summit of the coast, and went round a bend in order to descend to the bridge over the Brentola. Monsieur David coughed, stretched, yawned and finally quit his nonchalant posture. He looked at his watch.

"That's a strange story, my young lord," he said, suddenly fixing Julian with his eyes, which seemed more piercing beneath the shadow of his bushy eyebrows.

Astonishment caused Céleste to shiver.

"It's a story that the entire country knows," replied Julian.

"And this Manuele," said Monsieur David, "was in the Martorello when these extraordinary events took place?"

Julian did not respond immediately. His physiognomy, previously so mild, had an expression of umbrageous pride.

"Signor," he said, "that Manuele ought to be waiting for us on the road a few paces from here. The details that I was unable to furnish my young sister, you can request from him."

Monsieur David darted a rapid and anxious glance down the road. One might have thought, in fact, that he feared perceiving some frightful vision there. But the road was deserted. He pulled himself together and muttered: "After all, it's no concern of mine."

III. On the Highway

Henceforth, Julian and Céleste were mute. Monsieur David said, in a detached tone: "Every district in this fine region has its lugubrious story. One could make a ballad, in truth, with these knights of charcoal and iron! There are also the Companions of the Silence. All that has a fine ring to it, and gives little children gooseflesh. A little higher on the mountain, my young cavalier, I engage you to tell your charming sister about the actions and deeds of Il Porporato. You've heard mention of him, I'm sure?"

"Like everyone else," Julian replied, dryly, "I know that it's the name of a bandit."

"But what a bandit!" exclaimed Monsieur David, in a mocking tone. "Fra Diavolo resuscitated wouldn't reach his ankle! Oh, my young cavalier, this is a fine country, an excellent country for those who like old wives' tales. Our Calabrians supply the whole world with comic opera villains. But since the Calabrian bandit was invented, there has been none as illustrious as that splendid rogue Porporato. Our housewives are mad about him, and our Marquises dream about him."

He shrugged his shoulders again, that being, it appeared, his favorite gesture, and he plunged back into the corner of the carriage.

In the cabriolet, the newly-married Battista Giubbetti was responding as best he could to the questions of his mysterious companion, whose conduct inspired a certain fear in him. By chance, their conversation had also turned to brigandage.

"Then one readily encounters Il Porporato on these roads?" said Athol.

"There's no talk of anyone but him, Excellency," replied the coachman.

"And what do they say about Il Porporato?"

"They say that he's as terrible and strong as the thunder of heaven, as handsome as an angel and braver and more generous than a lion."

"Bah!" murmured the young traveler, smiling. "You Calabrians say that about all your bandits."

"Since the time of Rinaldini,[10] who was not the son of a man," said the coach-driver, with a convinced gravity, "there has not been a cavalier like Il Porporato in all Italy."   ·

---

[10] *Rinaldo Rinaldini, die Räuberhauptmann* (1797; tr. as *Rinaldo Rinaldini, the Robber Captain*) by the German novelist Christian August Vulpius, widely translated and enormously popular, became one of the archetypes in Britain of what Jane Austen dubbed in *Northanger Abbey* as "horrid novels": melodramas that had became enormously popular among female readers in the heyday of the

"And he sometimes comes to these parts?" asked Athol, negligently.

"I've never seen him, Signor," Battista replied, "but I can't say that he hasn't come. You know better than I do what they'd give in Naples to the man who brought his head."

"Exactly forty thousand ducats," replied the young traveler.

Battista winked. "That's written on the posters," he said, "but go to the police directory and say 'How much would you give me as a bonus if I brought the head of Il Porporato?'"

"Friend," the Chevalier interjected, "you're a well-informed fellow in business matters. Is he young, this Porporato?"

"Very young."

"I'd like to know where he hangs out, though, if only to avoid him."

"Signor, the entire kingdom of Naples is his domain. He raises contributions on the plateau of Abruzzo, and all the way to the Papal States, but his castle must be near here, since the song says..."

"Ah!" said Athol, laughing. "There's a song!"

"There are a hundred of them, but the one I mean has only been sung since last spring:

When the steward of Cosenza's daughter
Wants to see her friend from the mountains
She puts a white veil in her window,
And the sound of the horn says: "Where is Il Porporato?"

"Damn!" said the traveler, "but that resembles like two drops of water the stories of Zampa.[11] I'll wager that this Il Porporato plays the guitar!"

Every country has the eccentricity of its pride. The Calabrian defends his brigands with the same respect that the son of Marseille put into adoring his Canebière.

"Signor," replied the coach-driver in a piqued manner, "I don't know whether he plays the guitar, but I'd like to see someone laugh in his face at a hundred paces when he descends into the plain with his carbine. I'd wager a hundred carlins—and I'm not rich—that the joker would take off his hat."

English craze for Gothic fiction. It is one of the key templates of much generic fiction, including Féval's, although it took its own inspiration from previous dramatic works.

[11] Like the previously-mentioned Rinaldo Rinaldini, Zampa is a fictitious character, the hero of a French comic opera by Louis-Ferdinand Hérold, with a libretto by Joseph Duveyrier de Mélésville, *Zampa, ou La Fiancée de marbre*, first performed in 1831. Athol's reference is therefore technically anachronistic, although it would not have been had the opera been based on the career of a real bandit.

"There, there, Battista, my lad," said the traveler. "Don't get annoyed. Perhaps you're right. I'll only ask you one more thing. Is Il Porporato one of the Six?"

"If you're a master," replied the coachman, "how can you not know that?"

"I don't know it, but I am a master and I order you to reply." Athol had resumed his imperious gaze.

"Well, retorted Battista, "they believe so down there in the town. But when the forty thousand ducats was offered, a description was issued, and the description says that the brigand Il Porporato is twenty-two or twenty-three years of age. The youngest of our six lords is ten years older than that."

"Do they often come to the region, your lords?"

"Every year on the fifteenth of October."

At that moment the road formed a tangent to the semicircle formed by the coast.

"Stop!" said the Chevalier d'Athol, in English, with a very British inflection. "Friend, why are you no longer calling me Milord?"

"I'll call you whatever you like, Excellency, replied the coach-driver, pulling the bit, "but we aren't yet at the inn, and you won't find any house before the Brentola bridge." He interrupted himself and exclaimed, in a tone of sincere admiration: "San Gennaro! That's a fine leap for a gentleman!"

Athol had descended to the ground with a single bound, light and graceful. When Battista had handed him his small valise, around which a vast cloak was wrapped, the young Chevalier threw him a gold once, saluted him with his hand, and disappeared incontinently among the rocks.

"Ha! *Cervioli!* Ha!" cried the coach-driver joyfully, flicking his horses. "All roads lead to Rome. If the handsome cavalier wants to follow the beach all the way to Naples he has time. Ha! *Caprioli!* Ha!"

The Chevalier d'Athol had already been lost to sight, descending toward the shore from rock to rock. The horses trotted valiantly all the way to the bottom of the valley. They stopped of their own accord at the Brentola bridge. It was an obligatory halt. Julian and his sister got down. They went into the Osteria del Corpo-Santo, which was twenty paces from the road. In the ground-floor room there was a man of about fifty, with an honest and mild physiognomy, who was waiting for them.

"Manuele!" they cried, at the same time.

The man opened his arms and hugged them both against his heart. He had tears in his eyes.

"My beloved children," he said to them. "I haven't succeeded in my voyage. The powerful do not remember those who are dead. But one resource remains to us, and we'll know our fate tonight."

"Who will tell us?" asked Julian.

"If the deposit had been entrusted to a man I would have despaired of it," Manuele replied, "for I no longer believe in men..."

"Who has the deposit, then?"

"The earth."

Outside, Battista was preparing to give fodder to his horses. The head of the man in the silk bonnet emerged from the window.

"Hey, friend!"

"I'm all yours, Signor!" replied the coach-driver, pouring maize bran into a large wooden tray that the innkeeper of the Campo-Santo had brought him.

Monsieur David adopted a severe tone. "Come here when I speak to you!" he commanded.

"Oh!" said Battista. "Your Excellency is in a hurry!"

"My Excellency is traveling for the charcoal and the iron."

Battista immediately removed his cap. "It's the day...," he murmured, drawing closer.

"And the commerce is going well Milord?" he said. "Iron is strong and charcoal is black."

"There is something stronger than iron," pronounced David, extending his hand.

"It is faith," replied the coachman, who felt the traveler's fingers tracing a double cross on his palm.

"There is something blacker than charcoal."

"It is the conscience of a traitor. Your Excellency can command."

"Good. You can feed and water your horses when I get down. I'm in a hurry."

"And when will Your Excellency get down?"

"On the other side of the mountain. Get going!"

Without argument, Battista replaced his horses' fodder in the canvas sack that served as their larder.

"Hey, Pietro!" he shouted.

The innkeeper, a thin and jaundiced individual who seemed to have taken possession of all the malaria of the region, appeared on the threshold of his osteria.

"Take back your cup, Pietro," Battista said to him. "Next time I pass through we'll drink a glass of Sicilian wine. See you soon!"

"Bon voyage!" replied the fever victim.

The horses started climbing the slope at a rapid trot. A quarter of an hour later, at the most, the carriage went past the main gate of the convent del Corpo-Santo. It was an old and massive construction in the Italian style of the Middle Ages. There was a rampart, a few parts of which were falling into ruin. All the doors were closed, and the monastery, as big as a village, seemed abandoned. Battista made the sign of the cross, and then turned to ask: "Is this it?"

"Keep going," replied Monsieur David.

Half a mile further on, on the slope of the mountain, there was a bend that abruptly revealed a desolate horizon. There was no trace of any habitation.

"Stop!" shouted Monsieur David, though the window.

He got down, holding his cloak over his arm.

"Friend," he said, "remember carefully what I command you to do in the name of charcoal and iron. If the inspector questions you about the number of travelers you picked up in Palmi, you'll say: 'There were two men and a young woman.'"

"But…," Battista attempted to object.

Monsieur David put his middle fingerer under his nose, on which there was a ring of burnished steel.

"That's sufficient, Excellency," said Battista, in a tone of fearful submission.

Monsieur David turned his back.

Battista climbed back on to his sat. "Ha! *Colombi!* Ha!" he cried. Then, talking to himself: "It's the day…it's raining them! And, all things considered, a little lie to the inspector isn't a mortal sin."

Three or four hundred paces from the road a ravine commenced, which went in the opposite direction to the Martorello; the earthquakes had left such furrows in the terrain everywhere. Monsieur David whistled softly when he arrived near a hillock where cacti mingled their deformed serpentine stems. A similar whistle replied to him. One might have thought that he sound emerged from the tumulus. In fact, the stems of aloes and cacti moved aside, and the plume of a Calabrian hat appeared.

"Enter, Signor," said a coarse voice. "You're the first to arrive."

There was a large hole in the brushwood. The hillock was a smuggler's lair.

"How many carbines here?" asked Monsieur David.

"Eleven," was the reply, "and we're waiting for the Captain."

Monsieur David threw himself on to a chair.

"The Comte and his sister left Messina this morning," he said. They mounted their *calesso* at Scylla at about eight o'clock. Their escort is four armed valets and four men-at-arms. That's the information. The rest is up to the Captain."

Meanwhile, the carozza of the Monteleone coach-driver, lightened as it was of its entire burden, was traveling smoothly. Joyful thoughts came to our friend Battista. He thought about Giannina, his wife, who was watching for him while supervising the macaroni soup. Giannina was brunette and beautiful. Another two leagues, one hour, and he would see her, running toward him with her amorous smile.

"Ha! *Colombelli!* Ha! Ha!"

Suddenly, a man appeared at a bend in the road. He was a very tall man with a brown cloak thrown over his shoulder. He had a carbine slung over his shoulder slantwise and a feather in his hat. The road was completely deserted. Poor Battista was tempted to turn the bridle and start his "pigeons" galloping, but the man with the cloak put a little silver horn to his mouth that was suspended round his neck, and sounded an appeal that made our coachman shiver.

"And that's three!" he murmured "It's the day." He showed his animals to a walk.

While advancing, the man with the cloak intoned a fanfare whose motif was the song by Fioravanti: *Amici, alliegre andiamo alla pena.*

"All right all right," muttered the coachman. "Infernal song! How many times am I going to hear it today?" On seeing the man with the cloak stop in the middle of the road, she said "Does Your Lordship want to ride?"

"You're Battista of Monteleone," said the other. "You've married a beautiful girl, friend. How many travelers have you had in your carozza?"

"Three," replied the coachman.

"What sort?"

"Two men and a young woman."

"Aha!" exclaimed the stranger, laughing. "You've been made to promise not to say anything. The old fox doesn't like to leave a trail behind him. Is that it?"

"I don't understand, Your Excellency," Battista replied.

"No? What if I open the intelligence with this, comrade?" He brought his carbine forward.

"Oh, Milord!" cried Battista. "I'm only a poor devil...have pity on me!"

The stranger burst out laughing. He was a man of great height, at least five feet eight inches,[12] and built like Hercules.

"There!" he said. "Myself, I have no need to show my iron ring. But be at peace, comrade. I know where the pilgrim's coming from: straight from the hospital, and he'll go back there. Refrain from these pale faces—an honest man has blood under the skin."

He extended his hand toward Battista, who as still trembling.

"I don't make the cross in the palm, myself," he said, I don't talk about iron or faith, or charcoal or the conscience of traitors. I take the hand of a good fellow and I squeeze it—a little..."

Battista uttered a cry of pain, so violent was the pressure.

The giant uttered another loud laugh. "There's no danger," he continued, "of anyone disobeying me when they've felt that. Turn your bridle, my friend, you're wife will eat the soup without you."

"Why is that, Excellency?" asked the coachman, timidly.

"Because you're going to wait for me near here, at the bottom of the hill, like a good lad, and make a tidy sum for your money-box. I've come a long way

---

[12] I have translated this estimate of height as it appears in the version of the text I am translating, although it is an obvious error. We are told subsequently that the individual in question is six feet tall, but that is given as an approximate impression, not an exact figure.

and I'm tired. I don't resemble the old fox, me. If anyone asks you why you're there, you'll reply: 'For the Captain.' Everyone knows who that is. There's only one Il Porporato, and there's only one Captain. At midnight, my work will be done and you'll take me back to Monte Fama. God protect you!"

The giant threw his carbine over his back and plunged into the thickets bordering the road. Poor Battista remained in the same place, as if stunned. Then, his head bowed, with a resigned expression, he turned the head of his team toward the convent del Corpo-Santo.

"Let's go, my lambs," he said. "Patience! It's hard to wait until midnight, but it gives one pleasure to be a Calabrian when one sees such a fine bandit...believe me!"

IV. The Chevalier d'Athol

Meanwhile, the handsome young traveler who had come from Palmi in Battista's cabriolet had descended the stairway of rocks that led to the shore, and was marching rapidly, carrying his valise and his cloak under his arm.

There are people who are born for fighting, armed, in a sense, by nature, like those fine ships that the politics of States and private speculation have designed for racing over the seas. Nothing is neglected in the construction of those proud vessels, which only ought to carry men and gunpowder: no unnecessary surfaces outside; inside, no wasted space. The prizes follow in tow; the booty ought not to be carried aboard. The prizes follow with their vast holds, where aloes or sandalwood, pepper, cinnamon, cochineal, indigo and all the colors, perfumes and spices of India are piled up. They have to be large, those ship's lairs, which have to contain a great deal, but which cannot, alas, defend themselves. During the wars of the Empire, Surcouf,[13] with his brig carrying six canons and four carronades would take on entire fleets...

The young man, who was traversing the strand with a brisk and firm tread, head held high, had something about him that classed him in the family of the predestined men of prey. He was handsome, as adventurers are; his was an eagle's head, with eyes made for gazing at the sun. He had just taken off his broad-brimmed hat, and his curly chestnut hair with golden glints was floating around his bare neck: a white but muscular neck, a model of vigor and grace. A black velvet jacket was tightened around his slim waist and fell in numerous pleats over his black silk calzoni, which covered his boots of Siena leather, which came up to mid-calf. Our knock-kneed actors have dishonored that costume somewhat, which is remarkable elegant and swaggering when not worn by our actors. A black silk belt, knotted loosely around the jacket, supported two pairs of ebony-handled pistols. The wearing of apparent weapons was tolerated in the Two Sicilies until the reign of King Francis.

Where had he come from, that young man? Where was he going? Had he a precise goal, or was he one of those young gamblers who have decided to follow the current of destiny? He was dreaming, and smiling while he was dreaming. His lips, shaded by a thin brown moustache, were parted, showing the dazzling whiteness of his teeth, which seemed sculpted in alabaster. His gaze wandered over the spaces of the Tyrrhenian Sea. Did he see it as he gazed at it? Was he

---

[13] The privateer Robert Surcouf (1773-1827) was active in the Indian Ocean after 1789, and as successful enough to retire in 1801, after which he armed and advised other privateers on behalf of the Empire before equipping fishing vessels after the Restoration.

there to wait for one of the distant boats whose sails pricked the horizon like the wing of a gull? At what past was he smiling? Or at what future?

His forehead was proud and grandiose: a bold intelligence burst forth in the ensemble of his visage. I will tell you what was in it above all, though, and that was the supreme virtue of the man who is fatally bound to rise, just as lead plunges to the bottom in water; there was the sovereign quality of the elect of mortal life, the gift that makes someone lucky in love, in war, and everywhere: superb, serene insouciance!

It is almost an insult, that, in the language of our conversations: insouciance. But mistrust the things that our conversation disdains. Insouciance is a kind of faith; it makes adventurers bold and men strong. Look, for instance, at Il Porporato whose glory positively filled the Kingdom of Naples. People talked about him in the depths of the country as they did in cities, and it was not the poor village girls who listened most avidly to the strange stories of his exploits. A fine bandit, moreover, that one—a bandit as great as Robin Hood and as strong as Rob Roy! We French only know Mandrin and Cartouche, mere rogues. The thought has never occurred to our poets to put those bourgeois into a tragedy. But in Germany, Schiller has made *Die Räuber*[14] with the memory of Zaun, Schubry and Schinderhannes; in England Water Scott has found in Rob Roy a brow worthy of his immortal brush; and in Italy...that is the country of the modern Cacus![15] The Apennines produces bandits as the Lebanon produces cedars. And among the bandits of the Apennines, Il Porporato was like a cedar in the midst of the humble bushes that its shadow stifles.

No one knew his real name. They called him Porporato because of his purple blouse, the mere sight of which put carabiniers and policemen to flight. The man in purple, the bloody star of the Sila! The first time the red feather of his felt hat was seen and the sound of his carbine heard was at Lagonegro. The scaffold was set up. The priest was exhorting Giovanni Bertuzzio, a white-haired outlaw, to due. Suddenly, the sound of a trumpet fell from the bell-tower of the nearby church. The crowd opened up like the sea at the impact of a prow. The guards and soldiers fell or fled. Giovanni, who was already on the fatal platform, his hands bound, the rope around his neck, was seized bodily by a young man with a proud face whose graceful waist was tightened in a scarlet cloak.[16]

---

[14] *Die Räuber* (1781), known in English as *The Robbers* and in France as *Les Brigands*, was a classic melodrama of the German *strum und drang* [storm and stress] branch of what was later dubbed Romanticism. It was enormously influential in popularizing the theatrical figure of the heroic outlaw, forming the basis of three operas, including one by Verdi.

[15] Cacus was an anthropophagic giant of Roman mythology who terrorized Rome before being killed by Hercules.

[16] The French word *pourpre*, although it is the equivalent of the English "purple," actually signifies a dark red more akin to crimson than the *écarlate* [scar-

"Bravo, Porporato!" cried the enthusiastic crowd.

The name stuck. The purple cloak had its place among the flamboyant starts constellating the Italian mountains.

The next day, the deputy steward of Lagonegro put a price on Il Porporato's head. The day after, in the midst of a ball, Il Porporato came to bring his head to the official, in exchange for the promised reward. He had the reward, and took his head away. Along with his head and the reward he took away the deputy steward's diamonds, his cash and, if the chronicle can be believed, his young wife, whom he returned without ransom. The signora never complained about the adventure, and for a long time, she sighed while she gazed at the mountains.

Troops were sent against the young chief, whose renown, born yesterday, already filled all the principalities. Two pitched battles were fought in the foothills of the Apennines. It was not Il Porporato who was vanquished.

From that moment on, the balladeers took him under their protection. Guitars rang out at his name alone. From Abruzzo to the extremity of the Calabrias, all the *donne* revered his purple plume. Intoxicating descriptions were made of his beauty; he was a prime portrait by Raphael Sanzio, with his long hair framing an angelic face, and when the smoke of powder charged the breeze, he was the living lightning.

There was a castle in the mountains, God alone knew where—God and a few beautiful *signore*, who did not want to indicate the route. Prince Francis de Bourbon, heir to the throne of Naples, would have envied that radiant abode. It was in the depths of one of those cheerful valleys that sometime hide the rude summits of the Apennines. There was a beautiful lake in which lemon trees and flowering pomegranates were mirrored; a Greek palace in pink Sarraveza marble; serene colonnades, delightful gardens, arbors as obscure as those surrounding the Temple of Venus at Cythera. Inside, it was said, there were immense treasures.

According to public rumor, Il Porporato's band, composed of thirty elite men, was as invisible and undiscoverable as its chief himself. The other bandits of the Apennines had made efforts to join him, but he had disdained their alliance.

One strange thing that found a place in thousands of the legends running around that mysterious being is that the limits of the land were not the boundaries of his power. In the same way that kings have fleets to go in search of their enemies beyond the sea, Il Porporato had his navy. He was well known to the governor of Palermo, who had seen his city pillaged in broad daylight because

---

let] that the author employs as a synonym here, but I have translated it in this context as "purple" because the nickname Il Porporato would otherwise make no sense.

he had boasted at the court of Naples that he would bring Il Porporato bound hand and foot to the prison of the Castello-Vecchio.

That day, an elegant felucca which seemed to be playing with the wind, came to cruise under the harbor wall of Palermo. At the rear there was a rich tent under which the curious could see cavaliers and ladies seated around a served table. In the center was a young man wearing a purple cloak.

But why talk about bandits with regard to Athol? He had, it is true, asked for information about Il Porporato but that was such a common thing! No one talked about anything except Il Porporato. What could that handsome young man whose gaze was sometimes brilliant with hilarity and sometimes charged with reverie have in common with a bandit? We do not know. The truth is that the handsome Athol was manifestly one of those who do nothing by halves. He was an angel or he was a devil, and nothing in between.

The sun, three-quarters of the way through its career, was inclining toward the horizon behind the Aeolian Isles, which seemed to be swimming in a re-splendent conflagration. The evening breeze was beginning to rise, and, against the blue profundity of the sky, the delicate crescent of the moon was designed in the south-east.

Athol was dreaming and smiling. He said to himself, gazing at the dazzling brightness of the sky and the sea: *Since she is rich and since she is great, I shall be rich and I shall be great. I want that...if only for a day! A Prince, in order for her to be my Princess! And in that day, I shall live my entire life!*

He was in the middle of the narrow strand, two or three hundred paces from the fishermen's huts that were stuck to the cliff. He stopped, and his charming face took on an expression of arrogant challenge.

One day? he repeated. *Why not a century, if I wish it?*

He took from his bosom a small velvet wallet, and from the wallet a desiccated rose. His voice had changed when he murmured: "That name is necessary to that daughter of heaven: Angélie, Angélie!"

The flower trembled in the sea breeze. One of its leaves was detached, and started to fly away. Athol went pale. The sepal, borne away by the breeze, spun and went to fall in the sea, where it began to gloat, a tiny imponderable ship, on the caressant crest of a wave. Athol went into the water resolutely, fully dressed as he was. He did not want to lose that parcel of his dear treasure. The name *Angélie* fell from his lips. So superstitious is passion that it seemed to him that the event was symbolic.

If the leaf sinks, he said to himself, *the poor little leaf that the wind has stolen from me, adieu my hopes! My amour will never be fortunate.*

And he ran after the leaf, while the waves were already causing the fringes of his belt to float. It traveled, the leaf, driven by the waves, still virgin of any dampness inside, only touching the water at the extremity of its curve. Athol tried to seize it, but it played with him, the light and rosy conch, like the nacreous yawl where the nautilus displays its living flag. It fled, flirtatious and capricious...

The wind, again, took an atom of foam from the crest of a wave, and carried it into the tremulous conch, which trembled. Athol shivered: that knight who had laughed in the face of death so many times! He launched himself forward. The rose leaf took on water; it was now a boat too heavily laden. Athol seized it just as it was about to founder, and uttered a great cry of joy.

These lovers! Was everything not saved, in fact? He reunited the recovered sepal with the rest of the rose triumphantly and closed the little velvet wallet again. Then, looking at the sun, which took charge of warming him up and drying him out, he murmured: "Just in time. We only have two hours of daylight before us."

V. A Night in the Ruins

Athol put his hand in front of his eyes and gazed out to sea attentively.

The wind is contrary, he thought, *and we only have two hours...*

He headed at a rapid pace toward the hamlet formed by the fishermen's huts. His thoughts had changed direction. There was now a somber fire in his eyes.

Why this route rather than another? he wondered. *I don't know...but there's a secret in that. Something even stronger than my will is drawing me into this path. What, I don't know, I shall!*

The door of the first hut was wide open. He went in. The hut was empty. He reemerged in order to go into another, which was equally deserted. He called out. There was no response.

In the third hut, around which a small garden flourished, there was a spade and a pickax. He shouted again: no response again. As he was astonished by that silence, a thought occurred to him.

It's the fifteenth of October, he thought. *I know where they are.*

Having no hope of finding anyone to speak to, he took the spade and the pickax, for that was precisely what he had come to find, and he left a gold once and six ducats on the credenza in exchange.

Having done that, he resumed his route toward the north, still carrying his valise under his arm. He did not encounter a living soul between the hamlet and the coastguard watch-tower, which marked the entrance to the strand of the little river Brentola.

"That's our affair!" he murmured. "Poor saintly Monteleone! If I had had such a father...!"

Instead of going around the rock that formed the point of the natural causeway whose obstacle forced the Brentola to run obliquely as far as the strand, he scaled the rock and started looking round. To his right, the little river, enclosed, was flowing silently through gladioli; to his left, by contrast, it formed a broad fan, composed of a large quantity of little threads of water, which went to scatter in the sands.

A quarter of a league from here, he thought, *I'll find the barrage and the forges...doubtless ruins...but something, after all, if the devil is in it!*

Before quitting the little promontory, he went into the watch-tower and sat on a stone that the poor customs officer had doubtless placed in there in order to spend the hours of sentry duty more comfortably. From there one could overlook the sea and the islands.

"There are many mollusks," muttered Athol, "that would disdain such an existence. But I can hear from here the poor devil whose place I'm taking temporarily. He must say, in order to excuse himself: 'It's necessary to live!' A strange paradox. I prefer those austere monks who go about repeating to themselves: 'It's necessary to die.' To live!" he went on, getting to his feet abruptly. "To love! To shine...rapidly and a great deal! To die, of a thunderbolt, when the cup is drained..."

He went around the watch-tower and climbed on to the little flattened cupola that formed its roof. From there, he directed his attentive gaze again at the Tyrrhenian Sea, whose waters, turned crimson by the setting sun, were wrinkled by the breeze. A cloud descended over his brow, but suddenly, his gaze brightened. He had just perceived a light felucca coming about under the wind from Stromboli. It was exactly in the middle of the dazzling fan formed by the reflected rays of the sun. That was why Athol had not seen it immediately.

"Let's see whether they have good eyes!" he said, all his gaiety returning.

He attached his white handkerchief to the end of the handle of the spade and raised it above his head. The breeze seized the fabric and caused the pleats of the minuscule flag to flutter. A few minutes went by.

"Is Ruggieri searching with his telescope?" said Athol, laughing.

As he finished, a large black flag floated on the mast of the ship.

"Good, my lads, good!" Athol cried, joyfully. "If you hug the wind you'll arrive in time! He waved his handkerchief as if to respond to a signal, and leapt down from the watch-tower. A moment later he descended the hill and went up the course of the river. The path was greatly obstructed, even though it retained deep ruts, the signs of an ancient exploitation.

After ten minutes of walking, the soil of the valley ran out abruptly. The river had half a dozen successive cascades, some of two, others of three or four Neapolitan palms. At the height of the fifth waterfall, the marsh created by the old barrage began. The horizon broadened out at the same time, and large clumps of mulberry bushes, which certainly had not grown in a marsh, indicated the change that the soil had undergone. Athol looked at every object with interest. He was evidently trying to get his bearings, or rather, one might have thought that he was hunting, in a place that was unknown to him, for some mysterious marker.

"The worthy Battista wasn't lying," he murmured, finally, with a hint of disappointment in his voice. "There's nothing, absolutely nothing, in this accursed Martorello! Perhaps a former inhabitant of the valley might recognize it, but I'm wasting my time."

He stopped on top of a bank that overlooked the marsh, the other side of which was covered in serpentine aloes and flowering cacti. At the foot of the bank, a heap of white bricks was bathed in the mud, almost hidden in the midst of long grass. He took a dirty yellow piece of paper covered in tiny writing out of the reserved compartment of his wallet. On the other side there was a sort of crude ink drawing. It resembled a map. Athol examined it minutely.

"They were immense, those forges!" he thought aloud. "They were a true town. But how can they be found in this? There isn't an inch of wall remaining above the ground."

As he finished, his gaze was attracted by a gray mass lying among the rushes. He approached it. It was a stone cross, hollowed out at the intersection of the two branches, and carrying a little Madonna in that niche.

"The cross is on the map!" he exclaimed. "I have a point of departure; I ought to find it now."

He went back to the bank, which rose up, dusty and burned by the sun, in the middle of the sea of mud. He laid out his map there, and established the reference point. While he did so, he thought and said:

"My heart is beating rapidly. I'm more interested in this than is believable! From beginning to end, this adventure has had something strange and solemn about it! That's a fact; how can the fact be explained, given that I've passed without emotion through other adventures much more bizarre and much more gripping? How can I explain the efforts I've made, through such a tormented life, to find that obscure servant, that Manuele to whom the letter from the dead man was addressed? And how can I explain the puerile joy that I felt in depositing at his bedside, in the hostelry in Salerno, the letter that I had kept for seven years as an importunate deposit?

"He wasn't there. Didn't I wait for him for four hours? Haven't I regretted leaving without having seen him, as if it were a matter of my best friend? Why? What is he to me, that poor man, and what makes me do these things? I have nothing in common, nothing at all, with this Mario Monteleone. I never encountered him while he was alive; why has his phantom so often visited my nights? Why does his name make me shudder when it's pronounced? Why is his memory within me like that of a venerated master? Would he have recognized me as his disciple, a man who was pure, who was a saint?

"How is it that I, who have neglected so many important duties in my life, have had no repose or respite before having accomplished a command that rose up from the depths of a tomb? How is it that I, who have dissipated so many treasures, have kept this piece of paper, found by chance? How is it, finally, that I, forgetful and inconstant, have never lost or a single day the memory of the cell in mourning, where the last sigh of the just man remained? And here I am, after years, alone in this murdered town, running after I know not what, like a dreamer or a madman?"

He passed the back of his hand over his forehead, where there were drops of sweat.

"It's because," he replied to himself, "I'd try in vain to deny it, if I'm not acting against my will in this matter, I'm acting outside my will. A force that isn't myself, but which isn't hostile to me, since the idea of revolt has never occurred to me, is pushing me, and I'm going... it's destiny... it's God...and I'm sure that I'm facing something great here, and that something must be a treasure, or a secret!"

Initially, one talks like that internally, but then thought forces the pronounced words to emerge from the lips. Theatrical monologues are only a lie because they are commenced aloud. Athol had pronounced the last sentence ardently, and his emotion as at its peak.

People like him listen to their impressions. The unexpected, the impact of their life, throws them continually into scales unknown to sages. They hope more. Their existence, which is a work of fiction, incessantly expands the domain of reality.

It is certain that Athol was pursuing in that place one of those two things— a treasure or a secret—and perhaps both. A chill passed through his veins when he heard, in the midst of the reds and the long grass agitated by the evening breeze, a vague and prolonged sound that resembled a burst of laughter.

The sun was already hidden behind the mountain, and dusk was descending rapidly.

Is there someone there? he wondered, standing up straight.

There was no response. The wind alone seemed to be rustling in the long grass.

"When one is doing something childish," our adventurer murmured, "one becomes as fearful as a child. I'm looking for a needle in a haystack...it's entirely appropriate that I hear the gladioli laughing." He interrupted himself. "Let's see! The pleasure pavilion was in the center of the great wall, south-west of the forge. If I only knew where the forge was..."

"Here!" pronounced a voice, distinctly, emerging from a clump of mulberry trees to which Athol had his back turned at that moment.

He only needed one bound to reach the clump. The daylight had not yet declined sufficiently for it to be possible for anyone to hide in that place, which was more exposed than the rest of the marsh. However, Athol did not see anyone. On the other hand, he discovered to the right of the mulberries something that had escaped his attention until then: a vast parallelogram traced at ground level by the foundations of a thick wall. A very considerable edifice must have stood in that place.

"Goblin," he said aloud, "thank you very much! We'll end up finding it, if you can be a little obliging!"

The wind was freshening and crying in the branches of the mulberry trees. That was all. Nothing human was mingled with the sounds of the valley. Athol climbed the trunk of one of the trees, which was tilted at an angle because the damp had soaked its roots. He looked all around.

"The pleasure pavilion must have been there," he said, choosing with his gaze a small mound situate between the clump of trees and the bank on which he had left his map, his spade and his pickax.

"No," replied the voice of the invisible being who had spoken before, quite distinctly.

"Where, then?" asked our young adventurer.

As it had done once before, the voice pronounced: "Here!"

Athol's gaze followed the sound. He saw, with an indescribable amazement, a human form that seemed to be made of marble, so bright was its whiteness. It resembled a woman. The twilight was already no more than a vague glimmer. The woman was standing on the bank in the very spot where Athol had reposed a little while before.

"Stay! Don't run away!" he said, for it seemed that the dream was about to vanish.

At the same time, he moved toward the bank, no longer running, but at the timid pace, full of precaution, that children adopt in order not to frighten a brilliant butterfly, the object of their covetousness.

The vision did not budge. It was, in fact, a woman. By the last glimmer of twilight she could be seen, beautiful and tall, clad in a white dress and a sort of mantle of the same color. A white veil, which she was retaining with one hand, was floating around her pale head, covered with long black hair.

"Why would I run away, Signor?" she said, extending her arm toward Athol. "You were noble and good when I was alive...you loved me. Do I not remember that you had tears in your eyes on the day when we exchanged our hearts before the altar of the Virgin Mary in the church of the Corpo-Santo? You've remained young and handsome, Mario Monteleone...but except for you, everything here is like me...like me, who is dead."

A madwoman! thought our adventurer, who was in no mood to lull himself any longer with ideas of the other world.

And yet, the name of Mario Monteleone pronounced in that place produced an extraordinary impression on him. The madwoman, for she really was a poor insensate, went on slowly: "It doesn't astonish me that you don't recognize your wife, Comte...since you don't recognize your house."

The wind caught the white veil and caused its long pleats to float around her face. She folded her arms over her breast.

Athol was at the foot of the bank, contemplating her, said to himself: *How marvelously beautiful that woman must have been!* However, wanting at least to profit from her mania, he asked her: "The pleasure pavilion really was here?"

"Yes," she replied, with a sad smile. Then she added: "What can he remember, if he has forgotten that?"

"And beneath the pleasure pavilion," Athol asked, again, "there's a subterranean redoubt?"

"A fresh redoubt," murmured the madwoman. "On our wedding night, it was all embalmed with flowers..."

"By digging in the earth in the place where I am," said the young adventurer, "would I find that redoubt?"

The madwoman came down the bank. Her foot seemed to examine the soil.

"There!" she said, finally, marking a spot with the tip of her toe.

Athol seized his pickax and set to work incontinently. The moon, in its first quarter, showed itself among the branches of the trees.

The madwoman sat down on the bank.

"You were strong once," she said, "but the stones of the vault are so heavy. And for what have you come to search in that tomb?"

After a dozen blows, the pick sounded against marble.

"Isn't there an entrance?" Athol exclaimed, his forehead already bathed in sweat.

The madwoman smiled. "I never weep anymore," she murmured, "and for that it's been necessary for me to suffer a great deal...to suffer and to die...but I remember! How is it that you have lost your memory?"

Athol dropped his pickax and came to take her by the hand. She let him do it. Athol felt cold, as if in contact with a hand of stone.

"I beg you," he said, softly, "tell me where I need to dig in order to find the entrance..."

The madwoman looked at him with a fixed, dull stare. "What!" she said. "You don't remember? It is, however, you who had the door sealed on the day I died. You wanted the temple of our young amours to be sealed forever like a tomb. Oh, you loved me so much!"

Her head inclined over her breast and her long hair inundated her face.

"What are the motives of God?" she murmured. "The man who ought now to be an old man has silken curls around a face devoid of wrinkles..." Suddenly, she straightened up, and demanded: "Are you really Mario Monteleone?"

Before Athol could respond, a gunshot rang out, and echoed on the silence of the valley. Almost at the same time, a distant sound vibrated, sometimes swelling, sometimes dying, in accordance with the caprice of the wind, which was bringing it from the depths of the Martorello. It was the bells of the convent. They were ringing the knell.

At the gunshot, the madwoman shuddered violently. Then she started listening to the sound of the bells, while rubbing her eyes as if emerging from a dream. She looked at the young adventurer with a sort of terror.

"What is that?" he asked.

"It's vengeance," murmured the madwoman, "and it's prayer. Who is being avenged? A dead man. For whom are prayers being said? For a dead man..."

She was trembling in every limb, and she recoiled.

"The dead man who is being avenged," she pronounced, effortfully, "the dead man for whom prayers are being said...is you...is you!"

Athol saw her totter, and leapt forward to catch her.

"For you the murder," she murmured. "The knell for you. Now I remember! It's seven years since you were put in the earth!"

She put her head in her hands.

"Oh! Oh! Oh!" she said, in three heart-rending cries. I'm afraid of not being dead! What if I were only mad? My children! Who spoke to me about my children?"

Her arms fell back along her sides. The wind carried the sound of the bells with increasing clarity and strength.

"I'm coming! I'm coming!" the madwoman relied to that appeal. "They can't start without me. I'm the widow!"

Her white dress slid between Athol's hands. She vanished, like a vision. Athol, whose eyes were searching between the trunks of the mulberry trees, saw long veils floating in the wind against the rocks of the cliff. An instant later she had disappeared into the night.

Athol remain motionless. His pensive eyes lowered; then his head inclined. He was mute for several minutes.

"Her children!" he murmured finally. "There were children…yes…I knew that. The eldest is arriving at adulthood…the girl in still in the years of childhood. That woman is their mother…the one who lost her mind on the day when the marble of that door was cemented!"

His heel struck the stone, which rendered a dull sound.

His pickax was resting on the ground. He leaned on the handle, with no thought of further labor.

"Are they dead or alive?" he went on, after a long silence. "Were they killed? And why has that woman been left alive?" He made an effort, and laughed. "Ha ha! Am I here for myself or for others? Am I going to make myself, decidedly, a righter of wrongs and a Knight of the Round Table? Am I a guardian of orphans? Am I going to entangle myself in this diabolical story?"

He seized the pickax, angrily, but did not strike yet.

"And when will that be?" he murmured. "The first grave and good emotion that I felt in my heart, I owe to the testament of that saintly man, who is now a martyr at the feet of God. It was not addressed to me. I had it by the effort of my will, after seven days and seven nights of study to decipher that inscription in mysterious characters traced on the prison walls. It was transcribed there in my blood, for I had no ink in that dungeon, transcribed on the starched collar of my shirt. And I reread it often, because it tells me that there's a soul up there that is praying for me."

He took out of his portfolio a rectangle of starched linen, on which bizarre characters stood out in pale red. Those characters were disposed thus:

RA EL^2 A^{4}A3I3I^{2}A^{4}I ^{2} L^{3}NRNA^{3}OI^2 EI^2 E^{2}NA^{2}OI^{3}RI^2 NA^{3}I^{2}I^{2}M^{3}O
M^{2}NA^{5}M^2 RA OA^{4}NI^{3}M^{2}I^{3}I^{2}E^{2}I^2 DI^{3}I^{2}A^{4}A^{4}I^2
A INE^{2}DOI^{2}A^4 EI^2 RA DNA^{4}OI ^{2}

Below it, in ordinary letters, there was: *In the name of almighty God, divine yourself, or take these characters to one of the cavalieri ferrai. If you do that, whether you are a thief or a murderer, Monteleone will pray for you.*

"I did not address myself to the *cavalieri ferrai*," said Athol, with a victorious smile. "I searched; I had the time, I was a prisoner and in secret. I found the key to the mysterious grimoire, and I was able to read the words: *The last will of Monteleone is under the third stone counting from the door.*"

"Under the stone I found the letter addressed to Manuele with that piece of paper, on which the poor fellow had traced the map of the ruins, on the very night of his death. Lost child as I was then, I did not even have an idea of God, since the idea of God that suddenly surged forth within me astonished and revolted my pride. I remember that clearly. Who would have talked to me about God? Until that day I had been, sometimes with the zingari of the land of Bari, sometimes with the pirates of the Ionian Sea, and sometimes with the smugglers of the coast of France. But I knew the story of Monteleone, the benefactor of an entire people. The zingari had told it to me, and also the pirates, and also the smugglers. And it seemed to me that it was a sign of the will of Heaven that I had been the first to arrive in the dungeon of the Pizzo that had heard the last sigh of the just man.

"A just man indeed, for his supreme hour had been entirely devoted to submission toward the God who had struck him. He wrote that on the piece of paper deposited under the third stone:

I was too happy. God has truck me twice in my happiness. He stole my first-born when, rejuvenated by the love of an angel, I went to sleep in the bosom of an egotistical felicity. I awoke; I worked for those who surrounded me, but the wrath of heaven was not yet appeased. My children, my two beloved children, who were the heart of my dear wife, took away her reason. I saw those who loved me, my cousin Barbe and my other relatives, look at me in pity—me, whom they had perhaps envied. Thus did the friends of Job. Now that the compassion of God is calling me to him, because I no longer have anything to hope for in earth, is it the hour to murmur? In the eyes of the world, the punishment that is striking me is unjust, for I am dying faithful to Ferdinand de Bourbon, my lord and my king. In my eyes, it is the sword of clemency that is striking me.

I recommend my wife to my friends. She is no longer suffering. I hope to see her again soon in a better place. I shall find my children if they are dead: my elder son, who will now be a young man, and the two or little ones, the delight and martyrdom of their mother. If they are alive, may divine mercy provide them with a protector! I would like to bequeath them to Barbe, my pious relative, or to one of my friends; but God sometimes permits a stranger... I leave them in the care of the Savior and the Virgin Mary."

Athol had dropped the pickax. His eye was following the lines traced on the piece of paper. In the beautiful nights of southern Italy, one can read easily by moonlight. He read.

It seemed to him that those seven years had passed like a dream. Was it not yesterday that he had read the testament for the first time?

That was because Athol's life was, in fact, like a dream. Young as he was, he had already exhausted all sufferings and all intoxications. The days pass rapidly for those who existence is a whirlwind. Athol had lived a century in a few years, a century of perils recklessly braved, a century of mad orgies and amorous victories, a century of battles and soft sensuality. And that century appeared to him as a day.

They were rare, the hours in which he collected himself as he was doing now. Do not criticize his slowness, any more than one would criticize the Wandering Jew if he were able to deceive the eye of the angel and repose the fatigue of his eternal march momentarily by the side of the road. He was a rebel. The effort of his revolt had made him, until then, a blind man. He had driven straight ahead, like a wild boar piercing an impenetrable thicket. He had vanquished for the frivolous joy of vanquishing, without looking over an obstacle before breaking it. For him, the moment was solemn, not because he was now searching for his route, but because a superhuman finger had been able to show him to himself, in spite of himself.

It is necessary to relate things as they are, in spite of the danger of implausibility. Those natures are not like us; French romanticism is different. In that land of sulfur that melts in the sun, the soul has sudden impulses that we do not know, and languors that are incompatible with our courage. Italian beauty reveals that: a type simultaneously proud and effeminate.

Athol was in love; it was the twentieth time, and always wholeheartedly. He was counted among the fortunate elect whom passion cannot make blasé, and for whom every new cup retains the exquisite perfume of the first ambrosia. But the amour that he had now differed from his other amours. He gazed from beneath this time; he admired; he respected. That folly of a childish troubadour, that rose sepal lost and recovered, has shown him to us as he was. If we see him terrible and bloody one day, let us remember that rose-leaf.

Athol did not often travel in the humble carozza of a coachman with his valise and his cloak under his arm. It is necessary that the reader is not impatient, and thinks that he might see in the blink of an eye, from the outset, the thousand facets of his life. The child lost among the zingari of Bari, the smuggler of the French frontiers, the pirate of the Ionian Sea, the prisoner of the Pizzo, the adventurer who spoke the mystical language of the Companions of the Silence fluently, also frequented another society. It was neither in the mountains, nor on the sea, nor under the tent of the sons of Egypt that he had encountered that beautiful young woman, angel by name, by beauty and by heart, the noble and delightful creature the memory of whom made him kneel down. It was in Naples, and it was at the court. Athol went to the court, and you will see whether he was any prouder for it.

Since he had seen her, that Angélie, a profound change had taken place in him. A profound change, because the idea of abducting her had never even occurred to him. Now, we can certainly say that Athol had abducted women as beautiful and as noble as Angélie, and those women had adored him like a god. Jupiter, the most ancient of Don Juans, conducted himself thus, and all the Greek poets are in accord in recommending the advantages of that method. Athol had not thought of it. The thought of becoming great had been born in him: ambition, in the vulgar sense of the word. He wanted to raise himself up to the level of his idol.

A man is never a good judge of himself. Athol, in caressing that idea, scratched out his past at a stroke, as if life were a book from which certain pages can simply be ripped out.

Athol wanted to be great. The very fact of the labor that was operating within him had brought him back to that other shock, the already distant emotion that he had experienced, when very young, in confrontation with the mysterious legacy transmitted by the dead man: the testament of Mario Monteleone. He had suffered a kind of remorse.

And that was why he was wandering tonight in the ruins of the Martorello. For that, and for something else: for the dead man and for himself, for there was a vague hope within him of finding the first rung on the mystical ladder that would bring him closer to the heights where his dream was floating.

"Yes," he thought, his eyes fixed on the paper, on which he was divining rather than reading the characters, "he was punished...cruelly punished! And the punishment attained the happy mother who was still listening, the evening before, to the adored babble of two children. But if saints are struck like that, what punishment is reserved for those as culpable as me?"

I ask my first-born for pardon, Monteleone's handwriting continued. *For an instant, we have ceased to mourn him in contemplating two other cradles. I recognize that solemnly here, for my eldest son Mario, Comte de Monteleone. In the case that heaven has conserved his existence, I give him the guardianship of my widow, his mother, and my two dear children, his brother and his sister.*

The one to whom God will give the care of executing my last will can find in the place indicated below what is most dear to me in all the world: the fortune and the secret of Monteleone, the entire future of his race...

The plea followed to give a faithful servant by the name of Manuele, especially in the case that one could not fulfill personally the prescriptions of the testament, a sealed letter enclosed with the principal document. Then there were calm, precise, indications, which proved the liberty of intelligence the Mario Monteleone retained at that supreme moment.

Athol gazed at the paper for a long time after the reading was concluded.

"In order to escape from the cell where Monteleone died," he murmured, "I left fragments of my flesh on the bars...but I did not leave this. And yet, if the people up there can see us, the master must he saying to himself: 'Into what hands has my secret fallen? That man has been asleep for seven years!'"

He leaned his burning head against his hand.

"Seven years!" he repeated. "I was a child and I knew nothing. I've learned…I shall know now how to make use of the mysterious arms that accompany this missive…"

He straightened up and concluded, in a firm tone: "Don't mourn, Master, my route is yours! If I am late, I shall make up for lost time. I'm ambitious and I'm in love; I want to rise. If I rise thanks to you, your son and your daughter, if they are alive, will have a guardian, your wife a knight. I am taking possession of that part of your heritage which consists of protecting the widow and orphans. But this is a pact, Master; all trouble merits a salary, and I'm not a saint myself. I need a name; you will give it to me!"

He interrupted himself abruptly, and, with a gesture of impatience on listening to the bells, which seemed to be increasing the urgency of their appeal, he went on: "Oh, I hear you! I know that I ought to be there as well. Without me, the feast won't be complete! But we have time, and everything will have its hour!"

He turned the paper over in order to consult the plan, which was drawn on the reverse with a few strokes of a pen, and beneath which were a few more lines of delicate and closely-packed writing. The marble pleasure pavilion was marked distinctly. It was a hexagonal construction. The section of wall that faced eastwards was distinguished by a cross.

"The door is there!" Athol said to himself.

He got his bearings, and started digging in the damp soil a few feet from the place where he had been digging previously. After a few minutes, the superior cornice of the door was laid bare. But Athol understood the final words of the apparition then; an enormous slab of marble, sealed with pozzolana cement, blocked the opening.

"My pick can't do anything against that obstacle!" he said. "And I don't have time for a regulation siege."

He had shaken off his reverie as soon as it was a matter of setting to work, and now he was laboring ardently. With the aid of his spade he cleared the hole. The marble slab was revealed in full, the thickness of which had to be considerable.

Athol smiled, however, at the sound of the bells. He had the key to that insurmountable barrier. When he took up the pickax again it was to deliver little taps, always at the same point, in order to form a cylindrical hole by pulverizing the cement and the stone.

He wiped his brow more than once before finishing his task. At one moment he shivered, and placed his hand on his heart.

"Angélie!" he murmured. "My heart beat thus when it divines her…Angélie must be nearby…"

He blushed, and a skeptical desire came to his lips. The century has rubbed off even on the most romantic; they need at least to excuse their sentimentality with a little mockery.

"Fortunately," he said, "I'm smitten in this fashion once a month...it isn't dangerous." Angry with himself, he cried: "Upon my soul, if my valet Cucuzone spoke like that, I'd slap his head!"

That is the purpose of valets in comedies; to scold their masters' languor. When one does not have such rogues with one, one is not only obliged to serve oneself, but also to mock oneself.

Athol begged Angélie's pardon humbly for the impulse of mockery that had carried him away, and, making honorable amends, he swore on his salvation that he had never loved any woman as he adored her. As for the question of knowing whether he was breathing the same air as her at that moment, it did not appear likely. Angélie, one of the most beautiful and richest heiresses of the Neapolitan nobility, was doubtless on the balcony of her palace at present, gazing at the sparkling sea that bathes the shores of Capri, which the red lightning of Vesuvius sometimes illuminated with sudden gleams, or on the terrace of the other palace, the marvel of Palermo, the pride of Sicily, the white colonnade of which is mirrored in the sea opposite Capo Gallo.

Our adventurer was aiming high. Angélie, his idol, was the sister of Comte Lorédan Doria, the dear favorite of the King of Naples

But the bell of the convent of the Corpo-Santo was still ringing, and the point of the pick now disappeared entirely into the hole hollowed out by Athol. He picked up his manuscript one last time and read the lines that were under the plan

I adjure, in the name of God, the man who will render himself executor of my will, before entering the sanctuary where that which I hold most dear in all the world is buried, to swear an oath by Christ, if he is a Christian, on the head of his mother if he does not believe in the divinity of the Redemption, that he will only make use of the weapon hidden therein for the benefit of my children.

"Well, old Comte, rejoice!" said Athol, with a certain emotion in his voice. "Whatever the treasure might be, whatever the mystery you have buried so preciously, I am a Christian and I swear by Christ to employ it for the salvation of your race! Are you content?"

The hour of phantasmagorias had passed. The solitude had no voice with which to respond to that question. But it seemed that the sound of the distant bell, which was also the voice of the dead man, arrived more joyfully on the capricious wing of the nocturnal wind.

Athol opened his valise, took out his powder horn, and poured its entire contents into the hole that he had just hollowed out. Then he struck his briquette and lit a long strip of tinder, one end of which he plunged into the hole. The other extremity—the one he had ignited—hung down outside.

Athol lay down prone on the other side of the bank and waited. After two or three minutes, the ground trembled and a hail of stones stated falling around him. The echoes of the valley sent back the din of the explosion by turns; it might have been mistaken for an interminable roll of thunder.

Athol stood up. The stone slab had fallen. The moon's rays, penetrating through the large opening, illuminated a gracious nest of white marble, its walls clad with mosaics. There was a nuptial bed inside, and two cribs. Athol went in, with gratitude in his heart and his head bare.

VI. Brother and Sister

There were two other lost children, two children who had never known their mother or their father. But it was impossible to find debuts in life more different and making a more entire contrast.

For as long as Athol could remember, the tempest had raged around his boat. No repose: noise, movement and battle; orgy; the tent of the zingaris in the thicket, the caves that served as the smugglers' retreat, and the felucca dancing between two waves: such were his earliest memories; then the struggle, precocious amour, and then adventures...

For Julian and Céleste there had been none of that. In the distance of the past there was a humble and sad poverty, and then a ray of tranquil joy, and then an austere and almost claustral education. They had arrived in Sicily one winter evening. Céleste had not been old enough for her to remember that, but Julian retained a vague memory of it. The sky was black above the calm sea. A fine cold rain was falling. The earth seemed bleak, as if veiled. They had been told that at the end of the voyage they would find their mother, exiled like them.

They were in the charge of a man who forced them to call him their father. The man was often drunk; when he was drunk the man beat them and called them "Bastards!"

The man rented a wretched cabin in the vale of Mazzaro. Every month he went to collect a few écus from the nearby village. Céleste's earliest memory dated from the day that he beat her in order to make her till the soil.

In Calabria, and even in Sicily, it is the women who cultivate the fields. The stronger sex, in order not to lose its virile dignity, spends its time smoking and sleeping.

Julian and Céleste went to the fields. Between the two of them they earned a half-carlin of five grains per day, which is twenty-one centimes in French money.

Sometimes, the man who had them put a large brown loaf on the table and said: "Eke it out!" Then he went away, and sometimes remained absent for an entire week. The man's name was Thibaut. He was from Marseille. He had left a wife and five poor children back there.

During one of Thibaut's absences, Céleste and Julian, who were then eight and ten years old, saw a traveler coming along the road, exhausted by fatigue, his hair wet, and his shoes dusty. The traveler came to the cabin to staunch his thirst.

He was very pale when he came in, but when his gaze met Julian's, his face turned red. Céleste came in at that moment carrying water in a pitcher. The traveler took both of them by the hand and took them to the window. He looked at them for a long time, as nonplussed as they were. Then he started to question them, especially Julian, whom he devoured with his eyes. The stranger did not continue his journey any further. He said to Céleste and Julian: "Children, I am your father."

Thibaut came back drunk. When he was drunk, he had the custom of beating the children, saying to them: "I'd give both of you for a tari!" A tari is a small silver coin worth seventeen sous in our money.

The stranger had gone away when Thibaut returned. When the latter had gone to bed and beginning to snore on the straw, the stranger came back, holding two horses by the bridle.

"My children," he said, depositing a tari on the table, "come to your father, who has been searching for you for such a long time."

"Aren't you our father?" asked little Céleste, who loved him already.

"I'm your relative," the stranger replied, "but you have a father who is a lord."

"What is our name?" asked Julian, in his turn.

"My name is Manuele Giudicelli," replied the stranger.

"And our true father?"

Manuele hesitated momentarily, and then replied: "He has the same name as me."

"You're mistaken!" exclaimed Julian. "My father is a Frenchman...like our mother."

He had spoken too loudly, Thibaut stirred and turned over on his straw. Manuel seized Julian and put him on a horse. Then he put Céleste behind himself on the other, and they rode away at a gallop.

There was agitation in Sicily at the time. One only encountered soldiers on the roads. Everyone was talking about the imminent war. Ferdinand de Bourbon wanted to take back his Kingdom of Naples. It was the summer of 1815. Manuele traversed the entirety of Sicily with his two young companions and only stopped on the edge of the sea, two leagues from Catania. There was a convent near the village, and a good monk took charge of the initial education of the two children, who spoke an almost unintelligible patois, a mixture of Provençal and Italian.

At that time, Manuele said to them every day: "You will soon see your father."

Then, suddenly, there was the absence about which Julian and Céleste had talked in Battista's carozza; and when he came back, he bought them mourning dress. From that moment on, the character of the worthy Manuele underwent a transformation. He was sad, anxious and fearful. He kept the children in a sort of sequestration. He let them understand that they had powerful enemies who were searching for them. When they questioned him about their father thereafter, Manuele no longer replied.

"You know as much as me," he said to them one day. "You've come from France; you're French. But in your homeland, proscription weighs upon you. May God inspire you with the vocation to serve him!"

At other times he spoke vaguely about a great future, an opulent heritage.

As the children grew older they paid less attention to what the poor fellow said, whom they loved with all their hearts, but of whom the awareness faded in their eyes. They were two well-behaved and studious children, curious for knowledge; one could almost say that they were scholars by vocation.

The good monk who had begun their education was succeeded by the prior of the convent, Brother Geronimo, an erudite man of great ability, profoundly versed in theological studies, speaking several languages and not without certain lofty philosophical pretentions.

Geronimo had taken Julian in affection, which did not prevent him from declaring that Céleste had a greater disposition than him for dialectics. She was astonishing, little Céleste, taking on the grave Geronimo in moral or philosophical debates, while pursuing her needlework, without dropping a stitch or spoiling a point. Geronimo was annoyed when she beat him, but he adored her. He said willingly that Julian would make an estimable priest, but that Céleste, once she was a nun, would one day place herself, without a doubt, in the number of illustrious women. Her passion was to learn Greek.

Julian and Céleste were both quite determined from that time on to enter religion. Their sincere and gentle piety edified the entire village, and when Julian was received as a free pupil at the little seminary of Nola, Geronimo took him there personally, recommending him to the professors.

On the same day, Céleste entered the novitiate of the Ursulines of San Severino under Catania. Her brother had permission to go to see her there, and Brother Geronimo went with Julian. The visiting room of the good sisters was often witness to the forceful debates in which the girl embarrassed the worthy monk so well.

At that time Manuele was frequently absent for long periods. No one knew the secret of the preoccupations that absorbed him. He embraced the brother and the sister with tears in his eyes when he returned from his travels, and often said inconsequential things that seemed to reveal an increasingly apparent mental disturbance.

Sometimes, he praised the ecclesiastical estate and the repose of the cloister. At other times, when Geronimo repeated his usual refrain—"Julian will make a good priest; Céleste will be one of the luminaries of the convent"—a disdainful smile wandered over his lips. One might have thought then that he was dreaming of very different destinies for the two children.

He liked to take Julian to the sea shore. There, he told him long stories, exalting the grandeur of certain families and speaking about the duties of those who have power and wealth in their hands.

Julian thought that he understood that Manuele had left Italy in order to serve his father in the time of the wars of the French Empire, but that he had been born in the domain of Monteleone in Calabria, and that he had retained of the last scion of that illustrious family a memory that resembled a cult.

To Céleste, Manuele told the story of those chatelaines who are the providence of a region, and on that occasion the name of Monteleone often recurred. He had known the Comtesse de Monteleone, Maria des Amalfi, whom the people of Calabria called the good angel. But as soon as Julian and Céleste said: "Tell us about our father, friend, tell us about our mother," he lowered his head and fell silent.

When Julian reached his eighteenth year, he was a grave and gentle young man, very learned in all things that an old monk can teach, still possessed of the calm of the senses, regarding his future as a priest without joy, but without repugnance. The only scruple that he might have had on the subject of his vocation was the attraction that he felt towards tales of war. He willingly said: "I'd like to be like those knights of Jerusalem or the Temple, who accomplished the holy sacrifice of the mass with sword in hand."

That was all. No worldly or amorous idea came to trouble his profound quietude. In that regard, his sister resembled him. She was then sixteen years old. She was still a child, but for how long?

Céleste already knew reverie. All that one can say is that her reverie was devoid of an object. Perhaps she was not summoned as frankly as her brother to the religious estate. Her dreams went beyond what surrounded her. On the other hand, however, her genuinely superior intellect, her sincere piety and the precocious firmness of her heart responded for her resignation.

She was a strange girl. She had been able to retain all her virginal naivety in approaching her lips to the scientific cup. The pedantry that had touched her left her all her juvenile grace and all her delightful childishness; but the envelope was a trifle puritanical, and rendered her sudden mischievous impulses more charming.

She adored her brother; she even had a sort of respect for him. Such deferences sometimes come from superiority that divines itself. They were all the family that each of them had.

Physically, Céleste was more formed than is usual at her age, although the imminent spring would bring her a new beauty. Mentally, she had a simultaneously bold and reflective intelligence, rendered exceedingly subtle by an education not typical of her sex. She knew a host of things that women do not know. She was ignorant of many things that all women do know. The characteristic trait of her intelligence was precisely to go toward the unknown. What she did not know had the irresistible attraction for her of a posed enigma.

Such was the situation of the brother and the sister when an urgent letter from Manuele, who had been absent for several months, had caused them to undertake their journey.

Manuele had a paternal authority over them; they had not even debated his instruction. And who can tell whether that unexpected voyage did not respond in both of them, unknowingly, to a vague need for change and adventure?

They were in the hostelry of the Corpo-Santo slightly before nightfall, at the time when our knight errant, the handsome Athol, was going into the marshes of the Martorello with his pickax and his spade.

Céleste and Julian had questioned their good friend Manuele in vain; he had maintained his reserve, as was his habit. They knew no more than they had on their departure from Catania about the purpose of the voyage so imperiously demanded of them.

In front of the Osteria del Compo-Santo there was a trellised terrace, raised above the soil of the courtyard by three or four steps. Julian and Céleste were sitting under that trellis, finishing their evening meal, while Manuele was chatting with Pietro, the innkeeper. The bell of the convent had not yet begun to ring. The evening was silent and beautiful.

Manuele Giudicelli was now a man of about fifty, his stature a trifle stooped, his hairline receding. He had mildness and kindness painted in his features, but it seemed that God had given him too heavy a burden of suffering to bear. His eyes had lost the spark that Calabrian pupils never lack. There was something anxious, unhealthy—one might almost say defeated—in his gaze.

He had only taken a little bread and wine in the company of the two young travelers; then he had stood up, with no other purpose than to move around a little, as if it were impossible for him to remain still. He went back and forth in the little garden that surrounded the osteria. Sometimes, when he went behind a bush where he thought he could not be seen he took a piece of paper out of his bosom, which he reread avidly. He kissed it after having read it, and tears formed under his eyelids. Then he drew nearer to Julian and Céleste, and watched them covertly.

"The children have grown up," he murmured. "If Julian wants to be a priest, that's all right... I'd prefer to see him with a blade at his side and a feather in his cap, but we've had cardinals in the family, after all!

"And Céleste!" he went on. "All her mother's beauty! It's necessary for her to be happy. God is good...God has given them a difficult childhood in order that they'll sense the price of happiness better!"

At that moment, Julian was saying: "Poor Manuele! These few weeks have changed him a great deal, don't you think, my sister?"

"He seems to have aged several years," the girl replied, sighing.

"He toils," said Julian, "he strives, not for himself, but for us. He dreams wide awake of wealth and grandeur...as if all that were necessary, Lord God, to arrive at a Christian death, which is the goal of our miserable life!"

Céleste sighed again, more forcefully.

"The fact is," she murmured, with a hint of bitterness in her voice, "that we have no need of grandeur or wealth, for you to obtain the tonsure and me to take the veil and shut myself away in a cloister forever."

Julian looked at her. His expression was sad. "Will you regret the world, Céleste?" he asked.

"Since I don't know it..." the young woman replied, trying to smile.

"My sister," said the adolescent, in a grave tone, "one can regret not having known it."

Céleste lowered her eyes and took some time to respond. "Well, yes," she said, finally, blushing and smiling, "I would have liked to see what the world is, if only once."[17]

"Silly girl!" murmured Julian.

"And I'm sure...," said Céleste, looking at him out of the corner of her eyes.

"You're sure...?" Julian repeated, seeing that she had stopped.

"I'm sure that you've had the same idea."

Julian shook his head gravely. "I've sometimes tried to divine the world," he replied, "in accordance with what I've been told and what I've read...no, to be frank, mu sister, that hasn't given me the desire to know it better."

"And what have you divined, dear brother?" asked Céleste, drawing closer, curiously.

"Movement, noise, a vain excess of false pleasures, the satiety of which is remorse..."

Céleste pursed her pretty pink lips. There was, in truth, a little disdain in her smile, which was simultaneously mischievous and candid.

"You're right, little brother," she murmured. "It's in books that you've seen that."

"You have divined the world differently, then Céleste?" Julian interrogated, losing none of his air of superiority.

"For myself," the girl replied, "I don't know... I'd rather say that I don't know. 'Movement, noise, a vain excess...' Those words have no meaning for me. When people don't call things by their names, it seems to me that they're speaking a foreign language."

"But Céleste, my poor angel, neither of us knows the language of the world."

"We have ours, Julian," she replied, with mutinous vivacity. "The language of our dear conversations, the language of our heart and our reason. That's not the language you're employing. If you employed it, I'd understand you."

"However, my sister..."

---

[17] In this passage I have translated *monde* straightforwardly as "world," but if French it also mean "society," especially high society, and that ambiguity is crucial to what the author intends by the argument that Céleste voices for him.

"It's for that reason," she went on, animatedly, "that I have an empty soul and a completely dark mind after having read them, your treatises on morality and our pompous sermons! When you preach the word of God, Julian, I know, personally, that you have another eloquence. You've just spoken in order to say nothing, and that's a specimen, not of you but of your science. I've read that ten times, a hundred times: 'Movement, noise, vain excess, false pleasures...,' and all the rest."

"In that case, little philosopher," Julian interjected, curious in his turn, "since you're not content with my definition, give me yours."

Céleste's beautiful eyes became very pensive.

"I don't know what the world is," she replied, "but I believe I understand the reason for its attraction and its dangers. 'The world' isn't entirely a term devoid of meaning, like your 'movement,' your 'noise,' and your 'vain excess,' etc., but it's a word whose significance is entirely relative. The world only exists as a milieu. To express my thought better, the world is the supplement to every mundane personality, and I'd willingly liken it to the apparatus of mobile crystals that reflects, a thousand times over, the light of a chandelier..."

Julian looked at her in astonishment.

"I'll go further," she continued, sustaining his gaze valiantly, "and I'll hollow out my comparison, as our old professor used to say, so rich, exact and apt does it seem to me. Imagine, my dear Julian, an immense chandelier composed of many candles and countless reflective crystals. All that shines, isn't it? The candles by themselves, the crystals by means of the candles. That's the world!"

"Oh," said Julian, mechanically. "That's the world."

"A real brilliance," Céleste continued, "but multiplied by a mirage, an interested exchange of radiance. For, if an isolated candle burns in the emptiness of shadow, the night absorbs the light; it needs the crystals...but what becomes of the crystals, when the candle is snuffed out?"

"They need the candlelight," said Julian, laughing. "That's evident. I haven't seen that definition of the world in any treatise on morality. I haven't heard it in any sermon. But to judge its merit, it would be necessary for me to know the world. A vicious circle, little sister."

Céleste's dainty foot tapped the floor impatiently. "I've said too much," she said, "and I have difficulty forgetting that I once listened to the lessons of a professor of logic while doing my embroidery. The evil comes, my dear brother, from the desire I have to make you understand my thinking. There's a kind of education that consists of enveloping the intelligence in banalities, as one imprisons the poor limbs of babies in swaddling clothes. We've both had that education."

"That's a declared revolt!" murmured Julian.

"Alas, no, my brother. It's a protest, and that's sufficient for me. Now that I've shown how the commonplace wounds me as a stick does a donkey, I'd like nothing better than to submit; I surrender myself bound hand and foot."

"God doesn't want slaves in his house!" Julian interjected, in a severe tone

"God wants all those who suffer, my brother."

Julian took her by the hand and collected himself. He searched within himself for a few words that might appease the unexpected rebellion of that soul. It was a malady that had not shown any precursory symptoms to him. They had never quit one another for an hour, and yet it was only for a few minutes that Julian had known Céleste. He looked at her. Something in her seemed to have changed. She was a woman.

"Céleste," he said to her, softly, in a paternal tone, "in order to see so clearly the faults of the education we've received, it's necessary for you to have encountered an object of comparison. It isn't the good Manuele who has inspired these ideas in you."

"The good Manuele has always treated me as a child. You know full well that he reserved his long stories for you alone."

"Have you had other professors, then?"

That question was asked with a certain timidity. It was visible that Julian feared the response. But Céleste's smile was so modest and so pure, in spite of the sparkle in her large dark eyes.

"Have no fear, my dear brother," she said. "I've never had any other professor than yours. Except that, while I was embroidering and the good graduate Brother Geronimo accused me of indifference, I was listening too closely...and perhaps to avenge you on your enemy—how you yawned, poor brother!—I silently battered a breach in the graduate's arguments. That wouldn't have taken me very far, I admit, if I hadn't found a guide..."

"What guide?" cried Julian, sharply.

"One that can't frighten you. That guide was myself. Once I started to read the book that God has put into each of us, I no longer had time to listen to old Geronimo. I understood God and I understood myself."

"Are you quite sure, Céleste," murmured Julian, visibly anxious, "that there's no heresy in this?"

"Absolutely sure, my brother. I love my holy faith too much to examine it; it's the refuge...I'm only talking about mundane things; those are ours, they belong to us like an entire country to a conqueror. We aren't of the world; we never have been; in consequence, we can make nothing of it."

The grave and handsome adolescent who had recounted so sagely to his little sister the classic biography of Mario Monteleone, that serious student, freshly molded by the lessons of Brother Geronimo, was experiencing a complex emotion at that moment. He was tempted to admire his sister, and understood now why old Geronimo sometimes spoke with regard to her of illustrious women who had made their way in theology, philosophy and literature.

He was still—at least for today—at the age when one admires a knowledgeable woman. His sister appeared to him to have suddenly grown to the stature of someone who might, after her death, have a half-page article in historical dictionaries. But that joy was mingled with a certain chagrin. He had acquired the pleasant habit of being listened to as an oracle, and he certainly merited it by the irreproachable regularity of his conduct, but now his sister was standing up in front of him and challenging his legitimate supremacy. The girl was even permitting herself to embarrass him—him, who would soon be a doctor—to the point that he did not dare risk giving the discussion the appearance of a pitched battle, for fear of being routed.

He was very knowledgeable, good little Julian, and the worthy Brother Geronimo was not as unarmed as the inconsiderate scorn of the signorina might make one suppose, but surprise robbed Julian of a significant part of his means, and in any case, the syllogism is an awkward and heavy weapon, which softens against the smile of a girl. There is nothing a terrible as little girls who take it into their head to argue. One cannot say that there were not a few little traces of pedantry in that delightful pretty face, but Céleste was so young.

Until the age of sixteen I plead that extenuating circumstance explicitly: little girls have the right to philosophize any way they like. It is their privilege as schoolgirls. Julian, however, had studied his sister's thesis laboriously, like the student of theology that he was. It was, in the full sense of the term, a lesson in dialectics that he was getting.

"Well," he said, suddenly, following the series of arguments that he was posing to himself, "admitting that we're both types, you think that, suddenly placed on the threshold of the theater that is the world, my attention will be concentrated on the young men, while you'll only examine the young women..."

Céleste looked at him pensively. Her mind had overcome the obstacle that was stopping her brother a long time ago.

"You're still reasoning in accordance with the Geronimo system," she murmured, smiling, "so you're following a false route. Logic is the art of deceiving oneself."

"Didn't you say that?"

"I said that it's sufficient for me to know the world to see one young woman in the world...perhaps even to see a young woman of the world outside the world."

"By the same reasoning, it would be sufficient for me to see a young man in the world..."

"Or even a young man of the world...provided that you looked hard, with your own eyes, which are good, and not with the lying spectacles that enable scholars to see the stars at midday."

"So that," concluded he imperturbable Julian, "given your axiom thus formulated, one can only see outside oneself someone similar to oneself...one can only judge exterior facts by relating them to someone similar..."

"O Geronimo II!'" exclaimed Céleste, laughing.

"So that, as I was saying," the student continued, "the most perfect apparatus that the two of us could find for seeing the world would consist of a brother and a sister...some young comte and comtesse. I would dissect the comte, and you would anatomize the comtesse."

"They're the carriages of Comte Lorédan Doria," said a voice below them, "who is traveling with his sister, the comtesse."

Julian's speech was cut off. The laughter that had come to Céleste's pretty pink lips vanished. They looked at one another and murmured simultaneously: "That's strange!"

Céleste added: "The son and daughter of that Giacomo Doria..."

She did not finish. With a common movement, they got up and launched themselves toward the lattice of the trellis.

The trellis of the inn of the Corpo-Santo overlooked the road that went in front of it. At the back, the rectangular house opened its irregular windows. To the left was a small garden where, at that moment, the good Manuele and the innkeeper were chatting together. The latter, a tall, pale fellow, gaitered like Léopold Robert's reapers[18] and wearing a multicolored bonnet on his shock of black hair, was looking at his companion from time to time with anxiety.

The fellow's dreaming wide awake, he thought.

"Warnings have been seen," said Manuele, gripping him by the sleeve, "to emerge from the tomb!"

"Yes, yes," replied the hotelier, "there are drunkards who have encountered the late Comtesse Maria prowling among the grass in the arms of the Martorello. Me, I sleep at night and I don't go in for smuggling when the fever leaves me in peace."

"You weren't a servant of Monteleone, Pietro?"

"No, no...I came here after the death of the brave man...but I think the inn must have been better in the days when iron was forged here in the valley."

"And tell me, Pietro, what do you think of this?"

"Of what? Of the dead man's letter, received seven year after his death? I think that it's a joke, my old comrade, and you won't make your fortune with that."

Manuele lowered his head

"What does it say, the letter?" asked the hotelier, whose curiosity pierced his feigned insouciance.

"They're not my secrets," Manuele replied.

"What I'm asking," said Pietro, "is for you to give me an advice...but I'm winking my eye, my old comrade. You have two pretty children there, that's

---

[18] Louis Léopold Robert (1794-1835) established his reputation when "Summer Reapers at the Pontine Marshes" (1831) was bought by King Louis-Philippe. There is a significant reference to the painting in Alexandre Dumas' *Comte de Monte Cristo*, an important exemplar for feuilleton revenge fantasies.

certain. Put the boy in the army and marry the girl to some honest bourgeois from Cosenza, and you'll all live in peace."

Manuele stopped him short, squeezing his arm.

"Would you care to lend me a spade and a pickax, Pietro?" he asked, abruptly.

The other looked at him slyly and touched his forehead. "I'm damned if there isn't something cracked in there, Père Manuele. I'll lend you my spade and my pickax if you like…but you're as pale as a fever-victim the day after the bout. Come upstairs with me and have a glass of Sicilian wine to warm your heart."

The hotelier Pietro was a good soul. He had been expelled from the region of Otranto, where he had kept a smugglers' inn on the other side of the Apennines. Everyone in this world follows his vocation. Smuggling is a noble profession on the coasts of Calabria, almost as noble as brigandage. Between the mountain and the Martorello there was only the difference of the malaria for Pietro. But one lives with that fever before dying of it. Pietro took Manuele by the arm and made him go into the osteria. He went down to the cellar himself. Left alone, Manuele laid out the yellow and crumpled letter on the table. He started to reread it attentively.

It's certainly his handwriting, he said to himself, while reading. *I never disobeyed him while he was alive. May his will be done after his death!*

"What have we here?" cried Pietro in the courtyard, coming back up from the cellar.

Two men-at-arms on horseback appeared at the bend in the road. Instead of rejoining his guest, the innkeeper went to the doorstep. It was not every day that windfalls arrived at the Osteria del Corpo-Santo.

The two men-at-arms came into the courtyard. Behind them came two horsemen wearing bright livery and armed to the teeth. Then came a traveling caleche with four horses, on the cushions of which a young couple were reclining indolently. After the caleche came two more riders, a second carriage and two more men-at-arms, carbines in hand.

Céleste and Julian were no longer taking. Their souls were in their eyes. Both remained, in good faith, under the impression of the odd theory developed by the genteel pupil of the classic Geronimo. Julian was gazing at Comte Lorédan Doria; Céleste was devouring Comtesse Angélie with her eyes.

Does one know how these things happen, independently of all theories, old or new, academic or fantastic? While looking at the Comte, it was the Comtesse that our sage and savant Julian saw. Céleste, who believed that she was examining the Comtesse, encountered before her pupils the noble and charming visage of Comte Lorédan. It was truly as in tales of the marvelous. They had evoked the vision; the vision, meekly, appeared. Why was neither one of them thinking any longer of that cold study that ought to facilitate the "human apparatus," to employ Julian's expression.

The apparatus was perfect, and as they had desired; there was a young man and there was a young woman, a brother and a sister, not only of the world but of the elite race that floats above the world and whom the world envies: noble among the noblest, rich among the most opulent, the pride of the court, the flower of the realm!

Once, before the wars of the Revolution, the Neapolitans had said: "After Bourbon, Monteleone; after Monteleone, Doria!"

But while the great family of Monteleone had fallen and died, Doria was still growing, and growing all the more because the heritage of Monteleone had come to it by right of relationship. There was no more Monteleone, and Neapolitans could now say: "After Bourbon, Doria!"

Slowly, the caleche came down the slope that terminated the hill. For a moment, it almost appeared behind a hillock that the road cut through, and the summit of which, covered with a mane of brambles and a few young beeches. The daylight was declining, although the line of the horizon was still red, as if ablaze. When the caleche emerged from the shadow, Julian uttered a great sigh and straightened up involuntarily. Céleste went very pale. Outside, under the trellis, the staff of the inn were saying:

"They're coming from Palermo and going to Naples."

"The King wants to marry them both on the same day."

"The King has divided Mario Monteleone's domains between them equally."

Julian and Céleste exchanged a mute glance. The staff of the inn continued:

"The Doria of Rome is giving them all his palaces and two of his castles..."

"They don't have enough castles and palaces, then, in Naples, Palermo and Abruzzo, Calabria, Sicily and everywhere!"

A few bonnets flew into the air.

"*Evviva il conte Doria! Evviva la contessina!*"

Lorédan smiled and saluted. A profound sigh elevated Céleste's breast. Angélie waved her white hand and inclined her head idly. Julian placed his hands over his heart; his eyes widened involuntarily, and his stature suddenly straightened proudly, as if he were another man. On seeing the fire that suddenly lit up in his pupils, you would not have recognized the pale seminarian.

VII. Comte and Comtesse

Lorédan Doria was one of the admirable specimens of Roman beauty that evidently inspired the Italian school. There was such a noble serenity in the ensemble of his lines that one thought involuntarily of God made man. The beauty of Italy is a gentle, majestic, almost divine beauty.

Lorédan, Comte Doria, might have been twenty-eight or thirty years old. The curly masses of his marvelous black hair were separated over his white and pure forehead. When he smiled, his shadowed eyes, simultaneously profound and limpid, widely split but already fatigued by pleasure, gave the soul the sensation of harmony to which a beautiful masculine voice, or the distant sound of an organ, gives birth, as well as the severe and sweet odors disengaged by the shade of great woods.

It is not easy to depict the heroic mixture of nobility and strength that is seduction itself. Our men of the North do not have that. But remember that, under the tropical sun, giant trees as robust as our oaks bear, a hundred feet above the earth, garlands of flowers whiter than our lilies, pinker than our roses, and bluer than our azure convolvulus...

What it is necessary to renounce describing is the exquisite charm and the delectable grace of the young woman who was sitting next to Lorédan on the cushions of the caleche.

She was ten or twelve years younger than her brother. She was a smiler and a dreamer. It seemed that she might have had written on her forehead, in light, the divine name of Angélie, which made one think of heavenly poems. Her face repeated more delicately, but with a suave and infinite correction, the noble design of Lorédan's features. She was tall, as he was tall. Her figure had the chaste and voluptuous abandon of a creole virgin. Her chestnut hair, with softly pearly reflections, fell in opulent masses along her cheeks, paled by the fatigue of the journey. Her eyes, fringed with long curved lashes as black as jade, had a blue tint as obscure and frank as the vault of the firmament on moonless summer nights: the nuance that drowns rays of light even more profoundly than brown, in order to restitute them in a sheaf of fugitive sparks at the slightest caress of a smile. Her straight nose retained the Greek line of Genoese ancestors. As soon as she spoke, her mouth, sculpted coral, showed an array of miraculously delicate pearls, each of which seemed a key of the melodious harpsichord that was her voice.

She was not a Madonna; there was too much candid prettiness for that, too much dainty naivety in her sovereign beauty; she was the angel of blonde and dear amours, the child-woman, the woman that one would like to shelter day and night under one's wing, in order to preserve her from the brutal contact of earthly things. And she was also the young woman of our modern days, a budding grand dame, the perfect and select specimen of all our refinements and all our elegance. It was necessary not to see that lovely enchantress; as soon as she had been seen, the heart retained her ravishing image.

Julian, the poor solitary child new to any violent impression, gazed at her open-mouthed. He experienced the intoxicating sensation of a man born to some unknown sphere. His chest swelled beneath his humble soutanelle. His temples throbbed; dazzlements passed before his eyes.

While the caleche crossed the threshold of the courtyard at a trot, Angélie chanced to look up toward the trellis. For a moment, Julian could no longer feel his heart. He put his hands over his face in order to hide it. He was afraid and ashamed. He held on to the lattice of the trellis in order not to fall backwards.

She spoke. It was a proper name that fell from her beautiful nonchalant lips: a name that rendered Julian jealous to the point of distress; a name that would remain engraved in his memory if he lived to be a hundred

Angélie had said: "Prince Coriolani."

A name is nothing, and yet it is everything. There are names that are a novel or a painting, names that spread a perfume or sound like the resonant note of a horn. There are names to which one cannot attribute either old age or ugliness.

One is sometimes mistaken, but the astonishment one experiences, the disillusionment that wounds you, are still a tribute to the virtual sincerity of the first impression. Anger if one desired it, delight if one dreaded it, there is surprise, as in the moment when a sylphide, seen from behind and to whom the imagination lends such sweet charms, turns round and shows you a fifty-year-old face.

Julian saw that Prince Coriolani with a high head and flashing eyes, as handsome as a hero or bandit. Those two things do not differ as much in the Italian imagination as one might think. A hero: Angélie had smiled as she pronounced that name, so harmonious in her mouth. A bandit: Julian had clenched his fists and thought, for the first time, that at his age, other young men had a weapon at their side. He detested him, that Coriolani. He would have given ten years of his life only to see him.

Céleste had not done as her brother had. At the first glance cast at Comte Lorédan, her eyes were as if dazzled. But she could still see him; she could see him better through her closed eyelids. The emotion that she felt caused her a veritable fear. She would not have sold it for all the gold in the world.

They both stood motionless and mute for some time.

Céleste thought: *That man cannot be the son of a traitor.*

And Julian said to himself: *If Manuele had accused Giacomo Doria, I would not have believed Manuele.*

But their emotion did not take its principal source from the fortuitous fact of the indirect part that the handsome young man and the young woman had had in the recently recounted story.

The Comte and his sister had entered the osteria several minutes ago. The noisy comings and goings of hasty domestics were audible.

Finally, Julian looked at Céleste.

"What's the matter with you?" he said in a low voice.

She shivered, as if she had been caught doing something wrong.

"What's the matter with me?" she echoed

"Yes," said Julian, considering her with an astonished attention. "You've changed...you're more beautiful."

It was true. The awakening is a beauty. But it was especially true for Julian, whose eyes were illuminated for the first time and whose straightened stature took on, unknown to him, a masculine allure. So Céleste, contemplating him as if she had never seen him before, allowed these words to escape:

"It's you who are handsome, Julian! But that costume no longer suits you."

Julian was just thinking of the new graces that a less severe haircut might add to his sister's pretty face.

There was another silence. Both of them watched the valets and maidservants getting down from the second carriage. From the cellars to the attic, the osteria was up in the air.

"Well, Céleste," said Julian, "you got what you wanted."

"That's true," the young woman replied.

"Through so much beauty, so much opulence and so much nobility, have you found the world, Céleste?"

The charming puritan's breast swelled; her eyelids fluttered.

"Yes," she said. "I've glimpsed the world. Have you?"

"I don't know my sister. There are perfidious temptations. I've divined paradise on earth."

"Paradise," exclaimed Céleste, with vivacity, "would be to be *him*, would it not?"

Julian did not reply. Perhaps he had not grasped the meaning of the words.

"Did you imagine, my sister," he said, however, "that such a perfectly beautiful being could exist?"

"I would never have thought so, my brother."

"That gaze...that graceful elegance...that smile whose charm no words can describe..."

"And that indolent pride! That aureole of poetry! The forehead as pensive and white as that of a statue, beneath that silken hair, blacker than ebony..."

Julian gave his sister a sly glance. "You're talking about Comte Lorédan Doria," he murmured.

"And who are you talking about?" asked Céleste, naively.

"You said," stammered Julian, "You must remember, little sister, you said that if we suddenly had before us a young man and a young woman, a brother and a sister, of those that God has heaped with all the terrestrial joys, of those who shine in the world and who summarize within them the happiness of the world, that you would divine the world simply by looking at the sister."

"That's true," pronounced Céleste, in a whisper. "But didn't you look at the brother?"

"Alas," Julian replied, simply, "of the two of us, you're the philosopher. I didn't even see the brother..."

"And I only saw him...," sighed the young woman, as red as a cherry. She interrupted herself, seized Julian's hand abruptly, and placed it over her heart. "Feel that!" she said.

Her heart was leaping in her bosom.

"It's like mine," said Julian, sadly.

"And do you know what it is crying, my heart?" said the girl. "Wealth, nobility... splendor!"

"Ah!" said Julian. "That's not what mine is saying."

"What is it saying?"

Julian had both hands on his breast. He lowered his voice and murmured: "Amour."

Céleste threw herself into his arms and kissed him. They were both weeping, like the poor children that they were. Take note that less innocent individuals would have expressed their thought differently. Innocence always tells the truth.

"Dear brother," murmured Céleste, sobbing, "wealth, nobility, grandeur...that's what there is between them and us."

Julian pressed her to his heart.

Behind them, under the trellis, there was a slight sound. They turned round. Manuele was standing a few paces from the table where they had taken their meal. He was holding a spade and a pickax.

"Wealth, nobility, grandeur," he murmured, for he had only heard those words. "Poor children! Who has taught you to be jealous of that?"

Céleste and Julian remained still, their eyes lowered. Manuele, ordinary so calm and so mild, seemed prey to an extraordinary agitation. His face depicted a sort of feverish excitement.

"After Bourbon, Monteleone; after Monteleone, Doria," he pronounced, between clenched teeth. "Those people only come third in line."

He approached and kissed Céleste on the forehead.

"Yes, yes," he said, as if dreaming aloud, "grandeur, wealth, nobility. The bird whose wings have not been clipped will take off one day and go to seek the azure of the sky. It only takes an instant for Achilles to rip off his woman's tunic with disdain. Perhaps the time has come. Those who are traveling noisily are very noble and very rich...there are others as noble as they are...perhaps they can be as rich."

His second kiss was for Julian.

"You'll be a fine Comte," he murmured. "Look at me, Céleste. I've seen many princesses...you have the eyes of a queen. May God aid us, child! Old trunks flourish again every spring. I've met Dorias who were begging for their bread on the roads. People often rise to thrones on returning from exile. In Ferrara, I looked for a long time at the marvelous painting that represents the wheel of fortune. Those who have nobility sometimes go to bed wretched and wake up great. Sleep, children: Providence is awake!"

His hand extended over them in a gesture of benediction. His face had a solemn expression, almost inspired. He drew away slowly and went down the steps of the trellis without turning round. Céleste and Julian had their heads bowed. Far from stimulating their courage, the old man's words caused them to reenter into themselves. It was not the first time that he had made such strange speeches to them. He had suffered a great deal; suffering weakens the mind.

Sometimes, the brother and sister had gazed fearfully at that despoiled face and those eyes, alternately sparkling and dull. They had never dared to say it, but they had both had the same thought: poor Manuele's reason tottered at times, and he mistook certain dreams for memories.

Meanwhile, the sound and movement in the Osteria del Compo-Santo were increasing. Pietro, the hotelier, had set his cherished idleness aside and was multiplying himself. It was a matter of preparing supper for Their Excellencies, Their Highnesses, as you wish—in Italy, titles cost nothing. If Their Highnesses had testified the slightest desire, they would have been given Majesty. It is still the land of the Emperors who were made into gods while they were alive, before their throats were cut in order to allow them to enjoy immortality sooner.

Their Excellencies were very tired. The legitimate hope was nourished that Their Excellencies might sleep at the Corpo-Santo instead of going on to the town of Monteleone. What an honor for the osteria! Comte Lorédan and Comtesse Angélie were not entirely strangers in the locale. Although Naples was their habitual residence and the Dorias of Rome had left them immense domains in the province of Palermo in Sicily, they could also be placed at the head of the landowners of the second ulterior Calabria. Only the Monteleones had possessed more land and more manors in the time of their splendor. But there were no more Monteleones and no one henceforth, between Consenza and Reggio, could compete with the Dorias, who had inherited from the Monteleones themselves. It would almost be true to say, moreover, that the young Comte and the young Comtesse, who had lost their father a short time ago, did not yet know the exact tally of their possessions. That was the business of the steward general, who truly lived like a prince. The private stewards of Calabria, Sicily and Rome were also men of importance.

It would have needed a great deal for the Osteria del Corpo-Santo to be a palace. It was, nevertheless a house built of good stone, possessing several terraces, like almost all the habitations of southern Italy. One of those terraces overlooked the courtyard and, turning the south-western corner of the main building, had a view over the Tyrrhenian Sea through a gap. It was there that Lorédan and Angélie installed themselves in order to take their evening meal.

77

They were both in a charming humor, determined to take everything in good part during that encampment.

All those who had had the honor of contemplating Their Excellencies said that the contessina had already had already laughed like a madwoman a dozen times and that Comte Lorédan had started singing an arietta by Sacchini while lighting a cigarette It was certainly impossible to see two more cheerful Highnesses; the valets were more arrogant and the chambermaids even haughtier—which was the rule. They arrived on their terrace chatting and laughing. Fresh water had bathed Angélie's temples; she had left her somnolent languor in the depths of the carriage. She was lively and happy. She offered her brow to the perfumed evening breeze. She was as beautiful as the joy of youth.

Out of respect for Their Excellencies, the courtyard was evacuated and the bustle confined in the house. Angélie and her brother were really alone, if one made the abstraction of Céleste and Julian, forgotten behind the trellis. Who would have thought of those two poor children at such a solemn moment? The trellis would not have been enough to hide them if the hillock we mentioned, which was crowned by a sort of thicket, had not cast a shadow that was already profound, while the terrace, white and uncovered, remained brightly lit by the last rays of the sun.

Neither armed horseman nor men-at-arms could any longer be seen, but they could still be heard, at table in the low room of the inn. The horsemen had left their pistols and belts outside the stable door, where the grooms were taking charge of their horses. The carbines were leaning against the little wall of the trellis, outside, behind the table where Céleste and her brother were still sitting. They had both put their seats against the lattice, where rare broad vine leaves ran, hanging from old twisted stocks, as in the capricious but sober garlands that turn around the handles of antique vases. They were silent. They were gazing. Lorédan and Angélie were talking, but they could not be heard.

Sometimes, Angélie's smile was reflected on Julian's lips as in a mirror. At other times, that smile brought a cloud of sadness to the young man's brow. When Lorédan's distracted gaze passed over the trellis, Céleste held her breath. You might have thought, on seeing those two children, that they were spies paid to watch, their ears and eyes alert.

What were the Comte and Comtesse talking about? Their brilliant and noisy pleasures? Balls and fêtes? Or perhaps those they loved? How beautiful they must be, their fêted! And what adoration around them! A little while ago, someone had said that the King wanted to marry her to Coriolani! Prince Coriolani! That was doubtless the man who was to marry Angélie—so Julian thought.

No woman's name had fallen from Lorédan's lips, but did Céleste need a name to be sad? Did she not divine a garland of houris around that sultan? How could that be expressed? There was, however, some truth in Céleste's famous theory. It is quite certain that one cannot give the name of amour to the passionate disturbance that was making her heart beat. Lorédan was the pretext for that trouble, of which the hearth was Céleste herself. Perhaps she would love Lorédan, but at that moment, Lorédan was only the stone that is necessary to permit a steel to produce a spark. Behind Lorédan was the world.

Céleste was only mistaken on one point. She had seen the world in a magic mirror that was the brother and the sister; the error was only in the sex.

For Julian, the matter was quite different. Julian had been thunderstruck. Julian was in love. It is easy to observe that difference between a man and a woman. The man, being more naïve, loves at the first stroke. Passion is born within him in a single jet, and tends rather to decrease after the great dazzlement of the first sight. In the woman, especially a young woman, the impression produced is immediately complicated by an egotistical reaction.

The word "egotistical," in common parlance, implies a criticism; here it does not. It merely expresses the action of the self, and that action summons prudence and modesty. The rationale of that difference is providential. God has wanted woman to defend herself. It requires age or degeneracy to erode that instinct. The woman whom the first impression carries away irredeemably and irreversibly becomes a man. Julian had fallen in love. Céleste was still falling.

Julian was already suffering in the heart; he saw nothing but the idol. Céleste, as profoundly moved as he was, saw the paradise in which her god was enthroned—a paradise, alas, surrounded by insurmountable barriers. And while poor Julian incessantly divined on the beautiful laughing mouth of Angélie the name of Coriolani, which burned his heart, Céleste formed a dream. That dream could be expressed in three words: nobility, grandeur, wealth.

It was a beautiful autumn evening, calm and refreshed by the sea breeze. Suddenly Céleste and Julian turned their eyes away simultaneously from the contemplation that absorbed the, A flash of light had just struck them, unexpectedly. Something had shone on the summit of the hillock that the Monteleone road cut through.

The hillock was outlined in black against the carmine sky. The brushwood stood out like lace fringing the crest of the hill. Above it, swaying in the breeze, like the silhouettes of Chinese shadows, were the bright branches of birches and the heavier foliage of beeches. One divined behind the hill the rosy light that illuminated so vividly the terrace where Lorédan and his sister were smiling at the beautiful sky. It was from the bosom of the brushwood that the flash had sprung: a red and fugitive light similar to that which mischievous children send from a distance with a mirror.

At the same time, Céleste and Julian looked at the point from which the light had come. They saw nothing at first but an imperceptible movement in the brambles; the movement must have escaped the young couple seated on the terrace because of the glare of the sky, which put the summit of the hill in profound darkness. But, on looking harder, Céleste thought she could discern a human head in the blackness. Then, immediately afterwards, a second flash sprang from the brushwood.

Julian said: "Do you remember that hunter in Catania whose double-barreled rifle seemed to us from a distance to be a fire in the thicket? He was higher up than we were. The sun, which we couldn't see, was striking his weapon from below..."

"There are two men," Céleste interjected.

Julian did not continue his scientific explanation. He raised his hand to place it as a shield above his eyes.

"Two armed men...," he murmured.

Céleste felt herself trembling without yet knowing why. She gazed with all the might of her eyes, and was now able to make out two torsos protruding from the brushwood. "What are those hunters doing up there?" Julian wondered.

The man who was further forward was holding on to the trunk of a young birch in order not to fall down the slope. The other lay down and waited for his companion to adjust his position.

"They're not hunters," said Céleste, who had sweat on her brow. And she darted a glance of distress around, and saw the carbines of the men-at-arms under her feet. Julies had got up. Céleste closed his mouth with her hand.

"Don't call out!" she ordered, in a whisper, with a strange calmness. "The horsemen and the men-at-arms are at table. They've left their weapons outside. I sense that in a second, all help will be futile."

Julian's forehead was inundated by seat. A third flash sprang from the brushwood. It was the more advanced of the two pretended hunters, who had succeeded in straightening up and was raising his gun. There was no doubt about it. The two pretended hunters were aiming at the terrace. They were assassins.

Lorédan and Angélie were lifting glasses to their lips, chatting and smiling. Céleste had been right to close her brother's mouth. A cry would have doomed them. Between the appeal and the arrival of the escort, a minute would have gone by: a minute, each second of which would have sufficed for the crime to be committed.

Feeling faint, Julian leaned against the terrace. "If I could put my breast in front of hers!" he murmured.

"You can do better," said Céleste, who was pale but who was not trembling. At the same time, she seized the barrel of a rifle through the lattice of the trellis. She put the weapon in Julian's hands and concluded, in a form voice: "Kill them!"

The young seminarian had a kind of vertigo. A third shadow was outlined in the bushes, in the darkness that was about to thicken. He was seen to clap his hands—doubtless a signal.

"Kill a man! Me!" murmured Julian, whose legs, too weak, could no longer sustain is body.

The shadow had clapped twice.

"If you don't dare, give!" exclaimed Céleste, who surpassed him by a head at that moment.

She snatched the carbine from his hands and leaned the end of the barrel against one of the bars of the trellis. At the same instant that the shadow gave the last signal, the gun in the hands of the young woman fired. A second shot responded to hers, like an echo, from the summit of the hill. Lorédan collapsed in his sister's arms while the weapon dropped from Céleste's hands and she fell upon Julian's bosom.

At the top of the hill a human form stood up straight amid the brushwood. For an instant, a black silhouette stood out against the sky. Then the somber silhouette tottered, and a man fell, head first, into the dust of the road, fifty paces from the trellis. He had not fired. The men-at-arms and the horsemen brought by the sound of the double detonation found his loaded carbine beside him. His two companions—the other assassin and the shadow that had given the three signals—had disappeared, as if by enchantment.

Lorédan had a wound in his shoulder. As he fixed his ardent eyes on Angélie, who was wrapping her arms around him, Julian thought: *At the price of a mortal coup, I'd like to be in his place!*

Before falling in a faint, Céleste had seen the young Comtesse receiving Lorédan on her bosom, and her heart had murmured: *It isn't him that I've saved!*

At that moment, the bell of the Corpo-Santo started sounding the knell, at full tilt. And a few moments later, from the depths of the valley of the Martiorello, an explosion was heard, similar to the distant detonation of a large-caliber cannon. The dusk became black. The anxious escort had assembled in the courtyard. Everyone was wondering what was happening in the vicinity that night. On the terrace, a woman whom no one had seen come in suddenly appeared behind the group formed by Lorédan and his sister, who had sent away the innkeeper Pietro and his hasty servants. Lorédan's wound was slight; he had already recovered consciousness.[19]

The woman, the apparition, was wearing a white dress, and long black hair was floating beneath a veil around her pale forehead. She remained at the very end of the terrace. Her hand was seen to extend toward the distant towers of the convent.

She was heard to murmur: "The children of Doria are beautiful. Where are the children of Monteleone?" Then, in a loud voice, she said: "Do you hear the sound of that bell? Harness your horses; Death is here, in the vicinity. The shadows are full of the daggers of the Silence. It's the night of the fifteenth of October!"

---

[19] Like the explosion, this appearance is incompatible with the chronology of chapter V, unless the *"peu d'instants après"* [a few moments later] mentioned immediately after the bells begin to ring actually signifies a considerable lapse of time that has been drastically compacted within the narrative.

VIII. The Mass of the Twenty-Second Hour

Manuele was marching through the deserted valley when he heard the double explosion. He did not even look back. When the sound of the convent bells reached him, he bared his head and made the sign of the cross. Later, when the loud detonation made the earth tremble beneath his feet, he accelerated his pace.

"It's the night of the fifteenth of October," he said, also. "Prayers are being said for the accomplishment of the last will of the dead."

The obscurity was complete when he arrived in the ruins. Unlike Athol, our adventurer, he did not have to search for a long time. Memory guided him through the labyrinth of rubble buried under the vegetation. He went straight to the mound where Athol had seen the woman in white for the first time.[20] His heart was beating very forcefully and it was in a tremulous voice that he was talking to himself. But if a ray of light had suddenly appeared in that darkness, you would have seen hope illuminate that humble and virtuous visage.

"Yes, yes," he said to himself, "As noble and as rich... A reckoning is necessary...what some lack, the others have...I know, myself, that the Master had thought of everything before dying...!"

On arriving at the mound he stuck the spade in the ground and took the pickax in hand.

"Wealth, nobility, grandeur...," he pronounced, giving his voice a solemn tone involuntarily. "Everything is in there..."

But a cry of astonishment escaped his throat when he saw a gaping black hole before him.

"Someone has come!" he cried. "Who has come?"

He entered abruptly into the redoubt, whose threshold Athol had crossed with a sort of meditation. The odor of the powder was still inside. The moon, which had hidden behind a cloud, showed its silvery crescent, whose rays filtered through the opening. The low chamber suddenly lit up. There was no dampness within because the pavilion, built entirely in marble, had been built over a vault. It was a charming retreat, in the modern Italian style. The walls ornamented by light mosaic garlands, retained a singular freshness. It seemed that the artist had just put the final touches to the decoration. As there were no paintings or gilding, nothing had suffered, except that the bedcovers and the draperies were pale and faded. There was something strange in seeing those hanging tatters, dull and mildewed, amid the somber opulence of the paneling. A nuptial bed and two cradles, as we have said, formed the entire furniture of the chamber. For having been late in coming, the impression produced on Manuele was only

---

[20] Feval's serial appeared two years before Wilkie Collins' *The Woman in White* (1859).

more violent and more profound. He fell to his knees and his eyes were inundated by tears.

"Fourteen years gone by!" he murmured. "Instead of youth, beauty and happiness, death!"

His gaze was fixed n the bed with a sort of stupor. He took a piece of paper from his bosom and unfolded it slowly. He was facing the entrance, and the moonlight fell over his shoulder directly upon the handwriting. He read:

No one has entered that place since the day when all my happiness perished simultaneously. The door was walled up on Maria's bed and the two poor empty cribs...

Manuele stopped, because his tears were blinding him. He suddenly rose to his feet, griped by a tremor. "But someone has come!" he exclaimed.

For an instant, he had forgotten, so strongly had all his memories of the past gripped his heart. His gaze made a tour of the subterranean chamber. In that gaze there was more hope than dread.

"Those who have come," he thought, "didn't know the secret..."

Again, he consulted the piece of paper that he was holding in his hand.

"*At the head of the bed,*" he murmured, reading, "*the third panel, the one that bears the Monteleone escutcheon with the motto...*"

There could be no mistake. All the panels were similar except that one, which had, in addition to its light mosaic frame, a shield surrounded by the great cordon of the Golden Fleece. The shield was "azure with a heart of gold, transpierced by two swords in saltire," with the motto: *Agere, non loqui.*[21]

Manuele put his finger on the escutcheon that occupied the center of the panel and pressed. The panel immediately swung to reveal a rectangular cavity, like a cupboard, which only contained a sculpted steel casket.

Manuele uttered a cry of joy and took possession of the casket.

The lock had been broken by a pistol shot. It still bore the trace of the bullet. The casket was empty.

"Hola! Mariola! Madwoman!" cried a hoarse voice outside. "Have you made that hole to hide in? Come on, if you come back like a good girl, you won't be beaten, but if you make me run, you'd better look out!"

An expressive crack of a whip accompanied those last words. It was an old woman who was hobbling through the grass, with a lantern in one hand and a whip in the other: an old woman in the style of Rembrandt, with a long, meager face, bristling with gray hair, a trenchant nose that descended over the depressed mouth to the equine chin. Little gray eyes were blinking behind a thicket of rebellious eyebrows. She stopped in front of the entrance to the old pleasure pavilion.

---

[21] "Action, not speech."

"In truth," she murmured, "there's a bed one could carry away if it isn't too heavy. I've often gone past here without suspecting that there was anything inside..." She interrupted herself with a weary laugh, and then added: "La Mariola is capable of going to sleep in it, weeping over the two cribs."

The light of the lantern illuminated the corners of the chamber by turns. She could not see anything. One might have thought that she was afraid of going in.

"It's her knell they're sounding up there," she murmured. "I don't like coming out on the night of the fifteenth of October, and La Mariola will pay me for that." She resumed in a honeyed tone: "Come on, my good girl, when you spend the night running around, you know that the work doesn't go well the next day...you go to sleep over your spinning-wheel. And I ask God, do you earn the bread you eat? Come on, Mariola, come on, come on..."

She waited for a response momentarily. No response came.

"Will you come!" she shouted, angrily. "Or do I have to fetch you?"

The menacing whip cracked, but the response still did not come.

The old woman passed over the threshold with an unsteady step. She was afraid. The lantern was trembling in her hand. When she was in the middle of the room she perceived a dark mass half hidden behind the head of the bed. She approached. It was a man, holing in his clenched hands a steel casket, open and empty. The man was unconscious, as if dead. The old woman knelt down beside him and directed the lantern-light at his face.

"My nephew Manuele!" she muttered, with more surprise than emotion. "I must have grown old, since those I dandled on my knees are now old men!"

The old woman lived in a little cabin lost in the rocks a mile away, almost at the summit of the hill that separated the Martorello from the shore. Her name was Berta Giudicelli. She had been the nurse of Barbe de Monteleone, for whom she had retained a maternal affection. She alone knew the secret of Barbe's hopes of marriage to the deceased Comte; she alone knew the secret of Barbe's tears and despair when Mario Monteleone had taken a foreigner for a wife. However, Barbe had testified an ardent and urgent devotion to the new chatelaine from the outset. It was her who had obtained for her daughter the honor of nursing the firstborn of the Monteleones. After the catastrophe that plunged the house into mourning, when hope seemed to be smiling again on the master of the blacksmith knights, when Maria des Amalfi had given birth successively to a second son and a daughter, Berta had pressed around them like Barbe herself.

The children loved her because she knew beautiful songs and all the naïve tales the amuse village evenings. She called them her dear angels and attracted them to her cabin as often as she could. No one was astonished by that. Everyone in the vicinity adored the blonde cherubs, who were already good and gentle.

On the morning of the day when the Barbary tartan had been cruising in the gulf of Sant'Eufemia, the day when the second son and the daughter of Maria des Amalfi, Comtesse de Monteleone, disappeared, they had both been seen playing on the threshold of Berta's house...

As she was nearly eighty years old,[22] she had been left her cabin during the depopulation, as abrupt migrations ordered by the Italian government are called. She alone in the region had seen the heyday of the Martorello. The fishermen said that she was a witch. They also said that she had ill-gotten gold in some deep hole: the thirty deniers of treason. When she was far away and could not hear them, they called her the female Judas But they dared not refuse the fine thread that she produced on her spinning-wheel, which they employed for their fishing-nets.

She lived alone. When she went to take hr thread to the shore, her door remained shut. But there were vague rumors in the locale. Smugglers, while scaling the cliff one night in order to send a cargo of French cloth through the Martorello, had heard an argument in Berta's cabin. The old woman made threats; a whip cracked and there as a moan, something like the plaint of a woman.

In addition, the quantity of thread that she brought to the fishermen had seemed for a long time to be too considerable to be the product of her labor alone, even if she tormented her spinning-wheel night and day. But those who had chanced to pass the threshold of her cabin had always found her alone. She lived wretchedly. She bought exactly as much black bread as she needed to nourish herself. There are old people who talk in their solitude.

The new inhabitants of the village paid no heed to the surly and repulsive octogenarian, whom they did not know. The superstitious fear of men of the sea kept them at a distance, and Pietro, the hotelier of the Corpo-Santo, her nearest neighbor, was a halfwit who had quite enough to deal with by virtue of his fevers. Berta was therefore up there on her cliff as if in the middle of a desert. She did whatever she wanted. She had a slave in the middle of a Christian country, a slave she made to work with blows of a whip, in a hole. And if, from time to time, a stray passer-by encountered a phantom in the valley, it was because old Berta's slave had run away.

There were people who gave a name to the phantom, and who said that Maria des Amalfi, Comtesse de Monteleone, having died no one know where, returned by night and prowled around the ruins where the cradles of her children were.

That night, the slave had broken her chain, and Berta was looking for her, whip in hand.

Berta left Manuele lying motionless in the marble chamber and went out in order to go through the ruins again. As she limped through the vegetation she

---

[22] Berta's age increases later in the narrative, but even at nearly eighty, it would have been unlikely for her daughter to be young enough to have served as young Mario's nurse at the turn of the century.

called: "Come on, Mariola, my girl…come on, come on!" Sometimes she interrupted herself, and said: "My nephew Manuele is the last of the family. I saw that one as a child…he'll descend into the earth before me!"

At that moment it was a little past nine o'clock in the evening. The bells of the Corpo-Santo fell silent, but lights could be seen in the windows of the church at the top of the mountain. On the road, the traveling caleche of Comte Lorédan and his sister, now covered and tightly closed, was traveling at a great gallop in the midst of its escort. Pistols and carbines were loaded.

After what had happened, the leader of the men-at-arms had declared that the only safety henceforth was in the town, and Lorédan, in spite of his slight wound, had decided to depart.

Before then, however, the brother and sister had been informed of those who had saved their lives. To the great astonishment of the honest Pietro, Julian and Céleste refused to appear before Their Excellencies. That could have been explained by their timidity, but, but Céleste and Julian had also refused a purse full of ducats that Their Excellencies had ordered to be given to them. That was obviously madness, and Pietro could see that the two children had cracked brains like their father, old Manuele. Personally, the honest Pietro had thought that it would be the height of insolence to take the purse back to Their Excellencies, so, in order not to lack the respect due to Comte Doria and his sister, he had taken charge of their ducats.

Céleste and Julian followed the caleche with their eyes for a long time, and the cloud of dust that its escort raised from the road. When they finally lost sight of it around a bend in the road, Céleste threw her arms around her brother's neck. He remained motionless and bleak.

"My beloved Julian," she said, "I have shed blood. Is an entire life enough to do penance for that?"

Julian was absorbed "Am I a man, then?" he murmured. "My hand trembled…my heart failed…" He interrupted himself, excitedly. "Oh, Céleste, my sister, you did well! If it was a crime, I envy it!"

Céleste bowed her head. Her cheeks were so pale that one might have thought she was dead."

"You still love me, then?" she said. "You're not rejecting me?"

"You saved her!" Julian cried, pressing her to his heart.

There was a long silence between them. Céleste was praying. Julian passed his hand over his forehead.

"Who is he, this Prince Coriolani?" he said, suddenly, without knowing what he was saying.

Céleste looked at him, astonished, for she had never heard that name.

"My sister," Julian said, the blood throbbing in is temples and his eyes on fire, "if the altar was there, I would pronounce my vows at this very moment."

"I would like to be at threshold of the cloister," Céleste retorted. "I would cross it without hesitation."

"Is that true?" Julian exclaimed.

"It's true," Céleste replied.

"The doors of the convent of Catania will open again for you whenever you wish…and when I quit it, Geronimo said to me: 'Child, you'll come back; I'm waiting for you.' Shall we go, my sister?"

Céleste rose to her feet and said: "I'm ready!"

They took one another by the hand. At the same time, the two poor children with wounded hearts said: "The world is bad for us. We need God!"

In the twelfth century, Ugo de Monteleone had built the monastery of the Corpo-Santo for the relics that he had brought back from the Holy Land. It was one of those proud convents with battlements and towers, a few of which still exist in Southern Italy. In the Middle Ages, the Abbots of the Corpo-Santo had had religious and temporal jurisdiction over a large area of the region. The religious organization had soon abstracted itself from the authority of its founder, and Popes had covered the revolt of the vassal monks with their authority on more than one occasion. Nevertheless, the great escutcheon of Monteleone still remained in the center of the stone frontispiece that crowned the interior portal of the church. In spite of time, it could still be blazoned, shared as it was by Bourbon and Montferrat, and being above all the arms of the princes of Benevento, and in the heart, in the *tout du tout*, as the ancient heralds put it, were the proper armories of Monteleone: azure with a golden hearts pierced by two swords in saltire. The supports were two lions; around their mane unfurled the Latin motto: *Agere, non loqui.*

It was said that on the fifteenth of October 1815, Mario Monteleone had been executed at the Castello di Pizzo at nine-thirty in the evening, exactly an hour after Joachim Murat. At that time, the courts and the cloisters of the convent were all black. A somber and silent crowd could be seen confusedly on the parvis preceding the church. When the belfry sounded the fatal hour, nine-thirty, the doors of the church opened, projecting bright light into the courtyard. The voice of the organ rose up and pronounced the first bars of the gigantic funeral symphony that the old master Porpora[23] had composed, it was said, for his own funeral. The sound was prolonged, grave and soft beneath the vaults, while that mute crowd, previously assembled in the courtyard, mounted the steps of the perron.

The convent had been restored, repaired and embellished many times, but the church remained, and still remains, one of the finest examples of the Roman-Byzantine architecture of the end of the twelfth century. The painted murals, the

---

[23] The Neapolitan composer Nicola Porpora (1686-1768). The funeral symphony is fictitious.

polychromy of the entablements and the friezes, the arabesques of the ribs and corbels—in sum, all of the *struttura pittoresca*, as the style imported from Constantinople by the crusaders is known in Italy—had been restored by the munificence of the last Monteleone. The church seemed to have emerged from the hands of the architect.

There was a vast nave with an elevated or elliptical vault sustained by two rows of enormous pilasters, to which fluted columns adhered of the regularly cylindrical form particular to the Byzantine order. The capitals, infinitely varied—from a design crudely recalling the Corinthian form to clusters of bizarre leaves, nameless monsters, impossible palm trees, endless serpents enlaced like monograms—were fully gilded, standing out against a dark red background. Each of the pilasters had its general hue, which, although different, fell into harmony with the neighboring pilasters. The side aisles, pierced by profound chapels, the high arched windows, the sills of which, supported by Ionian columns, passed behind the choir and around the apse.

On the upper level, the windows, forming two arcs in their ensemble, were very high, enclosed in a common arch, ornamented by old Bologna stained glass. But it was the choir and the altar that could pass for models of that art, little changed in is magnificence, which recalled Babylonian boldness and profusion, to the extent that the eye searched for the porphyry basins, idols cover with gems, and monsters of gold and bronze that were also gods.

The lateral paintings of the choir, executed in fresco on a gold background by one of the splendid Greek illustrators who were precursors of Cimabue and Giotto, represented—without perspective, it is true but with incomparable colors—scenes from the Passion of Our Lord. The placement in the tomb completed the backcloth. The sparkling cupola reproduced the dazzle of the Ascension. The twisted columns of the altar, twelve in number, each formed by two interlaced serpents, one in black marble and the other in sanguine porphyry, separated by a gold cable, surrounded the tabernacle containing the holy relics. The tabernacle, which depicted a tomb, and the globe and the cross that surmounted the altar, were black basalt.

In one of the earthquakes that marked the end of the eighteenth century, the church of San Nicolao d'Andri had been engulfed. Since then, the basilica of the Corpo-Santo, open to all, served the area as its parish church. If the number of Christians spread along the coast had been quadrupled, the basilica of the Corpo-Santo would still have been too large for them to fill it.

Thus, the crowd that once encumbered the narrow parvis, disappeared, so to speak, as soon as it passed under the profound and opulent arch of the main door. Men and women spread out in the nave and the side aisles, hung with black. As soon as the organ fell silent a deathly silence remained in the immense vessel in mourning. The crowd that had just entered was composed of two quite distinct elements.

Firstly there were the local people, fishermen, smugglers and indolent villagers habituated to delegating the labor of the fields to their wives and children. Those people had been coming to that nocturnal solemnity for seven years, every autumn, as one goes to see a curious spectacle. Save for the small group of fishermen whose huts flanked the cliff south-west of the Martorello, those people had no link of memory or affection to the name of Monteleone. They had been transplanted. Another category, however, at least as numerous, was composed of travelers with sandals blanched by the dust of the roads. They came from far away, and were, for the most part, former inhabitants of the region expelled after Murat's abortive attempt. They did not mingle with the new residents of the neighborhood. They could be seen in groups in the shadow of the pillars, their cloaks over their cheeks. There were veiled women among them.

The lighting of the nave gave every facility, moreover, to those who did not want to show themselves. The altar was resplendent with the light of an enormous quantity of candles; the chandeliers of the choir were lit; and a double row of standing candelabras surrounded the great catafalque placed before the tabernacle; but that was all. Apart from the balustrade of the choir, there was not a single light in the church.

In the seven years that the ceremony had taken place, the agents of the central police had never made the slightest attempt to hinder it. It was not a seditious act, since Mario Monteleone has perished in consequence of a private treason. The order of clemency had been executed in good time by King Ferdinand. However, under every cloak in the silent groups protected by the shadow of the pillars, there was a weapon.

The catafalque bore a comtal crown and a cloak. There were also the insignia of the Golden Fleece of Spain, the Annunciation of Sardinia and Saint Ferdinand of Naples. On the face of the drape that faced the nave, a series of mystical emblems was embroidered, reminiscent of those employed in freemasonry. The principal emblem was a blacksmith's hammer placed on an anvil, and surrounded by this inscription, incomprehensible to the profane:

$AA^5A^4AA^3E\ E^2AI^2OA^3I^2$
EA^5
$IL^2AA^4MNA^3$
$I^2O\ EA^5$
$A^2I^2A^4$

$RI^2M^2\ INE^2DALA^3NM^2\ EA^3\ M^2I^3\ RI^3A^3II^2$

A black flag, which hung down from the vault, bore in silver letters the Latin motto that had been the dead man's, and which now belonged to the mysterious association whose members called themselves the Companions of the Silence: *Agere, non Loqui.*

At the very moment that the exterior door opened, the monks made their solemn entry into the choir. There were twenty-three of them, including the abbot and the two priors. Their costume consisted of a white robe, secured by a hemp belt. They wore the major tonsure, whose diameter is the line that connects one ear to the other. They were of the Order of the Celestines of the Temple instituted by Jean de Gaëte, whose rule differs little from that of Saint Bruno. Mute and grave, they arranged themselves in their stalls on both sides of the choir. The chaplain, who had fasted all day in order to say the mass of the twenty-second hour, soon appeared, clad in his ornaments of mourning and followed by his two servants.

When the chaplain's foot touched the first step of the altar, six men enveloped in their mantles and masked in black emerged from the shadows. They advanced at a slow pace and arranged themselves in front of the catafalque, standing in front of the balustrade of the choir. Their aspect caused a certain emotion in the semi-darkness in which the audience was drowned. A murmur could be heard, dominated by these words, pronounced in low voices:

"The *cavalieri ferrai*: the Six."

At the introit they knelt down, but their faces remained masked. The mass commenced, bleak and mute, we could say, for the priest and the servants seemed to be moving their lips without producing any sound. In the nave you could have heard a fly in flight.

Outside, there was the great silence of Italian nights, in which nature herself falls silent and sleeps: a silence so complete that the ear vaguely perceived the distant murmur of the sea, which, calm and slow, seemed also to be asleep on the deserted shores for more than a league in either direction.

After the first reading, and while the priest continued to officiate, there was a strange ceremony. A long file of men, enveloped in their cloaks, emerged from the darkness of the lateral aisles. They came one by one to kneel before the catafalque. Those who had been named as the Six covered them in turn with their extended hands decorated with iron rings. Each of the companions only bent his knee, and then got up to cede his place to another. They went to place themselves behind the Six, in two rows, in such a way as to occupy the entire central line of the nave.

In the meantime, the organ, which seemed to be a voice from the other world in the prodigious silence, played mutedly the motif by Fioravanti: *Amici, alliegre, andiamo alla pana...*

That lasted until the elevation. At the elevation, they all put their foreheads to the ground. As they did so, a voice suddenly fell from the vault. Mysterious as the ceremony had been made by design, that was not in the program, for everyone shuddered as they listened to it.

The voice said: "Why are you praying? The tomb is empty. It is not an old man that it has rendered. I have seen Mario younger, stronger, more handsome than in the days of his youth. It is only me who is dead..."

All gazes were directed simultaneously toward the vault, a somber dome of azure from which golden stars hung. A white form was seen, which glided slowly behind the trefoiled arcades of the high gallery. The bell tolled three great strokes, widely spaced. When the eyes turned again to the altar, there was a further astonishment. To the right of the catafalque, a tall man was standing, his back turned to the nave. A black cloak was draped over his shoulders and a velvet mask covered his face.

The Six counted one another. No one was missing from their ranks. Who, then, was the seventh?

IX. The Seventh Ring

Six lamps were burning around a coffin suspended by ropes above a gaping tomb. The seventh lamp was extinct. Its vase was gold. The other six were silver. Each of the six silver lamps bore a name engraved in the metal. The six names were:

Amato Lorenzo.

David Heimer.

Luca Tristany.

Felice Tavola.

Policeni Corner.

Marino Marchese.

The golden lamp bore the name of Mario Monteleone.

The crypt or subterranean church of the Corpo-Santo reproduced exactly, save for the elevation of the vaults, the design of the basilica itself. The suspended coffin occupied a place corresponding to the center of the choir where the catafalque was. In the coffin, there was an embalmed body with a noble visage, mild and calm in the pallor of eternal repose.

The light of the lamps scarcely extended more than a few toises from the bier. In the distance, the eye would scarcely have been able to divine the confused perspective of broad, short pillars. The crypt was deserted, and yet there were moments when one might have thought that movements and murmurs were audible behind that forest of pilasters. At intervals, the voice of the organ arrived like a dull hum.

A few paces from the open grave and the coffin, immediately underneath the altar of the superior church, a black drape was extended. Under the black drape there was an anvil, a blacksmith's hammer and a lump of charcoal. A crucifix dominated that symbolic table. And along the drape ran an inscription in four parts, separated by death's-heads. The characters and the skulls were embroidered in silver. The inscription was configured thus:

I^3R A^6A $I^4I2RI^4A^5I^2$ $IL^2NM^2I^2$ EI^2 DRA^5M^2 A^2N $A^4OI^4A^5I^2$ RI^2 $I^3AI^4A^{5\text{-}}A^4$.

II^2M^2O RA A^2NI^2.

I^3R A^6 A $I^2A^6I^2RI^4A^5I^2$ $IL^2NM^2I^2$ EI^2 DRA^5M^2 A^2N $I^3AI^2A^5I^2$ RI^2 $IL^2AA^4MNA^3$.

II^2M^2O RA $INA^3M^2II^3I^2AII^2$ EA^5 $OA^4AI^3OA^4I^2$.

That was the custom: every year, after the mass of the twenty-second hour, the six knights of the silence came to renew their oath around the remains of the deceased grandmaster.

There was I know not what secret apprehension among them that night when they descended the broad stairway descending to the crypt of the Corpo-Santo. The ceremony had been troubled twice. The mysterious voice that had let obscure and emphatic words fall from the vault remained in their memory like a threat. Another threat: who was the man, whom they had initially mistaken for one of them, who had stood up inside the balustrade beside the catafalque during the last part of the office? Where had he come from? How had he entered into that sealed enclosure, and by what right did he take the place of honor?

There was another thing, stranger still. After the benediction, as the crowd was leaving, the monks of the Corpo-Santo had come to arrange themselves in two files on either side of the unknown man, who, his head held high, had marched in their midst to the sacristy—with the result that the companions massed in the nave had murmured, wondering:

"Have we a grandmaster? Is that the heir of Mario Monteleone?"

And others said: "If he isn't one of the six lords, who can he be?"

That was certainly the thought of the six lords themselves while they passed, silently, under the somber arches leading to the crypt. Each of them said to himself: "There must be a grandmaster." That having been posited, each of them added: "It's me who is the heir of Mario Monteleone."

They went into the subterranean church together and arrived before the coffin without having pronounced a word. Among them there were four black-haired heads, one half-bald and one coiffed with white hair. He was the eldest. He said, in a low voice:

"Salut, lord and father."

And the others responded, in unison: "Salut, lord and father."

"I am," the old man resumed, "Amato Lorenzo, your companion and your servant."

The one whose head was half-bald said, with a pronounced Austrian accent: "I am your companion and servant David Heimer."

Then a sort of giant, whose forehead surpassed the others by a good four inches, said: "I am Luca Tristany, the Captain."

The other three, in turn, said:

"I am Policeni Corner, your cousin."

"I am Felice Tavola, your relative."

"I am Marino Marchese, your friend."

All six then extended their hands above the coffin, each of which had a similar ring on the middle finger: an iron ring with the motto *Agere, non loqui*.

"The seventh year is ending," said Amato Lorenzo. "Between the twenty-second hour of the last day and the new year, the silence is broken for as long as the hand remains extended. The master had the custom of saying to us at this moment: 'What do you want of me?' I am speaking in his name and I say, like him: 'Brothers, what do you want?'"

"To live free," replied the first, the giant Luca Tristany. "I've killed two men...two traitors. That's enough. I ask for the division. I'm retiring from the association, unless you make me grandmaster."

"I've given my time and my fortune," said David Heimer in his turn, "to the vengeance of the master...my task is complete. I want to be master or free, and I ask for the division."

"I'm a relative of Monteleone," Felice Tavola objected.

"I'm a closer relative than you," retorted Policeni Corner.

Amato Lorenzo said: "My white hair can no longer obey!"

"My black hair wants to command!" cried Marino Marchese, laughing. "Brothers, the comedy is played. The seventh year is accomplished. We're all rich. The time to enjoy it has come. Let's cut that rope and let our lord finally repose in the holy earth. Let's make the division and separate. Hasn't the promised land been given? Hasn't the sworn vengeance been accomplished?"

All the mouths were open in order to respond affirmatively, for that was the general sentiment, when a voice rose up, distinct and resonant.

"No," it pronounced, without any of them having spoken.

The six looked at one another through the holes in their masks.

"Who said no?" asked Marchese.

And all the others repeated: "Who said no?"

Then Luca Tristany said, in a provocative tone: "Man or devil, whoever said no is a liar!"

His rude voice was still resonating under the vault when the ropes sustaining the coffin between earth and heaven grated shrilly. Everyone saw the pulley turn around the winch, and the coffin began to descend, slowly...slowly...

At the same time, the black drape was agitated. The Six, plunged into an indescribable stupefaction, saw the silver lamps suddenly go out.

Amid the complete obscurity that reigned for a few seconds, a firm and sonorous tread was heard to strike the paving stones of the crypt at regular intervals. Then the light reappeared. But it was the golden lamp that was burning. The golden lamp was no longer suspended. It was in the hands of a handsome young man with a bold and proud face.

We would have recognized that arrogant bearing, and that eagle eye, the gaze of which was like a steel spike. It was Athol, our adventurer. But something had changed in his physiognomy. A grave emotion must have weighed upon him, for his features expressed a kind of meditation.

At the sight of him, the six recoiled; and, as if they only had one voice, they said: "Who are you?"

Their gazes were lowered toward the coffin, which was already at ground level. Their eyes went from the face of the dead man, pale and immobile, to the other face, radiant with youth. They seemed to be making a comparison—and the comparison led them all to a similar result. Their heads were bowed. There was not one among them who trembled. All of them had, however, given proof of resolution many times in their lives in the seven years that they had been gambling their heads every day.

The coffin passed the level of the hole. The shadow fell across the face of the dead man. Mechanically, the hands of the six remained extended over that cadaver, which sank slowly into darkness.

A seventh hand was extended on the other side of the grave. It was that of the newcomer. Like the other six, that hand had an iron ring on the middle finger—except that the ring was double, and bore by way of a bezel three diamonds disposed in a triangle.

As the coffin disappeared entirely, from the back of the black gaping hole, the newcomer pronounced, in a distinct and vibrant voice: "Adieu, lord and father!"

The six remand mute.

The stranger went on: "Luca Tristany, you're strong. Lift up that marble slab and cover this tomb."

"Who are you to give me orders?" demanded the giant.

"I am *the master*," responded the newcomer. He fixed his brilliant gaze on each of the six knights in turn. "Are you refusing, Captain?" he asked, smiling.

Next to the grave there was, in fact, a marble slab that had been lying in the dust for seven years. The giant measured it with his eyes.

"No man is capable of lifting that," he murmured.

Athol bent down, took the stone in both hands, pivoted it on one of its edges like a door that one is closing, and threw it over the grave. The ground resounded with a loud bang, which reverberated from arch to arch all the way to the back of the subterranean church.

"You're strong," said Luca Tristany, while the others still remained silent, "but while you were holding that stone in two hands, a child could have stabbed you in the back. You're not prudent."

Athol smiled again and pointed with his right hand, where the three diamonds were shining, at the overturned marble slab. Two words were engraved there in black letters: GOD WATCHES.

"We're six," pronounced old Lorenzo in a low voice, "and you're alone. You have the master's ring, it's true, but I've seen jewels stolen from the cemetery. We don't know what you want."

Athol replied; "I am the master. I've come from the cell where Monteleone lived his last hour. I want obedience."

"Are you even an initiate?" asked David Heimer.

Athol turned toward the black drape where the inscription was whose indecipherable characters we have transcribed above. He did that because Luca Tristany, the captain, Marino Marchese and Policeni Corner had all cried at the same time: "Let him read the inscriptions!"

"Up there on the catafalque," said Athol, I read the inscription: *To the grandmaster of charcoal and iron, the Companions of the Silence.*"

"And there, on the drapery?" said Lorenzo, who could not hide his aston-ishment

Athol immediately read: *"There is something stronger than iron; it is faith. There is something blacker than charcoal; it is the conscience of a traitor."*

"The key!" cried David Heimer. "The simple companions know that for-mula. Tell us the key, which is the secret of the masters!"

"No," replied Athol, "I will not tell you the key."

"You don't know it!" came from all directions.

"I know it."

"Then why do you refuse to say it?"

Athol picked up the piece of charcoal from the anvil. Instead of replying vocally, he wrote on the marble tablet of the tomb:

$$RI^2M^2 \; OI^2A^3I^2MA^4I^2M^2 \; I^2INA^5OI^5A^3O!$$

David Heimer leaned over, prey to a singular agitation, and read in a whis-per: "The darkness is listening!"

"He has the key!" said the other five. "In order to write, he must have the key."

"Each of us possesses it," replied David Heimer. "The grand master ought to know more than the knights."

Athol replaced the lump of charcoal on the anvil, seized the heavy hammer with one hand, and smashed the charcoal to smithereens.

"That's what I know," he said, suddenly drawing himself up to his full height. "I haven't come to talk. That's what I'll do to anyone who resists me."

And, as a murmur rose up among the six, Athol added: "I have six daggers for each of yours."

Involuntarily, the cavalieri ferrai plunged their fearful gazes into the distant darkness of the galleries. Some thirty paces away, they saw a somber and mo-tionless circle.

Athol applied the hilt of his Calabrian dagger to his lips. A shrill whistle-blast rang out, to which a grave and calm chorus relied

"We are here, Lord!"

"Well," said Marino Marchese, who was a cheerful fellow, "the darkness does more than listen, it talks. For more than a quarter of an hour I've sensed those worthy fellows behind me. Master, if you're the heir of Monteleone, I con-sent to obey you."

"Me too!" said Policeni and Felice Tavola, in unison.

"Speak," added old Lorenzo, "that we know our new lord."

Athol put his foot on the marble of the tomb. "You can see my face, but you don't know me," he said. "My gaze pierces your masks, however. I know your names, as I know your life. This man is entirely dead. His thought is dead within him. The companions of the holy martyr have become bandits, smugglers and pirates. So much the better! You're my men. Saints have scruples; I'm a bandit like you, an outlaw like you; it's outlaws and bandits that I need."

"To arrive where?" asked Mario Marchese.

"That's my secret," Athol replied. "I'll keep it."

"Are we slaves, then?" protested David Heimer

"Are you not already, since your life is in my hands? Since you are weak and I am strong? Since I am rich and you are poor? You're smiling? Under the pretext of avenging the master you've amassed a great deal. I know that. You were rich; just now you were talking about a division..."

He smiled too, and covered them with his mocking gaze. No one interrupted him again.

"There is in Sicily," he went on, slowly, "between Castro Reale and Santa Lucia, a large isolated house that was once a convent. Do you know it?"

The six had drawn together with a common movement. None of them replied.

"Now you're no longer smiling," Athol went on. "You're familiar, I can see, with that house, which has six masters. It's your treasure-chest, that house; it's your strong-box. Luca Tristany, it's said that the Marquis de Francavilla had diamonds worth six hundred thousand ducats. Trentacapelli was only a millionaire, but Samuel Graff, the secretary of the Duc de l'Infantando had enough to buy a kingdom. Isn't that so, Lord Felice Tavola? A fine vengeance, which brings in more than a hundred thousand gold ounces. Oh, certainly, there's something there to divide. And Lord David Heimer was a faithful guardian. When did you quit the large isolated house between Santa Lucia and Castro Reale, Meinheer David?"

"The day before yesterday, in the evening," replied the bald-headed masked man.

"That was too soon. I know that you had a double task. I know that you were watching for the departure of the son and daughter of Giacomo Doria, on the one hand, and on the other, for the arrival of two poor children, obscure orphans raised in the vicinity of Catania..."

David Heimer made a gesture of surprise.

"Don't be astonished," Athol interjected, coldly, "I've already been occupied with you for some time. And from the moment I began to occupy myself with you, you belonged to me."

"We can see that!" exclaimed Tristany, impatiently. "But why are you talking about the house between Santa Lucia and Castro Reale?"

"We'll get there, Captain. Before then, I have to tell you that if Lorédan Doria and his sister had fallen under your shots, not a single one of you would be leaving this place alive. Don't interrupt me again! Lorédan Doria and his sister are mine! I need them. David Heimer, you've sent twelve of your men in pursuit of them on the Monteleone road: either those men have turned back, or they're dead."

"Half one and half the other," said a voice from the depths of the subterrain. "Six fled, six dead."

"Good, Ruggieri," said Athol, while the *cavalieri ferrai* shivered. "As for the two children of Catania," he continued, addressing David Heimer, "if a single hair falls from either head, you'll answer to me for it with your life. I want no more blood! This tomb is sealed. Your oath is accomplished. Monteleone is avenged."

"You said the opposite a moment ago!" exclaimed Tristany.

"Monteleone is avenged," repeated Athol, "by virtue of the fact that I am taking charge of his vengeance. You are henceforth only the arm of the body of which I am the head; I am taking in hand the lever that the master left you: a lever capable of moving the world, and with which you have done nothing, because it was too heavy for you. You have struck right and left, in accordance with your hatred and your cupidity. After seven years, it needed a man to come to take over your unfinished task and give you alms. Alms, you hear! For your strong-box is in pieces and you only have a void to divide."

"Are you saying that our house has been pillaged?" asked David Heimer, in an incredulous tone.

The others murmured: "We're not children."

"Pillaged and burned," Athol replied. "I too have come from Sicily. When I went past Castro Reale yesterday, I saw the smoking ruins."

"Body of Christ!" cried Luca Tristany. "Only let me know the name of the man who has dared…!"

"It's easy to know," replied Athol, calmly. "It's being spoken aloud. It's Il Porporato."

"Il Porporato!" replied the six with one voice. Then they all fell silent. Even Tristany ceased tormenting the hilt of his dagger.

Athol was still smiling as he looked at them. "It pleases me," he said, "to make you richer and more powerful today than you were yesterday. Come closer. I'll speak for you alone; it's no longer necessary for the darkness to listen."

The six obeyed, mechanically. Athol lowered his voice.

"I have soldiers," he continued, in such a fashion that the mysterious Ruggieri and his companions could no longer hear what he was saying. "I need lieutenants; you fit my bill. I need men as skillful as David Heimer, as brave as Luca Tristany, as elegant as Marino Marchese, as venerable as Amato Lorenzo. I'm taking you to Naples,

"To Naples!" they protested. "That's impossible."

"There are prices on our heads," added David Heimer.

"Yours has five thousand ducats," Athol retired, coldly. "That's advertised. Felice Tavola's also has five thousand; those of Marchese and Policeni, four thousand each. That's very little; they're worth more than that. Lorenzo's has six thousand, the valiant Luca Tristany's ten thousand. In a month, I want Felice Tavola to be the most respectable banker in the Via Toledo. I want Policeni and

Marchese to put the dandies of the Villa Reale to shame. Amato Lorenzo's white hair will do well in the salons of the nobility, and I know no one who can wear a colonel's uniform better than Luca Tristany."

"But..." the six attempted to object.

"Silence when I speak!" said Athol, imperiously. "As for David Heimer, I'll keep him for a confidential employment, but the name of that employment ought not to be pronounced..." He interrupted himself and suddenly became animated. "My companions, you're in good hands, I assure you. Fie to those who said: 'Our work is finished.' Our work is just beginning. It will give birth to light and grandeur. I will give you, instead of these mute solitudes, beautiful Naples, the rich and joyous Naples. I will exchange your caverns for palaces; I shall extend beneath your feet, instead of this blasted and fissured soil, the delightful lawns of our royal retreats, all shaded by myrtles, orange groves and oleanders. In exchange for the depopulated mountains, there is a city of half a million souls. Enter without worry and without fear; you are at home, it is your domain."

"But once again," protested two or three voices, "we can't present ourselves in Naples; there are prices on our heads."

Athol counted them with his gaze. There was a prouder smile beneath his fine moustache. "Two times five, he said, "two times four, plus six, plus ten...that makes thirty-four thousand ducats for your six heads. For mine alone, forty thousand has been promised."

"Forty thousand ducats!" repeated Tristany

"There's only one head in the kingdom worth that price!" cried David Heimer.

And all together: "Who are you, then? Who are you?"

Athol parted his cloak, the flaps of which he threw backwards. He appeared dressed in a tight scarlet garment, laced with the aid of braid of the same color. His calzoni were black velvet, tightened at the ankle by red brodequins.

There was a single exclamation, contained, as if stifled by amazement.

"Il Porporato!"

"By San Gennaro!" added Luca Tristany, first. "I'll follow you to the ends of the earth!"

"A head worth forty thousand ducats!" added Marino Marchese.

"Were you go, Master," the others said, "we will go."

Athol held out his open hand. Each of the six other hands was placed in turn in his, in such a way that the iron rings clinked as they touched. It was the oath of the Silence.

Then Athol sad: "It's the fifteenth of October. A week from today, I give you a rendezvous in Naples, at the Teatro di San Carlo, at nine-thirty in the evening."

"The theater is large—where shall we find you?" asked David Heimer.

"Find the box of His Royal Highness Prince Francis," replied Athol, draping his cloak in order to leave, "and look hard at the man that you see sitting to the right of the heir to the throne."

PART ONE: BELDEMONIO

I. Peter-Paulus Brown of Cheapside

In 1823 there were still sailing ships providing a ferry service between Marseille and Naples. The *Pausilippe*, a pretty Levantine brig whose entire crew spoke the sonorous language that rejoiced the shores of the Canebière, doubled the mole with all sails aloft on a warm June morning and made its entry into the port of Naples.

For more than two hours, there had been a young man on deck who was impeding the maneuvers energetically, occupied as he was in gazing at Naples through a twelve-lens telescope patented by Dawson of Lincoln's Inn Field, "privileged supplier of Her Majesty the Queen and His Royal Highness Prince Albert."[24] The telescope was a respectable size. He carried it in a case under his arm, and every time that voluminous case caught some passing sailor, our man said with a scrupulous politeness and a solemnly comical English accent: "I beg your pardon, formally."[25]

The sailors laughed and cursed him.

Our man was an Englishman, and certainly looked the part. One aggravating circumstance: he had seen the crepuscular blur that the joyful English call daylight for the first time in Cheapside, in the heart of the City of London, between Fleet Street and Poultry. Gentlemen of commerce born in those famous latitudes are three times as English as the rest of the queen's subjects.

So, Peter-Paulus Brown of Marjoram, Watergruel, Brown and Company was aboard the *Pausilippe*. Mrs. Penelope Brown, the fifth daughter of Lysander Marjoram and Jocasta Watergruel, was also there, but in the cabin, where she was seasick.

Jack, Peter-Paulus' manservant, was standing not far from his master, carrying some of the utensils of which the gentleman made use on his travels. Melicerta, Mely, or simply Mel, Penelope's chambermaid, was cutting into four the lemons into which her mistress was biting.

---

[24] This is an unlikely advertisement in 1823, as Queen Victoria did not come to the throne until 1830 and did not marry Prince Albert until 1837.

[25] Whether he is supposedly speaking Italian or English, this character's dialogue is rendered in the original in an atrocious eye-dialect that is supposed to represent French spoken with a cockney accent. Obviously, that is untranslatable, and makes no sense, so I have been content to render his speech in ordinary English.

In the hours when she was not seasick, Penelope Brown was an adequately pretty blonde with a mouth that was slightly too large and enamel eyes. Mely was a tall girl, very well-proportioned. You know Jack, with his red waistcoat and bulldog face. Jack and Peter-Paulus were drawn from a number of exactly similar specimens.

On evening, after the cotton traders' market, Peter-Paulus finds his son William impertinent and his daughter Clary sulking. He perceives a goosefoot in the corner of Penelope Brown's eye. Spleen, that vampire of the banks of the Thames has slid into some corner of the nuptial chamber. It is lying in wait. The children weep, Penelope has a migraine. If Lysander Marjoram happens to drop in, they find him wearisome. Why had they not perceived it sooner? If grandfather Watergruel or Joky—alias Jocasta—the mother visits, they observe with astonishment that they are repeating today what they had said yesterday. Alas, they had been repeating yesterday the quotidian conversation of fifty-five years, but no one had noticed.

That is Italy! One goes to be in a bad mood; one dreams of the restaurants of the Palais-Royal or the corps de ballet of the Opéra. That is Italy. And first thing in the morning:

"Jack!"

Jack arrives with the tea.

"Go to the devil!"

Jack turns on his heel.

"Will you listen to me, wretch!"

Jack pricks up his ears. He has seen attacks of Italy before. At the first word, he knows.

"Jack, go to the foreign bookshop. Buy me a *Pocket Traveler's Guide to Italy*, a road-map of Europe, *The Description of Piedmont, The Antiquities of Rome*, an English-Italian dictionary and the *Storia d'Italia...*"

At this point, Peter-Paulus interrupts himself. He is smiling.

"The *Storia d'Italia*," he repeats, with that familiar accent. "I evidently have a disposition for learning languages!"

Jack has already bought all that for others. He knows where the pharmacist is—I mean the bookshop, which sells drugs for Italy disease. He comes back with a load of books. Peter-Paulus looks at them fearfully; he sends Jack to look for a suitcase in order to lodge that library. Then, putting out his twill coat, he goes to see G. C. W. Drake, S. Stevenson, J. N. Stewart and other cotton merchants, who have already had the disease and have brought back little lumps of Paestum marble. Unanimously, they say to him:

"The best hotels in Italy are the Albergo-Reale in Milan, the Imperial and Royal Hotel of the Two Towers in Verona, the Albergo-Reale in Venice, the Post-House in Parma, the Hotel d'Italie in Florence, the Northern Hotel in Livorno, The Grand Albergo in Bologna, the London Hotel in Rome and the Great Britain Hotel in Naples..."

"What about the curiosities, the sights..."

"In Milan the cathedral, in Verona the amphitheater, in Venice Saint Mark's, in Parma the Dome, in Florence the Campanile, in Livorno the Madonna, and the leaning tower in Pisa. In Bologna the museum, in Rome the catacombs and others, and in Naples, Vesuvius, Pompeii, etc."

"But everyone knows that!" Peter-Paulus Brown objects.

G. C. W. Drake, S. Stevenson and J. N. Stewart turn their backs and go about their business. Peter-Paulus heads for the Diorama in order to get a foretaste of Italy. He is shown Saint Peter's in Rome and the main square in Venice. He looks. He sees himself perfectly under the portal of St. Peter's; he recognizes himself even more clearly at the foot of the Lion Stairway. The painter has put him there, with his long legs, with the promises of his paunch, his narrow shoulders and his small-brimmed hat titled slightly backwards. That is providential. On his return he says to Penelope:

"You're in the second phase of phthisis. Dr. Temple prescribes the air of Italy."

Since early childhood Penelope has dreamed about phthisis. Penelope is one of those frail blondes who eat well at table and lock themselves in the room after dessert in order to devour two pounds of sandwiches.

Having learned with pleasure that she is phthisic, Penelope makes plan to spend all her nights writing her will in order to make Lysander Marjoran, Joky Watergruel and the grandfather dissolve in tears.

Some of Penelope's wills are masterpieces. They are reread in the families in the evening between two games of whist. They are made with pages borrowed in good faith from Young's *Nights*, Hervey's *Tombs* and Lewis' *Cemetery*.[26] The talent is in the filtration of these various ingredients. One could make a fortune editing a formulary of poetic testaments for young ladies. In the absence of such a useful volume, Penelope procured Lewis' *Cemetery*, Hervey's *Tombs* and Young's *Nights* and a few other poems off the graveyard genre

The question is whether William and Clary can be left in the care of Marjoram, Watergruel and company. Make no mistake, when Peter-Paulus feels the symptoms of Italy, he loses all his family virtues at a stroke and becomes a Byronian. He dreams of a brown and pale Marchesa with a jealous dagger. In two years he will return a good cotton merchant, an honest father and a faithful husband. Let the fever pass. At the time, no one can resist it. In his motionless face there is an aftertaste of ferocity. People are afraid of him. The children stay. Penelope weeps. Peter-Paulus makes purchases: an umbrella cane, also serving as a shooting-stick for sitting on and a lifeboat in case of shipwreck; a pair of

---

[26] The full versions of the first two titles are *Night Thoughts* and *Meditations among the Tombs*; the third title is imaginary, although the intended reference is probably to Matthew "Monk" Lewis, Féval's knowledge of English graveyard poetry presumably not stretching as far as a third genuine example.

rubber boots for traversing the Pontine marshes; one of those large purses full of copper coins that one throws at the brigands of Abruzzo; a morocco-leather traveling bag to attach around one's neck; a bag for Madame. A more voluminous bag for Jack and another for Mel; the famous telescope; the hammer necessary for breaking off fragments of ancient architecture; a portable kitchen; a tent; a hammock; several mechanical hats and large quantities of flannel vests. Those vests will be put on successively when one undertakes the ascension of a mountain, because of the gradual decrease in the temperature. Every day, the luggage increases. Finally, the hour of departure arrives; the goodbyes are heartrending.

The French route has been chosen. The ferry to Boulogne is ready to sail. From the height of London Bridge Lysander's cotton handkerchief agitates, while the tender Joky faints on the bosom of grandfather Watergruel. Let us flee these soul-wrenching scenes!

France is traversed. The *Pausilippe*, having departed from Marseille, has been at sea for four days. Penelope, exhausted by vomiting, has not been able to write a single line of her will, but she has eaten twenty-four dozen lemons Peter-Paulus Brown says to her: "That's nothing."

In fact, he is quite well; that is sufficient for his heart. Twelve league from the coast of Naples he has opened his guide-book and aimed his telescope. He is content. His guide-book is not mistaken. Naples is visibly situated on the coast of Italy, below Mount Vesuvius. The city is built in the shape of an amphitheater. That is good. Unfortunately, Vesuvius is not smoking; but it has smoked, and it will again.

Before closing this monograph on Peter-Paulus Brown of Cheapside, we think we ought to add that apart from a passion for lava trinkets and little pieces of stone extracted from monuments. A gentleman generally has two or three obsessions when he undertakes a voyage to Naples; they can vary, but not much. Ordinarily the three ideas are: (1) to observe the curious and little-known mores of lazzaroni; (2) to see a Calabrian brigand; and (3) to burn his soul in the fire of some Byronic passion, and, as a corolla, to receive a thrust of the Marchesa's dagger.

A veritably happy Peter-Paulus Brown is one who, after having slaked that triple passion, can still witness the ruination of some town assassinated by the volcano, but that is not given to everyone. Some have to be content with burning the tip of their cane in lava that is still hot and carrying that cane back as a trophy to Marjoram and Watergruel.

At the moment when the *Pausilippe* doubled the tip of the mole, Peter-Paulus had aimed his telescope at Vesuvius, searching for smoke at the summit of the volcano.

"Look out!" cried a sailor.

The cable of the master anchor was unfurling rapidly. It touched Peter-Paulus' leg, thin and clad in check trousers. Peter-Paulus fell over at the foot of the mainmast. First he looked to make sure that his telescope was undamaged.

Then he felt his ribs attentively. Thirdly, he saluted the sailor with his hand and said: "I beg your pardon…formally."

But his diaphanous nostrils flared abruptly while he amassed an abundant respiration in his chest. He drew himself up to his full height and took off his mechanical hat swiftly in order to look at himself in the little mirror that it had inside it. He thought, with the retrospective emotion of a man who has just escaped a terrible danger: *She didn't see me on the ground! I had already got up again when her head appeared at the top of the stairs…I'm sure she didn't see me.*

If she had seen him, that would have been shocking. I ask you! If she had seen him, legs in the air—him, Peter-Paulus Brown of Cheapside—rolling among the bales and the ropes! A ridiculous position, assuredly, for a gentleman well known in the cotton trade.

But what's up? you're wondering. Is it a matter of the dying Penelope? How little you know Italy in its relationship with Peter-Paulus Brown! Only the ferry, the ferry that brings him to Italy, is sufficient to change his lymph into molten lava. Yesterday's glacier is a volcano today. He needs his Marchesa. There is always a Marchesa on the *Pausilippe*.

From the stairway that leads to the first-class lounge, two women had just emerged. One divined the beauty of the first beneath the thick veil that covered her face. She was tall. Her bearing had pride, but also sadness. Her costume was that of widows at the most rigorous moment of their mourning. On considering that woman carefully, who was advancing over the deck slowly and pensively, there was something extraordinary about her. The sailors stood aside for her with a sort of respect. She did not seem to see that, but when a gaze met hers, she lowered her eyes precipitately. One might have thought that the light hurt them, or that she was experiencing the suffering of excessive timidity.

She appeared to be about thirty or thirty-five years old. The captain had been heard to call her Madame la Comtesse. Throughout the crossing she had kept herself apart in her private cabin and had not spoken to anyone.

The other was a young woman, a friendly and genteel brunette with dark clairvoyant eyes. It was not difficult to see that she occupied the rank of maid-servant in regard to Madame la Comtesse. But there was a Don Quixote in Peter-Paulus Brown, and we know the kind of prism through which that good knight saw his Dulcinea.

Peter-Paulus Brown had provisionally chosen the brunette Paola for his Marchesa. She had no suspicion of it. She found Peter-Paulus very droll. He had the gift of making her laugh out loud.

The captain came, his cap doffed, to meet the woman in mourning. He addressed a few words to her and escorted her to the rear, leaving her there in the charge of the brig's first mate. The mate, a somewhat bronzed but well built Marseillais, exchanged a smiling glance with Paola. Peter-Paulus closed his telescope carefully, even though he was in a bad mood, and put it away in its case.

On the mole and in the Strada Piliero there as a crowd—a Neapolitan crowd, a noisy, loquacious, gesticulating, a crowd that was shouting, stamping its feet and laughing, waiting for the passengers of the *Pausilippe* as if for a prey. At the corner of the Porto Piccolo and the corner of the street leading down to the mole an army of cabs could be seen, arranged in an orderly manner. The coachmen, bare-armed for the most part and seated on their carefully-folded blouses, were looking at the deck of the *Pausilippe* enviously, seemingly saying to themselves: "There's the forbidden fruit."

In fact, in 1823, a ship entering the port of Naples was not at the end of its difficulties. Almost all of the formalities that slowed down the disembarkation in those days have been abolished since.

Three small boats quit the bank simultaneously: the police, the customs and the sanitary inspectors. The Neapolitans remembered the plague in Marseille until 1830 or thereabouts.

As soon as the three boats reached the ship all was confusion on the deck. The police demanded passports, the sanitary inspectors tried to take everyone's pulse, the customs officers made use of their right, which is to turn all the luggage upside down.

Peter-Paulus turned to Jack and asked him for his Italian-English dictionary

"They're flattered when one gives them their titles," he murmured, riffling through the vocabulary swiftly.

"*Doganiere!*" he exclaimed, triumphantly "Signor Doganiere, how are you, Signor Doganiere?"

"Have you anything to declare?" demanded the later, having saluted.

Peter-Paulus riffled through his dictionary rapidly. "*Niente*," he replied. And after further research: "*Assolutomente!*"

The physician and the police inspector approached at the same time. The inspector demanded the passports. Peter-Paulus did not have time to check his title in the dictionary.

"Do you have any contagious disease?" demanded the physician.

At that question, which exceeded the boundaries of the shocking, Penelope turned green. Even Peter-Paulus clenched his fists, at the risk of staring a war between the Kingdom of Naples and the British cabinet.

"You are," he said, in bad Italian, "positively...unpolished." Then, fearing that he had gone too far, he murmured: "I beg your pardon...formally."

Have you any contagious disease?" repeated the doctor.

The veins in Peter-Paulus' temples swelled. "I said," he cried, "you are...an uncivil..."

"What an inelegant clown," said Penelope, at the same time.

Perhaps the doctor did not know English, but he had seen a great many Peter-Pauluses in his time, and he knew full well what was upsetting this one.

"It's a simple formality," he said.

"Oh!" cried the associate of Marjoram Watergruel, effusively. "Do you hear, milady? It was a formality!"

He seized the doctor's hands. "Look!" he said, opening his mouth were to display his long, strong teeth. Look at milady's teeth too…and Jack's, and the little maidservant's. All is proper…formally!"

They were in fact, twenty eight English teeth, capable of devouring a bull alive.

The doctor seemed content with his examination. Penelope wrote in her notebook: *Naples, teeth visited by health service, inconvenient and tyrannical.*

In the meantime, Peter-Paulus repeated, in order to calm his own suscepti-bilities: "Pure and simple formality."

Someone touched his shoulder lightly from behind. It was the police of-ficer, who said, in French and in a whisper: "Why isn't Gregory aboard?"

"Oh!" said Peter-Paulus, stupefied. "Did you say Gregory?"

"Is it you who has the Punjab?"

The doctor leaned over as he passed close to Penelope and murmured in her ear. "You'll be picked up this evening at eight o'clock."

And he drew away rapidly.

II. Riot on Board

While Peter-Paulus Brown as trying to understand the significance of those mysterious words and Penelope was following the course of her thoughts with a dreamy gaze, there was suddenly a great commotion at the front of the *Pausilippe*, which, in spite of the concluded visits, did not appear to proceed from the disembarkation of the passengers. A few minutes ago, an armoried carriage had stopped between the Teatro del Fondo, which is at the tip of the Castello Nuovo and the quay of the harbor. An elegantly dressed man had descended from it. He had taken a boat under the mole and had been rowed as far as the side of the *Pausilippe*, which he was just boarding. The captain had saluted him from a distance with a respectful haste. The customs officers, the sanitary inspectors and the police had similarly doffed their caps as they went past his boat.

The sanitary inspectors, the customs men and the police had climbed aboard as best they could. For the newcomer, one of the mobile ramps garnished with velvet had been deployed, which are only used in the navy or high-ranking officers. That was too much honor, it appeared, because the newcomer, young, nimble and equipped with sea-legs, leapt on to the deck without touching it. The captain was waiting for him, bare-headed.

"A fine young dandy!" the sailors murmured, between themselves.

The newcomer surely merited that qualification, given the supreme fashionability of his attire, and the gracious and slightly effeminate elegance of his manner, but he merited better still. A single glance sufficed to judge that. He certainly possessed, it is true, the ill-defined quality that badly brought-up men and chambermaids call "distinction," but everything about him was so far above that vulgar advantage that we only note it for the sake of memory.

He was handsome, with the great and audacious beauty that speaks of heroism or genius. Those eyes, now so calm and soft, must burn terrible in moments of passion. Power has its sign, visible, or at least sensible, even when it is dormant. That dandy, as the mariners of the *Pausilippe* called him, with white hands and silken hair, had not taken ten steps along the deck before the mariners changed their tone in his regard.

"At times, that one has red blood," said the helmsman.

"Damn!" said the second lieutenant, a man or garlic nourished on spices and bouillabaisse. "That fellow's all muscle!"

And others said: "Must be proud of that...he's hard!"

"She hasn't suffered from the voyage?" the newcomer asked the captain, holding out his hand.

"No, Prince," replied the latter.

"Well!" said the second lieutenant. "He's a prince!"

The two unknown women had stood up as the stranger approached. He took the hand of the Comtesse in order to raise it very respectfully to his lips. In spite of the thickness of her veil, an extraordinary emotion could be read in the beautiful face of the latter.

Paola was emotional too, but in her own fashion; her cheeks were as red as cherries. She lowered her gaze slyly, and a mischievous smile was born around her pretty mouth.

"I see, Madame," said the stranger to the veiled lady, "that Dr. Daniel has told you what you needed to know. This mourning-dress announced it to me."

"I know everything," stammered the passenger, who dissolved in tears, "everything that Dr. Daniel could tell me. It's you, Monsieur, who will tell me the rest, and make me the happiest or the most unfortunate of women."

The young stranger kissed her hand for a second time. "Repose today," he said, "business tomorrow."

"What!" cried the passenger. "I have to wait until tomorrow!"

"I have the letter of Dr. Daniel's prescriptions," replied the handsome young man. Then he added: "If you care to follow me, I'll take you to your palace."

"My palace!" repeated the astonished passenger.

Her interlocutor's eyes said: *Silence. We're being observed...*

She fell silent. He offered her his arm, and they went through the groups of passengers.

"Are they going to go away?" asked a fat merchant.

"Pity!" said a soap manufacturer from Marseille. To the captain, he said: "Are you going to let us go?"

The handsome cavalier, his companion, and Paola, who was laughing as she listened to the murmurs of the crowd, arrived at the front of the ship, where the boat was waiting.

The captain, not a little embarrassed, made a sign from a distance to two sailors, who moved in front of the young stranger, saying: "No one can leave."

"Good!" exclaimed the soap-manufacturer. "If I'm waiting, the King can wait!"

The groups of merchants clapped their hands

"What does this signify, Captain Bergasse?" asked the young stranger, turning to the commander.

The later came forward, cap in hand. "Prince," he said, "the regulations don't permit any exceptions."

"Not even for me, my lad?" the Marseillais soap-manufacturer put in.

"Not even for you!" said the other merchants, supportively.

And Peter-Paulus added: "That impertinent personage doesn't even have a case as exceptional as mine—I'm an English subject."

Those who had the honor of hearing Peter-Paulus Brown of Cheapside pronounce the words "English subject" understood the sublime emphasis of the ancient *Sum civis romanus*.[27]

The crowd of passengers had, however, tightened its circle in order to enjoy the confusion of the dandy who had thought that he could open a door closed to so many Marseillais merchants. The soap-merchant enameled his joy with all the flowers of the language born on the odorous banks of the Canebière.

In the midst of all that noise, the young stranger pronounced a name in a low voice: "Cucuzone!"

The cables of the port bulwark were seen to relax abruptly; a large hand touched the rail, and a tall fellow with a tanned face wearing the costume of the port oarsmen fell on to the deck like a ball.

"Excellency?" he said standing up in front of the stranger.

The audience fell silent, marveling at the savage agility of that odd individual.

"A very nimble acrobat!" observed Peter-Paulus, admiringly.

"Do you have the ticket?" the young dandy asked the mariner.

The latter took a piece of paper out of his bosom, which he handed to the captain.

"Let him pass," the latter immediately ordered, adding, with a respectful salute: "Prince, you'll pardon me for having done my duty."

The boat was resting against the side of the *Pausilippe*. Cucuzone leapt aboard with a single bound. Then the ladder was placed, and the young stranger helped his two companions down. Immediately, there was an uproar.

Peter-Paulus entered into such an agitation that Jack could not remember ever having seen him in such a state. He clenched his fists, he inflated his cheeks; his forehead and his ears, as red as blood, stood out amid the insipid yellow of his hair. He repeated: "I want to go...to go right way...it's intolerable! The torture of Tantalus! I'm an English subject, you hear?"

He mingled with the yapping crowd of passengers. The other crowd, swarming on the quays, laughed wholeheartedly, encouraging the riot.

Meanwhile, the boat was rowing forcefully toward the jetty, carrying the prince and his two companions, only one of whom turned round to address a mischievous glance at the passengers of the *Pausilippe*. Peter-Paulus took account of that glance, and his wrath increased. Among the cries that filled the deck of the ferry, the guttural voice of the cotton merchant could easily be distinguished, repeating his patriotic protest:

"I'm an English subject!"

The boat reached the quay. The prince, the veiled woman and Paola climbed into the armoried carriage, which departed at a gallop, and disappeared behind the Ministry of State.

---

[27] I am a citizen of Rome.

110

III. The Strada di Porto

Half an hour later, Peter-Paulus was installed in the Great Britain Hotel. An hour later he was wearing a costume that he had bought expressly in order to maintain his incognito in his travels, and, emerging quietly from the hotel, he went past the Villa Reale and up the Rua Santa Caterina, and then the Strada di Chiaia, in order to regain the vicinity of the port. It was after six o'clock, and the night was beginning to get dark. It was February.

Peter-Paulus marched with a long stride. One thought dominated him: he wanted to find the Marchesa. Peter-Paulus had letters of recommendation for the high dignitaries of the police. With a little help, in a few hours he would be able to discover the retreat of the woman he had chosen among all of them to adore Byronically.

Without having asked the way, he arrived at the Ministry of State, where the administration of the police was. The office was closed, of course. He went into the concierge's lodge and informed him that he desired to speak to Signor Spurzheim on a matter of the utmost importance. The concierge told him that Signor Spurzheim, who had been ill for four days, lived in a house in the Piazza del Mercato on the far side of the city.

Peter-Paulus had a cousin who was a physician employing sudopathic treatments.[28] He set off for the Piazza del Mercato, saying to himself: *Since the director is ill and I have a cousin who is a physician, I shall import sudopathy into this distant country.*

The vicinity of the mole and the Teatro del Fondo was deserted. There was no performance that evening, but as Peter-Paulus turned the corner of the Post Office in order to plunge into the old city, a truly extraordinary spectacle slowed down the vivacity of his pace.

The noise, the movement, the chatter, the cries, the jostling and the laughter that had extended along the mole when the *Pausilippe* had arrived seemed to have emigrated from that part of the city and to have been multiplied by a hundred. Thousands of lights could be seen shining and running around like will-o'-the-wisps. Fires were burning and smoking here and there in the middle of the road. At each gust of wind, an odor of cooking arrived, increasingly strong and

---

[28] Sudopathy [literally, sweat therapy] originated in the 1820s as an offshoot of hydrotherapy, which treated diseases externally by swathing the patient in wet cloths; it was pioneered by the German surgeon Vincent Priessnitz, who opened a clinic in Graefenberg in 1829, where he laid claim to an impressive clientele. Its fashionability was limited and brief. There are not known to have been any sudopaths in England in 1823.

penetrating. Peter-Paulus stopped under a street light and immediately riffled through his *Guide*.

The map indicated his position. He was at the entrance of the Strada del Porto, a long, fairly wide and irregular street poorly paved with slabs of lava, which enters profoundly into the old city, going around the commercial port and the small port at a distance of three or four streets. In 1823 that road led via the Vico Piccolo and the Sotto-Portico of San Pietro, to the principal entrance to the Castello-Vecchio, which was demolished in 1831.

Toward the entrance is the celebrated Fountain of the Three Virgins, near which Tommaso Anniello, upsetting his display of fruits and fish on 7 July 1647, raised the standard of revolution against Spain. It is said that the mascaron of the fountain represents the head of Masaniello.

This is what Peter-Paulus found in his Guide on the subject of the Strada di Porto:

This street, very lively and busy, full of open-air kitchens where poor people obtain their nourishment, offers a curious spectacle to strangers. Before going into it, it is prudent to put one's watch and jewelry in a safe place.

Peter-Paulus, always docile to the advice of his Guide, immediately sent the chain to join his watch in the depths of his fob-pocket. He put his brilliant cufflinks into his waistcoat pocket, fastened his twill coat from top to bottom and, thus armed, valiantly confronted the dangers of the street in question.

After a hundred paces he found himself drowned in the middle of a crowd so noisy that he was tempted to plug his ears.

The crowds of London are perhaps denser and certainly more brutal; one receives much sharper jabs of the elbow in the chest there, and more profound digs in the ribs. The crowd that presses silently during business hours on the sidewalks of the City is inhumane and homicidal; it stifles women and tramples children and passes on without looking back; but those thousand mouths do not screech, laugh and sing all at the same time. It has the advantages of the chronic sadness that is the repose of London; it keeps quiet.

In Paris, the crowd is noisier, but the crowd is benevolent. If it chances to crush someone, it is in despair. It offers twenty thousand arms to carry a sick child to the nearest pharmacy.

We do not hesitate to say, however, that Neapolitan crowds take the palm, as much by their gaiety as their amicability. They swarm miraculously, they shove artfully, fall, get up again, undulate, buzz, swirl, stagger and cackle in a truly inimitable fashion.

Among all Neapolitan crowds, the one in the Strada di Porto is renowned for the most jovial humor. It is a gastronomic crowd. Every evening, there is a banquet there with ten thousand guests, in which one does not see a single place setting. That shrill and comical feast is prolonged among the lazzi, and continues until eleven o'clock or midnight, depending on the season. Hundreds of fairground restaurants, doing their cooking *coram populo*, actively dispute public favor. The soup is on one side, the main courses on the other, the roasts a little further on. The desserts are held over the heads of merchants with bold and cheerful voices.

Only one stain soils the glory of that happy street, a rather large stain, which offends both the sight and the sense of smell of strangers, and that is the gutter.

Out there, the gutters do not flow. Whatever one gives them, they keep. They are little asphaltic lakes full of viscous liquid, yellow or black, which would certainly give the plague to the mighty porters of Les Halles. The filth of the times of the Spanish domination is still there. That mud could occupy the leisure hours of an antiquarian. As for the quality—first class! It is the quintessence of infection.

Peter-Paulus did not excite, to begin with, a very great attention. It was not like the street of the mole that morning. People go to the Strada di Porto to eat and amuse themselves, not to run after milords.

In any case, Peter-Paulus had his disguise—for an Englishman cannot undertake such an expedition without disguising himself profoundly by means of a wig and blue-tinted spectacles. Peter-Paulus resembled, make no mistake, those English petty officers who physiognomy is known the word over. What he called his "helmet" was a mariner's rubber-coated taffeta cap. It is rare that the port of Naples does not have some English ship in dock full of worthy men dressed exactly as Peter-Paulus was at that moment.

Everyone around him was making his purchases and eating them on the move, seasoning the lazzi repast. From time to time a small war broke out with slices of melon for missiles, but it was a trivial matter and Peter-Paulus was only hit in the face once.

"Very curious!" he murmured, wiping his face.

He moved slightly apart, however, and leaned on a boundary-marker thirty paces from the Fountain of the Three Virgins in order to consult his Italian dictionary on the subject of the multitude of cries that was deafening him. There was a street-lamp above his head. Nearby was a group mostly composed of women. They were all talking at the same time, and Peter-Paulus leafed through his dictionary furiously. He thought he understood that it was a matter of the imminent execution on the scaffold of a brigand, and that the brigand was named Baron d'Altamonte.

What a magnificent name for a brigand: Baron d'Altamonte! To arrive in Naples just in time for that!

The women were saying: "It's tomorrow!"

"Is he a handsome man?"

"Superb!"

"That's not bad! The last one was hunchbacked."

And they hurled their sales pitch at full volume over the heads.

"*Ostriche!*" they cried—meaning oysters—"*ostriche de Fusaro!* As fresh as roses!"

Peter-Paulus searched for *ostriche* in his dictionary, but was distracted before he had found it:

"*Lasagne d'Amalfi! Lasagne fondanti!*"

"*Ravioli dulci!*"

"*Macaroni di grano duro!*"

They are three kinds of pasta dear to Neapolitan palates; Peter-Paulus abandoned *ostriche* in order to search for *ravioli*,

"*Frittela calida! Frittiata! Frittume!*"

"*Carbonchiosi! Carnesseche! Carotate! Cestole! Scottate! Eselate! Megliacie!*"

Hot fritters, omelets, fries, grills, salads, stews, cutlets, cheeses, honey conserves, tarts, etc. Poor Peter-Paulus abandoned one to follow another and found nothing at all.

The tumult was increasing at every moment, and it seemed that the joyous turbulence of that population would soon surpass all limits. Suddenly, at the moment when the flame of a cooking-fire flared up brightly, stimulated by grease falling from the grill, the base of the fountain was illuminated as if by daylight, and Peter-Paulus saw a group that he had not yet noticed.

It consisted of three men, one of whom was leaning nonchalantly against the wall under the niche of one of the three Madonnas, the second sitting on the rim of the basin and the third lying down like a dog at the feet of the other two.

The first wore the costume of a fisherman, the only costume that was still clear-cut in Naples. He had tight calzoni of red wool, a round jacket and a belt. His red cap allowed the disorderly curls of his chestnut-blond hair with tawny reflections to escape. The man was magnificent. A painter would have wanted to seize his pose, nonchalant and virile at the same time. There was a poetry in his indolent pride so perfectly Italian that the sight of him made one think involuntarily of the superb types that art has conserved for us.

It was the head of which Veronese was fond, perhaps with more character and more effect. Illuminated at it was by that firelight coming from below, the protrusions of his aquiline features, of an extraordinary purity, were violently shadowed. The cap framed the powerful forehead squarely, which radiated intelligence. The neck, which supported that fine head with a kind of indolence, evidently had muscles of iron beneath its gracious contours. The torso was a composite of vigor and elegance. Tight calzoni had never designed a better-proportioned pair of legs.

But all that, the intelligence and the power, was casual. The man was relaxed, in the cherished idleness of southern populations. And all of it was dominated by the quality that we mentioned in the prologue of our story, the color, shadow or radiance known as insouciance: the insouciance that, in our meaning, is strength itself, or at least the consciousness of strength: faith in oneself. His gaze was staring ahead of him without seeing. His thought was only betrayed by the pensive smile that was playing over his fine lips.

The second man, the one sitting on the rim, had something of the mariner about him. He was short, thickset and broad, and he was smoking a meerschaum pipe voluptuously, the bowl of which hung down between his knees. He too wore a cap, but his short-cropped hair formed a sharp point between his eyes.

When our zouaves, those terrible killers, are confronted by the enemy and do not have time to shave, a similar point often appears beneath their turbans.

The third, finally, did not have any form or costume, to tell the truth. He was a bizarre mass covered in rags. He was lying in an impossible attitude, which a clown at our Olympic Circus could not have maintained for thirty seconds. His arms and legs, oddly tangled, eternalized I know not how, took away any human appearance from his body, rolled into a ball. His face, hidden under one of his arms, could not be seen.

Such was the group that emerged suddenly from the shadows and appeared momentarily to the astonished eyes of Peter-Paulus Brown. That group attracted his attention greatly.

A Peter-Paulus Brown, considered as a type or summary of various inhabitants of Cheapside afflicted with Italy disease, has almost always extracted from the *Guides* a certain sum of artistic knowledge. He knows that Italy is the fatherland of Raphael, Giotto and Titian. As he sets forth on the ferry that descends the Thames, he is not far from having a taste for the arts.

Peter-Paulus examined that group as an artist, and was content: content with himself, principally, because of the good taste he was showing. But of the three individuals, the one who struck him most, incontrovertibly, was the one who was lying at the feet of the handsome fisherman. He was an enlightened admirer of the indiarubber men and contortionists of Astley's Circus, but he had to confess that he had never seen anything as remarkable.

The flames died down; the ground reentered into darkness. The Sabbat round of cheerful macaroni-eaters redoubled the petulance of its movements

Peter-Paulus had almost forgotten the motive for which he had left the hotel, so occupied was he with that spectacle, described as "curious" by the *Guide* itself. He observed with a mixture of pride and astonishment the mores of that foreign land.

Two men passed rapidly before him, heading toward the upper city. Both were holding their cloaks in front of their faces. As they went past one of the two men pronounced words that Peter-Paulus could not grasp precisely, and then they went on.

The murmur of the two men gave Peter-Paulus an incredible desire to know. In any case, the Italian phrase contained a name that was sufficient in itself to make him feverish, a name that was in his Guide: the name of the most celebrated brigand in Abruzzo. The two strangers had been talking about Il Porporato.

He set to work. With the aid of his dictionary, he translated the sentence he had overheard. It was this:

"Il Porporato won't let him die; he swore by the Silence he'd rather scale the walls of the Castello-Vecchio himself."

IV. The Astonishments of Peter-Paulus Brown of Cheapside

Peter-Paulus was sure of his translation. The dictionary had given it to him word for word, and the Italian sentence remained engraved in his memory. What mystery there is in a single sentence! It was doubtless a matter of the Baron d'Altamonte whose execution was fixed for the following day. That terrible Porporato was in Naples, then! And what was the oath of the Silence?

The English mind is not easy to start in motion, and the atmosphere of the City of London does not develop the love of the fantastic. However, the fantastic of a certain genre—brigand poetry, if is permissible to express it thus—grips the British imagination forcefully. Ann Radcliffe, the celebrated cantor of so many bandits, was English.

A Peter-Paulus has devoured the Gothic novels of Ann Radcliffe; it is part of his education. In traveling to Italy, he always nourishes the slight hope of encountering in some corner the mysteries of the castle of Udolpho.

A Penelope also thinks about brigands, but she sees Rinaldo Rinaldini in a black suit and freshly gloved. Thus costumed, Antonio Rocca abducts her and takes her to a cavern in Apulia, where he shows himself particularly honest and gallant in her regard.

It was no longer a matter of the Marchesa! Peter-Paulus was even more anxious to demand the aid of the senior employee of the police to whom he had been recommended, but no longer to rediscover the Marchesa. The Marchesa had sunk. It would have been necessary, in order to return her to the surface, that she be unexpectedly mixed up in this new and tenebrous intrigue.

What Peter-Paulus wanted was the support of Signor Spurzheim, in order to be able to get into Baron d'Altamonte's cell; it was also to denounce the presence of Il Porporato in Naples and give an account of the words that chance had allowed him to overhear. He closed the dictionary and the *Guide* swiftly, in order to set a course for the upper city.

As he was about to set forth, the two men with the raised cloaks appeared again ten paces away. He became all ears. The two men seemed to be examining the crowd with a gaze that was more than curious. Some people saluted them; others got out of their way.

A third person, exactly similar to them, joined them just as they were about to go past Peter-Paulus again

"The chief they have tonight," said the newcomer, "calls himself Beldemonio..."

He was about to continue. The other two grabbed his arm, and all three stopped dead, looking at Peter-Paulus attentively. He heard one of them say: "That's the description."

The idea that they were policemen in disguise gripped him, and he was about to show them his passport when an object—a hand, he thought at first—fell on his shoulder. At the same time, a voice said to him, jovially: "Don't move, my friend, you'll bring me down. There! We're there! Thanks."

He turned round and saw that the object was not a hand but a foot. He had served as a support in order for a tall boy dressed in a miscellaneous fashion, to climb up to the cornice of a semi-ruined door. And that boy thanked him. Until then, it was quite simple, but the three strangers had disappeared again.

From the height of his improvised platform, the tall boy suddenly shouted in a tenor voice that dominated the surrounding noises: "Very exact and very interesting *notizie* regarding the pretended Baron d'Altamonte, captured by the royal police and condemned to death by order of the high court. His life, his crimes, his gallant adventures...documents proving that the bandit is the veritable Porporato of the mountains of Abruzzo...eight pages printed with care by Ducchino of the Street of the Booksellers, with a portrait of the brigand and supportive evidence...for sale at two grains!"

Before the boy had finished reciting that lesson an opaque and agitated circle had already formed around him.

"To me, Franconi! To me! To me!" people were shouting from all directions.

"To me!" said Peter-Paulus too, holding out a silver coin.

Franconi, being too busy, neglected to return the change. For his silver coin, Peter-Paulus had a small piece of wrapping paper folded four times, which did, in fact, produce eight pages. On the first of those pages was a thick ink-stain: the portrait of Baron d'Altamonte, alias Il Porporato. The veritable Porporato, for the royal police had already caught and the tribunals had already condemned four or five Porporati. The day after the execution, the diabolical Porporato had the custom of making some spectacular exercise of his métier, in order to prove that he was quite well, in spite of the work completed by the executioner.

"To me! To me! To me!"

The sale was going well. All arms were extended, and Franconi's pocket was swelling rapidly.

Placed in the center of the circle and captive of the crowd, Peter-Paulus tried to read his notice, but could not. The rags of poor appearance that are sold in the evening in the streets of Paris under the name of *canards* are Elzévirs by comparison with their Neapolitan brothers. Not being able to read, Peter-Paulus reflected. We know how commerce in cotton elucidates the mind. Peter-Paulus said to himself:

I'm evidently at the center of an ocean of mysteries. How can the tenor of this pamphlet be conciliated with the words pronounced before me by the two strangers who were passing by, and who, in parentheses, must belong to the police or the most dangerous class of society. If Baron d'Altamonte is Il

Porporato, it follows that Il Porporato is presently under lock and key, and is to be executed tomorrow. In that case, how can Il Porporato have promised, under the oath of the Silence—which seems to me to be a terrible oath—to scale the walls of Castello-Vecchio and free Baron d'Altamonte? There's obviously something about this that I can't grasp, and the shortest way is to go straight to the director of the police...

But the human wall tightened round him.

"To me! To me! To me!" was shouted incessantly.

And as soon as the sale began to slow down, Franconi's voice resumed with a new fervor: "Very exact and very interesting *notizie* regarding the pretended Baron d'Altamonte, captured by the royal police and condemned to death, etc., etc."

At that moment a cold hand touched the hand of Peter-Paulus and tickled it gently on the palm.

The associate of Marjoram of Watergruel did not like pleasantries. He turned round abruptly and saw before him a man of his own height, who was wearing a costume almost identical to his own. The man had his nose in the turned-up collar of his jacket, and his eyes were hidden by blue-tinted spectacles.

"It's hot around the Castello-Vecchio," the individual said to him, in a confidential tone.

Those words were pronounced in Italian. Peter-Paulus' first impulse was to consult his dictionary, but he was losing his footing in the midst of the torrent of adventures; he preferred to reach the bank, and replied in a surly tone: "I don't understand you."

"What?" said the stranger. "Do I have to dot the *i*s...?" and he added, leaning toward our gentleman's ear: "Iron is strong and charcoal is black..."

This time, instead of replying, Peter-Paulus pushed him away rudely. The other looked at him for a moment with a stupefied expression, turned his back, and disappeared into the crowd.

At that moment, there was a disturbance in the circle surrounding Franconi. A competitor had just established herself—it was a woman—on the neighboring boundary marker. She shouted in a contralto voice: "Official notices and the only ones authorized by the Ministry of State, concerning the brigand Felice Tavola, the so-called Baron d'Altamonte, also known under the name Il Porporato. Complete list of men he has killed and women he has abducted. Precise information regarding his band...the names of his accomplices...where to find the place and time of his execution, with his accurate portrait, drawn from life by one of our fashionable artists...eight printed pages...fine paper...five *calle!*"

Thanks to the oscillations of the crowd, which was abandoning Franconi to race toward La Marinaia, as the new pamphlet-seller was being hailed from all directions, Peter-Paulus was able to free himself. He found himself carried very close to her by a movement of the crowd, and extended his hand to obtain a notice. La Marinaia looked at him intently. Instead of giving him his notice, she grabbed his hand and drew him toward her.

"Why aren't you at the Maddalena?" she murmured. "Have you seen Beldemonio? It's nearly time…all the Englishmen are out there."

The Englishmen! That was another matter! There were Englishmen mixed up in this! What damnable conspiracy was being woven in the Strada di Porto, amid the thick smoke of these open-air kitchens, in the midst this deafening and hilarious joy?

Was the crowd, which was becoming more petulant and more excited by the second, part of the conspiracy? Peter-Paulus was inclined to believe so. He was now looking anxiously at the people surrounding him. He found their faces menacing. That laughter no longer appeared to be honest to him, and the gaiety seemed counterfeit. Behind that orgy of hilarity there was a mine ready to explode, with the consequence that Naples was positively between two volcanoes, of which Vesuvius was the less dangerous.

However, his efforts to pierce the crowd and run to the police superintendent relented. He allowed himself to go with the flow, so to speak, plunged into profound meditation.

At that moment, he found himself under an obscure portico some ten paces from the Fountain of the Three Virgins.

"Finally!" exclaimed a youthful and decided voice close by. "Someone to talk to! I've been searching for Beldemonio for a quarter of an hour."

An arm was passed familiarly beneath his own. What now? This time, it was something so extraordinary that Peter-Paulus nearly fell over backwards.

The woman who had just taken his arm was young, amicable and lively in appearance, and wore the costume of Neapolitan young women of the lower class. She had a basket of oranges in her hand. Beneath her little fur hat, garnished with black lace, which covered luxuriant hair, Peter-Paulus saw the laughing eyes of his Marchesa shining. That orange-seller was his Marchesa. He shivered so abruptly at that sight that he let go of his arm.

"What's the matter, Sansovina?" she said.

Then seeing that her companion was no longer moving, she snatched his cap away with a rapid gesture, Peter-Paulus' yellow hair was revealed, crowning his alarmed visage. The Marquesa was seized by a fit of mad laughter.

"The goddam from the ferry!" she cried, holding her sides. "The real goddam!" Then, suddenly becoming serious: "Why the devil have you raised your collar?"

Peter-Paulus felt drunk. He thought he heard someone nearby say, in French: "La Fiamma! We've been looking for you!"

He closed his eyes in order to collect himself. When he opened them again, the Marchesa was no longer beside him. A moment later, however, by a flash of light from a nearby cooking-fire, he saw the Marchesa again, at the foot of the fountain, with the three men forming the group that he had noticed earlier. The handsome fisherman had his back to the wall, the mariner was sitting on the rim and the prodigious acrobat was lying on the lava. At that moment, the face of the handsome fisherman was brightly illuminated.

Peter-Paulus started walking toward him mechanically and unconsciously. He rubbed his eyes; he thought he was dreaming. It was not the first time he had seen that proud face with the bold and aquiline features. It was the face of the unknown man, the dandy who had come aboard the *Pausilippe* that morning while the police, the customs men and the health inspectors had been deliberating while breakfasting, and in favor of whom a ticket of leave had been given ahead of all the passengers, without excepting Peter-Paulus himself, an English subject: the Prince, as the captain of the ferry had called him, respectfully; the man who had taken away the woman in mourning and the Marchesa! A prince in the morning, a fisherman in the evening, falling out of an armoried carriage into the fetid mud of the Strada di Porto. What was behind it all?

The reader will perhaps be wondering what effect the sight of his Marchesa in such company had on Peter-Paulus. For anyone who knows a little about Cheapside, cotton, Byronism and the mores of Italian brigands, the answer is quite simple.

First of all, the more unexpected, odd and eccentric the behavior of a Marchesa is, the more she enters into her role as a daughter of Satan, the more she is idolized. What would be the point of a Marchesa who behaved like a housewife and mother?

Make no mistake: however slightly a Penelope stumbles in the path of convention, it must be said, one would like to put a rope around her neck and sell her for a shilling in Smithfield Market. But every new slip makes the Marchesa more interesting. The Marchesa can caper about and walk on her hands, and still retain the fatal aureole that makes her Byronian.

Meanwhile, the pretty orange-seller was talking to the fisherman with vivacity. The latter had not forsaken his indolent pose, but his eyes were shining. The man with the meerschaum pipe, ceasing to swing his dangling legs, was advancing his neck curiously in order to hear better. Even the clown, unwinding the strange coil that his body had previously formed had raised his head like a snake.

Suddenly, the eyes of the handsome fisherman chanced to fall upon Peter-Paulus, who was still there, staring at him with all his immobile might, his mouth wide open. The fisherman touched the spirit Paola on the arm and whispered something in her ear. Paola turned round. Immediately, she gave voice to the frank, noisy laughter that the sight of Peter-Paulus seemed to have the privilege of procuring her.

The fisherman pronounced a few more words in a low voice. The clown came to his feet, lazily. He was a tall, handsome fellow, admirably limber, who must have made the perilous leap marvelously. The mariner slid off the rim of the fountain, as if regretfully, and put his pipe in his pocket. Peter-Paulus scarcely paid any attention to those preparations, so intent was he on the avid contemplation of the two principal characters in the scene: the fisherman prince and the Marchesa orange-seller. He was only able to observe that the mariner and the clown had disappeared.

There was a slight movement in the crowd.

Peter-Paulus heard a phrase pronounced several times: "*Alla girella...! Alla girella...!*"

Instinctively, he opened his faithful dictionary. But at the very moment when his dictionary informed him of the various meanings of the word *girella*, the crowd appeared to take responsibility for offering him a literal and striking translation.

Turnstile, reel, pulley, weather-vane, the dictionary had replied.

A shoulder touched Peter-Paulus' right shoulder without overmuch shock; but at the same time, another shoulder touched his left shoulder very gently. The first impact had came from in front, the second from behind. Involuntarily, Peter-Paulus was turned around, exactly half of a girella. While he was turning, a hand pushed his right elbow in; another pushed his left elbow out. The rotation was completed.

Have you ever seen a locomotive start moving? At first the thrusts of the piston and the puffs of steam are widely spaced. After a few seconds, they become increasingly closer together. However, one can still count them. Suddenly, however, there is no interval between thrusts. The same effect is produced on the hearing as a long line of street-lights produces on sight. The pulse of the machine soon becomes a continuous rumble, just as the lanterns present in perspective an uninterrupted line of light. Thus proceeds the fine Neapolitan game of the girella.

The timing of the movement we have indicated, right shoulder, left shoulder, left arm, and right arm, follows the descending scale of a geometric progression, until the moment when the gyratory movement reaches its maximum intensity—which is to say, when the victim of Parthenopean gaiety is spinning with the velocity of a German top. Then the merry crowd bursts in to immense, interminable Homeric laughter and shouts at the top of its voice, as it follows the human top: "*Alla girella! Alla girella!*"

Peter-Paulus, astonished by the first half-turn, offended by the second, worried by the third, tried to resist—but how? They are expert at that exercise, the joyful devils. The mariner had provided the impulsion to the first shoulder, the clown to the second.

"*Bravo, Ruggiero amico!*"

"*Bravo, amico Cucuzone!*"

Miterino was at the first elbow, Farfalla at the second—Miterino, the associate of a coachman city-dweller, to give him his place; Farfalla, an ambulant *frisore*.

"Bravo, Farfalla! Miterino, bravo!"

Then there was, in a double file—for it is necessary that the first steps be appropriately guided, Petruccio the cicerone, Masaccio the street-sweeper, Matteo the vermouth-seller, Russola the hotel bellboy and Gaspardo the fisherman in person—an important individual who had consented, that morning, to take charge of an umbrella during the disembarkation. Then all the Giovannis, all the Pietros, all the Carlottis and all the Vincentes in the Strada di Porto, and then all the bouquet-sellers who had flowered milady: Marietta, Giulietta, Antonietta.

"Bravi tutti!"

"Brave tutte!"

"Alla girella! Alla girella!"

After a dozen turns, poor Peter-Paulus had completely lost his head. He was sustained by the multiplicity of contrary impacts, and spun madly, extending his arms at random. The crowd, the shops, the fires and the lights whirled around him at a vertiginous speed. He could no longer see anything but a *danse macabre* of flames and faces, whose uniform laughter threw him into an extravagant anger.

Incessantly, he heard the cry that was like a spur to his fury: *"Alla girella!"* He made insensate efforts to cry out himself. He inflated his cheeks. He would have given fifty pounds sterling merely to be able to say to those cannibals: "I'm an English subject!"

But the words caught in his throat; and in any case, how could he make himself heard in the middle of that racket? He went on, he spun, piercing that crowd like the wind, in which every hand played the role of a whip on the hoof. His heart leapt, myriads of sparks formed a dust before his eyes. And always, always, there was that diabolical farandole round him, from which cries departed at a distance.

"Lasagne d'Amalfi!"

"Ostriche di Fusaro!"

"Frutti di mare!"

"Fritella calida!"

"Carbonchoisi! Frittume! Carneseche!"

And above all the great clamor: *"Alla girella! Alla girella!"*

How long did that last? Peter-Paulus was in no position to measure it precisely. However, after a long martyrdom, the cooking odors arrived less acridly at his poor upset stomach. The movement seemed less impetuous, the cries less deafening. The lights seemed to go out. Was it his eyes that were clouding over? Then there was something like a great night and a great silence, in which a few isolated bursts of laughter were grating. The laughter drew away in its turn. He sensed himself spinning in the void for a moment. He staggered like a drunkard about to fall, and then collapsed in front of a kind of luminous stairway that wounded his eyes.

The pavement of the street was wet and cold beneath his burning body. That woke him up. His groping hands found the gutter. As he raised his heavy eyelids, the ground shook beneath the gallop of a carriage that was arriving at full tilt.

"Look out!" cried the coachman.

Instinctively, Pete-Paulus dragged himself out of the way. The carriage went past. Fully awake, Peter-Paulus cast a glance around him. His condition resembled a heavy and torpid drunkenness.

At the solemn banquets of the Cotton Club, Peter-Paulus had often got into similar states, but then Jack had been expressly charged with carrying him off to bed. Where was Jack? Where was Penelope, whose thin hand poured, in such circumstances, the digestive, helpful tea?

As for Jack, Peter-Paulus could not answer exactly. But Penelope, oh, Penelope was very sagely tucked up in her bed at the Great Britain Hotel...

Certainly, the daughter of Jocasta Watergruel was not an amusing woman, but for virtue, for decency, for all that was "appropriate," Penelope left Lucretia, the most perfect type specimen of propriety, far behind.

Peter-Paulus had no idea where he was at present. It was a rather vast square surrounded by elegant and mostly modern constructions. A long well aligned and well lit street extended to his right. Above him was the bright light that had dazzled him at the moment of his fall.

It was the illuminated façade of a palace in the Greek style, ornamented with a double row of colonnades.

Peter-Paulus had crawled on his hands and knees as far as the corner of that square in order to shelter himself from carriages henceforth. A street-lamp illuminated two signs set at right-angles on the two faces of the corner. One said *Strada di Toledo*, the other *Largo dello Spirito Santo*. It was a case for consulting the map, but alas, the Guide and the dictionary had disappeared in the great storm of the *girella*.

Peter-Paulus' eyes returned to the glaring façade of the palace. The carriage that had nearly run over him had stopped in front of the peristyle.

Phantasmagorias are like misfortunes, which, it is said, never come alone. One can affirm that, once one has entered into the world of fantasies and astonishments, no one knows where the caprice will stop. It is a dream that, fleeing incessantly and always being transformed, bounces you through the domain of the impossible

Certainly, stupor had struck Peter-Paulus Brown many times since he had turned up the collar of his twill coat and put on blue-tinted spectacles in order to travel incognito in Naples, but this time it was the limit! The dream became a sickening nightmare.

Peter-Paulus saw a man about six feet tall, wearing a military costume, get down from the carriage. Nothing fatal in that—but after the giant descended a tall, slim woman with a sky blue satin dress, a pink mantle and an orange turban.

Strictly speaking, there could have been other women as tall and thin as Penelope. Peter-Paulus knew nine of them in Cheapside. But was there another for whom, on a day of munificence, Peter-Paulus had bought six aunes of sky blue satin? Had grandfather Watergruel, a wretched old man, made a present of that pink mantle to anyone else? And the orange turban with the tapering clasp, was it for anyone else that Jocasta had had it made, at great expense, by her own French milliner in Marylebone?

Penelope with a colonel! Dementia!

Delirium? Penelope was wearing the ball gown that she had worn last year at the big party at Smithson and Copperfield, the most honorable leather-manufacturers in Ave Maria Lane.

He called out to Penelope by name and launched himself toward the peristyle in terrible bounds. When he arrived, the tall thin woman in the sky blue dress, the pink mantle and the orange turban had already disappeared into the vestibule. No one remained but the giant. Peter-Paulus, transformed into a raging lion by rage, hurled himself upon him, called him a malefactor and accused him of kidnapping. The giant threw him into the middle of a group of lackeys with a sweep of the back of his hand and went inside.

"I want to go in!" cried Peter-Paulus, foaming at the mouth. "Arrest that corruptor! That was milady! I beg you, immediately! Oh, the detestable scoundrel!"

The lackeys surrounded him and blocked his passage, laughing.

He wanted to pay them, but his purse had flown away on the wings of the girella: his purse, his watch, his chain, everything that the *Guide* had advised him to leave in a safe place. He made an effort to launch himself forward, but the lackeys, seeing that torn and dirty costume and that distraught face, could not have any suspicion that they were dealing with the head of a textile firm.

"No one enters the Palazzo Doria," they said, "without having an invitation."

Peter-Paulus struggled momentarily; then he shivered from head to foot and suddenly became calm.

"That's all right," he said. "I'm content to know. The Palazzo Doria! I have my letter of recommendation. I'll send the police right away. He cleaved through the crown of valets and traversed the Piazza Spirito Santo at a rapid pace, gesticulating and talking to himself. He threw himself head first into the first cab he saw.

"The house of the director of the royal police!" he cried. "I'm an English subject...and I suspect milady! I beg you to hurry. I want to make an example...formally!"

V. Mariotto the Improviser

Since the epoch in which our story is set, the vicinity of the Strada di Porto has changed little, at least for the area between the principal street and the ports. In 1823, the Castello-Vecchio, the former residence of the Kings of Naples and the house of Anjou, which was destroyed by the great fire of 1829 and demolished two years later, still stood there.[29] The Strada di Porto ended at the Castello-Vecchio, not directly but via its prolongations. It also communicated with the various parts of the ancient edifice by way of several side-streets that formed branches along its trunk.

Evidently, the Castello-Vecchio was the center and the origin of the entire quarter. The tortuous tangle of its little streets has chosen it as the common terminus of their capricious and bizarre meanders. It was there, black and forbidding, but still robust in spite of the insults of time, in the middle of a veritable labyrinth. Since the advent of the Bourbons to the throne of Naples, it had served as a prison, and a large irregular square, which separated the eastern rampart of the Church of San Pietro Martire was the place where executions took place.

Behind the Fountain of the Three Virgins, where we previously saw the motionless group at which Peter-Paulus had looked too closely, to his misfortune, two side-streets opened, one of which rejoined the Largo San Pietro facing the church, while the other opened in front of the southern entrance of the castle in the Cortile d'Avilos.

Five minutes after Peter-Paulus had been carried away in the whirlwind of the fantastic girella that had made him see so many candles, the Strada di Porto no longer remembered him After approximately six minutes, the man with the meerschaum pipe came back to sit down on the rim of the Fountain of the Three Virgins. The clown, who had accompanied him as far as the Piazza Santo Spirito, where they had left Peter-Paulus comfortably seated on the lava, was not with him. He had been delayed on the way. He had seized in both hands the pole supporting the sign of a macaroni seller and performed the *bracchio ferrato*, to the great pleasure of the good lady's customers. The "iron hand," as everyone knows, is a feat of strength that consists of suspending oneself by both opposed wrists and stiffening oneself in a horizontal position by the strength of the biceps.

Cucuzone knew many others.

---

[29] Castello-Vecchio simply means "Old Castle," so it is not clear whether the author has an actual edifice in mind, but these data are not consistent with later developments in the story.

The queues around the kitchens were diminishing. Success henceforth went to four or five pamphlet-merchants selling the adventures of the famous Baron d'Altamonte, the brigand covered with crimes, who had murdered the Jewish banker Samuel Graff, the former secretary and steward of the Duc de l'Infantado. Above all, success went to two or three improvisers, who recounted, with infinite embellishments, the story contained in the pamphlets: the story of Felice Tavola, the so-called Baron d'Altamonte, Calabrian bandit and one of the seven Companions of the Silence.

There was, however, a schism between the various distributors of news.

Some claimed, as we have already said, that Baron d'Altamonte was the celebrated Il Porporato; others affirmed with a sort of conceit that the rope destined for that bandit king had not yet been woven.

After for the matter of the Companions of the Silence, there was a further confusion: as many orators, as many different opinions. One could even say that among the ten thousand habitués of that hospitable street, the Strada di Porto, there were ten thousand versions of the Companions of the Silence.

It was not only today that people were occupied with them. For three months the words "Companions of the Silence" had been in all mouths in Naples, but the more people talked about that mysterious brotherhood the less light was cast upon it. The rumors grew and, in a manner of speaking, piled up. In that incessantly growing mass of rumors, perhaps there was the truth, but it was lost in such quantities of exaggeration and fable that it would have required the eyes of a lynx to discover it.

There was, moreover, a good reason why the truth would not see the light of day. The very title that the members of the association of the Silence had adopted summarized their statutes and their law. Shut up: that was the Order's rule.

Everyone said it; everyone added that any indiscreet word was treason and that any treason was punished by death. Of those who were so well-informed it could be asked where their information came from, but when it is a question of secret societies the story is always the same, from the Mysteries of Isis to the Carbonari. No one has been able to pierce the terrible night that surrounds the agape, and yet everyone thinks he knows it. It is at the very moment when the mystery is declared to be impenetrable that it is unveiled to you, and that is precisely part of the mystery. As soon as an enigma is posed, everyone is passionate to find the key to it. When there is no enigma, we invoke the phantom of it.

The crowd was complicit, in the full meaning of the term, without knowing it and without wanting to be: not only the poor and ragged crowd of the Strada di Porto but the brilliant, elegant and gilded crowd that was presently filing the reception rooms of the Palazzo Doria. At the bottom, as at the top, you would have heard the same words: "Companions of the Silence," and the same name: "Porporato." Did anyone know, or not? Was he behind bars in the Castello-Vecchio? Was he still roaming the mountains? Or, more redoubtably, was he in

Naples, as was affirmed, powerful by virtue of his gold, his beauty and his audacity, as ungraspable as a vision, taking all forms, playing all roles, today a woman, tomorrow a priest, soldier, socialite or great lord, incessantly laying down a challenge to the proverbial skill of the royal police? Was he the enemy of the Companions of the Silence or was he their leader? If this Baron d'Altamonte was him, Il Porporato, would he be seen climbing the steps of the scaffold, the man who had shown his bloody coat at the last moment, even on the scaffold, so many times, in order to liberate the victim and disperse the executioners? The man who, speaking like the King, had said: "I no longer want the ax!" Would there not be some thunderclap at the last moment? Had the ax been forged that could cut the neck of that modern free-judge?

For he was a bandit, that was true; but these pages would swell by the size of a volume if it were necessary to list here all the wrongs he had redressed, according to public rumor, and all the crimes that he had punished. In his story, a strange epic and popular poem with a hundred thousand episodes, impossible by virtue of their very multiplicity, good was as abundant as evil, crime was juxtaposed with grandeur; stoical virtue appeared like a glimmer of light in the depths of the debauched night

That giant had, so the incessantly amplified legend said, everything that came from Heaven and everything that came from Hell. He was generous and he was cruel, lion and tiger at the same time. Like the god of Norse mythology, he held a sword in one hand and balm in the other.

If the noisy guests of the Strada di Porto had been convinced of the fact that their Porporato would be put to death the next day, one really could not say what the physiognomy of that crowd would have been. Most probably, it would have been in mourning, perhaps riotous. But the Neapolitan people make a joke of everything. They play with emotion. No one believed in the danger. One can say more: no one believe that the danger was possible. Il Porporato was, in the eyes of everyone, as invulnerable as Achilles. The man who was held in chains in the Castello-Vecchio must be some obscure affiliate, like those the royal police had already presented under the name of Porporato. And if, impossibly, he were Il Porporato himself, it is a long way from the prison to the scaffold! His familiar spirit was watching over him. No one had heard it said that his little Fiamma, the delightful daughter of the zingari, was a prisoner: Fiamma, his sister or his guardian angel, his slave and his queen, who remained faithful to him through the long orgy of his amours...

There were only one man and one woman in Naples as popular as Il Porporato and Fiamma. The man was Fulvio Coriolani, the magnificent prince with the ever-open hand, whose splendid carriage left behind a trail of gold when it passed through the poor quarters of the old city. The woman was Angélie Doria, the beauty of beauties, the providence of the unfortunate, the smile of the afflicted.

If Il Porporato had attacked Coriolani or Fiamma the beautiful Angélie, well, the petulant and passionate population of Naples would have abandoned Il Porporato and Fiamma.

But if Il Porporato had attempted the conquest of Angélie, and if Fiamma had loudly declared amorous war on Prince Corioliani, that would be a battle! The Neapolitans would have crowded the windows, ready to crown the victors! Between bandits and Italian princes, tourneys are made.

But that is pure fantasy. Coriolani alone was worthy of Angélie; no one but Angélie could fill the heart of the resplendent Coriolani. Naples entire had affianced Coriolani and Angélie.

In the noble world of which Angélie and Coriolani were the two stars, more was perhaps known about the Prince than in the Strada di Porto, but not much. The reasons for the singular favor that he enjoyed at court were a secret for everyone.

An anecdote had run around. Comte Lorédan Doria, the handsome Roman that we saw so close to death at the inn of the Corpo-Santo in Calabria, was Coriolani's friend and Angélie's guardian, but on the day when Coriolani came to ask him for his sister's hand, Lorédan had replied: "My sister is betrothed.

That was true. Angélie had been promised, since infancy, to the Romeo of the princes of Angri, the Marquis de Malatesta, her cousin, one of the bravest and most brilliant of the young noblemen of Naples.

Coriolani did not persist. But the same evening, he provoked Malatesta at the exit from the Teatro San Carlo and put him in bed with a thrust of his sword. The King knew about it, and forbade any pursuit of Coriolani.

Francis de Bourbon, the Royal Prince, did better, he summoned Lorédan Doria.

Lorédan said: "Even if Jean Malatesta and all the Marquises in Naples are put under ground, with all the Comtes, by the friends of our friend Fulvio, he will not be the husband of my sister Angélie Doria.

"Why is that?" asked Francis de Bourbon.

"Because we are the Dorias," Lorédan replied.

Francis smiled. "You think, then, that Fulvio is too petty a gentleman?"

"I don't know where he comes from," Lorédan retorted. "I don't know who he is. That name Coriolani might be good for the son of a king, since the custom is to give themselves fantasy titles, but from the sons of kings, when it comes to titles of caprice, one falls at the first step to adventurers."

The Royal Prince became serious and started to reflect. Then he said: "the Dorias are gentlemen...but Bourbon is also worth something, is it not, Comte Lorédan?"

"Milord is joking...," stammered the Doria.

"God forbid!" said the heir to the throne, almost solemnly. "I only want to tell you Comte Lorédan, that if, while remaining a Bourbon, I were not the son of a king, I would willingly give my sister to that Highness of fantasy, to employ your own expression, whose name is Fulvio Coriolani."

The rest of the conversation was not recounted. But a few days later people began to say that the King of Naples would sign the Princesse de Coriolani's contract of marriage. That was what people were already calling the beautiful Angélie.

The Marquis de Malatesta was a noble young man who had numerous friends. He formed a party against Fulvio, who did not even deign to accord a glance to that conspiracy. Light was to be cast on his life; they tried to delve into his past, but the curious and the hostile were thwarted at the first step. Behind the man's present there was darkness, absolute darkness: a night that no gaze could penetrate.

Muffled rumors went around then, not among the people, who did not know those drawing room anecdotes, but in the court itself. When malevolence and hatred came to a halt facing the unknown, encountering none of the ordinary purchase that every man encounters, malevolence and hared, momentarily disconcerted, ended up surpassing all limits. They went higher as the obstacle became higher. Malatesta's friends claimed that...

But it does not please us to say immediately what mad accusations the anger of the jealous and the vanquished brought against the lion of Neapolitan elegance. For us, it is now a matter of Il Porporato and not Fulvio Coriolani; it is not a matter of the courtiers of Naples but of our Companions of the Silence.

At the moment when the man with the meerschaum pipe and the clown came back from their expedition against Peter-Paulus Brown of Cheapside, the handsome fisherman had deserted the place he had previously occupied at the foot of the Fountain of the Three Virgins. No one could any longer be seen there but an improviser surrounded by an avid audience. But there was a silent coming-and-going from the streets behind the fountain to the principal street, and the handsome fisherman must not have been very far away, for the little orange-seller was showing her mischievous face continually at the opening of the Vicoletto Delfino or the Vico Sorrente. Those were the names of the two side-streets that went to join the Castello-Vecchio three hundred paces away, one to the left and the other to the right of the little square of San Pietro Martire.

The people who were going back and forth like sentinels resembled exactly, in terms of their costume, the eaters and drinkers of the Strada di Porto. But they were only lending a distracted attention to the emphatic narrations of the improviser, and that established a terrible difference between them and the crowd. The crowd was all ears.

In addition to the busy sentinels, a few individuals could be distinguished in the mass of the crowd with piercing and anxious gazes, seeking to thread a path through the group. We have already seen those prowling around the good Peter-Paulus momentarily.

In Paris, our police agents refrain from writing on their hats in visible letters, like La Fontaine's shepherd: "I am Guillot, shepherd of this flock." In Naples, one sometimes says in order to make people laugh, with a theatrical expression, that brigands have the custom of shouting: "Come see a brigand!" and the police agents are in the comedy, their uniform murmuring: "We're alguazils; have the kindness to chose the moment when we're passing by to confide your most important secrets to the evening breeze."

The individuals with piercing and curious eyes were agents of the royal police. They were known; they did not inconvenience anyone. Thieves gladly offered them a pinch of stolen tobacco, and our mysterious sentinels winked at them amicably when they crossed their path on the lava. That Neapolitan city is the capital of Arcadia; the wolves and the sheep fraternize there from dawn to dusk.

"As for being Il Porporato," said the improviser meanwhile, in pure Neapolitan patois, "he's Il Porporato, my dear friends. I swear to that on my eternal salvation. And there's Signor Onofrio over there who can tell you whether I'm lying. Good evening, Signor Onofrio!"

Signor Onofrio was one of the agents of the central police: a face as naively somber as that of a bit-part player in a melodrama. He was manifestly flattered by the remark, but he pulled the collar of his cloak over his mouth, murmuring.

"Hold your tongue, Mariotto," he said, severely, "if you want to live for a long time."

"Many thanks, Signor Onofrio!" cried Mariotto the improviser, when the agent disappeared into the crowd. "You saw, my friends, whether he said that I was lying! And why would I lie? God is my witness! It would be the first time in my life!

"Bravo, Mariotto, bravo!" called voices from all directions. "You've never lied, that's an article of faith!"

Mariotto assumed a tender expression.

"It's very pleasant, my dear friends, to receive that honorable testimony publicly. I'm poor and can't pay for flattery, so your words are sincere. In consequence, I'll tell you something you don't know."

"Speak, Mariotto, speak."

Silence fell.

Mariotto seemed to collect himself.

"My only friends," he went on, after a short pause, "one can't live on the air of the weather. I have a wife, two sons and three daughters. You'll find it very reasonable to give me a carlin for the news that I'm going to give you."

"If the news is good, you'll have your carlin, Mariotto."

"Better to hold than run after, my chosen friends," the improviser replied. "Fair's fair: the carlin for the news."

A Neapolitan carlin is worth ten grani or twenty Tournois deniers, about forty-two centimes. They knew Mariotto; the carlin was necessary in order to have the news. Denier by denier, the carlin was shelled out. Then, after having thanked his only friends, Mariotto spoke as follows:

"There's a ball this evening at the Palazzo Doria. It's me who's telling you that."

"Eh!" cried the disappointed crowd. "We all know that!"

"Have you turned thief?" asked a lasagna boiler, who had just put her finger on her nose.

And twenty irritated voices said: "Give us back the carlin, Mariotto, you scoundrel."

It was at that tempestuous moment that Mariotto Cigoli showed all his worth.

"If I've become a thief, Taddea, impenitent witch," he cried, "have I ever told the truth? That there are more worms than flour in your macaroni? Have I become a thief, the rest of you, you bunch of reprobates? Is it me who stole the Englishman's watch? Is it me who put a pillow over my wife's mouth, Miterino, bandit's bastard? Have I taken lessons from you, then, to become a thief, Farfalla, prison pavement, you who sing out there into the kerchief of our master Pietro-Gregorio Andrea?"

"Peace, peace, Mariotto!" said those who had not yet been named. "We were joking. Keep your carlin and earn it!"

"San Gennaro!" retorted the improviser. "I know full well that you were joking! And I too wanted to have a little laugh. Doesn't everyone know that Taddea, my old dear, cooks the best lasagna on the Strada di Porto; that Rizzolo has found the Englishman's watch, and that Miterino wanted to warm his wife up? It's just, my dear friends, that you spoke too soon. My news is worth ten carlins rather than one, and even a twelve-carlin piaster. Do you know why there's a ball at the Palazzo Doria this evening? No. And how would you know? You only see those people, my paupers, in carriages or in church."

"And you see them at close range, do you, Mariotto?" interjected Farfalla, who was still bearing a grudge.

"I don't flatter the great," replied the improviser, with dignity, "but I frequent them. I'm a cousin of Mario Caffaro, Lorédan Doria's second chamberlain. There's a ball at the palazzo tonight because the Contessina is going to be betrothed."

"With Fulvio Coriolani?" cried the crowd, with one voice.

"Right away, you've guessed it, my beloveds. And what's astonishing about that? You have so much intelligence. But even that isn't my news."

The circle tightened.

"My news," Mariotto continued, "isn't worth one piaster, it's worth twenty. Prince Coriolani was murdered his evening!"

VI. The Saltarello

You might have thought that that compact mass of attentive listeners had just received an electric shock. At first they recoiled, and the circle widened instinctively. That happened in a profound silence, the silence of amazement. Then a great clamor went up.

"Is it possible?"

"Coriolani murdered!"

"If it's Malatesta who's done that, by San Gennaro, Malatesta won't take it to paradise."

"Where was this murder?"

"When?"

"Are the murderers known?"

"La la la!" said Mariotto, proud and glad of the effect produced. "Do you know anyone else who'd have given you that for a carlin? My dear friends, when I say murdered. I haven't seen the body..."

There was a great sigh of relief in the crowd, for Prince Coriolani was adored in Naples.

"But," the improviser continued, "for what it's worth, I make you the judges. There was a great feast at the Palazzo Doria. The Prince was there, as is appropriate, seated beside the Contessina."

"Oh, said Masaccio, "a dear angel, that one!"

"As beautiful and gentle as the mother of God!" added a licensed street-porter.

Others cried: "Let him speak" Let him speak!"

"It was a pleasure to see them both," Mariotto continued. "The Prince was wearing his decorations and shining like the sun. Angélie, the beloved creature, was dressed in white and resembled one of those tender orange blossoms that open in the evening to perfume the breeze. But there was something else, my cherubs. There was also a feast at the Malatesta house, and God knows that there was no betrothal there. A dozen devils incarnate, all angry against that gentle lamb Coriolani because of the sword thrust he gave the Marquis and the love that the divine Contessina has given him. The feast took place on the pretext of celebrating Malatesta's recovery, who has been healed from the sword-thrust.

"They were there, all the handsome fellows that no longer shine since Prince Fulvio appeared in our city, all the stars that his star eclipsed so rapidly: Pitti of Florence, Ziani of Venice, D'Angri Vespuccio-Doria, Colonna and the two Doria-Panfili of Bologna, and others. All princes! There's no lack of princes in Italy, my only friends, but there are princes and princes! Find me another prince like Fulvio Coriolani!

"What were they doing at Malatesta's? You see, they're all enraged by jealousy, because His Royal Highness Francis de Bourbon—may God conserve him for a hundred years!—is at the betrothal, and because King Ferdinand himself—may he attain the age of Methuselah!—is to put his signature to the contract. Well, they were plotting.

"And this is what happened...I will tell you the truth, neither more nor less, I swear by my eternal salvation! One would have to be mad to lose one's share of paradise for a lie!

"At about five o'clock in the afternoon the feast at the Palazzo Doria was almost over. They had sat down at table at two o'clock. The Royal Prince was there, gazing at Angélie and sighing. A letter arrived. Where did it come from? You could chop me up like meat for pâté and I couldn't tell you, because I don't know. Shame upon the man who invents fables. The letter was for Prince Coriolani. On reading it he went very pale. He got up. He spoke in a low voice to the royal prince; they he went out, saying: 'I'll return...'"

Mariotto paused. A hundred voices cried, impatiently: "And he didn't come back?"

"Wait, my friends of choice! How do you expect to learn the end of the story if you don't let me speak? You know, don't you, that he went aboard the Marseille ferry this morning?"

"Yes, yes...aboard the *Pausilippe*," was the reply.

"We were there," said some. "He put two veiled women into his carriage."

"That's the advantage you have over me, my turtle-doves. I wasn't there...no...no one can be in two places at the same time... But if I had been there, word of a Christian, I would have found a way to know who the two women were. Anyway, no matter...he took them no one knows where, and that certainly complicates the adventure.

"You'll see. Half an hour passed out there at the Palazzo Doria, and then an hour, then two, and then the rest. Coriolani didn't come back.

All those who were at Malatesta's—you know, Pitti, Ziani, Colonna, Vespuccio, Panfili and company—had their invitations, as is only just, to the Palazzo Doria. They arrived at about seven o'clock, and they had Sicilian wine in the head, and French wine too, I swear it on my eternal salvation. Then all sorts of things were said. There was mention of the two veiled ladies, and the poor beautiful Angélie fainted in her brother's arms. But God in Heaven, there was talk of many others. There's no lack of beauties around the handsome Fulvio. And to tell the truth, the marriage isn't yet made; why reproach him already for his amours?

"Lorédan Doria listened and kept silent. He's a Roman; he knows how to shut up. Do you know, my doves, why all the intelligence in Italy has come to lodge in Naples?"

That question earned Mariotto a long and unanimous round of applause. That gave him pleasure, but he would have preferred a second carlin. He continued: "If you're content with me, my only friends, so much the better. I do what I can... So, the Royal Prince was very irritated. He went to Lorédan and spoke to him in a low voice. Lorédan replied in a loud voice: 'Until the sacrament, one can recant.'

"Meanwhile, some people had left in order to go in search of Coriolani. They were good men: Colonel San-Severo, who is six feet tall, the old banker Massimo Dolci, the cavalier Ercole Pisani, who was always with that scoundrel d'Altamonte...oh, if he had known that he was a bandit! And all the true friends of Bourbon and Doria. They had said: 'We'll bring Fulvio back, dead or alive!' Needless to say, the noble Marquis Andrea Visconti Armellino, the deputy superintendent of police, was with them.

"Some ran to his palace: no one there! Others went to the Villa Palmerini, where Belloni, the *diva delle dive* lives, the folly of all the young lords: nothing. Others went to the Palazzo Pallavicini, the home of the Marquise Aurora—and Prince Francis didn't know that... No Coriolani. Others, finally, went here and there, to the home of the Comtesse, the Baronne, the Princesse, the steward...nothing. Nothing! Naples is a great city, but Coriolani is as great as Naples, and it's as difficult to hide one as the other.

"The rumor suddenly ran round at the Palazzo Doria, my friends, that a pool of blood had been found at the Maddalena bridge. And it's becoming fashionable to find pools of blood by night. People said immediately: 'Prince Fulvio has been murdered!' And the Malatestas laughed as they replied...guess what! They replied: 'Murdered, no; murderer, yes.'"

There was a great rumor in the crowd, and Mariotto rubbed his hands. That rumor was pregnant with further carlins. The enticed crowd were going to empty their pockets in order to know.

"You're not telling us everything, Mariotto," chorused the crowd, in fact.

"You know more, Mariotto...there's a story."

"Ah, my true friends," replied the improviser, "One can't get anything past you! The Romans wouldn't have divined so quickly, nor the Milanese, nor the people of Florence or Turin. As for Venice the dead, we won't even talk about her. Yes, yes, my companions, there's a story...two stories...as true as it's necessary for me to work to nourish the wife and children...and you wouldn't want to have my trouble for nothing, my friends! I swear to that on my eternal salvation!"

"The story! The story! The story!" the chorus cried, tumultuously.

"Which one?" asked Mariotto. "I can tell you how our Fulvio was accused of murder in front of the Royal Prince in person...and I can tell you where he was seen two hours after leaving the Palazzo Doria..."

"The murder!" chose half the crowd.

"The Prince!" demanded the other. "Why did the Prince leave his own betrothal feast?"

"I can also tell you," Mariotto continued, "whose blood it was that was found at the Maddalena bridge..."

"Tell us, then, Mariotto!"

Mariotto hitched up the tattered red belt that was holding up his trousers. "It's a tari per story," he pronounced, firmly. A tari is two carlins.

Have you read descriptions of tempests in Classical tragedies? Crébillon père offers beautiful models of that sort. The sea hollows out its bottomless gulfs and sends its waves all the way to the heavens, no less. Well, the tempests of tragedy are mere squalls compared with the storm whipped up by the last words of Mariotto Cigoli, the celebrated improviser. The crowd stamped, blasphemed, cursed, shouted and howled. All the fists were clenched in order to threaten that rogue Mariotto, that thief, that ruffian, that forger! But after having hurled fire and flame, in all the force of the expression, the members of the crowd put their hands in their pockets, and the tari was made up.

Then Mariotto said, in a penetrating tone: "You'll have two stories for that one tari, my turtle-doves...two beauties, two fine stories, of which the devil won't see a drop. First of all, and this is extra to the bargain, there's the story of the Maddalena bridge. Oh, you want mysteries! Holy Trinity, we have them in stock!

"All afternoon, my friends, there has been an English sloop in the harbor. The launch of that sloop, of which no one knows the name, was moored at the quay of La Marinella not far from the harbor, and there were four fat Englishmen aboard with turned-up collars. What were they doing there, I ask you?

"The master has blue spectacles like the man you spun a little while ago. Twice the sloop made signals, twice the sound of a horn was heard at the end of the Strada Reggia di Portici...

"Look to see whether Signor Onofrio is within earshot..."

The crowd checked itself. Signor Onofrio and his colleagues were not there.

"Toward dusk, a man presented himself alone at the Maddalena bridge. Almost immediately afterwards, six policemen came toward him. The man pointed at the boat, as if he wanted to denounce the Englishmen. The officer gave him a purse. Then they went down under the bridge. People who were passing, when the night was completely dark, heard a cry. The boat drew away as fast as its oarsmen could row. People came running. Under the bridge there was neither a stranger nor any policemen, but a pool of blood and a dagger, on the blade of which three Latin words were engraved: *Agere, non loqui*.

"But this is this is the heart of the matter, my doves," Mariotto interjected, as the crowd was about to pepper him with questions, "this is the true secret...and God knows what will happen to anyone who goes to tell it at the Palazzo Doria! Come closer, and open your ears..."

There was no need for those oratory precautions. The crowd was devouring his words in advance.

"Prince Coriolani," he continued, "left the Palazzo at about six o'clock. At seven, I who am speaking to you saw him with my own eyes, not in his Highness costume but disguised as..."

"Disguised as what?" people cried from all directions, because Mariotto had stopped abruptly.

But the latter seemed to have been struck by amazement. One might have thought that he had perceived the head of Medusa there is the shadow of the Vicoletto Delfino. He stood there, open-mouthed and wide-eyed.

The impatient crowd repeated: "Disguised as what? Disguised as what?"

And as Mariotto's gaze remained fixed in the darkness at the opening of the vicoletto, all eyes turned in the same direction. They saw, in profile only, the fisherman of heroic stature who had previously been standing on the spot now occupied by Mariotto's audience, between the mariner with the meerschaum pipe and the strange individual lying curled up like a caterpillar.

Many of them wondered: *Who's that?*

A few of them exchanged rapid winks. Only one pronounced the word that we have already heard: "Beldemonio."

But the sight of the demon himself, whether he is handsome or ugly, is incapable of interrupting the impetuosity of Neapolitan curiosity. The interrogations addressed to Mariotto the improviser recommenced, and were already overlapping when a bizarre cry dominated all those noises. That cry, of a particular species, every Parisian has heard. Auriol, the glorious master of the perilous leap, always uttered it when he entered the arena. Auriol had borrowed it from Neapolitan clowns: the cry of the castrato, mocking and joyful, a weak but piercing cry that seems to emerge from the wooden throat of a doll.

A supple body, but of considerable mass, was seen to bound over heads, which ducked as best they could. Then a prodigious creature, having thus crossed the circle of the curious, started to execute utterly fantastic movements within the circle. It fell on its hands; it marched with its feet in the air and its head horribly inverted. The crowd, all those Neapolitan overgrown children, started laughing, and saying: "Bravo saltarello!"

The saltarello, who was none other than our clown from the fountain, launched his cry and saluted very respectfully with his feet; then, leaping on to the rim, and from the rim into the niche of one of the Virgins, he wedged his feet—I have no idea how—under the stone draperies that formed the Madonna's garment, and suddenly leaned backwards, sustained only by his heels. The crowd uttered a cry of fright and admiration. In that position, the saltarello's head was very close to Mariotto's ear.

In a whisper, he said: "One more word and your wife is a widow!"

Then he let himself fall on his hands into the basin, bounced like an elastic ball, made the Indian leap, the Chinese leap and the perilous leap on the spot, and, choosing at a glance the tall head of Gaspardo the fisherman, reached it with a sublime leap, placed his two hands upon it like a child playing on a vaulting horse, and crossed the curious hedge again with a miraculous leap. Gaspardo the fisherman could have sworn *Cospetto!* or *Corpo di Bacco!* as he chose; the saltarello had already disappeared.

VII. Il Porporato's Exploits

When the crowd had cried "Bravo saltarello!" loudly, it turned back to the improviser. It was his creditor. It wanted its story for its money. What could be more just? But the improviser was mute and utterly pale. He no longer seemed to have any enthusiasm for storytelling. His gaze, anxious now, scanned the circle that surrounded him, and, passing over the heads, sounded the increasingly dark depths of the Strada di Porto.

The fires were, in fact, extinct, and the candles too. The hour of the open air meal had passed; the mobile ovens could cool down. The concert of mercantile cries had lost its impetus and its vivacity. Nothing was being sold any longer but sweetmeats and fruits. Even they were the sweetmeats distained by the early arrivals, and the fruits left in the bottom of the baskets. *The belated get the bones*, as the schoolboy proverb has it, almost as ferocious as the Gaulish *Woe betide the vanquished.*

The facchini being seated, the fishermen's thirst slaked and the poor representatives of all those obsequious and importunate petty industries that allow Neapolitan idlers to survive having full bellies, they gazed with scorn at the overcooked meats, the punctured lemons and the invalid watermelons that the merchants were doing their best to persuade them to buy. God knows that it does not take much to fill Neapolitan stomachs. With the provender of a London coal-heaver you could give an ample dinner to half a dozen facchini

Those merchants who had finished their sale, having become men of leisure, mingled with the crowd, eating a morsel here and there on the move. The last clamors, uttered a long intervals, with a sort of discouragement, in that crowd once eager to buy, were like a sad echo of the final hour of the feast.

"For two grani," sang a watermelon seller in the distance, "you can drink, you can eat and you can wash your face!"

It was certainly not the transformation suffered by the Strada di Porto that was occupying Mariotto the improviser. That happened every day. One might have thought that he could see, among the ambulant groups with which the street as still filed, things that escaped the eyes of his audience, and which he had not noticed himself until then.

"They're all there," he murmured, as if talking to himself, "and the police too. What damned saraband are we going to dance tonight?"

A man, whom at first glance we might have mistaken for Peter-Paulus in person, stopped opposite him, a little way outside the circle. He had his hat pulled down over his eyes and the twill jacket of an English sailor with the collar turned up beneath the nose. His eyes were hidden by blue spectacles. That man made a hand signal to Mariotto, Mariotto responded by directing his eyes toward the Vicoletto Delfino, behind the fountain.

"Get on with it, Mariotto," cried the crowd. "Are you going to make us sleep here?"

There'll be more than one of them sleeping on the paving-stones tonight, thought Mariotto. Aloud, he said: "I'm getting there, my friends—it's that grasshopper who interrupted me. Don't worry, you won't lose anything—it's me who's telling you that."

Before telling the reader what Mariotto did to satisfy his audience without putting his wife in mourning, however, we are obliged to follow momentarily the individual disguised as Peter-Paulus, who was heading with a slow and heavy tread toward the Vicoletto Delfino. As he went around the fountain, the night suddenly became black around him. There were no street-lights in the back street.

"Hey!" he said, doing his best to feign an English accent. "If there's anyone there, speak to me—I can't see a thing!"

There was a burst of muffled laughter nearby.

"Hello, Sansovina," said a pleasant female voice. "Beldemonio's abroad tonight and is waiting for you."

"Will I speak to him?"

"No...but you'll speak to me, and it's all one." He saw a slender form emerging from the shadow of a low door.

"Oh," he said, "it's you Signorina? It's this evening?"

"It has to be, Sansovino, since there won't be time tomorrow."

"And everything is ready?"

"Everything will be. Beldemonio's putting his own hand to the task."

The young woman who was facing Sansovina put her hands on his shoulders and looked at him, laughing. "If you'd been here a little while ago, old wolf, you could have had a lesson in English jargon. I accosted a worthy fellow, thinking he was you, and we were obliged to make a girella to get rid of him. What's new?"

"A great deal. There's movement in the port; it's said that the guardians are on the alert."

"They are on the alert," said the young woman, coldly.

"A man was killed fifty paces from our boat, under the Maddalena bridge."

"God has his soul. We know that. What have you come to say?"

"I've come to say one thing and ask about another. We haven't seen Ruggieri all day..."

"Beldemonio needed him."

"And Cucuzone too?"

"Especially Cucuzone."

"That's all right...but our men are murmuring."

"Shut them up."

"I've tried. The thing I've come to tell you is that the boat has had to quit its post near the little harbor. There's a swarm of cops there..."

"We know that too. You moored at the mouth of the Sebeto..."

"And it's from there that we heard the scream of the murdered man. But there are as many cops in the Marinella as at the little harbor; this is what you need to know: I raised anchor. With our oars wrapped in straw we went out into the bay, doubled the point of the Castello dell'Ovo and moored to the west of the beach at Chiaia, in the rocks, between Virgil's tomb and the grottos of Pozzuoli."

The signorina remained silent.

"Did you hear?" asked the pretended English sailor.

"Beldemonio won't be content," she replied. "It'll be necessary to traverse the whole city to get to the boat."

"There are twenty surveillance launches between the port and the Maddalena," Sansovina replied.

"And the sloop?"

"The sloop has changed position too, because of a warship that's been cruising between Gaiola and Capo Miseno. The sloop had passed the Procida channel; it's anchored on the far side of the island, south-south west of the Foce del Fusaro... and God grant that it be left at repose there!"

"Is that all you have to say?"

"Everything," replied the English mariner.

"And what do you have to ask?"

"The hour when the boat will be sailing."

"If anyone apart from God knows that, Sansovina," the young woman replied, "it's the Master...and you can't talk to the Master, who isn't here at the moment. Return to your post and keep watch all night. Perhaps it will be soon...and perhaps you'll have to wait until daybreak. There are numerous obstacles that no one can foresee. The prisoner has been taken out of the cell whose bars were filed in advance and locked in the attics. He's being held in secret. The guards have been multiplied tenfold inside and outside the Castello-Vecchio. But what does all that matter, since the Master's will is that the prisoner be freed?"

"Beldemonio doesn't have wings like a bird, though," murmured the mariner.

The young woman's hand weighed more heavily on his shoulder. "He has wings like an angel," she pronounced, in a low voice, "or a demon..."

A minute later, the vicoletto was silent again, and apparently deserted.

"I swear on my eternal salvation," our improviser Mariotto said, at that moment, his audience pressing him very closely, "and would I damn myself for a tari? I ask you, my doves! Won't there be plenty of time to talk to you about Coriolani? Whereas the famous Baron d'Altamonte will be executed by the blade tomorrow morning at first light. No one can talk about him the way I can, my friends, Listen to me..."

"Return the money!" cried five or six rude voices. "You've deceived us. Nothing's happened to Prince Fulvio..."

"Nothing's happened! Spirito Santo! And it's to me that you're saying that?"

"Well, what's happened?"

The logic of that Neapolitan audience was surely overwhelming. Mariotto ranted like a man possessed.

"Is there any honesty on earth?" he cried. "Don't I know better than you do what's interesting in my news? Has anyone ever heard of people who plug their ears when someone wants to talk to them about Il Porporato?"

That name always had a great effect. There were still murmurs, however.

"That's all right," said the improviser, who saw the worst of the storm passing. "It's agreed—I won't tell you what's happening this very evening in the Castello-Vecchio. I won't talk to you about the tunnel that the Companions of the Silence have dug under the Vicoletto di Santa Maria in order to reach Il Porporato's cell..."

"A tunnel?" said the chorus, titillated this time.

"No, no," said Mariotto, "you don't want to know about that..."

"Yes we do!"

"Have I misunderstood, then?"

"Speak! Speak! Speak!"

"Listen, then, my true friends. I'm a Christian like all of you, and not a top that one spins with a whip. You'll surely give one carlin more for the tunnel, the companions disguised as jailers, and the manner in which all these things have been discovered."

The voice of Gaspardo the fisherman was not often heard. It was a basso-profundo as deep as a well.

"Give him to me," he said. "He's been mocking us long enough. It'll break him in two like a crust!"

"All right! All right!" cried Mariotto, swiftly, who saw himself already cut in two down the middle, like a wasp. "Don't you understand, my true friends, that I was joking. Is it forbidden, now to amuse oneself a little between comrades? This is it—and I'm the only one in Naples who can tell you this, I swear on my eternal salvation! When the treasure of the royal palace of Capodimonte was pillaged last winter, Bourbon was angry, and increased to ten thousand ducats the reward promised to whoever delivered Il Porporato. That made fifty thousand ducats—that's good to have; but no one put a hand on Il Porporato. Some time after that, the jewels of the Villa Regina disappeared, and then the silverware of the Villa Floridiana, where the King had his plate vessels, and then the archbishop's treasure. Another twenty thousand ducats was promised to whoever delivered Il Porporato, but how, my friends, can the ungraspable be grasped?

"One night, Bianca Barberini, the Duc's daughter, was abducted. There was mourning. An unsigned letter reached the old Duc informing him that, in exchange for fifty thousand six-ducat double ounces, the unique hope of his race would be returned to him. You know full well that he mounted up himself and rode to the indicated spot beyond Salerno, alone, as ordered. He advanced into the great plain between the two torrents that the Malaria, the Tusciano and the Selo throw off, all the way to the foothills of the Alburni, whose slopes are densely forested,

"He saw the herds of deer and wild boar that are no longer frightened by royal hunts. He saw the block of granite that marks the spot where the Roman consul defeated the army of the slave Spartacus. He saw, far away on the horizon, the old city of Paestum, deserted, silent and motionless, like a phantom, sleeping in its ruins for two thousand years. He saw that. The setting sun was reddening the long perspectives of Doric columns. The shadows were lengthening in front of him and carrying the gigantic shadow of the Temple of Neptune all the way to his feet. There was no one in the plain, no one in the city, until the moment when the sun, putting a wide crimson band behind the somber propylea, slowly drowned its disk in the gulf of Salerno...

"Then a man appeared, as crimson as the sun that had just set, from the plume of his Calabrian hat to the leather of his boots. His face was hidden behind a red mask. He pointed at the edge of the forest. Bianca Barberini was there, held by two men, with her arms extended toward her father. The old Duc counted out the fifty thousand ounces in gold and English banknotes. The man in purple, Il Porporato, didn't deign to bend down to pick them up. He only touches gold in order to deliver largesse. He returned Bianca to her father's hands, saluted like the lord he is, and disappeared into the woods. Since that time, those who love Bianca Barberini have never seen her smile..."

"That's what's said!" shouted Farfalla, while Mariotto drew breath.

"Ah," said Masaccio, pale with the emotion engendered in him by the poetry of the landscape and the tale, "Mariotto is a Neapolitan when he wants to be!"

"Thank you, Farfalla, thank you, Masaccio!" said Mariotto, proudly. "You know what's what! After Bianca Barberini, it was the turn of Preziosa Balbi, sixteen years old, the fiancée of Pisanelli of Mantua. That one, less rich, was ransomed at the price of thirty thousand gold ounces. Bianca Barberini is now a poor beautiful marble statue, Preziosa Balbi is a nun cloistered in the Carmelite convent of Capodimonte. That was what she wanted. After her, two at the same time: Jeanne Palliante of the Paleologue princes, the fiancé of Comte Doria-Doria, and Matilda Farnèse, goddaughter of Prince Ferdinand—may he live for a century! In order to get Jeanne back, it required Fulvio Coriolani..."

Mariotto interrupted himself abruptly at that point, and looked in the direction of the side-street into which the saltarello had disappeared.

"Go on!" someone cried. "Tell us how Coriolani got Lorédan Doria's fiancée back!"

On the improviser's face there was something like a reflection of the disturbance that had griped him during the saltarello's invasion.

"You know as well as I do, my turtle-doves," he replied, "that when one talks about Coriolani, it leads a long way. Just look at Giovanna Palliante when she goes past in her carriage, and tell me where her fresh colors have gone. Tell me also why the Palazzo Doria isn't celebrating two betrothals this evening..."

"Il Porporato's captives can be ransomed, but doesn't everyone know that the noble virgins don't bring back their souls from that palace he possesses, God only knows where? As for the beautiful Matilda Farnèse, no one was able to get her back—not even Fulvio Coriolani!

"You know, my friends, it would be a strange thing and as great as a combat of giants if Fulvio Coriolani ever came to grips, hand to hand, with Il Porporato! In the meantime, the King, weeping for his goddaughter, said: 'I'd give a hundred thousand ducats to the man who could deliver that demon to me!' If one thought of God, would one take so much trouble, my dear friends? God is powerful; what no man can do happens quite naturally by the will of God.

"One day last week, an old woman, the former maidservant of Samuel Graff, the rich man who had made his fortune in the service of the Duc de l'Infantado, saw a nobleman passing by as she came out of the church of Monte Oliveto. It's La Beata, whom you all know well, who gives alms meagerly in order to purify the good ducats once stolen by her master. On seeing the nobleman who was passing by La Beata uttered a scream and fainted. Why? Because she had recognized the murderer of the rich Samuel Graff..."

"That's true! It's true!" said several of the listeners.

"We know that!" replied others.

And the greater number: "Let Mariotto go on. He's in good form!"

"In good form!" protested the improviser, bitterly. "Are there days when others talk better than me to your liking, my lambs? I advise you to go listen to them, then."

"The next chatterbox that interrupts Mariotto," pronounced Gaspardo the fisherman, solemnly, will get a double girella from one end of the street to the other, there and back. And you, Mariotto, get on with it—you've been paid."

That double-edged sentence, worthy of King Solomon, was unanimously approved.

"Mine is a hard profession," the improviser went on. "I've seen times when people spoke more respectfully about people versed in letters who devoted themselves to the people of Naples. But no matter, my children, glory only comes after death.

"So, La Beata goes to the steward of her quarter, because Signor Spurzheim, the director of the royal police, was ill in bed. As true as I'm telling it, she reported the following facts:

"Some time before, a stranger came to the house of the rich Samuel Graff in Palermo, which is the capital of Sicily. The stranger was handsome and well-built. His name was Felice Tavola. He had letters from Spain and Graff received him cordially. Soon, Felice Tavola was one of the family.

"One night, La Beata woke up with a start. The house was full of noise and shouting. The rich Samuel Graff's guest had introduced southern brigands into his house, who called themselves the knights of charcoal and iron. The *cavalieri ferrai* had a vengeance to exact against the former steward of the Duc de l'Infantado. They had already killed the Marquis de Francavilla, Colonel Trentacapelli and many others. The house was pillaged from top to bottom. Samuel Graff, who was murdered, had a Calabrian dagger in his breast on which were engraved the Latin words: *Agere, no loqui*."

"The same as the one that killed the man at the Maddalena bridge," said Ruzzola, while a tremor ran through the crowd.

"The dagger of the Silence," pronounced Mariotto, slowly. Then he went on: "Old Graff's house guest, his Felice Tavola, disappeared with the bandits, and all Palermo recognized in him the terrible Il Porporato. Those are events of which one doesn't lose the memory. The nobleman that La Beata saw passing as she came out of the church of Monte Oliveto was Felicia Tavola. There it is. You know full well that he wore the name of Baron d'Altamonte at court, but it costs them nothing to change names. If one took the trouble to count, one would find more than a dozen of them for Il Porporato alone.

"Baron d'Altamonte laughed when they came to arrest him. He asked for the Cavalier Ercole Pisani, Colonel San Severo, the old banker Massimo Dolci, and Signor Johann Spurzheim himself, the director of the royal police, and also asked for Prince Coriolani. The King ordered that he be held in secret.

"The criminal court assembled, and witnesses were summoned from the Monteleone region and Sicily. The murder of Samuel Graff was proven beyond reasonable doubt. But one thing that wasn't proven at all was the identity, as they say, the identity of Il Porporato. The witnesses from Monteleone and Palermo certainly recognized Felice Tavola, as La Beata herself had, but they had never seen Il Porporato. Now, the law has been mistaken so often!

"Haven't you, to whom I'm talking, my gentle lambs, already seen five or six vulgar criminals go to the scaffold, proudly bearing the great name of Il Porporato, like Aesop's donkey who put on the skin of a lion? The day after the execution, the true Porporato always gave some terrible and bloody proof of his existence.

"The King wanted to know. There were five people in Naples who had seen Il Porporato with their own eyes and who couldn't say no. Firstly there were the three lovely creatures, Bianca Barberini, Preziosa Balbi and Jeanne Palliante of the Paleologue Princes After that there was Prince Fulvio Coriolani. The Duc had seen Porporato for his daughter Bianca, the Prince had seen him for Jeanne Palliante of the Paleologues, Doria's fiancée.

"The King ordered that Baron Altamonte, already condemned by the criminal court, be dressed in the purple costume that is the formal apparel of the Master of the Silence. He ordered that Felice Tavola, the so-called Baron Altamonte, be confronted with the three young noblewomen and the two noblemen.

"Do you think, my friends, that anyone but me could reveal secrets of State like this? If you think so, you're mistaken. Man is subject to error. There is no shame in saying frankly: 'I have made a mistake.'

"So, four carriages stopped outside the larghetto of San Pietro Martire. Bianca Barberini came with her father, Preziosa Balbi with the superior of her convent, Jeanne of the Paleologues with the Duchess of Luxemburg, née Princess of Bavaria, her aunt. Fulvio Coriolani was alone in the fourth carriage. Those who saw that said that Fulvio was pale-faced and had I know not what sadness under his eyelids.

"In the former armory of the Castello-Vecchio, the Royal Prince Francis de Bourbon, the Minister of state, the Superintendent of the Police, the President of the Criminal Court, the Archbishop of Naples and other great noblemen were assembled. As soon as everyone had entered, Baron d'Altamonte was introduced, dressed in a purple coat, with a scarlet feather in his cap and a red mask over his face. Bianca Barberini and her father were the first to approach him. 'In the name of the living God,' said the Archbishop of Naples, who was presiding, do you recognize Il Porporato here present?'

"Bianca put her head on her father's breast. Her gaze had turned momentarily toward Prince Coriolani. She no longer had any strength or voice. Does one know the number of those who have secretly adored the superb Fulvio?

"The old Duc answered for his daughter: 'We do not recognize this man as Il Porporato.'

"Preziosa Balbi advanced, sustained by the superior. What that one suffered, no one could see, because of her long, thick veil. It's said that instead of looking at Baron d'Altamonte, her motionless head remained turned toward Fulvio Coriolani. 'In the name of the living God,' repeated the Archbishop, 'do you recognize Il Porporato here present?'

"Behind the veil, a faint but distinct *no* was heard. Then the recluse tottered in the arms of the superior of the convent.

"It was the turn of Jeanne Palliante of the Paleologues. That one descends from emperors. She has the beauty of queens. As she went past Coriolani, her savior, she saluted him. 'In the name of the living God,' she said, before she was interrogated, "this man here is not Il Porporato.'

"Was she telling the truth? She fell in a faint at the foot of the tribunal.

"No one any longer remained but Prince Fulvio.

"When I recount, my dear friends, I invent nothing. The day when Baron d'Altamonte was confronted in the armory of the Castello-Vecchio, there were other witnesses than our great lords. There were ushers, there were guards. Do I need to tell you that I have friends everywhere? It's my estate.

"Some people have told me that since the beginning of the session, Altamonte had been staring at Prince Coriolani through his red mask. You have not forgotten, my doves, that Altamonte had asked to see the Prince at the moment of his arrest, as well as the director of the police and others, for he presented a fine face to the court.

"The Prince looked at him too, severely and coldly. He as doubtless thinking privately: *have I once shaken the hand of this vile scoundrel?*

"Something very strange is said. As Fulvio advanced to testify, Altamonte extended his head toward the cartouche above the door to the cloisters. If you don't know it, I'll tell you that in the days of the Spaniards, the Castello-Vecchio served as the palace of the military commander. The cartouche contained the escutcheon of the Medina Torres with their motto: *Beware!*

"'In the name of the living God,' pronounced the His Grandeur the Archbishop of Naples, for the third time, 'do you recognize Il Porporato here present?'

"The Prince immediately replied, in a firm and assured voice: 'Yes, I recognize him.'

"Altamonte bounded like a tiger, but his hands were tied. Bianca, Precioza and Jeanne, woken up, uttered a faint cry simultaneously. On the sole testimony of Prince Coriolani, the tribunal decided in its conscience that Baron d'Altamonte really was Il Porporato, but as no one, strictly speaking, had rendered him to the law, the reward of a hundred thousand ducats remained in the coffers of the royal treasury. What would La Beata, the poor old woman, have done with all that money?

"But let us note this: many people think that the Companions of the Silence have declared a vendetta against Prince Coriolani. They missed him today, by the grace of Almighty God, but will they miss him tomorrow? It would be as well for the respected lord to have present in his memory the motto of the Medina-Torres and to beware.

"Who are they, these Companions of the Silence? Never ask, my beloved brothers. Where are they? Here and there, near and far, everywhere. There are some in the circle that surrounds me, I'd swear by my eternal salvation, and some of you, in talking about me, a poor fellow, are wondering, *Perhaps he...*

"Now, the King is alert. In order to liberate Il Porporato tonight, it would be necessary to demolish the old fortress stone by stone. Will anyone try? The daylight will tell us.

"I speak no evil of the Companions of the Silence, my friend! And I pronounce the name of Bourbon with all the respect it merits. We are living in difficult times. An imprudent word can cause the death of the father of a family. But why would anyone kill me, who wishes only good to everyone? I say what is: the shadow of this night will cover a battle. Out there, on the other side of the fortress, there are movements in the shadows, and muffled voices can be heard. The attack is in preparation. The defense has weapons in hand. The entire regiment of the Swiss Guards is at the Castello-Vecchio. Did you know that? Squadrons of light infantry are behind the church. Dragoons are hidden in the houses around the parvis. I've seen bayonets filling the courtyard behind the courtyard of the old hospital for the poor, more bayonets in the garden of the Incarnation and yet more bayonets in the arena of Pallonari, at the end of the Sotto-Portico Sant'Antonio.

"As for conspirators..."

At this point, Mariotto's words were cut off by a whistle-blast that appeared to come from the terrace of a nearby house. Several other whistle blasts responded in the distance.

The Strada di Porto now presented an entirely new appearance. The majority of the lights were extinct. All the open-air shops had disappeared. The doors, however, remained open. There was still a crowd, but it formed half a dozen groups massed around improvisers.

At the whistle-blast, everyone did as Mariotto did. There was suddenly a great silence. In that silence, two vezzo-players of Abruzzo, placed at the two extremities of the street, started to play with energy, hastening the rhythm, Fioravanti's well-known tune: *Amici, alliegre, andiamo alla pena.* And immediately, there was a rapid movement in the crowd, a sort of triage. In every group a few men suddenly broke away, piercing the astonished and anxious throng with vigorous thrust of the elbow. Once free, they started running toward the top if the strada, led by a sturdy fellow with short legs wearing the costume of the mariners of the port, and a young woman dressed as an orange-seller.

All that happened in the blink of an eye. And it did not happen too soon, for at the same moment, from the openings of all the side-streets at once, bayonets glittered. The auditors of the eloquent Mariotto looked for him on his pedestal. He had disappeared. All the lights went out, as if by magic. Only a few smoky street-lamps remained suspended at long intervals from the top of the street to the bottom. Mute with amazement, the crowd heard arms being taken up in the side-streets, followed by the order: "Forward march!"

Two minutes later the Strada di Porto was bristling with bayonets, save for the little corner of the Fountain of the Three Virgins. There, the population was penned, silent and nonplussed, like a flock of sheep. But in that flock you would have searched n vain for Farfalla, Miterino, Ruzzola, Masaccio and others. It was not for nothing that the bagpipes had sounded. Even Gaspardo the fisherman had put to sea at that signal. And it was truly a flock of ewes that the soldiers of the King of Naples held imprisoned in the circle of their bayonets.

VIII. The Escalade

It might have been about ten o'clock in the evening when the armed force occupied the Strada di Porto. All the other avenues of the Castello-Vecchio were similarly and superabundantly guarded. The authorities had opined that an attempt would be made that night to liberate Il Porporato. They had taken their precautions in consequence, convinced that, given the circumstances, the audacity of the mysterious association, which seemed to have chosen the capital of the kingdom as its domicile, would go as far as laying its cards on the table and attempting a pitched battle.

Our comrade Mariotto has left us little to say about the brotherhood of the Silence, which had been causing such emotion in Naples for months and had ramifications even in the remotest provinces. We can, however, establish two facts.

The first is that no one knew whether the association in question, too redoubtable to be considered as a simple band of brigands, had a political foundation beneath it. That suspicion, above all, kept the government on the alert. The second fact is that very few people remembered the origin of the association, for the good reason that even the brotherhood seemed to have completely forgotten its point of departure. It was no longer a question of avenging Mario Monteleone. And if the murder for which Il Porporato was about to carry his head to the scaffold was connected with events recounted in the prologue to this story, it is because that murder, already old, went back to the times when the Companions of the Silence far from Naples and making their efforts in the southern principalities, gave the vendetta as a pretext for their crimes, and made use of the name of Mario Monteleone, the holy martyr, as a talisman with regard to the poor populations of Calabria.

Now, another direction had been imprinted on the subterranean endeavors of the brotherhood. We know that in the crypt of the Corpo-Santo, the Chevalier d'Athol—or, if you prefer, Il Porporato—had said that the thought of Monteleone had died with him, that he was to be allowed to rest in peace, and that he was avenged, since he was taking responsibility for his vengeance.

Those were proud words. We will doubtless know in due course whether Il Porporato had kept his promise. What is certain is that Il Porporato had not remained idle. For several months, unusual things had been happening in Naples In addition to numerous pillages, executed with incredible audacity, it had been found that the court and the city had been put to contribution for an enormous sum.

Only one circumstance, however, gives us the right to think that those bold nocturnal knights who had made Naples a conquered city were really our cavalieri ferrai of the valley of the Martorello: the name of Felice Tavola, whom we know to be one of the Six. Outside of that, we have not thus far seen anything. None of the wearers of the iron ring have been presented to our sight. We have not encountered old Amato Lorenzo, nor the wily David Heimer, nor the giant Tristany, even taller and broader than Gaspardo the fisherman, nor Policeni Corner, nor Marino Marchese, the two fashionable bandits, nor, above all, Il Porporato. None of them, in fact, had fallen into the hands of the law. Tavola was the first.

Tavola! But who could be sure of the identity of Tavola himself? Subalterns had often taken the name of Il Porporato and sustained the lie all the way to the scaffold. We know that. Why should Porporato, finally fallen into a trap, not have taken the name of a subaltern in his turn? He was, there could be no doubt, a man experienced in many ruses.

Let us go further. Would anyone in the world have been able to certify, in an absolute fashion, that Il Porporato, that giant of crime, really existed? That he was not a gathering of malefactors condensed, so to speak, under that collective name, a kind of hydra with twenty heads? With half of what was imputed to Il Porporato, who was nevertheless reputed to be a young man, one could have matched the legends of ten Fra Diavolos.

Deception is the greatest asset in these occult associations. Those men who pass voluntarily into the estate of wild beasts acquire the instincts of jungle animals. Hunters know that old stags and old wild boar always have some bodyguard who goes hunting in their stead in order to give them time to rest. The highland brigand Dougal Dhoe had three brothers with him, who resemble him perfectly, and all three of whom had themselves hanged one after another in order to spare him that supreme accident. Scotland is the land of romantic devotions and Italy, more egotistical, does not offer many similar examples, but without getting oneself hanged one can go a long way, if one only stops short of the rope.

Felice Tavola was not yet hanged. In any case, the organization, the rule, of a secret society, can, if necessary, replace voluntary devotion. It is not permissible to ignore the surprising tyranny that generally oppresses the members of similar associations. The rule of the Companions of the Silence was very strict, if the rumors running around could be believed. It was carbornarism perfected and brought to a monarchal condition. The master had unchecked sovereign power. The Six were not his ministers or his counselors but his immediate lieutenants. He consulted them when he wished. Below the six cavaliers came the companions engaged on oath, below the companions, a nameless proletariat that was paid and acted blindly. The oath of the Silence obliged them to die for the master.

The Castello-Vecchio of Naples, the plans and designs of which can still be found in specialist works anterior to 1830, was clear on five of its faces, each of which overlooked one or more of the small side-streets, or vicoletti, which we have mentioned. The main entrance opened between the Vicoletto Delfino and the Vicoletto Martinelli at the end of the sotto-portico bearing the name of Sant'Antonio, which prolonged the Strada di Porto. The sixth, seventh and eighth faces—for that castle formed an irregular octagon, of which one of the angles was indented, were encased by houses, and the three of them only presented a single exit, piercing beneath a vault a thick block of houses, and ending up behind San Giovanni Maggiore, not far from the entrance to the catacombs. Part of that vaulted passage still exists today. It is the most obscure sotto-portico, and the most malodorous that there is in Naples—and that is saying a great deal.

From the extremity of that vault to the larghetto, or small square, of Sant'Antonio, there is a road about a quarter of a league long, going around houses. The greatest width of that road is where the vault is pierced; it diminishes as one approaches the Larghetto Sant'Antonio, where the last of the dwellings is stuck to the rampart like a limpet.

That night, the Castello-Vecchio was invested by the garrison of Naples. There were veritable camps at all the exits, where those brilliant parade soldiers, who so rarely have an opportunity to prove their valor to foreigners, were bivouacked. The avenues of those strategic points were also guarded, and the Strada di Porto was a fortress. But in the long space between San Giovanni Maggiore and the Larghetto Sant'Antonio, as there was no issue, the precautions were naturally less exaggerated. Only five or six sentinels, placed within earshot of one another, were guarding that extent.

At about quarter past ten—which is to say, only a few minutes after the military occupation of the Strada di Porto—we shall conduct the reader to a small triangular area situated almost in the center of the façade of the series of houses masking the old castle. That small marketplace, known as the Piazzetta Grande, by comparison with some hole even more restricted, opened at one of its angles on to the Vicoletto Zaffo, one of the side streets that still joins the Strada dei Tribunali today. The side opposite that corner was formed by houses adjacent to the castle. In front of those houses passed the Strada di Mantua, a fairly broad but tortuous street cut by cul-de-sacs that entered into the block of houses.

Naples in 1823 was not overabundantly supplied with street lights. In the Piazzetta Grande there was only one, situated in the Strada di Mantua, at the southern corner of the square. What that street light, which could not see its colleagues, hidden by the abrupt bend in the street, illuminated was, first of all, a sentinel belonging to the Buffalo regiment of the regular infantry. That sentinel was walking back and forth at the opening to the square. Nothing in the surroundings, it must be said, was calculated to awaken the suspicion or the anxiety of that worthy conscript. The marketplace was empty. No sound could be heard in the Vicoletto Zaffo, which was the point to be watched. The neighboring house seemed to be asleep. In brief, the sentinel was coming and going in a veritable desert.

Perhaps someone more experienced than him might have conceived some anxieties precisely because of that. People are very fond of the night in Naples, even in winter. The population goes to bed late. The complete silence and that profound solitude at such an early hour might not have appeared natural. But our conscript of the Buffalo regiment did not go as far as that in his reflections. Romantic and amorous as he was, he was thinking about Nannetta, the watermelon seller, whose eyes were so dark and whose melons were so fresh. Will we ever know what our conscript liked best about Nannette—her eyes or her melons?

Apart from the sentinel, the street light did not illuminate any other human being. The dull and vacillating glow fell immediately upon a two-story house, low and old, which protruded on to the street and behind which rose another house at least twice as high. The roof of the first served the second as a terrace. The protrusion of the old building put in shadow the entrance to a cul-de-sac, at the other end of which was the coaching entrance of the second house.

We have said enough for the reader not to be astonished when we add that the conscript of the Buffalo regiment was not a subtle observer. If he had been anything of an observer he would have noticed something seemingly insignificant, but which might have a bearing on the present circumstances.

At the moment when our conscript had taken up his entry duty, the cul-de-sac had been illuminated by a smoky lamp placed in the niche of a Madonna. The lamp had now ceased burning. Darkness filled the cul-de-sac. Who had extinguished the lamp? There had been no sound of a door opening or closing, and no one had gone into the alleyway.

At the far end of the cul-de-sac, a large arched doorway gave access to a courtyard belonging to a considerable house, the third in depth, which was adjacent to the ramparts of the Castello-Vecchio. All the houses were terraced, like the first, and like five-sixths of Neapolitan houses, in fact.

The sentinel, therefore, was coming and going in all innocence. He was bored, which is the métier of the sentinel, and, in order to kill time, he was humming a tune from the Capitanata, which was his homeland.

At intervals, other sentinels called out "Who goes there?" Our conscript had not yet had to go to that trouble once. He was a sentry of leisure. While he was humming, dreaming about Nannetta's eyes or her melons, there was a confused movement in the shadows in the depths of the cul-de-sac, to the right of the large coaching entrance.

Two men were there, in the angle of the wall. One of them was slowly raising a ladder that had been lying on the ground and leaning it against the wall of the first house. He was unable to do so without making a slight noise. The sentinel came to the corner of the house and peered in.

Our two men were lying face down against the wall. The sentinel could not see anything but blackness, with the possible exception of the ladder. But his orders did not include investigating ladders leaning against walls. The good conscript turned round, and resumed his song.

As soon as he was out of sight, the two nocturnal prowlers got to their feet swiftly. One of them climbed to the top of the ladder with the agility of a cat. Then he let himself slide down the uprights and crouched down at the foot, saying only: "Too short by two or three palms."[30]

His companion made an energetic gesture of disappointment. In spite of the obscurity, his tall and proud stature would have been distinguishable; he was draped in a dark cloak. The other had his head in his hands and was maintaining a complete immobility. The man in the cloak looked at the ladder attentively.

"The cul-de-sac slopes downwards, he said, "the terrace in straight. Because of that the house is higher where we are than in the Strada di Mantua.

His companion pointed at the sentinel, who was going past the corner of the house at that moment, and then said: "There's the street light."

"Two things that inconvenience us," said the man in the cloak. "Let's get rid of them both."

He made a sign to the other to follow him, and traversed the street with a tread lighter than that of a little girl while the conscript had his back turned. Once in the square, the two men ran along the houses and disappeared into the Vicoletto Zaffo.

At that moment a voice descended from the ramparts and said: *"Sentinelle, guardatevi!"*

From the Larghetto Sant'Antonio to the vault, and going back along the Strada di Mantua, each sentinel had to repeat: "Sentinel, look out!"

The sentinel of the Buffalo regiment repeated that sacramental refrain, like all the rest, but he laughed in thinking that he only had to guard motionless walls and a street light.

Few minutes went by. The sentinel suddenly stopped walking. A sound had come from the vicoletto. It was, in fact, that of footsteps clearly resonating on the lava pavement. While walking the person was singing loudly; it was the voice of a woman or a child.

"Who goes there?" called our worthy soldier, striking the required pose.

The response was a burst of laughter. At the same time, a Neapolitan gamin—there are gamins in Naples, as in Paris—a ragazzo of the old city, with his bonnet over is ear and a bouffant chemise with tightly-belted calzone, emerged from the Vicoletto Zaffo.

"Who goes there?" repeated the Buffalo.

The gamin advanced boldly, his fist on his hip, still singing his sea shanty at the top of his voice.

One can't shoot at that, though, thought the conscript. Then he added: *Nannetta looked like that when she disguised herself as a ragazzo at the last carnival. Oh San Gennaro, what eyes! And what melons!*

---

[30] The Neapolitan palm was slightly over ten inches.

There was truth in what the Buffalo said. The gamin's figure was as slim and graceful as that of a woman, and the long curly hair escaping from his bonnet was falling in profusion on to her shoulders.

"Good evening, Comrade Pietro!" he said, when he was in the middle of the square.

"Go away, bambino," replied the soldier.

"Your name isn't Pietro, then, friend?" said the gamin, who was still coming forward. Good evening Francesco, Paolo or Andrea, then..."

"Go away I tell you."

The conscript raised his musket. The child stopped and held his sides

"Your implement hasn't been used for a long time, Jacopo, Rafaelle or Filippo!" he cried, in a mocking tone. "I'll wager that you don't even know how to load it."

"By the Holy Spirit!" muttered the Buffalo. "That's a girl in disguise, and a pretty one too, I say with a good heart." Aloud, he went on: "If you don't want to go away, Picciola, come here and give me a kiss."

"So, Carlotto," said he gamin, "you could tell that I'm a girl? Well, I'll kiss you, Ludovico, my friend, if you play along with me. I've bet two ducats, neither more nor less, that I can break the glass of that street light."

It was, in fact, the charming orange-seller of the Strada di Porto, the one who had accosted Peter-Paulus and sent the English mariner back to his boat. She rounded her arm and threw a pebble that she was holding in her hand. The glass of the street light shattered.

"Santa Maria!" cried the alarmed conscript.

"Ha ha!" said the gamin. "We daughters of Procida know how to throw stones. The wick now."

A second turn of the arm, a second pebble. The wick went out.

The idea of a treason sprang to the conscript's mind as soon as he was surrounded by sudden darkness. He seized his musket in order to raise the alarm, but two plump arms as soft as satin were wrapped around his neck from behind.

"Didn't I promise you a kiss, Tommaso?" said the girl's laughing voice.

And at the same time, his rifle was snatched away from front. A silk handkerchief rolled into a gag was stuck forcefully over his mouth. He tried to cry out but it was too late. A second handkerchief soon covered his eyes. Then he heard laughter and voices around him. Someone complained of not having any rope; someone made one with his own apparel, torn into strips His hands were tied, his legs too. Then he was deposited, thus carefully tied up like a parcel, at the foot of the wall of the house.

Poor conscript of the Buffalo regiment! There were four people around him: three men and the disguised woman. She and one of the three men went to stand as sentinels, one to the right and the other to the left of the Piazzetta Grande, in the Strada di Mantua. The other two went swiftly around the corner of the cul-de-sac and came back with the ladder.

The first threw off his cloak, and uncovered his rich and fine apparel. Underneath that he was wearing the costume of a fisherman, and we would have been able to recognize him, in spite of the obscurity, as the handsome idler previously leaning against the wall of the Fountain of the Three Virgins, between the mariner with the meerschaum pipe and the last of the lazzaroni coiled up like a snake on the lava: the mysterious Beldemonio. The second was the lazzarone in question, the saltarello whose advent had created such an untimely diversion to the narrations of our improviser Mariotto Cigoli.

That one was easy to recognize. He loved his profession. As soon as the ladder was posed against the wall of the house overlooking the square, he seized one of the uprights in both hands and gave himself the pleasure of doing a little iron hand.

"Hurry!" commanded the fisherman!"

He had scarcely had time to pronounce that single word when the saltarello was already at the top of the ladder. There really was a sensible difference of level between the ground of the Strada di Mantua and the part of the cul-de-sac where the escalade had been attempted previously. But the difference was not great enough, it seemed, for the clown let himself slide down again, as before, head down, fell on his hands, turned a somersault in order to put himself on his feet and said: "Two palms!"

"We need another two palms!" exclaimed the fisherman, stamping his foot. "Can't you cross that?"

"My mother is old," replied the clown. "I'm the sole direct heir to the name of Cucuzone. Ask possible things of me."

"Couldn't we find another ladder?"

"The streets of the old city are full of patrols. It's a miracle that we haven't run into trouble."

The fisherman bowed his head and reflected. Half past ten sounded on the clock of San Giovanni Maggiore.

"The sentinels are relieved at eleven," said the saltarello.

"Climb!" ordered the fisherman, throwing the beautiful tresses of his hair over his shoulders, with a determined expression.

"And afterwards?"

"Climb."

The clown obeyed. When he was at the top of the ladder, he felt it oscillate under a new weight. He turned and saw he fisherman following him.

"Signor," he asked, with profound astonishment, "Do you think you can do better than me?"

"I'm thinking of doing something different," relied the fisherman. "Hold firm."

The clown obeyed, stiffening himself as best he could by sticking his hands to the all. Immediately, he felt someone climbing nimbly along his sides, with precaution.

"Not bad, not bad!" he said, protectively. "Don't close your eyes—that makes your head spin. Keep looking up!"

A foot was placed on his right shoulder, then another on the left shoulder. The clown did not speak again, and held his breath. Cold sweat inundated his body.

"Damned if I tremble like that for my own skin!" he muttered. Then he added, in an imploring one, but without moving: "Come down, signor! Come down, my young master. I'll try again. If there's a head to be broken, it's better if it's mine."

"Shut up!" said the handsome fisherman, in a contained voice. "And don't weaken! There's someone on the terrace of the other house."

Another voice did, in fact, reach Cucuzone. It said: "There isn't a cat in these gutters. Let's go, lads! There are enough patrols on the roofs! We'll finish our night in the guard room."

"That's Lieutenant Frazer," murmured Cucuzone.

A forceful kick imposed silence on him.

From the height of the rampart, the watchman's cry descended for the second time: "*Guardatevi, sentinelle!*"

"Respond," ordered the fisherman, when the cry, going along the block of houses, had been repeated by the next sentinel.

"*Guardatevi, sentinelle!*" shouted the clown.

The echo was repeated at intervals all the way to the vaulted passage where the cordon of sentinels ended. Then everything fell silent. No one could be seen any longer on the terraces.

Cucuzone did not dare lift his head, but he experienced the precise reaction of all the efforts that his companion made to hang on to the edge of the terrace— efforts thus far impotent.

"It's too high," said the fisherman, finally. "I'm exhausting myself at a pure loss. Cucuzone!"

"Signor?"

"The day when we met in the main square you had a fifty-pound weight at the end of each arm...and you weren't trembling as you are tonight."

"That's true, signor...but I had both feet on Mother Earth's firm ground, and my fifty-pound weights couldn't break my ribs in falling."

"Don't worry about me, my friend. Let's see whether you still have arms as solid as before. Take one of my feet in each of your hands...do as you did with the weights...and by the grace of God...!"

The clown hesitated. "Signor," he said, "the ladder rocks. When I make the effort to lift you up, everything will tremble, the rungs and the uprights, and my poor arms more that the rest. There's no reason to try this, signor. Let me climb up in your place..."

"Do as I tell you!" ordered the fisherman.

Before obeying, Cucuzone passed the back of his hand over his brow, which was bathed by cold sweat. "May the Holy Virgin be with us," he murmured, making the sign of the cross rapidly. "I don't want to disobey you, but to save the rogue in there, is it worth risking my life?"

"Hurry up!" said the fisherman.

Cucuzone seized one of his feet, and then the other. He was a robust man hardened since childhood to all violent exercises, but emotion had certainly taken away a part of his strength.

What he had predicted happened. As soon as he attempted to stretch himself, an oscillating movement was communicated from his body to the ladder, which beat against the wall and began to creak. If he had dared he would have uttered cries of pain and anguish. His neck was taut, as if in a vice.

"Go on then, wretch!" snapped the fisherman.

Cucuzone made a supreme effort, his muscles contracting desperately. His companion's feet rose up, and he felt a terrible shock immediately. Then his hands were empty. The fisherman had leapt over the balustrade. The clown's arms fell. He had vertigo.

"Thank you," said the fisherman. "Leave the ladder there for as long as you can."

"What if they relieve the sentinel?"

"Fiamma knows what to do. You're all under her orders tonight."

From the summits of the Castello-Vecchio the watchman's cry arrived. The echoes followed the meanders of the Strada di Mantua. When the nearest sentinel had done his duty, it was the fisherman himself who shouted: *"Guardatevi, sentinelle!"*

The poor soldier of the Buffalo regiment could not complain. The task was performed conscientiously. But before the sentinels' responses were stifled by the distance, a low, subtle hiss like that of a snake resounded from the direction of the Vicoletto Zaffo. Almost immediately, and from the same direction, the heavy and regular tread of a patrol sounded on the pavement of the street. Cucuzone was already at the bottom of the ladder. The fisherman had disappeared into the night that enveloped the terrace. The young woman and the mariner with the meerschaum pipe were busy untying the conscript.

Before removing the gap from his mouth, the young woman said to him: "You haven't seen anything, comrade; as for what you've heard, listen: two ounces of gold if you keep quiet…six inches of iron in your breast if you talk."

"The surest way would be to start with the six inches of iron," muttered the mariner.

But the young woman replied: "The Master doesn't wasn't that."

A moment later, the three prowlers and the ladder were hidden in the shadow of the cul-de-sac. The leader of the patrol appeared at the opening of the Vicoletto Zaffo.

"Who goes there?" cried the sentinel.

"Good, good, Martino," said a voice. "We've just come to check up on you. If you'd been asleep, you'd have been in irons. Good watch—you'll be relieved soon."

IX. Journey Over the Rooftops

It was still a long way—a very long way—from the first terrace, where our young fisherman was, to the ramparts of the Castello-Vecchio, but one can say that the hardest part was done. The second house was, in fact, only one story higher than the first, and had protruding stones that rendered the climb easy. That house had a name; cicerones did not fail to show tourists the portal giving access to the cul-de-sac—which did, in fact, conserve a rather fine character.

"La casa del Folquieri!" said the cicerones.

Foulquier, Foulque or Foucher houses are equally common in west and south-west of France.[31]

The Folquieri house had been boxed in by more modern constructions, like the Castello-Vecchio itself. It occupied the greater part of the distance separating the fortress-prison from the Strada di Mantua. It was necessary to cross its entire width to get from one to the other, for its façade ran in the same direction as the cul-de-sac, perpendicular to the Strada di Mantua.

Our night-prowler waited for the patrol and its leader, whose speech was so unmilitary, to withdraw. As soon as there was no longer anyone on the Piazzetta Grande, he began to scale the northern corner of the Folquieri house. It was like a stone ladder. Our young man, agile and courageous, even though he did not have the gymnastic talents of his comrade Cucuzone, had soon reached the upper balustrade. He climbed over it and found himself in a monumental gutter, which made a tour of the old house. From there he was almost at the level of the ramparts of the prison, which formed a black mass in the distance. He could see the slow march of the lanterns that preceded the patrols.

No one was asleep in the Castello-Vecchio that night. All eyes there remained open. Our young man had only one danger to fear for the moment, and that was attracting the attention of the people living in the attics of the Folquieri house and being pursued as a thief. He therefore began to crawl cautiously along the wide gutter in order to make a tour of the old house. That was child's play for him, which a child could easily have accomplished.

In these eccentric journeys where one taken unbeaten paths, however, it is necessary never to cry victory too soon. As soon as our handsome adventurer had turned the southern corner of the gable that overlooked the Strada di Mantua, the aspect of things changed abruptly.

A family short of space had built an extension of their lodgings above the gutter. Our fisherman, stopped dead, sought a passage outside the balustrade. The edifice of planks constructed by the cramped family was literally hanging over the void. It would have needed wings to get over the obstacle. Beldemonio

---

[31] The French "Foulquier" is a slang term that refers to an old mariner.

allowed an expression of chagrin to escape, and turned back in order to go around the house the other way.

Without that intervention of chance our story would have been quite different. The fate of a man—and thus the fate of all those who depend on him—often hinges on the frivolous question of whether he will turn right or left. At this point, the bold prowler Beldemonio was forced to turn left. If he had been able to go to the right, firstly, he would have reached the goal of his nocturnal journey a quarter of an hour sooner. Now, during that quarter of an hour, a capital event occurred. Secondly, he would have followed his route directly, without distraction, because, in truth, he was not there to dart curious glances through widows and curtains. Now, he allowed himself to be distracted involuntarily. There are things at which one cannot help looking. To employ a worn-out expression, but one that is marvelously picturesque, for our life is like a woven fabric in which a single broken threat can vary to infinity all the designs of the weave, the weft of his existence was transformed. His life was like him, switching from right to left: unintentionally, it changed direction.

This is what caused Beldemonio's distraction and delay. He had already turned two corners and was following the ledge that crowned the anterior courtyard of the old hose when he saw a lighted skylight toward the middle of the main building. It was necessary for him to go past it. He stopped. The silhouette of a young woman was designed in black on the panes.

The young woman's head was leaning against the frame. She was dreaming, or looking out. In either case, it would have been folly to try to go past her without attracting her attention. Our young man was therefore obliged to halt and wait until it pleased the pretty sentry to desert her post. Was she pretty? He did not know, and it hardly mattered. All that could be seen of the girl was the delicate profile of her slim figure, slightly depressed by hunger or sadness.

Sadness and fatigue sometimes inhabit those poor floors, the closest to the heavens, where ingrate toil does not always provide daily bread: fatigue because one strives a great deal, and sometimes in vain, sadness because today's trouble will also be tomorrow's. What is heartbreaking in those dolors of the poor is the uniform, thick, implacable veil that prolongs into the future, hopelessly, the bleak mourning of the past. Sadness, fatigue...

Poets talk about the joys of indigent young. It exists, that joy, by the mercy of God, but in order to have it, it is necessary to have faith or insouciance, the virtue whose praises are unsung, which is the very flower of youth.

There are rose-bushes on which the sun never shines, and which have no flowers. There are youths full of shadow in which holy insouciance never blossoms. Poor stems and poor souls! When the sun comes too late, they lean forward, on the lookout; when amour touches them, they die...

One can well imagine that your young adventurer did not devote himself to meditations of that genre. The young woman inconvenienced him, that was all. We can scarcely say that he noticed the frail grace of her figure or the melancholy of which her attitude spoke so eloquently. After five minutes, she straightened up. Her face turned toward the heavens, her hands went to her face, and then she slowly went back into her room.

Although our young fisherman had not perceived her features, since her face had remained constantly in the shadow, the profound unhappiness there was in the gesture and the pose of the girl did not escape him.

"She's suffering!" he murmured.

Then, profiting from the route that was now open, he resumed his progress. The closer he came to the lighted window, the more he increased his precautions in order not to make a sound. Neither the young woman nor her shadow could any longer be seen, but Beldemonio knew that there were alert eyes and ears behind that casement.

As he went past the window he crept like a snake, without even daring to lift his head. No sound was coming from the lighted room. Why did Beldemonio stop before having completed that step, the most difficult of all? Why?

On turning his head slightly to make sure that no one was watching him, he had perceived, facing him, at the back of the room, a white form kneeling. It was the young woman. Beldemonio recognized her exquisite figure in its child-like slenderness, and even the appearance of discouraged weakness. She had turned her back to the window, doubtless in order to say her evening prayer. The lamp, placed on a little table, illuminated her oblique profile.

In those lines, pure, but lacking a little of joyful roundness of adolescence, nothing echoed the poor weaknesses announced by the depression of the torso. The forehead was high and crowned with adorable hair, which, devoid of any tie or band covered chastely veiled shoulders with its lavish curls. The brow-ridge, proudly sculpted, spoke of intelligence, and allowed the divination of the radiance it sheltered. The whiteness of temples, beautiful and broad, cased the lacy festoons of the tresses to stand out. The discouragement—for it is necessary to mention that again—was entirely in the poor neck, charming and flexible, which was tilted sideways, in the abandoned figure in the pretty pale hands softly joined.

What is there to say? The ensemble was both delectable and troubling. There was in that picture, so simple in appearance, an eloquent lament that rent the heart. And yet, our fisherman felt his heart contract; his rebellious heart was hammering.

He stood up, forgetting the precautions he had to take. He stood up straight, as if that new posture would have permitted him to see better.

What he saw in addition was a prayer book on the table and a small robe at the bottom of the bed. Hanging behind the bed was one of the little ebony crucifixes that nuns wear around their necks. He waited for a movement that would permit him to distinguish the features, which he divined to be charming. They young woman did not make any, except that her head inclined forward by degrees and ended up touching her hands. From that moment on she did not budge, any more than a statue.

Do you know what Beldemonio thought?

He thought: *If I encountered her tomorrow, I wouldn't recognize her*.

Suddenly, a noise, muffled at first and then loud, became audible in the vicinity, passing over the roofs. It was coming from the direction of the city, beyond the Castello-Vecchio, from the west. It was as if someone were nailing some vast carpentry, noisily. The young woman remained motionless. Did the fervor of her prayer prevent her from hearing? By contrast, Beldemonio shuddered from head to toe.

"The scaffold!" he murmured. "They're setting up the scaffold."

He scarcely had time to dart one last glance into the room—a regretful glance—and resumed crawling. But he said: "I'll come back."

In a matter of seconds he was at the end of the Folquieri house. The neighboring edifice was lower. With a light leap, he descended to its roofs, which he crossed at a run. Two buildings still remained between him and the rampart. He scaled them rapidly and then, reaching the nearest crenellation with a vigorous leap, he found himself on the very fortifications of the Castello-Vecchio. He could not help looking back beneath him.

His cheerful and bold face no longer bore any trace of his recent emotion. Had he already forgotten the pale kneeling girl? No. But he was one of those people who compartmentalize their impressions, repressing them one by one until the necessary time. That faculty is called sang-froid.

The part of the rampart on to which he had just climbed was a sort of platform. The view was limited to the north by a Gothic tower at the foot of which a guard-post was bivouacked, and to the south by a half-moon on which a sentinel was walking back and forth. A square building enclosed the semicircle within the platform, which it dominated by two floors. On the ground floor of that building, a lantern hanging from the wall illuminated the window of a cell blocked by thick iron bars.

I'm in the right place, Beldemonio said to himself. *Our man is there*.

There was, in fact, no doubt about it. The lantern, placed to illuminate any effort that the prisoner might attempt against the bars, is the supreme precaution employed in Italy. It is only taken against those condemned to death.

As Beldemonio got his bearing in that fashion, there was a movement at the foot of the tower, and the soldiers in the guard-post took up their arms. A patrol was passing. Beldemonio let himself down outside the crenellations, he held himself suspended by the arms from a projection of the stone. He heard the patrol pass. The soldiers were chatting and laughing at the excess of precautions taken in order to retain Baron d'Altamonte.

"Our chiefs can't believe," they said, "that the Companions of the Silence are going to attack us a hundred feet above the ground?"

The sentinel on the half-moon shouted his challenge, which was answered in the customary fashion. The patrol disappeared around a corner of the ramparts. It was scarcely a minute after the footfalls of the soldiers had ceased to resound on the paving stones when the sentinel suddenly found himself confronted by a young man of tall and proud stature, whom he had not seen approaching. His first impulse was to sound the alarm, but the unknown man had seized his hand and traced a double cross in the palm. The soldier darted a fearful glance around him.

"Here!" he stammered.

"Everywhere," replied the unknown man.

The soldier tried to see his face, which was covered by a mask. The stranger's costume was that of a fisherman. After having looked around, the soldier pronounced, in an ill-assured voice: "Iron is strong and charcoal is black."

There is something stronger than iron," replied the stranger.

"It is faith."

"There is something blacker than charcoal."

"It is the conscience of a traitor. What do you want, signor?"

"To free the prisoner."

"I'll answer for him with my life!"

"Your life is ours. Don't put yourself between the hammer and the anvil. You're here because we wanted it."

"In fact," murmured the soldier. "It wasn't my turn to stand guard…the sergeant…"

"The sergeant," the stranger interjected, "receives his orders from the lieutenant; the lieutenant obeys the captain, the captain the major, the major the colonel, the colonel the general. Who do you think the general obeys?"

"The King…"

"Me!"

So saying the unknown man put his extended hand under the sentinel's eyes. On the middle finger there was an iron ring ornamented by three glittering diamonds, which formed a triangle of fire,

"Order, signor," said the soldier. "I have my mother; I commend her to God."

"Death is against us," replied the other. "Life is with us, Have no fear."

He approached the window of the cell and called out in a soft voice: "Felice!"

There was no reply.

"Felice Tavola!"

The same silence.

Pale and trembling, the sentinel had resumed his pacing. At the moment when the unknown man turned toward him to question him, the watchword, as they say in Italy, passed from mouth to mouth along the line of the ramparts.

"*Niente nuovo!*" said each sentinel, successively: nothing new.

The poor soldier put his hands to his panting breast and replied, like the others: "Nothing new."

The sentry on the tower shouted for the external cordons: "*Guaradatevi, sentinelle!*"

"Bartolo Spalazzi!" said the unknown man.

"You know my name, signor?" murmured the soldier.

"You have done your duty," murmured the masked man. "Tomorrow you will have a corporal's stripes and your mother will be sleeping in a good bed. Reply and don't hide anything from me. Has anything happened in this cell since you began your watch?"

"Signor," replied Bartolo, "I made the oath of the Silence to the other soldier…on a day that my dying mother had no help. What I'm telling you is the truth. About ten minutes ago, someone went into Il Porporato's cell; I heard the sound of voices, then the clink of iron, then the door opened and closed again. Everything fell silent."

"A murder!" thought the unknown man, aloud. "That's impossible." Then he added: "Were those who went in policemen?"

"Yes signor."

"I need to know!" exclaimed the unknown man, who seemed to be prey to a terrible agitation. "How long is it between each round?"

"Thirty minutes."

"And when are you to be relieved?"

"At eleven o'clock."

The unknown man consulted his watch. "I have time."

He ran to the cell and took out of his bosom two small objects, which he fitted together by the light of the suspended lantern. The two combined objects, a circular file and a little wheel, formed an admirable machine invented by the celebrated English bandit Jack Sheppard, a man of science and talent. Sheppard's file, mounted on a gear moved by a strong Geneva spring, could saw through a bar an inch and a half thick in three minutes.

Think about poor Latude, who took thirty-five years to make his hole, and bow down before the progress of the century.

The unknown man employed his file, which only produced a slight hiss. He gripped the bar sawn through at the base with both hands, twisted it and lifted it up. An instant later, he leapt into Il Porporato's cell, holding the lantern, which he had =unhooked. The cell was empty. On the white wall opposite the window two lines had been traced in mysterious characters:

$$NA^3 E^2A \ NA^3MR^3I^2; \ EI^2 \ E^2I^2 \ L^3I2A^3LI^2!$$

The unknown man stood there as if struck by amazement. He could not take his eyes off those characters.

"Betrayed!" he murmured, while his arms fell alongside his body. "Ship-wrecked within sight of port!"

"Signor! Signor!" said the voice of the sentinel at the window of the cell. "People are coming from all directions at once."

The unknown man raised himself up to his full height.

"I'm still standing," he said. "Woe betide the traitors!"

He left the cell. The rampart was already full of noises. There was a general movement from the top to the bottom of the Castello-Vecchio. Voices were shouting from the other side of the half-moon

"They set up their ladder in the Strada di Mantua opposite the Piazzetta Grande. Martino was tied up and gagged. They put a blindfold over his eyes and gave him two ounces of gold to keep quiet."

"And Martino has talked?"

"His account is settled, poor devil."

"How many came up the ladder?"

"Only one. The others stayed with the disguised woman."

"He must be on the roofs, then."

"Or in the fortress itself."

"Alert! Alert!"

"Who's on duty over there?"

"Bartolo Spalazzi of the Trani regiment."

Footsteps approached, and the soldiers in the tower post took up their arms.

"I'm doomed!" murmured Bartolo.

Shout: "Who goes there?" ordered the unknown man, who had just extinguished the lantern, plunging the vicinity of the cell into darkness.

"Who goes there?" repeated Bartolo, mechanically.

"Shout louder!"

"Who goes there?"

"Arm your rifle...you're going to save yourself in saving...listen, they're turning the corner of the half-moon. Who goes there, again!"

The soldier obeyed. The unknown leapt on to the edge of the rampart.

"Take aim and fire," he ordered, as he dived.

A shot resounded, followed by an inexpressible tumult. More than a hundred men arrived on the rampart at the same time from different directions.

"Did you hit him, Bartolo Spalazzi?"

"This way! This way! A ladder! All the streets are guarded! We have him!"

X. The Chamber of the Dead

The words traced in hieroglyphic characters on the wall of Felice Tavola's cell were these:

I have been forgotten.
I shall avenge myself.

A terrible threat in the mouth of one of the *cavalieri ferrai!* But those who want to betray an association like that of the Companions of the Silence are always wrong to say: "I shall avenge myself." It is a long way from the threat to the delivered thrust.

Our handsome fisherman, Beldemonio, had traversed at a run the terrace-roof of the first house adjacent to the fortress. When the garrison of the Castello-Vecchio arrived at the crenellations from all directions, there was already no one in sight. Ladders were brought; people descended on to the roof. At the same time the order was given to double the guard at all the exits along the Strada di Mantua.

There really was little chance if the fugitive escaping. A complete battalion had been formed with those descending room the rampart on to the roof, which immediately set about furrowing the terrace in all directions. The chiefs had said: "Anywhere that you find a broken window or a forced frame, enter with bayonets forward."

There was a poor room situated in the attics of the old house known as the Folquieri house. A few wicker chairs, a round fir-wood table and a couchette surrounded by percale curtains composed all its furniture. In the corner opposite the one occupied by the couchette there was, however, a meager mattress extended on unwashed bars, polished by age. Between the table and the bed, there was a little stove, whose embers were being slowly consumed beneath white ash. Above the mattress, an image of the Virgin was stuck. On the nearby chair lay a thick Book of Hours, whose fatigued pages denoted long and frequent use. A scapular was attached to the bars of the sane chair. A soutanelle was hanging from a nail fixed to the wall near the mattress, affecting the long straight pleats appropriate to such a garment. Behind the bed was a holy water stoup, next to a little burnished copper crucifix whose cross was ebony. On the table, at the foot of the lamp that was about to go out, a piece of paper contained a few words. That was all.

One might have noticed in addition, however, that the unique window of that little room, denuded of any catch, was kept closed by the back of a chair leaning against the frame. Around that window, strips of white paper had recently been stuck over the cracks: a frail closure, but sufficient to guard death against life.

At first glance, in that mute chamber were the dying lamp cast uneven and vague gleams here and there, you would not have seen anyone. The mattress, set too low, remained in shadow; the bed was empty. In any case, slumber has its voice. The slow and measured respiration of someone asleep is easily audible. Here, no one was asleep. There was nothing but immobility and silence. But on looking harder, the eye, gradually adapting to the semi-darkness, would have distinguished two human forms: two creatures who seemed to be asleep, or dead. They were not moving, they were no longer breathing.

On the mattress, there was a pale and gentle adolescent, whose head was tipped back in the curls of his hair. He still had a smile full of sadness on his lips. Near the bed, in front of a chair that must have served as a prie-dieu for the supreme prayer, there was a very young and—alas!—very beautiful young woman. The last slumber had taken her while she was on her knees. She remained prostrate, but her poor charming body had slumped. Her pretty hands, half-knotted in her hair, were still holding her temples.

The stove was still burning, even though there was no longer anyone there to stifle; and the lamp, which had cast its silent and melancholy light over that double agony, out of oil and oppressed itself by the mortal atmosphere, was respiring effortfully, lifting its flickering flame, no longer having any but the blue light that makes objects livid. Two children! They were two children!

Is it the case, then, that some also suffer enough in that tender youth to have the courage or the cowardice to die? Had they never see their mother's smile? Were they alone in this world, into which God puts us in order to love?

Two children—two pious children!—one of whom had a crucifix by her bed-head, while the other slept under the gaze of Mary, mother of God. This was not chance. They had wanted to put an end to their days. Those strips of paper recently stuck to the cracks of the window were mute but irrefutable evidence.

Sixteen years old! Eighteen years old! That is the flower of souls! Everything is blue, sky blue! Everything is radiant! My God! They had wanted to die together, and yet far apart: the brother lying down in his bleak fatigue; the sister holding remorse at bay by prayer. They did not have their arms around one another!

The mouth of the brother was still open to murmur: "Adieu Céleste!"

The lips of the sister, also parted, retained the last words: "Julian, adieu!"

They were not stiffened by death. Two dead children! Two beautiful innocent creatures! That wrings the heart. There is a revolt. Hope is slow to extinguish. One says to oneself for a long time: *They will wake up!*

The house trembled, and the windows shook at the gunshot fired by the soldier Barolo Spalazzi a few hundred paces away. They did not wake up. And the lamp flared up, and then went out. Over the immobility and the silence, the night spread its crepe of mourning. It was a tomb. Adieu, Julian! Céleste, adieu!

They were running, all those soldiers hunting over the roofs around the Castello-Vecchio. They were shouting, animating one another at a distance. The tracked game could not escape them. The game was not running; it had a start, but it calculated its chances of salvation coldly, which were neither numerous nor good.

The summits of Italian houses do not present many coverts in which one can hide. There are flat terraces everywhere, devoid of chimney-pots. Only the roof of the old Folquieri house presented a few projections favorable to a fugitive. He was there, in the gutter running inside the balustrades. He followed the route he had already traveled. But it was easy to anticipate, given the slowness of his progress, that his intention was not to regain his point of departure. He knew that any issue in that direction was closed. He leaned over the balustrade two or three times. There was nothing there but a narrow ledge, and yet he said to himself: *It's not impossible.* Then, with a smile: *If I had them in the Apennines...*

Doubtless, he had a vision of sorts of those great forests full of refuges. He was thinking about the profound ravines, the rocks whose tutelary projections he probably know, the torrents that a desperate leap could cross but which stop a prudent army of mercenaries. It was a dream. And the footfalls of soldiers were beginning to resonate on the neighboring terrace.

Beldemonio looked behind him. He saw weapons glittering between the stone bars of the balustrade.

We are telling the truth: anyone who had observed that man at the moment of supreme peril would have searched his young and proud face in vain for any trace of anxiety. He held his head high; his gaze was free. He had intelligence and courage at hand.

There are people who win strange battles precisely because they do not believe that they can be vanquished. That is a presumption among the weak, and it serves them better than one might think. Among the strong, is a talisman. Our fugitive put the angle of the balustrade between himself and those pursuing him. He entered thus into the rectangle that formed the inner courtyard of the Folquieri house. When he had penetrated that courtyard before on the opposite wing, a light had been shining in one of the mansard windows of the building, and the gracious silhouette of a young woman had been outlined there. It was the same young woman that he had seen kneeling and praying. He searched for the lighted window and could no longer find it. The prayer had doubtless finished, and the young woman was in bed.

Beldemonio was now moving more rapidly. As he moved, he pressed forcefully, but soundlessly, on each of the windows that he passed. They were all closed. And he judged, from the sound of footsteps and voices, that the garrison of the Castello-Vecchio was in the process of scaling the balustrade. He drew his dagger, folded his cloak in a certain fashion that turned the collar down and gave it the form of a demi-hammock. If the cloak were solidly sustained by the flap and hanging in the void, a man, hanging from his hands and using the curve of the collar as a foothold, would have been able to remain there without too much fatigue, in a suspended sentry-box.

The bars of the balustrade were very close together; the dagger was long enough to serve as a lateral bar. And Beldemonio knew the temper of his weapon. He spitted the pleats of the cloak on the dagger.

"I've played this game before," he murmured, "to protect the honor of a comtesse. The wind swung me for two hours underneath a balcony. I can do it again. When one says *check*, the king escapes as best he can...

To be sure, that is a heroic means, and we recommend it to every Don Juan caught in an awkward situation. People search under beds, in cupboards and cabinets, and on balconies...but underneath? Here, for example, sixty feet above ground?

A good dagger and a cloak of honest fabric, which does not tear under the weight, two bars in which to wedge the apparatus—that's all that is necessary. One immediately becomes invisible, like those fortunate lovers of the time of Perion of Gaul who only had to put on Urganda's ring in order to be transformed into light vapor.

In the meantime, Beldemonio kept going, testing all the windows as he went past. The cloak was only a last resort.

In Naples, even in winter, windows are not very solidly closed. But this was an exceptional occasion. They all resisted the pressure of his hand.

The balustrade was illuminated in the direction of the Castello-Vecchio. The garrison had lit torches. It was time to make a decision.

At that moment, Beldemonio found himself in the middle of the main building. As he hesitated, torches appeared and the flood of pursuers, making a great noise, was turning the corner of the west wing of the Folquieri house.

Beldemonio immediately ducked and placed his head below the balustrade; but there was a window there. It cost nothing to extend his arm. Mechanically, Beldemonio pushed the casement, the frame of which immediately yielded, with a sound of tearing paper.

His face scarcely changed.

"Thank you, my star!" he murmured, laughing. "That's the decision re-made at a stroke!"

The cloak and the dagger were reserved for another occasion. Beldemonio went in and closed the window again, which he kept closed at the end of his arm, taking care to leave his head below the sill. He divined that the soldiers were doing as he had done and testing every window as they went past.

He was scarcely sheltered in that unanticipated retreat when the noise of footfalls and voices increased.

"Unless he throws himself from the top of the house to the bottom," said the leader, "we'll take him alive!"

"He's a bold rogue," responded another, "who must be one of their chiefs."

The captain stopped directly outside the window behind which Beldemonio was hiding.

"This one's well-closed," he said, after having tested the frame with a vigorous punch. Then he went on, in a confidential tone: "You'd have good feet and good eyes tonight, my children, if you knew the name of the bold rogue, as you call him...word reached us at nine o'clock from the Minister of State that Il Porporato had sworn an oath on charcoal and iron to attempt the liberation of Felice Tavola himself!"

"What! What!" Interjections came from all sides. "This Felice Tavola isn't Il Porporato, then?"

The captain shrugged his shoulders. "My children," he said, instead of replying, "remember that there's a hidden treasure somewhere on these terraces...a treasure of a hundred thousand ducats. If we find him, I'll give you twenty thousand ducats to share between you. Is that amiable? Forward march!"

There was a general *evviva*, so strongly was the captain's generosity appreciated. That worthy lion was offering them a fifth share.

Behind the widow-frame, the handsome Beldemonio laughed on hearing that. The soldiers set forth.

They had planted torches everywhere they passed, with the result that the western sector of the roofs was now illuminated. One torch had been placed on the balustrade almost opposite the window, and Beldemonio said: "That's what I call a delicate attention."

In fact, the torch cast sufficient light within the room for one to guide oneself therein.

Beldemonio tried to stand up when the soldiers had gone. As soon as he made the effort to do so, the torch in front of the casement seemed to throw off a thousand sparks, his numb hamstrings folded up, and he nearly fell over. He smiled again, for the last idea that could occur to him was being afraid—but his temples were throbbing and a hand of iron gripped them.

A convulsive yawn suddenly dilated his throat, while a strange dolor to which he could not put a name, which is the very anguish of death, rose from his icy feet to his burning brain. A great vertigo seized him. He felt himself spinning at an inconceivable speed, and saw a gulf beneath him. His hands touched his forehead and he drew them away soaked with cold sweat. His hair stood on end. Then, for the first time in his life, he felt the chill of fear in his veins. That unknown frisson laid him low. If one can express it thus, he was afraid of his fear. He did not know yet how death had gripped him, but he had no doubt that it was death.

At that moment, when his ordinary presence of mind abandoned him because the very heart of his intelligence was violently besieged, he had not remembered having smelled a singular odor on entering that room and having experienced a sensation overwhelming warmth.

It was instinct that took his hand to the window in order open it. But at that very moment he heard slow and measured footsteps. There was a sentinel a few paces away from him. He did not have the strength to fight. He did not want to die. A desperate effort came to his aid.

He went, crawling, dragging himself along, tottering and breathless, leaning on anything he could find in his passage, to the other side of the room, where he glimpsed a door. He stopped ten times, lacking breath. Between the table and the door he picked up an object whose form he could not distinguish. The object burned him. It was a stove, in which fire was still brooding beneath the embers. He was so low that that fact revealed nothing to his torpid intelligence. Only instinct floated within him. The door! He had to reach the door—perhaps to flee, because the idea of flight is in us all during any agony.

He fell before having touched the door so greatly desired, and his forehead rebounded from the tiles.

Everyone has a last vision when the moment of death comes; every lip murmurs a name that aids the completion of the supreme sigh. What did Beldemonio see in his supreme agony? A palace glittering with lights...young, beautiful, bejeweled women...and among them, a virgin with a saintly smile, and who seemed sad, and had the white crown of a bride on her head: Angélie.

That was true, Angélie Doria passed before his dazzled eyes, a radiant phantom. But he had another vision too. Our heart is full of strange mysteries! He saw, in a sort of cloud, a poor child whose oblique profile was framed by long loose hair: a kneeling child. That one, for him, had no name. She remained immobile there, while the tender bride held out her arms. It was not the bride that he was gazing at. He remained motionless for some time. His head was no more than two feet from the threshold.

Between the threshold and the door there was a slight air current, the only one that the suicidal solicitude of the unfortunate children had left. Beldemonio's open mouth drank that beneficent air from outside. After a few moments, he was able to take one more step, amid twenty attempts. He seized the door handle. The door was bolted. Then he plastered himself against the planks and hauled himself up like an earthworm climbing a stone wall.

He could not do it! His body collapsed. His muscles were made of oil! He put his mouth to the crack. He sucked in the external air through that narrow gap, and when his lungs were full he got up again, rendering a great murmur of triumph involuntarily. The bolt gave way, the door opened. He did not struggle any longer and let himself fall with a profound relief, his head outside.

His was a nature valiant among all. His prostration did not last long. The stairway communicated with the external air through several open windows. After ten minutes, Beldemonio opened his eyes and woke up. His first sensation was surprise; he had lost all memory of what had happened. What initially revived his memory was the burning sensation in his hand. Three of his fingers were raw.

The stove, he thought.

Then, having directed his gaze toward the illuminated window: *The soldiers.*

Then, finally: *There's someone dead in here!*

He got up without too much difficulty and shook off the fatigue that was overwhelming him authoritatively. In his belief, a long time had passed since he had entered that place. Now, apparently, time was precious to him that night, for he launched himself toward the window in order to consult his watch. He thought that his ach had stopped on seeing that it had only advanced by a quarter of an hour. He stuck it to his ear. The watch was going.

Two ideas were then in his head: to help the suicide; to run away and continue his work—for the struggle engaged that night was far from over.

To begin with, he seized the stove and carried it outside. Then he ran to the couchette, which he found empty. His eyes recovered their clear-sightedness. The sight of the couchette awakened a vague memory.

He got his bearings. He was not mistaken; this was the very place, at his feet, where he had seen the young woman at prayer. His gaze lowered while his heart contracted. At his feet there was a poor child collapsed in the floor. He took her in his arms and deposited her on the bed. She was not cold, but she already had a cadaveric rigor. He felt her heart. Hs own pulse was beating so violently that he could not tell whether the poor heart has stopped forever or not.

The torch planted on the balustrade was casting its light obliquely through the window-panes. A glimmer slid between Beldemonio and the curtains; it seemed to be caressing the pale and charming features, to which death had rendered an expression of smiling serenity.

He had played with death since childhood, but with death by iron, which drowns life in blood. This death, so different, this death of despair, which had not cut the flower that was leaning over, expiring on its stem, the death of a discouraged child, gripped his heart. Since he had become self-aware, no anguish as subtle had penetrated the most intimate recesses of his soul.

He was astonished. What was she, in sum? An unknown young woman whose gracious profile he had only perceived once, at a distance. That was all. In the victorious and cruel amours of his youth, had he not broken more than one young woman's heart?

He wondered, in his unexpected disturbance, whether it was not the collapse that he had barely escaped that was debilitating his senses or his reason. He tried to stiffen himself, but his soul melted; his breast heaved in sobs that his arms, violently crossed, tried n vain to suppress. Large tears rolled down his cheeks. He loved that dead child; he would have given his life to render her breath.

Was it one of those mad passions that add another flower every day to the garland of a Don Juan? No; desire fell silent before that virginal bed, which was a coffin. He would have liked, young as he was, to call that pale corpse "my daughter." "My sister" was not enough. And yet a sister, an adored young sister to whom one could render the caresses and the protection of a father who is no more...!

Who was he, this Beldemonio, to have such thoughts? You could have searched his conscience at that moment and you would not have found anything but exquisite delicacy and infinite purity. He could not take his eyes off the dead girl.

Have you ever seen a virgin with pale lips who has just rendered her last sigh—a sight so beautiful and so heart-rending? Have you seen the long hair in which the pallor of the face is floating? The eyes closed by a pious and loving hand? In modern art there is a work terrible and sublime in its concept: Tintoretto painting his dead daughter.[32] The canvas is beautiful. The canvas does not matter. Close your eyes and you will see the iron nail that is tearing that man's heart.

A father! The man who was so happy and proud the day before! The trunk from which that branch departed, the stem that bore that flower! A father!

In those cold veins, there was blood. There, under the collapsed veil covering the breast there was a heart; it was his heart. A father loves a son, but a daughter is the smile, the amour, the folly of a father!

There he is, Tintoretto: an old man, a robust and severe head bristling with gray hair. That hair says: *The child you have taken from me, O Lord, will have no sister...*

The delight of his hours of repose was to gaze at those young, chaste forms. He is gazing at them again, but it is the last time. Those grim and somber eyes have no tears. Oh, no, the desperate lack tears. He is gazing. He has given himself the task of seeking memories in death, the reflections of life. He is gazing. He is ashamed and terrified. That Titanic labor is crushing him, and I do not know what bitter sensuality is attaching and retaining him.

Alone as he is in confrontation with that funereal bed, a dream grips him: a sad and calm delirium. His brush is no longer moving. He is still gazing.

"Lord, you who make miracles! Lord, full of clemency and bounty, can blood not rise again to those livid cheeks? Can the smile not be reborn around those discolored lips? Lord, Lord, can that immobile heart not beat again at you behest? Who could sing the canticle of that mute fever, that motionless dementia? And who could also describe the anguish of the awakening?

But time is marching on and death moves rapidly in its labor of destruction. The model is about to escape the painter. To your brushes, old man! You do not have the time to moan!

The hour chimed in the belfry of the Castello-Vecchio: eleven o'clock at night. Beldemonio, returned to himself, shuddered swiftly. He darted a glanced

---

[32] The reference is Léon Cogniet's painting *Tintoret peignant sa fille morte* (1843).

around the room. The sheet of paper on the table struck his eyes. He seized it avidly, thinking that he might find a name, an indication...

There was sufficient light near the window to permit reading. Beldemonio read:

Dear Father, forgive us and pray for us...

"She's not alone!" he cried, silently.

And his eyes sought the other victim.

The corner in which the poor mattress was laid was the darkest in the room. Forewarned, however, Beldemonio discovered a recumbent form in the shadow there. He leapt forward. An adolescent was there, was stiff and straight as the statues that sleep on the tables of Medieval tombs. Beldemonio knelt down beside him. That face was in his memory. It was a noble head, with pure and slightly severe features.

Had he seen that child before, or someone resembling him? While he was interrogating his memory, a faint noise was audible from the direction of the couchette. It was like a sigh. Beldemonio launched himself forward. The young woman's hand had changed position. He put his cheeks against the dead girl's blue lips, and felt a breath...but so feeble!

Air was now coming into the room; the mortal vapor had almost dissipated. Our handsome fisherman put his hands together and his prayer rose toward God, ardently. It had been a long time since God had heard the voice of that man.

He waited, holding his breath. The young woman was no longer moving. Had he seen the supreme effort and collected the last sigh?

In his turn, the adolescent lying on the mattress made a slight movement. It was the time for aid; they might be saved!

At that moment, Beldemonio had no other thought. But suddenly, in the night that had become silent again, a voice rose up: a voice that recalled Beldemonio to himself, and threw him back into the strange and tenebrous milieu in which he spent his life. It was the sound of a horn coming from the old town. In spite of the distance, the motif of the fanfare could be heard distinctly; it was Fioravanti's song: *Amici, alliegre, andiamo alla pena!* He drew himself up to his full height, and frowned.

This time, the appeal was importunate. An idea of revolt was born within him against the mysterious slavery of his destiny. But it was only momentary. His gaze lowered toward the couchette. It was a pensive and altered gaze. Enthusiasm was no longer burning there.

"Anyone," he murmured, "a child or a woman, could bring the same help here as me. But who could replace me out there?"

His eyebrows furrowed, at the same time as a bitter smile came to his lips.

"What are they to me?" he went on, in a curt and harsh tone. "What do I owe them? Poverty is speaking here. They are among the vulgar desperate who can be cured with a little gold..."

174

He took a purse from his bosom and dropped it on the table. For a fisherman, that purse was too beautiful. It clinked loudly as it fell.

The distant horn repeated its fanfare, which came over the roofs.

Do you remember Athol responding impatiently to the bells of Corpo-Santo sounding the anniversary knell of Mario Monteleone? Beldemonio stamped his foot, and said, like Athol: "I hear you! I'm coming!"

Next to the couchette, on a chair, there was a commenced embroidery, and under that embroidery, scissors. As he said: "I'm coming!" Beldemonio had his plan made and was only searching for the route to take. With the aid of the scissors he briskly removed his nascent moustache, and then unhooked the poor soutanelle that was hanging on the nail over the mattress. He put it on, and buttoned it up from top to bottom. With a flick of the hand he smoothed his beautiful hair along his temples. At the third sound of the horn, he was ready.

Before leaving, he opened the widow. His eyelids lowered as he went past the couchette. Since he wanted to flee, he dated not look at the young woman again. His heart was beating rapidly when he crossed the threshold. What were they to him? to employ that harsh expression, chosen by himself. For any abandonment becomes brutal at pleasure.

They were nothing to him; but if someone had said to him: "You will never see that beautiful young woman again," perhaps he would have hesitated to go. He fled without looking at the couchette. He felt that a fishing-line wanted to catch his soul.

Several doors opened on to the corridor that led to the staircase. He turned the handle of the first and asked: "Is there anyone here"

A cry of fright responded. He recognized the voice of an old woman.

"Whoever you are," he said. "Get up and go into the next room. Someone needs your care, and here's your salary."

Two or three gold coins rang on the tiles.

Beldemonio was already going downstairs. But, a singular thing in so free a spirit—one might almost say so despotic—Beldemonio was no longer going where his thought wanted to go.

The danger had not diminished: quite the contrary. There is no need to have the genius of an adventurer, like our young fisherman, to divine that the garrison of the Castello-Vecchio, having searched all the terraces of the neighboring houses, would tighten the blockade around the block of houses adjacent to the fortress.

The fugitive had not been able to escape, that was certain. Therefore, he had hidden in one of the surrounding habitations. Therefore, the surveillance must be increased, especially in the Strada di Mantua and its cul-de-sacs, becoming a veritable perimeter. That perimeter, it was necessary to penetrate, and that would certainly not be an easy enterprise.

What astonished Beldemonio, and almost frightened him, is that instead of reaching toward that goal, his mind was going backwards, and was still in that poor room where the two children had tried to die. Until then, he had only ever required a single effort to shake off the most tyrannical preoccupations. Today, the preoccupation was stronger than his will.

He said to himself: *I would have saved them, I sense it! I'm sure of it...but will another do what I would have done?*

Incessantly, he saw the pale face of the young woman. He wept.

I would have had her first smile!

And when the features of the adolescent returned to his memory, he wondered: *Where have I seen that face before? Was it that of someone living or dead?*

His memory had no precise response to that question, but there was mourning in his vague recollections, as he associated the idea of that young stranger with some mysterious and austere silhouette of an old man.

It was not his mouth, this time, but his heart that cried: *I'll come back! I'll come back!*

It was necessary, however, to bring his reverie to an end.

"You can't get past, my young saint," said a soft voice to him, on the first floor landing.

He had picked up the stout prayer book at the same time as the soutanelle. An oblique glance showed him a middle-aged woman who was standing in her doorway, in night attire. He had no idea how the young saint whose role he was playing normally comported himself with that respectable neighbor, whose character seemed full of amenity. He lowered his head, holding his book in both hands, and got ready to murmur a few pious salutations, when the lady mumbled: "You can see that we're never going to know the color of his words!"

That was a very precious item of information. Evidently, the young saint had never spoken to the middle-aged lady, who was plump and well conserved.

Profiting from that confession, Beldemonio bowed profoundly and passed by in a modest manner, holding his stout book like a holy relic.

"God bless you, my poor Monsieur Julian," said the neighbor, with a hint of bitterness. "Don't forget me in your prayers!" Then she added, in such a way as to be heard: "He's too innocent, anyway, such a lamb!"

Beldemonio could not remember ever having been reproached for the excess of his candor.

He heard a lot of noise and movement in the vestibule below him. All the domestics in the house and some of the tenants were assembled there, chatting commenting and arguing. All of them had seen the lighted torches on the balustrade and the soldiers passing over the roofs like phantoms.

Two opinions, among the three hundred that were being produced, seemed to merit some credence. The first was that the prisoner, having strangled his jailer, had murdered the sentinel with a pistol shot—that had been heard—and passed over the bodies of the entire garrison, had crossed the rampart, the terraces and the street, and was already heading for the mountains. What was surprising about that, if he was Il Porporato?

The second was that the Companions of the Silence, several hundred in number, had scaled the terraces and were holding the garrison at bay. A pitched battle was imminent. There was a numerous artillery on both sides.

What cannot be described is the extravagant animation with which the true Neapolitan produces such nonsense. Men and women were all talking at the same time, sustaining whatever they were saying with redoubtable oaths and proposing vehemently that if they were lying they would lost all hope of eternal salvation.

It is possible, strictly speaking, to depict in writing the prodigious jabber of our friends and neighbors the polyglot English; it is easy to express the dull and fatiguing German accent; one can even understand the emphatic declamation of the twenty million souls who seems to be perpetually selling Swiss vulnerary[33] and who call themselves Spaniards, but Neapolitan volubility is ungraspable and untranslatable.

As soon as they perceived the "young saint," as the person whose soutanelle and prayer book Beldemonio had appropriated was known in the house, the racket of tongues cased. The young saint lived in the attics. He must have seen something.

The courtyard, solely illuminated by the torches placed on the balustrades sixty or eighty feet above the ground, was very dark. That was fortunate for Beldemonio, who had not found anything by way of headgear to hide his hair and face.

He was, moreover, slender and lanky. The young saint's soutanelle fit him like a glove. The fashion he had of arranging his hair, modestly flattened over the temples, the absence of a moustache, his timid and discreet gait, in the gloom and the disturbance that was keeping the house awake, all lent themselves to the illusion. It would only have needed the slightest suspicion for the deceit to be discovered, but no one had that suspicion

A few having asked, by way of acquittal: "Where is the *abbatello* going so late?" Fortunata Coccoli, the keeper of the house replied with the pride that distinguishes the honorable and redoubted class of porters in all lands:

"Don't you know that that angel goes out every night to sit with the invalids at the pauper's hospital?"

"Oh, the cherub of amour!" was exclaimed in all directions.

"Is he going to tell us whether he saw anything up there?"

"There's a torch outside his window."

"And the little sister? Isn't she afraid of remaining alone at night?"

The young saint passed through the groups without making any reply. He knew from the middle-aged neighbor that his double was not talkative. He also

---

[33] "Swiss vulnerary" was an old herbal remedy, also known as faltranck.

knew something else now: his double went out every night to visit the invalids at the pauper's hospital.

Addressing the audience, Fortunata Coccoli said: "Would anyone believe that you're reasonable people? I ask you without lacking politeness! To pester a young man of his estate like that! Rather solicit his benediction, sinners that you are!"

"Fratellino!" said the obedient assembly, immediately. "Bless us a little as you pass by!"

Beldemonio half-turned and designed a timid benediction, murmuring to himself: "May God forgive me! I have no intention of mocking holy things."

"Ah!" said all the tenants. "How well he blesses! That must be a heart!"

And Fortunata Coccoli, ever ready to reprimand her administratees, said: "That's enough! Don't make him proud!" She slid into his ear: "A word for me in your oremus, lamb of God. I've bought four numbers in the royal lottery. If the venerated mother of God grants me a good draw, I'll make a nice gift to the parish...without forgetting you, my seraph!"

Beldemonio was outside.

As we have said, the coaching entrance opened into the cul-de-sac of the Strada di Mantua, where the ladder had been initially set up for the escalade, before the misadventure of the good soldier of the Buffalo regiment.

Things had changed a great deal in a hour. The cul-de-sac and the Via Mantua were full of soldiers. At the first step Beldemonio took after the door closed again, s bayonet threatened his breast.

"No one can pass," said a burly Swiss Guard, who called himself Max Schoeffer, like all his comrades, in Fribourg Italian.

"Signor," replied Beldemonio, humbly, "I'm going to do my duty."

"I'm doing my duty!" pronounced the son of the beautiful valleys of Helvetia. "No one can pass!"

As the first Schoeffer had raised his voice, several other Maxes approached slowly and gravely, as stiff as pickets. There was an officer among them.

"Signor," Beldemonio said to him, "I'm expected at the paupers' hospital, where I ordinarily visit the sick."

"The paupers' hospital?" repeated the officer Schoeffer.

A few other Maxes repeated: "The paupers' hospital."

Upon which the officer looked at them and gave them an order: "Shut up!"

All the Maxes immediately put one hand to their face and the other to the belt of their trousers.

Schoeffer, the officer, approached the young saint and examined him attentively. Having done that, he uttered a good Bernese laugh, accompanied by the waddle that all the armories you know give to the illustrious city of Berne.

"You're an idiot," he pronounced sententiously, addressing the first Max, who was the cause of all that. "Can't you see that he's a sacristan?"

He laughed again. The other Schoeffers laughed even louder.

"March!" he said, pushing the young saint ahead of him. "when you can scale the walls, you, I'll give you your Queen Claude plums!"[34]

All the Maxes said in chorus: "Funny, Lieutenant! Ha ha! When he can scale the walls, we'll give you your Queen Claude plums!"

General burst of laughter.

Without hurrying, at an honest and discreet pace, Beldemonio crossed the Piazzetta Grande. As soon as he was in the Vicoletto Raffo, he started to run, unbuttoning his soutanelle, which he threw into a doorway. At the end of the street, he applied the hilt of his dagger to his lips, and a whistle-blast rang out. A similar whistle-blast was heard at the corner of the Strada Medina. Then the young woman disguised as a boy launched herself out of a sotto-portico where all the lights were extinct.

"There are five of us in there," she said. "We were going to attack…what should we do?"

"Where's my carriage?" asked Beldemonio, instead of replying.

"At the Monte Oliveto. What should we do?"

Beldemonio started to walk with a long stride toward the indicated place. An elegant light *calesso* harnessed to two magnificent horses was stationed behind the apse of the church. Beldemonio climbed into it.

At the window, the young woman repeated for the third time: "What should we do?"

Beldemonio took her hand and brushed it with his lips, saying: "Thank you, Fiamma!"

She blushed with pleasure. Beldemonio added: "In an hour, it's necessary that Matilda Farnèse is in Naples and ready to go with me."

"The Princesse Farnèse will be ready in an hour," the young woman replied. "And then?"

"Then you'll dress as a Duchesse, little Fiamma, and go to wait for me at the ball at the Palazzo Doria."

"Are we going to dance?" asked the young woman.

Beldemonio smiled. "Let the Comtesse find you nearby when she wakes up," he said.

"And the others?"

"Let them all go home, except for the men on watch round the Palazzo Doria. And let everyone by ready at daybreak!"

With his hand, he blew a kiss to the young woman. Then he leaned out and spoke to the coachman: "Is that you, Ruggieri?"

"Yes, signor."

---

[34] The fruit known in France as a *prune reine Claude* [Queen Claude plum] is usually known in English as a greengage, but the more literal translation has a certain flavor in this instance.

"Take the Via Tribunali as far as the Porta Capuana, go out of the city, come back through the Porta Notarea and descend to the Piazza del Mercato, to the house of Joann Spurzheim."

"Yes, signor."

The whip cracked; the horses set off at a gallop.

While the *calesso* was already racing over the paving stones, a man emerged from the shadows and leapt on to the back with a single bound, where he held himself in equilibrium, whistling a merry tune from the mountains.

PART TWO: THE DIRECTOR'S STUDY

I. Barbe de Monteleone

It was the evening of the same day in February 1823. Three windows were faintly illuminated in a large house on the Piazza del Mercato, situated at the eastern extremity of Naples, very close to the place that is now the common railway station of the lines to Capua and Castellamare. It was the house or palace of Signor Johann Spurzheim, an Austrian by birth, the director of the royal police. A police station occupied almost all of the ground floor. The director's family lived on the first floor. One of the lighted windows was that of Signor Johann Spurzheim's bedroom; the other two belonged to a drawing room where his wife was in conference with Dr. Pier Falcone, a young physician already illustrious for his knowledge.

Johann Spurzheim had not been in Naples very long—about three months. No one knew anything about his past, or the reasons for the great confidence that the court had immediately accorded him. But no one could say that that confidence had not been justified. There was only one voice on that subject. The new director of the police was a skillful and righteous man. Those who detested him—and he had many enemies—sought in vain for something of which to accuse him.

Nine o'clock has just chimed on the clock of Santa Maria del Carmine at the moment when we enter Johann Spurzheim's bedroom. That was the precise moment when the animation attained its peak in the Strada di Porto; but in the marketplace between the house and the church everything was calm, almost deserted. The shops were already shut, and the inhabitants of the quarter, too distant from the center, had the habit of going to seek their relaxations and pleasures elsewhere.

The bedroom was simple to the point of austerity, very high-ceilinged, and hung with somber fabrics. A single lamp illuminated it. The director of the royal police was lying on his bed, his head supported by a single horsehair pillow, for he affected stoical forms in all things. His features, visible in the light of the lamp, were pale and thin, but their design announced a keen intelligence.

There are faces that one does not forget, even if one has only seen them once. We would have recognized at the first glance in that dying man—as we shall willingly say, for he seemed no longer to have any breath—the taciturn and forbidding passenger of Battista Giubbetti's carozza, the man in the silk bonnet, Monsieur David, who occupied the two best places in the interior on his own, and had made a semblance of bring asleep while the seminarian Julian was chatting to his little sister Céleste; the man who had commanded Battista in the name of the charcoal and iron, and who had denounced to the smugglers united in their lair to the right of the road under the convent of the Corpo-Santo the departure from Palermo of Lorédan Doria and Comtesse Angélie.

History cites among the high dignitaries of the police men of head and heart, veritable knights who, combating evil hand-to-hand, go as far as penetrating the mysterious retreats of the enemies of society in order to strike them more surely. In Italy, Azeglio became a carbonaro;[35] in England the famous Templeton became the apparent accomplice of Watt Tyler. Perhaps Johann Spurzheim was one of those men. At least we have seen him in the crypt of the Corpo-Santo, around the cadaver without a sepulcher of Mario, Comte de Monteleone, in the midst of the Knights of the Silence. The reader divined him under the mask, in spite of the name of Heimer added to the forename David. It was him, the confidant and secretary of the first Grandmaster...

At other times, the contrary occurs. The imprudent and bold conspirator, by means of one of the thousand hazards that are life, can suddenly acquire power and dominate the same society that he attacked. Two roads are open to him in that circumstance: to deny his past or continue his work. What follows will tell us what the religion of the cavaliere ferraio David Heimer was in that regard, having become the director Johann Spurzheim. We shall know in due course for whom or against whom he was battling. What is certain is that, at the present moment, you would have judged him incapable of combating anyone.

His eyes were closed; his lips were pale, parted painfully, as if searching for the breath that was about to flee. His hollow and wan cheeks faded to black as they neared the eyelids. His entire body maintained a bleak immobility. He was not asleep, however, for, from time to time, and abrupt tremor agitated the corner of his mouth and creased the wrinkles of his temples. One might have said, in truth, that if he was not having a dream, he was listening to distant and mysterious sounds that a healthy man would not have been able to perceive. One might have thought that the conversation of two invisible individuals was reaching him. Extremity often involves such silent deliria, and some people claim that a prodigious subtlety of hearing is the last privilege of those who are about to die.

There was no one in the room at that moment, and no sound of voices could be heard outside. The two people nearest to Spurzheim were Barbe de Monteleone, his wife, and the young doctor Pier Falcone. Between the bedroom and the drawing room, however, there were two doors and a corridor. On the

---

[35] The Italian Statesman Massimo d'Azeglio (1798-1866) was not a policeman and not a Revolutionary, but he did write Romantic novels in imitation of Walter Scott. The reference to "Templeton" is enigmatic, but Wat Tyler, the leader of the 1381 "Peasants' Revolt" in England was featured in numerous literary works of the Romantic period.

night table, a few small bottles and glasses reposed in disorder among scattered papers and books. It was evident that the man, full of active thought and only being broken in the body, was obstinate in working until the final hour.

Under the covers passed the cheerful black head of one of those charming little animals that come to us from England, and whose royal origins have caused them to be given the name of a King Charles spaniel. A mania, we would say, if Johann Spurzheim had been capable of childishness; but we warn the reader in advance that it is necessary to rank him among those who do nothing by chance. If the black head, alert and dainty, was perceptible under the covers, it was because, for Johan Spurzheim, it was useful and necessary that the black head should be there.

We would say the same about another object that was visible beside him, next to the pillow, between the bed and the wall. It resembled one of those little horns that the dwarfs of chivalric romance carried suspended around their necks, about four inches in diameter. It was made of ivory. A rather long cable, more like a flexible tube, was attached to it firmly, the opposite extremity of which was hidden in a cupboard with an opening half a foot square, the door of which was open. That door had no lock, key or handle.

In the nearby drawing room, next to a fireplace—an unusual luxury in Naples—Barbe de Monteleone, the director's wife, was sitting with her feet at the fire. Doctor Pier Falcone remained standing before her.

Barbe de Monteleone was now about forty years old. Her face was beautiful, but too large for her body, as happens to people deformed at birth. That flaw was scarcely perceptible while she remained seated, the upper part of her body having sufficient length. As for the very apparent deformity that Barbe carried behind, which was a hump, since it is necessary to pronounce the word, you would have been able to spend entire hours in her drawing room without discovering it. Barbe had an armchair with a concave back and arranged herself within it with a certain aristocratic grace. She never stood up to receive anyone. Long exercise had so accustomed her to that nonchalant and relaxed pose that she retained the perfect liberty of her movements.

In that attitude, one can really only see the front of the figure; that was a matter for her dressmaker, and the noble regularity of her features was framed by entirely beautiful black hair. Fundamentally, that coquettish strategy did not prevent all Naples from knowing that Barbe de Monteleone was a hunchback, but it sometimes permitted that terrible truth to be forgotten—at least, Barbe believed so—in confrontation with a beautiful face and a conversation full of charm.

In fact, Barbe had no rival in the court of Naples for intelligence, eloquence and knowledge. The broad forehead, superiorly modeled, announced a vast and bold intelligence; the dark, sharp, profound eyes declared the subtleties of mind present and always ready for combat.

She had been in a dependent position early in life. Although she belonged to a princely family, the death of her parents and the absolute lack of a fortune had put her in the charge of her cousin Mario de Monteleone. The first spur that had stimulated her intellectual effort was the ambition to be the Comtesse de Monteleone.

Mario had seen her grow up near him. Mario loved her as if she had been his younger sister. Among Mario's entourage, her intelligence and her knowledge made her the queen. She hoped for a long time that her cousin's admiration might change into a more tender sentiment. She hoped in vain. If there is one route that does not lead to amour, it is that of admiration.

Barbe was not born wicked. We have already said that absolute wickedness does not exist. It is enough that there is interest and passion. Barbe was ambitious to excess. Her relative's marriage to Maria des Amalfi put the inferno in her heart.

There was a man in the Martorello who gazed at her from below. Barbe believed that she was adored. She said to herself: *That man will be my slave; I need a slave; I need an instrument; that man will be my instrument.*

That man was named David Heimer. He possessed all of Mario de Monteleone's confidence. Barbe made an alliance with him. Later, she married him. But it happened that David Heimer was at least as strong as Barbe herself.

It was a strange household. If there was conflict, it did not last. At the first impact, they measured one another and called a truce. Knights act thus when two lances, shattering into splinters, leave the joust uncertain.

Those two individuals, united in the same thought of ambition, did not detest one another, as is the custom. There was even a sort of amity between them, born of the perfect community of sentiment. One could say that they esteemed one another. And as the most hardened suspicion is not always alert, mutual trust had slowly been established between them. They believed in one another, all the more strongly because each of them believed himself or herself to be the more difficult to deceive.

The work that they pursued in common was arduous. David Heimer, whom we shall call henceforth by the name he had chosen, Johann Spurzheim, consulted his wife faithfully, and Barbe Spurzheim put at her husband's service everything she had of finesse, clairvoyance and prudence. It was a straight and honest alliance on both sides, insofar as there can be any honesty in two such souls. We should also say that in the court and throughout the city, Barbe Spurzheim was cited for the assiduous care that she lavished on her sick husband.

Barbe and the young doctor, Pier Falcone, had been together for about ten minutes. Next to Barbe, a massive folio volume was supported by a massive standing lectern. The folio was written in Latin, which Barbe could read fluently. Beyond the lectern, a small ebony table supported a small celestial sphere and a quantity of books, all of respectable physiognomy. A little further away there was an organ, with a book of musical scores open at Sebastian Bach's third fugue. On the other side of the room, were two easels, the first supporting a canvas by Tommaso di Stefano, a contemporary of Cimabue in the reign of Charles d'Anjou, the second a sketch for a painting by Barbe herself. The marble mantelpiece, in the Florentine style, had an antique garniture of severe simplicity. Two enormous amphorae in Etruscan clay flanked the extremities. Around the wood paneling hung six paintings by Lo Zingaro—Antonio Solario—and his pupils, the Donzello.[36] One of them, attributed to Donzello the younger, represented the death of Lazarus.

The eyes of Barbe Spurzheim and Pier Falcone fixed themselves at the same time on that last canvas. There as a silence. After a few seconds, Barbe's gaze quit the canvas in order to focus on the doctor.

He was a man of about twenty-eight, tall but too spindly and slightly stooped. His features, excessively pale, had beauty. His dark eyes expressed nothing at the moment save for an immobility of thought. Two or three precocious wrinkles furrowed his brow, where his hair was already thinning, as if burned. He might have been a thinker. He might have been audacious. There was no doubt that he was a man of great needs and great desires. As she looked at him, Barbe frowned.

"He's too young!" she murmured to herself.

Then, the doctor's gaze having met her own, she went on, as if to explain the involuntary movement of her physiognomy: "I thought for a long time that the painters of the old school knew how to render death-throes. I was wrong."

"However," replied Pier Falcone, "the agony of that Lazarus..."

"Exactly!"

"You don't find it horrible enough?"

"Too much and too little. Beneath and beyond. The masters who came later embellished death...these twisted and convulsed it. Johann Spurzheim is not like that."

Pier Falcone lowered his eyes before the frightening calmness with which those words had been pronounced. Barbe saw that, smiled, chose a pastille against coughing from a golden candy-box beside her, and went on: "If you could answer for saving my husband, Doctor, your fortune would be made."

"You know full well, Madame," replied Pier Falcone, "that that is impossible for me."

---

[36] This deliberately esoteric reference is to the brothers Pietro and Ippolito Donzello, to whom some fifteenth century documents refer as members of a Neapolitan school founded by Lo Zingaro. The text's earlier reference to "Tommaso des Stéphanie" is a trifle enigmatic but I have assumed that it refers to a contemporary of Cimabue's named Tommsaso di Stefano, better known by the nickname Giottino.

"What is science, then?" murmured Barbe, disdainfully. Then, suppressing authoritatively a cough that tried to burst forth, she added: "I would give fifty thousand ducats to whoever could say to me: 'Johann Spurzheim will live!'"

"That man would be lying, Madame."

Barbe placed her hands against her breast, flattening her dressmaker's lies with a convulsive effort.

"Oh, this cough," she said. "There are times when it seems that an ardent ember is going out in my lungs...others when I think I feel a heavy plug rising up and stifling me. Am I condemned, too, then, Doctor?"

"You think too much," retorted the physician.

"And thinking is killing me?"

Pier Falcone smiled. "If you offered me fifty thousand ducats to answer for you, Madame...," he commenced.

"You'd consent?" exclaimed the director's wife, swiftly.

"I'd stake my head on it," Pier Falcone concluded, in a firm voice.

Barbe extended her hand to him. It was cold and damp.

"Take another pastille," said the doctor. "You're going to have a coughing fit."

But the pastille had no effect. Barbe's chest suddenly heaved, while a vivid redness tinted the pallor of her cheeks. She had a slow, ripping cough, dolorous to hear. Her embroidered handkerchief, which she put over her mouth, was tinted by blood.

The face of the young physician remained impassive. Barbe showed him the red stain silently. He shrugged his shoulders.

"Will you believe me or not?" he said. "One doesn't cure consumptives, but I promise to cure you."

She drank a little water and remained motionless. For a moment, her eyes were veiled, as if haggard; but suddenly, the radiance beneath her eyelids was reignited.

"I'm well," she said, "very well. I wish to God that my husband were thus. Answer me, Doctor, on your conscience: is there no human means of saving him?"

"None, Madame."

Barbe lowered her gaze, and seemed to hesitate.

"And...," she continued, in a changed voice, "will it last long?"

Pier Falcone thought he had misheard.

As no response was forthcoming, Barbe raised her head. She looked the doctor in the face and repeated: "I want to know if it will last long."

"What, Madame?"

"The life of Joann Spurzheim, my husband," Barbe pronounced, distinctly.

"But Madame..."

"I want to know!"

"Science cannot be precise..."

"A week?" the director's wife interjected.

"It's impossible to affirm..."

"A fortnight?"

"In truth, Madame," said Pier Falcone, "such a question..."

"I have reasons for putting it to you, Doctor," Madame Spurzheim interjected. "I'm sure that you don't think that it can go on for another month?"

"No, Madame," Pier Falcone replied, this time. "I don't think so."

She lowered her eyes again, and murmured the words that she had pronounced before: "He's too young." Abruptly, she said: "Sit down there!"

Her long white hand indicated a chair with authority. The doctor sat down. Barbe closed her eyes, and said, after a minute of silence:

"Reflect before replying to me; what I have to propose to you is serious; I've thought about it maturely. Doctor Pier Falcone, would you like me to be your wife?"

II. A Strong Woman

It was a wise precaution to have obliged the doctor to take a seat. It prevented him from falling over backwards. He tried to say something, but Madame Spurzheim closed his mouth with an imperious gesture.

"I told you to reflect, Monsieur," she pronounced, severely. "You haven't yet had the time!"

She moved her armchair closer with a free and natural movement. Her face was still perfectly calm.

"While you reflect," she went on, lowering her voice, "I shall talk. Listen attentively. When I've spoken, you can reply to me in full cognizance of the cause.

"You're young, but you're ambitious, and, I believe, audacious. I have no amour for you...what I'm offering you is the title of Comte and the fortune of a king..."

The doctor's eyelids lifted slightly; he darted a suspicious glance at her, believing her to be mad.

"No, no," she said, with a smile, in answer to that glance, "I'm not mad. You're asking yourself, I can see: 'How can she give a title of Comte and a royal fortune, when she has neither.'"

"I know that you're rich," Pier Falcone tried to interject.

"Poverty!" she exclaimed, suddenly becoming animated. "Rich, me? Multiply what I have by ten...a hundred...by a hundred ten times over, and you'll still be short of the truth. The fortune about which I'm talking is immense!"

"But what fortune are you talking about?" murmured the doctor, stirred involuntarily.

"I'm talking about the fortune of the Dorias, added to the fortune of the former Comtes de Monteleone."

The physician's forehead was shiny, because droplets of sweat had formed there.

"Don't interrupt me again," said Barbe. "It will soon be the time when my husband wakes up from his evening repose. I need your response before we separate. You're a Companion of the Silence..."

In spite of the recent order not to interrupt, Falcone could not repress a cry of terror. It is necessary not to forget that the accusation was being made against him by the wife of the director of police, in the latter's own house.

"Madame!" he cried. "On my salvation..."

"Yes, yes!" she stopped him. "You're a Neapolitan, oaths cost you nothing. My poor doctor, it's a folly of youth: you've given your liberty to that mysterious association, and thus far, the association has rendered you nothing in exchange...at least, that's what you believe, isn't it?"

"It's true…," stammered the physician.

"A sad thing to see yourself at the orders of people you know and you don't. You've often regretted it…"

"Oh, very often, Madame!"

Barbe began to smile, and fanned herself slightly with her handkerchief.

"Falcone," she said, in a whisper, "iron is strong and charcoal is black…"

He sat up very straight, so profound was his surprise.

"I'll dispense you of the responses of your catechism," she went on, lightly. "I'll do more: I'll come to your aid immediately, for you're going to drown yourself in suppositions…to believe, for example, that Signor Johann Spurzheim, my husband, has revealed the secrets of the royal police to me, and that the royal police itself has discovered your secret…"

"The royal police has discovered nothing, my poor doctor. The brotherhood of the Silence belongs to the royal police…"

"Is that possible?"

"Let us put it better; there cannot be any trickery between us: the royal police belongs to the brotherhood of the Silence."

Falcone's arms fell along his sides. The smile around Barbe Spurzheim's thin lips became more mocking.

"A sad thing!" she repeated. "Not that the association has been sterile for you: it is not for anyone, and that will be its death. The association has given you the semblance of luxury and consideration that surrounds you. Without the association, where would your clientele be?"

"I thought…," the young physician said, with chagrin.

"Undoubtedly!" Barbe interjected. "One always attributes that to one's own talent. I'm not claiming that you lack talent, Signor Pier Falcone, but be kind enough to tell me who does lack talent nowadays. Yesterday the world was composed of a few lions of genius among the flock of Panurge's sheep…a few gold pieces in a heap of copper coins. Panurge would still find sheep, but before throwing themselves in the water, the clowns would explain why. As for lions, I believe the species is extinct. Our century, inheriting that fortune formed by gold pieces and copper coins, has made change of it all, which has produced a heap of small silver coins: carlins, tari, demi-piastres. In that, ducats are rare. I, whom am speaking, have only ever found one pistole, and it was fake!"

At that exact moment, in the silence of Johann Spurzheim's bedroom, there was a dry and painful burst of laughter. It was the dying man who suddenly entered into hilarity. Why? The burst of laugher lasted half a second; then everything became motionless and silent.

Barbe Spurzheim went on: "You have talent, Pier Falcone; would I have chosen you otherwise? But if you have crossed the threshold of this house in the capacity of a physician, it is because you had made the oath of the Silence, because someone had plans for you, and because you needed a clientele in order to get close to the palace of the Comtes Doria-Doria. You have therefore received, more rapidly and more abundantly than many others your salary as a companion. It's not for that reason that I am commiserating with you.

"You have done nothing yet; you have been paid. I classify you among our debtors.

"What is sad, Signor Falcone, is to feel that one is a slave and going blindly, without knowing, without understanding, always impelled by a mysterious will. Who can tell in what coin payment of your debt might be demanded tomorrow?

"What I am proposing to you is to lift the blindfold that covers your eyes and shine light into your night. What I am proposing to you is liberation, and more, for with me, you are going to become a master instead of a slave. You do not know anything; I can tell you everything. I am the dame of the Silence, and I am the only one..."

She removed from her middle finger a gold ring ornamented with three diamonds forming a triangle. Save for the metal, the ring was similar to Mario Monteleone's. It bore the Latin motto: *Agere, non loqui.*

Pier Falcone took it, examined it, read the three words of the motto and returned it, all in silence. He obeyed to the letter: he reflected. Barbe watched him with a contented expression, like a professor who approves of the conduct of a pupil.

"You're young," she went on, "and that is what has stopped me for a week...for I lost all hope of conserving my husband a week ago. But you're prudent, and I believe you to be bold...and I know that a vain scruple wouldn't hold you back.

"Before you link yourself with me in a narrow and irrevocable fashion, I can't tell you everything that it's necessary for you to know. I can only enable you to glimpse the future that I'm reserving for you. For that, two things are sufficient: to acquaint you with my past and that of the association.

"The association was founded by a saint; you've heard mention of Mario Monteleone, the master of the *cavalieri ferrai.* Its original goal was to do good, purely and simply. It had a second after the death of Mario Monteleone—two, I should say: one apparent, the other hidden.

"The first was the vengeance of the murdered grandmaster; the second was conquest. The first is a pretext and a flag. It will be our strength for a long time. The second would already have been attained, if there had been a lion among us, one of those gold pieces of which, alas, one only finds the change. But I haven't yet said everything, and there was a third phase, to which we are still subject today.

"A man came to us: a giant or a madman, I don't know. That man, I don't judge; I detest him. Perhaps he is the lion. If he is the lion, we will trap him.

"He's as handsome as a demigod. If I were young and beautiful, I'd want to crawl at his knees. But I hate him! I hate him!"

She pronounced that word twice, with a frightful energy.

"That man," she went on, lowering her eyes and her voice, while ardent patches tinted the pallor of her cheeks, "by means of a stroke of a magic wand, has made us what we are. We would owe him everything, if he hadn't acted for himself...for himself alone. Thanks to him, the city is ours...we surround the throne...

"But what that man wants for himself, without reason and without right, I want for myself. I shall have it. He incessantly looks above him; he will not see the net extended beneath his feet. I shall break him, I swear, not because he is our tyrant and has his foot on our heads, but because the wealth that he covets is my wealth, and he wants to steal my heritage. That heritage, I have bought with blood. I hold it...

"Pier Falcone, by what I say to you, judge whether you are mine!

"I will tell you one more thing: before calling myself Barbe Spurzheim, my name was Barbe de Monteleone."

"What!" exclaimed the young doctor "You are...?"

"I am the last of that name. Mario died childless; I am the unique heir. Don't ask me for explanations, Pier Falcone; you already know too much, and I no longer know myself whether you have the right to reflect further."

The doctor approached her respectfully, took her hand and kissed it.

"No, Madame," he said. "I no longer have the right to do so. I will not say that I accept—that would be too little. I give myself to you with delight."

Barbe fixed her half closed eyes upon him, from which a subtle and piercing gaze emerged. "That is well said, Signor Pier Falcone," she murmured. "You're an adroit and sage man."

"Madame..."

"Very adroit...very sage...you're capable of making a semblance of loving me, in the event..."

"Can you doubt it?"

""I don't forbid you that," Barbe interjected, smiling. "We'll need an excuse in the eyes of the world, when the time comes. Only amour can give it to us. Well, you'll be a fine Comte, Falcone. The imbecile and blind world will be able to say: 'The old woman is infatuated with that young man...'"

There was harshness, but no bitterness, in those strange words.

"The old woman will make sure," she went on, changing her tone, "that the young man will never be her master, that's all."

It was assuredly difficult for the doctor to maintain countenance in the face of such a lover. He did not know what attitude to adopt or what to say. She came to his aid.

"Falcone," she said to him, extending her hand to him with a kind of cordiality. "You will have a friend in me. You will be noble, rich, powerful...perhaps even happy. We will never play the comedy with one another. Let us be solid and sincere allies; nothing more, nothing less."

191

"You can count on me, Madame," the doctor pronounced, resolutely, "as the most faithful of servants."

"We'll see about that," she replied, "sooner than you think." She released his hand and became pensive. "What else do I have to say to you?" she murmured. "Perhaps you're wondering why I've hidden my name at Ferdinand de Bourbon's court—the name that the King has surrounded with so much favor...for Mario, my relative, was his best friend... I've hidden it because there are two living people between me and Mario's heritage: Comte Lorédan Doria and young Comtesse Angélie..."

The doctor's brow darkened involuntarily.

"Have you divined already," Barbe went on, "that it will be necessary for us to pass by a route where there is blood?"

As Falcone went pale, she went on: "I don't detest them: a handsome signor, a delightful child...but they bar our route. You're no longer saying anything to me, Signor Pier Falcone?"

"Madame," the latter stammered. "I dread understanding..."

"Dread nothing, understand!" said Barbe, dryly. "That's necessary. I have no intention, moreover, of posing you enigmas. I do not know words capable of burning my lips in passing, and for what I have to say to you, I will speak in good Italian. I chose you for a husband in the place of Johann Spurzheim, whom I regret sincerely and profoundly...whom I will always regret, understand that, because the two of us formed a couple, male and female: the same vocation, the same ambition, the same heart...I chose you to replace him in order for you to do what he had done, and this is what he had done: he had condemned three heads, Prince Coriolani, Lorédan Doria and Angélie Doria..."

The doctor's teeth clicked. The calm of that woman frightened him.

"Condemned?" he murmured. "How?"

"As the Silence condemns."

"Three murders!"

"You doctors, Signor Falcone, have other weapons than us...I will leave the choice to you."

For the second time, her chest heaved, and her cheeks became livid around the red patches that marked her cheekbones. She coughed. One entire side of her handkerchief was stained with blood.

As Falcone approached her with a glass of water, into which he had just poured a few drops of the contents of a phial that he had taken from his bosom, she pushed him away gently. She was suffering horribly, that as evident, but she smiled.

"No, no," she said, in a light tone. "Now that you're my future, I'm breaking all your engagements. You're no longer my physician."

Falcone, seeing a suspicion in those words, drank the glass he had destined for her in a single draught.

"There's nothing in that," said Barbe, coldly. "The fact is proven, but I don't want a physician who will be obliged to drink all my potions like that."

Falcone bowed.

"Without rancor," she went on. "To get back to business, have you ever killed anyone, Signer Falcone?"

The later took a step backwards at that unqualifiable question.

"In a duel?" Barbe went on. "In a case of legitimate self-defense? Involuntarily, in sum?"

"Never, Madame never," the doctor interjected.

"And yet," she said, as if talking to herself, "Gall's science is a mathematical certainty."[37]

"Dreams!" exclaimed Falcone.

Madame Spurzheim took him by the hand and drew him toward her.

"Bend over, please, doctor," she said.

He obeyed, mechanically. Barbe paraded her long, pale fingers over the posterior protuberances of his skull.

"Feel it yourself," she said, indicating a place behind the ear and slightly above it. Gall and our homonym, Dr. Spurzheim, called that organ, politely, destructiveness. Console yourself, Signor Falcone; if you haven't killed yet, you will."

As she said that, she covered him with a fixed and icy stare. Pier Falcone could not sustain that stare. And when he heard Barbe's voice, he shivered like a guilty man.

"You have killed," said that implacable and slow voice, "not in a duel, not in a case of legitimate self-defense, not by hazard and involuntarily. The science is true and you are a liar, Pier Falcone. You're a murderer..."

He uttered a long groan and let himself fall into an armchair, his head covered by his hands.

Barbe Spurzheim stood up. You would scarcely have recognized her, so much did she lose in quitting her wing-chair, the fortified place that defended her stature against the gaze. What there was in her, when she was seated, of nobility and dignity, disappeared as soon as she revealed the deformities of her person.

She was all upper body. The disproportion between the total height of her person and the enormous development of her head leapt to the eyes when she renounced the advantage of the posture that only put her torso in evidence. She limped on her unequal and short legs; her hips stuck out at every step. The sentiment she had inspired changed at that unexpected aspect. The grand dame, changed into a dwarf, immediately lost all her prestige.

---

[37] The reference is, of course, to phrenology, although that name was actually given to it by Gall's associate and eventual rival, Johann Spurzheim—hence Barbe's subsequent remark.

It is necessary, however, not to be mistaken; the sensation experienced was neither pity not ridicule. It was dread. There was something of the malevolent and cruel fay in that hunchback four feet tall. She showed her true physiognomy then. All the rest was stage-setting, illusion and deception. A fay! She was a fay! The sinister fay of the fine tales that made us shiver as children, the terrible fay who looms over the cradle of poor little children. Merely in seeing her, one understood the lugubrious history of Mario Monteleone's posterity.

That woman must have plotted dire projects in the shadows, with neither weakness nor remorse. The father's tears and the mother's sobs must have slid over her heart of steel. One also understood the mysterious terrors that she had inspired in the inhabitants of the Martorello. Out there, too, people had called her the fay. Everyone had believed that the future had no secrets from her.

When her window, always illuminated, was seen in the house of Mario Monteleone, a strange terror overtook belated passers-by on the road. What was she doing in those hours when others were asleep? What was the work in which she never relented? She knew everything, that woman; she was capable of anything! The poets of the marvelous, Boïardo, Berni and Ariosto, did not always create giants when they wanted to inspire terror; dwarfs are also terrible, and inspire fear. She scared people, that woman, and the man who had married her had to be the most impure of scoundrels.

"Falcone," she said, stopping before the doctor, whose visage was still veiled, "I knew that. I know everything. It is necessary that a man be mine, entirely mine, in order for me to speak to him as I have spoken to you. Johann Spurzheim was mine; that is why I regret him. You are mine, Falcone; that is why I am saying to you: *Look at me; you have never seen me.*"

She parted the doctor's hands herself. He raised his eyes toward her; he lowered his head after looking at her. What Barbe said was true: he had never seen her, for he had only ever seen her in her armchair or in her bed, where Barbe had the appearance of a woman.

Barbe's teeth caused blood to spurt from her lip. Coquetry is innate. Ugliness has nothing to do with it. Barbe required a violent effort in order not to show her mortal chagrin.

Nevertheless, she said in the free and detached tone: "Doctor, this is why I'm constrained to purchase a husband. Don't be revolted, as an imprudent or stupid man would be. Don't tell me that you're not for sale. I've kept the best arrows in my quiver; my response would be a thunderbolt. Remember this, in any case: it isn't you that I want, it's your aid. I don't need a husband, but an accomplice. I call things by their name. If I talk about marriage, it's because the sacramental form is necessary to give you the right to act for me, and in any case, without the sacrament, I have no pretext for putting the mantle of the Comte de Monteleone on your shoulders.

"I've had the dream of being the Comtesse; that dream will be realized; I wish it! Now you've looked at me, you won't ask me again why I don't go to the court. When the time comes, you will go to the court for me. The King knows me; I have letters from his hand. The King does not know that I'm the wife of Johann Spurzheim. I have only ever signed myself, in writing to him, Barbe de Monteleone. The King will make my husband the greatest lord in the kingdom."

She fell silent. After a moment's silence, Pier Falcone turned to her and said: "I accept."

"Unconditionally?"

"Unconditionally."

"Aha, my handsome doctor!" cried Madame Spurzheim, darting her sharp gaze into the depths of Falcone's soul. "Either you're even more ambitious than I thought, or you have a hidden agenda. If you're only ambitious, that's good; we'll go beyond your desires. If you have a hidden agenda, that's your business. A few people, in my life, have attempted to play a cunning game with me. They're dead."

As the doctor was about to reply, someone knocked gently on the door of the drawing room.

"Come in!" said Barbe.

A poor fellow whose costume resembled that of our Parisian bailiffs' clerks, with flat hair, gray skin and a gray shirt, appeared on the threshold. He bowed three times while caressing his pen, which was stuck behind his ear.

"What is it, Privato?" asked Madame Spurzheim.

"It's an Englishman," replied Privato.

"What Englishman?"

"Poor Privato had a position at two hundred piastres a year in the royal police. That is not enough to nourish an eagle. He gnawed his fingernails a little in order to give himself aplomb, and replied: "A thin Englishman with his collar turned up, blue spectacles and a paunch...yellow hair. He has letters for His Excellency."

"You know full well, Privato, that His Excellency is very ill and can't see anyone."

"Certainly, certainly," replied the employee, "but he's so astonishing, this Englishman...he jabbered a host of things at me. I understood that he's come about the great affair..."

"What affair?"

"The London affair...the diamonds..."

"Privato," the director's wife pronounced, severely, "beware of knowing too much."

The two-hundred-piastre employee immediately went back into his shell.

"Tell the man to come back tomorrow," added the director's wife, pointing at the door.

Privato did not budge. He was in suspense between the strong desire that he had to obey, and the need to accomplish his mission more completely.

"Madame knows the profound respect, and, I dare to say, extraordinary veneration that I have for her," he murmured, biting his fingernails to the point of drawing blood. "I'd rather leave my share of paradise to my most mortal enemy than displease Madame...but the Englishman doesn't want to go."

"What do you mean, he doesn't want to?"

"Have pity on me, your noble ladyship! He's already shaken me by the shoulders three times and put his fist under my nose five times..."

"What is this man's name?"

"A diabolical name...Peter-Paulus Brown."

"Brown!" repeated Barbe, shivering.

She took a pad out of her bosom, which she consulted.

"Brown!" she said, in a low voice. "I have the name but not the secret..." She went on: "Privato, you're an intelligent man. Introduce this Brown, under the pretext of enabling him to wait more comfortably, into the barred room in which nocturnal rioters are deposited. Lock him in."

The two-hundred-piastre employee rubbed his hands together energetically. "Good idea, illustrious lady!" he exclaimed. "That's what it is to have intelligence above the common run. In the cage, he can box the wall if he wants to."

So saying, he bit his nail again and ran away.

"What have you to tell me, Doctor?" asked Barbe, as soon as he had gone.

"Three things, Madame," replied Falcone. "The Punjab is a diamond extracted by a miner from the Mogul's quarries. It can only be bought by a King. The man who possesses it is named Brown."

Barbe was thoughtful. "In the week that Johann Spurzheim hasn't got out of bed, I've surprised many secrets, but I don't know everything yet...and I need to know everything. Down there in my husband's office there are three letters that I can't read became they're in a cipher that isn't ours. It's time for us to go and see Johann. Remember carefully what I'm going to say to you: forbid my husband to occupy himself with business; order him to stay in bed for the sake of his life; advise him to entrust to someone else the great interests that are preoccupying him in spite of himself, and which are killing him. Do you understand?"

"I understand, Madame," replied Pier Falcone.

"Now," said Barbe, "let's sum up what regards the two of us: on your part, the promise of marriage, under oath, and the end of the year of my widow's mourning. No need to put it in writing; I know how to force people to keep their promises. If you doubt that, Signor Falcone, inform yourself of what was found this evening under the Maddalena bridge.

"On my part, similarly, the promise of marriage. A share in the fortune that I shall have by right of succession, the title of Comte, which the King cannot refuse to the husband of Barbe de Monteleone.. Finally, on the day that Johann Spurzheim dies, his succession as *cavaliere ferraio* and his iron ring.

"Your arm, Doctor; let's go care for our invalid..."

Pier Falcone bowed silently and presented his arm to her.

If we transport ourselves now to the room where Johann Spurzheim is supposedly reposing, we will find a strange smile on his ravaged and singly leaden face. How can we put it? It was the smile of a mathematician who has just found the proof of an arduous and complicated calculation. It was the smile of a collector confronting a rare and precious object pursued for a long time. It was, above all, the smile that one only sees in theaters: the smile of the man who has followed the drama in good faith and who suddenly sees the Gordian knot of the intrigue severed: a smile of *denouement*, let us say. And that smile grimaced bizarrely through that agony.

There was, however, nothing there: no drama that could be seen or heard. The room was as deserted as it was when we left it. The drama was doubtless in the dreams of the feverish invalid. And yet, at the precise moment when Barbe said to her new knight: "Give me your arm," Johann had a sort of echo of the movement they made.

At the same time, the head of the King Charles spaniel emerged entirely from the covers, showing its large black and yellow eyes, gold framed in jet. It yapped quietly.

With his thin hand, which already had cadaverous tints, Johann caressed it, murmuring: "Good, Love, good!"[38] And he gave it a pastry hoop, which the dog went under the covers in order to nibble.

With a freedom of movement that one would not have expected, given his appearance, Johann Spurzheim extended his arm. He had the round ivory object in his hand that we have compared to the funnel of a wind instrument. The object, along with the flexible cable appended to it, was thrown rather violently to the back of the cupboard pierced in the wall. Johann then pushed the panel of the cupboard, which closed silently, so neatly that one would not have discovered any trace of it in the space beside the bed.

Having done that, Johann replaced his head on the pillow and closed his eyes, the bistre lids of which had the sinister black dot in the middle that causes fear and pity...

---

[38] The word Love is given here in English, presumably signifying the dog's name—but if so, the author must have forgotten it, for Spurzheim subsequently refers to the dog as Zora, and then as Trésor [Treasure].

III. Perfect Understanding

Scarcely had Johann Spurzheim closed his eyes, than the bedroom door opened cautiously. His wife Barbe came in, on the arm of Doctor Pier Falcone.

Beside the bed was one of those armchairs with a concave back for the use of Madame Spurzheim. It was always there that the doctor had seen her during her visits. She placed herself in it.

"Now I'm in my beauty," she murmured, smiling.

In fact, even though the illusion had been destroyed, Pier Falcone could scarcely understand how a human creature could be so different from herself. In the new pose that she had just taken, Barbe, of whom one could only measure the upper body now, lost the wretched and deformed appearance under which we have recently seen her. Her aquiline face appeared at the desired height. She was a woman.

Pier Falcone leaned over the invalid.

"I'm not asleep," said the latter, in a very faint voice.

"Is that a reproach, my good friend?" asked Barbe, with a cheerful affection. "I was delayed in the drawing room with our doctor, who was paining me a picture of what your convalescence will be as soon as the first good days arrive. It's a devoted servant that you have there, Johann. When he's returned you to health, I hope you won't forget him."

The lips of the director of police scarcely moved, but his reply was clearly audible: "When have I ever forgotten good or evil?"

Pier Falcone tried to take his pulse; he pushed him away, trying to smile.

"In a while," he said. Then, addressing his wife, he added: "Now you're in your beauty, Barbe, my dear companion—you said it; you're in your beauty, playing your role of good angel next to the poor condemned—I'd like to call all of Naples to this bed of pain to render witness.... You have been my beloved wife, Barbe, all the consolation of my last days!"

"Moderate yourself, signor," said Falcone. "Talking too much isn't good for you."

Johann Spurzheim addressed a submissive not of the head to him.

"My delay," said Barbe, had another reason. I'm doing what I can, my friend, in order that your affairs don't suffer too manifestly from your temporary indisposition..." She emphasized the word *temporary*, and went on: "...But your affairs, I'm not unaware, are in large part those that one cannot even confide to one's wife. If it's permissible for me to ask you the question, were you expecting a visit today from an Englishman named Brown?"

"Today? No," Johann replied, without hesitation.

"You were expecting him later?"

Johann Spurzheim nodded his head in a sign of affirmation.

198

"He's arrived."

"Good," was the invalid's only reply.

The hunchback still had her cheerful expression, but the devil lost nothing by it.

"I've had a good nap," said Spurzheim. "I feel astonishingly rested. Don't you both think that I have a better voice?"

"Yes," replied Barbe. "The doctor thinks that with a few weeks of rest, he'll reckon with the illness."

The doctor did not say anything. At that moment the doctor was suffering from the reaction of the mental shock that he had recently suffered. The doctor was thinking about the prodigious union offered and accepted; he was gazing at his wife...

That wife's husband turned toward him painfully.

"And you, Falcone?" he said.

"Me?" repeated the latter. "I don't know..."

The invalid had one of the smiles that the decomposition of his features rendered so lugubrious. "You don't know?" he pronounced, slowly

Then, addressing Barbe, who dared not look at her accomplice, Spurzheim said, forthrightly: "I'm sure, my dear friend that you sometimes wonder why I've given my confidence to this young man. A physician of twenty-seven or twenty-eight, in an illness as grave as mine...that's risky. And certainly, there are days when one might think that the young man doesn't have the use of all his faculties... Would you like me to give you the secret of his distractions, his reveries, his absences?"

"Signor!" Falcone interjected, with a kind of alarm.

"Talking too much isn't good for me, is it?" said Johann Spurzheim, whose smile was almost mocking. "Don't worry...I'm much better than you think. My face doesn't do me honor, that's all... So, I was saying that I can give you the key to the enigma, my good friend. Out dear doctor is in love!"

As he pronounced the final word, he closed his eyes complaisantly, as if to avoid seeing the gleam that shone in Barbe's eyes. The latter coughed slightly, to give herself countenance, but her chest did not like that game. The provoked coughing fit immediately responded to the appeal and put a new bloodstain on the handkerchief.

Pier Falcone remained as motionless as a guilty man awaiting his sentence. He knew what that woman's vengeance was worth. He had accepted the proposition, we could well say, because, in his mind, that woman, like her husband, was condemned to death. But death was not yet imminent enough for the woman not to be able to strike a terrible blow.

The reader will doubtless be wondering who that pale young man was, whose forehead had intelligence, whose eyes promised audacity, and whom, thus far we have seen easily dominated. Why did he stay there, between the tiger and the tigress, like an easy prey with which one plays, an assured victim for the teeth of the female or the male?

"Take one of those nice pastilles that do you so much good, my dear wife," said Spurzheim, his eyes still closed. "When you cough like that, it's as if my own breast were tearing. Oh, it must be a terrible grief, that of a widow searching in her excessively large house for the beloved companion who is no more! Fortunately for me, I'm destined to precede you on that great voyage..."

Barbe tried to protest.

"We're going to come back to that painful subject shortly," he went on. "I confess that I've delayed it until the last moment, because I knew that it would cause you so much chagrin... Look and learn, my friend Pier Falcone...you would search all Naples in vain for such a scene. This is the sanctuary of that great, that noble, that unalterable affection: conjugal love! Look at Barbe Spurzheim, who is dying because her husband is going to die."

The hunchback's cheeks were livid. "May it please God," she murmured, however, "that I can give you the few days that remain to me, Johann, my husband, in order to prolong your precious existence."

"Do you hear, Falcone? That's the treasure I'm losing! So, we were saying, my good friend," he resumed, abruptly, as if to shake off sad preoccupations, "that there was a reason for the reveries of this tenebrous beau. There he is, very embarrassed, for he doesn't know you. He doesn't know that you're made to understand his conduct...he's no ordinary lover...."

"In the name of God, signor!" the young doctor tried to interject.

"Let me speak!" said the invalid, forthrightly. "Barbe is a woman of a rare species. She will have more esteem for you when she knows that you have loved to the point of crime."

"Is the object of this amour alive?" asked Madame Spurzheim, who succeeded in feigning calm.

"Alive and beautiful under her veil of black crepe," replied Johann. "Our perfect lovers are waiting for the end of her mourning in order to become happy spouses."

Pier Falcone had cold sweat on his temples. Madame Spurzheim lowered her eyes and did not look at him. A gleam slid from the half-closed eyelids of the invalid. The blow had struck home.

Johann crossed his hands on the covers and adopted a tone of compunction.

"Barbe, my excellent companion," he went on "the emotion that the indirect allusion I've just made to my imminent demise had produced in you forbids me to treat a certain subject in your presence..."

Madame Spurzheim hastened to cover her face with her hands.

"It breaks my heart, Barbe," the invalid continued, "to see your suffering... What can I tell you, my wife? The separation will not be of long duration, and

200

we will soon be reunited, never to quit one another again, in a better world... I beg you to leave me alone with my physician."

"Do you no longer have confidence in me, Johann?" cried the hunchback, who had succeeded in shedding a tear. "Must I lose a few of these moments, so dear?"

Spurzheim held out his hand to her, which she kissed.

"Barbe," he said to her, "My confidence in you is entire; it is limitless. When the doctor has responded in accordance with his science and his conscience to the questions that I am going to address to him, I shall be more tranquil. I shall occupy myself then with ensuring the future of the only being who is truly dear to me in this world. You are a woman above your sex; assemble your courage, Barbe. Tomorrow morning, you will have nothing more to ask of me. Tomorrow morning, you will no longer have any curiosity or desire to satisfy..."

Finally, I shall know everything! Barbe thought, having difficulty containing her triumph.

"I owe you that, Barbe, my wife," Johann Spurzheim concluded.

She stood up, and went to deposit a silent kiss n the forehead of the sick man. A moment later, the director of the royal police and Pier Falcone were alone.

"I owe her that!" Johann repeated, as the door closed n her. Then, his voice took on an indefinable expression as he added: "Tomorrow morning, she will no longer have anything to ask of me." He interrupted himself abruptly: "What are you thinking about, Doctor?"

"I'm listening to you and awaiting your orders," Pier Falcone replied.

Johann smiled and said: "How much would you give, Doctor to get yourself out of the unfortunate predicament you're in?"

"I don't know what you mean, signor," the young doctor stammered.

Johann Spurzheim looked him in the face. "You were born lucky, Pier Falcone," he pronounced slowly. "In a single evening, a great fortune is going to be offered to you twice."

The doctor literally did not dare to pronounce a single word. He resembled a man who senses beneath his feet a terrain strewn with traps and pitfalls.

Spurzheim was enjoying his embarrassment.

"Doctor," the director of the royal police continued, "Let's talk about the only being who is truly dear to me in his base world. I just promised to occupy myself with their future. Have you divined who that privileged creature is?"

"Your wife, signor," murmured Pier Falcone.

Spurzheim uttered a brief dry laugh. "No, doctor," he replied, "it's myself. What do you think about my wife?"

"Signor..."

"Let's understand one another, friend. Quibbling wastes time, and we have such a terrible need of it this evening. I'm not asking you your opinion of the elevated perfections of Barbe Spurzheim. She's a masterly woman, we know that. I'm asking you how long you give her to live."

Pier Falcone remained nonplussed, thinking about the similar question that Barbe had addressed to him previously.

"Answer," said the director of the royal police. "I know that it's only a matter of time."

Falcone replied, unwittingly employing the same terms as he response to Madame Spurzheim. "Signor. science cannot be rigorously precise…"

"A week?" Johan interjected, his tine having become more incisive. It was a perfect imitation of Barbe's voice. Falcone stood there open-mouthed.

"A fortnight?" Spurzheim went on, with an inflexion so absolutely similar that the doctor began to tremble.

"I'm sure," Johann continued, repeating Barbe's final interrogation word for word, "that you don't think that she can last a month?"

It would be difficult to say what struck the doctor most violently. Was it the increasing bizarrerie of his situation, which was becoming fantastic? Was it the menacing and present danger? No nightmare had ever held his head in such a vice.

"You heard our conversation!" he exclaimed, unable to contain himself.

"Which of us is asking the questions?" pronounced Spurzheim, severely.

"Signor…," said Pier Falcone.

"Enough, my poor fellow," Johann interjected, closing his fatigued eyes again. "You said just now to my wife that science cannot be precise, that it is impossible to affirm…I believe it. Science is a simpleton, when it is not a charlatan; science moves me to pity. I've had that opinion for thirty years. But you're a lucky man, Pier Falcone…obliged to marry my wife!"

The doctor did not even try to protest, so utterly disconcerted was he.

"The request was abrupt," he director of police continued. "She's an admirable woman. However, I would have paid a hundred gold ounces to see your face when you said, Pier Falcone, with your twenty-eight years…when you said to that hunchbacked fay: 'Madame, I give myself to you with delight!'"

He laughed wholeheartedly this time. All things considered, it would have been impossible to have found a dying man in a better humor.

"Friend," he went on, in a whisper, "I shall regret my wife. She had great qualities. But if she lasted for a month, to employ her phrase, it would be infinitely too long. I'm even more of a hurry than my wife."

"Nothing announces that your impatience will be contented so soon," replied Falcone, who had finally pulled himself together.

"Nothing?" repeated Spurzheim. "You're a poor diviner, Doctor. My wife said to you, a little while ago: 'I have my reasons.' Who doesn't? Mine are admirable…and in order for you not to waste time searching for them, I'll spell them out. It's necessary that I'm a widower within twenty-four hours and remarried by the end of the week."

As he finished those words, three taps of a heel were heard on the floor above. At first, the invalid's expression took on an anxious and sly expression, but that was momentary. His smile returned almost immediately, and he tugged a little cord hidden in the folds of his curtains. A bell was heard to ring n the same place that someone had just knocked. Pier Falcone waited. Nothing could surprise him any longer—at least, he thought so.

The ceiling of the bed split and opened, forming a hole immediately above the invalids head. From that hole a small board descended, suspended by four silk threads.

"What's new, Beccafico?" asked Johann.

"Oho!" said a high-pitched voice from the ceiling. "There's a man there, Excellency."

"Don't worry about the man, Beccafico. What's new?"

"Nothing much, signor. There are more soldiers out here at the Castello-Vecchio than were necessary to take our Holy Father's estates in Tuscany. The scaffold is being set up nicely in the Piazza San Pietro Martire."

"Has nothing come from the Palazzo Doria?"

"Two couriers. They're looking for Prince Coriolani. The rumor's going around that he's been murdered."

"Murdered!" repeated Spurzheim and Pier Falcone, simultaneously. The latter attempted to catch sight of the mysterious Beccafico, but could not succeed. Only a black hole in the middle of the top of the ceiling of the bed could be seen.

The board, sustained horizontally by its silken cords, continued to descend. It arrived with arm's reach of Johann. He took two letters from it. His hand was trembling slightly but he succeeded in opening them.

"Hold the lamp, Doctor," he said.

Pier Falcone picked up the lamp and held it up so that Johann could read.

"We still don't know," Beccafico continued, "who struck the blow at the Maddalena bridge."

Spurzheim looked at Pier Falcone. "He knows," he said.

"Oh!" grunted Beccafico. "He's new! I don't know him."

At that moment, Spurzheim crumpled up the first letter, with annoyance.

"Nothing!" said Beccafico. "Bad business! Perhaps the second will be better."

Spurzheim read the second.

Beccafico went on: "I've seen the Englishman. But he's superb! He doesn't want either to go away or let go of his letters of recommendation. He's written on a large sheet of paper all that he has to ask of you, not to mention the State secrets he's going to reveal to you."

"You pronounced the word Punjab in his ear?" asked Spurzheim.

"Yes, signor. He blew into his cheeks and the tip of his nose went pale."

"What did he say?"

"That he wants his wife."

"His wife?"

"And the address of a mysterious unknown woman who was with him aboard the *Pausilippe*. He also desires to see a few lazzaroni, an eruption of Vesuvius and a true Calabrian brigand..."

Johann was no longer listening. He was reading the second letter with a singular attention. When he had finished it he reflected for a few moments.

"Bring the lamp closer," he said to Pier Falcone.

The latter having obeyed, he set fire to the two letters he had just received, and watched them burn one after the other.

"That purifies the air in a sickroom," he murmured. Then, aloud, he added: "That's good Beccafico. Go away."

The tray began to rise up again, soundlessly.

"Do you know Baron Altamonte?" Johann suddenly asked the doctor.

"No, signor."

"He's an amiable man. You're probably going to make his acquaintance tonight."

The tray had disappeared. The hole closed again.

At that moment, an idea occurred to Johan Spurzheim. He rang immediately.

"Present, signor!" said Beccafico's thin voice

Johan murmured, to himself: "Is the memory going? If Felice thinks he'll find me here he'll be on his guard. And yet, it's a task that it's necessary to do oneself! On what precise date," he asked, raising his eyes toward the roof of the bed, "was Baron d'Altamonte arrested?"

"The nineteenth of December, signor."

"And put in secret?"

"Seven days later, the twenty-sixth, on the order I carried myself on your behalf to the Castello-Vecchio."

"I didn't ask that," said the invalid, impatiently Then he went on: "On what date did we take possession of the palace where we are? Don't make a mistake, Beccafico!"

"The twenty-ninth of December, signor."

"You're quite sure?"

"Quite sure, Excellency."

"In that case, there's no response to the letters we've just received. Beccafico. All is well. Let the messenger go." To Pier Falcone, whose face expressed a profound astonishment, he said: "Help me to sit up, Doctor. "No physician has ever understood my malady well, and I believe that you're like all the rest. We're going to work together tonight; you'll see that I'm still good for something."

IV. Doctor Pier Falcone

When Falcone had helped Johann Spurzheim to sit up, the latter uttered a great sigh of fatigue.

"I'm very weak. Doctor," he said, "And I'm sure you're laughing inside at seeing me take so much trouble. *There won't be time*, you're thinking. *His days are numbered...*" He interrupted himself, half-closing his eyes, as was his habit. "There is no man, my friend, whose days are not numbered. I know my measure: save for poison or iron, I'll live to be a hundred. It's written."

"Signor," replied Falcone, "for me, in everything that I see here, there's something inexplicable and almost supernatural. This agony, by which even the men of the art are deceived, is a pretence, then?"

The director of the royal police shook his head disdainfully. "Give me a mirror, friend Falcone," he said "it's high time I looked at myself."

Falcone went to get a hand mirror from the dressing-table and brought it back. Johan put it in front of his face.

"One doesn't feign this livid pallor," he murmured, with a hint of sadness in his voice. "One doesn't hollow out the fleshless orbit of the eye like this oneself. One doesn't disguise oneself as a cadaver!" He pushed away the mirror and resumed his bitter smile. "The evil is there!" he said, pressing his chest with both hands. "I live with it, and I'm stronger than it is. I'm dying: science is right, poor blind thing—but what does it matter, if I take years to die!"

He placed his finger, moist and cold, on Pier Falcone's hand

"The illness is my accomplice," he said. "Understand that well. The illness is my safeguard and my shield. There is a man...a man that you hate, Pier Falcone, with all the force of your soul...a man who would have killed me a hundred times over if he didn't regard me as dead."

"A man that I hate?" repeated Pier Falcone, with an incredulous smile. "I'm very little, signor, to have such powerful enemies."

"You're nothing...but who knows the future? Just now, someone offered to make you a Comte and ten times a millionaire..."

The doctor resumed the stupefied physiognomy that he had kept voluntarily as a countenance since the beginning of the conversation. "You have a familiar spirit at your orders, signor," he murmured.

Everyone has his weakness. The wiliest man has a little corner accessible to flattery. Johann was waiting for that expression of admiration. He was content.

"I have no familiar spirit, Pier Falcone," he said, "And I swear to you that I haven't quit this bed for four days."

In consequence, he had not been listening at doors.

"If I may be permitted for to ask, signor...," the physician began.

"That is not permitted, Pier Falcone. But have you, who are a Sicilian, never heard of the ear of Dionysius the Tyrant?"

"If it please Your Excellency," Falcone retorted, hotly, "I'm a native of the Romagna."

"Is it me you want to deceive?" snapped the director of the royal police. "My poor companion, cleverer men than you have tried; it has bought them misfortune."

"I protest, signor..."

"Peace! Rather listen to a little story, which will amuse you incomparably. Three years ago, at the end of 1820, I was in Palermo on business...but in parenthesis, how did you like the tale I told Barbe Spurzheim? The tale of murdered husband and the marriage that awaits at the end of the year of mourning?"

"Signor, I've understood your intention..."

"You have the good fortune that Barbe's consumption is taking on a 'galloping' character, as you say in medicine. I wouldn't have given a ducat for your skin, my poor Falcone, if Barbe still had a week ahead of her...but let's leave the tale and get to the story. In the year 1820 there was great rejoicing in Palermo on the occasion of the sojourn that Francis de Bourbon, the royal prince, made there. There were many foreigners there, principally Neapolitans belonging to the noble houses of the court. The d'Angris were there, also the Barberinis; but Alizia d'Angri and Bianca Barberini, then too young, yielded the palm of beauty to Pia Frezzoloni of the Marquises of Mantua. Why are you closing your eyes, Pier Falcone?"

"Because the light is hurting me, signor," replied the physician, who, far from being troubled, was now allowing a sad smile to wander over his lips.

"Good, that gaze!" said Spurzheim. "You looked at me like a man. I didn't like your bearing a few minutes ago. If you're strong, my companion, we'll treat you in consequence."

"I don't know whether I'm strong or weak, signor," Falcone replied. "I'm waiting for the end of your story."

Johan winked, and continued. "It isn't a long story. There was a great fête given to the royal prince by the Comte de Ségeste, in his magnificent manor house, which is in the depths of the Gulf of Castellamare.

"While she was reposing on the grass. Pia Frezzoloni was bitten by a viper. She was carried back to Palermo dying.

"They have a way of curing viper bites out there. Someone condemned to death sucks the wound. The victim comes back to life but the condemned man dies. If, by chance, he escapes, the King grants him mercy.

"There was no one condemned to death in the prisons of Palermo. A letter from Francis de Bourbon, heir to the crown, was read to all the prisoners in the New Tower, which promised amnesty and five hundred ducats to anyone who volunteered to suck the wound of the beauty of beauties. Everyone refused except one. That one said: 'The five hundred ducats will be for my old mother…do you still have your old mother, Pier Falcone?"

A tear came to the doctor's eye. "No, signor," he replied, in a dull voice. "She's dead."

"Oh," said Johann Spurzheim, as if talking to himself, "that's true. Did you love your mother? Personally, I never knew mine…and I've never had a child. Is your son alive?"

"No, signor," Falcone replied, his head slumping on to his breast. "He's dead."

"The prisoner of Palermo," Spurzheim went on, "was named, if I remember rightly, Pietro Bertini."

"Pietro-Maria Bertuzzi," the doctor rectified.

"You know the story better than me, Falcone!"

"Signor," retorted the latter, with a strange inflection in his voice, "it pleases me to hear you tell it."

"Well, my companion," Johann Spurzheim continued, "that prisoner of Palermo, Pietro-Maria Bertuzzi, had, I believe, been smuggling in order to provide bread for his old mother. He sucked Pia Frezzoloni's wound, who was cured. The prisoner didn't die. But he had drunk the blood of the beauty of beauties; he was bitten in the heart by one of those passions that devour you, you Italians, and which other peoples are unable to feel. Such as you see me, Pier Falcone, I have never been in love…"

The young physician had a scornful smile.

"Good, that smile, comrade!" said Johann. "You still have Palermitain blood in our veins. With the five hundred ducats he received, Pietro-Maria Bertuzzi studied medicine. He had his plan. As soon as he was admitted to the first grade, he presented himself at the home of Doctor Gioja, who had the confidence of the Frezzolonis. He was handsome, that Pietro Bertuzzi, very handsome. You've aged well, Pier Falcone."

"That's the truth, signor. I've aged well."

"Doctor Gioja took him as a pupil. One night, when Gioja was ill or idle, Pietro Bertuzzi replaced his master summoned to the Palazzo Frezzoloni… I don't know exactly what happened…"

"Who can describe the joys of paradise down here, signor?" murmured Falcone, who had sweat on his temples.

"That lasted a year…"

"A century of happiness, which passed like a day."

"Pia Frezzoloni," Johann continued, "was a mother. The two lovers had no confidant and kept their secret entirely to themselves. One night…"

"A year after the first, to the day," the doctor put in, his face utterly transformed. It was somber, as menacing as Vengeance.

"Tell the rest, Falcone," said Johann. "My memory is failing."

"One night," the doctor pronounced, between grated teeth, "there was a fête at the Palazzo Frezzoloni…and Pietro-Maria was not invited to fêtes. He only had the right to hide in Pia's bedroom, which he had in full, for a priest had blessed their secret union. He was there, the lover and the husband, behind the muslin curtains. He was looking across the courtyard and the brightly-lit drawing rooms full of flowers. He had never found his wife so beautiful…

"The bedroom formed a corner of the palazzo. One of the windows in the other wall overlooked the gardens. That one was open. Pietro Bertuzzi heard someone talking under the balcony. The name of Pia reached him. He ran to it. A few young fools were chatting under the orange trees, and one of them said: 'I'll wager a thousand French louis that Pia Frezzoloni will belong to me before the night ends.'"

"Did you know that young fool, Falcone?" Johann interjected.

"I had seen him at the corso, signor," the physician replied, disdaining henceforth to make a distinction between himself and Pietro-Maria Bertuzzi. "He was the folly of the Palermitain grande dames, the invincible Don Juan, the romantic hero…the Chevalier d'Athol."

Johann nodded his head approvingly.

Falcone continued: "The others started to laugh. The bet was taken. Pietro Bertuzzi, or Pier Falcone, whatever you want to call him, signor, felt that a vertigo was about to seize him. He looked hard at that Chevalier d'Athol before his sight was troubled. He looked at him so hard that a hundred years of life could not make him lose the memory of those features."

"And what did he do, Pier Falcone?" asked Johann.

The doctor touched his temples with his handkerchief and drew it away bathed in sweat. "Signor," he said, "Pia Frezzoloni was as far above me as the Holy Virgin is above a Christian kneeling at the altar. I do not know myself why she took pity on my amour. What is certain is that the idea of losing my adored treasure made me fall into delirium.

"The thought did not occur to me, although it was simple, of plunging my dagger to the hilt in the heart of the Chevalier d'Athol. No, I was like a poor insensate: an obsession gripped me: I had to put a barrier between her and him—an insurmountable barrier. And I said to myself: *A mother's holiest safeguard is her child. Who would pass over a cradle?*

"I said that to myself. I went out. I ran. I went to fetch my son from the house of his nurse. I brought him, hidden under my cloak, and I put him in Pia's bed. The ball had finished. I went to take refuge in the garden where the companions of the Chevalier d'Athol had been talking and laughing. I was no longer a man. I let myself fall on to the grass. I didn't see what happened; but the following day, the whole city knew.

"All that foolish youth bore a grudge against Pia Frezzoloni, who had rejected their homages. Athol had bribed the chambermaid. Athol got into the room of which my folly had deserted the guard. As he did not come down, those who had wagered went up. Pia was asleep. Athol was playing with a little child that he had in his arms.

"I hate him, that man! Oh, I hate him! I'm telling the truth. He was playing with the child; he had respected the mother. I hate his generosity! I would damn myself in order to plunge him into the depths of Hell.

"Ten of them, perhaps twenty, had seen the child. Comte Frezzoloni came to present himself at his daughter's bedside the next day. He kissed her, and handed her a cup. Saying: 'It's poisoned.'

"Pia did not pronounce my name as she died, in order that my life would be saved. She was put in the tomb along with the poor dear child. And old Comte Frezzoloni, on one knee before Francis de Bourbon, who had tears in his eyes, demanded a combat against those who had killed his daughter with his honor.

"Francis de Bourbon replied that they had all left Sicily except three. The old Comte demanded combat against those three. They were dead. The Chevalier d'Athol had killed his three accomplices, in duels. Did that prevent him from being the murderer of my wife and my son?

"I was no longer in my right mind. I slept for a long time, and heavily. I woke up one morning to the sound of a coffin that was being nailed shut nearby. It was my mother's coffin..."

There was a silence. The doctor was straight and stiff beside the bed. His cheeks were livid, but his eyes were bloodshot.

"And when you woke up, Pietro-Maria Bertuzzi," Spurzheim took up the story, "your soul melted between those three tombs. You searched for the Chevalier d'Athol, but he was no longer in Palermo."

The doctor clenched his fists. A fringe of foam bordered his lips. Spurzheim smiled on seeing that.

"You set forth on the hunt," he went on, "like an ardent bloodhound; you traveled Italy and Sicily in all directions...and one day, you discovered that the Chevalier d'Athol was none other than the master of the Silence, the brigand as powerful as a king, the terrible and redoubtable Porporato."

"That is so, signor."

"And in order to get closer to him, in order to lie in wait for him, to choose the hour of your vengeance, you became a Companion of the Silence..."

"Yes, signor."

"And do you still want to kill him?"

The skin of Pier Falcone's face went red in places. His entire body trembled. His response was a roar.

"Sit down here, Falcone; you're the man I need. All the promises that Barbe, my dear wife, made to you, I will keep for her. You'll be rich; you'll be a Comte. Tell me, are you still capable of loving?"

"No, signor."

"Are you capable, at least, of marrying a young woman as beautiful as the angels, who will give you a fortune and nobility?"

"I'm ambitious, signor. It's my last passion."

"I have your wife. She's a third of the age of Barbe, tonight's fiancée. What did my sweet companion promise you?"

"The ring of the Silence."

"You shall have the ring of the Silence. Not mine, because it's necessary to die to cede that ring, and I have a presentiment that I shall bury all of you, but another, which will be free in a few hours. You see that I'm not mean. In exchange for that, what will you give me, Pier Falcone?"

"What are you asking of me, signor?"

"I'm asking for your strength, for that I don't have; your health, which I lack; your agile limbs, your piercing eyes and your subtle ears: you, in your entirety, in order that my intact mind has a body at its service."

"I will be your body, signor."

"You've understood fully?"

"I've understood fully."

"You no longer have a will...I am your soul."

"I no longer have a soul."

"Take my hand, Pier Falcone...tomorrow, you will be the king's physician, if you wish."

As their hands clasped, the same sound that we have heard before resounded above the bed on the floor above.

Johann immediately pulled the cord of the bell, which rang. The roof of the bed opened and allowed the tray suspended by four silken threads to pass through, as it had the first time.

"Well, well!" said the shrill voice of Beccafico. "The man is still there."

"What's new?" demanded Spurzheim.

"Someone has fired a rifle shot in the Castello-Vecchio. And Prince Coriolani has not yet reappeared at the Palazzo Doria."

Johann turned to the doctor. "Signor Pier Falcone," he interrogated, in a low voice, "have you ever encountered in your path the handsome Prince Coriolani?"

"Never, signor."

The tray arrived within arm's reach of Johann. He took a letter from it and opened it swiftly.

"Good!" he cried, as soon as he had scanned the first lines. "Has my wife returned to her apartment?"

"Her light is out, Excellency."

"That's good, Beccafico. Go and open the secret passage silently, and if any message arrives, bring it to my study."

As soon as the trapdoor closed again he said: "Friend, when one listens at doors, there are things that escape. Reply to me frankly. Barbe, my wife, isn't planning to hasten the course of events is she?"

"What do you mean, monsignor?"

"I'm talking about this mortal malady that will carry me off in thirty or forty years…and I'm asking you whether Barbe Spurzheim has any intention of giving nature a helping hand."

"I would not have lent my hand…," Falcone began.

Spurzheim frowned. "Do you think I would have bought you if I'd thought you were a man with scruples?" he said, harshly.

Pier Falcone bowed.

"Cards on the table!" said Johann. "I've made you my profession of faith. It isn't because Barbe Spurzheim might have wanted to steal a week or two from a moribund like me that I'd condemn Barbe Spurzheim. She's playing her game, she's within her rights. If I condemn my wife it's because my wife is inconvenient. Have you understood me, once and for all?"

Pier Falcone bowed again.

"Barbe has caught sight of affairs that I wanted to hide from her. You see that I'm not saying that those affairs don't concern her. Barbe has kept three letters from me. Take my pulse, Falcone…"

"It's agitated, signor," said the physician, having tested it.

"Those three letters, Falcone, could be our life or death. She hasn't been able to decipher them; so much the worse—that proves that they were important. One hope remains to me: she might have left them in my study."

"If you wish," said Pier Falcone, "I'll go get them, and bring them to you."

"Friend," relied Johann, smiling, "I promise you always to have confidence in you, because I shall never put myself in your hands. I need to go to look for those three letters myself."

"You?" cried the doctor. "That's impossible…quite impossible!"

Eleven o'clock chimed on the beautiful and severe clock on the mantelpiece. Johann pushed back his covers and revealed the frightful thinness of his limbs, unashamedly.

"Serve as my valet de chambre, I beg you," he said. "I'm going to get dressed."

Pier Falcone had seen clients die of starvation. He had never had before his eyes a cadaver as fleshless as that. It was composed of bones on which a diaphanous gray parchment was stuck. Nevertheless, he obeyed.

He sheathed those poor shivering tibias, which rendered a skeletal music when they chanced to collide with one another, in a warm pair of plushy and passed trousers. He shod the shriveled feet in furry slippers, and succeeded in passing over the arms, which he scarcely dared touch for fear of breaking them, the sleeves of a skimpy dressing gown, which would have been too tight for a child of twelve but was far too large for Johann Spurzheim.

While he was being dressed the latter coughed quietly.

There was a looking-glass facing the bed. "Lift the lamp up a little, my companion," he said. "I suppose I'd figure poorly in the guards' light cavalry regiment, but I'd still like to see myself."

Ferdinand I's cavaliers were the finest parade soldiers in the whole world.

Falcone raised the lamp. The mirror reflected something unusual: a wretched human appearance devoid of shoulders and a chest, over which that dressing-gown floated like the sheath of an umbrella.

Johan smiled contentedly. "I thought I was thinner than that," he said. "Much thinner. The malady still has something to eat!"

Falcone did not laugh. It was necessary not to know Johann Spurzheim to laugh, whatever he said or did.

"Let's go," he said, pushing back a few gray hairs in revolt on his shy cranium. "Take me in your arms, my companion, and carry me to my study; you can come back to fetch the lamp."

It is necessary to believe that Pier Falcone was not an extraordinary man like our great captain Luca Tristany, or even Gaspardo the fisherman. He was more elegant than robust. Without letting go of the lamp that he was holding, however he lifted Joann Spurzheim up with his right hand and carried him as nurses carry children fatigued by walking. The director of police was almost humiliated at first.

"You can rest on the way," he said.

Falcone could have made a tour of the city like that, but he had the good sense to reply: "You're much heavier than I would have thought, signor."

Taking advantage of his position, Spurzheim tugged his ear gently. "Not that way," he said seeing that the doctor was heading for the main door. With his finger, he indicated a second door on the opposite side of the room. Pier Falcone opened it, and they both found themselves in a dark cabinet, in the center of which was a turning staircase.

Pier Falcone began to descend the steps of that staircase with his double burden. At the bottom of the second flight there was a room similar to the dark cabinet on the floor above. It opened to a long corridor in which, at intervals, there were widows closed by strong shutters. As he traversed it, Pier Falcone thought he could hear footsteps sounding on the pavement. In his estimation, the corridor must run alongside the street or the market square.

At the end of the corridor was a locked door. Johan took a key from his bosom and gave it to his carrier, who introduced it into the lock. The door opened. They were in the study of the director of the royal police.

V. Cough Pastilles

Johann Spurzheim's sight was still piercing and sure, for as soon as they had crossed the threshold he exclaimed: "They're there!"

He meant the letters, all three of which were, indeed, reposing on an ebony desk.

The desk itself, and the multitude of papers that it bore, remained exactly as Johann had left them. If Johann had not had that singular machine in the gap between his bed and the wall, the ivory funnel attached to a flexible cable and enclosed in the little cupboard with the invisible door—the ear of Dionysius of Syracuse—Johan would have worn on oath that no indiscreet finger had leafed through his correspondence. But Johann had heard Barbe's confession.

"What a woman!" he murmured, with a sort of admiration, while Falcone approached the desk. "What a fay! See whether she's left a single trace of her passage! Friend, I certainly sense that I'll miss her!"

In front of the desk there was large leather armchair that had the form of a sentry-box. In seaports, merchants on the shore have seats like that to protect them from gusts of wind.

Johan's armchair was well-known in Naples. It was claimed that in addition to its principal and apparent mission, which was to protect the director of police from draughts, the armchair had other advantages even more precious. It was said that the armchair, which was a monument, obtained for him the result that diplomats of the old school demanded from blue-tinted spectacles and green eye-shades.

Johann willingly turned his sentry-box away from the light when it was a matter of an important interrogation. In the depths of that rolling house he was then like a priest in his confessional, or, better, like Zurbaran's monk, whose face can scarcely be divined in the deep shadow of his hood.[39] He could see, but he could not be seen.

Experts affirm that in current diplomacy and good police work, that detail has its value.

What is certain is that few people in Naples could have described the features of the director of police precisely. The citizens who frequented the offices of the police had glimpsed a shadow of sorts in the depths of that worthy armchair: a muffled body, a meager figure like the blade of a knife, so pale and thin that it appeared to be a phantom. That was all.

As for the aristocrats following the court, they were even less advanced. Since the King of Naples had had the good idea of entrusting the security of his

---

[39] Francisco de Zurbaran painted numerous monks, but the painting the author has in mind might well be his 1632 painting of St. Francis.

capital to the Austrian, who had a hundred eyes, like Argus, he had never been seen at royal celebrations. And if he had sometimes attended ministerial councils, it was in such accoutrement, and with such a luxury of precautions against glances that even his colleagues were yet to know him.

Pier Falcone put the lamp down on the desk; then, having both hands free, he undertook the task of placing Johan Spurzheim in his confessional.

The two lateral walls of the armchair were mounted on hinges, and could be opened in order for the director of police to have more air when he was alone and the weather was hot. When they were open, one could admire the intelligence that had presided over the construction of that monumental seat.

Each of the walls, well-lined, padded and quilted, had a compartment under its padded the sturdy lock of which protruded. What Signor Johann kept in those compartments, no one knew—not even Barbe, in spite of her strong desire.

The armchair only moved by means of its castors. For vigorous men would certainly not have been able to lift it up.

Johann Spurzheim uttered a sigh of relief when his carrier had installed him comfortably on the cushions.

"I'm a little out of breath," he said, "but that's not astonishing after the journey we've just made. Pass me my letters, doctor, and bring the lamp closer. You wouldn't believe how glad I am to see everything that surrounds me here...my papers my books, my old companions. And then," he added, with a wink that Falcone did not see, "up there, in that bed, I'm defenseless... This is a fortress, Falcone; it seems to me that I could fight a giant from here."

While he was speaking the doctor had moved the lamp closer and handed him the letters.

To begin with, he examined the three seals attentively, as if he were hesitating to look at the handwriting of the addresses.

"See, friend!" he exclaimed. "Three opened letters! I know that; she said it herself. Well, I declare that I'd search in vain for any trace of the operation in the wax or its surroundings. It was done with incomparable delicacy! You could search all of Italy, all of Europe, all of the world, and you wouldn't find a woman like her. There's only Barbe, my dear companion...I shall miss her, I know that full well; but those who know how to play piquet sometimes discard the ace. The fool who keeps everything loses the game."

He turned the three letters over one by one. Falcone saw his hands trembling.

The lamp cast an oblique radiance inside the confessional since it had been moved closer. Falcone was able to make out a singular agitation in Johann's face. Johann perceived his surprise.

"Friend," he said, "you will only ever know what I wish you to know, be persuaded of that. You'll be my confidant, it's true, but it's something of a sinecure. Never try to surprise me, believe me—that would bring you misfortune."

"Signor," said Falcone, "one piece of advice is worth another. I shall do, meekly and zealously, all that you order me to do...but don't go to the trouble of addressing threats to me; I have an ill-made character, and that might cause us to quarrel."

"Damn!" muttered Spurzheim. "We're treating as power to power, friend Pietro-Maria Bertuzzi!"

"Does that displease you, Signor David Heimer?" pronounced the doctor firmly.

Johann shuddered slightly on hearing that name. His mouth remained open momentarily. Then he began to smile softly, and he repeated: "Damn! Damn! We're more knowledgeable than we seem. That's good, Falcone, that's very good. We'll refrain from making threats. I can see that the two of us are going to be a couple of intimate friends. Turn the armchair round slightly, I beg you, my companion—not that I desire to hide from you, but I might have other visitors than you tonight."

Falcone grasped the armchair, and the heavy machine began to rotate on its castors.

"Enough!" Spurzheim ordered.

The lamplight no longer entered into the confessional.

"Falcone," said Spurzheim. "Do you know how old the name is you've just pronounced?"

"Three years, signor," replied the physician.

"Perfect, perfect. Bring up a chair I beg you, in such a manner that the person who sits in it will be fully illuminated. That's right... Now you're going to leave me, Falcone."

"Your Lordship has no further need of me?"

"Quite the contrary. I have a commission of the utmost importance to give you. But before then, be kind enough to unhook the curtain hanging in front of that door, and put it between that chair and my armchair."

The doctor climbed on to a chair and unhooked the door-curtain, which he placed in the location indicated.

"Let's see," said Spurzheim, as if talking to himself. "Have we forgotten anything? When you've gone I'll be alone, and I'll be a prisoner in this armchair..."

"I'll stay if you wish," said the physician.

"No, I don't wish...you have work to do elsewhere."

Falcone kept silent.

"Will you please give me a blank sheet of paper and a pencil," Johann said to him.

He crossed his meager legs and started drawing rapidly. What he drew resembled a map.

"This, Pier Falcone," he said, while drawing, "is the geography of my house you'll only recognize the drawing room, the dining room, my bedroom and this study. Tonight, you need to know the rest. Now, it's an old dwelling in which one can easily go astray in the tangle of galleries and corridors, all the more so if you have no lantern.

He added a final stroke and added: "But this is the conductive thread that will guide you through the labyrinth. We're going to study this together. Come closer."

Falcone obeyed. Spurzheim showed him his drawing, in which each linear compartment was dotted and marked with a letter.

"You see, my friend, we set off from point A, which is my bedroom. I hope that you can easily find my bedroom?"

"Yes, signor, easily."

"Very good. To the right of my bed is door B, which opens to the corridor BC, at the end of which is the boudoir of the woman who was my dear companion. Poor Barbe! I shall miss her! In the boudoir, you take door D and you go up the hidden stairway that leads to the second floor. All of the part of the plan that remains is on the second floor...do you understand?"

"Perfectly, signor."

"You take corridor EF, leading to Madame Spurzheim's drawing room, which is situated directly above the room we're in at present, two floors up. In that drawing room, this is door C, which it's necessary for you to take. It's the longest route, but you won't find anyone there. Three rooms, H, I and J are empty; they're guest rooms. You'll go through them, the third on tiptoe, for you'll be very close to the door of my dear wife, who inhabits chamber L, which you'll enter by door K."

"And why will I enter Madame Spurzheim's bedroom at this hour of the night, signor?"

"At the point where there two of you are...," murmured Johann Spurzheim, sniggering. But he interrupted himself. "Let's talk seriously; I shall regret her, I'm certain of that."

He handed the doctor a key. "Door K is locked," he said. "This is to open it."

"That doesn't tell me...," Pier Falcone began

Spurzheim interrupted him. "My dear Barbe ought to be asleep at this hour. She always has on her nightstand the candy-box that contains her cough-pastilles. The commission with which I'm charging you, my good friend, consists quite simply of removing that box, which you'll replace with this one."

He handed him a sculpted gold candy-box. Falcone's first impulse was to refuse it.

"You can see," Spurzheim said, without paying any heed to that reluctance, "that my box is exactly similar to poor Barbe's."

"What's inside it?" asked the doctor, who was paler.

"Why dwell on these painful details?" pronounced Johann Spurzheim, slowly.

216

"Poison!" murmured Falcone.

Spurzheim opened the box. "Pastilles," he replied, with a frightful calmness.

"But what if your wife wakes up?" said Falcone.

There was a chill in his veins as he heard Johann's response.

"Amour will be your excuse. You've stolen the key from me. You've gone upstairs silently...in sum, everything that gallantry can inspire in such cases. And you'll switch the candy-box anyway."

Falcone took the box, Spurzheim uttered a deep sigh and repeated once again: "I know full well that I shall miss her!"

"There is a pact between us, signor," said Falcone. "Wore betide whichever of us breaks it!"

He headed for the door. From the depths of his lair, Johann followed him with his gaze. "See you soon," he said.

"Soon," relied Falcone, who disappeared without adding anything more.

Spurzheim uttered a dry and broken laugh.

"I'll bury them all!" he murmured. "All of them! I'm thin...but there's life in there!" He gazed at his arms, which, in spite of the thick padded cloth of his dressing gown, looked like two sticks.

The presence of Pier Falcone, it appears, had deterred him from opening the mysterious letters that he was holding, for he examined them carefully as soon as the door was closed. The three seals were identical and bore a prominent escutcheon, of a golden heart pierced by two swords in a saltire, on a field of gules.[40]

"How did she not see that?" he thought aloud. "There are things that women don't see. The Monteleone escutcheon!"

He touched the seal on the first letter in order to open it, but changed his mind and placed it, with the other two letters, on a shelf inside his armchair.

I need to do my work first! he said to himself.

In order to do his work, the first necessity was to stand up. A terrible task! He thought for a moment that he would not be able to do it. His hands, convulsively clenched on the arms of his chair, made a great effort, but he could not lift his upper body, which always fell back. Finally, however, having been able to seize the side walls of the confessional, he hoisted himself to his feet and stood unsteadily on his tremulous legs.

"What strength I still have!" he pronounced, aloud, as son has is exhaustion permitted him to speak.

He would have liked to mop his brow, which was streaming with sweat, but he dared not let go of his supports. His head was spinning slightly in that

---

[40] Previously, the field of the escutcheon in question was azure, but it is gules [red] from now on.

perilous position, of an upright man supported to the right and the left, with a seat behind him and a table in front of him.

Our friend Cucuzone would certainly have been more comfortable perched on ne foot at the tip of the lightning-conductor of the San Gennaro cathedral; but Johan Spurzheim was content with very little. He was satisfied.

After having recovered his breath, he took one hand off the wall of his sentry-box in order to seize the rim of the desk. That was another triumph. With the aid of that new point of support, he took a step—which is to say that his right leg dragged itself forward by two or three inches. Immediately, he cried, with heartfelt joy: "Oho! They think I'm impotent? We'll see, we'll see!"

Dragging himself thus, and hanging on to all the furniture, he succeeded, with difficulties that would take too long to describe, in reaching the door through which Pier Falcone had just gone out.

He shot the bolt, saying: "And one!"

Then he recommenced his Herculean labor. It was a matter of crossing the room and reaching the other door, from which the doctor had removed the curtain in order to lay it on the floor between Johann's sentry-box and the chair placed for the visitor expected at that late hour of the night.

Joan stopped many times en route.

It's a long way, he said to himself. *What I'm doing here is enormous...and they think I'm impotent!*

When he arrived at the second door he did the opposite of what he had done at the first. The bolt was shot; he withdrew it.

And, believe me, casting aside all human respect, the director, sure that he was unseen, returned to his sentry-box on all fours. For him, everything was a matter of crying victory. He thought: *In this fashion I could go all the way across Naples.*

And they thought him impotent, the insensates!

When he had succeeded in replacing himself in his armchair, Johann Spurzheim uttered a long sigh of relief. He even caressed his meager chest, which gave him the sensation of a brutalized wound, and he rendered himself this testimony wholeheartedly: *I'll live for a hundred years!*

The first letter was unsealed. He had accomplished his task.

The first letter, written in a cipher that bore no resemblance to the one with which we are familiar, said:

In order to render myself worthy of the confidence that Your Excellency has been kind enough to grant me. I have set to work immediately. I am on the track. I can feel the threads of this mysterious and culpable scheme around me; I am sure that I can grasp them. Tomorrow, I shall have the honor of saying more to Your Excellency, to whom I declare myself, respectfully, etc...

That letter had been dictated two days ago, in the morning. It was signed with a simple cross and a number: 133.

There's not much in that, thought Johann. *He's searching, he hopes to find-that's regulation. Not a word about the two children. Let's see the others.*

Johann unsealed the second letter. That one was a little longer. This is what it contained:

I have been working hard since yesterday. I am still a novice in the métier of spy, and very old to make an apprenticeship, but the goal that is before my eyes sustains me. It is necessary that my master's children have bread. I have learned several things I judge that they will seem important to you. I will come to tell you what they are this evening.

"This evening!" Johann interjected. "Let see the date."

The letter was dated the previous day.

"Yesterday!" he cried. "He came yesterday!" There was a sharp anxiety in his one.

I beg you urgently, the letter continued, *to have me introduced to your presence. Yesterday, I knocked in vain at your private door...*

"He also came the day before!" Johann Spurzheim interjected, again; and he made a gesture of violent chagrin.

The letter concluded: *I have an absolute need of Your Excellency, or some other member of the king's government, to whom I can make my declaration. I kiss Your Excellency's hands.* And a cross for a signature, with the number 133.

"Or some other member of the king's government!" repeated the director, in a changed voice.

His hand was trembling so much when he picked up the third letter that he had difficulty unsealing it. With an avid eye he scanned it from beginning to end. It was dated the morning of that day. It said:

I have found Your Excellency's door closed again. I shall wait until this evening before addressing myself to someone other than you. Once this evening is past I have the intention of going directly to the Minister of State or the King himself....

You could have heard distinctly Johann Spurzheim's teeth chattering in the depths of his entry-box, for he had just read the following sentence:

At ten o'clock precisely I will knock on the little door of your study...

A blasphemy was stifled in Johann's throat.

"He's come!" he groaned. "At ten o'clock! It's half past eleven! He might be with the Minister of State at this very moment...or the King." He concluded: "I'm doomed!"

First he crumpled the letter, in a veritable rage, but, soon changing his mind, he smoothed it over his knee in order to finish reading it.

I have two reasons for acting thus, his mysterious correspondent continued. *Firstly I have kept silent for too long. I can say that I know everything. In the second place, I am in need, horribly in need. My master's children are starving.* Then came a cross, as in the other two letters, and the number 133. The cross and the number were at the bottom of the page.

Johann was about to tear up the paper furiously when he perceived below the cross, at the very edge of the letter, the letters inviting him to turn over. He turned it over; a few more words were written on the other side. Johann read:

If Your Excellency cannot wait for me at ten o'clock, I will make one last attempt and come back at half past eleven, knowing that the Minister of State and the King will be spending all night at the Palazzo Doria-Doria.

Johann Spurzheim breathed deeply. He darted a rapid glance at the clock, which, at that exact moment, chimed the half hour. Simultaneously, there were three timid and discreet raps on the door whose bolt Johann had just withdrawn.

VI. Number 133

Johann's first movement was to delve hurriedly in his bosom. His hand encountered a key there, suspended from a silk ribbon. His eyes gleamed. That was doubtless all he needed, for he pronounced in an assured voice:

"Come in!"

The door opened immediately, revealing a long and obscure corridor, at the end of which a distant street-lamp was perceptible.

The person who came in looked like an old man. On looking at him closely, however, one could have divined that his stature had been curbed more by fatigue and chagrin than by age. His eyes, timid and benevolent, retained a sort of youth under the graying tufts of his eyebrows, and his almost white hair framed a forehead exempt from wrinkles.

When the man had closed the door behind him, his gaze made a tour of the study, seeking the master of the abode.

That gaze was humble and fearful. The man's garments composed the complete costume of a Sicilian peasant, which showed the signs of excessively long service. They were clean but threadbare, ready to fall into tatters. He was holding his hat in his hand in the fashion that asks for mercy.

There was no need to be a keen observer to interpret the expression of that physiognomy and to give a meaning to the ensemble of that poor attire. In that man, everything spoke of lost hopes, of deprivation and suffering.

His gaze did not encounter anything but the somber hangings of the study, which was even more austere in its furniture, if that were possible, than Johann Spurzheim's bedroom. No one could be seen in the large mute room in which the lamp only found, to reflect its light, moldings of polished ebony and the ruddy frames of two or three old paintings of the Spanish school.

The newcomer, surprised by that solitude, stopped in the middle of the room and asked: "Is Signor Johann Spurzheim not here?"

A hoarse voice replied to him: "Approach the desk."

Where did the voice come from? The newcomer sought in vain to divine that.

"Approach the desk," Johann repeated, impatiently.

And as, while speaking, he had struck the walls of his niche, the latter moved. The poor man understood that there was someone inside it. He advanced, curbed in two.

"Sit down there, under the lamp," said Johann, harshly.

"Signor...," murmured the poor man.

"Sit down!" Johann repeated, imperiously. "I like to see the faces of those I'm interrogating clearly."

The poor man was able to think that Signor Spurzheim did not like to be seen himself. His timid gaze had, in fact, turned toward the opening of the sentry-box, in the depths of which an indistinct form was agitating. He sat down and put his hat between his legs.

In all lands, misfortune has the same gestures. One might say that it tries to gather itself, in order to take up as little space as possible.

"Lift your head," Johann ordered, "and look at me."

The poor man obeyed. The lamplight fell directly on his cranium, where spare hairs were whitening. It was one of those worthy heads of old servants, which one scarcely ever sees any longer except in paintings and books. The race of good old servant is extinct. They eyes of this one depicted mild and resigned sadness. He had handsome features, but energy was lacking. It required, in order to give birth to virile will in that benevolent creature, devotion pushed to the extent of heroism.

From the depths of his sentry-box, Johann Spurzheim devoured him with his eyes. Did he know him, and did that sight reawaken some distant memory in him? He passed his hand over his pointed chin two or three times. His pale lips moved without producing any sound.

He said to himself: *It's him! It's really him! Have I aged as much as that?*

To that question, Johann Spurzheim could only reply negatively. We know that he never paid himself bad compliments.

"You're number 133?" he asked, abruptly and aloud.

"Yes, signor," he poor man replied.

"You're the one who wrote me these three letters one after another?"

"Yes, signor."

"What brought you to make your first request to enter the royal police?"

"Necessity."

"Have you followed the métier of spy elsewhere?"

The head of police agent number 133 was suddenly raised, so proudly that you would have had difficulty recognizing it. But that movement of revolted honesty only lasted for a second. The poor man's forehead inclined again over his breast, while he relied, simply and softly: "No, signor, never."

"You're very old, friend, to commence your apprenticeship," Johan muttered, in his hole

"Signor," number 133 replied, "if it had only been a matter of myself, I would have died before undertaking it...but I have two children..."

"You're misunderstanding me," the director of the royal police cut in. "What do your two children and you matter to me? I'm saying that at your age, one no longer has the flexibility, the activity..."

"Will Your Excellency be kind enough to listen to my report?" the poor man said, interrupting in his turn. "I don't claim to be very skillful...but former relations...and chance...have served me to the point that I can put the King's government on the track of a whole army of malefactors..."

"At least you don't lack a good opinion of yourself, my friend," Johann sniggered. "Let's have your information."

Number 133 took an old worn portfolio out of his pocket, and opened it.

Before commencing," said Spurzheim, as if an idea had just occurred to him. "Did you find, buy or steal the seal that you use to close your letters?"

"My poor seal! By selling that, I could have had bread for the children...but that's all I have." His moist eyes were no longer able to read the writing traced in his notepad.

"Signor," he said, "I have a great deal to tell you, and I hope that you will treat an unfortunate favorably. I won't bargain; I'll tell you everything at a stroke, certain that a worthy magistrate like you won't abuse my good faith. Remember that I have a heavy responsibility..."

Johann stamped his foot. Number 133 immediately interrupted himself and began.

"At the moment when I'm speaking, signor, and if you hurry, perhaps there's still time to bring to order a bold young man who once roamed Sicily and Calabria under the name of the Chevalier d'Athol, and who is presently, serving or commanding the Companions of the Silence, prowling around the Castello-Vecchio in order to liberate the prisoner who is to be executed tomorrow. He is followed by a woman who is wearing the costume of an orange-seller, and thousands of mysterious soldiers are only waiting for a sign from his hand..."

"Pass on," said Johann, disdainfully. "The least of my agents knows where to find Beldemonio and his mistress, Fiamma."

"Why don't you take them, then?" asked the agent, naively

"You're not a good hunter, friend, if you can't distinguish the decoy duck from the wild duck."

"What!" cried number 133. "Beldemonio is with you!"

Joann burst out laughing. "Do you think we were waiting for you to have a police?" he said. "Your information isn't worth a Tournois denier. Pass on."

"I beg you to excuse me, ignore; the experience will come..."

"When the experience has come, friend 133," Johann replied, "you'll know that it isn't wise to threaten a man like me. In your letters, whose style would scarcely be pardonable for a child, you talk about the Minister of State and the King. All those who have tried to go to either one directly have ended badly, I warn you."

"Is it permitted for me to ask why, signor?"

"Because I don't like it," retorted Johan, dryly.

"That's sufficient, signor...I didn't know..."

"Get on with it, and hurry."

In a slightly tremulous voice, number 133 resumed: "When I dared to write to you the first time, signor, I had a plan. I knew that His Majesty King Ferdinand, Prince Francis and, in consequence, you were very preoccupied with that tenebrous and powerful association..."

"No big words, friend…facts!"

"In good Italian, signor," the agent retorted, jibbing under those harsh words, "I knew that the story of Mario Monteleone would surface again in the court."

"And you know about that affair?"

"A little, signor."

"That's not enough."

"Let me speak, I beg you. The King isn't unaware that the origin of the brotherhood of the Silence is in that. The King knows what brigandage is hidden under the mask of vengeance. The King is seeking the Companions of the Silence to punish them, but he's seeking the widow and the children of Mario Monteleone in order to render them their titles and their property."

"And do you expect to earn money spying on the King, friend?"

"Let me speak, signor," repeated number 133 in a tone that as submissive, but firm. "I expect to earn my money by serving the King in his desires and his wishes. You don't frighten me, because I know that your rudeness hides a noble equity as well as a profound devotion to our princes. Would you like me to talk to you about the widow and the children of Mario, Comte de Monteleone?"

Johann did not reply immediately, because he sensed that his emotion would trouble his voice. It was in such moments that the sentry-box rendered precious services. Without the entry-box, number 133 would have see his thin face quiver and a gleam light up in his eyes.

"Speak," said Spurzheim, finally, affecting indifference.

"The two children of Mario Monteleone had never received the slightest mark of interest from their father's pretended avengers, the Companions of the Silence…"

"How long ago did they leave Sicily?"

"Oh!" said the agent, nonplussed. "Your Excellency knows that they were living in Sicily?"

"My Excellency knows more than you about many things, friend, and you appear to me to be destined to see that it isn't easy to deceive My Excellency. I know that at one time, there was a boy and a girl in Sicily, who were being raised by a man by the name of Manuele Giudicelli. That worth fellow once took steps with regard to the court, but in order to claim a heritage it's necessary to have documents. This Manuele Giudicelli couldn't furnish any."

As he said that, Johann darted his keen gaze at number 133. I don't know what idea crossed the mind of the latter at that moment, but he would have given a substantial measure of his blood to be able to distinguish the face of the director of the royal police. A vain desire! From the two sides of the entry-box Johann had pulled the green silk curtains that supposedly protected his weak sight against the excessive brightness of the lamp. He was literally invisible.

"What one can't do one day, one can do another," murmured 133.

Which motivated Johann to ask a question: "Have you some acquaintance with this Manuele Giudicelli, then?"

"No," replied the agent, without hesitation.

And there was a silence.

"Is that all you have to tell me?"

"God forbid, signor!" cried number 133. "For I fear that, until now, I haven't earned my salary, and I need my salary…I need it at any price!"

"I'm listening…but tell me first whether the two young people about which we were speaking just now are presently in Naples?"

"Signor," replied number 133, "my two children and I, or, rather, the two children of my former master, were brought up near Catania in the same village as them. That's how I knew those young people, who were said to be Monteleone's heirs. I am only interested in them because of the amity that used to exist between them and my children. The last time I saw them was in the second ulterior Calabria, in the hamlet of Monteleone."

"What we you doing there?"

"It's on the road to Sicily. I was bringing my children from Catania to Naples."

"Your children are here, then?"

"Yes, signor."

"Pass on…and let's not waste our time."

Number 133 collected himself momentarily.

"If the king's government can deny the identity of the son and daughter of Mario Monteleone because they don't have their birth certificates," he continued., "I suppose it isn't the same for the noble Comte's widow."

"You know where she is!" exclaimed Johann, with a vivacity that he regretted immediately, for he hastened to add: "But twenty times over, impostors have spoken to us about her."

"I'm not an impostor," said 133, simply.

"And what do you want to tell me about Monteleone's widow?"

"I want to tell you that she's in Naples."

"Are you sure of that?"

"I'm perfectly sure of it."

"How do you know?"

"I've seen her."

"When did you see her?"

"This morning."

"In the vicinity of the Ministry of State?"

"In the port itself."

Johann put his finger on his forehead between his eyes, and fell into a profound reverie.

Poor Barbe! He thought. *It's not my fault…at the present moment my box of pastilles must be on her night-table.*

As if hazard wanted to reply to the doubt that was passing through his reverie, someone knocked lightly on the interior door of the study: the one though which Pier Falcone had gone out, and which Johann had bolted. He had no doubt that it was Pier Falcone returning.

"What's new, friend?" Johan shouted, from his place. And he added, as a precaution: "I'm not alone."

"Your commission has been carried out, signor," replied Falcone.

"That's good…that's very good, friend. Go and wait for me in my bedroom; I'll join you."

The doctor could be heard going up the stairs.

"What you're telling me must be true, comrade," said Spurzheim, addressing the agent, "but you're out of luck…someone else told me before you."

"Did that other also tell you where the Comtesse de Monteleone was coming from, signor?"

"No!" exclaimed Spurzheim, sharply. "I confess that that is new."

"I hope to tell Your Excellency even more important things," retorted number 133. "Maria des Amalfi was coming from France."

"Has she been there for a long time?"

"Since the day of November last when the anniversary of Monteleone was celebrated in the basilica of the Corpo-Santo."

"She was abducted that same night?"

"She was embarked the following day."

"And the voyage to France had an objective?"

"An important objective. There is in Marseille a celebrated practitioner, Doctor Daniel Bach, a pupil and compatriot of that immense genius Samuel Hahnemann, who has just created a new science.[41] Like his master, Daniel Bach has unknown weapons for combating the scourges of humankind: malady, madness, death…"

"Halt!" ordered Johann. He agitated in his entry-box. "Take a pen and paper from my desk," he added. "This physician has achieved good cures?"

"He has cured the Comtesse de Monteleone of her madness," the agent replied.

Jonathan allowed an exclamation of surprise to escape. If number 133 had been able to see him at that moment, he would surely have had difficulty in defining the expression of his physiognomy. There was both pleasure and embarrassment in it.

"This will be more difficult" he murmured, between his teeth. "I'll regret poor Barbe!"

"I have the pen and paper, signor," said the agent.

---

[41] Féval was a great admirer of the founder of homeopathy, Samuel Hahnemann, for the reason noted in the introduction.

"Write me legibly, and above all exactly, the name and address of this physician of Marseille. I know someone who is very ill...although he isn't threatened by death..."

The agent wrote: *Doctor Daniel Bach, 4 Rue de Chartres.*

Johann did not ask him how he knew that address. He said to him: "Friend, for this information alone I am your debtor; you will be recompensed. Continue."

"I've said all I know in that regard, signor."

"What!" Johan protested. "You don't know the name of the man who embarked Comtesse Maria for France?"

"I don't know it."

"And who brought her back?"

"The captain of the *Pauselippe*."

"On whose behalf?"

"I asked him, signor, but he refused to say."

"I'll interrogate him tomorrow."

"He's departed this evening."

"Was Maria des Amalfi aboard alone?"

"Alone with a chambermaid...or, rather, a demoiselle of the Company."

"Did you see her too?"

"Yes, signor."

"Her description?"

"Young, alert, lively, cheerful, brunette, very pretty."

"No distinguishing mark?"

"The underside of her eyelids marked like the daughters of the zingari race. Prominent eyebrows… stray hair above the lips."

Johann reflected. "You make good descriptions, comrade," he said. "And did anyone come to meet them on the mole?"

"Yes, signor."

"A man?"

"A young man."

"Do you know him?"

"No, signor, and I made vain efforts to recognize him."

"Have you been in Naples long?"

"A week."

"Then it's astonishing that you don't yet know the man about whom you're talking."

"You know him, then signor?" asked the agent, whose eyes expressed the keenest curiosity.

"Perhaps, comrade. What did he look like your young man?"

"Tall, elegant, proud, with a beauty I haven't seen before in anyone."

"Did the common people who were there share your ignorance?"

"On the contrary, signor. They knew him so well that everyone laughed when I asked his name."

"And how did they designate him among themselves?"

"They called him the Prince."

Johann smiled within the shelter of his sentry-box.

"Friend," he said, "I believe I know our man. But I engage you to beware. You're hiding something from me."

"You're mistaken, signor."

"Given the interest that you have on the Comtesse de Monteleone, an interest that you've let me see, it's impossible—impossible, you hear—that you didn't make an effort to follow our mysterious chevalier."

For a few minutes, the voice of the director of police had become increasingly veiled. In his obscure retreat there were little dry coughs. For an hour, that man, whom one would not have thought capable of reciting an *Ave* all the way thought, had been acting and talking without respite. In spite of the extraordinary valor of his mental nature, his weakness was getting the better of him.

"Signor," replied the agent, however, "you've divined correctly. I did try to follow the man they called the prince, and, in spite of the rapidity of his magnificent horses, I succeeded in not losing sight of it…but something happened to me on the way, and I was naturally about to recount that incident to Your Excellency. I have an old friend who is employed at the Ministry of State. At the Ministry of State, people are occupied with a very important affair."

"What affair, comrade?" asked Johann, negligently.

"They are occupied, signor, in assembling the evidence for a trial that is going to be held of a very powerful man who fulfills very high functions, and who is suspected of betraying the confidence of the government and the King."

The walls of the confessional shook, so violently had Johann shuddered.

VII. The End of the Interrogation

It appeared that Johann Spurzheim was interested in that highly-placed dignitary who was suspected of having betrayed the confidence of the government and the King, for he said:

"Tell me that in detail, comrade. Old employees are talkative. Your friend at the Ministry of State must have had a lot to say about this big affair..."

In spite of the shelter that hid him, and in spite of the tone of indifference there was in his voice, Johann would not have succeed in dissimulating his emotion if he had been facing an observer, but number 133 was not a very subtle observer. He was, in addition, in great haste to finish, for his presence was necessary elsewhere. Thirdly, it is certain that the alteration in Johan Spurzheim's voice has taken place gradually. Number 133 had perceived it some time before, and was able to confuse the increasing fatigue of the director of the royal police with his sudden disturbance.

"It's just that," the embarrassed agent murmured, "it was confided to me under secrecy, Excellency.

"It's very serious, then?" said the director.

"It appears to me to be extremely grave."

"Was the name of his functionary pronounced?"

"No, signor."

"Was his responsibility indicated to you?"

"In no fashion."

Johann respired in his retreat.

"Friend," he said, without having any need to play a part this time, "I'm harassed by fatigue. Our conversation has lasted too long. I don't want an agent like you, whose words have to be extracted from his body. You're refusing to answer my questions; in consequence, you don't merit any salary. Go away, and my God protect you."

Poor 133 was utterly devastated. Hs eyelids fluttered, burned as they were by tears.

"Signor, signor," he cried, "have pity on me! It's true that I'm not an ordinary spy...I'm selling my conscience at this moment, which I'll regret as long as I live, because I can't sell what remains of my blood. I tried to be a soldier, signor, but they looked at my bald head and laughed at me. I tried to be a laborer; they looked at my thin arms and my trembling hands and they laughed at me again. I tried to beg for alms, but I'm a poor beggar, no one gave me an obol. Lord, I'll tell you all I know; in the name of the God of mercy, don't send me away empty-handed!"

We may doubt whether Johann Spurzheim cared very much about the God of mercy.

"Speak, then, comrade," he replied, however, "and don't force me to interrogate you incessantly. I've told you: if I'm content with you, you'll be paid generously."

"Signor," number 133 continued, after collecting himself momentarily. "I'll tell you everything that happened between me and my old friend. I was following the carriage in question as best I could when, at the end of the Via Toledo, I heard someone call my name. You won't demand, I think, that I tell you that of the poor employee?"

"No, a thousand times, no. Cut it short!"

"'You're Calabrian,' he said to me. 'Would you recognize Battista Giubbetti, the former coachman of Monteleone?'

"I replied: 'I knew him at one time.'

"'Do you know where he lives?'

"'It's months since I've seen him. I didn't know that he was in Naples.'

"'The poor devil left the country after losing his wife, the lovely Giannina,' my former comrade said, 'who was abducted by one of those sinister rogues, the *cavalieri ferrai*.'

"'Which one?' I asked, for I knew the rogues of whom he was speaking.

"'The Captain, Luca Tristany.'

"'And why are you looking for Battista Giubbetti?'

"'Because he was a Companion of the Silence and he's sworn a vendetta against his former masters. I don't know him, but he might be able to translate a cipher for us by which we're gravely embarrassed.'"

"Write down that name Battista Giubbetti for me," Johann ordered, "under the name of the Marseillais physician. I must have encountered him during my travels through southern Italy. He was a cheerful fellow, wasn't he?"

"A handsome young man, signor, joyful indeed, like all those who have a clear conscience, before his happiness was killed."

"Write. I count on doing something for that poor Battista. And?"

"Your Excellency had a good heart," murmured the agent, moved. Then he continued: "I didn't know Giubbetti's address, but an idea occurred to me. In a very distant epoch, when the Companions of the Silence called themselves the brothers of charcoal and iron, I'd been initiated into their mysteries..."

"Aha!" said Johann, involuntarily.

"Yes, signor but it was then an association of Christians governed by a just man. There are still people in Calabria who remember that. The saint, Mario Monteleone, had only one enemy: poverty, the daughter of idleness and vice..."

"Pass on! Pass on!" said Johann.

"As I had only one thought," the agent continued, "to earn money by whatever means I could, I said to my man: 'If you like, I'll try to translate your cipher.'

"'You could do that!' he cried.

"'If it's the old cipher of the *cavalieri ferrai*,' I replied, 'yes, I could.'

"'And you'll give us the key to it?'

"I hesitated momentarily, signor, but as, in the final analysis, the people who are now making use of that cipher are odious bandits, I thought that I could do it in all conscience."

"Friend," said Johann, unctuously, "you're an honest man, and I approve of your conduct unreservedly."

"I'm very glad about that, signor, and the approval of a man like you goes straight to the depths of my soul. My old comrade had the pieces of paper on him, in case he succeeded in finding Battista Giubbetti. We went into the Corona di Ferro, which we were going past, and he showed them to me. It was definitely the cipher of the *cavalieri ferrai....*"

"And the documents?"

"The pieces of paper were four notes, two from London, one from Paris and one from Marseilles..."

"Addressed to whom?"

"To the high dignitary in question."

"Then you know his name?"

"Each of the pieces of paper, signor, must have been sent under seal, and I haven't seen the envelopes.

"A clever move, friend," said Johann, "if it isn't the truth."

"It's the exact truth, signor," replied number 133.

"How had these papers, about which we'll talk again shortly, come into the hands of our former comrade?"

"It's quite simple, signor. The high dignitary is absent from the Ministry of State, where he has his service. Some journey or other...I don't know. The pieces were addressed to the minister, and he first was opened in error..."

"The others by design?"

"Of course, like all those that will come henceforth.

"Perfect! Let's get back to the papers. You translated them there and then?"

"No, signor. It had been a long time, you see, since all those things had escaped my memory. I begged my friend to entrust the papers to me, as that I could draw up the key when my head was rested and make the translation."

"How much time did you request for that?"

"A day."

"You have to return them tomorrow morning?"

"Precisely, signor."

"Then," Johann exclaimed, with a singular accent of triumph, "you have them on you. Give them to me."

Number 133, caught in the trap of his own words, did not obey, however.

"Signor," he replied, "that's impossible for me. The métier I'm following at the moment can't be that of a man of honor, but I have honor. The papers don't belong to me. If someone tried to take them by force, I'd defend them to the death."

Johann's dry and hoarse laughter sounded in his sentry-box.

"Half spy," he muttered "half knight errant! You're a funny fellow, friend, and you amuse me. No one will take your papers by force, don't worry. But you're going to tell me what they contain."

"Signor..."

"Oh, no protests this time," pronounced the director of the royal police, harshly. As the poor devil hesitated, however, he added: "Fool that you are, do you think I don't know all these things better than you do? The employee who gave you those papers is old Benedetto Guerra. He's just left here, and it was because of his presence here that I let you knock in vain a while ago."

The agent had no way of knowing that the director was telling a brazen lie. It was indeed old Benedetto Guerra who had asked him for the favor. In that, Johann had guessed correctly.

"If that's the case," said the agent, with a residue of reluctance, "I no longer have anything to hide from you. There's no need to tell you the story, since you know it."

"The papers," sad Johann. "Show me the papers, or read them to me, as you choose."

Number 133 opened a section of his portfolio and took out five pieces of paper, the first of which he unfolded.

"This is the key," he said.

"Let's see the key," sad Johann, stifling a yawn.

What he said there was to support his role.

"The key is formed," said the agent, of the letters composing the first verse of Fioravanti's song, which also serves as the rallying call and the password of the Companions of the Silence: *Amici, alliegre, andiamo alla pena.* If your Excellency wants the alphabet, here it is."

Joann extended his arm from the sentry-box. At the sight of that gray, wrinkled, shriveled, horribly fleshless hand, which truly seemed to be emerging from the tomb, the agent dropped the piece of paper and uttered a cry of astonishment.

"Pick it up," said Johann, with his strident laugh. "I don't have plump fingers, it's true...but I'm all sinew, comrade, and I hope you live to be as old as me!"

Number 133 picked up the piece of paper and handed it to him. The sheet only contained the alphabet of the Silence, organized with the letters of the alphabet juxtaposed with the cabalistic letters, all of which were in capitals:

A = A, b = M, c = I, d = C, e = I^2, f = A^2, g = L, h = L^2, i = I^3, j = E, k = C, l = R, m = E^2, n = A^3, o = N, p = D, q = P, r = A^4, s = M^2, t = O, u = A^5, v = L^3, x = L^4, y = A^5, z = P

"Curious!" said Johann, after having darted a glance at it. "Very curious. It seems to me that I have several pieces of paper on me written in that fashion. It was Sanskrit to me. You're a very precious man, comrade. Henceforth, the king's government will easily be able to discover all the secrets of those wretches."

"One hopes so," replied the agent, who saw himself growing.

The cadaverous hand emerged from the shadow a second time. It held a piece of paper other than the one given to it by number 133.

"It's the same cipher!" exclaimed the latter, as soon as he had looked at it.

"They're brought to me from time to time," said Jonathan, in a forced manner. "Would you care to decipher that one for me; it was intercepted in the post a little while ago."

Number 133 spelled out the first words, and went pale.

"Well?" said the director of the royal police. "Read it aloud. I want to know."

His eyes, half-closed, studied the poor agent, who was trembling. Even so, he read it: "David Heimer is warned that Manuele Giudicelli is in Naples, with the two children from Catano."

"David Heimer!" exclaimed Johann, feigning surprise. "That's one of the blacksmith knights!"

"We'll find him, signor!" exclaimed the agent, for his part, with a singular passion. "By God, if he's in Naples, he won't escape us!"

"Do you know him?" asked Johann.

"Do I know him? Yes, I know David Heimer!"

"You have some personal animosity against him?"

Blood had risen to the agent's cheeks; he was making visible efforts to remain calm.

"My God pardon me," he murmured. "I can't lie: I hate him mortally."

Johann twiddled his thumbs gently in his confessional, and smiled. It was the smile of a tiger-cat.

"This is the first document, signor," the agent went on. "It's dated from London, It announces to its unknown correspondent, the important dignitary, that a diamond of inestimable value, the Punjab, extracted by a miner from the Mogul's quarries, has been offered to the King of England by the council of the East India Company, and that the diamond is being cut by a celebrated lapidary in Paris. It asks whether His Majesty King Ferdinand of Naples will buy the diamond, if it can be successfully deflected. The first letter is signed Brown. It must have required a response."

"I have a copy of the response," said Johann. He added, almost immediately: "Those poor fellows at the Ministry of State think they've made a fine discovery."

"I make the observation to you, signor," the agent replied, "that Their Lordships don't even know what it's about. I'm the one who has to take them the key to the enigma tomorrow. Their suspicions only bear on the important functionary."

Johann's laughter was heard.

"You're sure, then, that they don't have the slightest knowledge of the affair?"

"Not the slightest."

Johann took from his bosom the little key that was hanging around his neck on a silk ribbon. He approached it to a lock placed within the reach of his hand in the wall of the confessional, but he did not introduce it yet, and changed his mind.

"Let's see the other papers," he said.

"The second, replied the agent, "is from Paris and signed with the same name, Brown. It says, in substance, that it has cost fifteen hundred louis to have a fake diamond fabricated exactly similar to the Punjab, that the fake diamond has been substituted for the real diamond in the laboratory of the lapidary, and that they're waiting or the money to send it to Naples."

"Isn't there a small cross in red ink on the original?" asked Johann.

"It has passed before His Excellency's eyes!" exclaimed the agent, amazed.

"Oh, the King is well served by the clever men of the Ministry of State!" murmured Spurzheim, with a supreme disdain. "The third?"

"Dated from Marseille, signor and signed Brown. The fake diamond has left for London, the true one is on the way to Naples. It will be ceded to His Majesty in return for a sum of fifteen hundred thousand ducats, at an exchange rate of four francs twenty-five centimes per ducat in French money."

"Which gives six million three hundred and sixty-five thousand francs," said Johann. "That's not dear for a diamond of a hundred and sixty-six carats. Now let's see the fourth piece."

"It carries a note," said the agent. "*Must not be communicated to anyone, even the masters of the Silence.*"

Johann stirred in his armchair, and let slip the words: "I don't know it myself, that fourth piece!"

"The fourth piece," said number 133, "has neither a signature nor a subscription. It wasn't seized with the others. It was found in the lodgings of a mariner of the port, who couldn't be arrested, and whose name is Sansovina."

"And what does it say?" asked Spurzheim, impatiently.

"Something very strange, signor. It says that this Brown, already departed from Marseille and en route for Naples, sincerely believes that he is carrying the Punjab."

"And he's mistaken?"

"And he's mistaken. The true Punjab has been sold to the Emperor of Russia for the sum of four million rubles."

"Good!" exclaimed Johan. "We know enough, comrade. Put your papers in your pocket. I know what to do now. It's my turn now to tell you something. But before then, I want to pay you, for you've shown yourself to be an intelligent and submissive servant. Do you insist on hiding your name from me?"

"I insist absolutely on that, signor."

Johann's key grated in the lock.

"As you please, as you please," he said. "It's necessary, though, that I know where to address my messages to you, in case I have need of you."

"I have no lodgings, signor," replied the agent.

"You sleep under the stars?"

"Every night, at the sotto-portico San Antonio."

"A fine country, that of Naples," said Johann, turning the key in the lock, "which permits such habits. And if one wrote to your children?"

"That would reach me, signor."

"They don't sleep under the stars?"

"Oh, signor!" said the poor man, in a wounded tone.

"Where are they lodging?"

"In the Folquieri house, in the Strada di Mantua."

"Write that down for me, comrade, underneath the name of that Battista Giubbetti. I have no memory."

While the agent was writing, he heard the clink of gold coins.

And, his heart content, he thought: *Tomorrow the children will have bread.*

In his sentry-box, Johann Spurzheim had opened the interior cupboard or container that we have already mentioned. Instead of taking gold out of it, however, Johann had removed an object of rather considerable volume and of singular form. It was a kind of box terminated by a rod two feet long. Johann began maneuvering a screw set in the middle of the box. He had to return to it several times, because fatigue was overwhelming him. While working he talked.

"Those good people at the Ministry of State will be very surprised tomorrow when you tell them the contents of those pieces of paper."

"His Excellency had something to say to me," the agent interjected, having stood up after writing down the address of his children.

"That's right. You can take advantage of it if you wish. It was to me, comrade, to the director of the royal police, that the pieces of paper were addressed."

"To you, signor!" cried number 133. "But then...?"

"But then, my poor fellow, those incompetents at the Ministry of State will be humiliated. I already have this Brown and his fake diamond in my power."

He had supported the box against his shoulder, and was pointing the rod at the agent's breast. One might have thought, in fact, that the director of the royal police as taking aim at the poor man with that bizarre apparatus.

"That's not all," he went on. "In addition to the money that I've just counted out for you, and which you have earned so well, comrade, I can give you some good news."

With his left hand he stirred the gold in the bottom of the container.

The agent drew nearer, involuntarily, at that sound. He was very emotional, the poor fellow. A single idea filled his heart: his children. That shining gold was for his children! For his children, who were dying in desolate poverty.

"This David Heimer whom you hate and for whom you're searching," Johann went on. "He's ill, he no longer has anything but his breath. A gesture would suffice to crush him."

"You know where he is, signor?"

"He's here, comrade, two paces away from you. He's me."

The agent made a movement as if to launch himself forward. Johann pressed a protrusion, without ceasing to take aim with his strange machine. The agent fell, putting his hands to his breast and uttering a feeble cry—only one. The mechanism had produced a slight hiss, similar to the thrust of a piston in a pneumatic machine.

Silence—a deathly silence, one might say—reigned in the study of the director of the royal police for a few moments; then he was heard to sigh, and then to cackle again.

"I'm stronger than them," he murmured. "I'll bury them all!"

VIII. Johan Spurzheim's Crutch

Police agent number 133 had fallen exactly where he was when the mysterious thunderbolt had struck him—which is to say, between Johann Spurzheim's work table and the monumental armchair serving simultaneously as a fortress against draughts and indiscreet giving. After a few seconds, the dissected head of the director of police could have been seen to emerge gradually from the shadow, less than two feet above the ground. He was dragging himself on his hands and knees. Fatigue caused him to gasp. The lamplight, which now fell from above on his bald head, put livid parchment hues thereon, marbled with mat streaks the color of ash. It was horrible to see. He stopped frequently in order to respire, and his breath whined in his throat.

In passing, he put his hand on the agent's heart. "It's warm," he said, "but it's no longer beating."

The agent was lying on his side. His head was tipped back amid the masses of his gray hair. His eyes were wide open and staring. Johann looked at him very closely.

"Yes, yes," he muttered. "That man was well-conserved. He would only have had to lift a finger to knock me down. I'm dying, that's obvious…that's obvious."

And he laughed more loudly.

"So long as my dying lasts, here I am!" he went on. "And look at so many robust men that I've felled along my path! I'd rather have my malady than their health. I'd rather have my death than their life. I'll be like this for a hundred years!"

He rummaged in the agent's pocket and brought out the portfolio, which he opened. He took a few papers from the portfolio, which he scanned rapidly.

We'll look at all this with a rested head, he thought. *Today, we don't have time. Good! Here's the message seized in Sansovina's home. I take my property where I find it. And where's his agent's card?*

He opened the various compartments of the portfolio. The agent's card was in the last. It did not bear any name, but merely the number 133 with the police stamp.

Johann raised himself up on his knees, took the pen, in which the ink had not yet dried, and inscribed a name above the number. Then he put the card back into the portfolio, with the alphabet of the Silence and the translation of the letters signed Brown. The portfolio returned to the pocket of the agent's poor overcoat.

Still kneeling, Johann pushed his feet under the table, with great difficulty. He was obliged to make four of five attempts to lift up the curtain detached by Pier Falcone and cover the cadaver with it.

237

Perhaps the reader had thought that Johann Spurzheim had had the curtain taken down purely on a whim. We can affirm that the director of the royal police did nothing by chance.

When the body of agent number 133 had disappeared under the curtain, Johann got his breath back. But a glance darted at the clock doubtless reminded him that he did not have time to rest, for he resumed crawling toward his sentry-box with a new courage. He was an indefatigable specter.

He succeeded in replacing himself in his armchair, and immediately took possession of the bizarre machine, the mute lightning, with which he had felled a man so briskly. As he put it on his knees again, his gesture was almost a caress.

"One pays dear for rare and curious objects," he murmured, moving a little lever on the posterior part of the machine. "This one doesn't shine, but what utility!"

The machine creaked under the pressure of the lever, rather like a coffee-grinder at the first turn of the wheel.

"It's hard," Johann said then, "but I still have sinews!"

He took from his container a lead bullet of ordinary caliber, and introduced it into the long and narrow appendage that we compared to a rod. The bullet slid into it. The rod was the barrel of a rifle.

It remained to turn the central screw, but Johann Spurzheim's strength really was exhausted. He tried. His hand lost its grip, while his throat rendered a hoarse groan.

At that moment, numerous hasty footfalls became audible in the corridor by means of which agent 133 had introduced himself into the study.

Johann seized the screw again and turned it. His hand let go again.

"I can't do any more!" he murmured. "It's the work of a giant that I've accomplished this evening. I can't do any more; I need an hour of repose."

He heard someone stop in the corridor on the other side of the door. Then a voice asked: "To whom are you taking me?"

"It's him," said Joann, making a supreme effort. The screw could not move a single notch.

It's necessary, however, that I'm alone with him, Johann thought.

Someone knocked at the door it had to be the butt of a rifle that was ringing against the wood. Before replying, Johann had a consoling idea: *This one isn't free like the other. This one is in handcuffs. He can't revolt.*

"Come in," he pronounced, aloud.

The door opened at the moment when the clock marked eleven forty-five.

There were several men, among whom were four soldiers and a officer. They were conducting an unfortunate who had strong manacles on his hands and an iron ring on the right foot.

"This isn't the Ministry of State!" pronounced the prisoner, in a lamentable voice. "I only want to speak to the Minister of State or the King."

One would think that he scents me, dear Felice Tavola, Johann said to himself, recovering his grimace. *In any case, the lieutenant is ambitious; he'll remember my instructions.*

"The Minister of State changed location a long time ago," said the lieutenant, mockingly. "Come on, Monsieur le Baron, I humbly beg Your Excellency to take the trouble to enter." So saying he shoved him over the threshold, brutally and forcefully.

The prisoner did his best to resist.

"I protest!" he cried. "Before anyone but he Minister of State, I shall keep silent, even if I'm put to the torture."

"He scents me! He scents me!" muttered Johann, very softly. "That's sympathy!"

"His Lordship is there?" asked the officer, at that moment.

"Yes," Johann relied, disguising his voice.

"In the name of God, tell me where I am!" cried Felice Tavola, whom the soldiers pushed toward the table.

As soon as he was far enough into the room for Johann to be able to perceive him while remaining protected himself by the wall of his sentry-box, an expression of quietude spread over his features.

Even if he had been as strong as ten Hercules, Baron Altamonte would not have been able to rid himself of the enormous steel manacles that secured his wrists. Merely for the choice of handcuffs the intelligent lieutenant merited being promoted to captain. Altamonte, for his part, darted a sharp glance into the shadow of the confessional, but his eyes, dazzled by the glare of the lamp, could only see blackness within it.

"Does Monsignor want us to stay with him," said the lieutenant, "Or mount guard outside?"

"Outside," Johann replied.

At that word, Baron d'Altamonte lowered his head and no longer took the trouble to protest.

He's recognized my voice, Johan thought. *He's making his act of contrition, poor friend!*

The lieutenant was truly made to be a captain. After having pushed his prisoner as far as the heavy and massive table that served Joann as a desk, he passed a strong cord through the iron ring riveted around the Baron's leg and tied him tightly to the leg of the table.

"Monsignor," he said, as he stood up. "Remember that we're close by, behind the door, in the corridor. At the slightest sign, you'll see us arrive." Putting his hand on the prisoner's shoulder, he went on: "This man is Il Porporato. As his companions didn't come to liberate him, he asked to make revelations in order to save his life. May God protect Your Excellency."

He went out with the servants of the prison and the soldiers who had brought Baron d'Altamonte.

The latter was a rather handsome bandit of thirty-five or forty. One could easily have taken him for a gentleman of the court of Naples. Among the *cavalieri ferrai*, before the arrival of the Chevalier d'Athol, who had made himself their sovereign mater, Felice Tavola had possessed an influence equal to that of David Heimer himself. They were enemies.

When the door had closed on the lieutenant and his soldiers, Felice Tavola said, without raising his head: "I know you're there, David. You've made me fall into the trap; kill me without making me languish, that's all I ask."

Johan laughed dryly and replied, with a snigger: "Don't you have important revelations to make to me, my poor Felice Tavola? Don't you want, illustrious Baron d'Altamonte, to tell the Minister of State, my superior, or the King, my respected master, via my unworthy channel, that a rogue has usurped their confidence, and that the Neapolitan police are in the hands of a bandit?"

"Kill me," said the blacksmith knight.

"And how would I do that, my friend Baron?" replied Johann. "I have neither arms nor legs myself, you know that. How many times have you laughed after drinking, while calling me the cadaver? Alas, Tavola, my poor companion, it's the executioner who is going to lose his head—you, full of strength and life!—while I, the moribund, the cadaver, will remain in this vale of tears, where I promise to pray for you very devotedly."

"Kill me," pronounced the prisoner, for the third time.

"As we are," said the director of the royal police, unctuously, "it's as well that your hands are tied; if you could only take one step, you could crush me with your own weight. I'm defenseless, as you know, like an invalid in his bed, like an infant in his crib. I wouldn't even have time to cry for help, for you have all your strength, Felice. I've never see you more handsome than today!"

"You're not a man, David," grated the prisoner, between his teeth, "You're a tiger."

"That's what we are, Felice, my dear brother. If you'd stayed in your cell for five more minutes you'd be free. Beldemonio, that madman who has wings when he wants, scaled the walls of the Castello-Vecchio!"

"Can it be!" exclaimed Tavola. "Me, who accused him."

"I can give you the joy, my dear brother, of rendering justice to him before dying. He did what he could; the sentinel of the platform was gained; that young hero Beldemonio got all the way to the window of your cell, through dangers that would be very gripping in a book. He sawed through the bars and got into your prison."

Felice uttered a gasp of anger, but—how can I put this?—that that gasp was a trifle forced. One might have thought it the dramatic gasp that actors find in the depths of their chest in the fifth act of a drama, the traditional gasp that makes the audience shudder.

Johann ought to have paid attention to that gasp. Shakespeare said: Well roared, lion!" He would have been able to say: "Well gasped!" But Johann was triumphant, and nothing is as dangerous as triumph.

"He found nothing in your prison, Baron d'Altamonte," he went on. "A quarter of an hour earlier, you had received my letter, which promised to save your life."

"It was you who wrote that to me then, David Heimer?"

"Who but me could have touched the chink in our armor, Baron?"

Felice Tavola's hands clenched. This time it was because Johann laughed.

"But that's another matter!" he continued. "I don't only need your death, my dear brother, I need to doom that young hero Beldemonio. Now, it's known that I'm envious and malevolent, which aren't petty sins in this world of imperfection and misery. It's known that Beldemonio does more than hinder me, that he oppresses me. Any anonymous denunciation would be attributed to me, that's evident. I've therefore arranged, my dear brother, for the denunciation to have a signature, and that it should be yours."

"You've counterfeited my signature?"

"Of course not! Forgeries are always discovered. I count on living to be old, my brother, and I want tranquility in my old age. No, no, no forgery, at least as you understand it. Read this, I beg you."

He put out his hand and thus placed in the lamplight a sheet of paper bearing these signs:

$$NA^2 E^2A \ NA^5M \ RI^3I^2 \ EI^2 \ L^3I^2A^3LI^2$$

Felice Tavola read fluently, accustomed as he was to the characters: "I've been forgotten, I shall avenge myself." Then he added: "What does that mean?"

"Think about it, my brother. Prisoners all show the same weaknesses. As they have no one to talk to, they chatter on the walls of their prison. It soothes them.

"I didn't write anything on the wall of my prison," said Felice Tavola.

"And yet, our Beldemonio found something there.

Felice Tavola went pale, and this time, it was genuine fury.

"Oh, you'd like to have your hands free, my dear brother," said Johann.

"Wretch! Infamous scoundrel!"

"Our Beldemonio fond that inscription there," Johan continued, cheerfully, "with the consequence that, when you're dead and his little secrets are known, the most handsome of the Greeks will say: 'It's that wretch Tavola who has betrayed me!' What do you think of that naïve plan, my dear brother?"

Johann had just finished that question, in a mild and sly tone, when he experienced the greatest astonishment that had ever struck him in his life. It was unbelievable.

The face of the prisoner, possessed by impotent rage a moment ago, gradually relaxed. It appeared that irresistible laugher was about to take hold of him.

Madness sometimes arrives like that. Johann wondered whether his "dear brother" was going mad. He was not afraid, however. If he had only remembered the gasp that had not rung true a little while before, he would have been afraid.

Felix Tavola stared at him intently. In spite of the certainty that Johann had regarding the impossibility if the prisoner, placed in the light, being able to see into the depths of his shadow, that gaze irritated and embarrassed him. Instinctively, he took in hand the machine that had hissed at the moment when police agent number 133 had fallen dead. Felice Tavola was still staring at him, and mute laughter was around his lips.

"David Heimer," he said, finally, without moving from the spot but suddenly drawing himself up to is full height, "you're a curious rogue. In truth, I don't hold it against you, any more than I hold it against a viper that its bite kills, because God had put venom in its gums. But article 7 of the rule says that any blacksmith knight who discovers treason must kill the traitor. You have committed treason, and I shall kill you."

That had the appearance of an extravagant boast. The corridor was full of guards and the prisoner, retained by the leg, had both hands shackled; but there was such an expression of security on his face that Johann gathered his breath in order to shout for help.

"Don't shout!" said Felice Tavola, who divined that. "You said just now that if my hands were free, or if I could only free my keg, no one would have time to come to your aid. You're as defenseless as an invalid in his bed, as an infant in his crib—those were your own words. I could crush you with my weight alone."

Tavola made an abrupt movement. The two steel handcuffs around his wrists fell away at the same time. They had been sawn through in advance. Johan gripped his heart, which was failing. He did not cry out. Tavola picked up a rich dagger, which was on the table to serve as a paperweight, and cut the cord securing his leg.

One might have thought that Johann was dead in his sentry-box. His breath was no longer audible, and he was not making any movement. The prisoner took a step toward him.

Then a lamentable voice emerged from the shadow. "Have pity on me Felice, my good brother," begged the director of the royal police. "I was wrong to toy with the anxiety of a friend. But you weren't duped by my foolish pleasantries? You know full well that in setting foot in here, you were saved!"

"Shut up!" Tavola ordered. "You make me ashamed and disgusted."

"Oh, but my beloved bother," cried Johann, "I can't leave you in this fatal error."

"Shut up! You have only one means of not making instantly the flea-jump that separates you from Hell, where a place is reserved for you, and that's to conduct me through your house to the door of your garden that opens into the Vicoletto Ognisanti. Get up and walk!"

Joann uttered a groan. It resembled the cry that escapes weakness in a supreme effort.

"I can neither get up nor walk," he replied, in a muffled voice, but a little less altered by fear. "You know that full well—no one is unaware of my wretched condition. But by the holy name of God who judges us, it isn't to refuse you, Felice, my old companion. Approach, take me in your arms; you can walk for me, and I'll guide you."

"Did you call, Signor Director?" said the voice of the lieutenant who had just become a captain, from behind the door.

"Answer!" ordered Tavola.

"No, my lad no," Johann Spurzheim replied, in fact. "Stand easy."

The prisoner was now in front of the entry-box.

"What's that?" he demanded, discovering the object that Johann was holding in his hand.

"Are you afraid of the impotent?" said Johann, laughing. "Don't worry, Felice, my friend; it's my crutch. Look, one puts it under the arm, like this, as if one were shouldering a rifle, for it's to help the most wretched creature there is in the world to crawl around inside his apartment. You see, the end that is close you your breast touches the floor. I had it made in metal so that it would bite and not slide."

"Hurry up!" Tavola interrupted, opening his arms to seize him, as had been agreed.

And for a second time the dull and brief hiss as heard. The unfortunate prisoner tottered, put his hands to his heart and fell, his head upon the cadaver of the agent.

"What's the matter, Felice, my friend?" said Johann, fearing that he might not be dead. He slid toward him. And when the prisoner's brief convulsions had ceased he said: "Yes, yes, I had it made in metal so that it would bite."

IX. The Dark Alley

Johann had undertaken a great task: to lift up Baron d'Altamonte's head in order to lift up the curtain that was underneath it, with which to cover it. He had grasped the abundant hair of the dead man and hauled it aloft, as mariners say, with all his strength. Sweat was running down his face, but he was joyful.

"It's true," murmured, "that I'm not very robust. But what use was their vigor to them? I reckoned with both of them, one after another. They fell in a row, like dominoes. I've beaten that one in a duel, one might say, and what a shot! The bullet must have gone straight through the middle of the heart!"

The curtain was finally freed. He put Felice Tavola, his dear brother, under the same cover as the poor devil stamped with the number 133, and raised himself up again, adding: "I nearly wasn't able to turn that bitch of a screw. I must put some oil on it!"

"No one can pass," pronounced the voice of the soldier who was doubtless standing sentinel at the entrance to the street.

Johann pricked up his ears sharply, in order to seize the response. There was no response.

"The other one, now!" he said, dragging himself toward his sentry-box. "Let no one say that I'm a man of leisure! Oh, poor Barbe understood me. It saddens me to think that I won't be able to tell her everything I've done tonight. I'll miss her!" He interrupted himself, and added, incapable as he was of not mocking his victims: "But how is it that my poor Barbe, who was a fay, didn't foresee what would happen to her tonight?"

He caressed his chin, smiling in spite of his melancholy.

We are obliged to leave for a moment the study in which Johann Spurzheim had employed his time so actively in order to go and see what was happening in the street between the sentinel and the newcomer whose presence still seemed to be awaited by the terrible director of the royal police.

Perhaps the crutch was going to hiss and strike for a third time. It was a curiosity, that crutch. Similar ones had been fabricated in Rome in the time of Cosme Libranius, who sent the first air rifle to the Prince de Condé under Henri IV. Air rifles, of Roman origin, are loaded with compressed air by the combined effect of a wheel and a pressure-screw producing the effect of a pump.[42]

The man to whom the soldier had just said: "No one passes!" had descended from an elegant and rich carriage harnessed to two fine French horses. The

---

[42] It is not known who invented the first air rifle or when, but the oldest known specimen does date from 1580 or thereabouts, shortly before the reign of Henri IV of France, so Féval was perfectly free to invent a fictitious supplier in that era.

carriage had arrived some fifty paces away, in front of the main door of the director's residence.

The narrow and long alley, into which we have darted a glance, and at the end of which a distant street lamp was shining, was not, of course, that main entrance. It was not even the normal entrance to the offices and outbuildings. The former owners of the house had had it pierced through the billings overlooking the square for the service of a private bathroom, which Johann Spurzheim had made into his study. Several doors communicating with the offices opened on to that avenue, however.

The rumor ran around Naples that many great lords went into that dark alley after nightfall and went to talk to Signor Johann in private. There was mention of healthy and solid beatings administered with canes to a few impertinent individuals who had slipped into it simply out of curiosity, to see what was there.

A password or a number was required.

The Neapolitan imagination, which is never at a loss when it is a matter of inventing bizarre details, had paved that passage with traps and obstacles of all sorts. As it was almost as dark in broad daylight as it was at midnight, and never—absolutely never—had any light been seen to shine within it, the boldest idler would not have braved the hazards of such an excursion. People looked into it as they passed by, but saw absolutely nothing—because of which, a multitude of things was divined.

The carriage had remained in the guard of a valet in front of the main entrance. The master had headed with a long stride toward the dark alley. The coachman and the footman, a big fellow dressed in a miscellaneous fashion, had gone into the offices arm in arm.

The master wore, moreover, a uniform that one is not accustomed to finding in such sumptuous carriages. He had the tight red calzone if the port fishermen, a belt and a shirt, and that was all. No headwear covered his beautiful tawny blond hair, which he seemed to have wanted to stick modestly along his temples.

Such was, if we have retained the memory correctly, the costume that Beldemonio had been wearing underneath the soutanelle that he had borrowed in the mansard of the two children whose death he had prevented: the soutanelle of the young saint, the good little abbé who had the custom of going to visit the sick at night at the paupers' hospital. In order to discover the deceit the worthy Swiss lieutenant would only have had to part the flaps of the soutanelle, but he had not bothered to do that.

The master of the rich carriage introduced himself into the alley, dark and strewn with ambushes, that led to Signor Johann Spurzheim's study.

His present costume scarcely lent him the appearance of a great lord, and yet he had a noble bearing, in spite of his shirtsleeves and his fisherman's calzoni. Either because he was unaware of the supposed perils of the dark alley or because he was scornful of them, you would have seen him go into it without hesitation at a rapid pace. He did not go far. A musket placed sideways blocked his progress almost immediately.

"Who goes there?" he asked.

The man holding the rifle began to laugh. "I'm the one who's supposed to ask you that question, friend," he replied.

"I'm expected by the director of the royal police."

"That's possible, but we have our orders."

Beldemonio seized the rifle and tried to move it out of the way. At the sound of the struggle, four or five rifle-butts immediately rang on the paving stones of the alley, and it was then that the lieutenant called out: "No one passes!"

Beldemonio let go of the rifle that he was already holding in both hands and said: "Who's in command here?"

All the men stationed in the alley for half an hour had eyes adapted to the obscurity. They were able to make out the newcomer's costumes and took him for a man of the people who had entered in error, or, at the most, for a low grade agent.

"What!" said the lieutenant, insolently. "This clown isn't permitting himself to ask us questions?"

By contrast, Beldemonio could see nothing around him but darkness. "You're the leader," he went on, in a tone that scarcely went with his costume. "I need to talk to you."

"Do you know who I am?" replied the lieutenant, angrily.

"I believe I recognize the voice of Lieutenant Spinosa," said Beldemonio. "I have to talk to him about things that happened last night between the Teatro San Fernando and the Porta Capuana. If Lieutenant Spinosa desires, I can say those things out loud."

Not only did Lieutenant Spinosa want to be a captain, but it also appeared to be in is interest not to have the things that had happened the night before between the Porta Capuana and the Teatro San Fernando discussed too loudly. He shoved the soldiers aside in order to get closer to the newcomer. The soldiers and the prison staff murmured to one another in low voices: "What's happened last night?"

"And why is the lieutenant making a mystery of it?"

In the meantime, the lieutenant had joined the newcomer. He grabbed his arm and gripped it forcefully. "Whoever you are…," he commenced

The arm slid from his fingers. A hand weighted upon his shoulder and an arrogant voice pronounced in the shadows: "I engage you not to lose respect."

Everyone heard that. All ears opened avidly. Unless it was an extravagance of a drunken man, what could those strange words signify? A man who resembled a port fisherman or a port rogue, engaging Spinosa, a lieutenant in the royal guard, not to lose respect! And doing that with a calm so full of authority that the lieutenant, a young parade soldier of proverbial impertinence, remained mute and silent henceforth before him.

There was a silence. The newcomer leaned toward Spinosa's ear and pronounced a word: a single word, according to all appearance. Spinosa was seen to straighten up immediately and put his hand to his helmet.

"Highness…," he murmured.

"Silence!" Beldemonio cut in.

But the effect had been produced the men from the prison and the soldiers had heard him called Highness. They all leaned forward and made vain efforts to see his face.

Who was the Highness who was coming to lose himself at midnight in the menacing corridor heading to Johan Spurzheim's private study?

"Make way," ordered the lieutenant.

They obeyed, and maintained silence. Beldemonio passed through two motionless hedges, which he could only divine by the sound of contained respirations. When he was on the threshold of the study he turned round and said: "That's all right, Lieutenant Spinosa. You've heard mention of me. You can withdraw."

"Signor," replied the officer, embarrassed. "My orders forbid it."

Beldemonio opened the door abruptly. "Johann Spurzheim," he pronounced, in a loud voice. "Will you please command these men to withdraw."

The soft and broken voice of the director of police immediately rose up. "Withdraw, my friends," it said. "We have no further need of you."

"But the prisoner…," said Spinosa.

"The prisoner is in a safe place, and remember, Lieutenant, that I only have to account for my actions to the King."

Spinosa had advanced as far as the door and had darted a rapid glance inside the study. He had seen that the prisoner was no longer there.

"Forward march!" he commanded.

The soldiers went along the corridor in silence. They were not yet at the end when the lieutenant, incapable of containing himself, muttered between his teeth: "Il Porporato must be far away if he's still running."

"What!" cried voices from all sides. "You think…?"

"My lads," said the lieutenant, "I have no desire to end my days in an Austrian prison. Let's not get mixed up in these things!"

They fell silent. But the lieutenant muttered, from time to time: "If the King knew! If the King knew…!"

Beldemonio had gone in. He closed the door behind him and shot the bolt. He crossed the room at a rapid pace.

Ordinarily, as we have repeated several times, those who conversed with Johann Spurzheim did not see him. Whether it was day or night, it was the same.

By night the lamp was placed in such a fashion as not to shine into the sentry-box, while the light fell directly on the face of the person who was conversing with the director. By day, the same result was obtained by the fashion in which confessional was placed relative to the windows, which never let much light pass.

It appeared that Beldemonio did not want that. As he arrived at the table he picked up the lamp and placed it directly opposite the opening of the sentry-box. The light fell directly on Spurzheim's face; he blinked painfully, like an owl surprised in its hole in the wall by a ray of sunlight. Beldemonio sat down opposite him, with his back to the light.

The roles had changed, as well as the stage setting. This time, it was not the director of police who was interrogating.

"Why are you not in bed, David Heimer?" Beldemonio demanded.

"Master," Johann replied, respectfully but calmly, "I knew that you would come."

"How did you know that I would come."

"Calculation isn't forbidden to members of the association, I suppose, Master. I'm very ill, but I have my head."

"Are you really very ill, David Heimer?" pronounced Beldemonio, in the tone one adopts in order to address questions to oneself in solitude.

"In the days when you called yourself the Chevalier d'Athol, signor," Johann retorted, "we met twice. Would you have given me the three or four months that I have lived since then?"

"That's true," said Beldemonio.

Johann Spurzheim smiled sadly "Those who wish me dead," he murmured, "will not have time to lose patience..." He interrupted himself and changed his tone. "But I can't believe that you wish me dead, signor, who know my devotion and fidelity so well." He had a slight coughing fit.

Beldemonio looked him in the face.

One could only experience pity for that wretched and debilitated creature, whose lips always seemed ready to let the last breath pass. It was, I tell you, a painful contrast to see that cadaver, animated by a residue of vegetation, facing that noble and brilliant type-specimen of Italian beauty, the Chevalier d'Athol, or Beldemonio, whatever you want to call him—or Il Porporato, since he also had that redoubtable name.

Thus, clad only in a short damp with his sweat, a pair of tight trousers and a woolen belt, Beldemonio had nothing to envy in the most opulent costumes. His forms appeared in all their virile perfection, and also the bold and supple graces of his youth. Illuminated from behind, his fine stature gave him the appearance of being scarcely twenty years old. It was necessary, in order to bring back the idea of the fully-made man, to measure with the eye the development of the temples, to admire the virile squareness of his shoulders, and, above all, to hear the masculine and sonorous timbre of his voice.

"If I wanted you dead, David Heimer....," he commenced. He did not finish.

"You'd accomplish your wish very easily, wouldn't you, Master?" said Johann, quietly.

Beldemonio turned his eyes way with a sort of disgust. That was a mistake, for at that moment, Johann darted at him the glance of a serpent.

"Master," the latter continued, "I would like to tell you this, which is the pure and simple truth. I had calculated that the association would have need of me tonight."

"You believed, then, that my enterprise would not succeed?"

"Your enterprise, Master, could not succeed. Events have proved that."

"And do you attribute that failure to hazard, Johann Spurzheim?"

"Only hazard, Master, could be stronger than Il Porporato." Involuntarily, there was a hint of sarcasm in his tone. Beldemonio looked at him again.

"Did you know that Felice's cell had been changed?" he asked.

"Yes, signor."

"Is it you who informed me of it?"

"You know full well that it was me, Master."

"Did you know that someone had propositions of mercy sent to him in his prison?"

"Word of honor," cried, Johann, "I did not know that."

"Word of honor," repeated Beldemonio, bitterly. "But I want to believe you, David Heimer. Only reflect on one thing: if you can be ignorant of such events, it's dangerous for the association to rely on you."

"You're severe, Master."

"I'm just."

"The state of malady in which I am…"

"It's not an invalid that we need in the position you occupy."

Johann's livid cheeks were animated imperceptibly. His eyes closed momentarily and his lips quivered. However, the replied calmly: "I do my best, Master. If you know of anyone more skillful and more active than me, I'm ready to cede my place to them."

"We'll see about that, David," said Beldemonio, coldly. "There's no peril for the time being, and I don't believe you're made enough to fight against me. To each day it's work; let's talk about today's. Is it via your garden door that you allowed Felice Tavola to escape?"

"No, signor," Johan replied, his voice lowering involuntarily.

"You told him," interrogated the new Athol, "that Sansovina's boat had to change location, and that it's now stationed outside the city, in Chiaia, opposite Virgil's tomb?"

"No, signor, "Johann relied for the second time. "I had no need to tell him that."

"He knew it?"

"I don't know."

"What does that mean?" cried Beldemonio, already fixing his suspicious and anxious gaze on him. "Has some misfortune happened to Felice Tavola?"

"Master," pronounced Johann Spurzheim, slowly, with his head held high. "Felice Tavola is dead."

X. The Two Cadavers

Beldemonio had not expected that. The announcement of that death struck him violently. He paled at first, and then the veins in his forehead swelled.

"You had him murdered?" he pronounced, so quietly that Johann could scarcely hear him.

The anger of that man was terrible, but Johann, that frail creature whom death already held by the throat, was able to deploy at times the composure of heroes and a prodigious courage.

"You're mistaken, Master," he said, tranquilly.

"You knew that I loved him, that he was my right arm and my best confidant."

"Yes, Master, I knew that. We all knew that."

"You're going to tell me, I divine, David Heimer, that the soldiers of the guard only brought a cadaver here."

Johann smiled disdainfully. "You divine poorly, Master," he said, folding his arms over is meager chest. "Felice Tavola arrived in this room alive, and as I have only done my duty, I do not need to search for a subterfuge. Felice Tavola died on the very spot where you are."

Beldemonio could not repress a slight shudder.

"Killed by whom?"

"By me."

That was something so improbable that Athol was momentarily incredulous. Tavola, a young, vigorous, agile, valiant man, put to death by that dying old man!

Athol considered the skeletal arms, and that poor hollow chest, which wheezed at the slightest effort. But an idea occurred to him, and he changed his mind.

"He was in chains," he said.

"Another error, Master," retorted Johann Spurzheim. "The English files you sent has sawn through his handcuffs; his hands were free." His finger pointed at the table. Athol could in fact, see the prisoner's cut irons.

While he maintained silence, Johann went on: "Article Seven of the rules orders every knight to administer justice himself in the case of treason."

Beldemonio's eyes were lowered; he seemed to be plunged in thought.

"I only struck him," added Johann, "at the moment when Felice Tavola, traitor to his brothers, proved to me that he also intended to unveil the Master's secrets."

"And what proof do you have of that treason?" asked Beldemonio.

"The Master's conscience will be my witness."

"Explain yourself."

"The Master has seen the threat. I have seen the execution of the threat. Who would dare to doubt the combined word of Il Porporato and David Heimer?"

Athol had no reply to make, having once accepted the mores and customs of the association of which he was the chief. He had a voice within him that was saying: "There is treason, but Felice Tavola was not the traitor." But nothing supported that belief.

Johann had acted within the rigorous measure of his right. More than that; Johann had done his duty.

That threat, so perfectly appropriate to a prisoner abandoned by his accomplices—a prisoner who, from the depths of his cell, could hear the blows of the mallet beating the planks of the scaffold, that threat written in the alphabet of the Silence, it was Athol himself who had read it on the wall of Tavola's prison: *I have been forgotten; I will avenge myself.*

But how could Johann Spurzheim know that that threat existed, and that Beldemonio had read it? That idea crossed Athol's mind in a flash.

"That's good, David," he said. "Our rule condemned the unfortunate Felice Tavola to death; you became his executioner, doubtless reluctantly."

"Yes, Master, reluctantly."

"It was your duty; the council will judge you. I've wasted my time; I'll try to make better use of the rest of the night."

He stood up, affecting a tranquil countenance.

"Master," said Johann, "We haven't finished."

"What do you want of me?"

"Article nine of the rule attributes to the blacksmith knight who has punished a traitor the right to choose and present to the council the man who will wear the iron ring in his place. I claim that right."

"It belongs to you," replied Athol, who made a movement to leave.

"Does Your Lordship not want to know the name of the companion I have chosen?"

Athol turned round and replied: "If he is my friend, what does it matter? If he is my enemy, woe betide him. Adieu, David Heimer. I repeat in leaving what I said to you just now: I do not believe that you are foolish enough to dare to fight me."

He was heading for the door when Johann Spurzheim repeated for the second time; "Master, we haven't finished."

Athol stopped, and darted a glance at him so piercing, that Johann felt a chill in his heart.

That one is stronger than me, he thought, at the first moment, *it's him who will kill me!* But the mental strength of the man seemed to be in inverse proportion to his astonishing physical infirmity.

He went on, in an assured tone: "We haven't finished, because we haven't yet talked about you."

"About me?" Athol repeated.

"Master," said Johann, "you charged me with various missions. I have acquitted them."

"People are waiting for me," Athol murmured, his gaze slipping toward the clock. It was past midnight.

"They have been waiting for you for such a long time, signor," replied Spurzheim, with a sort of bonhomie, "that a quarter of an hour more or less will make no difference henceforth to the affair."

"Has someone come here?" Athol asked.

"Several times, and I ought to tell you that strange rumors are running round on your account at the Palazzo Doria. As it's impossible for you to admit the task in which you have employed your night..."

"Perhaps I've accomplished more than one task, signor David," Athol put in, with a proud smile.

Johann inclined his head, silently, after which he went on: "I know that Your Lordship rarely has need of aid. That is not the subject about which I want to talk to Your Lordship. I want to say three things. The first regards the two children of Catania."

Athol immediately drew nearer.

"They're in Naples," Johann went on. "Before tomorrow is finished, I'll have them put in your hands."

"If you do that, David," cried Athol, ardently, "many sins will be forgiven you."

"I didn't know, Master," retorted the other, coldly, "that I was in need of your noble clemency."

"I have the certainty of being understood when I speak," said Athol, dryly. "And?"

"The second communication I want to make to you, signor," the director of the royal police went on, "regards the widow of my former and beloved master Mario, Comte de Monteleone."

"Ah!" said Athol, who could not help smiling. "And what can you tell me regarding the widow of Mario Monteleone?"

"The same thing as regards the two children from Catania. She is in Naples."

"Are you quite sure of that?" Athol turned his head away as he asked that question.

Johann Spurzheim replied with great seriousness. "I'm sure of it signor. As I am that one of the chevaliers of the Silence went to receive her this morning aboard the *Pausilippe*, that the chevalier in question has not made any report to the council and is thus in the circumstance foreseen by article three of the rule."

"Pass on," said Athol. "The chevalier of the Silence to whom you are making allusion is above the rule."

"The rule is above all," pronounced Johann, gravely.

"I said pass on," said Athol, stamping his foot impatiently.

"I am obedient to you, Master," murmured Johann, lowering his eyes. He went on immediately: "The third communication relates to a man for whom you have often ordered me to search. I have no need to remind Your Lordship of the indefatigable zeal that I have always put into executing his commands."

"What man are you talking about?" said Athol.

"I'm talking about the Calabrian Manuele Giudicelli."

"With a bound, Athol was beside him.

"You've found him?"

"Signor," replied Spurzheim. "I understand now the interest you had in taking possession of this Manuele. I cannot claim the merit of having discovered him; it was pure chance that threw him into my hands."

"I hope you haven't let him escape."

"I refrained from doing so, signor."

"He's in your house?"

"He's here in this room."

Athol's gaze made an involuntary tour of the room.

"Lift that curtain, signor," said Johann, showing him the drapery extended in front of the table.

Athol obeyed, and took several steps backwards on seeing the two cadavers. That of poor agent 133 was lying in the shadow of the table. Only his pale face could be seen, framed by long gray hair. The head of Felice Tavola, placed further forward, was resting on the agent's hip, as if on a pillow."

"Manuele! Manuele!" cried the Chevalier d'Athol, with a profound emotion. "Yes, that must be him! That's exactly how I imagined the last servant of Mario Monteleone!"

"Master," Johann Spurzheim interjected, feigning misunderstanding, "have no fear. I know Manuele Giudicelli in the Martorello. It's him, I can affirm it."

Athol turned toward him. His gaze was fiery. "David Heimer," he said, pale with the effort he was making to contain his anger, "you will answer to me for this murder."

Johann remained immobile and made no reply. After a long silence, however, and while the kneeling Athol was feeling the breast of the unfortunate Manuele, he went on: "You described that man to me, signor, but you did not tell me your secrets. I should have been able to see from the outset that this man was your enemy, and, in consequence, the enemy of our association."

"You murdered him for my benefit, did you, David?" said Athol, bitterly.

"I killed him," replied Johann, "because my anticipations were far surpassed. Not only was that man your enemy and ours, but I can say that we had no enemy in Naples more dangerous than him."

"But how did you kill him?" cried Beldemonio, standing up abruptly. "How did you kill them? Tavola, young, vigorous, terrible in a fight, Manuele weaker and already diminished by age, but who could have knocking you down simply by blowing on you?"

"When it's a matter of our interests, Master, and that of my brothers," Johann replied, "I am strong."

And as Athol gazed at him in the fashion that one looks at reptiles that are both despicable and terrible, he continued, smiling: "There is a man stronger than Tavola, stronger than Tavola and Manuele combined, stronger than ten men, than a hundred men. That one has not yet found his equal, the bravest know him and fear him, the most boastful have pallor in their cheeks and a chill in their veins when his name is pronounced: the name of Il Porporato, Master, the name that is our honor and our flag. Well, that man, that giant, threatened me just now, me, a poor earthworm. Is it not as if I were crushed in advance? I have, therefore, since he threatened me, and his strength almost equals my weakness, the right to defend myself. Signor, I tell you this: it would have been as easy for me to take the life of a giant as it would be for the giant, at the moment, to use our own expression, to knock me down simply by blowing on me. You have belonged to me in the same fashion as Manuele, in the same fashion as Felice Tavola. You owe me your life."

So saying, he stood up on his tremulous limbs and extended toward Beldemonio the crutch whose virtue he had so rudely proven that night.

"This is lightning," he added. "Silent lightning, which strikes without advertising the blow. You turned your back to me for more than a minute, and it only takes a second to aim. I repeat to you, Master, that you have belonged to me, and if there are not three cadavers there instead of two, it is because it pleased me to spare your brilliant youth, even at the risk of the few unfortunate and tottering days that I still have to pass upon the earth."

Athol took the crutch and examined it.

"Master," Johann Spurzheim went on, taking advantage of the moment to plead his cause, "one judges a man by his actions, doubtless, but also and above all by the motive that was able to determine those actions. I am delivering to you but my actions and the motive that was able to determine them. May it please God that I am as irreproachable and pure in the eyes of God, who will soon summon me to his tribunal, as I am before you and my brothers. I have killed, I whom am about to die—do you think that my heart did not quiver? I have killed a man who was my companion, I have killed a poor old man who never did me any harm? Why? For myself? What would be the point, alas? What are things of this earth to me, henceforth?

"I have killed in spite of myself; I have killed for you. I have killed because the treason of the first and the revelations of the second were about to deal you an equally deadly blow. Felice Tavola, for vengeance, Manuele, for a little gold, had sworn the doom of the association. Tavola did not know to whom he was talking when he came in here; your name was the first to emerge from his lips, and it is as a delator that I punished him. Manuele was a police spy. Search him and you will find his card, his number, and the secrets he had already discovered. Article eight of the rule condemns a spy, no matter who he is. It was not reproaches and threats that I expected from you, Master; I have the right to praises!"

While he was speaking thus, Beldemonio had opened Manuel's poor jacket and rummaged in his pocket. He drew out the papers through which Johann had riffled before him.

Johann was defending himself. The care of his speech for the defense had taken away a little of his habitual vigilance. Otherwise, he would have seen that Athol, in taking the agent's papers, had suddenly shuddered—very slightly, since it had escaped Johann, but, in sum, he had shuddered And the back of his hand had remained applied to Manuele's breast for an instant more than was strictly necessary to take possession of his portfolio.

Johann could not see Athol's face. The latter's features had been subjected to a sudden and remarkable change. The emotion that they marked now was new, and of an entirely different species. There was an unexpected hope in his eyes. His heart was beating faster, He had sensed a movement under Manuele's damp shirt. Felice Tavola, struck first, already had the rigor of death. Manuele was still warm. There was only one cadaver there.

Athol turned round, holding the portfolio in his hand

"Read," said Johann, "and judge whether it was possible for me to allow the man to live who brought to the director of police, for a first reward, the alphabet of the Silence."

Beldemonio opened the portfolio and read a few pieces of paper at random. His thoughts were elsewhere now.

Among the pieces of paper that Johann had not had time to examine there was one whose mere sight caused Athol's heart to leap in his breast. He had recognized it at a glance. It was a letter of which the paper, softened and worn, spoke of a long time elapsed. It was the letter that Athol had forwarded himself to the address of the good Manuele at a hotel in Salerno, executing very belatedly the mission with which he had been charged in the Castello di Pizzo. It was the letter written by Mario Monteleone in his cell during the solitary and sad hours of his last night.

"David Heimer," said Athol, "you have acted in accordance with duty, I recognize that. What you have done disrupts my plans, but you did not know my plans. I said one day—do you remember?—'I want no more blood.' I add today: 'The association has no need of blood.' Your conduct will be submitted to the council."

"I have my conscience, Master," replied Johann, brazenly. "But don't go, I beg you," he said, interrupting himself, seeing that Athol was putting Manuele's papers away and preparing to leave, For the third time, I tell you, we haven't finished."

"What more is there?"

"Your Lordship, in the circumstances we're in, owes me aid and protection. I'm too weak to make hose two dead bodies disappear."

Perhaps he was expecting a refusal. The readiness with which acceded to his proposition troubled him. Athol, in fact, seized Manuele's body and loaded it on to his shoulders. Before that, he had taken Felice Tavola's iron ring from his finger.

"This is what you have earned, David," he said, handing it to him.

He headed for the door, carrying his burden. Manuele's blood was trickling over his shirt.

"For the other," he said, as he passed the threshold, "I'll send you Cucuzone."

Johann did not reply. He was watching Manuele's blood trickling. His hands clutched his breast, and he murmured, letting himself fall, exhausted, into the depths of his sentry-box.

"I've done nothing. That man isn't dead!"

XI. The Legend of San Gennaro

Peter-Paulus wanted to consult his watch when he woke up on his bench in the police station, but the girella had refrained from leaving it to him. He looked at the clock in the waiting room. It was after midnight. It was the hour when, every day for twelve years, he had emerged from the Cotton and International Club in order to return to the bosom of Marjoram, Watergruel and Company. A clause in his contract specified that he must never return at an undue hour.

But how easy the return was on emerging from the Cotton and International Club! Here, on the contrary was the solitude of darkness and the unknown.

What route should he take to get back to the Great Britain Hotel? What perils might the obscurity hide, in this accursed city, where Peter-Paulus had already had so many misadventures.

Certainly, there was a means of not braving the perils of nocturnal Naples, and that was to sleep in the police station. Peter-Paulus preferred the street.

"Am I a prisoner here?" he said, in a low voice, to Privato, the sole companion he had in the office.

Privato shrugged his shoulders and continued writing. Peter-Paulus refrained from repeating his question. He slid toward the door.

There was no longer a single street-lamp illuminated on the Piazza del Mercato, which was as black as an oven. No light was shining behind the windows. However, Peter-Paulus could see distinctly what was happening a few paces away from him because of the lanterns of a carriage stationed outside Johann Spurzheim's house.

Next to the door, the bizarre individual who was searing a whimsical costume, the clown of the Fountain of the Three Virgins, was helping another individual to load a heavy object of considerable volume into the carriage, of which Peter-Paulus struggled in vain at first to recognize the nature.

Cucuzone's companion was in short sleeves and was standing in the shadow. Peter-Paulus heard him say: "Be careful, you'll bump his head on the wheel."

"Since he's dead...," Cucuzone replied.

That word sufficed to remove the scales from the Englishman's eyes. The confused mass took on a form for him: it was the body of a man. And such things were happening outside the very door of the director of police! Peter-Paulus still wanted to doubt, so impossible did the thing seem, but doubt was no longer possible.

"How he's bleeding," said Cucuzone. "The cushions of the vehicle will be stained."

"Push," ordered the other person. "Come on, firmly, we're there!"

At that effort, the garment of the poor deceased gave way in Cucuzone's hand. His companion let a cry of terror escape. The head of the cadaver suddenly hung down, only sustained a few inches from the ground.

"Damn!" murmured the acrobat. "Don't worry—the poor devil won't die twice."

In that new position, the light of one of the lanterns struck the head of the dead man obliquely. Peter-Paulus distinguished with horror the features of an old man, whose long gray hair swept the pavement for a moment. He would have liked to flee, but it was as if his unsteady legs were paralyzed.

Finally, the body went into the carriage.

The man in shirt-sleeves went to talk to the coachman in a low voice, and his face was illuminated brightly in its turn, placed close to the lantern as he was. Peter-Paulus shivered with astonishment amid his terrors. He recognized the man, and it was like a sudden flash of light in his memory. The entire group of the Fountain of the Three Virgins, at the entrance to the Strada di Porto, was there.

The man in shirt-sleeves was the handsome fisherman who had been leaning against the wall beneath the Madonna, and, in consequence, the gracious, elegant, brilliant dandy who had come aboard the *Pausilippe* in the morning: the man they had called "the prince."

The coachman was none other than the mariner with the meerschaum pipe sitting on the rim of the fountain. The man in the fantastic costume was, as we have said, the clown rolled up like a caterpillar at the feet of the other two. In truth, all that was lacking was the orange-seller.

Peter-Paulus did not even try to attribute a meaning to that bizarre reunion. He gave up, as children playing charades say. Everything that had happened to him hat night surpassed the limits of the possible to such an extent, in his view, that he let himself go, like a spectator relaxing into the changes of scene in a phantasmagoria. And if he had wanted to search, he would not have had time.

The handsome fisherman of the Fountain of the Three Virgins only said a few words to the coachman, in fact. Immediately afterwards, he climbed into the carriage where the dead man was. The acrobat went to the door, and the handsome fisherman said to him: "Now go and fetch the other."

The other what?

The carriage pulled away and departed at a gallop.

Cucuzone had no suspicion of the presence of the Englishman. The carriage, carrying its lanterns, left the square in complete darkness. Peter-Paulus heard the clown grumble: "That scoundrel Privato has closed the shop!"

That was true. During the brief scene that we have just reported, Privato had quietly closed the shutters of the police station. Everything in the vicinity was as black as ink.

Perhaps Cucuzone was brave, but there are various genres of bravery. The commission that he had been given was evidently not to his liking. Peter-Paulus heard him sigh as if the thermometer were six degrees below zero.

Fear, as everyone knows, is contagious. Our Englishman, also very brave, had a commencement of colic.

Cucuzone wanted to sing in order to give himself courage, but his hoarse and tremulous voice put a chill in Peter-Paulus' veins.

Having not found relief in music, Cucuzone made his decision and headed, with an evident reluctance, toward the narrow dark alley that led directly to Johann Spurzheim's private study. It was there, in fact, that it was necessary to go in order to pick up "the other." He muttered as he walked, saying: "Damnable work! Some luck! It had to happen on a bitch of a night when there's no moon!"

He passed within a few feet of Peter-Paulus without seeing him. God knows, he was no long thinking about Peter-Paulus! On the threshold of the alley he hesitated momentarily, but he finally went in it, after having made a large sign of the cross.

The alley was long. Cucuzone's teeth chattered more than once on the way, and the noise added to his fear; he thought he could hear the rattle of dry bones in that lugubrious sound. The night filled with phantoms or him. God, the Virgin and San Gennaro, whom he evoked fervently, did not seem to be listening to his prayer.

At that moment, he heard the distant footsteps of Peter-Paulus, who was going past the opening of the alley. A cold sweat pierced his skin.

An instant before, he had been wishing passionately to hear a human sound, Now, the sound that he heard frightened him. He had asked all the saints in paradise for a glimmer of light in order to rejoice his eyes, drowned by the darkness. When he perceived the light that was filtering under Johann's door, he nearly fell over backwards. He arrived, however, more dead than alive, and knocked very gently.

"Come in!" said Spurzheim's broken voice.

Cucuzone turned round, thinking that someone had spoken behind him.

All the specters that populate the darkness of large subterranean spaces, abandoned cloisters, old churches and cemeteries—all of them—were there, arranged in an interminable line along the corridor. Cucuzone saw them, thin and white, hiding their death's-heads under profound hoods. They were motionless; but when Cucuzone moved, he saw them oscillate slowly and all together, like ripe ears of wheat swayed by the wind. They were here! They were there!

"Lord Jesus! Virgin Mother! San Gennaro! San Gennaro!"

All those veiled white heads inclined. The wind that blew through the phantoms was moist and icy.

"Come in!" repeated the cracked voice, impatiently.

Cucuzone would not have turned round for all the gold in the world. He backed up to the door and sought the handle by groping behind him.

Do you know what the specters did? They laughed in the depths of their hoods, showing, from one end of the alley to the other, those great shiny teeth no longer covered by gums. Oh, the laughter of the dead!

The door opened. A great sigh of relief escaped Cucuzone's breast.

The broken voice said: "What do you want with me so late, friend?"

Cucuzone mopped the cold sweat from his brow.

With an expression of anxiety, the hoarse voice said: "Who are you, friend? Have you nothing to say to me?"

"Iron is strong and charcoal is black," replied Cucuzone in a plaintive tone. Then he added: "Not as black as that infernal alley!"

"Approach!" ordered the broken voice. "You're very belated in replying!"

Cucuzone came to stand next to the table. The lamp had been moved away again. Nothing but shadow could be seen in the director's confessional, but the light that reigned in the cabinet was sufficient to render Cucuzone all his effrontery. He would have laughed at his fears, but for the idea of traversing that terrible corridor again.

"It's not you that it's necessary to take away, then, Master?" he said. "If I'm very late it's because I wasn't in a hurry. Would you like me to give you some news? I'd rather be in my bed at this hour than in your respectable company."

"Why have I been sent this clown?" muttered Johann.

"Because there was no choice, Excellency. If you care to take a little stroll, you'll see that there aren't many people in the street."

He shivered at the memory, and turned a couple of somersaults in order to restore a suitable circulation to his blood, but they lacked enthusiasm and gaiety. He had the idea of the corridor to traverse, thus time with a cadaver over his shoulders.

"Enough follies," said Johann. "Go draw the bolt from that door." He indicated the one by which Pier Falcone had exited two hours before in order to go to Barbe's bedside. Cucuzone carried out the order by means of a series of sideways Indian leaps, which finished soothing his completely. He removed the bolt with the tip of his foot, with his hands on the floor.

If only an intelligence like mine had the strength and agility of that man at its service! Johann thought.

Cucuzone braced himself, attained the summit of the sentry-box in a single leap, went over it with the vigor of the wrist and came down in front of the director, trembling at having seen that body pass over his head.

"Friend," he said, dryly, "I've seen monkeys that climb and leap even better than you."

"Excellency," Cucuzone replied, "you want to render me jealous, but I warn you, that fruit smells rotten here…where is my package?"

"Here," replied Johann, pointing at the curtain.

"Where is it necessary to take it?"

"To the beach."

Cucuzone lifted the curtain.

"Oho!" he said. "It's poor Signor Felice. He drank a good glass of Greek wine. That must be heavy!"

"You're robust."

"When I'm paid. What is there for the commission, signor?"

Johann handed him a gold once, and Cucuzone murmured: "It's only healthy people who are generous." However, he loaded the body on to his shoulders.

"Remember this," Johann said to him. "If you encounter a patrol on your route and anyone finds out where your burden came from, you won't wake up tomorrow morning."

"Excellency," replied Cucuzone, "I know the mores of your dear little community. My God protect you!"

He headed for the door, and crossed the threshold with a firm tread in spite of the weight of his burden.

Johann could hear him counting as he marched: "One, two, three, four, five, six, seven, eight..."

Then the door closed again. Cucuzone was on the ninth pace.

Now, there is a legend in Naples—the famous legend of San Gennaro—which says that that a man carrying a dead body is doomed if he takes a hundred steps with his burden. And poor Cucuzone, trembling and seating copiously, resumed his route trying to gain a foot with every stride. If he had had a pickax he would have hollowed out Felice Tavola's grave in the middle of the alley.

To die before the end of the year! Him, Cucuzone, who performed the handstand, the Chinese leap and the iron hand so well! In spite of all his efforts, he had taken eighty paces before he arrived at the end of the long corridor. A capital of twenty paces remained to him, and there was no means of eluding the task that had been imposed on him. The brotherhood of the Silence did not joke. Cucuzone knew that from experience.

When he emerged on to the Piazza del Mercato he stood Felice Tavola's body, which was beginning to stiffen, against a wall and used his hands to mop his brow, with was streaming with sweat. He lay down on the pavement, curled up in his favorite position and started to reflect.

He had been there for nearly a minute when he heard precipitate footsteps crossing the square. It was a bare-headed man, running as fast as he could, moaning as he ran.

The man launched himself flat out into the Vico Albanese, a narrow, winding street that made a circuit around the square, like certain corridors designed to serve in the interior of houses. All the houses and habitations on the eastern side of the marketplace had an exit on to that back-street.

At first, Cucuzone only paid slight attention to that incident. He was too seriously embarrassed to pause over such trivia. Twenty paces! One more and he was fall into the circumstance of the legend of San Gennaro. And if he fled, leaving the cadaver here, as he had a strong desire to do, they would not wait for the end of the year to send him to the grave.

For a second time, those precipitate footsteps became audible in the square. The running man seemed to be very weary. The moon, in its final quarter, was rising behind the hoses in the direction of the old city. The night was already much less black than it had been before. By that vague glow, Cucuzone was able to see the person passing rapidly by, running with a sort of fury. His plaints were more distinct. As he had the first time, he disappeared into the Vico Alabanese.

Cucuzone was no longer thinking about him; but, a veritably strange thing, after a further minute the same course recommenced. It was becoming fantastic. In Naples, people rarely make wagers. It was definitely the same man, but more fatigued.

Cucuzone leapt to his feet and picked up his burden. He had recognized Peter-Paulus Brown of Cheapside.

The rest can easily be divined. Penelope's husband, somewhat dazed by his misadventures and frights, had tried to find his way back to the Great Britain Hotel. He had chanced to go into the perfidious Vico Albanese, which had faithfully returned him to his point of departure, circling the square.

Everyone knows how deceptive obscurity is. In the darkness, the curvature of the street had escaped him, partially; in any case, it was as if the poor English subject were drunk. When he had made two or three circuits, panic had seized him. Fear, fatigue and anger had gone to his head. He had the confused idea that he was the victim of some kind of malevolent enchantment. Naples, that enemy city full of tricks and ambushes, was personified for him; he saw the houses positively advancing to bar his passage. And he was trying obstinately to find a way through, in that street that always brought him back to the Piazza del Mercato.

He was suffering, he was sweating, he was moaning, but he kept going. His ideas were increasingly disordered; he was going mad.

Cucuzone's plan was made in the blink of an eye. He turned a somersault on the spot, and felt his heart lighter than a feather. He loaded Felice Tavola on his shoulders and reached the center of the square in fifteen vigorously spaced steps. He thus retained a margin of five paces for unforeseen necessities.

The place he occupied barred the passage of the fanatical runner. The latter soon reappeared on the far side of the square. His progress was now convulsive and gangling. He was panting hard. He could not see anything, distressed as he was, and, his yellow hair disordered, he was about to run straight into Cucuzone when the latter cried, in a thunderous voice: "Stop!"

Peter-Paulus could have asked for nothing better, but the shock he experienced at the sound of that voice, which rang in his ears like a thunderclap, far from halting his surge, caused him to lose his balance and he slammed into poor Tavola, whom Cucuzone opposed to him in the manner of a shield.

"You've killed him," said the latter, dropping the body.

"I beg your pardon...," murmured Peter-Paulus.

"You've killed him," repeated the clown. "Do you hear me?"

Peter-Paulus emitted a loud moan. "That's the ultimate misfortune!" he sobbed. "I'm a murderer...formally."

He stood there, arms dangling, as motionless as a boundary marker. Cucuzone, profiting in a cowardly manner from his advantage, picked up the cadaver and loaded it on to Peter-Paulus' shoulders, saying: "May God forgive you! There's nothing you can do except throw him in the water."

Then he fled as fast as he could, happy and proud, for he had five paces to spare.

Peter-Paulus remained all alone, drunk, crazy, bewildered and flabbergasted, no longer having legs, arms or a head, in the middle of that deserted square, with a dead body on his back.

Johann Spurzheim had remained alone in his study. He listened momentarily to Cucuzone's lurching footsteps, drawing away along the dark alley.

At the moment when everything fell silent in the direction of the street, someone knocked on the interior door.

"Come in!" shouted Johann.

When the physician had crossed the threshold, he said: "Come in, come in! We've been working for you, my friend, and working well, I can say without boasting. Zora doesn't lack anything?"

Zora was the King Charles spaniel that shared Signor Johann Spurzheim's bed.

"Zora doesn't lack anything," Pier Falcone replied. He was pale and distraught. Johan noticed that.

"What's the matter, friend?" he asked.

"It's a terrible night," murmured the doctor.

"A fine night!" said Johann, rubbing his hands. "A fine night! Pick up that curtain and hang it over the door...I like everything to be in order. Oh, Falcone, my companion, it has served well this evening, that curtain." He laughed weakly. "When you've reattached the curtain," he added, "push the bolt. We're going to go back upstairs. We're going to go to bed and to sleep like a good little saint."

While the doctor obeyed, with a bleak expression, he went on: "Not you, friend, not you. Your work tonight isn't finished yet. Damn! You were born lucky...I'm inviting you to a ball. You're going to be dancing soon at the Palazzo Doria-Doria, my comrade."

"I'm tired," said Pier Falcone, in the manner of a refusal.

The director of the royal police burst out laughing.

"Look at them!" he cried. "I alone am indefatigable! If you'd only accomplished half my work, you'd be dead, my poor companion!"

Pier Falcone came back, after having hung up the curtain and shot the bolt. "Two hours ago," he murmured, "I heard the gasp of a dying woman..."

Johann's physiognomy changed suddenly. He adopted a mournful depression and murmured between his teeth: "Poor Barbe! I'll miss her!"

There was a silence.

Pier Falcone was standing in front of the desk, his arms folded over his chest.

"Did she suffer a great deal?" asked Johann, his eyes lowered, speaking very softly.

"She's still suffering," replied Pier Falcone,

A nervous tic agitated Spurzheim's face. "And she can be heard crying from my bedroom?"

"Distinctly, signor."

Johan reflected for a second, and then said: "No one sleeps in that part of the house. There's no danger."

Pier Falcone felt a chill in his veins.

"Let's leave that," said Johann. "It's necessary...necessity has no law. I'll miss her." Then, suddenly changing his tone: "Put this ring on your middle finger," he said. "Its possession makes you a master chevalier, and you have in Naples, at his moment, an army of twenty thousand soldiers. Tomorrow, you'll be the King's physician, if you wish. The secret of the masters of the Silence is triple. The master of the silence knows where the treasure is; he possesses the key to the characters; he knows the names of his peers. Come closer."

Falcone advanced.

Lowering his voice, Johann continued: "The treasure is in Abruzzo, at the foot of Mont Laurea, in the subterrains of the Purple Castle built by the Borgias of Rome, which was part of the Monteleone domain. The key to the characters is on this piece of paper; take it; you'll be as knowledgeable as me. Your peers number six of which one grandmaster has your life and ours in his hands: that man is Il Porporato. He has the name. Five masters remain. After me comes my lieutenant, Andrea Visconti-Armellino, superintendent of the royal police; his real name is Policeni Corner. The third in importance in Colonel San-Severo, a Hercules, a giant; we'll see his end. His real name is Luca Tristany, his bandit soubriquet Il Capitano. The fourth is old Massimo Dolci, the court banker. He won't inconvenience us. His real name is Amato Lorenzo. The fifth, the cavalier Ercole Pisani, is devoted to Il Porporato. He was the friend of Baron d'Altamonte, whose ring you have. We'll kill him as soon as he gets in our way. His name is Mario Marchese. Armellino wants my place; that will bring him misfortune; San-Severo is too strong; that wounds my sight. Friend Falcone, if you wish, we'll remain alone, both rich and as powerful as kings!"

"What is it necessary to do for that?" asked the doctor.

Johann looked him in the face. He uttered the sarcastic laugh whose effect was so bizarre on that ravaged face.

"First," replied Johann, "It's necessary to take me in your arms and carry me very gently to my bed. I'm sleepy."

"Signor," said Falcone, "if you go back to your bedroom, you'll hear the groans."

"Not for long," said Spurzheim, calmly. "The pastilles are well made."

He held out his hands, as tired children do when demanding the assistance of their nursemaid. Pier Falcone lifted him up. He went back up the stairs with the same facility with which he had descended. Johann hoped until the last step that his carrier might became short of breath, but there was nothing.

"These long breaths aren't the best," said Johann.

When they entered the bedroom he pricked up his ears. There was a distant moaning, but so faint!

"It was much louder a little while ago," said Falcone.

Johann uttered a deep sigh, and burrowed beneath his bedclothes, where the King Charles spaniel greeted him fraternally.

"Open the top drawer in that chest," he ordered Falcone. "There's a piece of paper on the right. Pick it up."

The doctor was about to bring it when Johann stopped him, saying: "It's for you. Look at it."

Pier Falcone unfolded the piece of paper, which was a letter of invitation decorated with delightful vignettes drawn by hand, which is still the custom in Italy.

Lorédan Doria and Comtesse Angélie, his sister, begged Signor—the name was blank—to do them the honor of attending that evening's celebration.

"Write your name," said Johann.

"And what shall I do at the Palazzo Doria?"

"You'll observe."

"It's very late."

"The man for whom I'm sending you will not arrive until after you."

As the doctor was about to respond, Johann made him a sign to listen. A profound cough was heard, followed by a faint cry. Then silence reigned in the house.

"Poor Barbe!" said Spurzheim. "That must be her last sigh."

"Signor…," stammered the physician.

"Good, good, friend…opinions are free. If I believed in God, I'd have masses said for poor Barbe. Lower the lamp and go away, Falcone. I'm sleepy."

The doctor turned the switch. The lamp did not go out, but only cast a faint light. Johann wanted it beside him.

Before turning over, he said to Falcone: "Friend, didn't you say to me that you knew Prince Fulvio Coriolani?"

"On the contrary, signor; I've never met him."

"No? That's surprising; everyone knows him. Listen carefully, Falcone. When Prince Fulvio Coriolani is announced tonight at the Palazzo Doria-Doria, look at that young and brilliant nobleman attentively. When you've looked at him, Falcone, you won't wonder any longer why I've sent you to that fête. Go."

It was half an hour later, Johann was asleep. The King Charles spaniel suddenly emerged from the bedclothes and stood up on its short legs. A noise came from the door. The spaniel started yapping angrily.

Johann heard, for he was a very light sleeper, but it always took him several minutes to vanquish the numbness that paralyzed his limbs when he awoke. Many people afflicted with nervous maladies suffer that cataleptic symptom every day.

Johann heard, and made impotent efforts to shake off his torpor.

His face was turned toward the wall. Someone had just opened the door. Terror covered Johann's entire body with a cold sweat. The little dog started howling ad leapt off the bed. There was the sound of a struggle, followed by two gasps. Silence returned. Two or three minutes of terrible anguish followed. Johann recovered the use of his movements. He turned round. Everything in the room was still.

By the feeble light that escaped the lowered lamp, however, Johann thought that he could see the door open and a dark mass before the threshold. He turned the switch of the lamp. The room filled with light.

The door was, indeed, open, and the body of his wife, Barbe Spurzheim, was lying there, next to the strangled King Charles spaniel.

Johann shivered in all his limbs.

He got up as best he could. He dragged himself across the parquet, pushing the lamp in front of him. He arrived. Barbe's left hand was still clutching the throat of the little dog, which had bitten her furiously. In front of her twisted mouth, which was kissing the floor, there was blood: the blood of the supreme coughing fit, which had choked her. With that blood, her right hand had traced a few words on the parquet. Johann read:

Next week, at the same hour, I'll await you in Hell, murderer.

Johann looked at the clock, which marked half past midnight.

"She knows the future!" he said, letting himself fall, exhausted, next to the cadaver.

Soon, however, he raised himself up again.

"Poor Barbe!" he murmured. "She wanted to avenge herself. It's to frighten me...I shall live a hundred years!"

The carriage in which we left the Chevalier d'Athol, Beldemonio, traversed the streets at a gallop, and then turned into the courtyard of an elegant and magnificent palace situated in the high city, near the middle of the Strada Nuova di Capodimonti. Beldemonio leapt nimbly out of the carriage. As soon as he had mounted the perron, the courtyard was full of movement and sound. The stables opened, and a splendid court carriage emerged from the garage. Ruggieri, directing an army of valets, had four beautiful French horses harnessed to it.

At about the time that Barbe and the King Charles spaniel, all that Johann Spurzheim loved in this base world, died together, torches were seen to appear at the top of the marble perron. The Chevalier d'Athol appeared, in a court costume, wearing the sash of the Annunziata and that of Isabella the Catholic, giving his hand to a young veiled woman. Both of them climbed into the coach and the Chevalier d'Athol said to Ruggieri, who took his position on the seat, in full livery: "To the Palazzo Doria-Doria!"

PART THREE: PRINCE CORIOLANI

I. Colonel San-Severo

Everyone was there that night: in the drawing rooms and the galleries, on the terraces embalmed by flowers, among the flower-beds and the arbors, along the illuminated staircases that went up to the light and bold Chinese hat known as the Belvedere, and in the depths of the grottoes where a mild half-light reigned. The court was there, brilliant lords and beautiful ladies.

When Doria gave a fête, people came from far and wide. You would have heard all the dialects of Italy spoken under the orange trees: the grave language of Rome; pure Florentine; Piedmontese, already Teutonic; and Venetian, which has taken its words from all the idioms of earth.

There was scarcely any great family in the peninsula that did not boast of being allied with the Dorias. Merely with his noble relatives, Doria could have filled his galleries, his drawing rooms and his gardens.

It was February, the heart of the carnival. During the carnival in Naples, masks are worn everywhere. One does not give masked balls, one gives balls. Everyone is costumed according to whimsy, provided that the costume is beautiful.

They were passing by, therefore, those queens, already fatigued by pleasures, for the night was advancing. They were passing, in gracious and laughing groups, from the spectacle hall, where the company of the Teatro San Carlo had been singing all evening, to the covered and open air dance halls, from which the appeal of orchestras departed incessantly. Others were descending the mysterious pathways leading to the grottos and the arbors, on the arms of their cavaliers.

Among the latter, we would have recognized Penelope Brown, the imprudent wife of Peter-Paulus. She was still accompanied by her colossal sigisbeo, Colonel San-Severo of the Roman Guard.

That superior officer, six feet tall, had not quit her, and was paying assiduous court to her. But let us refrain from allowing the reader to believe for a single instant that the daughter of Marjoram and Watergruel had the slightest wrongdoing for which to reproach herself.

Penelope had learned of her husband's departure from Jack. Her suspicions had been alerted in advance by the inconsiderate conduct of Peter-Paulus aboard the *Pausilippe*. Penelope knew at a stroke the extent of her misfortune.

"I'm betrayed," she said to Melicerta, her faithful confidante.

"All men are alike," Mel replied, shrugging her shoulders.

269

"Do you truly believe that I'm betrayed?" asked Penelope, who had hoped for a contradiction.

"Someone is asking for Milord Brown," said a hotel servant at that moment, sticking his head round the door.

"Is it a woman?" cried the jealous Penelope

"No, milady, it's a man who has come about the affair you know about."

"Dissimulate!" Mel whispered in her ear.

"Have him come in," said Penelope.

A man six feet tall, wearing the rich costume of the Roman Guard, was introduced. Penelope adopted the grim attitude of the Englishwoman who knows her "decencies." As the stranger bowed, she said to him, in French: "You're the first man who has entered my bedroom. I'll tell you the reason. I want to avenge myself on milord."

The colonel did not understand a word of French. He saluted milady, and, taking her hand in order to kiss it, he drew a double cross in the palm. Penelope, tickled, retreated all the way to her bed, shrieking like an eagle, in English: "Shocking! Very shocking indeed!"

"It's the habits of the country," Mel told her. "A fine fellow of a man!"

"Ah!" said the colonel, in Italian. "Has there been a mistake? I thought you knew about the affair...but if I'm inconveniencing you..."

He made as if to withdraw. A sign from Mel retained him.

"I'd like to stay," muttered the colonel of the Roman Guard, "but I'm damned if I know how to make them understand.

Penelope and Mel looked at him. He searched the room with his eyes and saw a jewel-case on the night-table. He pointed his finger at it.

"Diamonds?" he said.

"I understand," replied Penelope, in French.

"You have them?" asked the colonel.

"Yes, yes," said milady, "to go in the evening to the ball."

"Exactly!" cried the fine fellow of a man. "To the ball!"

"And milord is there?" Penelope interrogated.

"The Punjab?" said Colonel San-Severo. "Diamonds...ball...this evening!"

"I understand. I'll surprise Monsieur Brown and avenge myself...positively."

"Monsieur Brown!" exclaimed San-Severo. "That's it! We understand one another!"

They had absolutely no idea what they had said to one another, but each of them had an obsession.

San-Severo—who, as the reader already knows, was the terrible Captain, Luca Tristany—having learned that an Englishman named Brown had arrived on the *Pausilippe*, had connected that to the affair of the Punjab. Penelope vaguely understood that a handsome military man wanted to take her to a ball, where Peter-Paulus was already in breach of her conjugal rights.

"Milord," she said, "I will confide myself to your honor, in order to surprise Monsieur Brown and avenge myself."

"That's it!" cried Luca Tristany. "Monsieur Brown...exactly!"

She held out her hand. He took her waist, casually, and made a turn, repeating the word "Ball." I believe that his moustache even brushed Penelope's chaste and immaculate forehead.

"It's the habits of the country," said Mel, opening the trunks.

The handsome colonel, seeing that the prestigious costume that we have already described was being taken out of the trunks, the various components of which had been purchased by Peter-Paulus himself in the most elegant shops in Fleet Street, approved warmly and said: "Perfect! You will show it to the Royal Prince and His Majesty himself."

He was talking about the diamond.

Mel took the colonel by the hand and conducted him to Peter-Paulus' bedroom, which was empty. The colonel kissed her on both cheeks. When she had gone, he put various small objects that were on the furniture into his pocket. He was not a petty man, but there are old habits.

Penelope dressed rapidly and cheerfully. The marriage of the vivid colors—pink, blue, orange and amaranth—was arranged in accordance with the most severe rules of Cheapside taste. When Mel went to fetch the colonel and he saw that tall woman dressed in rainbow colors, he offered her his arm eagerly. A carriage was stationed at the door. On the way, the colonel patted his companion's pockets a little, to see whether he could feel the case of the Punjab.

"My honor is in your hands," Penelope told him. "I am a feeble gentlewoman. I want to savor my vengeance...but I want to preserve virtue preciously!"

San-Severo, the worthy giant, only wanted the Punjab.

Penelope had two principal occupations at the fête at the Palazzo Doria: to find Peter-Paulus, her infidel husband, and to avenge herself. To tell the truth, she did not succeed in either. We know whether the poor English subject was on a bed of roses! As for the colonel, who was naturally charged with aiding Penelope in her vengeance, he acquitted his employment very poorly. He was there for the diamond. Penelope's jabber was beginning to exasperate him. He had dragged her from one drawing room to another, telling everyone that she was the wife of the richest jeweler in London, but all his efforts to obtain the slightest information about the Punjab remained absolutely fruitless.

Those who passed close to him congratulated him on his conquest. At the end of an hour, Penelope weighed a hundred pounds of his arm.

Toward midnight, she could see a certain unusual movement in the drawing rooms and the gardens. Her colonel was accosted successively by several people who whispered a few words in his ear. From then on the colonel became, if possible, even mote taciturn and cold with regard to his beautiful companion. He accosted a cavalier abruptly, whose chestnut hair Penelope admired in a melancholy fashion, and asked him a question in a low voice.

The cavalier said to Penelope, in English: "The colonel desires to know whether you have the diamond on your person.

"Oh!" exclaimed the daughter of Marjoram, and continued in French: "It's very pleasant to hear the language of one's native land so far from England."

"What did she reply?" asked San-Severo.

"Nothing," said the unknown cavalier.

The Colonel frowned, and pronounced, harshly: "Tell her to respond, blood of Christ! We don't have any more time to waste!"

"The colonel begs milady to reply," said the cavalier. "Does milady have the diamond?"

"What diamond?" said Penelope.

When the cavalier had translated that for Colonel San-Severo, the latter let go of milady's arm, sat her down in an arbor, got up, and said: "I'll return." After which, he disappeared with his companion.

Scarcely had he turned the corner of the hornbeam hedge, leaving Penelope as desolate and embarrassed as Ariadne, than she saw the unknown cavalier coming back. He sat down beside her.

"Don't reply to me," he said in English, "and pay close attention to my words. If it's your husband who has the diamond, let him refrain from showing it. Leave for Marseille tonight, if possible. It's a matter of life and death!"

The cavalier stood up and went away. Penelope was petrified. She heard a voice behind her in the bushes.

"Let's speak in Italian as little as possible," said the voice, in French. "We're being watched. The Royal Prince and the King are bewitched."

In spite of her slightly masculine appearance, Penelope was a daughter of Eve. Curiosity prevailed over her fear. Gently, she parted a few branches of the jasmine that closed the back of the arbor, and slid a glance into the bushes. There were six black dominos there: six bearded masks. It was impossible to see the faces. By their voices alone, Penelope divined that they were young men.

"What if he doesn't come…?" said one, expressing a doubt and a dread.

"He'll come!" put in another.

"Then it's up to us," said one of those who had not yet spoken

"If you have the courage, Marquis!" was the reply.

The Marquis extended his hand. "I swear," he said, with all the energy of Italian hatred, "that if it depends on me, the man will only leave here dishonored or dead."

"Even if it's necessary to give your own honor or your life?" said another.

The man who had been addressed as the Marquis first drew himself up to his full height, and then lowered his head and pronounced in a dull voice: "Even so!"

II. Through the Fête

Penelope was more dead than alive. She was trembling in every limb, but her terrors consoled her somewhat for her abandonment. How can one not hope for a little romance for oneself is the midst of all those romantic things?

Penelope was only asking for that: a little romance; a pirate to stab her while uttering the cries of Othello; even an Albanian, a simple Albanian, to abduct her in a tartan. But time was passing, alas. Around Penelope the appearance of the ball was becoming increasingly mysterious and dramatic, and none of those mysteries were for her! One might have thought that all those dramas had been given the password to leave her out.

The dominos in the bushes drew away, taking their somber conspiracy elsewhere. Busy groups appeared. They were speaking Italian. Penelope was enduring the torture of Tantalus. In order to counter her fever she took out her notebook and inscribed a few judicious remarks, the fruit of recent observation:

Naples, continued. Great stature of colonels. They come to look for foreign ladies in hotels to take them to balls. Slightly mad, talking incessantly about diamonds. Women's costumes shocking. Women ugly. Not enough rum in the sorbets.

There was a pause in the dancing in the drawing rooms; the couples, fatigued by pleasure, were scattering along the pathways between the orange trees and myrtles, among which enormous camellias were displaying the splendid bouquets of their perfume-free flowers at ground level. It was winter, but winter in Naples is more beautiful than spring in our harsh climes.

Penelope had I know not what English malady in her vision that prevented her from seeing pretty women, and yet she remained open-mouthed in contemplating one young woman who was passing by.

That one had no domino or mask. Her white muslin dress, simple and designing the adorable contours of an eighteen-year-old figure, bore no other ornament that a light and sober garland of blue convolvulus. She also had a few of those mild nocturnal flowers in her hair. She wore no jewelry. She was so beautiful thus that Penelope dropped her notebook.

The young woman's hand was supported on the arm of a tall cavalier who was as handsome as she was beautiful. There was a family resemblance between them.

While Penelope was contemplating them, jealous of that pearl of beauty and envying her superb cavalier, as much for the color of his hair as for the calm ad profound gaze of his large dark eyes, the couple went around the arbor and plunged into the same clump of bushes where the dominos had been conversing in low voices shortly before.

"Angélie," said the cavalier, raising the young woman's hand gently to his lips, "I'm your brother, but I'm also your guardian and protector. I'm the head of the Doria-Doria family. Let me speak to you as our noble father would speak to you, if God had not given him his place in paradise."

"Loredano, my beloved brother," Angélie replied, "I am listening to you as if you were Giacomo Doria, my venerated father."

They sat down on a grassy bank. Lorédan collected himself before going on.

"My sister," he said, holding Angélie's beautiful little hand in his, "you are the most beautiful, the richest and the noblest of the young women of the court. You are also the best and the most worthy of being adored. I have searched around me for a long time for the man who might be your equal. I have not found him. He is not..."

"That is pride, dear brother," Angélie interrupted, blushing and smiling at the same time.

"That's the truth, my sister...and there's a singular thing. Do you remember those fine Spanish comedies we read together? The heroic journeys of Lope de Vega and Michel de Cervantes? Our grandmother was a Medina-Celi, my sister...there's Castilian blood in our veins."

"Why are you telling me this, brother?"

"Because...but you were as passionate as me in contact with that proud poetry. Do you remember that?"

"I remember."

"The soul of all of that is honor...umbrageous and armed honor...honor that protects itself with the dagger and the sword."

Angélie was pale. "But why are you talking to me about that, brother?" she repeated, lowering her voice involuntarily.

As if he were dreaming aloud, Lorédan went on: "Did you notice, Angélie, that in the comedies of Vega and Cervantes, the sword that watches over the family mirror, in order that no foreign breath should tarnish it, is always in the brother's hand?"

The beautiful young woman did not reply. Her eyes lowered, and her soft smile vanished.

"Angélie," continued Lorédan, whose voice was softer and graver, "don't interrogate me, for I can't explain myself yet, but believe me, my heart tells me that there is a threat hanging over the house of Doria...and I have never measured as well as I do today the responsibility that my title as head of the family causes to weigh upon me..."

Voices became audible in the gardens.

"The Comtesse!" they were saying. "His Royal Highness is looking for Comtesse Doria!"

Angélie made a movement to respond to that appeal. Lorédan retained her.

"You really love him, then?" he murmured, so quietly that his sister had difficulty hearing him.

A hint of scarlet came to Angélie's cheeks as she replied: "I love him as much as one can love."

Lorédan abandoned her hand, his brow furrowing.

At that moment, it would have been curious to observe those two faces, so perfect in their various beauty. Lorédan's anger was sad, as if paternal. Angélie's eyes had just looked up, expressing an unexpected pride, entirely ready to revolt.

She was a gentle young woman; everyone said that her name depicted her soul. Thus far, she had never resisted her brother's authority. Those who knew her compared the suave and cheerful equilibrium of her character to the cloudless azure of a May sky.

"I love him so much," said Angélie, whose soft voice was not trembling, "that if you had something to say to me against him, my brother, I would refuse to listen to you."

"Is it you who are speaking thus, my sister?" stammered the Doria..

"It's me, my brother. It is Princesse Coriolani."

Lorédan swiftly lowered his eyelids in order to hide the somber flame that he sensed igniting in his pupils.

"You aren't yet Princesse Coriolani, Angélie," he pronounced, in a contained voice.

"The man who prevents me from being," the young woman pronounced, distinctly, "will be declaring himself my most mortal enemy."

Doria shuddered, and looked at her. "Has he cast a spell on you, like the others?" he said, in a tone into which anger put something provocative.

"My brother," said Angélie, trying to take back the hand that he had withdrawn, "don't pronounce words that you would soon regret. You're good, you're noble and you love me…what is in me, you don't understand, and I don't have the power to make you understand it. I have no need for anyone to feel sorry for me, and I don't want anyone to insult me."

In nearby pathways people were laughing and chatting. The joyful sounds of the fête were coming from all directions. Opposite the grassy bank, which was hidden behind laurels and arborescent camellias, two paths intersected, forming a crossroads, at the center of which was a Medici Venus.

A domino, whose heavy tread announced a great age, stopped at the foot of the statue. He remained alone momentarily at the crossroads. Angélie and Lorédan could see him tearing a page from his notepad, on which he had scribbled a few words in haste.

He clapped his hands three times, then twice, and then once. A masked man appeared at the corner of the path and took the piece of paper in his hand.

"I don't know that one!" murmured Doria.

"The old man…," Angélie began.

"The old man is Massimo Dolci, the court banker, but the other..."

At that moment, the one who had just been named as Massimo Dolci said to his masked companion: "It's necessary that they know this...and right away. Go; I'll wait for them here."

Almost immediately afterwards, Massimo Dolci was surrounded by three other individuals, among whom was Colonel San-Severo. Lorédan named the other two: Andrea Visconti-Armellino, the superintendent of the royal police, and Cavalier Ercole Pisani.

"Only Johann Spurzheim, the director of the royal police, is lacking," he said. "We'd see all Prince Fulvio's friends gathered."

That was a provocation. Comtesse Doria did not respond to it.

Massimo Dolci and his three companions conversed briefly in low voices. What they said could not be overhead.

Everything has been foreseen," sad Visconti-Armellino, however, in response to a question from the old banker. "Johann Spurzheim will interrogate Felice personally."

Lorédan smiled bitterly on hearing the name of the director of the royal police pronounced.

Massimo Dolci drew way, leaning on the arm of Ercole Pisani.

He had a fine financier's head, the aged Dolci. His broad and firm forehead was crowned with long white hair. In Naples, and above all at the court, he had the high commercial renown that is almost glory. His immense fortune had been made, it was commonly believed, in England. From his old age, by virtue of a laudable patriotic sentiment, he had wanted his native land to profit. For three months, every time there had been a crisis, everyone had willingly spoken of him to direct the finances of the State. The question of whether he was worthy of it was resolved in advance by his limitless credit and skill, but it was feared that he might not accept.

Ercole Pisani, his companion, a man of great relations and fine company, was a Venetian. For a long time, alas, Venetians had had no need of an excuse to leave their homeland. Ercole Pisani occupied a considerable position at court, supported as he was by Prince Fulvio, Massimo Dolci and Johann Spurzheim. There had been mention of him lately as a potential Secretary of State for Foreign Affairs.

Armellino-Visconti, still young, even more elegant, if possible, and above all more insinuating than Cavalier Pisani, occupied a position all the more important because his immediate superior. Signor Spurzheim, was hovering between life and death.

As for Colonel San-Severo, his path to court had not been made all alone. Intelligence did not shine excessively in that Herculean head. His friends did not scorn him, because he could do much with a thrust of his hand, but he was not good for political intrigue, in which the association had found itself unexpectedly involved by the sovereign will of its grandmaster.

Lorédan Doria retained momentarily the sad and bitter smile that was around his lips. "It's necessary that the Royal Prince and His Majesty must be bewitched," he murmured. "There are four adventures who are, at the present moment, the foremost in Naples!"

"I don't know them and I'm not defending them, "replied Angélie. "I know Fulvio, and I'm defending him."

"You know him!" Lorédan repeated. But he retained the irritated speech that was on his lips, and went on in a melancholy and tender tone: "Poor dear child! You are our joy and our pride. I have no rancor against you. That man has dominated you, like so many others. And have I not been his friend myself?"

"Why are you no longer, my brother?"

"Because you love him," replied Doria, without hesitation. Then he continued, explaining his thought in an affectionate and noble tone: "The two of us were alone in this world, my sister. We had wealth, we had power, but God, who never gives everything at once, had made a void around us. Our father was dead, our saintly mother had preceded him into the tomb. Do you know how many times, a young man as I already was, I sat down next you your child's cradle, pensive and discouraged? Do you know how many times I contemplated your smiling sleep with tears in my eyes? I tell you this, Angélie, I have loved you more than anything down here, even more than the tender, beautiful and unfortunate young woman that I once named my fiancée..."

A furtive tear came to Angélie' eyes. She drew her brother's hand to her lips and kissed it silently. Lorédan leaned over her forehead, which he brushed.

"No," he cried, "on my honor as a gentleman and my faith as a Christian, it wasn't jealousy. Fathers are sometimes jealous of their daughters at the age of loving, and I am your father, dear, child, my little sister. I loved you enough to be jealous, but it's not that, I swear; you know whether I'm lying. Only, I have had for you the clairvoyance that was lacking for myself. I have looked that man in the face to whom I had given my amity blindfold...and I have seen I know not what cloud over his present; I have shivered; I have made my investigations regarding his past. There, on all sides, darkness!"

"I can answer for his past, my brother," pronounced Angélie, in a whisper.

"You're a woman. Women easily abuse themselves when they're in love. You're young; youth is easy to deceive."

"The King is an old man. The Royal Prince is a mature man!"

Lorédan passed the back of his hand over his forehead. "You'll support yourself on the authority of our princes in order to resist me, my sister?" he murmured

"I'll support myself on you, my brother. I'll address myself to your heart."

"What if I were to say: 'I don't wish it'?"

"I'd respond: 'I'm in love.'"

Lorédan's had fell on to his breast. "It's very powerful, then, amour?" he pronounced, without knowing that he was speaking alone. And as if, from the depths of his heart, a new sentiment, scarcely admitted, were making a mystical response to that question, his lips agitated and he added: "Yes, it's very powerful."

But Angélie did not hear that. Angélie was prey to an extraordinary agitation. She went pale and red by turns. Lorédan felt her huddle against him, as if a sensation of fear or anguish had traversed her heart. He saw that her eyes were full of tears.

"I'm suffering and I'd like to die!" she said.

She said that as that other poor child had said it: the child as lowly descended on the rungs of the social scale as she, the radiant and adorable Angélie, was highly elevated. She said it as the daughter of Sicily had: little Céleste, the sister of the seminarian Julian.

And as Lorédan looked at her fearfully—for men have no way of understanding such a plaint—a more vivid incarnadine came to her charming cheeks, and her eyes shone with pride. "I'd like to die," she repeated, "for his amour alone can save me, and I don't know whether he loves me."

Lorédan took her in his arms. "Save you from what, my sister?" he cried.

Angélie hesitated. Her charming bosom rose up two or three times, as if she were on the point of busting into sobs. But suddenly, raising her head in a provocative manner and interrogating instead of responding, she demanded: "My brother, what were you doing last night at the corner of the Strada di Mantua and the Piazzetta Grande, opposite the old building called the Folquieri house?"

Lorédan shivered violently and looked at her in amazement. She stood up. This time, he did not try to retain her.

"There is an enigma in me," she said, "that you cannot divine, my brother. I'm wasting my time. I'm suffering, but have no fear for the honor of our name. I shall die before failing it."

She disappeared through the bushes, as lightly as a sylphide. In the depths of the bush, a burst of stifled laughter was audible. Lorédan bounded to his feet. Another white dress was running behind the orange trees.

"It's that demon Nina!" murmured Lorédan, letting himself fall back on to the grassy bank.

"Comte," sad a voice nearby, "I'm glad to find you alone."

The newcomer was one of the six dominos that we saw holding the mysterious council behind the arbor where Penelope Brown was sitting. It was the domino to whom his companions had given the title of Marquis, the same one who had sworn that, at the price of his own honor or his own life, he would dishonor or kill a man tonight.

Lorédan turned to him and said: "What do you want with me, Cousin Malatesta?"

"I want to ask you two things, Cousin Doria. First, will you plead my cause with regard to your sister Angélie?"

"I have pleaded it."

"And the result?"

"Angélie will never be your wife."

Malatesta had a smile that was both proud and hateful.

"Let's pass on to my second question, Cousin Doria," he said. "The King is master everywhere, but you are master in your own home. Would it displease you if an arrest was made in your palace tonight, in the name of the King?"

"That depends," said Lorédan. "If it's for the service of the King himself, I consent, on one condition. If it's a ministerial affair, I refuse."

"It's for the service of the King himself. Your condition?"

"That the person threatened is not my friend..."

"He's your enemy!"

"I was about to add, Cousin Malatesta: "or my enemy.""

"When you know his name..."

"I divine it. You will not have my sister, Marquis Malatesta. We Dorias do not like those who fight thus."

"I've fought Fulvio Coriolani with the sword!" sad Malatesta, stiffening.

"That's good...and you were vanquished. Perhaps I'll have the same fate, Cousin Malatesta. But if Fulvio Coriolani is attacked under my roof, I shall defend him with my sword."

III. The Grotto of Endymion

The one thing for which one can reproach the marvels of Italian opulence is a mythological coloration that it a little too uniform. Private art has not been able to become Christian so close to the cradle of pagan theogony, which furnishes so many charming subjects. Italy is still Greek; only the churches are romantic or Christian. Are not the churches, even, full of antique memories? The majority of them are built with marble conquered from Jupiter, Minerva or Neptune, and almost all the holy water fonts are baptized ancient basins that one contained lustral water. In the palaces Olympus reigns in mastery, and only has a rival in Tainaron;[43] Homer and Virgil are there in the boscage. One sees nothing but nymphs, dryads or Bacchantes. Not one modern image; the chisels of sculptors only know how to shape the gods.

Half way up the slope, not far from the Belvedere, illuminated by a thousand colored lights like precious stones, there was a grotto, the opening of which was formed by large rocks extracted from the flanks of the Posillipo, covered with green moss and flowery creepers, promised solitude and coolness. Two young women were there, all alone, and both so beautiful that a master of the brush would have been inspired by the sight of them.

Contrast, that mysterious enchanter, set them off against one another, and added to the charm of each one. It was impossible, in fact, to encounter two faces more charming or more dissimilar.

One was tall, ample in her noble grace, generous in race and in blood, borrowing her exquisite seduction from the perfect lines of the most radiant visage had admired in a hundred years: the smile of an angel, a celestial gaze, the bearing of a queen. The other, as small and robust in her suppleness as an African black panther, had nothing regular, and acquired her charm in I know not what bizarre boldness of design and contours, in the unexpected and the strange.

The gestures of the latter were sometimes abrupt and almost virile, and sometimes of a softness so exquisite that merely seeing her gave birth to reverie and rocked the soul in a sudden languor. She had large dark eyes veiled buy curves fringes, a faceted forehead crowned with prodigious hair; a pert nose, whose mobile nostrils were flared by passion; a cruel mouth in which the gay smile sparkled; the feet and hands of a fay. A slim figure, and yet so strong! There was a little of the Spaniard in it, but the burnished gold of that complexion was from further away than Spain. Only those who have erected striped gypsy

---

[43] Cape Tainaron, on the southern tip of Greece, is nowadays known as Cape Matapan; it is quoted here because a cave there was reputed to be the entrance to the Underworld employed by Heracles and Orpheus, among others.

tents on stormy nights in the deserted plans of southern Italy would have been able to tell the race to which that delectable creature belonged.

The tall, the beautiful and the noble one was Angélie Doria. The other was the Nina that Lorédan had called a demon. Under that name, we do not know her yet, but she did not only have that name.

We have seen her aboard the *Pausilippe*, plying the role of lady companion to the mysterious unknown woman, the Comtesse. There she called herself Paola. And Peter-Paulus Brown of Cheapside had chosen her officially as the Marchesa of his Byronian dreams. We have seen her again in the Strada di Porto, in the costume of an orange-seller. We found her again in the Strada di Mantua, opposite the Folquieri house, disguised as a ragazzo, in order to extinguish street lights under the nose and bead of the unfortunate conscript of the Buffalo regiment. And, I do not know on what occasion, we have heard the bold adventurer whose nocturnal adventures have occupied so many pages in this story call her Fiamma.

Now, out there in the Strada di Porto, has not Mariotto, the brazen improviser, told us that Il Porporato had a servant, a mistress, a farfadet, a goblin, a fay named Fiamma? But how can one believe that the familiar spirit of the bandit Il Porporato, Fiamma, had an entry into the noble palace of the Doria-Dorias?

From the place where the two young women were, the illuminations outside could not be seen. It was not dark, however, because the light of the gardens, where myriads of odorous candles were burning, was reflected along the walls and making, in the depths of the grotto, a sort of gentle chiaroscuro. That semi-daylight allowed the sight of the shepherd of Caria, a grandson of Jupiter, who was the lover of the chaste goddess. The grotto had two issues, one of which opened under the belvedere above the statue. In the same way that Diana, jealous of her happiness, chose the somber hours of night to visit her beloved, at certain moments, the moonlight, filtering through the upper issue, still came to caress the marble Endymion with its silvery radiance in the depths of the grotto.

Angélie and Nina were sitting on a mossy bank with their backs to the pedestal of the statue. Nina's hands were playing with Angélie's soft hair while the latter's nonchalant head was leaning on her shoulder.

Nina was the niece of old Massimo Dolci, the banker of the court of Naples. She had the rank of maid of honor with regard to Her Royal Highness the Princess of Salerno, the wife of the King's younger son.

"I've read a beautiful book," she said. "It's the romance of Amadis,[44] which he priest in *Don Quixote* mocks so roundly."

_____

[44] *Amadis de Gaula*, the most famous of the pastiches of French chivalric romances that enjoyed an enormous vogue in Spain at the beginning of the sixteenth century, and were ruthlessly parodied by Cervantes in *Don Quixote*. The French knight Amadis is in love with Oriana, daughter of Lisuarte, king of Great

"Have you nothing else to say to me, Nina?" murmured Angélie.

"No," replied the brunette, putting a kiss one the Contessina's hair. "I want to talk to you about Amadis. But before anything else, beautiful Oriana, have you done everything that I recommended?"

"Yes," Amelie replied, in a low voice."

"Have you launched the stick into the wheels of the powerful King Lisuarte...?"

"I don't understand you, Nina," Angélie interjected.

"That's because you haven't read *Amadis of Gaul*, my adorable princess. Lisuarte was a king of Great Britain, magnanimous and without faults, as is said of your august brother Loredano Doria..."

"Are you making fun of my brother, Nina?"

"God forbid, Highness! This Lisuarte had for a daughter the eighth wonder of the world, the celestial Oriana, whom you resemble like two drops of water. The faultless Lisuarte did not want Oriana to marry the terrible Amadis, of whom our Fulvio is the living portrait, but Princess Mabila, whom I resemble slightly..."

"Mercy, Nina, talk seriously!" said the young Comtesse.

Nina took her two hands and applied them to her lips. "Do you love me even half as much as I love you, proud daughter?" she said, suddenly. And as Angélie looked at her in astonishment, she went on: "Listen! I'm taking about that mad novel, that superb novel, because I've found my portrait in it. Answer, I beg you: do you love me and do you love him?"

"Don't you know that I have no better friend than you, Nina?" Angélie replied.

"That's not enough," said the petulant girl, whose pose became more abandoned, while her eyes, darker than jade, were full of dreams.

The Princess of Salerno's maid of honor was far away. In the half-light of the grotto, next to the pure and suave visage of La Doria, it really was the head of a zingara that was tipped back amid the undulating masses of that long ebon hair, whose curls scattered more blackly over the white marble of the pedestal. Lorédan had spoken the truth; there was something of the goblin in the laughing and dreaming Nina.

"No, that's not enough," she repeated, "but let's only talk about him; how much do you love him?"

Very pink, Angélie put her companion's hand on her heart.

"When I love," Nina murmured, "my heart beats differently." She fell silent, pensive and suddenly sad.

"I have a secret to confide to you, said Angélie.

Britain, and is protected in his various adventures by the fay—i.e., enchantress—Urganda.

The zingara leapt to her feet, lighter than those of Taglioni or Elssler;[45] then she suddenly knelt down before La Doria, placing her pert head on her knees.

"Secret!" she said. "Oh, I know too many secrets! But you'll talk later, beautiful Comtesse. What did King Lisuarte say when you talked to him about the Strada di Mantua and the Folquieri house?"

"Lorédan went pale."

"Poor King Lisuarte. If he were only as shrewd as he is handsome, brave and generous! But the horizon is darkening around us, Angélie, my darling. And if the wise fay Urganda wants to protect us, it's necessary that she hurry."

"When you'd like to explain yourself clearly...," murmured the young Comtesse, with a gesture of impatience.

"Perfect Oriana," the zingara continued, "why have you not deigned to read the most charming of all books of chivalry? There is a scaly monster in it whose breath reeks of the cemetery, who is named the Endriago, and who reminds me of the venerable invalid Johann Spurzheim, from whom your brother now obtains almanacs. Amadis killed the Endriago, but not without difficulty."

"In the name of heaven, Nina...!" Angélie commenced.

The zingara raised herself up with an abrupt movement and threw her arms round Angélie's neck. She began rocking Angélie's head gently, as if she were rocking a baby. And she sang, in a voice as soft and sweet as the organ register known as *celeste*, the song of young Sicilian mothers:

Sleep, little flower of my heart,
Perfume of the garden of love,
Of the garden that is ours!
Portrait of the father,
Joy of the mother,
Angel without wings, by the grace of God,
For you would fly up above
If God had given to you wings.
Sleep, little soul,
My life is in you;
When you smile, I weep;
It seems that you are smiling at Heaven
Because the earth is very sad,
Little girl, lily bud!
Joy of the mother,

---

[45] The ballerinas Marie Taglioni (1804-1884) and Fanny Elssler (1810-1884), both stars of the Paris Opéra in the heyday of Romanticism. The latter famously had an affair with Leopold, Prince of Salerno—a minor character in the present story—in 1827.

Portrait of the father,
He is absent; she is sad.
Dream that they are united!
God will reunite them!

Her voice died away. She sat down in the place she had occupied before. Her physiognomy became serious.

"I'm his sister," she said. "He is half of myself. When we were small, he fought one day to defend me against a wild dog of the Apennines. The dog got him down beneath him. I picked up his knife, which he had dropped. I plunged it entire into the gaping maw of the dog, whose breath was burning me. The dog foamed red and rolled down to the bottom of the mountain.

"Our hearts awoke at the same time. Comtesse, you are more beautiful than me, but I love him more than you. He has no more need of me to be happy, let him be happy without me! But if he is to suffer or to die, I will be there, to die or to suffer!"

"You still love him, Nina!" said Angélie, lowering her eyes.

Nina burst out laughing. "I had pride!" she said gaily. "I believed that I was the only one of my species. But beautiful Oriana, there is nothing new under the sun. Behold, I'm as old as the world! My portrait is in a dusty book. Don Quixote, the priest, and his housekeeper, knew me three hundred years ago!"

She interrupted herself in order to strike the consecrated pose of the story-teller.

"Amadis," she continued, "son of Perion, King of the Gauls, and Oriana, the daughter of Lisuarte, King of Great Britain, had a son whom the sage Urganda named Esplandian, because he dazzled like a sun.[46] That Esplandian, a hero from childhood, conquered the forbidden isle with his sword, and put to death the impure family of the enchanter Arcalaus. Don't yawn Comtesse, here is my living portrait.

"Her name was Carmella. She was beautiful, but not like you happy and perfect creatures; she was as beautiful as a young tigress of India, graceful and savage, like the magnificent golden serpent of the Australian isles, which fascinates herds of caimans, coiled up as they are in the sun among the pale flowers of marshes.

"She was sixteen years old. She saw Esplandian for the first time asleep in the hermit's cell, and as she had been snatched from the race of Arcalaus she seized from the hero's bedside the sword of the forbidden isle, in order to pierce his bosom with it.

---

[46] Garci Rodriguez de Montalvo cashed in on the success of the four-volume 1508 edition of *Amadis de Gaula* credited to him (which was probably not the original) by issuing a fifth, featuring the story of Esplandian, in 1510; other writers added half a dozen further extensions and sequels.

Esplandian, who was dreaming, extended his arms, as white and round as a woman's. He smiled softly in his sleep. Carmella allowed him to escape the enchanted blade whose touch alone caused death; she fell to her knees and her lips sought Esplandian's lips in spite of herself.

"It was not about Carmella that the son of Amadis was dreaming. A name escaped his lips. It was not Carmella's name. Esplandian was dreaming about the beauty of beauties, Leonorina, daughter of the Emperor of the Greeks.

"Carmella waited for him to wake up. When he finally opened his eyes she summoned him, on his honor as a knight, to grant a gift to an unfortunate damsel. Knights could not refuse that. Esplandian granted her the gift.

"'I shall not ask for your amour,' said Carmelle, with tears in her eyes, 'since your amour is for another. Only let me follow you and love you.'

"The young hero could not take back his word. Carmella followed him, and loved him.

"Do you understand, Angélie, that there are souls—sick people who do not want to be cured—who prefer martyrdom to absence? Do you understand that? The physicians of the heart say to them: 'Forget.' Those souls do not want that. At the price of a thousand tortures, they want to love, and to love incessantly. They cling to their dear suffering. Do you understand that?"

"No," replied Angélie, who was now listening with avid attention. "For myself, I would flee. But in a little while, Nina, I will tell you things that perhaps you won't understand either."

"Me, I understand everything," said Nina, whose mischievous and bold smile shone through her melancholy. "Carmella followed her Esplandian. Carmella loved him, and Carmella, one might say, lived and died for that love.

"That is beautiful, you understand, Comtesse. That is great, that is true. Your Italian poetry has nothing similar, I know that. But if Dante had found that idea, he would have made it sublime. There are women like that, in whom love is a kind of worship, the devotion of a religion. They love in order to love. They love so much that their passion, sanctified, floats above the human inferno. Even jealousy is extinct in those purified hearts. The women of whom I speak can love and serve their rival: love them well, and serve them faithfully...."

She fell silent. A slight sigh elevated her charming breast. She drew Angélie to her bosom and kissed her hair for a long time.

Angélie straightened up, because she had felt a tear fall on her forehead. Nina was weeping.

"You're unhappy, then?" murmured the young Comtesse.

"No," replied the young zingara. "I see him every day."

She stopped. Both of them had lowered eyes, the two charming creatures, so differently beautiful.

Nina, a character inexplicable in her sudden eccentricities, seemed to regret the words she had pronounced. She did not look up at Angélie, because she feared that she might have wounded her; for she was good, and her love for the young Comtesse was very genuine.

The latter was profoundly thoughtful. Her dream went far beyond the present subject of the conversation. Mechanically, her pretty white fingers tapped out the measure of a German waltz that the distant orchestra was playing.

"I know what you're thinking about," said the zingara, in a whisper.

"Is that true?" said Angélie, shivering.

"You're thinking about the trees of the Pamfili palace in Palermo."

Angélie did not reply.

"It was during that waltz that he spoke to you," said Nina.

The young Comtesse had forgotten that. Her eyelids fluttered. Nina thought that she was about to weep. "Oh, you love him!" she said, passionately. "You love him! It seems to me that I would give all my blood for you."

Angélie's physiognomy became sad. "There are moments," she murmured, "when I would like him to love you."

Then, without transition, and as if it were impossible to delay any longer broaching the new subject, she said: "Answer me, Nina; you've been treating me like a child for too long: why did my brother shudder when I spoke to him about the Strada di Mantua and the Folquieri house?"

"Curious!" said the zingara. "So it wasn't Fulvio that you were thinking about just now?"

"Answer me!"

"Comte Lorédan shivered when you mentioned the Strada di Mantua and the Folquieri house to him because true love, driving love, the love that he has never felt in his life before, found the chink in his armor a few days ago."

"An intrigue?" murmured Angélie, smiling.

"An entire destiny," pronounced the zingara, slowly.

"Do I know the person?"

"Perhaps, perhaps not. You must have seen her. Perhaps you've forgotten her."

"Her name?"

"She has no name."

The beautiful Doria formed a little scornful moue.

"Tomorrow," Nina continued, "she might have one greater than yours."

"Oho!" said Angélie, who rarely mocked. "It's at least three days since you've taken your sibylline tone!"

"And I won't keep it long, Comtesse. Let it suffice you to know that the august Lorédan, your brother…the man who finds that the marriage of his sister with Fulvio Coriolani would be a misalliance, has just fallen in love with a poor young woman who occupies, with her brother, a little room in that huge Folquieri house. I say madly in love…respectfully in love…prowling like Almaviva under Rosine's windows—which are, alas, on the fifth floor!—not daring to write, not daring to show himself or to speak In brief, as amorous as a page, at the majestic age he has!"

"Is she beautiful?" asked Angélie.

Nina's gaze slid from her companion's forehead to the suave and proud fall of her shoulders.

"There is nothing as beautiful as you, Comtesse," she said, "but the young woman is adorably beautiful. If I were in love, I'd be afraid of her." While she pronounced those last words there was something somber in the zingara's voice.

"And you wouldn't be afraid of me?" said Angélie, smiling.

Nina was serious. "Listen," she said, lowering her voice without knowing it. "What your Fulvio does not know himself, I know. I can see into his heart better than he can. It has been such a long time that I have sensed everything that he experiences that the thought radiates from him to me, as if I were only the reflection of his life. I'm not afraid of that young woman for myself, being condemned; I'm afraid of her for you."

Angélie remained silent for a moment; then she repeated the words that she had pronounced before her brother. "Then, I would die," she said, "for he is the only one that can save me."

The zingara's astonishment was the same as Lorédan's. Like him, she asked: "Save you from what?"

Before La Doria had the time to respond, a broad and growing shadow appeared on the wall of the grotto. Then a man showed himself, clad in black and wearing a mask. He was walking with precaution. The zingara put her hand over her companion's mouth.

The newcomer tried to see what was in the depths of the cave, but he was in the light; the shadow deceived him, and he did not discover the two young women. He stopped twenty paces away, at the place where a bend in the subterranean path still permitted a sight of the garden, while hiding, or partly hiding, a person standing as sentinel. He took off his mask in order to breathe, and a cry was stifled in the throat of the zingara.

IV. Another kind of loving

From the mossy bank where Angélie and Nina were sitting, the oblique profile of the newcomer, whose face was fully illuminated, was distinctly perceptible. He was a man still young, but whose hair was already sparse; seen from behind by the light from the garden it seemed etiolated on his cranium. He had a pallor of marble. His pose made it obvious that he had no suspicion of the gazes fixed on him from behind, and that he was in ambush there.

"Do you know that man" murmured Angélie.

Nina nodded her head affirmatively.

At that moment, there was a loud noise outside. Suddenly, a shadow emerged from one of the lateral paths that cut across the path to the grotto. The man replaced his mask hastily, because a hand had just been placed on his shoulder from behind. Angélie heard the distinct words: "Iron is strong and charcoal is black..."

The other replied in a whisper, and they drew away together, precipitately.

At the moment when the second of the two mysterious individuals had come into the light at the bend in the path, Angélie had recognized the superintendent of the royal police, Andrea Visconti-Armellino.

"What does this mean?" she said.

"You'll see many things tonight that will seem inexplicable to you, Contessina," her companion replied.

"Am I not mistaken? Was that really the superintendent?"

"It was him."

"And the other?"

"The other is a man seeking revenge."

"On whom?"

"On you...on me, and all those who love Prince Fulvio Coriolani."

"I beg you, Nina, explain yourself!" cried the young Comtesse.

"Have I ever hidden anything from you, ingrate girl?" retorted the zingara, curling her companion's beautiful hair with a distracted hand. "Do I know why I love you, you who are, relative to me, like those elder brothers who take the entire family heritage, you who are crushing me with your beauty, you who are happy with all my lost happiness? Ought I not to hate you and fight you, I who cherish you and serve you? Let all these things go, and have no fear. It is not given permitted to me at present to pierce for you the mystery that surrounds you. In this house, Comtesse, your magnificent palace, you are a slave and a prisoner. Your destiny and many others will be decided tonight. But know this: you can do nothing either to attack or to defend yourself. In this strange tragedy, whose prologue was played far from here and whose last twists and turns are about to burst forth before your eyes like lightning, you have no role. You are like those princesses in magical tales, always exposed but always defended by the good spirits that watch over them."

"Can you hear that? Can you hear it?" exclaimed Angélie, who had stood up in order to listen.

The rumor outside was increasing. Nina lent an ear. "It's not the Prince yet," she said. "It's news coming from the Castello-Vecchio."

"What news? Do you know it?"

Nina resumed her nonchalant pose. "The noble crowd that is cluttering your drawing rooms and gardens, Contessina," she said, "resembles far more than it thinks the other poor and ragged crowd that I traversed tonight."

"What other crowd?"

"I took a stroll after supper on the Marinella beach," replied the zingara, negligently. "There was a tumult like that around the Maddalena bridge, where a cadaver had been found."

"Yes," said Angélie, "I heard mention of that. One could believe that Naples is in the power of an army of malefactors.

"One could certainly believe that," murmured Nina.

"What are you saying?" said the young Comtesse, turning toward her sharply.

"What everyone is repeating," replied the zingara. "And do you know what rumor is running around down there? It's being said that the dead man is Prince Coriolani."

Angélie went as pale as a corpse.

Nina burst out laughing. "It will be the arm of a giant that will wield the dagger when my beloved brother Coriolani falls," she pronounced, raising her head proudly. "How could one of those dwarfs that surround us combat the man that pagans would have adored as a god? I opened the door of my carriage in passing and I threw my purse to the crowd, saying: 'This what Fulvio Coriolani gives to his good friends in Naples to prove to them that he is not dead...' And the cry of joy of those poor people rose all the way to the heavens...and the wheels of my vehicle were lifted up. 'Where is he?' they demanded. 'Where is the great Highness?' 'At the Palazzo Doria,' I replied, 'for his betrothal to the Comtesse Angélie...'"

The young Comtesse seized her arm. "You did that?" she said.

"With the result that," Nina went on, placidly, "at this moment, all Naples believes that the betrothal is being made here under the auspices of the King and the Royal Prince...." She interrupted herself in order to cut off her companion's speech, and added: "Oh, your majestic brother will have difficulty vanquishing us. The people are with us; the court is with us...and I know not what black jealousies that are conspiring in the shadows will sooner or later give us the opportunity to engage in a battle that is won in advance!"

"But it's war that you've declared on Lorédan, my brother!" murmured Angélie.

"Let him marry his beautiful unknown!" replied the zingara. "The fashion is for misalliances…and at least you, Comtesse, will be misallied with a prince!"

She stopped in order to listen.

"Can you hear?" she said. "The name of Baron d'Altamonte is being pronounced on all sides. It's a long time since our pretty ladies have seen the execution of a gentleman! To see a lord who danced so well die is a curious thing!

"A little further along than the Maddalena bridge," she continued, "there was another crowd: the Strada di Porto. Holy Virgin! Save for the accent and the odor of macaroni, which replaces out there the exquisite perfumes of your gardens, Comtesse, it was very similar—two names, as here: Coriolani, Altamonte; the condemned and the victorious. And, singularly enough, people were asking down there, as they are here, why Coriolani had left the Palazzo Doria in the middle of the fête, on the same day when His Majesty King Ferdinand I, King of the Two Sicilies, was to solicit the hand of the beautiful Comtesse on his behalf…"

"They already knew that, then?"

"They know everything in the Strada di Porto. Naples is like the immense house of a great lord. Here we're in the drawing room; in the Strada di Porto they're in the servants' parlor…and since when can the staff be accused of knowing less than the masters? Except, they've sometimes known it for longer, and in the Strada di Porto, it's being said that our pretty ladies won't see the execution of Baron Altamonte."

"Altamonte! Altamonte!" responded the voices from outside, like a distant echo. "Baron d'Altamonte!"

Nina had a bitter smile. "I'm beginning to find that Fulvio is very late," she murmured.

A hint of pallor came to Angélie's cheeks. "And yet," she replied, "the Prince said to me: 'Tomorrow, you shall know everything…' And until now, you have protected me against anxiety. If you're beginning to dread…"

"Oh, I'm not afraid," said Nina. "Everything he does is done well. If there's a battle, so much the better: he'll be victorious!"

"A battle?" Angélie repeated.

But the capricious zingara was no longer in a mood to explain herself. In her turn, she put her brunette head in her friend's knees, and murmured her cradle song for a second time, like a child who wants to go to sleep.

Sleep, little flower of my heart,
Perfume of the garden of love,
Of the garden that is ours!

"But why did you say that to me?" she said, interrupting herself and suddenly sitting up.

"What?"

"Why did you say that he alone can save you?"

Her large dark eyes, curious and bright, were fixed n Angélie's. The latter's eyelids lowered their long lashes over her cheeks, to which a slight blush rose.

"Did I say that?" she stammered

"Come on! I was asking you why you needed to be saved when the doctor suddenly showed himself."

"What doctor?" asked Angélie, instead of replying.

"The man who has sworn to kill Fulvio."

"And you're calm in saying that?" cried the beautiful Doria, already shivering.

"There are twenty who have sworn that oath," replied the zingara, in a disdainful tone, "and twenty who have died trying. But answer me, answer me quickly!"

Her petulant little foot stamped on the gilded sand of the grotto.

Angélie did not reply immediately. Her charming face expressed a painful embarrassment. She would have liked to speak, but dared not. She needed to open up, but something closed her mouth authoritatively.

"You don't trust me, then, Comtesse?" said Nina, offended.

La Doria still maintained silence. Then, suddenly, her beautiful hands covered her face, and shone, inundated by her tears.

Nina put her arms around her. "Darling, darling!" she said, as tender and good as a mother, "don't cry...you're going to be happy...whatever they do. I swear to you that you'll be happy!"

"Oh, Nina!" stammered Angélie, her voice intercut with veritable sons. "If you knew...!"

"Tell me everything...quickly, very quickly."

"I can't...I'd never dare..."

"Dear fool!" And she added, all smiles: "Wouldn't one think that she had some enormous sin on her conscience?"

At that word, Angélie hid her burning face in her friend's bosom. "I haven't done anything!" she cried, as if to deny an accusation had wounded her in the utmost depths of her heart. "Do I know what there is in me? I'm mad!"

"But what's the matter, Comtesse?" said Nina, finally frightened and serious.

"She has a brother," Angélie stammered, so quietly that the zingara divined rather than heard it.

"A brother!" she repeated, perhaps understanding already, but doubting her own intelligence. "Who has a brother?"

"That young woman," murmured Angélie, whose mouth stifled her words in the folds of Nina's blouse.

"What young woman?"

"You know very well who I mean."

"The young woman of the Folquieri house?"

"Yes."

That *yes* was lost in the flowery gauze. There was a silence. Angélie felt her friend's heartbeat and sat up.

"I don't love him!" she cried. "No! I'm ready to swear it...and how could I love him, since he belongs to God? I don't love him...but I'm very unhappy."

Her eyelids lowered under Nina's gaze, which depicted a profound stupefaction.

"Oh!" she said. "You don't love him...!"

Then, with a kind of severe indignation, for the idea of any rivalry between Coriolani and another man revolted that enslaved heart: "But what about him? What about Fulvio?"

"Oh, him I love!" cried Angélie. "I'm sure of it! And I've loved him for a long time! Did I even know that the heart beats before having seen him? He came toward me, I've told you that often...the music of the waltz had plunged me into a kind of dream. I could no longer see anything, and the ball became a confused dazzle before my eyes.

"Our cousin Malatesta was sitting beside me. He was telling me that I was beautiful. The words that were falling from Malatesta's mouth I put into the mouth of the man who was coming toward me, so pale and proud that I thought I was seeing a hero of ancient legend.

"And—do I know how to say it myself?—so much gentleness amid his pride...his eyes were on mine and by means of their radiance, his entire soul flowed no mine...to capture it, Nina, my poor childish soul, to take it away, to leave I know not what anxious and dolorous void that his presence changes into joyous plenitude.

"I no longer remember. Did he speak to me? Why would he have spoken to me? His eyes had taught mine the unknown and mute language. Oh, I already knew full well that I was his! He carried me off like a prey. I can still see the glance of hatred that Malatesta darted at him.

"I hate him, that Malatesta! I cherished him like a brother; we had been brought up together.

"When I hear that waltz, I feel myself dying. My heart signs involuntarily. Nina, believe me, I love him, I love him! My head leant on his shoulder. I felt his heartbeats. Oh, mine was racing! Once, the wind of his breath came into my hair. His arms lifted me up then, for I was collapsing, dying..."

The zingara wiped her brow, which was bathed with sweat. A profound sigh elevated her breast.

"You love him," she said, as if talking to herself. "There is something in you that I didn't suspect...you've never shown me the corner in which your heart scintillates."

"Nothing!" Angélie went on. "Not a word...after the waltz, I didn't see him again. A month later, on the Messina boat, he said to me: 'If God comes to my aid, my beloved, my wife, your life will be paradise.' And since that time, we've been betrothed before the Lord. He's my master, and all my hope is in him..."

"But then," said the zingara, "If you love like that...like the beautiful and ardent soul that you are, darling...why did you talk to me about the brother of that young woman?"

"Because I'm suffering, Nina...because there's something incomprehensible and fatal. Fulvio's absence leaves me defenseless...when he's no longer there, I doubt him and myself."

"Explain yourself..."

"Just now, I said that to you," murmured the beautiful Doria, who had a melancholy smile amid her half-dried tears. "Just now, I also said to you: I don't understand, and perhaps soon, you won't understand me yourself. How can I explain the inexplicable?"

"You're talking about doubt..."

"Yes, doubt...it's only via that word that you'll arrive at my thought. Myself, I don't know the Fulvio that I love...I don't know him, Nina, my dearest friend. When he's no longer there, I don't know, I'm afraid...that mysterious past frightens me...what I know about it, that life of temporary amours and mad passions."

"Isn't it a beautiful lot and a beautiful role," the zingara interjected, "to be the salvation of that great lost soul?"

"Oh yes! And God is my witness that it's my consolation and my pride. But...but you haven't understood me yet, Nina."

"I've understood everything that you've said, Comtesse." That was pronounced in a colder tone. And, as Angélie was silent, the zingara continued. "If it's necessary to divine..."

"No, no!" said Angélie, swiftly. "What I'm asking of you is to have pity for me. I'm suffering, I tell you."

In her turn, the zingara remained silent

"Well," the beautiful Doria went on, wiping her eyes with a melancholy resolution, "I'll speak, then. I've seen that young woman. I agree with you...she's more beautiful than you and me, because there's I know not what divine aureole around her candor. I saw her, one evening at benediction, at the San Gennaro hospice for the poor. I asked who she was. They replied: 'She's the sister of the young saint...'"

"Aha!" said the zingara.

"Don't mock!" ordered Angélie. "I won't suffer any mockery in his regard."

"Oho!" said Nina, in a different tone.

"That's the way it is...judge me as you please. I'm in pain, but my conscience has nothing to hide from the Virgin Mary, the consoling saint of the afflicted. When they replied to me: 'He's the sister of the young saint...'"

"You wanted to see the young saint."

"That true. He was shown to me. He was kneeling near the balustrade. His long blond hair, flattened against his temples, fell in strands over his poor straight and stiff soutanelle. He can't be much older than me, and his virile development hasn't yet come. And I even made a comparison within myself between that humble, indigent and pious child prostrate in his faith before the Lord...between that modest, gentle, tranquil seminarian, whose soul had only ever had thoughts of mercy...and the brilliant cavalier who is to be my husband..."

"Comparisons have their danger," murmured Nina.

"You're mistaken, my girl...and although you'd like to mock, you'd be mistaken...my heart was calm while I made that comparison. I only said to myself: 'There are some who have their paradise in this world...'"

"Which of the two has paradise?" asked the zingara.

Angelique was astonished. Evidently, in her first thought, the word paradise was applied to the brilliant existence of Fulvio Coriolani.

"You're right," she replied. "That's a good question...and now that I think about it, I'll go further: it isn't even a question. The other manifestly has the advantage, down here, as on high."

The zingara bit her lip.

"But let me speak," Angélie went on. "Do you know why they've given him that name: the young saint? No, you don't know. No one knows that, except the poor. As he has nothing on the earth, the pious child, except his soutanelle and his prayer book, it's his life, his health and his slumber that he gives as alms to the suffering. The great San Gennaro, the great patron of our cathedral, buried the dead, and that was all. This one has devoted is nights to the indigent sick; his repose belongs to them. Every evening, he's seen to quit his humble attic in order to run to the hospital, where his place is marked at the bedsides of the dying and the desperate. At is approach, the evil angel flees; the good angel is there...and when Death does not want to yield her prey to his ardent prayers, it is consoled and conciliated souls that fly up to heaven."

"That's beautiful," said the zingara, "but who told you that?"

"A saved soul! A poor old beggar-woman who was dying blaspheming, and who is now alive, bearing her heavy cross without a murmur, her gaze fixed on the celestial realm, where the last are the first."

"And it's that miracle of the young saint that has troubled your heart?"

Angélie did not reply directly to that question. Her voice became softer, and a veil of reverie descended over her charming face.

"I told you," she murmured, "that he was kneeling near the balustrade of the choir; his back was turned to me. His head was bowed over his joined hands, and his entire pose spoke eloquently of the Christian favors that filled his soul. I looked at him, it's true. On seeing him, I remembered my pious mother, whose forehead was inclined like that when her thoughts rose toward God. I envied that faith, that ardor, the delights of that sincere devotion. Suddenly, the hour chimed. He awoke from his ecstasy; he turned round..."

"Is he handsome?" Nina asked.

Angélie was very pale. Her voce trembled. "It seemed to me that I was having a dream," she said, passing her hand over her eyes. "You're asking me whether he was handsome? How was Fulvio, the most beautiful man that I've encountered in my life, in the days of his candid adolescence? You know that, Nina; I don't."

Nina smiled, and her eyes shone. "The head of Sanzio and the body of Meleager," he said.

"Look at the young saint if you find him in our path," La Doria went on. "Look at Julian..."

"Ah!" said Nina. "You know his name!"

"Yes," Angélie replied, simply. "I only heard it once, but I shall never forget it. Look at Julian, as I say, and you'll see what I saw: Fulvio's features rejuvenated, Fulvio's features, not embellished, but softened, and crowned with I know not what seraphic aureole. He's Fulvio adolescent, Fulvio timid and pure. Listen! If it were possible for my heart to beat for a child consecrated to altars, Fulvio would again be the cause of my misfortune...it's Fulvio that I love in him..."

Nina was no longer laughing. Her half-closed eyelids hid the radiance of her large dark eyes.

"Is that all?" she said.

"No, that isn't all," replied Angélie. "Julian also perceived me, placed as I was not far from the lamp of the Virgin. When our gazes met, he tottered as if a blow had struck him in the heart. He stopped. He held himself up on a column. Then, lowering his eyes and paler than the marble of statues, he fled."

"Is that all, this time?"

"Not yet. A memory awoke in me. It wasn't the first time that I'd seen him. Last year, during our passage through Calabria, we were at the inn of the Corpo-Santo..."

"Could it be him...?" cried the zingara.

Angélie looked at her, astonished.

"Don't open such wide eyes, Contessina," said the zingara, resuming her jocular tone. "It isn't from today that I love you and I'm not unaware of anything that concerns you. I'm asking you whether it's him who fired at the assassins?"

"Not him, but his sister."

"Oho! That's a young saint and a beauty with whom it's necessary to occupy oneself!" said Nina, as if talking to herself. "There's a destiny!" Then, taking Angélie's hands in hers, she said, gaily: "We young women are all mad for at least one day in our life. You're in your day, my lovely Comtesse. I'm trivial myself, you know, and I remember a fable in which one sees an honest dog in suspense between his prey and a shadow. The dog releases the prey, and repents of it, because he didn't even have the shadow..."

They both shivered, and the zingara's speech was suddenly cut off. The grotto was filled by a sudden din. Hundreds of detonations had just burst forth simultaneously outside, echoed and inflated by the subterranean walls.

"The fireworks already!" exclaimed Nina, getting up. "They were only to be fired when the King entered. The King is here!"

"And Fulvio?"

"Fulvio is doubtless looking for you. Come on, let's hurry."

They took one another by the hand and headed for the entrance to the grotto.

Close to the entrance, a man was standing. Angélie recognized him as the masked individual who had previously introduced himself into the grotto, where the superintendent Visconti-Armellino had joined him. As they went past him, the zingara said, in a light and sarcastic tone: "Greetings, savant doctor Pier Falcone!"

V. Peter-Paulus' Hundred Thousand Ducats

The two young women had replaced their masks before quitting the grotto. The man whom the zingara greeted by the name Pier Falcone remained completely impassive.

"He hasn't budged," said Angélie. "You're mistaken."

Nina released her arm and advanced resolutely toward the unknown man. "I'll know what color his words are!" she murmured. And taking the masked man's hand in accordance with the ritual that we have already described several times, she whispered in his ear: "Iron is strong and charcoal is black."

There was no response, except that the masked man showed her his hand, where there was an iron ring. Nina recoiled.

She returned to Angélie, very pensive, and said to her: "You're right; I was mistaken." But she added to herself: *It's definitely him! What's happened? He's Barbe Spurzheim's doctor. Has Johann died tonight? Has he stolen his ring of the Silence?*

She turned round in order to look at the masked man again. He had disappeared.

Meanwhile, the aspect of the garden of the Palazzo Doria-Doria had changed completely in an hour; the vicinity of the grotto of Endymion was now deserted, and the crowd of guests was massed on the far side of the belvedere, where the fireworks were being let off.

It is from Italy that we obtain that fashion of playing with fire and transforming conflagration into a savant keyboard capable of producing for the eye the ecstasies that an orchestra provides for the sense of hearing. Volcanoes have doubtless taught humans that prodigious art of scoring the lightning and tying tamed thunder in sheaves.

The entire north side of the garden was a vast dazzle, and against that splendid background, the belvedere profiled the light arabesques of its oriental architecture. Toward the south, by contrast, everything was pale. The moon, in its last quarter, was rising as deformed and truncated as the unpolished medallions that are found in the foundations of ancient monuments. Its irregular disk was half-revealed behind Mount Somma. The vapors of Vesuvius, which had been threatening an eruption for several days, gave it a somber and funereal tint.

It was impossible to find a more violently emphatic contrast. Here there was a glory in which inexhaustible radiance sprang forth, there a dull sky veiling its livid moon behind a shroud.

Nina felt Angélie's arm shudder under hers.

"What's the matter, darling?" she asked.

The beautiful Comtesse pointed at the sinister firmament and murmured: "One might think it a threat of misfortune."

Nina forced her to make a detour. "In life," she replied, "it's always necessary to look on the bright side. What does a mourning matter that one doesn't see?"

As they drew closer to the place where the fireworks were, they found the crowd again. But the crowd did not seem to be paying much attention to the firework display, which was lavishing its ardent rains and its bouquets of light in vain. The crowd was agitated and anxious, whispering. It had divided into groups, like the people in the streets during the fatal hours of revolutions.

As they traversed the groups, Nina and Angélie heard what was being said.

"Doria is as somber as a stormy day."

"The King hasn't come..."

"Unless he's here incognito."

"The Royal Prince hasn't been seen."

"Coriolani hasn't reappeared."

"Malatesta's friends are waiting for him."

"What's going on here tonight?"

Angélie trembled.

Suddenly, there was a more general rumor. A name ran from group to group with lightning rapidity. In her turn, Nina shuddered. That name was Il Porporato.

"Il Porporato," someone said, "was murdered yesterday evening."

"In his prison?"

"In the street."

"He had been taken out of his cell?"

"He had escaped."

"Has his corpse been found?"

"Was that Baron d'Altamonte really Il Porporato?"

"Who did it...?"

"The police...?"

"The Companions of the Silence...?"

All those questions, which had no responses, overlapped.

Scarcely had Angélie Doria and Nina, her companion, quit the Grotto of Endymion, than the cries of a frightened peacock were heard in the subterranean path that descended from the belvedere. A woman hurtled into the grotto—a woman dressed in bright rose-pink, celestial blue, amaranth and orange. She was being pursued by a domino as long as a greasy pole, who was taking enormous strides and breathing more heavily than a blacksmith's bellows. The woman had a start, because the maladroit domino was hampered by the long pleats of his silk garment. Just as he was about to seize the fugitive, a burst of stifled laughter was heard a few paces away from them. They saw two dominos emerge from the shadow, arm in arm.

"That officer!" cried Penelope, blushing.

"That malefactor!" said Peter-Paulus Brown, for his part.

The two newcomers pronounced in unison, and gravely, in pure English: "Iron is strong, charcoal is black!"

"Gentlemen," Peter-Paulus replied, politely, "what you say is quite true."

"Make the response," ordered the shorter of the two men, still in English.

"I have made the response, Gentlemen," replied Peter-Paulus. "I said that your formula is incontestably true."

"You can't say anything but that?"

"Oh, I've said everything, Gentlemen."

"Do you have the diamond with you?"

"I bought a diamond, Gentlemen, for five hundred and eighty-six pounds sterling, for the occasion of milady's marriage to me."

"It's very romantic and theatrical," Penelope murmured, in her companion's ear.

The latter replied: "I beg you to shut up for the moment."

The fact is that the moment was solemn. The shorter of the two dominos, the one who was versed in the language of Pope and Milton, raised his finger in a threatening gesture.

"All this is unclear," he pronounced, severely. "The association has no confidence in you. I warn you that from this moment on, all your actions will be watched. If you attempt to dispose of the Punjab to anyone but us, it will cost you your life."

"I'll give you the Punjab!" cried Peter-Paulus, with tears in his voice. "And the entirety of Hindustan! I'm an English subject, Gentleman, and a member of the Cotton and International Club! I'll tell my government positively that you've attempted to play with me...and milady! I'd like to get out of this abominable country!"

"We forbid you to do that" retorted the shorter of the two men.

"Oho! I'm free!" said Peter-Paulus, whose cheeks were inflated and whose nose was flicking from right to left like a weather-vane in a variable wind. "I'll defend my liberty to the last drop of my blood, by God!"

"Oh! Shocking!" said milady, at that oath.

"I said, shut up for the moment. I'm talking to these gentlemen."

The two dominos consulted one another. The shorter one put an end to the discussion by saying: "Be prudent, and above all keep quiet about everything that has happened tonight, if you want to avoid misfortune. Even if you're not the person we were expecting, you belong to us, since you've divined a part of our secrets. Go back to your hotel, don't come out again, and tomorrow, the council will inform you of its will."

The two dominos withdrew, marching at he measured pace that actors permit themselves in great circumstances.

"I say!" cried Penelope. "That was very dramatic."

Peter-Paulus let himself fall on to a grassy bank in order to wipe away the sweat that was bathing his yellow hair.

"It's prodigious!" he murmured, with discouragement. "Voyagers, the guides and the itineraries are criminal for having kept silent about the dangers of this surprising land. I said to you, milady, shut up. I want to reflect...formally!"

Outside the din of the fête had ceased. The fireworks had extinguished heir capricious dazzlement, and the belvedere now designed its illuminated lines against the black sky. Toward the west, the moon was rising slowly in the sky behind the menacing vapors of the volcano, which as veiled by mourning. Only a few rare groups were circulating here and there in the pathways between the myrtles, orange-tress and oleanders. The garden was almost deserted. On the other hand, the orchestras had fallen silent. Through the colonnades surrounding the palazzo, the immobile an mute host of guests was visible n the drawing rooms. All of them were there.

For anyone who had witnessed the noisy beginning of the fête, the sight of that noble house, still brilliant with light, but now silent, would have seemed full of sorrows and threats. Something was happening over there, something terrible, which had caused both the suave voice of the musical instruments and the insouciant laughter of the crowd to fall silent. Among those hectic joys, tragedy had shown its pale mask, and pleasure, terrified, had fled...[47]

---

[47] Something is obviously missing from the story here, especially given the provocatively enigmatic title of the present chapter. In the version of the text that I am translating, no information is ever given as to how Peter-Paulus disposed of Felice Tavola's body, how he acquired his black domino and how he got into the grounds of the Palazzo Doria. I suspect that a section of the original text is missing from the Phébus edition, but the issues of the *Journal Pour Tous* in which the story was serialized are not on *gallica*---they are presumably missing from the Bibliothèque Nationale collection—and no copy of the 1857 book edition issued in Paris in 9 volumes by A. Cadot is accessible either, so I cannot be certain that the missing text was present in the serial, or when it went missing from subsequent texts if it was.

VI. The Marquis de Malatesta

There was also a décor of tragedy: immense drawing rooms in the broad and open style that modern Italy has borrowed from antique memories; outside, long white colonnades whose pure pedestals were surrounded by flower-baskets, and terraces with Attic balustrades, which the nocturnal breeze perfumed in passing; inside, marble paneling with severe and gracious moldings, ceilings illustrated by the hands of masters, the treasures of art, paintings or sculptures, with which Italian wealth is so prodigal.

Everyone knew that the King of Naples was incognito that night at the Palazzo Doria. No one had greeted or seen him, but his arrival had given the signal for the fireworks. As for the princes of the royal family, they had all shown themselves several times that night. The hereditary Prince, Francis de Bourbon, had been seen, as well as his younger brother, Léopold de Bourbon, Prince of Salerno, and the princesses, the king's daughters.

Although royal etiquette was not in force that evening, because of the King's incognito, a relative silence reigned in the august enclosure and its surroundings. The ball had reached its conclusion, and an army of valets was serving the Roman liqueur in which snow refreshes the ardent tafia of the Antilles.

Around the princesses, a grave circle of Statesmen was arranged. The princesses were talking about sermons and opera, as practiced in Italy and elsewhere. God knows that the Statesmen were talking about. The Statesmen of Naples do not weigh much in the balance of European destinies. The King does everything in that land, where a number of things are not done well. I do not believe that the name of a single Neapolitan minister has crossed the Tyrrhenian Sea to strike continental ears for thirty years. Perhaps they were talking about the police—that is a big thing out there—or perhaps horses, for the leprosy of the English conquest is beginning to take hold in southern Italy; or perhaps gaming, for the Neapolitans are gamblers. Whatever they were talking about, the voices were discreet and contained. No outburst troubled the calm conversation of the princesses and their court.

The conversation was even quieter in the drawing room to the left, the Giorgione Room. Here, eight or ten young men, all masked, were gathered.

At first sight, it would have been difficult to say what they were doing massed in the darkest corner of the gallery. Were they conspiring? Against whom? Were they nor rather preparing to stage, to employ the theatrical expression, some dramatic work.

They were talking, they were gesticulating, and they seemed, in truth, to be distributing roles. One of them, a very handsome young man, to whom the principal employment reverted, had parted the lining of his domino and was displaying a costume as rich as it was gallant. The others were addressing him as Marquis, and we would easily have recognized him as the mysterious conspirator who had made the bizarre oath in the bushes: "He will only leave here dishonored or dead, even if it's necessary to give my honor or my life for that!"

In the drawing room to the right and those that followed, people were playing an infernal game.

"A hundred gold ounces!" cried someone at the nearest table. "Vicente Capelli is lacking a hundred gold ounces. Will you make them up, Malatesta?"

The man who had been so often addressed as Marquis, who was Giulio Doria d'Angri, Marquis de Malatesta, turned his head, but one of his companions answered for him.

"Malatesta's playing another game tonight."

"You're spoiling him, Sampieri," someone said. "What will become of Malatesta if he corrects his vices?"

Sampieri retorted, testily: "Mind your own business, Balbi, believe me…leave us to ours." He turned to his companions and added, lowering his voice: "If he doesn't come, so much the better. You know the proverb: the absent are always wrong."

They were all young men of the highest Italian nobility; the previous evening, they had held an orgy at the Palazzo Malatesta and had come to Lorédan Doria's house after drinking. One cannot say, however, that they were drunk. The orgy, already distant, had left no other traces in them but fatigue of the brain and the somber fever that faithfully follows excesses of the table. If they had taken off their masks you would have seen all those young faces pale and drawn. But their pallor was not only a reaction to drunkenness.

Those lords were called Sampieri and Mareschalci, both from Bologna and both princes; Vespuccio Doria and Pitti, of Florence; Colonna, of Rome; Ziani, of Venice and Gravina, of Naples. There was not a single name there that was not historic and illustrious. And although passion was driving them, the passion that has the most subtle sting of all, conscience, told them that what they were about do would not add to their glory. Sad work for the sons of Italian chivalry! Great hatred and venomous and moral rancor founded on too frivolous a motive!

Certainly, the Italian conscience does not have a very loud voice. It is a long time since the heroic age came to an end out there. And yet, those young men, who were the sons of giants, were ashamed. That shame, however, which wrung their hearts, did not have the strength to stop them.

They had united there against a man. It was emperors and kings that their forefathers had fought; they were in league ten against one, and they were also calling treason to their aid. Sword in hand, each of them was brave. They had come together to commit a cowardly and tenebrous act. They had come together in order to stage—we used the right word just now—one of those homicidal comedies that kill other than and better than the dagger.

Their stage-setting was regulated in advance. They were taking their positions; running through their final rehearsal. And why where they taking up the abject weapon of cunning, those men who were young, who were strong, who had shown themselves sensitive twenty times in their lives to what they called so naively points of honor? Because they were afraid of their adversary? Certainly, none of them would have admitted it. But perhaps, in fact, they were afraid of their adversary; they had reason to be.

That man was one of those whose life marches like a triumph: a habitual victor who did not yet know, after a hundred battles, the meaning of the word defeat. He was the happy and glorious conqueror, the unknown of yesterday whose name sounds like a fanfare today in all deafened ears. He was the living splendor, the human sun whose radiance put all rival renown in the shade. He was Prince Fulvio Coriolani, the folly of the Neapolitan people and the star of the court: the man whose mere presence made the smile of all those beautiful princesses softer and more pensive; the demigod that all young marquises saw in their dreams; the noble and courteous intelligence who set the pace of high society, as they say in London; the fulgurant épée whose thrusts no rapier had yet been able to parry.

That man was the pride of his partisans, the sultan of changing and ever-fortunate amours, the favorite cavalier of the Queen and her daughters; the friend of the Royal Prince; the favorite of the King.

No, it was not entirely out of fear that our conspirators had thrown away the word in order to take up the net in that desperate hunt. It was by virtue of excess of hatred and in order better to ensure their coup.

But what had he done to them, that splendid young man? Why so much irreconcilable aversion? There was an unpardonable crime.

Before the advent of Fulvio Coriolani, all those young lords, Malatesta, Sampieri, Mareschalci, Vespuccio, Pitti, Colonna, Ziani, Gravina and others, had shone. What becomes of the poor stars when the sun rises over the horizon? What place is left for the vanquished population of secondary stars by the insolent radiance of Phoebus Apollo?

Malatesta was evidently the principal actor in the drama that was about to be played. His companions were surrounding him and encouraging him. It appeared that his role was difficult.

"I'd prefer to have him there in front of me," he said, replying to Sampieri's last words. "I don't like attacking people from behind."

"You weren't fortunate, Marquis," replied Colonna, "when you attacked him from the front."

Sampieri hastened to speak, in order to avert the bitter argument that could not fail to break out. "Peace, Colonna!" he said. "You, Malatesta, listen. The lot fell to you; it's you who must strike the great blow. But if you don't have the heart, say so. I'll put our names back into the urn and we'll draw again."

"Any of you who thinks himself braver than me," replied Malatesta "has only to come to the right of the Porta Capuana at daybreak. If he comes back, he'll give you news of me."

"Take care, Marquis," said Grimani and Gravina at the same time. "Those who boast are afraid."

Sampieri interposed himself again. "It's not a matter of bravery," he said. "Everyone is brave with a rapier in his hand. What we need is firmness, composure, and presence of mind. At the present moment, Marquis, do you have all that?"

"I have all that," Malatesta replied.

"Show us your face," said the Florentine Pitti, "for your voice is trembling and you aren't upright on your legs."

Malatesta took a step backwards and raised his hand. Sampieri stopped him again. For an observer, it would have been easy to divine that all those young hotheads were exciting Malatesta, as one does for bulls before a contest.

He took off his mask with a convulsive movement. His face was livid but his eyes were burning. He was a handsome young man of twenty-four or twenty-five. Without the stigmata that the orgy too so commenced had left on his features, his resemblance to his cousin Lorédan Doria would have been striking. The spur became unnecessary; everyone could see that clearly. The bull was sufficiently excited.

Sampieri smiled behind his mask on seeing the fringe of foam blanching those convulsively contracted lips, and the bloody line bordering the eyelids. "Good, Marquis, good!" he said, extending his hand to him. "I knew, personally, that the son of your father could not tremble."

"I forbid you to talk about my father here," murmured Malatesta, lowering his eyes. "But," he added, "if my father had had that man facing him, perhaps he would have done as we are doing."

"Certainly! Certainly" was cried on all sides. "Our case is good, Marquis; no scruples!"

An hour after midnight chimed on the clock of the Palazzo Doria.

"It's time," said Sampieri. "The King might leave."

Two or three voices asked: "Are you ready, Marquis?"

"I'm ready," Malatesta replied.

"Have you learned your role?"

"If my memory fails," said Malatesta, with a bitter smile, "you have only to prompt me, my brothers."

There was an instant of hesitation in the group.

The Marquis had just passed his hand over his forehead, bathed with sweat.

"You're trembling with fever, Marquis!" murmured Pitti.

"You don't dare, Malatesta," said another.

He raised himself up to his full height. "Signors," he said, with a certain nobility in his voice, "you've detested that man for longer than I have. If he hadn't taken the heart of the woman I love, I sense that I might have been his friend. There's only my blood here that has reddened his sword. He has stolen my happiness. Let me pale if I am ashamed, let me tremble if I'm afraid; one can strike while trembling; I swear that I shall strike."

All hands sought his, and someone cried: "Bravo, Malatesta!"

That was like the signal for a battle long prepared. There was a movement among the conspirators, who traversed the hall in small groups and took up various combat posts, some inside and others outside the high vaulted door of the Albano drawing room, where the court was. In the later drawing room, almost everyone was unmasked, out of respect for the princesses.

Sampieri, in the second lead role, especially charged with responding to Malatesta, remained with him under the vault. Colonna and Mareschalci went into the drawing room; Pitti, Ziani and Gravina formed the center of three groups. There was a great silence, during which the conversation of the princesses could be heard. They were talking about the handsome, the great, the seductive, the incomparable Coriolani.

"Do you hear that?" whispered Sampieri. "Each of our words will strike like a thunderbolt. Are you ready?"

"I'm ready."

"Begin."

Immediately, Malatesta adopted very loudly, and better than might have been expected, the one of a discussion already begun.

"If you don't believe me," he said, "I'll prove it to you."

"How will you prove it, Marquis?" asked Sampieri, similarly in a loud voice, and in a provocative tone.

A few indifferent individuals were already turning their heads to discover what difference was about to surge forth between that hothead Malatesta and that other hothead Domenico Sampieri, Comte Sampieri della Romana.

At that moment, the Princess of Salerno said: "But what can have become of him tonight?"

"It's evidently a very serious matter," replied the Comte de Castro-Giovanni, a cousin of the king privileged in Sicily, "to retain our dear Fulvio way from the Palazzo Doria at this moment."

While saying that he looked at Comtesse Angélie.

The Princess of Salerno made and affectionate sign to the latter to approach. Angélie obeyed.

There was a murmur of admiration in the Albano drawing room when people saw the respectful and gracious fashion in which the beauty of beauties approached the princess, the daughter-in-law of the King. The latter embraced her, smiling, and whispered in her ear: "My dear cousin, extract us from embarrassment and tell us where he is."

Blushing from her forehead to her breast, Angélie lowered her eyes and replied: "Highness, among the secrets that the Prince doesn't tell me, it's necessary to place the good that he does. Only God and he know."

Nina Dolci, sitting at the feet of her mistress, blew her a kiss. The Princess made room for her beside her.

In the meantime, Malatesta and Sampieri were arguing in low voices, with an increasing vivacity. Others were beginning to draw nearer and mingle with the argument. The curious opened their ears.

Suddenly, Malatesta cried: "A thousand gold ounces if you wish!"

"Two thousand if you like!" riposted Sampieri.

"What is it? What is it?" said the bystanders. The court had not yet paid attention.

"I tell you that I know it!" said Malatesta, with a hint of bitterness.

"What is it? What is it?" repeated the curious, whose anxious circle was thickening around the door.

"Sampieri sustains that he has the right to call himself thus," replied Colonna, entering the stage in his turn.

"But who are they talking about?"

"What!" said Colonna. "Don't you know?"

"They're talking," replied Pitti, shrugging his shoulders, "about Prince Fulvio Coriolani."

"That's absurd!" added Ziani.

And Gravina added, sententiously: "That Marquis de Malatesta is incorrigible!"

"Blood of Christ!" cried Malatesta. "Why isn't he here? You'd see the figure he'd cut!"

"Don't insult someone who's absent!" said Balbi.

"If Signor Balbi wants to take in hand the defense of a wretch and a bandit," cried Malatesta, in a voice that was suddenly thunderous, "he's free to do so: I stand by what I say!"

It was necessary for the court finally to pay attention. A hundred people were massed around the door.

The Princess of Salerno demanded, as many others had done before her: "What is it?"

"If it please Your Royal Highness," replied Mareschalci, bowing respectfully, "someone is accusing Prince Coriolani of having stolen his name."

The Mareschalcis are great lords.

"And who dares to advance such an insolence?" exclaimed Marie-Clementine of Austria.

Mareschalci replied: "It's our Lorédan's cousin, Giulio Doria d'Angri, Marquis de Malatesta."

"And he's saying that seriously?" said Comte de Castro-Giovanni.

"Very seriously, Highness. He's even saying things much graver...also very seriously."

All the faces of the ladies of the court were uniformly painted with indignation. Angélie Doria was as pale as a corpse. As for Signora Nina Dolci, the reader must suppose that she was the most indignant of all, but we are obliged to say that she did not seem so. She was leaning familiarly on the arm of her mistress' chair, fanning her smiling and charming face with an air of perfect tranquility.

There were only three people mingling with the crowd, and assembled by a corner of the vaulted the door, who were as calm as she was at that moment. They were Andrea Visconti-Armellino, the superintendent of the royal police, the great banker Massimo Dolci, Signora Nina's uncle, and the cavalier Ercole Pisani. Behind them stood the old soldier, Colonel San-Severo, who seemed, on the contrary, to be prey to a violent agitation

"Where is the Comte, then?" asked the Princess of Salerno. "It's necessary to put a stop to this scandal."

"If Her Royal Highness desires…," commenced Castro-Giovanni.

But he did not finish. A hand fell on his shoulder from behind, and a voice murmured in his ear: "I'm here, Signor, and I'm listening!"

He had recognized Lorédan Doria, masked and confounded in the ranks of the court.

Meanwhile, as always happens in these circumstances, a great silence had gradually fallen around the two principal interlocutors. Each of them desired to be heard henceforth. Even the court, in spite of its prejudices in favor of the handsome Fulvio, fell silent and became attentive

"I'm sorry," Malatesta was saying at that moment, with an evident intention of sarcasm, "that the matter has gone so far. I wanted to talk, but my intention was not to make a public accusation…"

"You won't take it any further, your accusation!" grunted San-Severo, between his teeth. Armellino made him a sign to be quiet.

"You've said too much, Marquis, replied the Venetian Ziani, with an apparent severity. "Retract, or give us your proofs."

"You're talking loudly, Signor Ziani!"

"I talk as I must."

"Think…."

"I'm thinking of the place where I am. Everyone at this fête has united more than once the name of the man you're insulting with the cherished and respectable name of Comtesse Angélie Doria."

All that had been agreed in advance. They wanted to set fire to the mine from all sides at once.

"That's true! That's true!" said some. "Ziani is right!"

"Ziani is wrong!" said others. "Why mingle the name of Doria with these quarrels of scatterbrains?"

Sampieri whispered: "Courage, Marquis! The Princesses are listening!" Then he added, in a loud voice: "You've talked a great deal, Malatesta, but you haven't yet said anything!"

"I've accused," Malatesta went on, "the pretended Prince Fulvio Coriolani of having led exactly the same life as that titled rogue who is to be executed tomorrow."

"Oh! Oh!" protested the assembly. "What! Comparing Fulvio to Baron d'Altamonte!"

"Weren't they a pair of friends?" cried Malatesta.

"Who is there among us," objected Sampieri, the good apostle, "who hasn't previously shaken the hand of Baron d'Altamonte?"

Among the courtiers, however, voices said: "What? What? What relationship are you establishing?"

"That Altamonte always had the effect on me of a knight of industry, and I often said, you might recall: 'That Baron d'Altamonte will finish badly.'"

Sampieri had struck home. It gave Malatesta, in fact, the opportunity for this simple reply, which he launched hotly at his adversary: "So, I've said something, Signor Sampieri, since I've advanced...and since I maintain, that Altamonte and Coriolani, Coriolani and Altamonte, are two of a kind!"

There was a new and great murmur. Two new persons were in the front rank of the crowd: a domino with his shoulders curbed by age and an elegantly-clad young man who wore a bearded silk mask. Those who were around the old man stood aside respectfully, save for one companion who was there to support his tottering steps.

The young man had placed himself not far from the four Chevaliers of the Silence. Signora Dolci only needed one glance to recognize him as the mysterious individual who had slipped into the Grotto of Endymion while she was conversing with Angélie Doria: Doctor Pier Falcone.

Malatesta, standing up to the rumor that was disapproving of him from all sides, cried: "I'm mistaken; they're not the same. Altamonte is worth more than Coriolani, because Coriolani had a name: a bandit's name. His name was Felice Tavola...while Coriolani doesn't even have a rogue's name!"

That new outrage remained unechoed.

Malatesta wiped his forehead; his task was rude.

"Courage!" Sampieri whispered to him. "You'll soon be at the end, Marquis. The King is listening!"

VII. Lorédan Doria's Glove

Malatesta had his back turned to the old man, whose curbed spine was hidden under an ample domino of black silk. He had not seen him. When Sampieri said to him: "The King is listening," he shuddered from head to toe.

"Corpo di Bacco!" grunted the tall San-Severo, behind his three colleagues. "I'll become enraged if you don't let me strangle that accursed Marquis!"

"It's the Master's order," replied old Massimo Dolci, half-turning toward him

The Princess of Salerno was quivering with rage. That scene, in the presence of such a gathering of princesses, daughters and daughter-in-law of the King, assuredly had an inexplicable character. It was not hazard alone that could have favored the offensive developments. It was necessary that there was a hidden protection around that insulter.

The Princess heard a supplicant voice in her ear. She turned round. Angélie collapsed in her arms.

"Madame," she murmured, no longer able to hold back her heart-rending sobs, "Lorédan Doria, my brother, is the enemy of Prince Fulvio Coriolani!"

That was a flash of light for Marie-Clementine of Austria. She stood up, searching with her eyes for some high dignitary who could execute her orders. Nina, who continued to fan herself graciously with an air of complete indifference, said to her: "Highness, if it were permitted for me to give you advice, I would suggest that you remain silent."

"Can I suffer that in my presence…?" the proud Austrian began.

"Highness," the zingara interjected, "the Prince, your husband, is here; I've just see him."

"If the Prince of Salerno judges it appropriate to remain silent…"

"The Royal Prince is also present," Nina interjected again.

"Even so…"

"Highness, please look…you will recognize the King behind the Marquis de Malatesta."

The princess fell back into her seat, overwhelmed by amazement. She had, in fact, recognized the King.

It was easy to see, moreover, that the sentiments of the assembly had changed. People were no longer listening with anger, but with a sort of interested curiosity. The news that the royal persons were present behind masks had circulated from mouth to mouth. That took away part of the responsibility from everyone. No one else felt called upon to judge, where the King was. But that increased the interest of the scene enormously.

This was no longer an ordinary duel, such as one can see every day in high places, where interests and passions collide incessantly. It was a matter of one of those solemn combats where the lists are public, where trumpets sound the fanfare to the four winds, where banners are deployed in the sunlight, while the champions make a tour of the barriers with their lances held high and their visors raised. It was an antique joust, with its entourage of princes and noble ladies. It was the ancient judgment of God. For it often happened, in those splendid and barbaric solemnities, that only one of the champions was present. The word that expresses the fact has remained in the mildewed vocabulary of our men of law. The other champion was "in default." And then, after he had been summoned three times, duly and sufficiently, by horn, by cry and in all the customary fashions, the one present, declared the victor, had won the cause: one more proof in favor of the good old proverb: "The absent are always wrong."

Nothing was lacking the tourney, neither the sovereign, spectator and judge, not the noble crowd of witnesses. Everyone that remained in the Palazzo Doria was gathered in the Albano and Giorgione drawing rooms.

In order for the aspect of that brilliant crowd to recall the amphitheater, heads were seen raised in the distance, because the last ranks of the curious had taken possession of benches and chairs.

The guests of the feast of hate that had taken place the day before at Malatesta's house had wanted to cause a sensation. Hazard had come to the aid of their efforts. They had succeeded even beyond their desires.

There was, however, a great silence in the two drawing rooms and the neighboring galleries. The indifferent remained silent henceforth. They were waiting! It was necessary for one of the conspirators to devote himself to giving Malatesta the necessary reply.

"When one accused an absentee," said Colonna, "vague allegations are insufficient."

"Are you appointing yourself Coriolani's defender, Prosper Colonna?" said Malatesta. "I will reply that I have been seeking someone here to whom to speak for some time. My vague allegations, as you call them, repose on positive facts. But to plead a cause, it requires a tribunal. I hoped to find here the august presence of His Majesty King Ferdinand. I would have spoken before the King."

Everyone knew that the King was present. There was a long murmur, but no voice rose up among the guests of the Palazzo Doria to say: "The King is here!" The etiquette, out there, is to respect the royal incognito. It was the King himself, the old man draped in a black domino standing behind the Marquis de Malatesta, who touched his shoulder and said to him, in a low voice: "Marquis, you have judges here. Since you want to speak before the King, speak."

It was in Malatesta's role to feign great astonishment, but he did not have time to make many grimaces. The King went on: "Don't turn round and get to the facts. I'm in a hurry."

There was emotion in the King's tone. Malatesta sensed it, but his boats were burned, and, above all, his lessons were learned. He half-turned, as if involuntarily, in spite of the King's order. His gaze sought courage in the eyes of his colleague Sampieri, and after collecting himself momentarily, he went on:

"Since those who are around me desire that I explain myself, I will do so, even though I have not prepared, and do not have the habit of speaking. I have only one wish, which is that Coriolani appear in our midst before I have said all that condemns and dishonors him. His nocturnal task is finished. He is free henceforth. If he has friends here, let them warn him and let him come.

"I have said and I repeat that Fulvio Coriolani had stolen his name. I have said and I repeat that Fulvio Coriolani is a malefactor disguised as a gentleman, the accomplice of Baron d'Altamonte, one of the members of the mysterious and sanguinary association, the Companions of the Silence."

A stifled cry was heard from the part of the room where the princesses were. It was Angélie Doria, who was struggling against a violent attack of nerves.

Nina Dolci leapt toward her and took her in her arms. "Have no fear!" she whispered in her ear.

Lorédan Doria, who had quit his place, took a step toward his sister. He had unmasked himself since the King had ordered Malatesta to speak. Without intending to, and perhaps without being aware of it, he had gradually drawn nearer to the center of the circle.

The Marquis de Malatesta had pronounced those last words in a precise and assured tone. The emotion of the assembly was great but mute.

In sum, no one could say anything about the past of the brilliant Prince Coriolani. He was like a dazzling meteor who had illuminated the court of Naples a few months ago. But where did he come from? The favor of the King and the royal family was worth as much as a genealogy; that was all. Those meteors always emerge from the clouds.

The King was listening, motionless, under the vast hood of his domino. None of those escorting him had made a gesture.

Opposite the King, Armellino, Ercole Pisani and the rich Massimo stood impassively. One might have thought that they were perfect strangers to what was happening. Colonel San-Severo, by contrast, was furious, and murmured; "Where will this take us? Corpo di Bacco, I don't know how to fight with thrusts of the tongue… But if that fellow is a police spy, Corner, you must know him."

Superintendent Armellino, responding to the name of Corner, commanded him to be silent, "by the will of the Master."

A few paces away, Pier Falcone, his arms folded over his breast, was conscientiously carrying out Johann Spurzheim's orders; he was observing.

"That's good," said Sampieri to Malatesta, who was drawing breath. "Get to the facts right away."

The other conspirators were saying, in the groups: "Is there really something serious underneath this?"

The hardest work was done. Malatesta paraded his gaze over the assembly, and seemed to be provoking its recriminations. He resumed, in a calm and clear voice: "You were all surprised, lords and noble ladies, to see Fulvio Coriolani disappear tonight in the middle of a fête of which he is, in a way, the hero. He could not get out of it. The tenebrous brotherhood to which he belongs punishes the slightest disobedience with death. He received a message at the end of the meal; he left. From that moment on, he belonged to me. I had him followed; I know what he did."

"What did he do?" asked the King.

"Everyone knows" Malatesta replied, "that a man was murdered tonight on the Marinella beach, at the Maddalena bridge. The rumor ran around that the murdered man was Prince Coriolani...the improvisers have said so in the public squares. Even here, in the Palazzo Doria, which he has long soiled with his assiduities, it was repeated, and I saw that beauty go pale, the poor young..."

"I forbid you, Marquis Malatesta," Comte Lorédan interjected loudly, "to make any allusion to my sister Angélie Doria."

The Princess of Salerno squeezed Angélie's hand. "You've misjudged your brother," she said to her.

A voice rose up and said: "Well said, Loredano!"

Better than anyone, Malatesta would have been able to affirm that the voice belonged to the King. A cloud passed before his eyes.

"The wretch has bewitched them all!" he muttered, with a blasphemy.

"Courage, Marquis," replied Sampieri. "We have them, I tell you!"

Malatesta assembled all his firmness in order to continue: "Why was it said that the man murdered at the Maddalena bridge was Coriolani? Because Coriolani had been seen on the Marinella beach, talking to an unknown man in the costume of a mariner. Thus far, no crime, is there? But who was that mariner? That mariner, by the name of Sansovina, as the Minister of State could tell you, boarded a boat moored at the beach, which was waiting for a passenger and was due to set sail for the coast of France. The name of that passenger, you have divined: it was Felice Tavola, alias Baron d'Altamonte."

The man who was next to the King removed his mask. Everyone recognized Francis de Bourbon, the heir to the throne. "Uncover your face, signor," he said to the man standing to his right. That mask, removed, allowed the sight of Carlo Piccolomini, Minister of State.

The Royal Prince added: "Speak, I beg you."

"Highness," replied Piccolomini, "thus far, the Marquis de Malatesta has told the truth: the mariner Sansovina has escaped us, but he was manning a boat intended to favor the escape of Baron d'Altamonte. At eleven o'clock, the boat, aware that it was being watched, raised anchor in order to make a tour of the ports and moor on the far side of the city."

"That's strange," people were saying in all parts of the drawing room.

Nina Dolci whispered in the ear of the reanimated Angélie: "Do you trust me? I swear to you, on my share of paradise, that whoever attacks Fulvio Coriolani will be broken!"

"May God protect him!" murmured Angélie.

The words of the Minister of State had, however, produced a great effect. On listening to them, the superintendent of police had allowed a start of surprise to escape him. It had been the affair of a moment, however. An instant later, Andrea Visconti-Armellino has resumed his attitude of calm indifference between his two impassive companions.

Only Colonel San-Severo, curbing his tall stature in order to put his mouth at the level of the colleagues' ears, repeated in a tone of profound amazement: "How the devil can he know all that?"

Pier Falcone, the observer, began to watch him from the corner of his eye.

"I am glad," continued Malatesta, in a manner already triumphant, "That His Excellency Signor Carlo Piccolomini has deigned to corroborate my words with his irrefutable testimony. I did not expect to receive that aid and, if I dare express myself thus, I had no need of it. What it remains for me to reveal will, in fact, be published tomorrow, and contains grievances that are much more important. The man that I am forced to call Coriolani until we have learned his real name as a malefactor, has committed a murder tonight, perhaps two..."

The entire room was agitated. Angélie Doria uttered a great sigh and fainted in the zingara's arms. The King made a gesture. The Minister of State ordered silence. Something singular was then seen. The Princess of Salerno, who was the favorite among all the young women and daughters-in-law of the King, traversed the entire length of the room, supported on the arm of the Comte de Castro-Giovanni. She came as far as the sovereign and kissed his hand, saying: "I know that it's you, Father, and I beg you, in the name of your tenderness for us all, to put an end to this odious scandal.

The King pushed her aside coldly and said to Malatesta: "Continue!"

"A murder! I'm sure of it," the accuser went on. "Altamonte is dead; I have seen his cadaver; a bullet has traversed his heart. Two murders, I believe, for the man whose blood as shed at the Maddalena bridge was a Companion of the Silence,"

"That is true," said the Minister of State, "But how do you know it?"

"Yes," cried San-Severo, involuntarily, "how does he know it?"

Carlo Piccolomini directed a piercing gaze at him, which also embraced Massimo Dolci and Ercole Pisani. Then he leaned toward the King's ear. Those who were close by thought that they heard the name of Johann Spurzheim pronounced.

That incident gave Malatesta time to collect himself. One is never ready for everything. He had not prepared a response to the question he had been asked.

Given what we have already put into his mouth—and he had not finished—the reader can already be persuaded that Malatesta and his noble comrades knew at least as much as the Minister himself. Perhaps they knew much
more. But from what mysterious source had they obtained that information?
That is what they doubtless could not say.

Old Massimo Dolci stepped heavily on the toes of the good Colonel San-
Severo.

"Would you like to be called by your true name of Luca Tristany within
ten minutes?" he murmured. "Would you like to be hanged at daybreak from the
gallows built for Felice Tavola?"

"I made a mistake," replied San-Severo. "But that rogue David Heimer
must have played us a trick of his trade."

Sampieri saw Malatesta's disturbance.

"We'll find something," he said. "Keep going."

And Malatesta went on, driven by the need to go forward.

"How do I know that, signor? I know other things too...things that might
perhaps surprise you, you who watch over the security of the royal persons, the
court, the city and the realm. Until the last moment, the brotherhood of the Silence maintained Baron d'Altamonte in the hope of being liberated; they had
had succeeded in getting a file to him in his subterranean cell, and the measures
had been so well taken that he would have escaped this evening through the old
tunnel communicating with the crypts of San Giovanni Maggiore if the governor
of the Castello-Vecchio had not transferred him suddenly to the cells of the upper tower. His accomplices learned that. He was convinced that Felice Tavola
would be liberated by force or murdered in his cell.

"That is the rule; at the last moment, even the most hardened sometimes
confess. It was necessary to avoid that. One of the Masters of the Silence was
therefore chosen to accomplish that prodigious tour de force of penetrating into
the fortress, in spite of the garrison, multiplied tenfold, in spite of the guard
posts and the patrols that were defending all the avenues. For that, a demon was
required. They had Coriolani; the fortress was scaled."

Pier Falcone made a movement.

Nina, holding a bottle of smelling salts under Angélie's nostrils, said:
"Highnesses, what will be the punishment of this madman?"

The princesses made no response. They did not believe as yet, but each of
them was thinking: *Not one voice is being raised to defend Prince Fulvio, who is
the King's favorite.*

That was certainly a very strange symptom. And before that symptom, the
apparent extravagance of the accusation vanished, to a large extent.

Malatesta's friends, working hard, were saying: "Who would have thought
it?"

And Sampieri, encouraging him with his gaze and his gesture, murmured:
"Courage, Marquis, we have them!"

It was not courage that Malatesta lacked.

"The fortress was scaled," he went on, "and Signor Piccolomini also knows that. What Signor Piccolomini might not know is that the bandit found his comrade's cell empty.

"Who are you calling the bandit?" demanded the Minister of State.

"Coriolani," replied Malatesta, without hesitation. "He arrived ten minutes too late. The alarm had been given. Two thousand men pursued one single man, and could not catch him. I tell you that the manikin with which children and little women afraid, Il Porporato, has stolen his specter and his crown. The true king of the brigands of Naples is not Porporato but Coriolani."

"Have you finished?" demanded the Minister of State.

"No, signor…and you suspect as much, since ten minutes ago, I heard the sound of bayonets in the gardens of this palace, where all was previously joy, sensuality and harmony. I haven't yet finished, because I haven't yet said how Coriolani killed his brother and friend Baron Altamonte in a cowardly manner."

"Tell us!" ordered the Minister of State.

"Baron Altamonte," replied the Marquis, left the Castello-Vecchio at eleven o'clock. As it was known that Your Excellency was at the Palazzo Doria, he was taken to the house of Signor Johann Spurzheim in the Piazza del Mercato. I need not tell anyone that director Johann Spurzheim's study is preceded by a long dark corridor pierced through the buildings of his house. Baron d'Altamonte was seen entering that corridor…and Prince Coriolani was seen coming out of it, carrying a cadaver over his shoulders."

"Are you accusing Signor Johann Spurzheim?" demanded Piccolomini.

"God forbid!" replied Malatesta. "I'm accusing Fulvio Coriolani, and only him. Fulvio Coriolani has paid his debt to the Companions of the Silence; it was necessary that his friend Altamonte should be free or dead that night. He could not free him, so he murdered him.

Malatesta fell silent. The great and muffled rumor that curiosity had suppressed rose up again.

It is necessary not to place oneself at the standpoint of our French mores to judge the accusation brought here.

Twenty authentic historians, going back no further than the beginning of his century, could be cited, and prove superabundantly the frequency and audacity of the usurpation of names in Italy, Here, these things happen, and no one has forgotten the famous adventure of Colonel Pontis de Sainte-Hélène, arrested in the middle of a review at the head of his regiment in the courtyard of the Carrousel.[48] He was an escaped convict who bore the large epaulettes in a regiment

---

[48] The impostor posing as Philalgo Pontis, Comte de Saint-Hélène was really Pierre Coignard, a volunteer in the Revolutionary Army who had been convicted of theft, but had escaped from the labor camp at Toulon and joined the Spanish guerillas fighting the French. He allegedly acquired the identity papers of the

of the royal guard! But what is in France such a rare exception that it falls, in a sense, into the improbable domain of romance, becomes out there an event that is, if not habitual, at least frequent. The physical constitution of the country, the character of the inhabitants, the proverbial weakness of governments and I know not what tradition that gives the métier of brigand an almost epic coloration, combine to elevate the bandit. The bandit, in southern Italy, is quite naturally a lord. The Apennines have their mysterious chronicles, which swarm with analogous examples. The bandit, who is a king in his mountains, cannot, under pain of grave derogation, descend into cities without taking the title of prince, or at least Comte.

The enterprise of Malatesta and his companions was, therefore, neither absurd nor devoid of chances of success. Only, they were attacking a strong party, and, although there was a certain solidity in their allegation, proving that they were not striking at hazard, there was one capital question to which the Marquis had not responded.

"How do you know all that?" the Minister of State had asked

The good Colonel San-Severo would not have been embarrassed to respond. At that very moment he was saying to his colleagues, who had made him every sign they could to shut up: "I tell you it's that rogue David Heimer!"

In spite of the scant subtlety of his intelligence, Luca Tristany divined the hand of Johann Spurzheim here. Three shrewd individuals like Marino Marchese, Policeni Corner and old Amato Lorenzo, who had become superintendent Armellino, Cavalier Pisani and the royal banker Dolci must, with even more reason, have recognized the intervention in the circumstance of the director of the police, but their role, it appears, was to abstain.

Piccolomini returned to the royal persons who were following him and appeared to take their orders. They were seen conversing in low voices.

In the camp of the princesses there was the silence of stupor. Angélie Doria slowly recovered her senses in Nina's arms.

"What are they saying?" she said. "Have their infamous calumnies been tolerated?"

---

deceased Comte from his mistress and made use of them when taken prisoner by the French, offering his services in return for a commission. He accompanied Louis XVIII in his exile and was promoted to Colonel after the Restoration. He allegedly resumed his criminal career in Paris, secretly directing a gang of burglars headed by his brother, but was denounced by a former convict who had known him in Toulon; he was returned to prison in 1819, where he died in 1834. A play by Charles Desnoyers and Eugène Nus based on his exploits was produced at the Ambigu-Comique in Paris in 1849, which Féval presumably saw; details borrowed from the story are employed in several of his novels, including the Habits Noirs series as well as the present narrative.

"You love him well, Angélie," replied the zingara in a whisper. "You'll love him better in a little while. Have you sometimes seen the sun emerge victorious from the clouds after a tempest? You will see Fulvio Coriolani...he is coming...I can sense him coming!"

But what would certainly have attracted the keen attention of that noble crowd, if each agitated and loquacious group had not been arguing heatedly in the two drawing rooms, was a rapid and highly charged scene that had taken place between Malatesta and his neighbor Sampieri. They had been talking in whispers since the moment when Malatesta had ceased speaking to the assembly.

"Can't I tell them the truth?" demanded the Marquis. "Can't I show them the anonymous letter I received tonight?"

"All would be lost," said Sampieri. "No one believes anonymous letters."

"However..."

"I'll only ask you one question: do you believe it?"

Malatesta seemed to hesitate. Sampieri increased his effort. "Do you believe," he said, "that Fulvio Coriolani, the friend of the King, the fiancé of Comtesse Doria, quit this Palazzo in order to murder Felice Tavola? Do you believe that Fulvio Coriolani is a Companion of the Silence? Do you believe that?"

"No, in truth," replied Malatesta, finally. "I don't believe it. And yet, I'd give three pints of my blood for it to be true."

"Who will believe it if you don't?"

"What are we going to do, hen?"

Their voices lowered further.

"You swore," Sampieri said, "to dishonor him or kill him, at the price of your life or your honor. Your life can do nothing, it only requires your honor..."

"Explain yourself."

For a moment, they whispered so quietly that even the murmur of their voices could no longer be heard.

"Blood of Christ!" cried Malatesta, suddenly, his eyes shining and blushing. "I won't do that!"

"If you don't do it," replied Sampieri, "You're doomed."

"Then I'm doomed, by the death of God! Doomed a hundred times over. I won't do it!"

"Marquis Malatesta," said the minister Piccolomini at that moment, in the midst of a great silence, "where did you obtain the facts that you have advanced?"

"From a good source, Excellency," replied the young marquis, with a wild expression. Sweat was pouring from his temples. It was easy to see that a terrible combat was taking place within him. That did not escape the audience, in whom a reaction was taking place.

"He can't answer!" Colonel San-Severo was the first to cry.

And ten voices repeated: "He can't answer."

"You're agonizing, Malatesta," murmured Sampieri.

"This has gone on long enough!" said the Royal Prince.

And the Princess of Salerno, perhaps ashamed of being momentarily shaken, said: "I hope that man's punishment will be exemplary."

"Malatesta," murmured Sampieri again, "you now have only two seconds to choose between life and death."

Malatesta was livid, and there was foam at the corners of his mouth.

"Answer!" said Piccolomini, for the second time. "You heard; everyone believes that you can't answer."

And the rumor increased. Malatesta's friends were already lowering their heads.

"Answer!" said the Minister of State, for the third time.

"*De profundis!*" whispered Sampieri.

But at that moment, the Marquis raised his head.

"Be content," he said to his accomplice. "I'll dishonor myself!"

There were gray circles around his eyes. Cold sweat was sticking his hair to his hollow cheeks. He was frightful to behold.

"Majesty," he said, addressing the King himself, in a jerky and strangled voice, "you are the first gentlemen of the realm, you will understand why a Doria d'Angri has been slow to respond when it is a matter of soiling the name of his family..."

"Silence! Silence!" was uttered from all directions.

All heads were seen to lean forward, all mouths agape.

Malatesta put his hands to his breast.

"Have you not remarked," he went on, "that Béatrice Doria, my sister, was not at the fête tonight?"

"Good," said Sampieri, who respired deeply.

The princesses quit their seats.

"Coward!" said Nina Dolci, whose eyes were shining.

Pier Falcone had taken a step forward, not to listen, but to look at a domino of tall stature that was standing motionless facing him.

"Let's go," said Sampieri.

"Majesty," said Malatesta, "my sister is the mistress of the bandit Coriolani, who has deceived her...and my sister has betrayed the bandit Coriolani."

There was an inexpressible tumult in the two drawing rooms. Angélie had uttered a long cry of distress. Malatesta, who was tottering, sustained by Sampieri, suddenly saw the haughty and calm figure of Comte Lorédan Doria in front of him. The latter removed his glove slowly.

"Where the King has his mask, he is not the King," he said. "Malatesta, you have lied! Malatesta, you are a coward! Malatesta, since Béatrice Doria has no brother, I, Doria-Doria, the head of the family, become her brother, and I shall avenge an infamous and slanderous accusation."

He raised his arms and flung his glove in the face of the Marquis, while the princesses and the crowd cried: "Bravo, Loredano!"

But the glove did not reach Malatesta's face. A hand advanced and stopped it in flight. That hand belonged to the tall domino that Pier Falcone had been examining with such great attention for several minutes. No one else had noticed it until then. With an abrupt movement, he threw off his costume of floating silk and appeared in a rich court costume.

It was a violent *coup de théâtre*. The cries fell silent, and all that feverish agitation calms down at the sight of the magnificent young man with the stature of Apollo and the head of a king who had unexpectedly revealed his pensive and arrogant face, over which a calm smile drifted.

A name ran from one extremity of the drawing rooms to the other: a dull and profound murmur, in which there was admiration, envy, tenderness and respect.

"Coriolani! Prince Fulvio Coriolani!"

VIII. The King of the Day and the King of the Night

In the drawing rooms of the Palazzo Doria there were only three men whose physiognomies had not changed. They were the three Chevaliers of the Silence, the banker Massimo Dolci, the superintendent Visconti-Armellino and the cavalier Ercole Pisani. They remained as impassive as before. But around them, an inexpressible agitation grew, and the fourth master of the Silence, Colonel San-Severo, took part in it wholeheartedly.

"Corpo di Bacco!" he exclaimed. "That Doria is a worthy signor, and that rogue of a Marquis has his reckoning!"

The exclamations were lost in the general tumult. To give an idea of what that tumult could be, in spite of the noble status of the majority of the actors on stage, we shall recount a rapid incident of which that honest San-Severo was the hero.

Pier Falcone, at the sight of Prince Fulvio Coriolani, had recoiled as if a violent nervous contraction had drawn him backwards. "It's him!" he said, in a whisper,

And that statement: "It's him!" had a terrible expression of hatred in his mouth. So calm a little while before, and so cold and grave in the face of the strange adventures of the Spurzheim house, he seemed prey to a kind of sudden rage. He slid his hand into the lining of his costume and drew out a Sicilian dagger with a blade as slim and sharp as a needle. Certainly, at that moment of disorder, nothing would have been easier than to launch himself forward and strike. That was his intention. There was no mistake about it. But at the moment when he set forth, an iron hand seized him by the throat, while another equally vigorous hand twisted his wrist and forced him to drop the dagger. Falcone stifled the cry of pain that tried to escape his throat.

The iron hand, which was that of San-Severo, went there in good faith. The doctor's face was already injected with blood when the colonel's gaze fell upon the unknown man's right hand, which had previously held the dagger. On the middle finger of that hand was the ring of the Silence.

San-Severo let go. He dragged the doctor as far as the three chevaliers and showed them the ring.

Armellino said: "We knew that."

San-Severo lowered his head, and reflected momentarily. "My companions," he said. I'm beginning no longer to understand...and the day when I no longer understand anything, beware!"

Armellino and Falcone exchanged a sign. Falcone lost himself in the crowd.

All that had not lasted a minute. Not a word had been exchanged in the group of the principal characters, who maintained their respective poses, as happens on solemn occasions. In this instance, the theater, which is not habitually accurate, copies the truth, and that is why the method of presentation known as a tableau almost always has such a great effect on spectators of good faith.

Doria was to the right of the Marquis, whom Sampieri was containing, and who seemed to be prey to an attack of epilepsy. To the left, Coriolani, his head high and his arms folded over the decorations that scintillated on his chest, was standing upright. The King and the princes surrounded that group.

At the other end of the room, the Princess of Salerno and her companions were applauding with veritable transports. Where passion is, etiquette disappears. Angélie was weeping with joy in Nina's arms. The latter smiled and murmured in her ear: "What did I tell you! It's to misunderstand Fulvio to fear for him."

And yet, in reality, nothing had happened. No response had been opposed to Malatesta's accusations. The King had not said a word; the princes and the Minister of State were mute. But there was in the newcomer a power so communicative, a charm so great and victorious, that it seemed that his presence alone would win his cause.

He looked at Malatesta, smiling. Malatesta, his face marbled with livid patches, his eyes haggard, and foaming at the mouth, was making futile efforts to meet his stare.

The first word pronounced emerged from the King's mouth. The King threw back the hood of his domino and uncovered his handsome Bourbon face, crowned with hair as white as snow, which, in spite of certain actions of his public life, still inspired a sincere respect in the people of Naples.

The King said: "Doria, you are a gentleman. Your father would have done as you did; you have done well."

Lorédan bowed profoundly.

The Royal Prince came to him and embraced him. It was on the arm of the Royal Prince that Ferdinand de Bourbon had leaned throughout the scene.

The King's other companion was his second son, the Prince of Salerno.

Fulvio Coriolani bowed to the King in his turn.

"Welcome, Prince," he King said to him. "You have been accused in your absence; I hope that you are going to defend yourself."

"I will endeavor to do that, sire," replied Coriolani.

All hearts were already with him.

Before continuing, he turned to Lorédan. "Comte Doria," he said, "I thank you and I offer you my hand."

Lorédan bowed, but his hand remained motionless by his side. "Prince," he replied, coldly, "you owe me nothing; I was defending the honor of my house."

"The honor of your house is mine, Comte," said Coriolani, "since I am going to be your brother."

Lorédan replied in a glacial tone: "The future is God's. My sister is free, under the good pleasure of the King, her master and mine."

He bowed again, and broke off the conversation ostentatiously.

Coriolani handed him his glove, silently, which he took back. Having done that, Coriolani straightened up and said, addressing the King:

"Sire, saving the respect that I owe Your Majesty. The Marquis de Malatesta has lied wickedly and in a cowardly manner. Shame upon the man who has lost the memory of his mother to the extent of outraging his own sister!"

"Well said! Well said!" was cried on all sides.

The Archduchess Marie-Clementine, wife of the Prince of Salerno, said: "Prince, in the name of my sisters and the entire court, I thank you; you have expressed our thought nobly."

Coriolani put his hand on his heart. His gaze, in rendering thanks to the princess, lingered, full of amour, on the pale and beautiful face of Angélie, who nodded her head, smiling.

"Are you dead?" whispered the implacable Sampieri, in Malatesta's ear.

"Sire," said the latter at that moment, his speech embarrassed and slow, "saving the respect that I owe Your Majesty, this bandit, who has given lessons to the gentlemen of your court in your presence, is not worth the trouble of a Doria d'Angri responding to his denial. I stand by what I say, and I accept the challenge of my cousin Lorédan Doria, who is at least a gallant man."

Sampieri squeezed his hand furtively.

Malatesta went on, with more assurance: "Since this man has bewitched you by turning the heads of all your wives, all your sisters and all your daughters, O great men of Naples, my former friends I no longer have much hope of removing the blindfold that covers your eyes. I shall therefore limit myself to asking two simple questions: With what task has he been occupied tonight? In what country of the moon is the principality of Coriolani situated?"

As he finished that speech, Malatesta had recovered all his insolence.

"Sire," said Prince Fulvio, "it is not to this man that I am addressing myself; it is to Your Majesty, who has testified the benevolent desire to hear my response."

"Benevolence, yes, Prince," said the King. "We do not believe you culpable until there is proof."

Coriolani took a step toward the King, put one knee on the floor with the noble grace that he possessed to an incomparable degree, and kissed his hand, saying, in a low voice: "I render this homage to the King who loves me. I render it above all to the friend of my noble and beloved father."

Around the room, people asked one another: "What is he saying? What is he saying?"

"I believe, God forgive me!" exclaimed Malatesta, sniggering, that that son of hazard mentioned his father."

The Royal Prince made a sign.

The butts of twenty muskets were heard to resonate loudly on the paving stones. All astonished gazes turned toward the vestibule, which was seen to be full of Swiss Guards.

Malatesta wanted to speak again, but Sampieri, judging that he was irredeemably doomed, put his hand over his mouth. "Let it go," he said. "You've done enough."

"To blow my brains out as soon as I have a pistol," replied Malatesta. "You're right."

"Sire," Fulvio Coriolani said, in the midst of the silence, reestablished as if by enchantment as soon as he opened his mouth, "I saw, a few weeks ago, a great mourning in your august house. This is to respond to the first of the Marquis de Malatesta's questions, which challenged me to say what my task was tonight. Your Majesty had close at hand a noble young woman whose veins contain imperial and royal blood, Matilde Farnèse, whom you had held over the baptismal font..."

"Do you have news of her, Fulvio?" cried the King, vehemently.

It was known at the court that the King adored his goddaughter. It was even said—and not as one of the thousand rumors that run around the camarillas—that the beautiful Matilde Farnèse held her godfather by bonds tighter than those contracted by the first of sacraments. Matilde's mother had died young, and Ferdinand de Bourbon had loved her.

Colonna said to Mareschalci, whom he had rejoined in the crowd: "The wretch is dealing us a master blow there!"

Mareschalci replied: "What if the anonymous letter that set us on campaign was a trap?"

They both had their heads bowed, and dared not look in the direction of Malatesta.

Coriolani went on: "Could I do too much to recognize the gracious hospitality that Your Majesty has deigned to accord to me? Those who say that they saw me tonight on the Maddalena bridge and on the beach are not mistaken; I went there. I went further; a boat transported me across the Bay of Naples I went past Cajola, doubled Capo Miseno and crossed the channel of Procida...on the far side one the islands, opposite the Foce del Fusaro, there was a ship at anchor; I went aboard..."

"And you have news of Matilde?" asked the King, for the second time.

"Yes, Sire."

"Good news?"

"Yes, Sire."

"May God recompense you, Fulvio! Tell us what that ship was."

The circle around Coriolani had tightened, and room had been made for the princesses, who were now in the first rank. Malatesta's companions had been reduced to protesting by their incredulous and mocking silence.

"That ship," replied Prince Fulvio, "belonged to the redoubtable chief that your police incessantly believe that hold, and who always escapes them."

"Porporato!" That name, pronounced in low voices, ran from one end of the room to the other.

"Baron Altamonte, who was to be executed tomorrow, isn't Il Porporato, then?" said the King.

"No, Sire."

"Prince Coriolani said the contrary, formally, during the confrontation," observed the Minister of State.

"Excellency, if I had not seen Il Porporato with my own eyes tonight aboard his felucca, I would still say now that Altamonte is Il Porporato...they resemble one another feature for feature. On this point, I am afraid that there has been a fatal and very regrettable error. I believe that the law and the police were mistaken. I believe that Altamonte was innocent."

Andrea Visconto-Armellino took a step forward. "My resignation as super-intendent of the royal police," he said, "was deposited at the Ministry of State yesterday. The reason for my resignation is that I share the opinion of the noble Prince Fulvio Coriolani."

"Oho!" whispered the tall San-Severo in the ear of the banker Massimo Dolci, who remained alone in the place previously occupied by the three chevaliers of the Silence, for Ercole Pisani had just gone to the vestibule. "What comedy is this, old Lorenzo? Will I spend my entire life without seeing a glimmer of your schemes?"

"This is strange, Piccolomini," said the King to his Minister. "I've already received, tonight, a letter on that subject from signor Johann Spurzheim, who, ill and dying as he is..."

"Early tomorrow," the Minister of State interjected, "I intend to submit important communications to Your Majesty."

The King looked him in the face. "Woe betide those who seek to deceive me!" he pronounced in a low voice, frowning. "I'm the oldest sovereign in Europe, but by the Holy Virgin, I still have a sound head and a long arm."

It is impossible for us, at this moment, for us to make the conduct of that joyful dying man Johann Spurzheim comprehensible. In this battle, he had dealt a deadly blow to Piccolomini, and yet he was not with Prince Fulvio. He was working for himself alone, directing his batteries from the depths of his alcove and mixing with pleasure the tangled confusion of his intrigue. He was a fanatical diplomat.

We only know one of his agents at this point, Pier Falcone, but who can tell how many unknown colleagues Pier Falcone had in the drawing rooms of the Palazzo Doria?

The real battle, it is necessary to say, was between Johan Spurzheim and Fulvio Coriolani. Even Malatesta, unwittingly and involuntarily, was Johann Spurzheim's instrument.

"And what did you do aboard the felucca, Fulvio?" asked the King.

"I spoke to Il Porporato, Sire."

"It was the second time you had spoken to him?"

"It was the second time."

"And now you'd no longer be mistaken? You'd recognize him?"

"I would recognize him, Sire."

"Why did he approach our coasts thus?"

"He's a strange individual, Sire. He also says, in speaking of the shores of the Kingdom of Naples: *my coasts*."

The King had a constrained smile. "We are two for one kingdom," he murmured. "I am the king of the day; that brigand is the king of the night. All that will change, if God aids me. I've snatched my heritage from the hands of Murat, who was a soldier…why should a bandit stand up to me?"

Everyone was able to see Prince Fulvio's eyebrows furrow suddenly at the name of Murat, pronounced unexpectedly.

"Sire," he said. "Il Porporato had, according to him, two motives for approaching your capital."

"Let's hear the motives of His Nocturnal Majesty," said the King.

"Firstly, to liberate Baron Altamonte, not out of amity, because he affirms that he does not know him, but out of sympathy: Il Porporato does not want any more executions."

"Ah! Damn!" cried Bourbon, bursting out laughing.

"San Gennaro," Fulvio continued, placidly, "gave himself the mission of burying all cadavers without a sepulcher. Porporato has sworn an oath to liberate all those condemned to capital punishment."

"This time, at least…," the King began.

"If it is permitted to me to respond to Your Majesty," the Prince cut in, "Porporato had anticipated the eventuality. He said to me, in his own words 'One of two things will happen: either he will be murdered, or I shall liberate him.'"

In is turn, the King frowned.

A murmur of astonishment ran through the room. This Porporato was growing to the stature of a power.

"And what was His Diabolical Majesty's second motive?" asked Ferdinand.

"The second motive was quite different, Sire. Il Porporato is in love with a young woman of your court."

There was a shiver in the ranks of those ladies.

"Ah!" said the King, having great difficulty conserving his forced smile. "He knows our court, then?"

"Very well, Sire."

"Does he do us the honor of coming here sometimes?"

"Often."

Ferdinand went pale, and his anger showed, involuntarily. "By the death of the Savior!" he cried. "I want ministers who can protect me from such insolences! Has any sovereign been toyed with as outrageously as that?"

"Sire," said Coriolani, coldly, "I have not accused Your Majesty's ministers."

There was a silence between the King and Prince Fulvio, but the entire room was filled with whispers. The King greatly regretted having begun that conversation in public. He changed the subject abruptly, and with ill grace.

"Tell us about Matilde, our goddaughter, Prince," he said. "How much does that man want to sell us her liberty?"

"A barter, Sire," Fulvio replied. "Il Porporato wants the woman he loves in exchange for the noble Matilde Farnèse."

"He hopes for that?" cried the King, indignantly.

"He pronounces the name of Your Majesty with an appearance of profound respect. He does not request anything. What he desires, he is able to take."

There was a further silence. This time, it really was stupor.

"But what about my goddaughter?" said the King.

Coriolani turned toward the vestibule, where the Cavalier Ercole Pisani was standing, in front of the Swiss Guard. He made a sign. Pisani disappeared into the midst of the soldiers, whose ranks opened to let him pass.

"I am reporting Il Porporato's own words to you, Sire," Fulvio said. "Il Porporato said: 'I am returning his goddaughter to the King of Naples without ransom. Tomorrow, the woman I love will be in my power.'"

Lorédan Doria, who was next to his sister and who was fixing Fulvio with an attentive and somber stare, made an involuntary movement, as if to take hold of her and protect her. Angélie did not see that, for she was also looking intently at Prince Fulvio. She was very pale, and her heart was beating forcefully.

The King did not have time to respond.

Ercole Pisani came through the ranks of the soldiers again. He was holding by the hand the veiled young woman that we saw in the courtyard of the palace where Beldemonio had descended after leaving Johann Spurzheim's house. Fulvio advanced toward her, took her from Pisani's hands and led her to the King, who held out his arms to her with tears in his eyes.

"Is Your Majesty satisfied with my employment of this night?" said the Prince, without raising his voice.

Matilde Farnèse was already receiving the caresses of the princesses. The King held out his hand to Fulvio, who tried to kiss it—but the King pulled him toward him and gave him the accolade. The princesses and the court applauded, with a veritable transport, Angélie was dazzled, and as if intoxicated.

Nina smiled, and there was a bitter disdain in her smile.

Lorédan Doria interrogated himself with the anguish of a man who senses madness entering his brain. The three chevaliers of the Silence, Andrea Visconti-Armellino, Massimo Dolci and Ercole Pisani, were united again, forming a motionless and impassive group in front of Colonel San-Severo, who was utterly lost in the middle of that sea of enigmas.

"Signor Armellino," said the King, "we do not accept your resignation."

"In that case, mine is at Your Majesty's feet," said Piccolomini, swiftly.

The King smiled. "Tomorrow's sun," he said, "will see many things. I want a minister who puts the daughters of my noble friends and servants in security. In the meantime, it is necessary that justice be done. Since your resignation is at my feet, Excellency, I shall appoint a Minister of State for the future. Be at the palace early, Fulvio."

Prince Coriolani bowed.

Everyone could see that Piccolomini's portfolio was his if he wanted to accept it.

"Hey! Baumgarten!" cried the King.

The major of the Swiss Guards came in immediately. The King whispered a few words in his ear.

Sampieri, guessing, made a movement toward the door. He felt a hand retaining him. Doctor Pier Falcone was between him and Malatesta.

"My young signors," said Falcone, "you've played a valiant game; you've lost. I offer you your revenge."

"Signor Mareschalci," said Baumgarten at that moment, "I arrest you in the name of the King."

Malatesta gazed feverishly at Angélie Doria, whose eyes seemed to be appealing to Prince Coriolani, to whom the King was no longer speaking.

"In the name of the King," said Baumgarten, then, "Signor Gravina, I arrest you."

"All my blood for a revenge," growled Malatesta, whose hand, passing inside his coat, tore at his breast.

"Are you quite determined?" asked Pier Falcone.

"If the Devil offered me his aid," replied the vanquished man, "I'd make a pact with the Devil."

Falcone smiled.

Baumgarten had just arrested Ziani and Colonna.

"We only have one more minute," said Pier Falcone. "Pitti is being arrested in his turn...but it's anticipated. The others will be too. Remember this, Sampieri, and you, Malatesta: you have an ally. At whatever time and in whatever place the name of Johann Spurzheim is pronounced in your ear, be ready!"

"Johann Spurzheim!" repeated Sampieri, amazed.

And Malatesta added: "I only evoked Satan."

Baumgarten was facing them. He said: "In the name of the King, Domenico Sampieri and Giulio d'Angri, Marquis Malatesta, I arrest you."

Falcone lost himself in the crowd.

At that moment, Fulvio Coriolani went to Angélie Doria and kissed her hand respectfully.

As the Princess of Salerno was summoning him, he let fall these words rapidly:

"Comtesse, it's necessary that I see you tomorrow, alone and without witnesses. On that interview will depend, if you love me, your future and my happiness."

"If I love you...!" repeated Angélie.

He went past, marching toward the princesses, who were waiting for him to make him a triumph.

Angélie leaned on Nina, who had exchanged a sign with Coriolani. She tottered.

"Come," she said. "My heart is hurting...I'm stifling...it seems to me that I'm going to die!"

PART FOUR: MARIA DES AMALFI

I. Djabel the Great Scorpion

Nina Dolci, the Princess of Salerno's maid of honor, was sitting beside the bed. Angélie Doria, lying down, her face pale and distraught amid her scattered blonde hair, had her eyes closed. A lamp was burning on the marble table, but first light was already blanching the muslin curtains. It was three or four hours after the end of the fête. Nina Dolci was watching over Angélie, who was ill.

All that simple and grand luxury can invent of the suave and imagine of the delightful, while respecting the virginal color that is the necessary ornament of a young woman's bedroom, was there. It is impossible to describe the exquisite freshness of the furniture and the wall-hangings. Everything in that charming redoubt was smiling—everything except poor beautiful Angélie.

Not long ago, she had taken so much pleasure in ornamenting her retreat with ever-renewed flowers. Not long ago, she had watered so faithfully, morning and evening, the camellias stained with blood and the crimson cacti that carpeted her white marble terrace.

Had she even spent a single morning, before the two months that had just passed, without admiring the pupation of charming tropical birds that were pecking and fluttering in her aviary? That aviary, a jewel, was her amusement and her care. And so many other pastimes! Pastels, in her artistic fingers, had velveted rose petals so softly; the piano sang so cheerfully!

Does it only require one day to change the dear joy of young women into melancholy?

Angie was sad, and the delicate coquetries of her redoubt smiled in vain around her. Angélie might have been as beautiful as an angel, noble among the most noble, richer than the richest, but she was sad. She often wept.

When the keys of her abandoned piano, less white than the ivory of her fingers, broke their long silence, it was to play some slow and melancholy tune, the echo of the languors of her soul.

That night, Angélie Doria had gone to bed with an ardent fever. Her heart was full of aches and fears; her head was burning. Painful and crazed thoughts absorbed her while fatiguing her. She had said so to Nina, her nurse. She had said it blushing, with her beautiful eyes full of tears. She was losing her reason; she no longer understood her heart.

Still filled as she was with the radiant victory that had just been won by Fulvio, her great friend, her hero, her fiancé, she no longer wanted to think about anything but him. But the fever, with the patient obstinacy that enervates and exhausts, incessantly brought her another image. Another? Is that the right word? An exactly similar mage, but younger, more humble, more gentle: a Fulvio who was not her Fulvio, a timid and sad adolescent, whose long blond hair hid his pale cheeks while he prostrated himself before the Lord's altar. She chased it away, that image, but the image always returned.

During the four hours that she had been there, she had not been able to find an instant of slumber. Sometimes, her eyes closed, as at present, and Nina thought that she had fallen asleep, but Angélie's faint voice soon broke the silence. She said, in the plaintive tone of a fearful child: "I'm not asleep. Talk to me, I beg you. Defend me against my dreams!"

Then Nina spoke.

At first she had spoken about things regarding her companion. She had tried to calm her by clarifying the disturbance of her soul, by treating as childishness and folly the scruples that were tormenting her, but that had only augmented the trouble.

"They're here!" Angélie said. "Both of them...between you and me...Fulvio and Julian. I only love Fulvio! Why is it always Julian that leans over me, caressing my cheeks with his curly blond tresses?"

"It's the fever," Nina murmured.

"I'm going mad! I can sense it already. When I close my eyes, it's Julian who approaches. Why does Fulvio remain back there, in the shadows? There are moments when he's so far away, my Fulvio, that I can no longer see him!"

Sometimes, while she listened to those incoherent thoughts, which were neither reason nor delirium, a strange smile wandered over Nina's lips. She loved Angélie, however—but can one ever silence completely the stubborn voice of the heart? She had tamed her passion, that valiant and bizarre young woman; she had said in good faith, counting on her as-yet-indomitable strength: "I shall be Fulvio's sister..."

But does Vesuvius—to compare the tempest of the heart to the cataclysms of nature—the extinct Vesuvius, the slumbering Vesuvius, the Vesuvius that allows tranquil crops to grow along its sides, and amber vines from which flow, drop by drop, the miserly sap of Lacryma Cristi, the golden wine—have no more fire in the depths of its crater for all that? There is fire there. One night, the subterranean fire is reignited, the mountain shudders with the interior seething of lava, the earth trembles, the sea foams, and everything disappears, vines, gardens, crops, cheerful houses and proud palaces, beneath the torrent of fire that is the volcano's reawakening.

Nina smiled. Nina willingly cradled herself, as she had told us herself, in the bold and impossible poetry of romances of chivalry. She compared herself to Carmella, the hopeless lover of the young Esplandian. Well, in that same *Amadis de Gaula*, a grotesque and sublime mess, there is the story of a sword that lives, thinks and is faithful. Balan's sword can only serve Balan. It turns against any stranger who wants to make use of it to fight. Smiling, Nina thought:

This amour is like Balan's sword. God has given it to me. It turns against those who steal it from me.

"Talk to me," murmured Angélie. "In the name of Heaven, talk to me."

Nina collected herself, and, pretending to search for the story of another in her memory, she recounted a few strange episodes of her Bohemian life. She had seen many things, that young zingara whom hazard had made into a great lady. Angélie listened to her. Sometimes Nina thought she had fallen asleep, and resumed her reverie.

The lamp was between them, illuminating those who different beauties with a similar radiance: Angélie, as pale and gentle as Raphael's Holy Virgins; Nina, brown and bearing in her boldly sculpted features the bronze tint of which the masters of the Spanish school were so fond.

As the first light of dawn slid timidly and palely through the window panes, Nina stopped talking and Angélie remained silent for a few minutes. The zingara's eyes were beginning to close, and it was at that moment that one could have remarked, especially in those ravishing faces, the violent contrast of races.

Suddenly, however, Angélie shivered and cried: "They're both there! As soon as you're no longer talking, Julian's face is there, very close to mine!"

"I want to keep talking," said the zingara, feigning joviality, "but your phantoms are more difficult to chase away than Saul's. What can I tell you? I don't know many more stories."

"A long story...long!" said Angélie, whose tone was becoming increasingly similar to that of little children.

"A long, long story!" repeated Nina. "Let's see, I'm searching...there is one long, long one. It's that of Il Porporato."

Angélie opened her eyes very wide. "You know him, then?"

"Better than anyone," Nina replied, unable to help smiling.

"Why do you say that: 'Better than anyone'?"

"Because Massimo Dolci, my uncle, has a country house at the foot of Mount Sila, where the Purple Castle is said to be."

"Oh!" said Angélie. "The Purple Castle! Does it exist?"

"And because," the zingara continued, "my uncle Massimo Dolci is the friend of the superintendent of police, who lent him the dossiers on the famous bandit."

"And you've read them?"

"With more avoid curiosity than the most interesting of romances. Judge, Comtesse! The official documents complemented the poetic stories that I heard so often in my childhood. I rediscovered there, officially established, all the fantastic tales that had frightened and charmed my young imagination."

"And you never told me about that!" Angélie put in.

"I couldn't have guessed," retorted Nina, "that the noble Doria was interested in the deeds and feats of Il Porporato."

"That name," murmured the young Comtesse, "has always produced a bizarre effect on me. What I've been told about him is so strange. He appears to me to be as great as Don Juan...or like the Spirit of Evil himself..."

"There is something of Don Juan in him," Nina replied, "but there's good amid the evil, and his career, proscribed by law, is full of generous heroisms."

"Begin quickly, Nina. I'm listening."

Comtesse Angélie turned sideways on her pillow. Her reanimated face expressed a singular curiosity.

"Have you ever encountered in the plains of southern Italy," Nina asked, "those wretched caravans of zingaris who pitch their tents far from villages and always seem to be stealing the water of the springs from which they drink and the air of heaven that they breathe?"

"I remember having seen those people two or three times in my childhood," Angélie replied.

"Well," Nina went on, "perhaps you've encountered without knowing it the wandering family of the tzigane Djabel the Great Scorpion, in which the childhood of Il Porporato passed, and also the childhood of Fiamma, his close friend."

"Ah!" cried Angélie. "You're also going to talk to me about Fiamma?"

"It's impossible," replied Nina, with a twinge of pride, "to talk about Il Porporato without talking about Fiamma. They're the shadow and the body...or rather, the body and the soul.

"Djabel the Great Scorpion, a red-haired tzigane from Moravia, was traveling through the land of Bari at the beginning of the century with his family, or tribe, as numerous as that of Priam.

"Time marches on, Contessina, and prejudices decline. Those races, so long proscribed, will one day have their place at the great feast of humanity. Here, that will come belatedly, because we're slow to let go of old customs, but in England, a land of merchants, which has its qualities and its faults, there are a Duke and a Viscount among the members of the House of Lords who have wives of the gypsy race. In Russia, Prince Nikolai Tolstoy married a *cigana*, originally from Portugal,[49] and it's said that the Bohemian princess in question is not the least among the ornaments of the emperor's court.

"The two first-borns of Djabel were named Horeb and Baissa. Horeb knew the art of reading the stars; Baissa tamed snakes and cured fevers by laying on hands. Djabel himself was endowed for scorpions and tarantulas. He had a song that charmed those maleficent animals, which circled around his forked stick and fell dead when he said to them: 'Die!' He was small, thin and pale; his gray hair bristled on his head. When he stared at dogs, the dogs howled and went

---

[49] This reference must be to Nikolai Aleksandrovich Tolstoy (1761-1816), who was master of ceremonies at the Russian court, but the reference would be anachronistic if the wife in question had not survived her husband.

mad. The peasants of the land of Bari paid him a fee in order to him not to stare at their flocks. Djabel's father had known the secret of the Purple Castle."

"What is the Purple Castle?" asked Angélie.

"It's the mysterious terrestrial paradise of the sons of Achingan, who was the first king of the tziganes, and, it's said, gave then their name. It's situated in the heart of the southern Apennines, in an inaccessible place covered with impenetrable forests. It's said that sometimes, on the paths of the valley, distant songs and he sounds of feasting can be heard. They're noises descending from the Purple Castle, the palace of marvels. The mountain people believe in its existence, but no one has seen it. It's the location of the treasure promised to the disinherited races, the inexhaustible treasure, like the water of the sea and God's bounty."

The dubious daylight that the closed curtains allowed to pass was already paling the gleams of the light. An almost infantile curiosity was legible on Angélie's face.

Nina's features had become animated while she spoke. There was a kind of aureole of mysterious poetry on her forehead, and her eyes were shining with an extraordinary gleam. She was in her element, the daughter of oriental imaginations, the friend of impossible splendors and of the marvelous full of mystery. She continued.

"The seventh ancestor of Djabel the Great Scorpion died searching for the secret of the Purple Castle. His name was Pharam. He was the seventh nephew of Ptolaum, the stem of the tribe, who had come from the land of Chal—that's Egypt. It was Pharam who built the Purple Castle.[50] When he was pursued by Christians he spread on the path of exile the dust of red marble that served to build the palace.

"Pharam's descendants swore by him. And among the Romichal—the men of Egypt—the sons of Pharam are now the first. They say that the marble dust spread in the mountain gorges by Pharam, their ancestor, was enchanted. The wind doesn't have the power to disperse it, the rain can't dissolve it. Where the ancestor put it, it stays. And anyone who finds a particle of that red dust would only have to follow the trace to arrive at the Purple Castle, where the treasures of the son of Ptolaum are. So, as long as there's a descendant of Pharam, there will be a man who will devote his entire life to the search for that treasure.

"Djabel the Great Scorpion and his tribe were wandering incessantly in the land of Otranto and the land of Bari, without ever surpassing the Capitanata. They were trying to get closer to the summits of the Apennines, from which armed force always drove them back. The zingaris are feared in the mountains, in fact, because the mountain makes the brigand.

---

[50] The text is inconsistent on this point, but Nina/Fiamma is obviously reporting legend and unreliable hearsay at this point in her story, whereas her subsequent account is mostly based on her own experience.

"Djabel grew old; his sons grew up; his race multiplied to the point that famine often reigned under the tents. There were ten tents, which always drew apart by considerable distances in order not to alarm the region.

"Under the tent of Horeb, the eldest son, there was a child of the Christian race, who was hidden with care. The tziganes called him Beldemonio, because of his precocious boldness..."

"Beldemonio!" repeated Angélie. "Where have I heard that name?"

"In Naples everyone repeats it. But the same name belongs to several people, in the same way that some people have more than one name. Let me continue.

"Under the tent of Baissa, the second child, there was a little girl, Djabel's niece, who was the gaiety of the entire tribe. Her name was Mani, but the Christians, who liked to see her dance the gira and the tarantella, had nicknamed her Fiamma."

Angélie leaned on her elbow on her pillow. "And it's this Beldemonio who became Il Porporato?" she interjected

"Wait," said Nina. "Fiamma was beautiful, as the daughters of Bohemia are. Her hair was black; her eyes shone like diamonds under the somber arches of her eyebrows. It was easy to take her waist, already supple and fine, in the hand. But I can't tell you, Comtesse, how Beldemonio resembled the angels. He was tall; his long blond hair famed his candid and pure face. His eyes had a celestial softness; if, like Achilles, he had worn women's clothes, he would have had no rival.

"Fiamma did not know that Beldemonio loved her; they were two children. This is how Fiamma began to love Beldemonio:

"The two tents of Horeb and Baissa came together not far from Brienza, in a valley through which the torrent of Organa flows. The young people of the two tents were sent into the mountains to gather simples, for all tziganes are physicians. Hazard bought Beldemonio and Fiamma together. Fiamma saw that Beldemonio ran out of breath climbing the steep slopes; he dared not speak to Fiamma.

"They both followed the bed of the Organa, which descends from the mountains in abrupt cascades. They arrived thus near the summit of a crag, the ledge of which overhung the foaming waters of the torrent. Above them was an inaccessible slope where stunted myrtles grew here and there and cacti with crimson flowers. Two turtle-doves, parents, were fluttering around a crevice in the rock uttering plaintive cries. Fiamma and Beldemonio were sitting on the moss.

"Fiamma said to Beldemonio: 'Why are they weeping?'

"Beldemonio was in the process of contemplating Fiamma, and his eyelids were damp. He looked up at the summit of the crag, were the thorny spines of the cacti were agitated. 'They're weeping,' he said, because there are chicks in the nest, and two children are creeping up toward the crevice.'

"Fiamma uttered a cry. She had just perceived the cruel heads of the little hunters. 'I'll kill them if you like,' said Beldemonio, picking up a pebble.

"A stone launched by the hand of a zingari goes straight to the target like a musket-ball. 'No, no!' cried Fiamma. 'Don't kill the children, but save the poor turtle-doves' chicks.'

"At the moment when Beldemonio launched himself forward to climb the slope, the hand of one of the children reached the crevice. Fiamma uttered a cry of joy. From the crevice, one of the two turtle-doves emerged and took off, in a poor, timid flight, which dipped in such a way that the turtle-dove passed close to the little girl, who put out her hand to seize it.

"At that moment, a falcon fell from the sky like a thunderbolt, caught the little bird in flight and carried it away.

"Beldemonio still had the pebble in his hand; the stone whistled. The falcon fell head first into the torrent, while the turtle-dove, flapping its little wounded wings, disappeared into the bushes. 'Thank you,' said Fiamma, 'but the other? I'd like the other.'

"The other emerged from the crevice just then, avoiding the hands of the chagrined children, and sank toward us in its uncertain flight. 'The hawk did well,' said Beldemonio, and he leapt, the amorous and crazy child; he caught the little title-dove in flight and fell into the torrent without letting go.

"Fiamma let herself fall on to the moss, half-dead.

"A moment later, Beldemonio was at her knees with the little turtle-dove, whose beautiful pearl-gray feathers were scarcely damp. Beldemonio was bleeding from several wounds.

"From that day on, Fiamma was Beldemonio's slave. She had looked at him more closely. She had recognized, under the blond hair of a seraph, the powerful head of a lion..."

"Strange child!" murmured Angélie, in a dream. Then she added, in a lower voice: "Fulvio would have done that for me."

"I don't know," said the zingara, who was hiding the flamboyant pride of her gaze beneath the beautiful fringes of her eyelids. She went on: "Fiamma and Beldemonio were fourteen. That's the age at which tzigane girls become women. There were battles around the tents. There were already disputes over Fiamma's heart. Djabel the Great Scorpion, old as he was, said: 'I want her!'

"He was the chief and the father; no one had ever resisted him. Beldemonio resisted him. Beldemonio came to the tent where Djabel was, with five of his sons around him and he said: 'Master, you're too old for Mani, who has given me her heart.'

"The sons raised against him the Egyptian weapon, the pum, which is a large lead ball at the end of a leather thong, a silent weapon, almost always mortal. Beldemonio tore up one if the spikes that fixed the tent-ropes. He broke the arm of Pharam, Djabel's third son, and this is what happened:

"The leather thong brandished by Thiphare, the fourth son, broke. The ball struck the head of Djabel the Great Scorpion. Djabel said: "That is fate!' And he fell face forward.

"As his sons launched themselves upon Beldemonio all together, he stopped them with his dying voice and said: 'Don't touch him! He's the one who will find the way to the Purple Castle.' And he rendered his breath to the wind, for there is no God for the tziganes.

"The will of Djabel the Great Scorpion had always been respected while he was alive, but why should one obey the dead? They took hold of Beldemonio, who was alone against all of them. They bound his hands and feet and threw him in a corner of the tent.

"Horeb was the eldest and the chief, but Baissa counted more partisans, because he was braver and stronger. He said to Horeb: 'I could expel you. Give me Fiamma and you can remain the chief.'

"Horeb replied: 'I want her.' Baissa killed his brother Horeb with a blow of the pum.

"There was a feast in that tent, where there were two dead men. After drinking, the drunken tribe fell asleep pell-mell amid the debris of the feast and the empty bottles. Fiamma was to marry Baissa the next day. She took a knife and cut Beldemonio's bonds. They fled together.

"Then a life of strange adventures and incessant perils commenced for them. The six tents of Djabel's sons united against Beldemonio, who, having no protection for which to hope from the Christian authorities, was tracked in the mountains like a wild beast. That lasted a year.

"If Beldemonio's life and that of Fiamma surpass a century, neither of them will ever rediscover those dear and charming hours spent between the threats of death and the smiles of amour. They loved one another. Fiamma was the daughter of the land of the sun: blood of fire and a heart of diamond, capable of keeping the first imprint received for eternity.

"Beldemonio...but what can I tell you about that young lion? Beldemonio loved his Fiamma so much that he had forgotten that he had no wings on the day when she had manifested her first desire! Beldemonio had fallen sixty feet that day into a torrent bounding over the rocks, and he had not injured the turtle-dove, because his Fiamma had said: 'I want to have it!'

"They loved one another; they were alone in the world. God gave them his beautiful sky for a roof; God threw beneath their feet his grass and is flowers, splendid carets, and the music of the mountains the wind that sings in the cente-narian fir-trees celebrated their wedding feast. They were free; they were strong; they loved one another.

"Baissa, the new father of the zingari, the sons of Pharam, had said: 'Whichever of our sons takes possession of Mani will have her for a wife. Whichever takes possession of Beldemonio, the predestined, will have whatever he requests.' He called Beldemonio the predestined because father Djabel had said that he would find the way to the Purple Castle.

"The hunt was rude. When passion grips them, the men of Chal are patient, courageous and indefatigable. They all traveled together in pursuit of Fiamma and Beldemonio. Twenty times, Beldemonio and Fiamma were on the point of falling into their traps.

"At that time, Beldemonio had no weapons. When he could not avoid the Romichal he fought them, like the knights of ancient days, with branches torn from the mountain trees, or with pebbles picked up from the dry beds of torrents. He lacked David's sling, but he only needed his sure and vigorous hand.

"Finally, after ten months, the implacable enemies of Beldemonio and Fiamma, always tightening the circle traced around them, had cornered them on the peak of a sterile mountain in the most deserted region of the Apennines. It was in the Basilicata, beyond the sources of the river Agri.

"Fiamma and Beldemonio went three days and three nights without taking any nourishment. In the distance, they could hear the songs of their persecutors' orgies. On the third night, they were both sleeping in the hollow trunk of an enormous green oak. Fiamma awoke with a start. There was a devouring fire in her entrails.

"Until then, she had suppressed her plaints, but one is weak at the moment of awakening. Fiamma allowed a groan to escape. Beldemonio heard it, and got to his feet.

"Beldemonio was about to reach his fifteenth year. He had the gracious beauty of Apollo, but he had the indomitable vigor of Hercules. 'I'll bring you bread,' he said. To seize his club and bound to the path that led down the mountain was the work of a single instant.

"Fiamma would have liked to retain him, but how to retain a lioness that hears the cry of her hungry cubs! Fiamma followed him. After a few seconds, she had already lost sight of him.

"Four fires were burning at the foot of the mountain. A profound silence reigned. The sons of Pharam were asleep, trusting in heir sentinels and their vigilant dogs. But their dogs knew Beldemonio; they came to lick his hands, and the sentinel did not have time to raise the alarm. Scarcely had he seen Beldemonio than he fell, his skull broken by a blow of the club.

"It was the first time that Beldemonio had killed. The sight of blood shed by his hand intoxicated him. Fiamma heard him utter a terrible cry, which challenged the tziganes to combat. He disdained surprise; he wanted living men for adversaries. A fearful murmur responded to his cry, and then a great tumult: plaints, clamors, gunshots and howls.

"Fiamma hastened her course, but ran out of breath. He was alone, they were twenty; but he was Beldemonio, the man whom no human force has ever resisted. He was Beldemonio, the living thunderbolt; Beldemonio, before whom

Italy entire would soon tremble; Beldemonio, who was of age, and who would be called Il Porporato.

"When Fiamma was within visual range, she perceived one man standing alone in the middle of an open tent. Ten bloody cadavers lay around the man. The first that Fiamma recognized was he giant Baissa, the master of the tziganes. Baissa's head, split open, was leaking brains and blood. Beldemonio's club was entirely red.

"Fiamma had bread..."

Nina interrupted herself and put her hands to her heart. The daylight was increasing; the dull lamp had lost its glare.

"What's the matter?" asked Angelie. "Are you in pain?"

"No," the zingara replied. "I like lions."

"Would you have been able to love Il Porporato?" asked Angélie.

"I have loved the man that my destiny chose for me," the zingara replied. "Do you want to sleep?"

"Oh, no!" cried La Doria. "Keep talking, Nina, I beg you."

The zingara passed the back of her hand over her forehead, where droplets of sweat were forming. She smiled bitterly, because she heard Angélie murmur: "Fulvio is a lion too!"

"The most beautiful of lions and the most terrible," pronounced the zingara. After a brief silence, she continued.

"In the town of Potenza there was a steward named Antonio Basili, Marquis de Casanuova. He was like a great lord of comedy, powerfully rich, and very jealous of his wife, but not given to fidelity. The Marquise de Casanuova was young, charming and reputed to be very virtuous. "Poor Fiamma scarcely suspected that her first rival would be so highly placed.

"Beldemonio had become a chamois hunter. He had acquired two carbines and ammunition from Baissa's tent. He and Fiamma took possession of an abandoned hut in the gorge of Mount Gaudente. They lived happily, thanks to Beldemonio's skill; he never came back empty-handed.

"It was to Potenza that he went to sell his hides. One day, when he was going there, carrying his burden on the end of a knotty stick, he encountered an escort of three policemen who were conducting a poor devil with his hands tied behind his back.

"In those days, there was something of the knight errant in him. Although, strictly speaking, he was not yet a rebel against society, since no cause for war had been offered to him, he regarded the law as a club destined incessantly to spare the strong while crushing the weak.

"It must be that there is a special genre of vocation here, since we have so many bandits who pose as free judges. Without knowing it, Beldemonio was a free judge in embryo. He was like Don Quixote de La Mancha, when the mirror of chivalry fell on the Santa-Hermandad in order to liberate the Biscayan. He attacked the three policemen without warning and set the poor devil free. A staff against three carbines might seem improbable to you, Comtesse..."

"No," Angélie interjected. "I believe that Fulvio, without arms, could fight ten armed men."

Nina started to laugh. "And Julian?" she said.

Angélie closed her eyes and went horribly pale.

Nina fell upon her hand. "I'm a fool!" she said. "I should never have mentioned him to you...The poor devil, however, was not of the same opinion as you. He was utterly bewildered by the flight of the policemen. As soon as Beldemonio had removed his bonds, he made a large sign of the cross at hazard, in order to ward off the enterprises of the sorcerer he had before his eyes.

"The sign of the cross having not caused Beldemonio to vanish, the fellow recovered his courage. In order to testify his joy he executed a prodigious somersault, and, launching himself to the top of a tall beech tree in three of four bounds, he started turning around a branch with the rapidity of a rattle moved by a child's hand. That done, he let himself slide down to the ground and walked on his hands as far as the ditch beside the road, which he crossed with a perilous leap.

"The names of Il Porporato's companions are popular knowledge in Naples. That poor devil was the acrobat Cucuzone, who has never quit him since then. He came from Evoli, where the police had arrested him in the public square because he did not have the steward's permission.

"Having sold his skins in Potenza, Beldemonio returned to Mount Gaudente, but he did not find Fiamma there.

"This is what had happened. Antonio Basili, Marquis de Casanuova, also liked hunting. While Beldemonio was in Potenza, the Marquis was roaming the forest with his pack and his beaters, forcing a beautiful fallow deer. He encountered Fiamma, who was wandering alone in the wood while waiting for her friend. He abandoned the deer for the girl, and began another hunt.

"You're aware, Comtesse, of the cowardly complaisance of our Italian servants. The Marquis' men cried 'Tally ho!' and helped him shamelessly to track the young woman like a wild animal.

"If Fiamma had had time to reach her hut, she would have defended herself with her friend's carbines, because Fiamma was as valiant as a man, but she was soon surrounded. There was no other issue available to her than a precipice open at her feet. She threw herself into it, invoking the name of her idol. The branches of a spiny fig-tree retained her between earth and heaven. The Marquis' men seized her...

"It's said that the men of Orli and Bajeta heard Beldemonio's cries, calling to Fiamma from the summit of the mountain. The lion was roaring.

"Shepherds told him that the steward of Potenza had taken his companion away. He resumed he route to Potenza. A galloping horse could not have overtaken him.

"That evening, at nightfall, the acrobat Cucuzone was turning somersaults in the public square. Suddenly, he saw a pale face among the spectators whose flamboyant eyes were looking at him. He packed up his luggage immediately and went to the ditches of the town, where Beldemonio was waiting for him. 'What do you want of me, Master?' Cucuzone asked.

"'You have wings,' Beldemonio replied. 'I want you to lend them to me in order to penetrate into the steward's palace.'

"'And what do you want to do there, Master?'

"'To take back my wife, who has been stolen from me, and steal his, in order that the law of talion can be executed.'

"Cucuzone looked at him. The idea pleased him. That night, they both penetrated into the palace via the terraces. Fiamma was liberated and the Marquise was abducted. And Fiamma knew tears.

"Beldemonio sent the steward's wife back after a day and a night, and challenged him. The steward put a price on his head.

"I shall not describe, Comtesse, all the battles that Beldemonio fought against the steward's henchmen in the Basilicata and the neighboring principalities. He was a bandit from the day that the Marquis de Casanuova declared him an outlaw. Fiamma disguised herself as a man and often fought by his side.

"In this country, out of every ten bandits, six are made by the stupidity of stewards.

"Just now I pronounced the words 'free judge.' As soon as he was a bandit, Beldemonio issued sentences. If one believes the unanimous voice in the regions where he exercised that kind of knight errantry toward and against everything connected with the government, he was a great and generous soul with a heart of gold. What he took from the State he rendered to the poor. We women are given to excusing these madmen whose heroism leads them astray and stands them up in opposition to an armed society.

"Beldemonio was soon known throughout the southern provinces. He did not want an army; he was alone with his valet Cucuzone and his mistress Fiamma.

"One evening, he encountered a poor wounded man at the foot of the mountain. His pity was excited. He loaded the wounded man on to his shoulders in order to take him to a nearby osteria. It was a trap. The osteria was full of the steward's henchmen. The doors closed on the unsuspecting Beldemonio. He was captured, put in chains and taken to the Castello di Pizzo, the somber fortress that had previously seen the last moments of Joachim Murat. It was, in fact, the end of the year 1815.

"Beldemonio had the cell in which the great Comte Monteleone, your father's friend and the friend of King Ferdinand de Bourbon, had died."

The beautiful Doria's eyelids were heavy with slumber.

"Are you listening to me, Comtesse?" Nina asked.

"I'm listening to you," Angélie replied, half-opening her beautiful veiled eyes again.

The zingara continued: "It's said that mysterious things happened in that cell, where the saint Monteleone, grandmaster of the chevaliers of iron, had died. I've often heard it recounted by the people of the south that the saint appeared to Beldemonio during the first night of his captivity, and that he traced unknown characters with a luminous hand on the wall of the cell. That is a fable.

"The truth is that the Comte de Monteleone, perhaps foreseeing his tragic end, had left a sign, incomprehensible to the vulgar, on the walls of his prison. The brotherhood of the Silence had its language if initiation and its alphabet. The police dossiers say so.

"Beldemonio should only have quit his cell to go to his death, but he got out alive with the secret of the Silence. Beldemonio had divined the enigma posed on the wall. He had found, buried in the floor of the cell, the saint Monteleone's testament.

"A few months before, one evening when Fiamma and her fine friend were allowing their boat to drift on the blue ways of the Gulf of Tarentum, not far from the mouth of the Aradano, they heard cries of distress from the sea. There was a ship there whose captain was in the process of giving the *calata umida* to one of his sailors. The *catala umida*, so called by opposition to the mortal *calata secca*, is one of those barbaric tortures that is conserved in spite of all humanity in the Levantine navy.

The *calata secca* consists of precipitating the victim from the top of the main mast on to the deck. The *calata umida* consists to hurling an unfortunate sailor into the sea from the summit of the topgallant, having previously attached a forty-eight pound cannonball to his feet. In the *calata secca* one hardly ever picks up anything but a frightfully mutilated cadaver, but it sometimes requires three or four *calata umidas* to put an end to a robust man.

"When Beldemonio arrived in the waters of the Sicilian ship, they were on the second ordeal, the mariner having resisted the first. He still had the strength to cry out and ask for pity. Fiamma and Beldemonio heard the dull and profound sound of the second fall. The movement imprinted on the sea caused their boat to dance. Beldemonio drew his dagger, put it between his teeth, and dived head first.

"The officer of the watch ordered the maneuver to raise up the victim. The extended cable was reeled in. There was no longer anything on the end of it.

Beldemonio had cut it under water with his dagger, after having freed the sailor from the cannonball attached to his feet.

"At the first cry of astonishment from the Sicilian mariners Beldemonio brought the poor victim under the boat, and Fiamma helped him to haul him aboard. The boat was hailed, but there was a calm, and it was able to draw way by the force of oars.

"The sailor's name was Ruggieri. His life is Beldemonio's. Like Cucuzone, he is devoted to him until death. There were, therefore, three people who were wandering around the Pizzo during Beldemonio's captivity like souls in torment: Fiamma, Cucuzone and Ruggieri.

"By means of a ruse, Fiamma succeeded in introducing herself into the fortress. She was able to pass the captive, her lover, a file and a letter. Cucuzone scaled the supposedly insurmountable walls of the castle and attached a rope to the bars of Beldemonio's cell. Ruggieri was waiting at the bottom of the cliff in a boat. That is how Beldemonio recovered his liberty.

"He said to his companions: 'Henceforth, I have a mission down here.' But his life was like a dream. It was a long time before he could accomplish the last will of the saint Monteleone.

"During the six years that went by between his escape from the Pizzo and the execution of Monteleone's last will, Beldemonio fought relentlessly. Twenty times…what am I saying?—a hundred times, the reports of the stewards are there to prove it—he arrived, braving lines of soldiers bristling with bayonets, at erected scaffolds; he arrived, and the executioner's blade did not drink blood.

"It was in 1817 that he first acquired the name of Porporato. There was a cut-throats' den at the foot of Mount Sila where a number or travelers had lost their lives. The neighboring populations complained, but the innkeeper, enriched by those crimes, paid off both the brigands of the mountain and the police of the pain. He was left in peace.

"Beldemonio came to sleep in that inn, all alone, in the costume of a gentleman traveler. About midnight, when he extinguished his lamp…."

At this point, Nina interrupted herself in order to ask, softly: "Are you asleep, Contessina?"

"Oh, no!" stammered Angélie, whose eyes were closed and who was already in the land of dreams, "I'm listening."

The zingara looked at the brightening daylight, and her black eyebrows frowned slightly. She extinguished the lamp.

"What happened at midnight?" Angélie asked.

Nothing is as strange as the persistence of attention in people who go to sleep while listening to a story. A confused perception survives their waking state, and what is said to them is incorporated into their dream.

"What happened," Nina went on, "is that the master of the inn, seeing a traveler so richly dressed, believed it was a windfall. He sent a child that he had to see whether the stranger was asleep.

"The child scratched and asked: "Signor, do you need anything?'

"Beldemonio heard, but did not reply. A few moments later, the staircase creaked under a heavier tread. It was the innkeeper and his two oldest sons, who were coming to do their work. The door was only closed by a latch. They came in. By the vague light that moonless nights have in our beautiful Italy, they could see that a man was lying in the bed, motionless and doubtless plunged in a profound slumber.

"'Strike first, in order to get your hand in,' said the father to his younger son. All three of them were armed with cudgels.

"The adolescent struck, and the head of the sleeping man rendered a cracked sound. 'Success at the first blow!' exclaimed the father. 'He didn't even have time to say *God have my soul!*'

"In order to acquit their conscience, the father and the older son each struck a blow, and then they went to the clothes scattered over the furniture.

"The father heard a sigh in the darkness, then two. 'What's the matter, lads?' he asked. There was no reply. And in the darkness, a third sigh was heard. After that, the father did not speak again. Beldemonio had struck three times."

"I knew that he wasn't in the bed," murmured Angélie, without opening her eyes, but with a smile. "I've heard that story told before."

"What! You aren't asleep, Comtesse?" said Nina, disappointed. "Beldemonio took the little child out, set fire to the house, and returned to the mountain.

"The child was weeping and walking ahead of him. 'Where are you taking me?' he asked.

"'To my castle,' said Beldemonio.

"'Is it yours,' asked he child, 'the great red castle that I saw once through the trees?'

"'Where?' asked Beldemonio.

"'Somewhere at the top of the mountain.' The child replied, 'but I couldn't say where. When I mentioned the castle to my father and my brothers they said that I was dreaming.'

"Day was breaking. Beldemonio chanced to look at his feet. He saw that the earth had something like large bloodstains at intervals. Involuntarily, he remembered the red dust that Pharam had dropped all along the road after his expulsion from the Purple Castle. He had been brought up in a Romichal tent, and the impressions of infancy are indelible.

"Always going upwards, he followed those patches that resembled blood. Having arrived at the summit of one of the peaks that crown the Sila, a prodigious spectacle struck is eyes.

"The path had not been beaten for a long time, Beldemonio was walking through dense brushwood, but on the ground, as gray and powdery as ash, the red marks were visible every twenty paces.

"It was like one of those magical stage sets that come into view in plays when the action is frankly led by spirits. On emerging from a narrow gorge whose overhanging walls scarcely left visible a narrow strip of sky, Beldemonio suddenly found himself facing a fertile basin where trees of every species attained a surprising height.

"In the middle of the basin was a tranquil lake, as bright as a looking-glass. Herds of fallow deer were wandering freely around the edges on lawns of magnificent thick grass, and roe deer were bounding in the nearby woodland. In the foliage, brightly plumaged birds were chasing one another and chattering, while on the lake, a flotilla of majestic swans was moving between the islets. All of that was full of life, movement and joy. Only humans were lacking.

"The child cried: 'I knew it wasn't a dream! There's my big red castle!'

"It was an immense castle—or, rather a palace—the scarlet colonnades of which were profoundly shaded from the midday sun, and fortress too, with those heavy squat towers that the Syrians built around their cities, and which saw the Biblical battles: in sum, something marvelous, and so completely unexpected, in spite of the advertisements of tradition, that Beldemonio stopped dead, his eyes dazzled and his heart constricted.

"It was the Purple Castle edified by Pope Alexander VI; it was the Canaan of the sons of Pharam, the promised land of the red tziganes, the descendants of the first father Ptolaum.

"There was no longer a path to reach the lake. For centuries, no human foot had trod the soil of those impenetrable woods. The arrival of a human being was saluted by a melancholy cry drawn from all the creatures of that terrestrial paradise.

"Aided by his dagger, Beldemonio traversed the thickets. He drank the fresh, pure water of the lake. He crossed the marble perron and made the massive doors, armored with robust steel plates, turn on their hinges.

"In the vestibule, open to all the winds, six Egyptian statues with the heads of woman and the bodies of lions were crouched on porphyry pedestals. On each step of the gigantic stairway, a jasper vase still retained the dusty skeletons of the flowers it had contained.

"You would have thought that the magic wand of an enchanter had touched that colossal magnificence, and that all of it was sleep, like the azure palaces on the sea bed. In the rooms—those Borgias were so rich!—paintings by masters were lined up in a crowd. There were masterpieces there whose existence was one reordered in archives.

"In the midst of all that, Beldemonio, the young barbarian, was disdainful and superb. His victorious heel struck delicate and expert mosaics, every square foot of which had cost a great deal of blood and gold, and said: 'Fiamma will like it here!'

"Fiamma, whose retreat, the previous night, had been a crevice in a rock or a hollow tree! As there is not an inch of land in our old European countries that is not owned, the Purple Castle had a master. It was part of the domains of the Comtes de Monteleone, who descend, via the distaff line, from the youngest son of Alexander VI, Gioffre Borgia.[51] But the Purple Castle and that delightful plateau of the Sila had remained unknown to their own lords for several generations, and its existence had been relegated to the rank of the fables that are too often published by old family charters.

"The next day, Fiamma and Beldemonio's companions were at the Purple Castle. It was then that Beldemonio became the veritable king of the Apennines, the terror of bandits and henchmen, the providence of the indigent and the abandoned.

"Comtesse, from the ruins of Paestum to the Gulf of Tarentum, you know as well as I do, all the mandolins sing the glory of Il Porporato.

"The first time he was seen in his crimson costume was at Cerignola, where the King's men had erected a scaffold for the old smuggler Isaac Birbante.[52] Isaac was a Jew; he had no consoling priest to accompany him to the summit of the fatal climb. The people lamented on seeing that poor figure curbed by age and that white beard. Suddenly, the rumor spread that a cardinal was coming along the Ascoli road. His crimson cloak and is scarlet biretta had been seen in the distance. The executioner was already brandishing his sword at the moment when the pretended cardinal emerged into the square of Cerignola. The people and the dragoons knelt down.

"The cardinal leapt on to the scaffold. 'He's going to convert the Jew!' someone cried. 'Brava, Eminienza!'

"The Eminence seized he poor bound Jew in his muscular arms and carried him off under the eyes of the stupefied executioner; and the people cried: 'Bravo, Porporato!'

"Isaac Birbante, lying across Beldemonio's horse, was already galloping along the road to the mountains.

"They followed Il Porporato; they tried to discover his retreat; but all research was futile. Only hazard or treason could reveal the bizarre and mysterious path leading to the gorge.

"Now, hazard is with Il Porporato; he has his star. And as for treason, he defies it. They are not servants who are around him; they are fanatical followers.

---

[51] Gioffre Borgia (1482-1517) married Sancia of Aragon, the daughter of King Alfonso III of Naples, obtaining as part of his dowry two estates within that kingdom, immediately before it was invaded by the French. Gioffre retired to live in his Neapolitan estates in 1504, and contrived to hang on to one of them, Squillace in Calabria, which was inherited by the son of his second marriage, and could, in theory have been passed down to the Comte de Monteleone— although history, obviously, has no record of it.

[52] This is not the name cited in the version of the anecdote related in the prologue, but what was reported there was, of course, hearsay.

His companions numbered forty to begin with, and never surpassed that number until he made himself master of the Silence. Now he commands an innumerable army.

"He blocked the two southern issues with rocks, only retaining the southern gorge and two subterranean tunnels, one of which opens on the southern slopes of the Apennines, the other to the north-west. The openings of the tunnels are hidden by rocks and brushwood. They are defended by horizontal grilles and precipices traversed with the aid of drawbridges. Each contains more than twenty obstacles, every one of which is insurmountable...

"That was his base of operations for several years. He often departed, always accompanied by Fiamma, who was his shadow, and almost always followed by his valet Cucuzone and the sailor, Ruggieri. France, England and Spain remember that young foreign lord, who dazzled them with his magnificence. All women adored him. Fiamma saw the ephemeral reign of her rivals passing, like as many summer clouds borne away by the wind. She remained the best beloved...

In 1821, Beldemonio saw the woman who, for the first time, put jealous anguish into Fiamma's heart, the one who changed the destiny of Il Porporato and threw into his soul the seed of a new ambition. He wanted to be at court, because she shone at court; he wanted to be a prince, because she was a princess.

"The testament of the saint Monteleone was not yet executed. Beldemonio came to the coast of Calabria with a double objective, and this time, Fiamma was not included in the voyage...."

For several minutes, Nina's voice had been weakening gradually. It was now a murmur. Angélie Doria was asleep, her head supported on her beautiful white arm. The first rays of the sun struck the embroidered muslin curtains.

Nina got up silently. She leaned over her companion's bed. "It was you, poor dear child," she murmured—and there was neither hatred nor rancor in her voice. "It was you, so beautiful, so gentle, so saintly...you, La Doria, who broke Fiamma's heart. Others had passed, you stayed; and I believed that he would love you with the great amour that only ends with life..." She had a pale smile. "I believed that, and I thought of dying," she went on, "but the daughters of Pharam are able to consult the mysterious book of the future. It is me who will die with him. His last kiss, his last smile, and his last sigh will be for me."

She remained very pensive for a moment, her lips parted and her eyes lowered.

While she remained silent, Angélie stirred in her sleep, and murmured a name: "Beldemonio!"

She was dreaming the story that Nina had just told her.

Nina raised her eyes to look at her, the large dark eyes from which, when she wished, a magnetic fluid flowed. There was a kind of imperious command in her gaze. Under that gaze, the slumber of the beautiful Doria became more agitated. Again her lips parted, and another name escaped:

"Julian!"

The zingara raised herself up so proudly that you would have thought her a queen. "There is only me to love him," she thought aloud. "God created our souls together. He is mine, and mine alone...for life and for death."

She leaned over Angélie's bedside and deposited a sisterly kiss on her forehead.

A few moments later a carriage was carrying her at a fast gallop toward the palace in the Strada di Capodimonte from which our nocturnal adventurer Beldemonio had departed the previous night to go to Lorédan's Doria's fête. The door opened before her, and numerous valets made way for her as if she were the mistress of the house.

She went under the arch of white marble on the frontispiece of which the inscription *Palazzo Coriolani* was traced in golden letters. She went up the stairway embalmed with flowers, and reached a door on the first floor on which she knocked gently.

A valet came to open it, and said to her: "He's asleep."

She went into the splendid bedroom of the king of Neapolitan elegance, and the valet closed the door behind her.

Fulvio was lying on a bed that was a masterpiece of magnificence and taste. He was, in fact, asleep, and it was impossible to see anything but the noble head of a pale young man, amid the burnished masses of his hair, into which the oblique rays of the rising sun put tawny reflections.

Nina knelt down next to the bed and kissed the dangling hand of the prince for a long time. There was, on the part of the zingara, a sort of pious meditation. She listened to his calm and gentle breath. She smiled; her eyes moistened. Then, suddenly, as she had done for Angélie, her gaze became fixed upon Fulvio's brow, imperious and piercing .

Almost immediately, the latter began to stir in his sleep. His lips parted, but it was not a name that escaped them.

"So young!" he murmured. "So beautiful!.... Poverty and death!"

The zingara's face expressed a sudden surprise. Her lips trembled and went pale.

"Has he seen her again?" she thought aloud. And soon afterwards: "That's the one he'll love... If he loves her, woe betide her!"

She took from her bosom a little ivory-bound notebook whose cover was strangely constellated. She opened it. On the first leaf, which she tore off, she wrote two names: *Fulvio, Céleste*. She separated the sheet into two and drew two lines on the parquet of the bedroom. Having done that, she put the two names in the palm of her hand and blew on them. The two pieces of paper flew away, separated, and came to fall together within the drawn lines. The zingara's cheeks and lips went pale.

"It's destiny," she said. Then she knelt down, her head in her hands, on the carpet, in front of Fulvio's bed. Her charming face expressed a profound discouragement

"He'll love her," she said, again, between her tears. "When I cast the lots for Angélie, the two pieces of paper separated as they fell, so I wasn't afraid of Angélie...I love her...but this one...oh, this one I hate!"

She opened one of the compartments of the notebook that she was holding. There was a microscopic deck of tarot cards inside. They were cards quite different from those whose usage has been consecrated in various civilized countries. Each of them bore several strange figures, with captions in the Roma language. Nina shuffled them and laid them out before her on the table, in threes. Then she raised her eyes, literally bathed by tears, toward Fulvio.

"I've never read," she murmured, in a tremulous voice, "I've never dared interrogate the book on the question of life or death...but I'm suffering too much...it's necessary that I know the term of my torture. Since your death belongs to me, Fulvio, my adored idol, I want to know when death will render you to me."

Her finger counted the cards, disposed as we have said. She picked them up in nines, and mingled them seven times. Then she lined them up in a single row and consulted them with a rapid glance.

Her eyes were veiled by blood. Her arms fell. There was an expression of unspeakable horror on her distraught face.

"Seven days!" she pronounced, her teeth clenched and her throat breathless. "That's impossible!"

She picked up the cards and arranged them again, after having shuffled them. Her entire body was shuddering with violent spasms.

When the cards were aligned, she closed her eyes, as if she were afraid to read the sentence rendered by the oracle. Finally, she looked, and her twisted hands struck her knees, which impacted convulsively with the floor.

"Seven days! My God! Seven days!"

The zingara remained motionless, as if annihilated, for a long time. The idea of that mortal threat, whose term was so imminent, crushed her. But soon, there was a fugitive reflection of a smile around her lips. Her eyes were reanimated. She picked up her cards and laid them out for the fourth time.

"For me?" she murmured, leaning avidly over the tarot cards,

And her face suddenly brightened with a radiant expression, while she put the hand of the sleeping Fulvio to her lips, saying, from the depths of her consoled heart:

"God is good! Seven days, for me too. We shall die together!"

III. Berta Giudicelli

We shall see the day break again, this morning, in two other bedrooms, very different from the fresh redoubt of Angélie Doria and the splendid retreat in which Prince Fulvio Coriolani was asleep. We shall return first to the home of our old acquaintance David Heimer, the director of the Neapolitan police under the name of Johann Spurzheim.

That gallant man had the coquetry of never admitting strangers to his awakening. He claimed that sleep pales and that a handsome fellow does not show himself advantageously at the beginning of the day. Even the domestics had orders not to enter his room unless they were summoned. It is, however, necessary to note one consented exception in favor of Beccafico, the employee of ambiguous appearance who wore the costume of a marchesa so well.[53] Johann received him every morning at eight o'clock.

In fact, Johan still had a few hairs, of which he was very fond. It was also necessary for him to be shaved, in order to have freshness, and on days when he had to receive ladies for the good of the State, he had a little rouge applied. Beccafico would have been able to say how mild, and even agreeable, the commerce of the director of the royal police was. He had child-like joys. His only fault was paying too much attention to local gossip.

That morning, Johann Spurzheim woke up well before the time when the chamberlain Beccafico usually came to visit him. When he ceased sleeping, the first gray gleams of twilight had scarcely appeared behind the panes of his windows. He took ten minutes, as was his custom, to gather his self-mastery. During those ten minutes he reflected, and sensed his heart light as he thought about the events of the previous night.

The hardest part is done, he thought. *I haven't regretted Barbe as much as I would have thought. It's astonishing, there are monsters of all kinds...poor Barbe had all the vices, and I ought to have occupied myself with her some time ago.*

After that funeral oration, he felt cheerful enough to try to turn over.

One loss, he went on, moaning at the effort he was making, *is Treasure! I'll need to buy another spaniel. I'll send for one from London. It's certain that if Barbe had been able to get as far as me, I'd be a dead man.*

He interrupted himself in order to utter a sigh of relief; he was more than half turned over.

---

[53] This remark has no basis in the text as presented here, but might relate to something in the text missing from the subplot featuring Peter-Paulus Brown. Beccafico might well have been involved in the solution to the problem of Tavola's cadaver and smuggling Peter-Paulus into the Palazzo Doria.

Oof! he said. *Every day I have more difficulty raising myself up, that's evident...I'm at a critical age...when this is over, I'll run like a deer, I'll jump like a kangaroo, and if I die at hundred, it will be in consequence of my excesses. Unfortunately, I have too sensual a nature; that will doom me.*

He stuck his hand, which seemed to have been dissected by a meritorious laboratory assistant, under his pillow, and drew out a little box of Russian platinum. He opened it effortfully. He took out three grains of Spanish tobacco, which he sniffed voluptuously, but with precaution. A sneeze caused an explosion throughout his machine, and nearly dispersed its various components.

He remained still momentarily, fearing a renewal of that shock, but the second explosion, which might have blown him up like a mine, did not come. Naturally, he took that opportunity to offer himself further congratulations.

Yesterday, he said to himself, *I sneezed twice, the day before, three times. It's astonishing how I'm gaining strength. Tobacco produces many effects, even on the most vigorous men, and poor Barbe always engaged me not to abuse it, in my own interest.* He interrupted himself. *Oh, my lad, how you'll be able to release the bonds on our passions when you've overcome this crisis, which comes uniquely from age! You're naturally vicious, don't try to say anything different. I know you're not a man to refuse yourself anything!*

He finally turned his eyes, with an anxious and slightly sad expression, toward the threshold, where Treasure, the King Charles spaniel, and poor Barbe had yielded the last sigh.

He must have suffered a great deal, the cherub, he thought. *Poor Barbe had bad moments. She was abrupt. Decidedly, I won't miss her as much as I believed.*

A slight creak was audible above his head.

"Are you asleep, Excellency?" asked a voice that seemed to emerge from the awning of the bed.

"No, no, my lad," replied Johann. "I'm here, awake, like a mouse, nimble and well, thank God. Has Beccafico arrived?"

"Not yet, signor. It's me, Privato, who was on guard in the box last night."

"And what's been thrown into the box, Privato, my poor fellow? You're not in good health…"

"All the reports of the signors from the fête at the Palazzo Doria have been thrown in the box," the clerk replied.

"Oh yes, the signors," said Johann, laughing. "Proud gentlemen, believe me! Send down the apparatus, Privato, and go to bed."

The tray supported by four silk threads, which we have already seen serving as a postal service during Johann's conversation with Doctor Pier Falcone, started to descend slowly, and came to a halt a few inches from the bedclothes.

"You don't need anything, signor?" asked Privato.

"No, my dear fellow. Did you hear Madame Spurzheim coughing last night?"

"Nothing was heard in the offices."

"That's frightful, Privato, my friend. We're going to lose her, you'll see. Go ahead!"

Johann had taken a handful of papers from the tray; it began to rise again, while Privato said: "My respects, signor."

He returned to his hovel, where he was finishing a libretto for Signor Magrezza, the incomparable maestro to whom we owe *Aminta e Clori Il Minotoro*, and *Citerea nell'isola di Pafo*.[54] He returned to work.

> *Pietà! Idol mio...!*
> *Delizia del cuore...!*
> *Crudel beltà...mi perdona...!*

For in every Italian opera one begs for pity and pardon from the introduction to the finale.

Johann took the papers and examined them summarily one after another. He laughed quietly, the cheerful companion, and muttered: "Two comtes, three barons, two cavaliers and a vicomtesse! And they claim that civilization is declining in our beautiful Italy. Unjust writers! Ingrate philosophers! Our great lords and noble ladies are employed for the good of the State that's all. Because one had ancestors in the crusades, is one forbidden to serve one's country? Let's see old Rigoglio's work first...it's always drafted with care...and it doesn't cost much."

He turned up his lamp and opened the first envelope.

"Oho!" he said, after scanning two pages. "Malatesta has conducted himself like a worthy little marquis! Anonymous letters are overly neglected. When one mentions anonymous letters people turn their heads away and say: 'Ugh!' but everyone reads them avidly, and everyone believes them, a little."

He fell silent and pulled a face on finishing the report. He had just seen something therein that did not please him.

"Another," he said "Let's see Comte Stellacci. Another very worthy lord. ... What!" he interjected, on arriving at the middle of his reading. "Why the devil are they making so much fuss about this Englishman and his diamond? Do I need to get mixed up in it. Good! Now there's an Englishwoman! The Englishman has brought his wife! It's astonishing...every time I pronounce that word I think of poor Barbe."

He darted an oblique glance toward the threshold.

---

[54] This is wordplay; *magrezza* means thinness and both cited titles refer to the minotaur and the labyrinth of Paphos—thus, metaphorically, to Spurzheim, to whom the pleas for pity and forgiveness included in the invented lines are tacitly addressed.

"She would have read me all this nonsense," he murmured, "and how well she would have punctuated it while reading. But a reckoning was necessary, and regrets can't be eternal."

"On to the vicomtesse! There's an honest and decent manner of paying for one's dresses! Oh, feminine pathos! Prince Fulvio resembles an immortal! I'll take charge of demonstrating that he's mortal, me Johann...and that the vicomtesse can go to the devil." He crumpled the third police report, which was written on satined and scented paper, angrily.

The fourth that he opened remained unfinished; his pushed them all away, wearily. "Our starlings are in prison," he muttered, twiddling his thumbs under the bedclothes, "that rogue Athol is truly strong...very strong. There's pleasure in taking on a player like that!"

His eyes clouded over. He reflected.

"I ought to have expected that theatrical exhibition of La Farnèse," he muttered, after a pause. "It's in the mores of the character, who's an actor to his fingertips. He would have earned a living, that handsome fellow, playing leading roles at the Teatro del Fondo. His stage setting is irreproachable. But patience! We're on a stage where there's more than one trap-door. Since he likes noise and glare, I'll arrange a plot-twist with petards and fireworks. He'll have the consolation of being applauded as he dies."

He made an effort to raise himself on to his elbow, but could not succeed. "You're attempting the impossible," he said to himself, in a paternal tone. "Wait a few days."

Then he fell back into his meditations.

"A fine player," he murmured, "who has good cards! He has all the princesses for him, who are all mad, with the Princess of Salerno in the front line, who is utterly mad. All the ladies of the court follow him like a pack of spaniels... He's a handsome fellow!" he interjected, caressing his pointed chin benevolently, "but that's infatuation. If I weren't here, me, the dying man, the cadaver, the son-in-law would be, in truth, the master of Naples!"

A key was introduced into the lock of the door situated behind the bed-head. Johann Spurzheim's face brightened. He rubbed his hands together slightly, which rendered a rattle of bones.

Here's my friend Pier Falcone, he thought, *a rather fine acquisition, I believe, who's arriving just in time. I was beginning to be slightly embarrassed by the corpse of my poor Barbe.*

Aloud, he went on: "Come in, Doctor, come in, my dear friend. I'm admirably well this morning. Come here—I'm content with you."

It was, indeed, Pier Falcone, who had taken the time to put on his town costume.

"Have you already had news of the fête, signor?" he asked.

"Already?" Johann repeated. "My friend, when you want to inform me of something, it's necessary to make more haste. It's three hours since the fête ended. I know everything. I even know that you nearly fell over backwards when you saw the face of the handsome Prince Fulvio Coriolani." He adopted a severe tone: "But don't carry a dagger with you any longer in society, my dear doctor. A friend of Johann Spurzheim must maintain decorum. Doesn't our colonel have a memorable wrist?"

"When I saw that man…," stammered Falcone, whose lips were trembling.

"Good, friend, good! We all have our little rancors, that's certain. That man did you a bad turn, I don't deny it…"

"And the man's unassailable!" exclaimed the doctor.

"Really?" said Johann, who had the sly smile so typical of him.

"I've seen it with my own eyes!" cried Falcone. "He's supported from above, supported from below…"

"Oh! Poor fellow!" murmured the director of the royal police. "How young you are, still! Look me in the eyes. Today—today, you hear—I, Johann Spurzheim, a poor phantom that one could cause to vanish by blowing on him, will make that colossus dance like a two-carlin marionette…dance on his feet, dance on his hands, on his head, until that marionette, that colossus, ends up breaking his neck!"

Falcone looked at him with an incredulous expression. Johann plunged his trembling hands under the bedclothes, saying: "The mornings are cold." Then, in a suddenly saddened tone: "I've suffered a loss, Falcone—two losses, I could say, counting my poor Barbe…"

The doctor shuddered. That memory had also been lost in the midst of the night's emotions

"Is Madame Spurzheim…?" he commenced.

"Alas, yes," Johann interrupted. "She's over there in that corner, my veritable and dear friend."

Falcone had not yet looked in that direction. He recoiled several steps at the sight of Barbe's body, illuminated by the nascent daylight.

"As you see," Johann went on. "Don't try banal consolations on me. Poor Barbe had her faults like everyone, but she was a woman above her sex. That accident only hastened her death; you know full well, doctor, that you'd condemned her yourself. I hope she didn't suffer much…a dozen spasmodic coughs…that's the least one can dread…"

He paused, and resumed, in a penetrating tone: "This sad world is regulated thus. The hour of separation arrives. I've already occupied myself with the interment, which I want to be decent, even brilliant…she was a Monteleone. …and I'd like people to say, on seeing the cortege: 'Signor Spurzheim does things well.' But it's my poor little dog hat I'm going to miss, Doctor!"

Falcone approached the threshold.

"Do you think she was coming to kill you?" he asked.

"There's no doubt about it, friend. Treasure saved his master's life. Take them both away, I beg you, for the day's progressing and someone might come."

A vivid repugnance was manifest on the doctor's face.

"Friend," said Johann, placidly, "it's necessary never to refuse me anything. If anyone ever finds out hat poor Barbe died from eating pastilles. I'll be forced to confess that you gave her that golden candy-box..."

"What!" cried the doctor. "You'd dare...?"

"Tell the truth? Always, friend, always. Load poor Barbe on to your shoulders and put her in her bed. Arrange things as necessary, placing her bloodstained handkerchief near her mouth. At the same time, bring me back the candy-box. As for the spaniel, throw him out of the window. Take him away! The sight of him renews my regrets incessantly."

He punctuated that little speech with a gesture that did not admit any reply.

Pier Falcone lifted up Barbe's body, which was cold and stiff. Johann looked t it and murmured: "I thought that it would have more effect on me. Adieu Barbe, adieu, my dear friend, Treasure!"

Pier Falcone disappeared with his double burden.

Johann resumed twiddling his thumbs under the bedclothes. When Pier Falcone came back he said to him: "Put a rug over the place where there's blood. You're a skilful chemist, you'll be able to choose me a reagent to get it out of the parquet. We'll deal with all that tomorrow. Today, we have other work to do. Sit down and let's chat. I'll give you my instructions.

In the conversation that followed, Pier Falcone was able to recognize that the director of the royal police knew as well as he did what had happened at the fête at the Palazzo Doria. Johann knew, for example, that Falcone had approached the Marquis de Malatesta and had spoken to him in a low voice at the moment of his arrest

"Although I'm content with you in general, friend," said Johan Spurzheim, on that subject, "I'll criticize you on one particular point. This is the inflexible rule: never act without orders. Malatesta is one of those allies who are no longer worth anything on the day when they know the secret of the alliance. It's necessary never to show the puppets the strings with the aid of which one makes them move. Consider yourself warned in future."

"It's sufficient, signor," replied Falcone "I hope that I'm not telling Your Excellency anything is saying that among the Princess of Salerno's ladies-in-waiting there's a very intimate companion of Angélie Doria, and that the young woman in question..."

"Friend," Johann interjected, "I sent you out there or your particular instruction, not mine. You now know what positions Il Porporato and his mistress Fiamma occupy in the Neapolitan court. Take advantage of it. But with regard to that Fiamma, remember that she's one of those individuals that one never attacks from the front. Also remember that all our thrusts must be directed, until further notice, in such a manner as never to attain the brotherhood of the Silence. That would be to strike ourselves. That's precisely the difficulty of the situation. Do you understand that clearly?"

"Perfectly, signor."

"So much the better. Also understand this: in the entire world, there is only one man capable of maneuvering in the narrow and dangerous space in which we are forced to do battle...only one man, you understand, who knows where to place the foot safely and toward what target to direct the artillery. That man is me."

Pier Falcone bowed.

"Me!" repeated Johann, with all the naïve pride that contrasted with the profound shrewdness of his nature. "Me, who will put my name, before dying, at the head of the greatest diplomats in the world...me, Johann Spurzheim, who will be Comte de Monteleone and prime minister of the Kingdom of the Two Sicilies...me, who will make of you, good friend, a Comte, a Duc, a Prince, whatever you wish, provided that I watch over you. Extinguish the lamp and prop me up on my elbow."

The doctor obeyed.

Johann commanded him to be silent with a gesture, and started on the chapter of instructions. That complete man, the foremost diplomat in the world, omitted one detail, however. He forgot to ask Pier Falcone for the gold candybox. And Pier Falcone had not reached the bottom of the staircase when he was already regretting it.

"It's necessary to find a way to take care of that," he murmured, scratching his ear. And he agitated he little bell that corresponded with the floor above, violently.

We shall quit the bedroom of the director of police in order to see day break one last time in the poor mansard at the very top of the Folquieri house, where Beldemonio had taken refuge in order to avoid the pursuit of the garrison of the Castello-Vecchio during his journey over the rooftops.

That episode—which already seems distant, so many events being concentrated in this story, without there being any effort or even desire in our part—was only a few hours away.

It was the previous evening. The woman arrived at the ultimate limits of age whom Beldemonio had paid to replace him in his good work, was sitting next to the young woman's bed, sleeping the slumber of old age that is punctuated by frequent and incessant awakenings. Céleste was reposing on the bed. Julian was in a kind of torpor on the mattress.

The reader has already recognized the two children of the inn of the Corpo-Santo, the adoptive family of poor good Manuele Giudicelli. The old woman is also known to us, less intimately, it is true, but also bearing the name of Giudicelli, belonging to an entire clan of old servants of the Comte de Monteleone. We saw her on the night when Athol and Manuele came successively to the valley of the Martorello to visit the buried ruins of the pleasure pavilion, the nuptial temple of the Comte de Monteleone and Maria des Amalfi:

the pavilion with walls of white marble where two empty cribs still remained. We saw her in the middle of the dark night; she was looking for someone in the valley. She was looking for the poor insensate who was like the spirit of the destroyed village and the dead solitude, replacing the life of a happy population. We heard her calling: "Mariola! Mariola!" and promising the fugitive not to beat her. She had a whip in her hand. She was old Berta, the mother of the nurse from whom the Monteleone children had been stolen.

She had not changed since then, Berta Giudicelli: she still had the same long, stiff figure, bent in two under the burden of the years, the same earthen face in which myriads of wrinkles mingled their confused tangles. She was only a few months older, and her eyes, covered by bristling eyebrows, had the gaze, anxious in its fixity, which announces the death-throes of tottering reason. She had not had a living person in the Martorello, save for Mariola the madwoman, with whom to talk.

On the autumn night on which our story began, she had searched for the Mariola in vain. She had not found her. Someone had taken the Mariola away.

She took her staff and ran after her slave, her madwoman, whom she made to work with blows of a whip. She had dragged herself along the roads, and slowly—very slowly—got all the way to Naples.

She asked to speak to the King. On the way, she had gone into a chapel. A priest had received her confession, one day when she believed that she was going to die. The priest had ordered her to continue her journey as far as the court.

"Sinful woman," he had said, "the mercy of God has no limits. You will not die until you have discharged your conscience. Go and repair the evil that you have done."

The King had received her at the palace because of her great age. When Berta was before the King she searched her poor head and found nothing there. She no longer knew why she had come. Since then, her vacillating reason had been renewed at intervals, only to be veiled again almost immediately. She was in the situation described by the saddest of phrases: second childhood.

That night, however, she had done her duty with regard to Julian and Céleste. Thanks to her, the two children had had fresh water. They were both saved; but they were both in the grip of a leaden sleep.

There was no lamp in that poor room. The light that had served Beldemonio as illumination, the torch planted on the terrace by the soldiers of the Castello-Vecchio, had been consumed long ago. When the first rays of the morning twilight came to attack that profound darkness, Berta, waking up for the twentieth time, stood up, muttering unintelligible words. She put her cold, dry had on Céleste's breast; she felt her heart beating there.

"Ah!" she said. "If only I had died at sixteen!"

Then she crossed the room, unsteadily, and came to feel Julian's breast, in his turn.

"It's beating," she said. "He's warm. How long is it since I've no longer had a heart?"

Then, pulling herself up almost upright, she said: "Ah! Who, then, told me to talk to the King? I need to talk to the King. I can't die without that."

She went back to her chair, where she fell asleep. After five minutes, she woke up again. She had lost the memory of recent events momentarily.

"I'm sleeping in a chair, then," she muttered. "Is it because I have no bed?"

Then memory returned to her. "I'll soon be sleeping underground!"

The light, brightening, was already casting vague gleams through the open window. The old woman started shivering.

"I'm cold," she said. "Hell must be cold. Burning isn't suffering."

There was a rosary hanging on one of the knobs of Céleste's bed. The old woman picked it up. "On the day of my first communion," she said, with an idiotic laugh, "the priest gave me one of these. I don't even know how to pray with it any longer. Let's see, though..."

She made a violent effort to summon the consecrated words to memory. But it had been too long. She could not do it. She replaced the chaplet on the bed-knob. As her eyes were about to close again it seemed to her hat something was shining vaguely on the table. Immediately, her physiognomy changed. She had an avid and sly expression, like a cat stalking a prey. She approached the table very quietly. She looked to the right and the left, to see whether the children's eyes were closed. Then her hand, like the claw of a bird of prey, closed upon the shiny object. It was a purse. It was the purse that Beldemonio had deposited on the table as he left.

A joyful gasp rasped in the old woman's throat. She had recognized gold by its feel and its sound.

She drew away from the two beds and went to the window in order to open the purse and count. There were twelve double ounces in the purse and three or four single three-ducat ounces. A triumphant smile burst forth among old Berta Giudicelli's wrinkles. Her intelligence seemed revivified in the radiance of that treasure.

With a strange clarity of reasoning, she said: "It isn't theirs, since they wanted to kill themselves for poverty. It's the other who left it...they don't know that they have it."

She emptied the purse into the palm of her hand, careful not to make any sound; then she put it back on the table. She had only left one of the small gold coins in it.

"The other!" she repeated, however, while her eyes took on a wild expression. "His voice entered into my heart...and his face...oh, God always sends me people who resemble them!"

That did not give her the idea of restituting the stolen sum. On the contrary, she knotted it in a corner of her handkerchief. On looking at the chair, however she said to herself: "Yes...yes...it's necessary that I speak to the King."

Scarcely had she sat down than her head fell on to her breast. Heavy slumber had overtaken her again.

Broad daylight was filling the room when she awoke. Her gaze turned toward Céleste, whose charming head was resting on her folded arm. Her sleep was that of an angel. The old woman rubbed her eyes.

"Oh!" she said. "I'm dreaming!" She pushed back her chair. It was as if a specter had appeared to her fearful eyes. "I'm dreaming! I'm dreaming!" she repeated.

And, as if the vision were still here, before her bewildered gaze, she fled to the far side of the room, where the young saint Julian's mattress was. Her eyes encountered the pale and handsome face of the seminarian. She uttered a stifled cry and fell to her knees, which struck the tiles dryly. Her entire body was trembling like a leaf.

"They've emerged from the ground!" she said, with an accent of profound terror. "I've seen all three of them…all three last night. Have pity on me, Lord Jesus! I'll speak to the King! I made a vow to speak to the King!"

She dragged herself as best she could toward the door. When she arrived at the threshold she darted a double glance of fright toward the bed and toward the mattress. She held her shivering hands before her eyes. She went out as one takes flight, traversed the landing and came to fall in the middle of her poor mansard, muttering through her chattering gums: "I'll speak to the King…I promised the priest…I made a vow to speak to the King!"

IV. The Awakening

After the exit of old Berta Giudicelli, the bedroom of the two children remained silent. Nothing could be heard any longer but the alternating sound of their breathing. Everything was, moreover, as it had been at the moment when Beldemonio, finding the window poorly closed, had pushed it inwards in order to seek a refuge there. Except for the soutanelle and the large prayer book, which were missing, and Céleste's change of position, now recumbent on the bed, nothing had been disturbed, and Berta, obedient to the mechanical need for order that is innate in all old women, had brought the stove back in. The pious images stuck or hung on the walls were distinctly visible now that it was daylight.

On the evening when the brother and the sister had taken their meal together under the trellis of the Osteria del Corpo-Sancto, the evening when the gentle Céleste had fired the carbine in order to defend the life of the handsome Lorédan Doria, a bleak discouragement, we recall, had succeeded the exaltation produced by the sight of the danger. Céleste and Julian, proud in their indigence, had felt profoundly humiliated by the offer of payment. Had not Angélie's dear smile already repaid Julian sufficiently? And what price was above the glance that Lorédan had darted at Céleste?

They departed for Naples. Beautiful dreams come as soon as one is no longer searching for them. All along the road they had beautiful dreams. How many times had Julian and Céleste, catching one another pensive, said in a low voice, blushing: "Are you thinking about her?" or "Are you thinking about him?" Julian blushed more than Céleste

They smiled, and did not reply. But their hearts murmured: "We'll see them again."

That was the first thing they attempted, on arriving in Naples.

While the good Manuele searched for a room for them, they escaped, asking in the street where the Palazzo Doria was located. The Palazzo Doria was not difficult to find. They soon arrived on the Piazza Spirito Santo, in the middle of the magnificent Via Toledo, which is the pride of Naples. They saw the Palazzo Doria and dissolved in tears. The passers-by did not know what was wrong with the two children: a girl, genteel in spite of her poor dress, and an adolescent wearing is humble black soutanelle with pride, who were both weeping.

Facing them, the Palazzo Doria rose up, arrogant and splendid. All the nobility of that opulent race was radiant on its frontispiece. When the portal opened, one could see the noblemen going up and down the florid perron. The brilliant horses of ten carriages were striking the lava paving in the courtyard. The two children wept

Alas, who would have suspected such a joke? The adolescent with the soutanelle was in love with Angélie Doria, whose hand princes dared not solicit. The girl loved Comte Lorédan, who had not yet found the princess destined to bear his name. Alas, alas! Céleste and Julian, the two poor little fools!

They only quit the Piazza Spirito Santo after having seen Angélie and Lorédan emerge in their carriage in order to go to the court. Both smiled through their tears.

Céleste said: "I haven't seen him so handsome…"

"She's become even more beautiful," murmured Julian, pressing his heart with both hands.

Old Manuele had been waiting for them for two hours at the rendezvous. He had rented, for them alone, the mansard in the Folquieri house.

"I have lodgings elsewhere," he said. That evening, he lay down under an arch in the port district, but the two children had good beds.

The next day, Manuele set forth to realize the promises he had made.

But do you know why Julian immediately acquired that ardent devotion for the invalids at the hospital for the poor? And do you know why Céleste close the church of Santa Maria di Monte Oliveto to accomplish her daily duties of piety?

She really was as pious as a little angel, that poor Céleste, in spite of the naïve revolts of her physiognomy; she had a heart of gold and an elite mind. Julian's charity was equally sincere. And yet, there was a reason for Céleste's assiduous devotion and Julian's charitable excesses.

Lorédan was one of the protectors of the church of Monte Oliveto, his parish.

Angélie has told us herself, in her conversation with Nina, the fake niece of the court banker, of the effect that the sight of the young saint had had on her.

As for Céleste, this is what had happened:

One evening, she was followed when she returned to her lodgings. A gentleman approached her and said: "Tomorrow, if you wish, you can have a palace. The Doria has noticed you…

Céleste had great difficulty climbing the stairs to regain her room; the distance that separated her from Lorédan had never struck her in such a crushing fashion. That was the day when Lorédan had almost fallen ill because his gaze had met Angélie's. They did not exchange their secrets. But Céleste no longer went out, and Julian only left the house when the time came to mount vigil over the sick. They remained face to face, mute and bleak.

The sadness of Manuele, who came to see them every day, visibly augmented at the same time. He came three times without bringing the daily bread. Céleste and Julian were hungry. But what is bodily suffering? Once they heard neighbors talking, who said: "Doria is going to marry Giovanna Palliante of the Paleologue Princes, and this evening, the engagement is being celebrated of Dona Angélie with Prince Coriolani."

There were no more tears. Julian's brain was on fire. Coldly and firmly, Céleste said: "The good Lord will forgive us."

She blocked the gaps in the window while Julian lay down on his mattress, moaning and gasping, for his heart was dying before his body. Then she lit the stove and set about praying.

There was dancing at the Palazzo Doria. Manuele had become a police agent in order to bring bread to his children, who, in despair, were taking refuge in death.

The window of the mansard faced eastwards. The first ray of sunlight that passed over the interior block of the Folquieri house, came to attack the open window obliquely, and slid as far as the bed where our little Céleste was asleep. Beldemonio, that connoisseur, would have stopped at that moment to contemplate her, so delectably beautiful was she. Her head, covered by scattered hair, had rolled off the pillow. Her agitated sleep had uncovered the birth of her cleavage and her young shoulders, which seemed a small-scale reproduction of an ancient fragment of sculpture. Her cheek was still a little pale, but her lips had recovered their red color and, slightly parted, revealed two rows of pearls framed with pink coral.

Beldemonio would have dreamed for a long time before that ravishing tableau. But who can tell whether Beldemonio was not seeing that ravishing tableau in his dreams?

When the sun came to brush Céleste's eyelids, she quivered slightly. Morpheus, as the Italian poets, who are frenetic mythologists, would say, struggled momentarily with the mischievous caresses of blond Phoebus, but Morpheus was defeated. Our lovely Céleste agitated under her sheets, uttered a profound sigh and opened her beautiful eyes slightly, enfeebled by repose. At first it was her everyday awakening, with a smile. Unhappiness is so foreign to childhood that even an unhappy child wakes up smiling. It requires a kind of intimate labor, a reflection, to render consciousness of distress.

But Céleste's smile did not last, and deserted her suddenly pallid lips. An idea had just crossed her mind.

"I had a dream," she said to herself.

That word, for her, signified everything: the distress, the despair stronger than faith, the suicide. The suicide in that room full of God and the Virgin Mary, could only be, in fact, a dream.

And yet...

That was her reflection. Céleste's features contracted. Her timid and sly glance slid over the floor and encountered the stove. She uttered a heart-rending cry:

"Julian might be dead!"

With one bound she was out of bed. Another took her to Julian's side. But her blind eyes could no longer see. She knelt down next to the poor mattress. She called out, in a stifled voice: "Julian! Julian!"

No response.

He's dead! she thought.

Her breast rose in a heart-rending sob. She hurled herself upon her brother, repeating again; "Julian! My Julian!"

Immediately, the seminarian woke with a start.

"What's the matter?" he asked, rubbing his eyes.

It was a deluge of kisses that replied to him. Céleste laughed. Céleste wept; Céleste was crazy.

"What's the matter with you, little sister?" asked Julian, bewildered. That abrupt awakening held him in a state of mental imbalance. He had lost all memory of what had happened.

"Oh, how good God is, Julian, my dear brother!" Céleste cried. "You're alive! There you are! I can see you! The Holy Virgin hasn't permitted our insensate crime to be accomplished!"

"Our crime!" stammered Julian, sitting up. Then, memory was suddenly born in him. "It's true! It's true!" he added, horror painted on his face. "We would have been damned! Damned forever! God has worked a miracle."

They were no longer speaking. Julian kissed his sister's forehead, and then took her by the hand. They both knelt before the crucifix. Julian recited a prayer, from the depths of his heart, in a loud voice, to which Céleste provided the response.

God must have listened to that orison, simultaneously ardent and serious, in which two poor broken hearts begged his forgiveness for having lacked the strength to suffer, and thanked him at the same time for have left them the life that was a martyrdom for them. God must have smiled, reconciled, in seeing them both strike their breasts in the bosom of their misery and promise, two repentant and contrite children, knowing that they would bless henceforth the hand of the sovereign master that was weighing upon them so harshly.

For a long time they remained kneeling, with tears of gratitude in their eyes. Children's tears, those—good tears! But those that came later were the tears of a man and a woman. They were in love, alas, and their similar wounds were bleeding again, copiously.

Prayer is the supreme remedy. They got to their feet consoled, with I know not what hope smiling for them in the future. God's gaze was upon them.

They both sat down on Céleste's bed, still holding hands.

"It's a miracle," said Julian, "a true miracle. There's the stove, still. Oh, my sister, we deserve to be punished."

"Our hearts were hardened, my poor Julian. When I think that we stuck strips of paper over the cracks in the window!"

Julian raised his eyes to Heaven. Céleste collected herself internally.

"Every miracle is the work of God," murmured Julian, whose curiosity was returning, "but how was this one accomplished? Was it you who had the strength to open the window?"

"When I woke up just now," Céleste replied, "the window was wide open."

"And the chair had been removed...the chair that closed the casement?"

"The chair was where you see it. I haven't moved anything."

"It was someone who came in from outside, then? With what purpose?"

Céleste did not reply. She seemed to be making an appeal to vague and uncertain memories.

"Perhaps a thief," said Julian. "Providence often works in strange ways."

"We have nothing that anyone could steal," said Céleste smiling sadly.

Julian had just risen to his feet abruptly. He ran to the mattress. "My soutanelle!" he cried. "And my prayer book!"

Céleste opened her eyes wide. Her gaze, like her brother's, made a tour of the room.

"The soutanelle has been stolen," Julian said. "Someone has taken my prayer book."

There was no way of denying it, and yet Céleste shook her pretty head, with a doubtful expression.

"Listen, Julian," she said. "I don't know how to express this...they're not memories...it's like a confused sensation of a dream that's imperfectly engraved in the memory...and yet, as I speak, it seems to me that it's all becoming clear and taking on substance... Did you lose consciousness immediately?"

"Immediately. I stuck my mouth against the mattress in order to have less air. I must have been insensible in a matter of minutes."

"You didn't suffer, then?"

"There was a sort of dull anguish...I could almost say: no, I didn't suffer."

"Oh, not me!" cried Céleste. "I suffered a great deal, my dear Julian. And I also experienced something like a sensation of strange and exalted pleasure. I struggled for a long time. I thought at first that the carbon vapor wasn't doing anything to us, and I thought, when I looked at you: 'He's asleep...he'll wake up tomorrow to suffer...'

"I quit the place I occupied at the foot of my bed. I traversed the whole room without tottering, I remember that clearly...and I even put my forehead, which was burning, against the window panes. The first thing that made me sense that my reason was about to fail is that I thought I saw a kind of shadow sliding along the balustrades of the gallery I passed my hand over my forehead, where there was cold sweat. The piece of paper we'd left on the table to beg our father's pardon seemed to me to double and triple. I felt joy: that was the beginning. But I wasn't tottering yet, and that astonished me.

"I knelt down in front of the chair that was at the head of my bed. I prayed, asking for celestial pity for you and for me..." She interrupted herself. "You know, dear brother, it's astonishing how precise and clear my memories are at this moment... While I was praying, I heard a noise coming from the direction of the window...but I continued talking to God, and the noise ceased..."

"And me?" asked Julian. "How was I?"

"You were immobile. You seemed to me to be sleeping a calm and peaceful slumber. A few minutes after hearing the noise, the mist began to thicken around my thought. I felt a pressure on my temples, my ears were ringing shrilly, a chill was rising from my feet to my brain, that three or four times in succession, at rapid intervals. It was as if I'd been plunged into water feet first. At the same time, sparks were playing around the corners of my eyes. My stomach tightened, and I felt a sharp pain in the back of my neck. I wanted to put my hand to it, but my arm was made of stone. 'So this is how one dies,' I said to myself, for my intelligence remained entire. 'So my hands and arms are already dead!'

"I went back to the prayer. At that moment, you uttered a great sigh. I called to you in a loud voice; you didn't reply to me. I couldn't pray any longer, though: puerile, but also tenacious, ideas were laying siege to my brain. The cold I felt in my feet preoccupied me, and I said to myself: 'We've forgotten to block the crack under the door...'

"Then I saw our father with his poor benevolent face, so gentle, and his white hair scattered over the forehead. He was weeping. I had no tears myself. Then, again, in a luminous place full of white light, I saw a saint who was smiling at us, and who said: 'My Julian! My Céleste! My children!' It was our mother...and how beautiful she was, dear brother! I tried to launch myself toward her in order to put my head in her bosom, but there was a kind of weight that still retained me to the earth.

"She called to me with a gesture full of love and her sweet smile. Oh, it seemed to me to be a long time, the time one takes to die!

"Then, again, I saw him: *him*, tall, proud, happy... He went past...he didn't even see me. 'Lord, my God,' I prayed—and that was my last thought—'may Lorédan Doria be happy...!'"

She interrupted herself again; a tear was balancing on her eyelashes. Julian lend toward her and kissed her silently.

"I'm sure," she murmured, "that you saw Angélie pass, white in the black cloud that had just covered your sight..."

Julian truck his breast and said: "I want to tear that image out of my heart."

Céleste shook her pretty pale head again.

"There was something like an icy hand," she said, "that suddenly weighed upon my head and plunged me into darkness. I lost consciousness...but not entirely, as you'll see. From the depths of that inert slumber, which I mistook for death, I heard someone open the window..."

"Ah!" said Julian, suddenly becoming more attentive.

"The strips of paper," the young woman continued, "squeaked as they tore. The chair, disturbed, grated on the floor. I think I can affirm that, at that mo-

364

ment, my head touched the lava tile. It was cold. It was hard. Doubtless I'd collapsed beside my bed. What I can certify knowingly is that I wasn't in bed…but that when I woke up just now, I found myself lying on my bed…"

"And did you see the man who opened the window?" Julian interrogated.

"See?" said Céleste. "I don't know if one can call it seeing…a confused shadow in a dense cloud…"

"Was it a man?"

"Yes, it was a man… But let me…the light is marching step by step in the darkness that is behind me…don't ask me any more questions…hold on! This struck me like a flash! I saw a bright light outside, on the terrace…a crowd of men running past the window. They were shouting and calling out to one another. The light showed the man who had come in. He was crouching down and seemed to be hiding. I'm trying in vain to take account of what that light was…"

"I'll tell you!" Julian exclaimed, having just darted a glance outside. "There's the debris of torches at intervals along the gallery. Some prisoner must have escaped last night from the Castello-Vecchio…and the man who entered here really was a thief!"

Céleste looked at the extinct torches.

"Yes," she said, "perhaps you're right; but it astonishes me to see how the sensations I experienced are coming back to me one by one. Just now it seemed that I was recounting a dream…now I can see the man. He was seized after a time by asphyxia. He fell on his hands. He crawled to the door…and I heard…yes! I'm sure I heard his hand bump into the stove and his flesh quiver as it was burned by the hot iron."

Julian picked up the stove by the handle. On the side turned away from the bed there was a large stain, still damp.

"He must have a wound!" said Julian.

Céleste pressed her head with both hands. "He didn't cry out," she continued. "No, I didn't hear him cry out…. He opened the door…with a great deal of difficulty…and then…but now I can no longer remember. Is it him who put me on the bed?"

The desperate effort she was making was legible on her face, anxious and bathed with cold sweat.

"Is it him?" she repeated, twice. "Is it him? I can see his face close to mine, but…oh, this is inexplicable, Julian, my dear brother! They're your features…it's you…more virile and stronger…with a few more years…."

Her head inclined over her breast. She was no longer trying to tame her rebellious memories. An invincible fatigue gripped her. However, she went on:

"No, no, he's not a thief. A thief couldn't resemble you, Julian…you, who are an angel…"

"My dear sister," said the young saint, after a brief interval employed in meditation, "what fills my heart is gratitude toward Providence. I see in this the inexhaustible benevolence of God. Have courage, my beloved Céleste. What is this time of proofs, so quickly passed, that we call life...?"

"Something in me cries that our life is going to change," murmured the young woman, whose eyes were half-closed and fixed. She was speaking like a somnambulist. Before Julian could reply, she continued, abruptly: "The purse! Where's the purse?"

Julian looked at her anxiously. Had the repeated shocks, after long and bleak suffering, affected the poor child's reason? "What purse?" he asked, softly

Céleste's impatient foot struck the tiles. She suddenly launched herself toward the table, moved the piece of paper, and seized the purse that old Berta had slid underneath it. Julian stood there, stupefied.

"It's him who left the purse!" said Céleste. "No, no, he isn't a thief!"

At that moment, a shadow came to stripe the tiles of the corridor two or three feet from the door. The stairway was illuminated by a narrow and high window; a man must have been between the window and the threshold; but his approach had not been announced by any noise; perhaps he had been there for some time. Céleste and Julian had not noticed that shadow, which was now motionless beyond the threshold.

Céleste lifted up the purse and said: "I told you that something fortunate was about to happen!"

It had been beautiful and rich, that purse, but old Berta's larceny had made it very light. Julian looked at it while Céleste lifted it up, playing with it, above her head.

"There are letters of pearls," said the young saint. "We'll know the name of our benefactor."

Céleste tried to read. Immediately, she went as white as the fabric of her collaret.

"What is it?" asked Julian.

He took the purse from his sister's hand. She tried to hold it back. At the first glance, he knew the name formed by the elegantly interlaced pearls. All his blood rose to his cheeks.

The pearl letters formed the name: FULVIO CORIOLANI.

"Coriolani!" he pronounced, between clenched teeth. "Why has that Prince Coriolani come into my house?"

At that moment, the shadow on the other side of the door moved. The immobile and pale face of Pier Falcone became visible on the threshold.

V. The Separation

Pier Falcone had emerged from Johann Spurzheim's bedroom costumed as a cavalier: black frock-coat and trousers, his cloak folded over his arm.

The question of how long he had been listening in the corridor is idle, since we are certain that he had heard enough.

The sight of him arrested Julian's anger, which had burst forth. The color returned to Céleste's cheeks; she knew her brother better than he knew himself. She knew that he was gentle, generous and obliging, as good as the angels, but she also knew that in an unknown covert of his heart he had a treasure of unoccupied strength, of idle courage, saved up, as it were, which could explode as a given moment with an indomitable and savage violence.

Julian was a saint. In all the world, only Céleste knew that that tranquil surface hid a fiery temperament. She had watched Julian closely, because she loved him with all her heart. She had fathomed that sick heart. She had found in its depths only one evil sentiment: an implacable hatred, a furious jealousy, against Prince Fulvio Coriolani. That hatred was born of the amour that filled Julian's existence.

The first words that Julian had heard fall from Angélie's beautiful mouth were that name: "Prince Coriolani." Angélie loved him; Julian knew that. Prince Coriolani was publicly considered as Angélie's fiancé.

Before killing himself, Julian had thought of killing his rival, whose radiant happiness insulted his misery. And perhaps that idea had occurred to Céleste; perhaps Julian had only fallen as far as the thought of the crime of suicide in order to save himself from a greater crime, murder.

Céleste had never seen Prince Fulvio Coriolani. The vague memories of the previous night, the dream of sorts, of which she retained a confused memory, were not preoccupying her at that moment. What had made her go pale was Julian's anger. What caused her to rejoice in the arrival of a stranger was the providential diversion it brought to Julian's wrath.

Pier Falcone came in then, without asking permission, and came straight to Julian, who was holding the purse of pearls in his hand. Pier Falcone examined it and said, harshly: "Does this Prince Coriolani have the habit of coming to see you at night?"

Without waiting for a response, he picked up the stove and considered it at length.

Julian looked at him, stupefied. He knew nothing about the ways of society and did not have the words necessary to chastise such insolence.

It was Céleste who replied. "Signor, you have not yet told us what right you have to interrogate us."

Pier Falcone put the stove down.

"The right hand must have retained the trace of that burn," he said, quietly. Then he turned to Céleste. "Young woman," he said, "hazard enabled me to overhear the last words you pronounced. You said: 'Something in me cries that our life is going to change.' That voice has not deceived you. You are in the presence of the man who is going to realize your presentiments. Your life is going to change, it is changing, it has changed, because, from this moment in, your past is no more than a painful dream, and you can turn your gaze without dread to the smiling future..."

A suspicion crossed Céleste's mind. She said to herself: *It's another emissary from Lorédan Doria.*

Julian crumpled the purse convulsively between his fingers. He was only thinking about Prince Coriolani. What is more cruel in this world than alms falling from the hand of an enemy?

Pier Falcone continued, addressing Julian: "It's necessary to come with me, young man."

"Come with you?" repeated Julian. "Why?"

"Manuele, your father, is waiting for you."

All of Céleste's suspicions vanished at that name. Julian drew nearer to the stranger.

"You've come on the part of our father?" he asked.

Pier Falcone nodded his head affirmatively.

"And is my sister not to come with me?" asked Julian

"Your sister is only a woman," replied Pier Falcone. "The burden that is to be placed on your shoulders requires a man to carry it."

"What burden? Can you not explain yourself more clearly?"

In a solemn tone, Pier Falcone pronounced: "Young man, I have no mission to instruct you. Someone more powerful than me will announce the good news to you. But I can tell you this: a great name is a heavy burden."

"A great name!" repeated the brother and sister, in chorus.

Céleste's eyes shone. Julian remained cold, as if nonplussed.

Pier Falcone went n: "You have demanded a new life. I am appearing before your eyes like the spirit messenger of marvelous tales; I am bringing you that new life: an entire past that is not yours, and which it is necessary for you to espouse: loves and hatreds, a family and a vengeance."

"Speak! Speak, in the name of Heaven!" cried the young woman.

Pier Falcone smiled at her. Then his gaze turned toward Julian with a challenge in which there was scorn.

"Is it you who are the man?" he murmured. "And what is he?"

There was a somber fire in Julian's eyes when he replied: "Loves and hatreds? I have my hatreds, and my loves."

Pier Falcone pointed with his finger at the purse that Julian was still holding in his hand. His other forefinger pointed at the greasy stain that was still on the side of the stove.

"That purse and that stove are two double-edged weapons for you," he said. "They will serve your love and your hatred. Come."

Julian took a step toward his mattress. Then he stopped. "I no longer have any clothes," he murmured. "They've been stolen from me."

Pier Falcone unfolded his cloak and threw it over his shoulders.

"When you are before the man who will interrogate you and instruct you," he pronounced, slowly, "you will tell him why you are presenting yourself thus clad; that will be your third weapon, and that one will kill your enemy. Come."

Julian hesitated.

Céleste put her arms around his neck. "We have never separated, my dear brother," she whispered to him. "I don't believe in this man, but I believe in God, and my heart tells me that this moment is solemn. Go; I'll wait for you; come back quickly."

They maintained the embrace for a long time. Then Julian raised his head decisively.

"I'm ready. Let's go."

Pier Falcone bowed to Céleste. "Signora," he said, as he went out first, "you won't have to wait long. Follow the man who comes, like me, in the name of the good Manuele Giudicelli, your adoptive father."

Céleste listened to her brother's footsteps drawing away. She sat down at the foot of her bed, where Julian had been beside her a little while ago. Her room seemed enormous and utterly empty. It was the first time that she had been alone. All the hopeful ideas that had excited her before vanished. She repented of having let Julies depart; and her distress was exhaled in words that filled her eyes with tears:

"What if I never see him again!"

VI. Poor Mother

The Palazzo Coriolani was as far above the Palazzo Doria as Florentine marvels are above Neapolitan elegance. Built by Luca-Mario Silice, on plans by the great Brunelleschi, it had served as a house of pleasure for the viceroys under the Spanish domination, and the Marquis de Pescaire,[55] in particular, had enlarged and embellished it with the aid of Tuscan architects. Prince Fulvio Coriolani, rich among all the great lords of Italy and possessing artistic taste to a higher degree, had restored that masterpiece, which was now he jewel of Naples.

Although Prince Fulvio Coriolani was not married, he had given magnificent fêtes in his house at which the entire court had gathered. The presence of the King and the princesses of his family had sanctioned more than once those exceptions to social etiquette, which, moreover, are not nearly as rare in Italy as they are in France.

Prince Fulvio was, in the full force of the term, the friend of the King, and the favorite of the princesses. No star on the horizon of the court shone as brightly as his. As always happens, the hateful opposition that formed around him and the jealousies that tried to bite his heels served his glory, and added to the infatuation that all Naples felt for that nobleman, so young, so handsome so opulent and so generous. Even calumny, far from harming him, enveloped him with a kind of romantic mantle that added to his stature.

No one knew his past, as we have said several times. The best-informed put about two versions that had some plausibility. The first version gave the prince a Franco-Italian origin. He had the age required for that. He was said to be the son of a Republican general and a Piedmontese princess. The second version presented him as a child of the Greek archipelago. He certainly had the grandiose air, the beauty, delicate and broad at the same time, that still distinguishes certain descendants of the proud Hellenic race In addition, the isles of the Archipelago are almost as fertile in princes as the naïve soil of Russia, where Highnesses grow in open ground, without any care or cultivation.

In the former version he had had adventures in the mountains: a little heroic brigandage, that which does good. In the second, he had had maritime adventures: a little of that grandiose patriotic piracy under the starry skies of the Oriental seas, the piracy that is so poetic and so well-draped. That suited him even better

One certainly would not have believed that if one wanted to maintain decorum, but is there not an aftertaste of mystery in those romanticizing countries that immediately puts a kind of precious aureole around the head?

---

[55] Fernando de Avalos, Marquis de Pescaire, or Pescara (1489-1525), was a soldier in the army of Charles Quint during the Italian wars.

Prince Fulvio's enemies had tried many a time to undermine the confidence of the King with the aid of those more-or-less authentic stories. In those cases, the King had smiled in the wrinkles of his great Bourbonian face. The Royal Prince also smiled and shook his head, like a man who is not saying what he thinks. The princesses exchanged knowing looks and smiled. And Fulvio's favor was augmented.

In the Palazzo Coriolani the morning sun was arriving obliquely in a rich room in which no wall-hangings except for a few light sheets of embroidered muslin hid the splendid nudity of the paneling. The luminous rays arrived there filtered by the delicate foliage of the myrtles and double pomegranates that made the neighboring terrace a cheerful and cool boscage. The breeze was coming in too, impregnated with the fresh perfumes of the orangery and royal magnolias.

The ceiling, in a cupola, representing Apollo in the midst of the nine Muses, his sisters, was signed by Calabrese. The panels, framed with mosaics, showed the Muses again with their various mythological attributes; they had been painted by Ghirlandaio and Pietro Novelli. All of that, mosaics and paintings, while maintaining the depth and the harmony that time alone can give to works of art, nevertheless had an exquisite freshness. It is only in the lands of the sun that brightness can be wedded to harmony.

Through the foliage of the thousand shrubs ornamenting the terrace, the admirable landscape presented to the north of Napes was visible. We have already seen the southern aspect: the gulf, with its enchantments, the islands, Vesuvius in the east, Pozzuoli to the west, behind Posillipo; and, in the distance, beyond Mount Gaudo, the horizon of the other sea. Here, there was the hill of the Two Gates and the hill of Sentillo, the Camaldoli, the Villa Legina, Nozaretta, the royal palace—which would be sufficient in itself to delight a vast countryside—Capodimonte and its enchanted woods.

Naples is beautiful; Naples is superb; Naples is the amour of Italy, whose pride is in Rome, Florence and the dishonored ruins of Venice.

There was a woman in that drawing-room. We would have recognized that woman easily as the one who had excited so much respect and curiosity aboard the ferry *Pausilippe*: the one who was called "the Comtesse."

She was still wearing mourning-dress. Her pale face, with regular and mild features, still retained the expression of sad and almost savage timidity that we noted in her at first sight. She was holding a letter in her hand—an open letter.

That letter will at least tell us her name. It was addressed: *To Maria Maddalena des Amalfi, dowager Comtesse de Monteleone.*

She was, therefore, the widow of the saintly man, the great citizen, the benefactor of an entire region who had lost his life for an act of heroism, very rare in our interested civilizations: for having had pity on a fallen enemy. She was Maria des Amalfi, Comtesse de Monteleone, the mother of the two children missing from the two poor cribs in the pleasure pavilion out there in the feverish marshes of the Martorello; the mother afflicted three times in her children, who were her entire heart; the martyr who had gone mad by dint of weeping all her blood in her tears.

We have seen her during the autumnal night on which our story began, amid the mysterious evolutions of the chevaliers of iron. We have seen her twice: once in the depths of the valley, in the ruins, saying to the handsome Athol, who was looking for the sealed door of the pavilion; "It's here!" and disappearing like the pale mist of warm nights at the distant summons of funereal bells; the second time, in the church of the convent, under the Byzantine vault restored by the Comtes de Monteleone; we heard her voice, which troubled the Companions of the Silence around the empty catafalque. She was mad then and captive. It was her that old Berta was pursuing, whip in hand, along the overflowing Brentola. It was her, the Comtesse de Monteleone, who spun fishing nets in the sealed cabin, under penalty of being beaten!

We have had to recall all that, because there was a great distance, in truth, between the poor insensate fleeing her jailer's whip, and the beautiful and proud woman who was at home here and who resembled, amid the magnificence of the Palazzo Coriolani, a queen in mourning. Had it not been for the hint of fearful sadness that sometimes added something grim to her gaze, one might have thought that her past madness had not left a trace on her mild and charming face; one might even have said that age had stopped for her, omitting from the tally of her years the days lost to her dementia. There was, in fact, a singular youthfulness not only in her movements and in the entire attitude of her body, but also in her facial features.

She was sitting on a sofa facing the terrace. She was crumpling the piece of paper she was holding distractedly. Her eyes seemed to be gazing without seeing the admirable landscape that was before her. A tear suddenly came to her eye and trickled down her cheek.

That exaggerated suddenness of impressions was symptomatic in her, evidence that the disturbances of her brain had left her weakened against any external or intimate shock.

"Out there," she murmured, "the wind arrived thus, charged with embalmed savors. It seems to me that it was yesterday... Oh, my poor memory! It requires a physical object to strike me to awaken many dormant memories! Those perfumes speak to me: the bitter perfumes of myrtle, the warm perfumes of the orangery! Out there, it was the sea that one saw through the flowering pomegranates. Mario, Mario! I, your widow, have spent years without saying a prayer for the repose of your soul. I no longer knew how to pray, and I was even unaware of my mourning..." She interrupted herself, passing the back of her hand slowly over her forehead. "But I want to reflect! It's necessary that I reflect. This letter...who put it by my bed-head? The writing is unknown to me. It speaks to me about my children."

That word inclined her pensive head over her bosom. She repeated, as if it were a plaint: "My children!"

Her heart could be seen beating violently beneath the black silk of her dress. She unfolded the letter and reread it. It was thus conceived:

An old friend, a relative of the noble Maria des Amalfi, is sending her these lines, in order that she has at least one good advice in the extraordinary and dangerous situation in which she finds herself at present.

There is a vast intrigue around her, but there are also open eyes that are watching to her advantage.

If Maria des Amalfi bears in her heart the mourning that her attire proclaims, let her be prudent and let her deflect with her own hand the hand of the murderer.

If Maria des Amalfi is a mother, let her be vigilant; let every word pronounced in her ear be engraved in her mind. Her children are not far away. Her children will ask her for the name of the murderer. And the murderer will betray himself...

In a few hours, Maria des Amalfi will receive further communications.

There was no signature.

Poor Maria wiped the sweat from her brow, for she was making a desperate effort to comprehend that sibylline message

"There is only him," she murmured, finally, "him toward my heart goes out so ardently. If this is against him, I don't want to hear it. I believe in him, I hope in him. As soon as he comes I'll show him this letter..."

Her gaze, which chanced to fall on the letter again, discovered there the sign that orders the turning of the page. There was something written on the other side.

All will be lost, said that postscript of sorts, *if Maria des Amalfi allows the man she knows by the name of Prince Coriolani to see this letter.*

She shuddered, not because of that threat but because of a voice that she suddenly heard behind her. The slightest sound struck her.

It was one of the three chambermaids charged with serving her, the senior one.

"His Highness puts his respect at the feet of Madame la Comtesse," she said. "His Highness asks whether Madame la Comtesse will consent to receive him."

Maria blushed like a young woman.

"The Prince can come whenever he wishes," she replied. "I will always be happy to receive him."

The chambermaid bowed. Maria des Amalfi added: "Has Signora Paola returned?"

"Signor Paola is with His Highness," replied the chambermaid, who bowed again and withdrew.

Maria started to tremble, so sharp was her emotion. She made an effort to calm herself. She had already recognized Fulvio's footsteps at the far end of the galley.

Fulvio was, in fact, coming along the terrace. Nina was accompanying him. He said to Nina: "Folquieri house, the top floor, a little room that overlooks the reigning terrace. It's necessary that I see that young woman. I want it!"

Nina looked at him sadly. "And Angélie Doria?" she murmured.

"Angélie Doria's fate is in her own hands," Coriolani replied.

Ah!" said Nina. "I wasn't jealous of that one, Fulvio, my master...my master! I know your heart even better than you know it yourself. You haven't yet loved anyone but me..."

Fulvio smiled.

Nina's black eyebrows frowned. "Are you saying the contrary?" she pronounced, in a tone of sudden menace.

"No," replied Coriolani, mildly.

"No one!" said Nina, her eyes ablaze. "You could say it, but I wouldn't believe it, because I'm in your heart. But listen to me, Fulvio: that young woman, you'll love as much as me...you'll love her more than me! And you'll be broken in that amour, Fulvio...broken by her, broken by yourself...and you'll return to me to die in despair!"

"Beautiful witch," said Coriolani, passing his fingers through the zingara's silky hair, "life is heavy and slow. May you speak the truth!"

They were in the midst of the boxes of the orange-bushes, the shiny foliage of which hid them from all gazes.

"Oh, may God hear me," she murmured, with an indescribable passion, "The moment of dying with you will by my entire existence!"

Coriolani sustained her in his arms, He gazed at her, charming and tremulous. His lips brushed her forehead twice. And he thought aloud: "Yes, it's true... we were happy." But he straightened up almost immediately, saying: "Go, Fiamma...and hurry!"

"You want it?" stammered the zingara, all of her soul in her eyes.

"I want it!" repeated Fulvio, in a firm tone.

She escaped from his arms. "Let your will be done, Master," she said. "I know the talisman that the beautiful unknown will bring you."

"You know..." the Prince began—but Nina interrupted him.

"Has old Manuele Giudicelli recovered the power of speech?"

"Who told you?" exclaimed the Prince, amazed.

"I'm a witch," said the zingara smiling. "Just answer me."

"No," said Fulvio. "Manuele is still mute...although the surgeon answers for his life."

"Well," said Nina, "when he can talk, interrogate him. You'll know what my talisman is."

She disappeared behind the flowering shrubs, kissed the hands of the Comtesse in passing, and fled.

Fulvio continued his route at a slow pace. An usher preceded him and said at the entrance to the drawing room: "The Prince!"

The Comtesse rose to her feet in order to receive him. Her emotion was at a peak, and was certainly disproportionate, at least in appearance, to the circumstance. That emotion made a complete contrast with the perfect calm of Prince Fulvio Coriolani.

It is here, above all, that the distinguished and noble beauty of the latter appeared in its full light. He did not need the animation of a fête or the prestige of lights. He offered the exquisite type of our modern elegance, while retaining the valiant amplitude of form that is the cachet of perfections. He was Alcibiades, the Greek who would have worn our black frock-coat so well.

Prince Coriolani was wearing a simple and gallant morning-suit, exclusively French, with none of the baroque tendencies that the English conquest has imposed on the fashions of all nations. For modishness, a grave symptom of decadence, is now called "fashion" everywhere, the English noun having no more genre than a true gentleman has brains.

Prince Coriolani advanced toward Maria des Amalfi and took her hand in order to brush it respectfully with his lips. He led her back to the sofa and sat down there beside her. The Comtesse looked at him, tried to speak, could not, and dissolved in tears.

"Has something here displeased you, Madame?" asked Fulvio, astonished.

She placed her two hands against her heart. Then, as if someone had expressed a doubt in her regard, she said: "I swear to you, Prince, that I have all my reason...all my reason. In the presence of the King himself I would not experience such emotion. I would have liked to present you with a tranquil face, but I cannot. No, I cannot. I expect everything from you without knowing any of what you will do for me. Doctor Daniel, my savior, had moist eyes when he spoke to me about you. That he gave me excellent and expert care, to the point of working a miracle in my favor, was for love of you; I know that, he told me so. Paola, that dear child you placed beside me, whom I have not seen again during my sojourn in Naples, and whom I love already like my sister or my daughter, had a tremulous voice and a swollen heart when she pronounced your name...

"Everyone loves you, Prince, and that is not saying enough: everyone adores you. Why have you extracted me from my misery? What reason did you have for making yourself my visible Providence down here? Answer me I beg you, for my head is still weak and my heart is reaching out to you. It seems to me, on seeing you, that my entire past is about to be reborn. I have had the dream—understand me and don't mock me—the intoxicating and charming dream that you were my son, since my entire being trembles at the sight of you, that you were the son of my beloved, Comte Mario Monteleone, since your features are his and you have his beautiful soul. I have had that dream, and, in the sincerity of my heart, I tell you this: I would give, hour by hour and day by day, all the years that remain to me to live, if that dream could be realized for one minute...in order for me to see you, arms open and eyes moist, in order for me to finally hear your voice, which reminds me of another voice, so dear, stammering in saying to me: "Mother! Mother!"

All of that was pronounced with an extraordinary and almost delirious exaltation. The very efforts that the Comtesse was making to calm the surge of her passion brought it out and gave it impetus. She was a mother, this was her son. To thwart that immense desire, which was changing of its own accord to certainty, would be to strike the poor woman with a very cruel blow.

While she was speaking, Fulvio had changed color two or three times. It was evident that all the calmness that he had maintained when entering was only apparent. As Maria finished, her arms extended and her knees already bent, ready to adore the mercy of God in the idolatry of the son who had been returned to her, one could have seen Fulvio's lips contract violently, while the veins in his temples swelled.

"I beg you, Madame," he replied, a low and hoarse voice, "not to take away my courage at the beginning of a conversation on which much depends for me. I know that you have all of your reason. I can prove it to you by saying: look at me and see what a terrible conflict is going on within me at this moment."

"That's true!" exclaimed the Comtesse. "A conflict, indeed, a terrible conflict! One would think that your heart were being wrung. But why that conflict? Is it so difficult, then, to say to one's mother: *I am your son; open your arms, here I am?*"

At that moment, Fulvio was the athlete prepared to meet a savage lion, who finds a submissive dog at his feet. His eyes lowered before that tearful mother. He searched for words and could not find any.

She thought that it was necessary to redouble her eloquence and plead that dear and sacred cause with all her heart. The poor woman put her hands together and said: "Oh, why reject me, my son? For you are my son, I sense it with all the impetus of my heart. Am I an obstacle to you in some way? I don't know, myself; I've forgotten so much about society. Perhaps you're ashamed of me, you who are a prince, you who are said to be the pride and the folly of the court? Well, you'll only say it to me...and I'll keep your secret. You'll have me here, in a corner of your house. If that's asking too much, I'll go...but let me go with my son's kiss on my forehead...and let me hear, before going, the name that would make me die of joy if it fell from your lips: Mother!"

"Mother!" Fulvio repeated, finally. "What would I not give to be able to call you by that sweet name, Madame!"

She bowed her head, and her voice changed. "I believe I'm going mad again," she murmured.

Fulvio put his hands on his heart. He had not divined that suffering.

"Doctor Daniel told me," the Comtesse went on, looking at him through her tears; 'You will find happiness and repose out there.' My God, you who have stricken me so cruelly once, at least you gave me a coffin in which to sleep alive. I ask you my God, if I only have my reason to suffer like this, render me my madness!"

Pale as he was, his eyes hollowed out by a moral torture, the reason for which the Comtesse certainly could not divine, Fulvio murmured: "Madame, you have two other children."

She sat up very straight. "Oh!" she cried. "May they forgive me! It's the dementia again! I loved you so much that I had forgotten them!"

VII. Tête-à-tête

There was fear and there was anguish. Prince Coriolani had cold sweat on his temples. Was an instant about to destroy the miracle of science operated by Doctor Daniel? Was that woman about to fall back into the depths of her madness? He had come because it was necessary finally to explain, clearly and simply, the mystery of that strange situation. He had come to lie to that woman and make her the instrument of his supreme elevation. He had come to say to her: "Here I am; I am your son!"—to say precisely what the poor abused woman expected with such a passionate desire, and what she was requesting with so many tears!

He needed a name. He needed a family in order to be the husband of Angélie Doria, the daughter of princes. He had said one day: "I shall elevate myself as far as her!" And everything that man said, he did.

But that plan, made by the adventurer Athol, in the middle of the solitary night in the ruins of the Martorello; that plan, which the papers found in the depths of the marble cupboard in Mario Monteleone's pavilion had rendered not only practicable but facile; than plan, whose execution had been so valiantly launched by Il Porporato facing Monteleone's tomb, hazard had just undone.

Athol, Porporato and Prince Coriolani were one and the same lion, a lion of amour, a lion of valorous pride, a lion of honor and generosity, in the very depths of the tenebrous path that he had chosen. His was a great heart fallen, the soul of a hero gone astray in a bandit's breast. Fulvio Coriolani no longer wanted to deceive hat kneeling mother. The lie, at that solemn and poignant moment, horrified him.

"Oh!" said the Comtesse, suddenly looking at the Prince. "Do you know what Doctor Daniel said? He said: 'Reason often has its madness; madness often has its reason.' I understand that very well. When my mind was lost, I had vague memories. and now, at present...I remember that I saw one night...among the ruins, on the edge of the water...my husband, the Comte de Monteleone...as young as I had ever seen him...and it seems to me that that was you."[56]

"It was me," said Fulvio, in order to guide her through the labyrinth in which her feeble intelligence was about to go astray. "It was me that you saw in the Martorello."

"And why," she interjected, abruptly, "do you resemble Monteleone so much, if you're not our son?"

---

[56] This feat of remembrance is not consistent with the theory of the double memory subsequently invoked in order to cover up one of the cracks in Spurzheim's intricate plan, which was presumably an improvisation made on the wing.

"I will tell you who I am, Madame," the Prince replied. "On my honor, I will not hide anything from you..."

He pronounced those words in the tone that one adopts in order to calm feverish children."

The Comtesse smiled, bitterly. "I know how people speak to the mad," she said. Then she went on, volubly: "But what does it matter to me? Do I really know whether everything that is happening around me is not a dream? Never quit me, signor, don't send me back, that's all I ask of you. I won't say any more to you about this subject, which seems so painful to you. When my fits seize me, my fits of maternal transport, I'll retire, alone, to my apartment. There, no one will be able to mock me. I'll recall, weeping, the beautiful joys that seem to me to be yesterday, and which so many years separate us. My first happiness, my dear little Mario, who had the features and he name of his father...then, when he was no longer here, the double treasure that the Virgin had sent me to console me: Julian and Céleste. I'm afraid of seeing them again. What if they, too, were to say to me: 'You aren't our mother.'?"

Time had marched on. The sun, turning around the palace, was no longer sending its rays into the drawing room, but it was still shining at the extremity of the orangery and the myrtles arranged on the terrace.

Prince Coriolani and Maria, Comtesse de Monteleone, were still sitting next to one another on the sofa, but the roles had changed: Maria was listening attentively and open-mouthed like a naïve child to whom a great story is being told.

Coriolani was speaking.

"...There is no hope," he said, continuing an explanation that was already long, "that I shall ever know the secret of my birth. I came into the world over the sea; that is all I know. The ship that bore my father, and perhaps my mother, was captured by pirates between Zante and Cephalonia.

"I was very small. The pirates came to sell the cargo in a port in southern Italy. I was given to a tribe of wandering tziganes,

"Madame, when hazard or Providence rendered me master of the secrets of your family, I was seized by a great and profound pity for such cruel misfortunes. And my mind, for an egotistical man relates everything to himself, sought complaisantly for relationships between my position and that of your son.

"Something strange happened within me, I must say; I had eyes full of tears in touching the floor of the cell that still bore traces of the blood of Mario Monteleone. I put a certain passion into divining the enigma posed to me by those completely unknown characters traced on the wall of the cell. And when I divined the enigma, I was triumphant in my heart...

"But you're weeping, Madame. This old story, in which I am only telling you about me, speaks to you about your dear husband. The dolor that you did not experience before, because the blindfold wrapped around your mind hid the full extent of your misfortune from you, you are feeling today. The mourning of your soul is like that of your garments, belated but prolonged...

"I am not your son. Too many signs tell me so. I am not your son, although there is the devotion and respect of a son within me for you. I am your guardian by the will of God, who put the testament of Monteleone in my hand. If your first-born is alive, I will be his brother and his friend, I swear it. And I will be the father of your two rediscovered children. For all that. I demand a salary..."

He stopped there, and the Comtesse shook her head slowly. He had seen a singular depression in her for a few moments.

Lowering her eyes she stammered: "It was my best hope...it was my dearest dream." Then, with a sudden force, she cried: "I am not a bad mother, Prince! I would give all my blood for my Julian and my Céleste." Letting her head fall upon her breast however, she added: "But if I had found a son like you..."

Coriolani looked at her intently. "You do not know me yet, Madame," he pronounced, sadly. His physiognomy expressed a slightly haughty coldness while he added: "The mercy that I ask of you is not to judge me when you only know half of me."

In her turn, the Comtesse looked at him with astonished eyes. "Judge you, Prince!" she repeated "By what right? Am I not uniquely obliged to you? Are you not my benefactor?"

"Have you not understood me, Madame?" relied Fulvio. "I have just said to you: for the little that I have done, I demand a salary."

"No, Prince, I haven't understood."

"Madame," said Coriolani, gravely, whose gaze suddenly became dull and cold, "I beg you to listen to me henceforth without interrupting me. Time is passing, and, in more ways than one, the fate of my entire life will be decided today. It is possible that my words will excite surprise in you. It is possible that you will be offended or even indignant. It does not depend on me to change what I have to say to you. Only remember one thing: you are free...free to accept, free to refuse. And in one case as in the other, I engage myself now, under oath, not to do anything against you or your children."

Fulvio put his hand over his eyes, as if he needed to collect himself. The Comtesse looked at him, both curiously and fearfully.

Fulvio suddenly straightened up and said: "I am not a Prince. I am only an orphan child who does not even know my family name. In two hours, I have a meeting with the King. In two hours, if I do not have proof, documents in hand, by the testament of my father and the testimony of my mother, that I am the eldest son and heir of the late Mario, Comte de Monteleone, I am doomed."

The eyes of the Comtesse shone, and then became clouded. She changed color.

"But...," she said, prey to a sort of spasm, "I've misunderstood...or I'm going mad! Say one word, and the testimony of your mother will not be lacking!"

"I will not say one word, Madame," replied Coriolani, severely, "because that word would be a lie. I have been able to lie in my life and fall short...but what I said and what I did had the reason, or at least the excuse, that I was engaged in a valiant struggle. My enemy was stronger than me. I was battling with society entire. Today, when I am only facing a woman in mourning, that pretext vanishes, the excuse is lacking. And I am a strange bandit, Madame: I only strike the strong!"

"A bandit" repeated the Comtesse, going pale.

"A soldier, if you prefer, for I have not renounced my self-esteem and I claim that my cause is just, by the same title that makes war between peoples, or between kings equitable. I was humble and poor, I have made myself rich and great. That is, in brief, my entire history...and since the beginning of the ages, it has been the history of all conquerors."

"Prince," murmured Maria des Amalfi, "it's necessary to have pity on my intelligence, which is tottering. Your words dazzle and strike me, but I sometimes try in vain to discover their precise meaning. Speak to me as you would to a child...my reason is recent, like that of a child."

Coriolani attached a gaze to her in which there was so much tenderness, both protective and filial, that a smile shone beneath the moist eyelids of the Comtesse.

"Oh yes," he murmured, "that would have been paradise! I too, in certain aspects, am a child, since I remain new to the holiest joys of existence. I do not know what a mother's kiss is...and it seems to me that God can add nothing to the felicity of a son who reposes his weary brow on the maternal bosom.

"I was alone, without support or counsel. Does God, who gives strength to the lion, tell him not to use his strength? I had passions of iron, and menacing death made me smile...

"Let me speak, Madame, let me speak, my heart has never overflowed! I did not have friends to replace the absent family. There was beside me, since I sensed that I was alive, a beautiful and tender girl...but amour has spoiled the union of our souls...I would give my right hand to call her my sister..."

"Paola?" murmured the Comtesse.

"Paola...Fiamma...Nina...," replied Fulvio, whose smile was bitter, "we have so many names, those of us who do not have a name. You've heard mention of her and me...perhaps you'll deny her at the same time as me..."

"Me, deny you, Prince?"

"And why not? Even if you were only told the truth, Madame, you would have the right."

"I swear to you..."

"Let me speak." Fulvio said, "as if you could understand me. You are good, you are generous; my words. I know, will go straight to your soul and will be engraved thereon. Later, when you have grasped the meaning that escapes you today, you will say to yourself: 'That which was noble in him was his...the rest was the crime of his destiny...'

"Yes, yes," he went on, becoming animated, "you will say that, widow of the saint that I have chosen for a patron in Heaven, widow of Mario de Monteleone, who has come to visit me so often in dream, and who has said to me so many times: 'Protect her! Protect them! My wife and my children! You cannot be saved on earth, but that will be your salvation in Heaven.'

"O my beloved and respected sister, my mother, you asked me, the first time I took you by the hand: 'Why those tears in your eyes?' Why those tears in yours, gentle lady? Does one know why, at certain solemn moments, the heart melts and breaks? In a few minutes, I shall be as cold as marble, and hard as steel, but now I am weeping...we are weeping...friends yesterday, does it not seem to you that we have spent our entire lives loving one another...?"

"Yes, Fulvio," murmured the Comtesse. "I love you with all the strength of my soul. I love you so much that I am requesting God or a miracle. Be my son! Be my son!"

He let himself slide to his knees, and put a long kiss on her joined hands.

"If I were your son, Maria," he said, "I would take you my arms and carry you away like a prey...far, far away from Naples and Italy...so far that you would no longer be able to hear the voices of those who, in a little while, will perhaps tell you who I am..."

"But who are you, then, in the name of Heaven?" cried the Comtesse.

"I am," replied Fulvio Coriolani, with calm sadness, "the friend of the King of Naples. In two hours, I might be, for you, the sanguinary and cowardly bandit who tightened the silk cord around the neck of Mario Monteleone, your husband."

"By the very name of Monteleone, and on my eternal salvation," cried Maria, exalted, "I defy anyone in the world to make me believe that infamous calumny!"

VIII. The Promise

Fulvio had resumed his bitter smile. And certainly, his conduct today had been in contradiction with his entire life. That man, who had won so many impossible victories by the very effect of that active and misunderstood strength, insouciance, who had always risen merely by gazing at the star in the sky that he called his star; the favorite of fortune, who had played the most terrible of all games of hazard since the age of fifteen without ever losing—Beldemonio, the tzigane vanquisher of his entire tribe, the Chevalier d'Athol, the fortunate adventurer, Il Porporato, the king of nocturnal legend, and finally, Prince Coriolani, the nucleus of beautiful elegance and noble grandeur in the court of Naples—felt gripped by weakness at the moment of delivering his final battle, and spoke like Pompey on the night of Pharsalus.

What, then, had happened within him, and why did he no longer have the same heart? That is the very mystery and the key to those organisms. Doubt breaks them more surely had anything else, because the condition of their existence is faith. Their passion is the beacon that guides them and the strength that sustains them. If they cease for an hour to desire ardent, they collapse and fall.

Fulvio Coriolani had piled Pelion on Ossa in order to elevate himself to the level of Angélie Doria, the beauty of beauties. Angélie Doria had determined an entirely new phase in his life. He had emerged from his mountains, which recognized him frankly as suzerain; he had entered with resolution, gladly and courageously, into a civilization that is not that of Paris, but which is civilization nevertheless. Not only had that civilization accepted him, but he had dominated it. In a matter of months, he had taken the city, and the old court that is the proudest in Europe, by storm.

Armed with the secret obtained the cells of the Pizzo, he had made himself a redoubtable general staff. In those drawing rooms, which admired in him the young and brilliant lord, the arbiter of taste, the king of fashion, there were twenty fanatical followers obedient to his slightest gesture. He held Naples by the top and bottom. If he had wanted to, he could have made a revolution in Naples. Those who were attacked by him, vanquished and broken, attested to his strength and adorned his triumph...

One day, with a marvelous rapidity, the rumor had spread in Naples that a foreign prince had just arrived, as rich as the Torlonias of Rome or the Rothschilds of Paris, as noble as the King, very young, as brilliant and beautiful as a star. The crowd formed mobs to see his carriages pass by, more opulent, and, above all, more elegant than those of the court. And suddenly, the scaffolding was removed from around a splendid palazzo that had been under restoration for some time. The palazzo appeared, brilliant and magnificent, bearing on its frontispiece the name of Coriolani inscribed in golden letters

There are names that are resplendent; no knows why, names in which there is gold, rubies, flamboyance and fanfares. The unknown name of Coriolani sounded loudly and majestically. It seemed that it had always been seen on the fronton of that royal palace. And the first time that the Prince's carriage passed through that portico in order to descend, at the gallop of its magnificent horses, the great Via Toledo, there was a hedge of spectators all the way from the Palazzo Coriolani all the way to the King's palace. From that day on, Fulvio Coriolani was the idol of Naples.

But kings, it is said, old kings, do not allow themselves to be seduced as easily as peoples. What talisman had Fulvio Coriolani employed with regard to old Ferdinand de Bourbon? There were the princesses, but that might not have sufficed.

Let us remember two things. Let us remember, first, what Francis de Bourbon had said, addressing Comte Lorédan Doria. Doria had manifested repugnance at the idea of the marriage between Fulvio and his sister, Francis had replied that Bourbon was as good a name as Doria, and that if he were not on a throne, a Bourbon would not have believed it a misalliance to give his sister or his daughter to the man we know as Prince Coriolani.

Beneath those emphatic words there was assuredly some great secret.

Let us remember, now, that King Ferdinand had loved Mario, Comte de Monteleone, paternally, and that his son Francis had had no dearer companion in his youth.

On the day when the Chevalier d'Athol, wandering on the beach at Sant'Eufemia, had taken from his bosom the dried rose of which one sepal had flown away on the waves, the Chevalier d'Athol had said as he threw himself into the sea in order to recover that frivolous and precious reassure: "I shall rise as high as her...I shall be her equal!"

The proverb in the land of Naples was: "After Bourbon, Monteleone; after Monteleone, Doria."

The evening of that same day, the Chevalier d'Athol, emerging from the marble redoubt in the valley of the Martorello where the nuptial bed and the two empty cribs were, had a name, a weapon and a point of departure. After Bourbon, Monteleone!

A Bourbon, speaking to a Doria abut a family that did not involve an misalliance, could only be alluding to the house of Monteleone.

Coriolani was the son of the martyr of the Pizzo. The King knew that, and the Royal Prince too; they were awaiting the promised proofs. The promised proofs were the testimony of the living mother and the testament of the dead father. Coriolani had the father's testament.

It only required a miracle to obtain the testimony of the living mother, who was mad. Coriolani had worked that miracle; the scales had fallen from the eyes of poor Maria des Amalfi, which had reopened to the light of reason.

Was all not said? Had that conqueror not crowned all his successes with a supreme triumph? Perhaps. Everything was in question because he no longer knew himself. He was the man of caprice and attraction even more than the man of destiny. Amour had regulated tyrannically every facet of his life. Fiamma had made him a man and free. The wife of the steward of Potenza had made him a bandit. Angélie Doria had made him a great lord...

But now a poetic and ravishing vision had suddenly appeared to him at the moment when his fate seemed fixed. Hazard—the great god of that man's variegated existence, had thrown into his path a young woman with an angelic face, and a dead woman whom he had resuscitated. And since then, his soul had wobbled, hesitant and disenchanted with the radiant goal that had previously intoxicated him. It was a new soul, a very young soul, for whom the pure seductions of the family were suddenly nascent.

The filial dream that absorbed him at the moment, the passion for the family that was growing within him, attached him by a mysterious bond to the young woman in the Folquieri house. Oh, what delightful and holy purity he had seen in the soul of that child, for whom misery and misfortune made an adorable crown! To render her fortunate, to contemplate her in her young happiness, to revive her smiles of a suave virgin, to watch over her naïve desires, to adore her kneeling, to be intoxicated by her devotion...what do I know? He was made thus; a dream replaced a dream within him. There are insatiable souls.

The man that everyone in the world had the right to name a bandit had within him, at that moment, all the delicacies of a virgin heart. His ambitions of the previous day made him ashamed. He was entirely ready to break, with his disdainful heel, the pedestal erected by so much effort, which put his head so far above the vulgar...

"Madame," he said to the Comtesse, "I am not one of those who do not believe in devotion and who deny gratitude. You are speaking in good faith, I am sure; it seems impossible for you to have scorn and hatred for me..."

"Oh" cried Monteleone's widow. "For you, Prince! Hatred or scorn...!"

Fulvio took her hand and kissed it. "Calumny is skillful," he said, "and you are surrounded by enemies as powerful as they are implacable. I say you and not me, Madame, because it is you that they will try to strike in my person...you and the heirs of Monteleone. What can they do against me, who is weary of everything and will go willingly into their traps?"

"But why this fatigue, which resembles despair?" asked the Comtesse.

She understood, vaguely, that incomprehensible nature. Perhaps she understood it better than she would have had her reason been firmer, her intelligence less shaken.

Fulvio did not reply. After a pensive silence, he went on: "Madame, I could defend and refute in advance the attacks that will lay siege to your confidence. But for that it would be necessary for me to make accusations myself, to argue, to combat. I do not want to make that effort. I will tell you what concerns you. What concerns me personally is of little importance

"Hazard, as I have already informed you, rendered me master of a secret, at the age when the head is ardent to the point of folly. Perhaps I took too long to sense the importance of that secret. The secret belonged to Mario Monteleone, and to you, Madame, as his widow and his heir. When I had the secret, I swore an oath. I took years before accomplishing it.

"One day, ambition came to me. It was because of ambition that I remembered my oath. The accomplishment of my oath did, in fact, open a new path to me. Those are my veritable crimes, Madame. If there can be an excuse for ambition, that veritably human—which is to say, egotistical—sentiment, it is amour, I had that excuse. It was amour that made that ambition.

"I was in love—oh, ardently in love, Madame! That amour rendered me so strong that I was victorious in an insensate struggle.

"I remade in myself the work of God. The man who had come into the world humble and or placed himself among the great of the earth, by the sole power of his will. Were my desire to impel me, tomorrow I would be the prime minister of the King of the Two Sicilies, unless you barred my passage. But you will bar my passage, Madame, and my desires are dead..."

He interrupted the Comtesse, as she was about to protest, with a gesture full of fatigue.

"Only a few moments remain to us," he said, "and I have not yet told you the objective of this conversation. I mentioned to you a salary that I have to demand of you. In order to merit that salary, I will render your two children to you. I know that they are in Naples. I am on their track..."

Maria des Amalfi went pale, and began to tremble.

"My Julian," she murmured, "and my poor little Céleste."

"My belief," the Prince continued, "is that I alone am in a position to recover for you all that you have lost. I have the King's ear; the ministers fear me; the Royal Prince likes me, and the sovereign's entire family is with me. In addition, I possess the titles confided to me by the Master's testament: the birth certificate of Mario, Comte de Montefiore, your first-born, the birth certificates of Julian and Céleste. Lastly, I know each and every one of your enemies.

"The salary that I request is this. I have told the King, the Royal Prince and the august princesses that I am Mario, Comte de Monteleone, your son. I have not told you that, Madame. If I had told you, you would have believed me.

"I have made myself strong enough to take to the King today, in the palace of the Princes of Salerno, where the royal family is assembled, the proofs of my birth: my dead father's testament and the testimony of my living mother. Will you aid me in sustaining that lie?

"Don't reply before I've finished completely. I'll finish by saying that whatever your determination might be, even if you refuse my request, I shall accomplish my duty as the executor of the your dead husband's testament. I shall put the two Monteleone children in your hands, and I will restore the three birth certificates that I found in the marble cupboard in the pleasure pavilion in the Martorello."

Prince Fulvio fell silent.

Maria des Amalfi's face expressed an indescribable surprise. "Is it your secret desire that I refuse, then, signor?" she murmured. "In all this you seem to be pleading against yourself."

"Passion," replied Coriolani, "causes one to pass over certain obstacles. One does not even see them if the passion is violent or ardent. If the passion dies or is dead, the obstacles loom up again. There are some such that one experiences, in overcoming them, a certain sentiment of repugnance. The idea of hearing a noble lady, a mother, affirm a lie, and call someone her son who is not, is one of those obstacles for me...and my passion is dead."

"You no longer have ambition, then?"

"I have another ambition...and I would like to be able to say that I no longer have amour."

Perhaps the image of Angélie Doria passed before his eyes at that moment, the image of Angélie, so sweet and so beautiful. He lifted his gaze toward the heavens; his features were painted with a mortal sadness.

"I do not know whether I would have understood you once, signor," said the Comtesse. "Today, it's true, your benevolence has rendered me thought, but my poor head is very weak, and I would be wasting my time trying to fathom enigmas. I do not know why you are losing courage, I do not know the cause of this sudden change that has so visibly taken place in you since the beginning of our conversation. I do not even know the name of the woman who was like the soul of your ambition; I only feel sorry for you if you no longer love her, for I sense inside me that she loves you...or rather, I sense that it is impossible to cease loving you. For myself, even if I lived to be a hundred, I could not forget how my heart beat faster at the idea that I was your mother.

"Now that you have disabused me, signor, now that you are proposing to me coldly, almost disdainfully, I know not what bargain of which you are ashamed yourself, I feel sad, but I have no rancor. I regret you, who would have been the glory of our restored house. I regret you, and I cherish you.

"Perhaps I cannot grasp as well as you the scope of the bargain that you are proposing to me. At least, I do not blush in saying to you: I accept."

"You accept, Madame?" cried Fulvio, astonished. A little blood rose to his cheeks, previously so pale.

The Comtesse looked at him, smiling. "Why should I blush at calling you my son, Fulvio," she said, "since my dearest wish was to hear you call me 'Mother.' And may it please God that it is possible to renounce a bond so soon broken. If I had my daughter with me, I would say to her: 'This is the man that it is necessary to love.'"

387

The Prince raised his head sharply, but he repressed the words that were on his lips. And the same smile of bitter melancholy returned to sadden the noble beauty of his features.

"I will say this, Fulvio," the Comtesse went on, "as I will say it to King Ferdinand de Bourbon, since you wish it: 'This is the elder son of Mario, Comte de Monteleone, my husband!'"

IX. Father-in-Law and Son-in-Law

It was about midday. The house of the director of the royal police, Johann Spurzheim, was hung in black outside, and the clergy of Santa Maria del Carmine, his parish, were maintaining a vigil in the room of Barbe Spurzheim, transformed into a chapel of rest. Everyone felt sorry for the unfortunate husband, who was too weak and too ill to come to pray beside his dead wife.

It had been a good marriage, one of those solitary and withdrawn marriages in which the man is everything for the woman and the woman everything for the man. The priests said to one another: "The worthy signor will not wear his mourning for long. God will unite in Haven those who loved one another on earth."

Johann Spurzheim had done things well. He had wanted to prove once more the tenderness that he had for his dear wife by giving her a splendid funeral. The clergy of Santa Maria del Carmine could not doubt that a household composed of a wife so well buried and a husband who buried so well would by happily reunited in a better world.

In the meantime, Johann was in his bedroom, in the company of the young and good doctor, Pier Falcone, to whom he was more attached with every passing moment. They were having lunch together, Johann sucking a slice of marzipan dipped in a glass of tokay, and Pier Falcone, less immaterial, washing down a duck pâté with a bottle of Sicilian wine.

Johann thought, mildly: *To think that that handsome fellow is like all the rest! The stomach is a chink in the armor for men of appetite.* He added: *Poor Barbe scarcely ate; she must still have had strength to have strangled Treasure.* He interrupted himself and said: "Friend, remind me to buy another spaniel. And give me back, I beg you, the rest of the pastilles that were in the golden candy-box."

Pier Falcone raised his glass and saluted him, saying: "To your health, signor. You are a hundred per cent better than yesterday."

Johann swelled with pride. "Poor Barbe certainly believed that she was certain to wear a widow's mourning," he replied. "I shall miss her, Falcone...but not as much as I thought. Give me the candy-box, please...."

The doctor took a large gulp of tokay. "Signor," he replied, "I'm making a collection of those bagatelles. I've put your golden box on my shelf, with Barbe de Monteleone's."

"The pastilles inside?"

"The pastilles inside. They're so perfectly similar that seeing them side by side like that, one wouldn't be able to detect any difference. There's nothing as eloquent as material objects, signor."

"Are you already seeking weapons against me, Pier Falcone, my son?" murmured Johann, in a penetrating tone

"There are two kinds of weapons, signor," replied the physician, coolly, and not missing a bite; "there are offensive weapons and there are defensive weapons: the sword that strikes, the buckler that parries he thrust. Frankly, against you, I don't think I need a sword...but last night's events have given me a great idea of your capability. I don't disdain the buckler."

"Ah!" said Johann, sighing. "The world is always the same. Acquire a fine affection for a man, and you're sure to find an ingrate. Keep your buckler, Falcone, my poor friend...personally, I don't want any against you."

The doctor helped himself to a chicken wing.

"Signor," he said, "be just and be frank; isn't it better that I can always sit down at table beside your bed without anxiety...and drink your wine, which I declare to be excellent?"

"What!" cried the director of the royal police. "You suppose...?"

"Ha ha, signor...on condition of regretting me, like poor Barbe."

Johann's little gray eyes blinked, He smiled.

"You're cheerful this morning, my worthy comrade," he murmured. "What I like most about you is your joyful character. Come on, let's talk reasonably. The young man is here?"

"And he's already impatient at not seeing his Manuele. He wants to return to his sister."

"He wants! He wants! It's a strange story, you know: that suicide, that window opened by an escaping bandit, that purse bearing the name of Coriolani, that providential burn...we're going to be rich and powerful, Falcone."

"I've been weak and poor for a long time, signor."

"And you've suffered a cruel insult..."

"I haven't forgotten it, signor."

"When one is powerful and rich, friend, one can avenge oneself!"

"Be tranquil, signor; rich or poor, powerful or weak, I shall do what is necessary to avenge myself."

Johann had finished his marzipan. He experienced the bliss that follows a copious and well digested meal.

"Good, good, my excellent companion," he said, twiddling his thumbs above his bedclothes, on which the crumbs of the pastry remained. "Last night, you wanted to go too quickly..."

"Let's not return to that," said Pier Falcone.

"Don't let it take away your appetite, comrade," Johann went on. "I don't hold it against you. As for the vengeance, it's dormant within you, like the fortune, as long as you don't try to deal as an equal with the man who is your master."

"Who, then is my master?" asked Pier Falcone, smiling.

"A poor invalid," replied Johann, "whom you could knock down simply by blowing on him..." He interrupted himself to add, in a strident voice: "And who will break you like a dry straw torch, Doctor Pier Falcone, if you try to resist him."

Falcone started to rise to his feet, but he sat down again and filled his glass.

"Keep your two boxes, naughty child," the director of the royal police went on, without taking the trouble to hide his disdain. If I weren't better than you—or, let's talk frankly, if I didn't need you—your two golden boxes would take you to the gallows. But have no fear; I like you and you'll never be strong enough to hinder me. Let's get back to business. How do you like the girl?"

Pier Falcone retained the morsel suspended between his plate and his mouth. His eyes shone.

"You love her already?" cried Johan.

"No," replied Falcone, "but better than that: I think Coriolani loves her."

"There are two, then," said Johann. "Lorédan Doria and Fulvio Coriolani. I know more than one princess who would like to be in that little girl's place. But see how everything is working out, Falcone! There isn't even any need to take a hand! Those two men, who are in our path, will devour one another some day, and we'll be tranquil spectators of the battle. The blind will say; 'It's chance,' but there will be at least two people, friend Falcone—you and me—who will know that chance has another name here, and that poor moribund Johann Spurzheim has struck a fine blow. What did he seminarian say on the way?"

"He only talked about his father Manuele."

"And the girl?"

"I don't bring the girl."

Johann started under his covers. "And you say that Coriolani is in love with her?" he cried. "Ring, wretch! Ring quickly!"

The doctor immediately agitated a bell-cord hanging down over the mantelpiece. The bell rang clearly on the floor above. Almost instantly, the ceiling of Johann's bed opened.

"Why!" said Beccafico's high-pitched voice. "The man from yesterday is still there. Good day, Excellency. How are you feeling?"

"Better and better, my lad. My convalescence is making giant strides, thank God. Send down a blank warrant with the correspondence."

"There's something else as well as the correspondence," said Beccafico.

"Send everything."

The tray began to descend slowly. At the same time, in spite of the carefully closed windows, the bells of Santa Maria del Carmine could be heard ringing at full tilt.

"That's poor Barbe's knell," muttered Joann. "This time yesterday, she was here, at my bedside. That's life!"

On the tray there were several letters and a small cubic package. The blank warrant was also there, with a pen and ink. First, Joann filled in the warrant.

"Go yourself, immediately," he ordered Beccafico. "Take two agents, and have the girl here in half an hour."

The tray went up again. Johann had put his correspondence and the square package wrapped in paper next to him on the coverlet. He felt it, and began to smile, looking at the doctor from the corner of his eye.

"You're not strong, friend," he murmured, "not strong...fortunately, the poor moribund has intelligence enough for two. The girl was implied. Another time, doctor, I'll dot the *i*s for you. Damn it! You have, however, paid for knowing that the Chevalier d'Athol doesn't beat round the bush."

Pier Falcone's face suddenly darkened. He put his knife and fork down.

"No, no," said Johann. "Eat well! Drink better! We still have a lot of effort to make today."

While speaking, he undid the square packet. The doctor heard a metallic sound. He even saw a shiny object disappear beneath the director's sheet, but there was never much daylight in the room. You might have thought it the boudoir of an old coquette.

Johann's smile became more and more joyful. However, he had not yet opened his letters; it was, therefore, the square package that was entirely responsible for that contentment.

"She's said to be as beautiful as the angels, that girl," he said.

"Very beautiful," replied Falcone, laconically.

"See the luck that you have, friend," the director of police continued. "Poor Barbe was over forty. She was frightful and repulsive—said without offending her memory. You're gaining by the exchange, firstly by not having poor Barbe, and secondly by having the other, a jewel of sixteen who will bring you a princely fortune and the honor of being the son-in-law of Johann Spurzheim, future Comte de Monteleone and prime minister of His Majesty the King of Naples."

"To arrive at all that," asked Falcone, looking him in the face, "isn't it necessary that Monteleone's widow consents to marry you, signor?"

"Yes, my dear child," replied Johann, winking maliciously, "yes, my dear son-in-law Falcone. That frightens you, doesn't it? You consider it to be impossible that a woman would consent to marry a moribund like me..."

"Signor," the doctor put in, "I only consider to be impossible that Maria des Amalfi could ever marry David Heimer."

Johann did not lose his smile. "When you pronounce that name, dear friend," he said, softly, "speak in a lower voice if you don't want anything unfortunate to happen to you. Any yet, fundamentally, that name is as good as any other. The man who bore it started from a very low position...he played more than one difficult game...he never lost any of them..."

His gaze took on the expression of conscious satisfaction that was habitual to him. No man had ever been more imperturbably content with himself than the good signor Johan Spurzheim.

"So, my son-in-law," he went on, making the doctor a tender little threatening gesture, "we know the story of the Martorello in detail?"

"Yes, signor," replied Falcone.

"May one ask by what channel?"

"I know—what does the rest matter?"

"There's reason in that. And what do you think of the expedient employed by David Heimer?"

"Odious, signor," replied Falcone, without hesitation. At the same time, he pushed away his plate and his glass.

"Ha ha!" said Johann Spurzheim. "You're a severe moralist, my beloved son-in-law. Personally, I declare the method bold and remarkably ingenious. It's one of the most subtle stratagems of which I've ever had knowledge in my life. To make use of a madwoman to set fire to the powder is adroit, prudent, and leaves no trace."

"But it's necessary not to take it into one's head to marry the madwoman," said Falcone rising one's feet.

"Come and sit down here at the head of my bed, like a pious son my son-in-law." said the director of the royal police, cheerfully, "and let's have a little chat about medicine, since it's your specialty. Have you studied the fundamentals of madness a little?"

"Enough to discuss it with you."

"Ha ha! That's to tell me that I'm a poor ignoramus...but I have an excellent character and we'll make a very close little family when we're treated. If you've studied madness fundamentally, you must know the theory of the two memories."

"I know it."

"Take the trouble to explain it to me, please."

"Its authors have established," Falcone replied, "and experiments have proved, "that a madman, in his periods of dementia, has the memory of events produced successively during his various crises."

"Very good."

"And that once cured, or traversing a lucid period, the madman has the memory of events occurring before his illness or during other lucid intervals."

"Perfect. And the two memories never mingle?"

"That seems authentically demonstrated."

"Marvelous! Then you must understand that I have absolutely nothing to fear in approaching Maria des Amalfi, the widow of the Comte de Monteleone. In order for her to remember the weapon that I put in her hand on the night of the thirteenth of October 1815, it would be necessary for her to go mad again...and when mad people talk, people do not believe them, my son-in-law!"

He opened one of the items of his correspondence at random.

Falcone started coughing, with a doubtful expression. Johann put his hand under the bedclothes, swiftly, as if he wanted to take something out, but changed his mind, and his hand came back empty.

"How those bells are ringing!" he murmured. "No one can say that that isn't an appropriate funeral…!" He interrupted himself as he scanned the first letter that had come to hand. "Uh oh! Our friends at the Maggiore prison have made difficulties."

"Who do you call our friends at the Maggiore prison?" asked the doctor.

"Those marionettes I made dance last night at the Palazzo Doria," replied Spurzheim. "Malatesta, Sampieri, Colonna and the rest. They've tried to recoil! But when I hold someone, friend Falcone, I hold them hard. Our men have returned to better sentiments. In an hour, they'll be free. In two hours, they'll play the second act of their comedy."

"May I know…?"

"No need. Your role will be whispered when the time comes... Another story! A wounded man was taken to the Palazzo Coriolani last night...an old man. That's Manuele Giudicelli, indubitably. At ten o'clock his morning he hadn't recovered the power of speech. His physician is Doctor Antonio Doni. Do you know him, my son-in-law?"

"I'm one of his pupils, signor."

"Bravo, friend!"

"Why bravo?"

"Because it's necessary that Manuele Giudicelli doesn't recover the power of speech."

"And in what way does my relationship with Doctor Antonio Doni…?"

Johann opened a third letter.

"Oho!" he said. "You know a great many people, my dear son-in-law. I'll answer your question shortly. Permit me to ask you what kind of relationship you have with the charming young woman known at the court of Naples under the name of Nina Dolci?"

"That's my business, signor," replied Falcone.

Johann darted a rapid glance at him, so piercing that the doctor lowered his eyes involuntarily.

"Come, come!" said the director of the royal police, with a sudden bonhomie. "I don't want to penetrate your little secrets, my son-in-law. Here's a fourth letter, which speaks to me about my noble fiancée, the dowager Comtesse de Monteleone. She too spent the night at the palace of the glorious Fulvio. Everything is going all the better because he thinks himself fully armored. He's an intelligent fellow, one can't say the contrary..."

Suddenly, he stopped talking. Then he collected himself momentarily, his head in his hands.

"The two of us," he resumed, after a pause, and in a manner that contrasted by virtue of its seriousness with his habitual sarcastic tone, "are going to occupy ourselves with our marriages!"

"In order for us to be happy husbands," Johann Spurzheim, "you of Monteleone's heiress of Monteleone and me of his widow, two things are necessary. Firstly, it's necessary that Manuele remains mute, and I only know one paralysis that is sure and good, which is death. Secondly, as I can't go to pay my court to the noble Maria des Amalfi, it's necessary that the noble Maria des Amalfi takes the trouble to come to find me in my poor house. Those are two delicate and difficult precautions. I'm counting on you to carry them out successfully."

"Kill Manuele Giudicelli and abduct the Comtesse?" pronounced Pier Falcone, coldly.

"Exactly!" retorted Johann. "You reduce things to their simplest expression. I don't detest that."

"Signor," said Pier Falcone, "I call things by their name in order that there's no ambiguity. I can't kill Manuele and I can't abduct the Comtesse."

"Bah!" said the director of the royal police. "Why can't you, my son-in-law?"

"Because they're both dangerous, signor, and I don't want to expose myself to any personal danger."

"Good idea!" said Johann, smiling. "I like that better than scruples. What if I asked you nicely, though?"

"It would be futile."

"And if you were threatened a little?"

"Try," said Pier Falcone, who put a toothpick between his lips.

Johan looked at him with the sly and amiable smile that we have described. For the second time, the doctor coughed. It was doubtless a fashion of maintaining countenance under the mocking gaze of the director of the royal police. But the latter did not take it that way.

"It's necessary to look after that cough, my son-in-law," he said, in a tone of affectionate interest. "It reminds me to much of poor Barbe's cough."

Falcone frowned.

Johann put his hand under his bedclothes, swiftly, and added, with a deep sigh: "I've neglected nothing for her funeral."

This time his hand brought back a small object that glinted in the half-light of the alcove. He held the object out to Falcone, simply saying: "It's for the cough, my son-law. Poor Barbe had great confidence in it."

Falcone seized the object hastily. His cheeks, and even his lips, went pale.

"You've sent your agents to my home!" he exclaimed.

"A pastille," Johan repeated, "for the cough..."

Falcone shot him a bloody glance. He had recognized at first glance one of the golden candy-boxes. Johann, who was still smiling, plunged his hand under the bedclothes and pulled out an identical box.

"Would you prefer to take one from this box, my friend? I can't remember, exactly, which is the good one."

He threw the second box on to Falcone's knees. The latter was quivering with wrath.

"Remember this, my son-in-law," he murmured, his smile becoming lop-sided. "I'm very strong...and you're only an apprentice as yet."

"But now that the two boxes are in my power...," Falcone tried to say.

Johan started to read aloud a piece of paper that was among his letters.

"*Report addressed to His Excellency the director of the royal police by Jacopo Civetta, inspector third class, regarding the seizure carried out at the domicile of Signor Pier Falcone, doctor of medicine of the faculty of Bologna. The said seizure consisted of two golden boxes bearing the monogram of Dona Barba Spurzheim, wife of the signor director...*"

Falcone's fists clenched and he uttered a dull groan.

"I'm very strong," said Johann, interrupting himself and resuming his smile. "Don't you agree, my son-in-law?"

There was a sudden noise above the bed.

"The Minister of State's carriage has just stopped at the door to the offices," said Beccafico's voice.

Joann had a tremor, soon suppressed.

"On your feet, Falcone!" he ordered. "And to work!"

The doctor stood up, involuntarily.

Addressing the invisible Beccafico, Johan continued: "Since His Excellency deigns to visit a poor man who is about to die, have all doors opened for him. Arrange for him to pass through the chamber of mourning. Don't hide it from him than I'm very low...very low, alas! The unfortunate and premature death of poor Barbe has administered the final blow. Go!"

The trapdoor closed.

"Friend," said Johann to Falcone, "this isn't chance. I'm very strong. Say a few words to the seminarian in passing to bid him to be patient. We'll have need of him after my conversation with the Comtesse. You need to be at the Palazzo Coriolani in ten minutes."

"But in the name of Heaven!" cried Falcone, with a veritable distress. "How do you expect me to do that?"

Johan shrugged his shoulders. "Doctor Antonio Doni," he replied, "left this morning for Salerno. That isn't by chance; I put my hand to everything...but it might seem to be chance...like the minister's visit..." He laughed dryly, and went on: "That's for Manuele. As for the Comtesse, she received a love letter this morning, and you'll find at the door of the Palazzo Coriolani a carriage exactly similar to those of the glorious Fulvio. The rest is up to you. Damn it! Physicians replace one another; that's the brotherhood. And when one is dealing with a poor mother in quest of her children...but here comes His Excellency. Go! Go!"

Pier Falcone left by the corridor that led to the former study of Barbe Spurzheim. It was in that study that Julian was waiting, already anxious, and saddened by being separated from his sister. Falcone went into the study at a run; he had the appearance of a madman. He paled and stopped at the sight of the vast armchair in which Barbe had been sitting the previous evening.

Johann had hastily opened the little cupboard hidden between his bed and the wall. He put his ear to the instrument composed of an ivory funnel retained by a flexible cable.

"Have you come to fetch me?" Julie asked Falcone.

Let's see how he replies, thought Johann, who had heard the question clearly. *He isn't strong...but I don't like people who are too strong.*

"It's not a matter of you!" Falcone replied. "This is the house of the devil!"

Johann started to laugh, shrugging his shoulders. The ceiling of his bed creaked slightly; a piece of paper fell on to the covers, while Beccafico's voice said: "Privato is taking His Excellency via the mourning chambers."

The piece of paper contained these words: *The young woman was no longer to be found in the Folquieri house.*

Johann put his finger to his forehead. He heard footsteps in the nearby corridor.

"It's necessary to profit from this," he muttered, closing his little cupboard again. "The good player profits from everything...and in the fifty years I've been on earth I haven't encountered a player as skillful as me."

Having thus rendered himself full justice, Johann Spurzheim arranged himself on his pillow and got ready to gasp plaintively, because the door was opening.

"Will His Excellency please proceed gently," said Privato, who appeared on the threshold, his pen behind his ear. "His Lordship is very low...very low!"

Johann privately awarded him a ducat of gratification; he did not abuse gratifications, but he sometimes had the intention of recompensing virtue. History does not record whether the thin and emaciated Privato, distinguished poet, ever received his ducat.

"It reeks of death here," murmured the minister, as he came in.

Privato closed the door behind him.

Signor Carlo Piccolomini, Minister of State to King Ferdinand of Naples, took a few steps forward, guiding himself with his cane like a blind man. He had a mixed expression on his haughty face, in which suspicion and repulsion were combined in almost equal doses.

"Are you in bed, Signor Spurzheim?" he asked, as he arrived next to the table where Doctor Pier Falcone had previously taken his morning meal.

Johann's only reply was a long and feeble groan.

Signor Piccolomini took another three steps.

"Have you no one to watch over you?" asked the Minister of State.

Johann uttered half a dozen stifled plants, and then replied: "Oh, Your Excellency! Worthy Signor Piccolomini, your conduct is that of a Christian and a true gentleman! You've come to visit a poor subaltern who is packing his bags for the other world. That's fine…one might even say sublime, in this century of egotism and hardness. But you've always had an elite heart, Signor Picolomini, my dear and beloved master. Oh, Lord Jesus! Oh, Virgin Mother, is it necessary to suffer so much, then, in order for the soul to quit this miserable prison?"

The minister was at the bedside. His eyes, gradually habituated to the obscurity, were beginning to distinguish the pale, shriveled and cadaverous face of the director of the royal police. He thought, privately: *There's a poor fellow who won't last the day.*

"Your Excellency thinks of everything," Johann went on, between two groans. "Your Excellency has deigned to ask me why I'm alone and without a nurse in his extremity. Oh, Lord Jesus, savior of the world!...we were such a close couple...I couldn't suffer anyone beside me other than my poor Barbe. Could I ever have imagined that she would precede me where we were both bound? I'm alone, in fact, alone and abandoned down here, Excellency…and I wouldn't have any consolation if I didn't know that my hours are numbered. Sit down, Excellency; the head is still sound, since I've been able to think of Your Excellency's interests."

"Please, signor director," said the minister, "let's only talk about you."

"About me!" Johann protested. "I've fulfilled, thank God, my last duties of religion, and I have nothing more to do on earth. Lord Jesus, and Saint John, my patron, when I think that I've been accused of being ambitious for the position of which Your Excellency is the ornament!"

"I never believed that, Signor Spurzheim."

"For a long time, Signor Piccolomini, I've no longer had any attachment to the things of the earth. I wanted to give my sovereign and you one last proof of zeal by thwarting the projects of an association of malefactors gathered to exploit royal good faith with the aid of a diamond supposedly extracted from the mines of India…"

"Ah!" said the minister. "You have some particular notions about that..?"

"Excellency, I have even pretended to enter into the conspiracy..."

"That is to take devotion a long way, Signor Johann."

"My life was the King's, my honor too, Excellency. Everything necessary to follow the affair will be found in my papers. At the moment, I want to talk to you about matters that are far more important. If you don't put your foot on the head of Fulvio Coriolani today, Coriolani will be prime minister tomorrow, and the traitor Armellino will be sleeping in Your Excellency's palace."

What gave Johann strength was that for some time, already, Signor Piccolomini had felt the ground of the court trembling under his feet. The impression of what had happened the previous night at the Palazzo Doria was still fresh in his mind. From the political point of view, Signor Piccolomini was between life and death. Johann knew that very well, having hollowed out the mine with his own hands.

"My dear signor," said the minister, hiding his emotion as best he could, "I am touched by the devotion that you have to the person of our royal master—profoundly touched, I assure you. As for the interest in me that you have just been kind enough to attest, that is only justice, or I have always been one of your most ardent partisans. You have enemies…I have done my best to protect you. But have the kindness to tell me how I could attack that man today. Yesterday, he emerged victorious from a battle…"

"A skirmish, Excellency," Johann interjected, "A skirmish engaged in order to make him emerge from his positions. You had to maintain neutrality in that conflict of advance guards, I understand that. But the blow carried, believe me; the public is attentive now, because it has heard the noise of the fusillade…"

"Ah!" said the minister, following that series of martial metaphors with some astonishment. "For a dying man, you're talking miraculously well, Signor Spurzheim."

Johann let two or three groans escape. "I alone know what it costs me, Excellency," he said. At the same time he made an effort to raise himself on to his elbow in order to move his face a little further into the light. The minister looked away; Johann never failed in his cadaverous effects.

"Listen to me, signor," the director of the royal police went on. "I am giving the remains of my strength to his conversation. It's without regret, I assure you. Is it necessary to tell you that I can't be suspected of working for myself? What do the things of this world matter to me henceforth?"

"My dear Signor Spurzheim," said the minister, in a tone of affectionate compassion, "I'm all ears. Lower your voice in order not to fatigue yourself too much, and be as brief as you can…"

"I'll follow your good advice, Excellency, and set aside what I wanted to say about the reports directed against me, the petty intrigues, and the calumnies spread in your offices on the subject of the Brown affair…"

"What!" said the minister. "You know…?"

"Signor, the King's government is suspicious of me…of me, devotion incarnate. Coded letters have been seized, an entire secret correspondence. Tomorrow, when I am no more, the King's government will offer apologies to my memory. My last day will have been precious to the State. I shall bequeath it the secrets of the brotherhood of the Silence."

"Is that possible?" cried the minister, avidly.

"Justice is gladly rendered to the dead," Spurzheim pronounced, in a melancholy tone. "Envy and hatred fall silent before a coffin. Perhaps I shall have a few lines in the glorious page of history recounting Your Excellency's administration."

"Can you not reveal that secret to me?"

"You will know it this very day, signor, if you do not recoil before my proposition."

The minister moved his chair forward, and said: "Speak."

Johann rendered his little contingent of groans, and then continued. "Between two and three o'clock, the entire royal family, the Dorias and the Pamfilis will be gathered at the Villa Floridiana, in the home of Her Highness the Princess of Salerno."

"I know that."

"Do you know the reason for that gathering?"

"To regulate the conditions of the marriage between Fulvio Coriolani and Dona Ageie Doria."

"And to recognize Fulvio Coriolani," added Johan Spurzheim, "as the direct and legitimate heir of Mario, Comte de Monteleone, whose domains will similarly be restituted by royal prerogative."

The minister started on his chair. "Are you telling the truth?" he stammered.

"I'm telling the truth...and I'll continue. Coriolani, an adventurer, favorite of fantasy, fabulous prince, was more popular in Naples than you and your illustrious colleagues. What will Coriolani be, I ask you, twenty or a hundred times a millionaire and the cousin of the King?"

"But is he really Monteleone's direct here?"

"No."

"Then..."

"He's the son of the Devil, signor, as the southern tziganes call children of hazard. But he's also strong, clever and as bold as the Devil, his father. He has obtained proofs of his pretended birth...and there's only me in all the world, Johann Spurzheim, capable of thwarting him."

"And you're nailed to your bed!" exclaimed the minister.

"By mortal illness," concluded the director of the royal police, coldly.

The minister's arms fell along his sides. "What can we do?" he murmured. Those words escaped the minister's mouth like a cry of distress. Johann forgot to groan, and replied:

"You closed the door of the Maggiore prison yesterday on six or seven gentlemen who were, without knowing it, agents of my department."

The Marquis de Malatesta and his companions?"

"Yes, signor."

"My hand was forced."

"I'm not criticizing, Your Excellency...I'm merely telling you that those young lords are at liberty."

The minister straightened up.

"And they're waiting for Your Excellency," Johan continued, softly, "at the palace of the Minister of State."

"With what objective?"

"What time is it, Your Excellency?" Johann asked, instead of replying.

The minister looked at his watch and replied: "Two o'clock."

"It's necessary," said the director of the royal police, "that Malatesta, Sampieri and the others should be at the Villa Floridiana in a quarter of an hour. They know their role. They have the supporting proofs, and if those proofs aren't sufficient, the *deus ex machina* will appear at the appropriate moment..."

"Signor Spurzheim!" cried the minister, at the peak of agitation, "these are enigmas for me. I can't go forward blindly."

"Every minute you waste, Excellency," Johann retorted, "gives a terrible advantage to your adversary."

"But..."

"I have spoken. Let the responsibility for any delay fall on your Excellency."

The minister stood up and headed for the door. He was like a drunken man. Johann followed him with his most mocking gaze.

"If you don't find me alive again," he added, by way of adieu, "I beg Your Excellency not to forget me in your prayers..."

The minister was already going downstairs in a hurry. Johann uttered a small burst of laughter, which procured him a prolonged fit of dry coughing.

My chest sounds better than usual, he thought. *The convalescence is making evident progress. It's written: I'll bury them all!*

He took a pencil and a sheet of paper from beneath his pillow.

"Let's recapitulate!" he said to himself. "That's the gunshot. I'm like the spider at the center of her web. If I forget a single thread, adieu the ensemble. But I won't forget anything. What a chess player I would have made!"

He moistened the lead of the pencil and traced a few words on the piece of paper.

I still have beautiful handwriting, he thought, incapable of missing an opportunity to pay himself a compliment.

The task with which he was occupied consisted of giving a name to each of the threads of his spider's web.

"The seminarian is here," he murmured, scribbling. "The little girl is at the Palazzo Coriolani, I'm sure. We'll utilize that. The minister is running to his post. Malatesta, Sampieri and company are at theirs. Poor Barbe! Oh, she wouldn't have been able to refuse me her admiration; she understood me so well. I've arranged the Brown affair and the cipher. I've done the necessary for Manuele. Pier Falcone won't embarrass me much, he's a poor fellow. There remains the Comtesse. That will be the bouquet! A masterpiece!"

He rubbed his hands first; then he opened his little cupboard again, and put his ear to the ivory funnel.

"He's walking around, the little cherub," he said. "He's getting impatient. God forgive me! I believe he's talking to himself... Angélie! It's an amorous monologue! I'll take personal charge of curing him radically of that amour!"

He picked up his piece of paper again and wrote the name Lorédan Doria there: another thread of his web. The door grated on its hinges. Pier Falcone appeared on the threshold. Johann put his hand over his eyes in order to see him better.

"My son-in-law." he said, jovially, "you have a perfectly lugubrious physiognomy, so you must have succeeded all along the line. Speak quickly, we're in a hurry."

"I've succeeded," the doctor said, in a low voice.

"Manuele?"

"Manuele won't talk again."

"The Comtesse?"

"The Comtesse is downstairs, in the carriage."

"You're decidedly worth your weight in gold, my son-in-law!" cried Johann Spurzheim. "Come and help me; I want to get up. We need to play a little preparatory scene. The most important person here isn't the dowager Comtesse de Monteleone."

While Pier Falcone helped him to get out of bed, he said: "You'll have the Comtesse come in via the apartments to the right. It's necessary for her not to see too much mourning-dress. All must be rosy and the color of smiles on the eve of our happy betrothal..."

XI. The Monteleone Escutcheon

Julian had been alone for more than an hour in the room of which we gave a description in one of our previous chapters, which had formerly served as the study of Barbe de Monteleone, the wife of director Spurzheim.

Julian had been told that his father, Manuele, was waiting for him. He had also been told that his fate was about to be decided. Julian had arrived there with his heart full of vague and romantic hopes. It could not be for nothing the Providence had miraculously conserved Céleste's life and his own. In vain he defended himself against the inexplicable movements that sincere faith calls superstition, and which his young philosophy reproved, but does the heart listen to such reasoning? His heart was quivering with optimism; Céleste had said to him that that a new life was opening. They were about to be happy! And what could happiness be, if not Angélie, the dazzling vision that had awakened his childhood?

Certainly Julian could not yet see the mysterious ladder whose rungs, once climbed, would raise him up as high as her, but his mind was emboldened to make that impossible dream. He remembered clearly. Out there in the church of the San Gennaro hospital, Angélie had looked at him. And how beautiful she was, Holy Virgin! And how Julian's heart had contracted under her gaze! She had blushed; that was not an illusion. Then, suddenly, pallor had replaced the redness in her cheeks, to the extent that Julian had wanted to launch himself forward to sustain her.

Those things he had not even told Céleste, his dear and sweet confidante. A smile, with regard to those things, would have broken his heart.

Why had she blushed, and then paled, that divine young woman? Had the violent and mute appeal of Julian's soul touched hers? Oh, how he had prayed that night and the following days! What ardent charity he had lavished on the poor guests of San Gennaro. And if he had wanted to kill himself, it was because that evening his despair and his discouragement had said to him: "You're mistaken; she didn't blush; she didn't go pale; she didn't look at you."

It was austere, the furniture of that room. Certainly, nothing invited the voluptuous reveries that twenty-year-old imaginations nurse in a woman's boudoir. While alive, Barbe Spurzheim had scarcely been a woman. Those bare walls with somber and straight moldings, those rare master paintings representing tragic or religious scenes, those folio volumes open on oak lecterns darkened by time, all took Julian back to the familiar severities of the holy dwellings he had frequented in his childhood. But his mind had no need, at that moment, of the assistance of external objects to launch itself into the chimerical land of dreams.

He was sitting in the armchair in which we saw Pier Falcone sitting on the previous evening. The open harpsichord was facing him. Above the harpsichord, a Saint Cecilia by Antonietta Pinelli, her eyes raised to Heaven, seemed to bathe his senses and his soul in a mystical harmony. That was enough. A vision more beautiful than the patron saint of pious symphonies, a blonder, sweeter, more inspired angel, came to sit down for him at the harpsichord, slowly moving her fingers over the mute keys. And Julian listened ecstatically to I know not what delightful concert, which was the voice of young amours.

Once, that dream became reality. The wind bought him real, grave and lugubrious songs. He got up to go to the window. The window overlooked the courtyards. Julie saw opposite him a door hung with black, and priests going up the perron intoning a funereal hymn.

There was a death in the house. When Julian returned to his place, his ideas had changed direction. The priests would not have come like that to sing for poor Céleste. The brother and the sister would both have been taken away, without a fuss, to the nearby chapel, and from there to the cemetery.

Would Angélie have even noticed the absence of the young seminarian from the services at San Gennaro?

As he returned to his place, Julian said to himself: *What can be keeping our father Manuele? Céleste is all alone and waiting for me.*

His gaze fell upon the back of the huge armchair that was facing him. It was Barbe's armchair. The fabric, embroidered, represented an escutcheon. Julian was versed in the study of heraldry.

"Gules with a golden heart pierced with two swords in a saltire," he murmured. "The escutcheon of the Comtes de Monteleone."

Was that chance? Family furniture sometimes leaves extinct houses to be scattered in other dwellings at the hazard of the auction. Julian looked at the room more closely.

Of all the stories that had cradled his childhood, the story of the saintly Mario, Comte de Monteleone, was the one that had struck him most forcefully. He knew all the details of it. The suspicion had often occurred to him that Manuele Giudicelli his adoptive father, had been mixed up in the drama of the Martorello. Many a time he had thought about those orphan children born in opulence, who now relied on the grace of God. Monteleone had doubtless sat in that armchair.

Mechanically, and unwittingly, his hand extended toward a small table beside him. His hand encountered a little book bound in brown shagreen with golden clasps. He picked it up and looked at it. The Monteleone escutcheon was stamped on the cover of the little book, with the motto *Agere, non loqui.* Julian opened it. It was an *Imitation of Christ.* On its first blank page, two lines were inscribed in feminine handwriting: *Maria has given me to Mario, on the day of Santa Maria, 25 August 1808.*

Tears filled Julian's eyes.

The two children, in those days, were still in the happy house. Maria des Amalfi had given that pious present to her husband on the day of their common festival. A beautiful day, on which so many caresses were doubtless exchanged around the two cribs!

But what was this house, then, in which the memory of Monteleone was thus alive? Julian became agitated. The hours were passing. Poor Céleste, anxious and sad, must already be listening for his footsteps on the stairway of the Folquieri house.

Julian started marching back and forth in the room. It was at that moment that Johann Spurzheim, opening the little cupboard beside his bed, was interrogating his ivory funnel.

As the minutes went by, Julian's impatience increased. Finally, he could no longer keep still. He went to the door in order make enquiries about Manuele, in whose name someone had come to fetch him. As he arrived at the door, it turned slowly on its hinges. Julian recoiled all the way to the middle of the room, so extraordinary and unexpected was the apparition offered to his eyes. On the threshold, sustained by the cavalier who had come to fetch him from the Folquieri house, a living cadaver was tottering and trembling

Julian had never occupied himself with the frivolous reading that charms our early years. He knew nothing of the fantastic and misty imaginations that are peculiar to certain German and English spirits. If Julian had been one of our schoolboys, whose desks are always full of works of fiction, he would have recognized at first glance one of those fantastic individuals whose skeletons are heard creaking in the tales of Hoffmann.

He was no longer anything but skin and bone: poor, feeble and ill-attached bones; a skin as gray and wrinkled as that of a desiccated snake. He was small; literally, one could have knocked him over by blowing on him.

It was broad daylight, and yet Julian was wondering whether he was really awake.

Johann Spurzheim—for the reader cannot have failed to recognize him—stopped on the threshold. His blinking and uncertain gaze went in search of Julian, and hen lowered almost immediately.

"There's too much light here," he murmured, in a stifled voice.

"Here is the young man," said Pier Falcone.

"There's too much light, Johann repeated. "It's hurting me." He closed his eyes and shivered.

Pier Falcone closed the door behind him, propped him up in a corner like an inert object, and ran to draw the curtains over the windows.

When he came back, Johann said: "See how I can stand up on my own!"

Julian waited, motionless and mute with surprise.

"Let's go," said the little specter, clutching his conductor's clothes. "A helping hand, friend. Forward! I don't want to be carried."

Pier Falcone gripped him under the armpits, and the specter began to move, slowly.

He was draped in a sort of quilted dressing gown, the lining of which, when it opened up, allowed a glimpse of the frightful anatomy of his legs. He arrived, panting and moaning, close to Julian, who did not budge. He succeeded in putting his clenched hands on his shoulders and he looked at him, for a long time.

Julian felt a kind of uneven and convulsive tremor throughout that wretched body; but the cadaver's face remained calm. His eyes were bright; a cruel and chilling smile wandered over his discolored lips.

"He resembles him greatly...greatly!" he murmured, half turning toward the doctor.

Julian was embarrassed; the man's eyes were boring into him.

"Signor," he said, "Am I not going to see my father Manuele?"

"Greatly!" repeated Johann. "He resembles him greatly!"

"I have a sister," said Julian, "who is alone in the house. She's waiting for me. I'd like to go back to her."

"Put me in that armchair, friend," said Johann to Pier Falcone. "I'm very tired. Don't carry me! I don't want to be carried!"

Pier Falcone helped him drag himself to the embroidered armchair that bore the Monteleone escutcheon. As he dropped into it, Johann said: "Poor Barbe! She mentioned seven days...but that was to frighten me. She had a little malevolence in her character." He went on: "Put something over my head, friend; I'm cold. Drape something over my feet—look, poor Barbe's shawl, hanging up over there. God knows that I don't bear any rancor toward her memory, even though she mentioned seven days..."

When Pier Falcone had arranged him comfortably in the armchair, Johann raised his voice. "Bring the young man here," he ordered.

Falcone brought Julian. Johann fixed his cold, hard gaze on him.

"Manuele won't be coming," he pronounced, in a strident voice. "Manuele is dead."

Julian uttered a cry. "Dead!" he repeated. "Manuele! My father!"

"He resembles him greatly," mumbled Johann, for the third time. "It's his eyes...and his eyes took on that expression when someone came to tell him: 'Your children have been abducted...!'"

Julian did not understand. As he was about to speak. Johan closed his mouth with a curt gesture.

"Shut up," he said. "We'll chat later. You have time. You wouldn't find your sister at the house any longer. Your sister has been abducted."

Julian bounded, and wanted to run toward the door.

"Stay," said Johan, imperiously. "You have only one friend and one protector here, and that is me."

"My sister! My sister!" sobbed Julian, wringing his hands.

"Open the door of that cabinet," Johann ordered the doctor.

The latter obeyed.

"Go in there, young man," the director of the royal police went on. "Keep track attentively what is happening in here. Listen carefully. Whatever you hear, not a word, not a sigh! You're about to learn your history. Your history is terrible. When you leave here, you'll be a man. When you're a man, I'll give you the weapon that will avenge your tears and your blood. Go!"

It was as if Julian were drunk. He allowed himself to be drawn into the nearby cabin, of which Pier Falcone pulled the curtain. Johann said: "Bring the Comtesse immediately."

A moment later, Maria des Amalfi, dressed in mourning and veiled, came into Barbe's room. Pier Falcone had remained outside. Julian, hidden behind the curtain, pressed his breast with both hands, and held back his sobs.

XII. Johann Spurzheim's Speech for the Prosecution

With the curtains closed, the room was so dark that Maria des Amalfi could not see anything at first except a confused motionless mass in the large armchair in front of the table.

Julian, on the other hand, placed in an even darker location, and whose eyes had adapted to the gloom, was able to distinguish the noble figure and the kind face of the unknown woman, for she removed her veil as she came in.

In spite of the profound distress which the news he had just learned had plunged him, sensed a powerful interest born within him, which astonished him. He had never seen the woman, and yet it was with a kind of anxiety that he waited for the sound of her voice, as if he hoped to recognize it. But that first impulse vanished very quickly. Manuele, the poor old man who had raised him in his childhood; his sister, his cherished sister, his only companion: his entire family...Manuele was dead! His sister had been abducted! If the words of that man, who seemed to be the master here, had not given him the vague hope of knowing something, nothing could have retained him in that place.

In a low voice, as soon as she was a few paces from the door, Maria des Amalfi said: "Am I before His Majesty here?"

That question dispenses us from explaining to the reader the stratagem that Pier Falcone had used in order to lure the Comtesse to the house of the director of the royal police. She did not know Naples, and the sight of the places had not been able to disabuse her. She believed that she was at the Villa Floridiana, the dwelling of the Prince and Princess of Salerno, where the King ought to be to-day.

But there was a rather strange repercussion. Julian, the poor child who came from the depths of Sicily, did not know the King. A great disturbance created a diversion for the suffering of his heart. Was it the King, the bizarre individual who had spoken to him with so much dryness, while declaring that he was his sole protector on earth? Was it the King who had announced to him so coldly two crimes at the same time? He cocked his ear avidly to listen to the response of the specter who was Ferdinand de Bourbon.

The response did not come. It pleased the pretended King to maintain silence.

In the middle of the confused tangle of intrigues, in which that singular person was so amorously pleased with himself, this was an important and decisive act. Its stage setting had to be careful. To fail in his effect here was to risk losing the entire game. And he was playing a great game, that redoubtable and grotesque moribund. He was playing almost the same game as Fulvio Coriolani, with more chances of winning because he had fewer scruples.

"Please come closer, Comtesse de Monteleone," he pronounced, after a long silence.

Julian shivered violently in his redoubt. It was, therefore, his destiny to find himself mixed up in that tragic history, whose prologue had so greatly moved him once. That woman was Maria des Amalfi, the dolorous mother whom the loss of her children had rendered mad.

Julian looked at her more closely; he found her more beautiful, and nobler. He would have knelt before her and given her his faith with his heart, as young knights of the lance had once done, consoling the mourning of dispossessed widows. That was not incompatible with the religious and austere education that had been Julian's. Nowadays, there is no longer anyone but the priest to recall, distantly, the valor of ancient chivalry. But Julian was already no longer a priest.

For several days Julian had lowered his eyes many a time, shivering, at the sight of the young and brilliant soldiers of the royal guard, whose flanks were beaten by swords. He dreamed about a sword every time the image of Angélie came to visit him. The sword was for him, who lived in the past, the insignia of liberty and nobility, like the long hair that distinguished our Frankish ancestors from the vanquished Gauls. Yesterday, he had wished for a sword in order to conquer Angélie; today, he wished for a sword again, to defend and raise up that widow.

Obedient to Johann's order, Maria des Amalfi took a few steps forward.

"If you are the King," she murmured, "I beg Your Majesty to listen to me and render me justice," she murmured. "I have found the beloved son of Mario Monteleone..."

"You're lying, woman!" Johann interrupted, rudely

The Comtesse straightened up and took a step backwards. Julian would have liked to kiss the hem of her dress.

In a milder tone, Johann went on: "I beg you to excuse me, Madame; when you see with whom you are dealing here, you'll understand that I don't have time to choose my words. You are not at the Villa Floridiana, and I am not the King."

"Has my ignorance been abused?" cried Maria des Amalfi. "Does someone want to prevent me from seeing the King?"

Julian made a movement as if to launch himself forward, but he was retained by Johann's response.

"Someone has taken advantage of your ignorance in order to save you, Madame. It is, in fact, necessary that you see the King, that you speak to the King, that you demand justice from the King...but it is necessary beforehand that you know the name of the man who killed Mario Monteleone, your husband, in order not to commit the sacrilege of giving the name of son to the man who made you a mother without children and a widow!"

Pale and tottering, Maria was obliged to lean on the table in order not to fall over. She understood, or rather she divined, but she did not believe. This was an accusation against Fulvio.

Julian did not understand yet.

"It's you who wrote me a letter?" murmured the Comtesse.

"It was me, Madame."

"Who are you? I don't know you."

Johann sensed clearly that this was the solemn moment. His heart tightened against his hollow chest. He assembled all his courage to say: "I can't come toward you. Come toward me and look at me."

The Comtesse obeyed, urgently, for curiosity impelled her. She approached Johann, who turned his face toward the pale light filtering through the crack in the curtains. The Comtesse had an instant of alarm at the sight of those horribly ravaged features,

"No," she said. "No. I don't know you."

"Ah!" said Johann, with a sigh that, this time, was heartfelt. "I've changed a great deal then!"

The chagrin that he felt at that was strong enough to combat his anguish; but he thought: *All those people who looked healthy have died before me!*

"Look at me," he repeated. "A dying man doesn't resemble a man in good health. The letter you received is from a relative and a friend. Have you so many relatives and friends, then, Comtesse de Monteleone?"

"Seemingly," murmured Maria das Amalfi.

"Have you forgotten your cousin David Heimer, the late Comte's best servant?" Johann pronounced, lowering his voice involuntarily.

Maria felt a tremor throughout her body. Johann sensed a cold sweat forming. Was Maria about to remember?

She passed her hand over her forehead two or three times. One might have thought, to judge by the horror that appeared momentarily on her face, that her memory was making an effort to be reborn. But science had not lied. The memory of madness was not reborn in reason. Johann was saved. The memory of the night of the thirteenth of October 1815 remained in darkness.

The Comtesse said: "I remember David Heimer, the companion and friend of Mario Monteleone. Are you really David Heimer?"

Instead of replying he extended his hand, which she took, but the contact of which made her shiver slightly.

Julian searched his memories laboriously for the name of David Heimer. He was sure of having heard it pronounced by his father Manuele.

"Many years have gone by, my noble cousin and mistress," Johann continued, in a tone that was both respectful and affectionate, "since the time when I was happy in your happiness. Thunder has burst more than once over the house of Monteleone. But the clement God, the good God, has not wished that I would quit this earth without giving one final proof of my devotion to the beloved companion of my benefactor. Sit down here in front of me, Comtesse. I hope that my weakness will not betray my determination. My last words will be for you...and if you wish, the last act of my life will be the best and the most glorious, since it will have saved the posterity of Mario, my relative and my master."

Maria des Amalfi took the seat facing Johann. Behind the curtain, Julian's attention was redoubled.

"You can clearly see, can you not, Madame," Johann continued, his voice seemingly weak, "that my hours are numbered? You know, and cannot doubt, that it is a dying man who is speaking to you? God wants my words to have, relative to you, the authority that the words of a dying man never lack. I shall see accomplished the sole wish that it remains for me to make in his world.

"I'll begin, and I beg you not to interrupt me, out of regard for my extreme weakness.

"Your elder son is dead, murdered by the same man who killed your husband."

The Comtesse uttered a stifled groan.

"There are precocious monsters," Johann went on. "Mario Monteleone's murderer was barely sixteen years old. Madame, I am going to remind you of events that our cruel malady has perhaps expelled from your memory. It is necessary; it is an imperious duty that I am accomplishing. The excess of such perversity sickens your heart. So much the better! You will thus escape the fascination of the most dangerous individual in the world."

"Prince Coriolani is my benefactor," said Maria, feebly. "It's through him that I recovered my reason."

"My strength is ebbing away, Madame," said Johann. "I no longer have time to argue. I shall recount. Do not miss any of my words. They have the price henceforth that is attached to rare things. I do not complain of quitting this life, in which I have suffered a great deal, and the only grace I ask from God is that he will give me one more day in order to ensure the safeguard that I have prepared for the widow of my very dear master. She has need of it: great perils menace her. If I can put her in shelter, not behind me, who is no longer of his world, but behind my memory, I shall be content to go to rejoin the man who was my first protector and my best friend."

He paused on that vague phrase, of which Maria des Amalfi certainly did not grasp the true meaning. It was a matter of preparing the ground.

"Madame," he continued, adopting the grave and precise tone of a man who is going to make an important narration, "you have already lost your three children, two of whom will be returned to your kisses if the Almighty helps us. The saint Mario, as we all called our excellent and dear master, was living in solitude and dolor. He was weeping for his children, his wife and his homeland: his children stolen, his wife martyred and deprived of reason and his children from which the upstart soldier who the governed the kingdom of Naples had just been expelled.

"Mario was in Sicily, with the very august Ferdinand de Bourbon, his friend and his master. Vague as it might be, you must have retained some memory of that time?"

"None," Maria replied. Her voice expressed the disturbance—or, rather, anguish—that grips people whose intelligence has been attacked when they try to lift he heavy veil that, for them, covers the past."

She's mine! Johann thought. *They think I'm dead, and I'm moving mountains!* He had great difficulty dissimulating his triumph.

"No!" he repeated, in a chagrined tone. "I ought to have expected that...but the strength of the truth is such that I have no need of your memories. One night, Madame—it was the thirteenth of October 1815..."

He paused, and his piercing gaze interrogated the face of the Comtesse. That face remained calm. Johann's last anxiety vanished.

"On the night of the thirteenth of October," he continued, "we were gathered in the Martorello in order to celebrate the master's return. The restoration of Ferdinand de Bourbon had reopened the doors of his house. Suddenly, in the middle of the nocturnal meal, someone came to tell Monteleone that a stranger was asking for him.

"That stranger was Joachim Murat, the ex-King of Naples, his enemy and his persecutor. The King of Naples had come to ask him for shelter against the Bourbonian troops that were pursuing him. Mario Monteleone was a knight, as you know very well..."

"Oh, yes!" murmured the Comtesse, who had tears in her eyes. "Mario Monteleone was a knight, I know that. He would have given shelter to his enemy."

"You have said it, Madame. Mario Monteleone gave shelter to Joachim Murat. Apparently, there was no danger in that for him, for we were all there. However, there were three strangers at the table. I will name them for you, Madame, in order that you can repeat them to your son. The son must avenge the father; in Italy, that is the law of our love and our hatred.

"Firstly, there was Comte Giacomo Doria. Then there was Lorédan Doria, his son. Finally, there was the man you call your benefactor..."

"Prince Coriolani" exclaimed the Comtesse.

"In those days," said Johan Spurzheim, "I do not think that the name Coriolani had been invented. At any rate, our man was not a prince. He sat humbly at the foot of the table. He was a traveler named the Chevalier d'Athol, to whom Monteleone had chanced to accord hospitality."

"And it's him that you're accusing?" asked the Comtesse.

No words can describe the passionate avidity with which Julian was listening henceforth.

"Monteleone was betrayed," replied Johann. "That much is certain. Choose between proven servants and the three strangers...between those who would lose everything by his death and those to whom his death gave a great fortune...for the two Comtes Doria inherited Monteleone's wealth...and that Athol, having become Prince Coriolani, is about to marry Angélie Doria, who possesses half of your children's wealth."

Maria des Amalfi bowed her head in silence.

Johann continued: "But the proofs I will give you, Madame, will not be simple inductions. I know that you are prejudiced. I will do as God did with Saint Thomas: you will touch the wound with your finger.

"One thing of which you seem to be ignorant is that you were yourself the terrible and fatal instrument of Mario's loss."

The Comtesse straightened up, indignantly.

All this is in conformity with the stories of our poor father Manuele, Julian said to himself. He believed it, so happy was he to put the crime on the conscience of his detested rival.

"Madame," Johann Spurzheim went on, "It required necessity to constrain me to cause you that pain. I repeat, you were, unknown to yourself, the fatal weapon that delivered the first blow. It was a ruse so odious, a stratagem so abominable, that I have a cold sweat merely in talking to you about it. You were mad, Madame; the word must be pronounced here. Your madness was the loss of your children. That night, a man slipped into your retreat and said to you: 'Madame, the scoundrel who abducted your children is in this house; his name is Joachim. Go! Run!'

"And you went, poor mother. And you ran...and to the first people you encountered that night in the valley, where you were wandering at random, you cried: 'Joachim! Joachim!' You were followed, for the country and the shore were full of soldiers, and all those soldiers were looking for Joachim. Joachim was King Murat.

"The soldiers entered the Martorello, to which you led them. Murat and his noble defender were taken prisoner together.

"We were all there, Madame, but the two Dorias and the Chevalier d'Athol had vanished..."

Johann Spurzheim paused.

The Comtesse pressed her forehead with both hands. "That's horrible!" she murmured. Then she said, as if inspired: "How would the man guilty of such a crime dare to present himself before me?"

It would have been evident to a observer that Johann expected that objection, and was even awaiting it impatiently. A sad smile contracted his lips.

"God has strange ways," he said. "I've pursued that man for years, and I haven't found him, because he had changed his face and his name. It is you, Madame, you again, who enabled me to find him."

"Me?" repeated the Comtesse.

"We will come to the murder of Monteleone shortly," said Johann. "I'm only talking at present about the odious crime of the night of the thirteenth of October. I was searching. Toward the end of last autumn I was drawn to France by the renown of the celebrated physician Doctor Daniel Bach; you can see, Madame, that science has not been as strong as my malady…I was condemned, since he was not able to cure me…"

At the name of Dr. Daniel Bach, Maria des Amalfi's attention had redoubled.

"On the day when I consulted that prince of science for the first time," Johann Spurzheim went on, "he was in his garden, in conference with a foreigner…a foreigner who came from Italy. I had been left free to wander in the garden. I was walking at random when I suddenly heard two voices talking on the other side of a hedge. I listened, Madame, I must accuse myself of that; I listened because, in passing, I had heard the name of the noble widow of my master pronounced."

"My name!" said the Comtesse. "Then it was the prince who was there!"

"It as the Chevalier d'Athol; and this is what I heard the Chevalier d'Athol ask: 'Is the theory of the two memories true, Doctor?'"

Johann Spurzheim interrupted himself. "I beg you, Madame," he said, "to make me repeat if you don't understand, for this is the manifest and palpable proof. I did not know then, as you perhaps do not know today, what the words 'the theory of the two memories' signified.

"Doctor Daniel replied: 'It's a fact that now seems perfectly demonstrated by experience.'

"'In that case,' said Athol, 'supposing that the woman were able to recover her reason, she would not remember events contemporary with her madness?'

"'She would not remember any of them.'

"'Even the most striking.'

"'Even the most terrible.'

"I could not see the Chevalier d'Athol, but I sensed his smile. The physician continued, speaking in good faith and from the viewpoint of science: 'When she has recovered her reason, what will be restored to her will be the memory of events anterior to her madness.'

"The Chevalier d'Athol bowed and took his leave. Have you understood, Madame?"

Oh, thought Julian, in his retreat, his fists clenched and his brow furrowed, *I've understood! I've understood!*

The Comtesse wiped the sweat from her forehead. "It's impossible," she murmured. "God would not suffer such perversity!"

We can see that Johann was making good use of the information that Manuele had furnished him regarding Doctor Daniel.

"A similar perversity, Madame," he continued, "is indeed difficult to admit. However, it is necessary to admit it, since Prince Coriolani, fortified by the doctor's response, has presented himself to you with his head held high.

"In rendering you reason, he took away memory. The pretended benefit for which you are so grateful was a further ruse. The proof is that he must have proposed to you some bargain, some infamy."

The Comtesse's breast rendered a groan.

"He was on safe ground," Johann continued. "In order for you to recognize him, it would have been necessary for you to go mad."

"Oh," said Maria, covering her face. "That will happen. I shall go mad again!"

If she had looked at Johann at that moment she would have seen a sudden expression of alarm in his features.

"Let us pass on to the murder, Madame," he continued. Here it is chance—which is to say Providence—that has spoken. I am the director of the realm's police. I know everything, even what is said in the King's cabinet. I learned that there was a man in Naples who was claiming to be the elder son of the saint, Mario Monteleone, but who, for the public, possessed another name, and who had promised His Majesty and the heir to the throne to furnish complete proofs of his birth: his father's testament, to employ his own words, and his mother's testimony."

The Comtesse shivered in every limb.

"I see that you understand, Madame," he said.

"No," she replied, in a muffled voice. "I still don't understand."

Me, I understand! I understand! thought Julian, who was biting his bloody handkerchief in order to retain the cry that was trying to escape his breast.

"Beware!" murmured Johann, severely. "You are the wife and the mother of his victims. I have said enough to enlighten a sincere conscience.

Julian found that he was right. But the Comtesse said: "Say more."

"The King," said Johann, "once loved Mario like his own son, and Mario was the dearest companion of Francis de Bourbon, the Royal Prince. Those two august individuals took the impostor's cause in hand. Who in the world is easier to deceive than the great? They became the champions of the pretended prince Fulvio Coriolani. They gave him their guarantees with regard to Lorédan Doria. If you do not want to be persuaded, finish your work. Fulvio Coriolani has his father's testament, the testament he stole from the murdered Mario. Go and give him the testimony of his mother."

"Have pity on me, signor!" Maria stammered. "What proofs do you have of that crime?"

"What proves the theft," cried Johann, who almost succeeded raising himself up, "if not the stolen objects? Monteleone was held in secret in his cell in the Castello di Pizzo. Only one man penetrated the cell, and that was the murderer. One single man could take possession audaciously of his remains…that is the murderer."

Maria let herself slide to her knees.

"He has the testament," Johann went one, finding, I know not where, the strength to speak vehemently. "He has the birth certificates. He has everything, and as long as the breath is not torn from that cowardly breast, Mario Monteleone will demand vengeance from the depths of his tomb!"

Three o'clock in the afternoon sounded at that moment on the beautiful renaissance clock that was on Barbe Spurzheim's mantelpiece. Johann's livid head reared up like that of a snake.

"On your feet, Madame!" he cried. "The murderer, of whom I have not yet told you the true name, the brigand Il Porporato, who bears so audaciously the title of Prince, is before his judges at this moment!"

"Il Porporato!" repeated Julian and his mother at the same time.

Johann continued: "On your feet, Madame! This is the moment when your husband's murderer is taking possession of the name and heritage of your children. On your feet! Or be accursed, widow devoid of memory, mother devoid of entrails, accursed by your husband, accursed by your posterity!"

Maria stood up, her gaze wandering in the void. "What is it necessary to do?" she stammered

Johann clapped his hands. Pier Falcone appeared on the threshold.

"Have the Comtesse de Monteleone," he said, in a loud voice, "taken immediately to the Vila Floridiana. If anyone attempts to attack her, because she is a widow and alone, say that the director of the royal police has chosen her for a spouse…that will be her aegis!" And, turning to the stupefied Maria: "The hand of a dying man can be accepted," he said, sadly. "I have nothing to give but that. My master, who sees me from on high, can read the depths of my heart!" It seemed that tears came to stifle his voice. The Comtesse's emotion was at its peak.

Johann concluded: "May God leave me on this earth for one more day. My noble mistress and her children, if she does not disdain to accept, for a few hours, the name of a faithful servant, will be delivered forever from their cruel enemies." He interrupted himself. "Go, Falcone! The King is waiting. The Comtesse will speak henceforth in accordance with her conscience."

He extended his cold and trembling hand. Maria took it. Then, bending down abruptly, she kissed it.

Pier Falcone dragged her all the way to the carriage.

Scarcely had the Comtesse and her guide disappeared than Julian launched himself out of his hiding place.

"I knew all that!" he cried, like a madman. "I knew all that! Blessed be the bounty of God, which puts men like you, signor, in opposition to scoundrels like this Coriolani!"

Johann seemed literally exhausted by the long effort he had just made.

"In the name of Heaven, signor, reply to me," said Julian. "Is it that man who has abducted my sister?"

Johann opened his mouth to say yes, but changed his mind. Johann's paths were always tortuous, and he had more than one adversary to strike.

"No," he replied, in a whisper. "Do you think you have only one enemy, you who are the first in the realm after Bourbon?"

Julian stepped back, bewildered.

"Beware of Doria!" pronounced Johann, even more softly.

"What did you say?" asked Julian, trembling. "Me, the first in the realm after Bourbon."

"Were you listening?"

"Yes, I listened hard."

"Then get up and go where your duty summons you, Julian de Monteleone. That woman in mourning, who was used a dagger to kill, is your mother. The martyred saint who died in the Pizzo was your father."

Julian extended his arms and uttered a loud cry. Then he drew himself up to his full height.

"A weapon!" he pronounced, between clenched teeth.

"You have a weapon," replied Johann, coldly.

Julian felt his side, like a soldier. Johann started to smile

"One does not punish such sins with the sword," he said. "The scaffold is required. You have a weapon to send Il Porporato to the scaffold. It is sufficient to prove that Fulvio Coriolani was in the Folqueri house last night."

"I will say so."

"Rather prove it. You have a weapon."

"What weapon?" cried Julian, beside himself,

"The purse embroidered with pearls."

A gasp escaped Julian's throat. He seized the purse between his clenched fingers, raised it above his head and departed like an arrow.

Johann, left alone, closed his eyes and extended himself comfortably in poor Barbe's armchair.

"The earthworm has killed the lion!" he murmured, as a blissful expression spread over his meager face. "I shall be Comte de Monteleone... and I shall bury them all!"

PART FIVE: THE MOUNTAIN AND THE VOLCANO

I. A Heart Pierced by Two Swords

In the immense gardens of the Palazzo Coriolani there was a pavilion, a model of rich and graceful elegance, which was known as the Romitorio Dolci. The venerable court banker had his pleasure apartments there, which he did not abuse, to tell the truth.

It was not entirely the same for Nina, his charming niece, the maid of honor of the Princess of Salerno. Nina loved that delightful redoubt, sufficiently separate from the principal palace for malicious gossip to have nothing to bite. She was, moreover, in an exceptional position at the court of the King of Naples. She was treated there as a lady, because she made manifested the very determined intention never to marry. Her bold character, her intelligence, simultaneously charming and redoubtable, the fortune of her uncle, Massimo Dolci, which was presumed to be enormous, and the admitted favor of the Princess of Salerno all kept the stings of malice at a distance.

Nina did what she wanted. Chagrined or jealous individuals who had wanted, from time to time, to hinder her free whim, had always repented of it. Under the cover of her uncle's name, she frequently resided in that pavilion when her service did not retain her at court; it was her battle station. The Princess of Salerno's maid of honor became Fiamma again, the genteel and powerful lieutenant of Beldemonio.

She had made the Dolci pavilion a charming little temple. She pleased herself there. Often she spent long hours there alone, entertaining herself with her memories.

In order to go from the palace to the Dolci pavilion it was necessary to traverse the entire length of the garden.

At that moment, it was not Nina who was in the boudoir ornamented with delightful paintings; it was Angélie Doria. Angélie was waiting for Fulvio.

She was calm—or, rather, there was I know not what somber resolution within her that was not in her nature. She often gazed at the path bordered with oleanders that plunged and wound through the bushes.

It was by that route that Prince Fulvio would come. And Prince Fulvio was late, in the estimation of Angélie, for whom everything down here had thus far been smiles, and who had not yet learned the hard science of waiting.

Fulvio had left the palace on the heels of Nina, who had announced Angélie's presence to him.

The profound shadow in which his hopes and aspirations had drowned momentarily was about to brighten. He had become himself again. Daylight had dawned for him, and, in accordance with the versatility of his nature, all the things that he had just seen sad and veiled in mourning were now colored, as if a cheerful ray of sunlight had suddenly struck them.

As he quit the drawing room where his conversation with the widowed Comtesse de Monteleone had taken place, he immediately took the path to the Dolci pavilion. He had only one thought at that moment: to kiss Angélie's hand and thank her on his knees.

But have you noticed something singular and curious, and as incontestable as the light of day? Have you observed the phenomenon of the maturation of an idea? The idea suddenly surges forth, as a ripe fruit is suddenly detached from the tree.

It was a long way from the palace to the Dolci pavilion: a charming path, shady and florid, along which, here and here, white statues smiled amid the dark foliage. Between two of them was the labyrinth, the tangle of hornbeam hedges that mythological gardens never lack. For want of Ariadne's thread, in order to find one's way in that miniature maze, it was at least necessary to look ahead.

Prince Fulvio had set off at a fast pace. After a minute, you would have found him in the heart of the labyrinth, his head inclined over his breast, pensive, lost, and heading in reverse of his initial direction. The idea had ripened; it had just come to light. But the circumstances rendered that idea so implausible, that Prince Fulvio was obliged to reject it at first. It was romance, it was comedy, it was double romance, triple comedy.

Fulvio did not want it, that idea, which gave for the denouement of his life an overly subtle and vulgar plot-twist. He stiffened himself against it with all the force of his repugnance. It could not be. The career of a man of his magnitude, to whom God had given indomitable vigor, audacity and faith, everything necessary for him to fight and vanquish, could not end the petty, stupid imbroglios that amuse the crowd in popular theaters.

He shrugged his shoulders disdainfully, the handsome Fulvio. He had a scornful smile on his lips. He murmured, in the sincerity of his heart: "It's insane. It's impossible."

But a blush rose to his face. Then a pallor soon came to replace the redness of his cheeks. He was emotional, anxious, almost tremulous. He sometimes stopped mechanically, and you could have seen beads of sweat on his temples.

Why didn't I think of it sooner? he asked himself.

Fulvio stopped in the bushes. He sat down on a bench and took out of his bosom the portfolio in which the papers of which he was to make use at the Villa Floridiana to consolidate his imposture were prepared and put in order. Those papers were the ones he had found in the marble cupboard during his nocturnal visit to the ruins of the Martorello.

They comprised six loose sheets. The first was the birth certificate of young Mario, Comte de Monteleone, the elder son, with the name of his father and is mother. The second and third were the birth certificates of Julian and Céleste. The fourth was the certificate of Monteleone's marriage with Maria des Amalfi. The fifth, composed of two parts written several years apart, contained the story of the abduction of little Mario, and then the story of the abduction of the brother and the sister; it was notarized. Mario Monteleone had added a few observations to it in the margin. Finally, the sixth, entirely in the handwriting of the late Comte, was his testament, addressed to his elder son, in case the bounty of God ever permitted him to execute it.

Fulvio had read the various documents many times, and yet, he was scanning them at that moment with a particular avidity. Evidently, the meaning had changed for him. Evidently, he had discovered something that had escaped him thus far.

"The man sensed that he was surrounded by enemies," he murmured, disposing the papers on the beach. "One divines that by the precautions he took. Doubtless he would have taken other precautions, which were futile, and which I don't know."

He crossed his hands over his knees, and began to reflect.

"He would have been my age," he went on, thinking aloud—and this time, it really was his famous idea that was translating itself without him knowing it. "He was very nearly my age...exactly, even...at least, everything leads to that belief. He came into the world at the beginning of the century...and I can't be more than twenty-three years-old, although my life already seems so long! He was abducted by pirates, accomplices of a domestic treason. My infancy was spent at sea..."

He picked up one of the detached sheets. It happened to be the birth certificate of the elder son of Mario and Maria. His fingers began to crumple it. He went on:

"I've interrogated my memories...I can't see, in the distance of my first years, a great house, nor a white-haired father, nor the gentle face of a mother..." He interrupted himself angrily. "Madness! Madness! I can't be taking all that seriously!"

His smile wanted to be disdainful and mocking, but there was so much sadness in his eyes!

"The tziganes once came to the bay of Sant'Eufemia," he went on. "Did my heart beat faster? No..." He interrupted himself again, with a sudden animation. "But my heart beat faster in the cell of the saint Monteleone! And how many times have I interrogated myself with astonishment, asking myself the reason for that motiveless interest, those strange emotions!"

His head inclined over his breast. "Have I ever heard the name of Monteleone," he said, as if he were arguing against his own skepticism, "without shivering in the depths of my heart? Perhaps the cause of my disturbance, the unknown cause, was a vague memory!

"And out there, in the valley, when I came, full of the thought of my beautiful Angélie, ambitious and ardent, ready to break any obstacle with my foot, what anguish gripped my soul as I penetrated into that refuge where two individuals unknown to me had enjoyed a simple and tranquil happiness...!

"Unknown!" he went on. "Can one apply that word to those who were already the best friends of my dreams: Mario Monteleone and Maria des Amalfi, the saintly man and the gentle martyr!

"But it's no longer a matter of me. One deceives oneself. It's a matter of an individual deprived of reason, a poor madwoman who mistook me for her husband, rejuvenated by a miracle, and who greeted me by that name, which I'm about to take wrongfully today: Mario Monteleone!"

Fulvio was subject to a law; Fulvio was prudent for the first time in his life. His desire pleaded for the belatedly arrived idea, which was plausibility. His reason laughed and mocked. And a fever rose to his brain because all of that was outside his battle plan, and he had not counted on the agitations that threw themselves across his effort.

He had need of all his composure. He sensed that. His seething head already no longer had the calm necessary in the first hour of a battle.

Time was pressing; the hour of the royal rendezvous as about to sound, but it would have been impossible to extract himself from the reverie into which he had entered with so much disdain.

"Mario!" he went on, still crumpling the birth certificate in his burning hands. "She called me Mario. She asks me why the years, far from blanching my hair, had brought youth back to my face...

"And later, when I saw her again on her return to France after the miracle operated by science...what trouble in her gaze! And during that entire conversation, the memory of which will remain engraved within me if I live to be a hundred, how many times did her heart not launch itself toward mine...?"

He stopped short, and resumed: "There's more. In spite of her denials, I'm not sure that she doesn't still believe that she sees in me her lost son, the legitimate heir of the Comtes de Monteleone!"

He fell silent. Other memories arrived in a host, among others, the words that had escaped the Companions of the Silence when he entered the crypt of the convent of the Corpo-Santo. Those words struck him more vividly than they had at the time when they had been pronounced: "They're the same features!" the knights of charcoal and iron had said. In their mouths, that was like a confession extracted by evidence. He thought he saw again the astonished gazes of those men moving from his face to the face of the dead man. In spite of his ignorance at the time, in spite of his insouciance, that had been a solemn moment for him. The impression was reborn intact today.

He appealed to his memory, and said, in the depths of his consciousness:

Yes, they're the same features! I'll return to the convent of the Corpo-Santo, I'll lift the marble of that tomb again...the same mirror will reflect the features of my face, and those of Monteleone. I shall see! I shall see!

He tried to put down the paper, which he felt dampening between his fingers, bathed in sweat. But, his gaze having fallen by chance on the part that his clenched fingers had covered, a stifled cry escaped from his breast. Between the lines of the birth certificate, other mysterious lines emerged, pale but sufficiently distinct for the characters to be divined.

There are secrets of which an adventurer cannot be unaware. Fulvio knew the virtue of certain chemical agents, which are known in Italy as *tinte di sapienta*, and which form an ink invisible until the appropriate reagent makes them appear to astonished eyes. Some of those inks appear on simple contact with water, others require heat in order to be reborn.

Abruptly, Fulvio opened his waistcoat and shirt, He applied that already warm paper to his burning chest, and felt beneath it is precipitate beating of his heart.

"That man knew that he was surrounded by enemies," he pronounced, for the second time, while his fingers quivered with impatience. "Doubtless I only know part of his secrets. Struck by an invisible hand with blow after blow, he multiplied his precautions at hazard..."

His gaze rose toward the sky, and he went on, with a profound impulse of piety: "Let there be light, Lord! I have sworn to protect the posterity of Monteleone and I have sworn to avenge them. I am ready; even if I must break my own pedestal, I want to accomplish my vow!"

Beneath those words there as a cry of his soul, which was repeating: *If only it were me! If only it were me!*

It was slowly, and almost timidly, that he removed from his breast the paper introduced to it with such vivacity. He held it open for an instant without daring to look at it. Finally, though, his gaze lowered; his entire body experienced a shock. His eyelids fluttered, and his cheek changed color twice.

There were only two lines traced in the sympathetic ink. The warmth of Fulvio's breast caused the characters to revive distinctly. The two lines said:

The elder son of Mario, Comte de Monteleone, bears the escutcheon of his house engraved on his left arm.

Those kinds of tattoos, so common among the popular class in France, are employed out there in great families. Mountain-dwelling servants are skilled in the art. It is not rare in southern Italy and in Sicily to see children bearing their name tattooed in full on their breast or around the arm. The astonishing quantity of kidnappings that take placed on the coast and in the mountains has doubtless perpetuated the custom. But it is an established fact that tattoos, which leave almost indelible traces on adults, are effaced for children at about the age of puberty, in consequence of the great work of elimination that the crisis of the age brings abut. So, that precaution or childishness is not without inconvenience. The year in which he beard grows removes those henceforth useless labels.

Fulvio stood up, dropping the piece of paper.

"A heart pierced by two swords," he murmured, "on the arm. I never thought of that!"

His eyes had something wild in them. He took off his jacket precipitately, rolled up the left sleeve of his short and looked at his arm. The white and delicate skin still retained a few traces, but so vague!

Fulvio slapped his arm where those marks were almost completely effaced. The skin reddened, the traces remained white; but it was impossible to rediscover in those confused lines a heart pierced by two swords.

"And you, I have to know!" cried Fulvio, standing up, his arms folded over his breast. "It's necessary that I know whether I have a mother, a sister and a brother...and of the dead man lying out there in the crypt of the Corpo-Santo is my father...the dead man who is not yet avenged!"[57]

---

[57] This is surely odd; even though the effaced tattoo can no longer serve as evidence capable of convincing anyone else, Beldemonio must surely have seen it a thousand times in his childhood and must know what it depicted. How, then, could he still be in any doubt?

II. Manuele's Slumber

In order to know, there was a means: to interrogate Manuele Giudicelli.[58]

Prince Fulvio hastily repaired the disorder of his attire and headed at a rapid pace toward the part of the palace where the poor wounded old man had been sheltered.

That was in the east wing of the former house of the Avalos. Manuele had been laid down in a ground floor room whose shaded window overlooked the bushes. Coriolani had recommended him particularly to his servants; he was surprised not to see anyone in the vestibule. The room preceding that of the wounded man was similarly deserted.

At the moment when Fulvio traversed it, the head of a young woman, dazzling in its charm and beauty, lifted the curtain closing the doorway. Fulvio recognized at first glance his dear vision of the previous night, the young woman of the Folquieri house. She put a finger over her pretty mouth, and said, as if she were talking to a friend: "Shh! He's asleep."

Fulvio stopped to look at her, and his face was painted with a sort of enchantment.

"I recognize you," she said, in a whisper. "It's you who left the purse...you're the Prince..."

"Have you seen me before, then, dear child?" Fulvio asked, advanced toward her.

"His voice too" she murmured, suddenly becoming serious. "My brother Julian's voice!"

That speech, enigmatic for any other man, entered so well into the current of ideas that was filling Fulvio's brain that he took her by the hand, saying to her with a sudden and great emotion: "You find that I resemble your brother Julian?"

"You're more handsome than Julian," the young woman replied, with a hint of pink in her cheeks, lowering her gaze.

"Do I frighten you, Céleste?" the Prince asked, then.

"No," she replied, her eyes still lowered. "You've been our good angel...and you're so far above us!"

She raised her bright gaze again, in which a delicate smile was shining.

"It was in a dream that I saw you," she said, replying to the prince's first question. "If you didn't resemble my brother so much, I wouldn't have been able to recognize you."

Fulvio put his face in the daylight.

---

[58] This too is odd. How can Manuele possibly help him to establish his identity? It is perhaps as well that the question soon becomes irrelevant.

"Look at me carefully, dear child." he said, "That resemblance…"

"Oh, like that," Céleste interjected, "at such close range, one no longer sees it. And then, I've never seen my poor Julian dressed like you…and then again, as I told you, Julian isn't as handsome as you."

The valet charged with watching over Manuele came in at that moment. "Highness," he said, "I was looking for you. Doctor Doni couldn't come. He's in Salerno, but he sent one of his friends and pupils in his place."

"What is his name?" asked Fulvio.

"That imbecile Petruzzi wasn't able to tell me that, Highness."

"And what did this doctor do with the patient?"

"What all doctors do, Highness… felt him, looked at him, grunted, blinked, shook his head…"

"Didn't he give him any medicaments?"

"Yes, and a good one, for the fellow's been sound asleep ever since."

"This medicine was doubtless in a bottle?"

"Yes, Highness, in a bottle."

"And the bottle must be on the night-table?"

"As for that, no, Highness. The bottle is in the replacement doctor's pocket. I'll tell you why. The savant doctor simply had the mouth of the wounded man opened, and put two or three drops of is cordial in it. He also poured a few drops on the wound, which he had unbandaged."

An anxiety seemed to enter the prince's mind, and that sentiment was immediately reflected, as if in a mirror, on the young woman's face.

"How did the wounded man look?" asked Fulvio, after a pause.

"Highness," replied the valet, "I wouldn't like to speak ill of a comrade, assuredly…it will be the first time in my life…but Petruzzi is three-quarters idiot, everyone knows that. He told me that the doctor had turned the wounded man's face to the wall himself, saying to him: 'Sleep!' And that he added, addressing the guardian: 'Take care that no one wakes him before I come back. That would be dangerous…perhaps mortal."

"Mortal," repeated Céleste, fearfully.

Fulvio indicated the door to the valet, who went out backwards, bowing profusely.

As soon as the valet had left, Céleste approached the Prince confidently.

"It's you who saved our father Manuele, signor, isn't it?"

Fulvio took her by the hand and led her to the sofa, where he sat her down.

"Child," he said pressing her little soft white hand against his heart, "if you had a brother like me, would you love him?"

Céleste did not seem astonished by that question; and yet, that question was very strange, addressed by the powerful Prince Fulvio Coriolani to the poor orphan from the Folquieri house.

"I'm ready for anything," she murmured. "Do you know what they say, Highness—since they call you that—along the edge of the warm blue sea out there in the town of Catania in Sicily?"

Fulvio contemplated her, smiling and affectionate. "The sound of her voice, the unexpected and suave poetry of her speech, and everything else about her, attracted and enchanted him.

"No," he replied, as one does to beloved children. "I don't know, Céleste. What do they say in the town of Catania?"

"They say that God suddenly protects those that he has extracted from a great danger."

"And the danger was great from which God has preserved you, little girl!"

"God and you, Highness. So great that I shudder every time I think about it. Not for me, but for my beloved Julian. I'm pale, aren't I?"

"You're pale, Céleste," said the prince, whose smile had taken on a hint of melancholy involuntarily. "So you love him a great deal, your Julian?"

"When one is one of two, Highness...." She blushed, and her expression had a sly gaiety.

Fulvio leaned over to kiss her forehead, as a good father would have done to a precociously genteel child. But the child, who was too old, thought the father was too young. Céleste recoiled and stopped smiling. Her lovely face took on an expression of mild but firm dignity

"I'm not annoyed," she murmured, "but I'm sixteen, Highness."

Fulvio actually stammered an apology.

She did not let him finish.

"Since this morning, as I said, Highness," she went on, "I'm ready for anything. God is good, our life is about to change. You aren't my brother; I don't believe that. That would be too much happiness..."

"Truly!" Fulvio interjected, his heat beating rapidly "That would make you happy? You'd love me, then, Céleste?"

"I already love you without that," she replied, without hesitation. "How could I not love you? You're our savior."

Fulvio frowned.

"Well," said Céleste, "don't be irritated, Highness. If you hadn't saved us, I believe that I'd love you anyway." Then, with volubility and in an affectionate tone: "but you're not my brother, and my hopes don't go as far as that...no, that would be a fairy tale. At least, I'm sure that you know our father and our mother..."

As Fulvio did not reply quickly enough for her liking, she drew closer to him and took his hand again.

"Speak!" she said, with a delightful little moue.

Fulvio finally replied, in a staid and thoughtful tone: "Your father is a saint in Heaven,"

Céleste's eyelid lowered, moistened by a tear, but she said: "And our mother?"

"Oh," said the prince, who seemed to be smiling at some dear and radiant vision, How you're going to adore her, child, your beautiful, sweet mother!"

The tears that were on the edge of Céleste's eyelids suddenly overflowed on to her cheeks. "My mother!" she repeated, twice. "My mother!"

That was all she said. Her face, previously so mischievous, expressed a grave and profound ecstasy.

"And when shall I be in my mother's arms?" she asked, after a brief silence.

"This very day," replied Fulvio. "I promise you that, Céleste."

For the second time, he forgot the hour and his rendezvous with Angélie. A great and calm shift had just taken place in his existence. He had set forth a little while ago, not even in doubt, but in the most complete incredulity. His idea, as we have called the voice that had suddenly spoken in the depths of his heart, had only awakened disdainful objections in him.

No event had occurred to modify Fulvio's beliefs. Since the moment he had said "It's impossible!" nothing had come to combat his incredulity; nothing except the muffled argument of the heart, more powerful than all the proofs in the world. The revolution had been accomplished so naturally and so quietly that he did not realize it. Perhaps he would still have been capable of saying: "It's impossible," like those sly lovers who refuse the kiss severely when it is already conquered. But that impossible thing was implicitly accepted. It became henceforth the principal element of his life. He had a mother, a sister and a brother! His soul, too full, could scarcely contain all his delight. He looked at Céleste, who was weeping, no longer having any words. The young woman's joy added to his own joy. She was his sister, that young woman, whom he had been afraid to love. And was there not the hand of Providence in all that?

Since the moment when he had seen her for the first time, that child who was nothing to him, and to whom he could not even put a name, he had felt himself magnified and becoming better. Implicitly, he had broken with his past, at least in his heart. And at the moment when a word would have been sufficient for him to conquer the testimony of Monteleone's widow, he had recoiled, gripped by shame.

Céleste left her lovely little hand between his. They were both dreaming. And it was certainly a strange thing to see them next to one another like that: her, confident and no longer feeling the timidity of a savage child; him, already habituated to the calm contentment that his heart had not known the previous day. One might have thought that they had always been together.

Suddenly, Fulvio seemed to wake up, He drew Céleste's hand to his bosom.

"And why all that great despair?" he asked, following the train of his thought. "There was, however, a pious image at your bed-head."

Céleste blushed and lowered her eyes.

"We have begged God's pardon," she murmured. "I know that we were committing a great sin."

"But why" Fulvio insisted.

The young woman's embarrassment redoubled. "Julian wanted to be a priest," she murmured, "but amour came..."

"Has he pronounced his vows?"

"No...oh, no...he's free"

"Then why?" repeated the prince, for the third time.

"When one has raised one; gaze too high…," said Céleste, with a singular expression of sadness.

"He loves a rich young woman?"

"Very rich...but it's not only that."

"What is it, then? Noble?"

"Yes. Even more noble than rich." She uttered a deep sigh. Was that sigh for Julian?

"Would you like to tell me the name of that young woman, Céleste?" asked the prince, softly.

"That's my brother's secret," she replied.

The prince smiled, and said: "And you, Céleste? Have you no secret?"

Red s she was, she went very pale. Two beautiful tears sprang from her eyes, while she replied: "Oh, no, I have no secret."

"And you wanted to die, Céleste?"

She raised her moist gaze to Fulvio, and then turned her head away.

"Is he very rich too?" Fulvio asked. "And noble?"

"How did you guess that I love him?" Céleste cried, naively.

The prince kissed her hands. She went on: "He's noble, and he's very rich. He's as far above me as the stars that shine by night are above the humble glow-worm that shines on earth on a blade of grass..."

"And you can't forget him?"

A kind of indignation was painted on the mobile features of the charming girl. "Forget him!" she repeated. "That's impossible." Then, fixing her limpid and resolute gaze on Fulvio, she added: "I'm able to suffer. I no longer want to die."

There was another silence. No noise was coming from the room of the wounded man.

"Céleste," said Fulvio, in a tone so soft that you might have thought it was a mother with her child, "no matter how highly placed the woman is whom your brother loves, and no matter how brilliant and great the man is on whom you've fixed your gaze, there cannot be any insurmountable obstacles between you."

"Is that the truth?" stammered he poor child.

"It's the truth, but I'm not saying enough. Even if that young man and that young woman were sitting at the foot of the throne..."

"They are sitting at the foot of the throne," Céleste interjected.

"Even if they were the first after the King, your father's name would place you above them."

Céleste was open-mouthed. After a few seconds of reflection, she shook her blonde head incredulously.

"You're a Prince," she murmured, "and there is the beautiful radiance of frankness in your eyes than I love so much in the eyes of my dear Julian...but I'm only a poor child. Why would you want to deceive me?" Then, after a sudden reflection, she said: "Have you said all this to Julian?"

"I haven't seen Julian," replied the Prince.

She was not anxious immediately. The surprise came before the fear. "What have they done with him, then?" That seemed an inapt question. As the prince did not reply to it, Céleste went n: "Why is it that I haven't found him next to our father Manuele?"

The prince's face expressed a sudden keen attention. "You hoped to find your brother with Manuele?" he asked.

It was Céleste's turn to look at him; she was astonished. "But...," she said, her voice trembling already, "someone came to fetch him before me..."

"On whose part?" demanded Fulvio.

"Don't you know?" cried Céleste. "Since someone came to look for me afterwards on the same part?"

The prince reflected. Céleste heard him thinking aloud: "I promised that mother to return her two children..."

"Isn't he with you?" she said, frightened. "And if he isn't with you, who could have set a trap for my brother Julian?"

"We don't know yet that it is a trap," Fulvio replied, summoning up all his calmness in order not to frighten her further. "Do you know of any enemies?"

"Yesterday, I believed that we were two poor children, signor, orphaned and abandoned. Yesterday, I would have replied: 'No, we have no enemies.' But you pronounced words just now so strange that I no longer know what to think. If you weren't toying with me...if all this isn't a dream, Julian and I must have enemies."

Fulvio nodded his head to approve that conclusion.

"You know that we have enemies?" said Céleste, and immediately added: "Do you know who our enemies are?"

She stood up, quivering, because a sudden idea clutched her heart. "In the name of God," she cried, "what do you fear or my brother Julian?"

The prince agitated a bell-cord hanging behind him. At the same time he took Céleste's hand in order to invite her to sit down.

"What time did someone come to look for your brother?" he asked.

"In the morning," she said, "about ten or eleven o'clock."

A valet appeared in the doorway. "Send Cucuzone to me immediately!" the prince ordered.

When the valet had gone, he added, addressing Céleste: "Can you give me a description of the man who came to your home?"

"Tall and handsome," replied the young woman. "Cold expression, face fatigued and pale."

"Did he have an accent?"

"A Sicilian accent, it seemed to me."

The bell rang a second time, more loudly. Another valet came to the threshold. In spite of the noises made so close to the wounded Manuele, no sign seemed to announce his awakening.

"Ruggieri! I want Ruggieri immediately!" commanded Fulvio.

At his imperious gesture, the valet left at a run.

He turned back to Céleste. "Tell me," he said, "whether you noticed anything particular about that man."

"Nothing," replied the young woman, who interrogated her memory laboriously, "except that his words, like yours, signor, seemed to announce some great and abrupt change in our existence. But I beg you, explain to me what you fear..."

At a movement of impatience that escaped Fulvio, she added, with tears in her eyes: "Signor...I only have him to love!"

The Prince softened and kissed her hand "Céleste," she said, "I am strong enough to protect your brother. Have no fear. But to fight as it is necessary to fight, I need to know. Don't hide any detail from me."

"I'm searching...," said the young woman, almost distraught

"Did he pronounce any other name than that of your father Manuele?"

"No."

"You're sure of that?"

Céleste pressed her forehead with her hands, then replied: "I'm sure." She suddenly cried: "Oh! I remember. When Julian said that he had no clothes to go with him, the man said: 'Remember that circumstance; it will kill your enemy!'"

"Your enemy?" repeated the prince. "You've hidden something from me, then? You have an enemy!"

"Not me," replied Céleste, blushing and smiling involuntarily. "It's Julian who has an enemy."

"And you don't want to say his name, Céleste"

"It's Julian's secret. Listen...all this is so confused in my mind that I can't see any longer. Another man than you came to our house last night. It wasn't you, was it, who took my brother Julian's soutanelle?"

"I ask questions, Céleste," retorted Fulvio, with a hint of severity in his voice, "but I don't answer them."

"No, no," she said. "What would you have done with that poor garment, you who seem so rich? But it was really you who burned your hand on the stove."

Fulvio's right hand was still gloved

"And besides," said Céleste, "the purse…"

"Did you mention that to the man in question?" asked the prince.

"We were talking about it, Julian and I, when the man came in. I don't know whether he was listening at the door, but he told Julian to bring the purse with him, and to be sure to remember the burn."

Fulvio's head was inclined over his chest. "Were you alone," he asked, when you woke up?"

"Quite alone."

"How much was in the purse?"

"A simple gold once."

The prince made a gesture of astonishment.

At that moment, a somber mass irrupted into the room through the open window overlooking the garden. Céleste uttered a cry of fright. The somber mass was a man, or rather a baboon, for he had fallen on to his hands, with the aid of which he was walking, waving his legs in the air as if he wanted to salute the company politely. Having taken a few steps in that unusual position, the man folded himself, his body suddenly rounded like a ball, and ended up motionless and vertical, his entire body supported on one of his hands, which was hanging on to the knob of a chair.

The door opened and another individual came in, this one on two short and slightly bowed legs, walking like a mariner, with his knees braced. He had his cap under his arm and he was digging his incombustible thumb into the bowl of his pipe in order to extinguish it.

"Down, Cucuzone," said the prince, severely.

The baboon-man immediately fell on to his feet and stood before him in the stance of an unarmed soldier.

"It's astonishing, all the same," said the mariner Ruggieri, "that a man of his age can't keep still!" He addressed Fulvio: "Which doesn't prevent him being a fine fellow when he occasion demands. But as for costume…" He finished his sentence by shrugging his broad, square shoulders.

Cucuzone made a clownish gesture and replied: "Everyone can't be decked out as an ambassador, like cousin Ruggieri."

"Peace!" said he prince. "Who was at the Piazza del Mercato this morning?"

"Me," replied the mariner.

"What's new?"

"They're burying the hunchback."

"Barbe de Monteleone is dead?" murmured the prince, surprised.

"Last night…while people were dancing at the Palazzo Doria."

"And?"

"Pier Falcone came to make his report."

"And?"

"Johann Spurzheim sent men to his house to seize two golden boxes, both bearing the monogram of the dead woman."

"What was in the boxes?"

"One would think it was candy."

Fulvio murmured: "Barbe was poisoned. And?"

"That's all."

"You don't know whether he sent anyone to the Folqueri house?"

"If it pleases Your Highness," put in Cucuzone, "I can answer that. I was giving a little performance this morning at the Castello-Vecchio. The poor comrades were delighted with me, to the point that they made a collection on the rampart and I made fifteen or twenty carlins. I wanted to see something of what was happening out there."

"And what did you see?" asked the prince.

Cucuzone drew nearer with an abrupt movement, and replied in a low voice: "I saw the cell where you'll be this evening, Master." And, without giving him time to reply, he added, aloud: "If it pleases Your Highness, I saw extinct torches all along the balustrade of the Folquieri house. And as I didn't think I was doing any harm. I can say that I darted a glance into a certain attic. I saw a very pretty girl there, who has a right to all my respects, since she's now here in your illustrious company."

He laughed slyly.

Ruggieri, solidly camped on his broad base, remained imperturbably serious.

"You didn't see anything else?" said the Prince

"I saw the young man. We've known one another for a long time, Highness. Well, if I'd encountered him four or five years ago, that child, or his double, out there, toward Potenza, I know what name I'd have called him by..."

"What do you mean?"

"But, the acrobat went on, placidly, "there are funny resemblances like that in the world. Anyway, not to make you languish, I also saw the man."

"What man?"

"The man sent by our worthy friend in the Piazza del Mercato."

"By Johann!" cried Fulvio

"And from where did you see all these things, friend?" asked Céleste.

"Excellency," replied Cucuzone, "I was hanging by the feet from the roof of your skylight, and my head descended as far as the upper panes. I noticed a head. One never looks at the upper panes, under the pretext that only the birds can look through them. That's a mistake."

He bowed deeply to the young woman, and resisted the desire he had to walk on the ceiling a little.

"And did you recognize Johann's envoy?" interrogated the prince.

"Perfectly, Highness."

"Who was it?"

"Your best enemy."

Fulvio stamped his foot impatiently.

"The man from Palermo," added Cucuzone.

"If the Master had wanted it," muttered Ruggieri, "that one wouldn't be getting in our way..." He caressed his dagger inside his sailor's jacket.

Prancing gracefully, Cucuzone went on: "There's no time to lose. I'll take care of him, if the Master..."

"Peace!" interrupted the latter. "I forbid you to touch a hair on his head."

The mariner and the acrobat immediately fell silent.

"It's not me who orders that, lads," he went on, changing his one and speaking in such a way as not to be understood by Céleste. "It's the rule, Pier Falcone has the ring of the Silence."

"Has he stolen it?" Cucuzone could not help asking.

Fulvio's gaze was mute.

"The young man from the Folquieri house," the Prince continued, "must be with Johann Spurzheim now. It's necessary for one of you to go and keep watch outside, and for the other to get into the house, no matter how."

"That's my affair!" exclaimed the acrobat. "The building has chimneys."

"If anything happens to that young man," Fulvio concluded, raising his voice and looking at Céleste, "you'll both answer to me for it with your lives."

III. The Portrait

Angélie was still alone. The beautiful clock-face, supported by the emblematic chariot of Diana Lucifera declared the slow passage of time. Angélie was sad. Angélie was waiting. It was the first time.

Around her the odorous trees were mute; no footsteps sounded on the golden sand of the pathways. In the silence, Angélie listened for a sound. Her beautiful pensive head was resting on her hand. The sound did not come. Only the dormant breeze murmured occasionally, swaying the idle braches of the oleanders. Nina had not come. And Fulvio was not coming.

In that charming boudoir there were a few gracious master paintings and, in front of the windows, two antique groups forming a pendant. There was also a modern canvas, a portrait in the manner of Van Dyck.

It was a young man—a very young man—dressed in the fashion that it is conventional to call German, which the Germans do not follow. Out in the depths of the second ulterior Calabria, on the shores of Sant'Eufemia, we once saw the original of that portrait. He came from far away, that handsome young man, we know not where. He was going where the mystery of his destiny called him. Alone on that radiant and deserted beach, he took a spade and a pickax from the abandoned cabin of a fisherman and turned the corner of the Brentola, searching for the submerged ruins of the Martorello forges.

What portrait could be in Nina Dolci's boudoir except that of Fulvio, her good friend? It was a portrait of Fulvio, but of Fulvio adolescent, such as he was in the happy times of battles and amours, the man whom the tzigane Fiamma had adored on her knees.

Do you remember? The original of that portrait was the Chevalier d'Athol whom we saw for the first time in the carrozza of Battista Giubbetta, the coach-driver of Monteleone, marching dreamily along the shore, bathing his gaze in the bright horizons of the Tyrrhenian Sea. He took a desiccated flower from his wallet, against which his heart was beating; he adored that flower like a holy relic, and pursued into the water the sepal that the wind stole from him. The games of amorous children!

Well, that Athol, so young and handsome, had a few years more than the portrait. His hair had darkened, his eyes no longer retained the feminine softness of the adolescent gaze. The face of the portrait stood out white against a dark background, which outlined the blonde hair, soft and smooth. The face in the portrait was beautiful and poetic. You might almost have thought it the face of a woman, or, better still, one of those young recluses who die in worldly life and pass, sad and gentle, from the school benches to the priest's stall. That severe costume, that somber velvet, buttoned up to the collar, lent itself to the comparison. It had the look of a soutane.

Angélie was sitting directly facing that portrait. Her eyes had fallen on the canvas many times, and her gaze had always turned away with a fearful expression, we might almost say anguished. She was suffering. It was not her pride, wounded by the waiting, that was her principal suffering. You could have seen that when her hands suddenly went to her heart and her cheeks became very pale. She was suffering, but she sometimes stood up indignantly, as if she were ashamed of her malaise. Then her lips parted and a few words emerged, wearily.

"I've disobeyed my brother," she murmured. "I've doubted my brother. Lord! What is there in the depths of my soul?"

The poor beautiful head curbed under I know not what remorse, too feeble against her passion. But what was her passion? And why did her gaze turn away from that portrait? Fulvio must have been eighteen when that portrait was painted. Angélie knew someone who resembled that portrait more than Fulvio himself. Angélie was afraid, and dared not contemplate those features, which spoke to her of someone other than Fulvio. In her troubled soul, she said to herself:

I am very sure of this. If he loved me, I would be strong.

And amid the clouds that obscured her conscience, a question came to light involuntarily.

And what about me? she thought. *Do I have the love for him that I had before?*

In order to respond, it was necessary not to look at the portrait, for the white face that stood out from the dark canvas was no longer Fulvio. It was the adolescent with the melancholy and suave face that Angélie had encountered in the church of San Gennaro, the one who had put his hand on his failing heart one day when she had passed close to him: the young saint that she had mentioned to Nina Dolci at the ball at the Palazzo Doria. It was him, feature for feature. And that resemblance had, for Angélie, something supernatural about it. She saw a kind of predestination in it.

It was Fulvio who troubled her poor heart in that new form: Fulvio as she would have liked him to be, as she would have loved him more, Fulvio retaining his young and virgin soul, Fulvio without his gallant history, his past of a fortunate Don Juan.

And today, when she was alone in her fiancé's house, when she had risked that step, resolutely and decisively, in order to rivet more securely the chain that bound her to Fulvio, Angélie did not experience the calm that ordinarily follows any great determination. Her heart was constricted in her breast, and her eyes were filled with tears,

She no longer dared look at the fascinating portrait that spoke to her mysteriously of someone other than Fulvio. In order to flee the thoughts that were obsessing her and oppressing her, she was obliged to take refuge in her profound pity and say to herself: *He belongs to God!*

She spent a long time thus, motionless, with her eyes closed. Why was Fulvio not there? Why was he not defending her against herself? Her burning head was heavy. She put her beautiful hands over her face, and a groan escaped her beast.

"I'm going mad!" she murmured.

Through her closed eyelids and her beautiful hands, spread like a veil, she could still see that suave and seraphic smile...

The sun was already descending toward the horizon. Its rays, which were passing through the bright foliage of acacias planted in quincunxes in front of the pavilion, came to play upon Angélie's forehead.

Suddenly, there was a shadow. Angela divined that someone was between her and the window. It was Fulvio for whom she was waiting; it was Julian of whom she thought; for her, it was Julian who was standing there—or rather, for her fever was throwing her into fantastic spaces, it was the living portrait, detached from the canvas, who was about to part her hands in order to force her to contemplate him again.

"Angélie," said a grave and soft voice in her ear, "why are you weeping?"

The dream vanished like the crazy mists that the breeze chases away in the month of May. All her vague terrors disappeared at the same time. She uncovered her face, suddenly smiling. Fulvio always saved her from herself; it only required, in order to return her to reason and happiness, the presence of Fulvio, just as it only required the first ray of dawn to chase away all the phantoms of the night.

"Thank you for having come!" she murmured, extending her hand to him.

Fulvio bent his knee in order to raise that hand to his lips.

"Prince," the young woman said to him, in a reproachful tone in which there was no anger, "I didn't know what it was to wait."

Coriolani did not apologize. His lips remained stuck to Angélie's hand. She was smiling, paler now, and her heart was beating rapidly.

There was something admirable to see in the face of each of those creatures, so perfectly beautiful, those two proud masterpieces of God. It was impossible not to say, on looking at them, that that superb virgin was made for that young man of heroic bearing.

They loved one another; their eyes said so, and it seemed that nature ought to celebrate that splendid betrothal.

"Fulvio, Fulvio," said Angélie, "You said to me yesterday that it was necessary for you to see me. I also needed to see you. I'm sick at heart and tormented. Be my physician, Fulvio, cure me!"

She lowered her eyes because she wanted a word that would encourage her confidences. Fulvio had not come for that. He remained kneeling before her and said: "I asked you why you were weeping, Angélie. You haven't responded, and you've done well. What need is there? I am the source of your dear tears, and I would like to dry them up with kisses. You have disobeyed your brother, whom you cherish like the best of fathers...and while resisting him, you have opened your heart to some of the suspicion that are in his. You're suffering. You have a kind of remorse. Isn't that what I've divined, Angélie?"

She bowed her head. Such ought to have been her preoccupation, in fact. But she had not only been thinking about her brother.

Fulvio contemplated her with an admiration full of amour.

"I've never seen you so beautiful, Angélie," he murmured.

A tear rolled between the young woman's eyelids. Her lips were very pale.

"Fulvio," she pronounced, so quietly that he could hardly hear her. "I would give my life to be sure of your amour."

"I would give more than my life to be sure of yours, Comtesse," replied the prince, whose voice was sad.

She raised wide astonished eyes to look at him. They remained thus for a moment, looking at one another."

It was far away, the strange image that was fatiguing the dreams of that virgin. Fulvio was there, her Fulvio, her conqueror. She loved him ardently, profoundly. She was happy. Fulvio sensed reborn within him the holy fever of his initial tenderness. It seemed that no human force could henceforth bar the florid route of their felicity.

"Angélie," said Fulvio, "I have put in you, in you alone, all my hopes for the future. If you love me, I shall have paradise on earth. If I am mistaken, everything is finished for me; I sense it…and I wish it."

"If I love you…," stammered La Doria, whose beautiful eyes clouded over. "Holy virgin! He asks whether I love him!"

Fulvio continued as if he had not heard.

"If you loved me, Angélie, that would be the most beautiful joy of my days. The suspicions I mentioned just now, your brother's suspicions, would fall, for he is a noble heart and I know that he would not try to deny the light when the light were manifest…if you loved me…"

"But I don't want you to talk like this, Prince," Angélie interjected. "I am in your house and I am leaving you at my feet."

There was a hint of bitterness in Fulvio's smile. "Forgive me," he said, raising Le Doria's hand to his lips respectfully. "It is because love, as I understand it, is rare. I don't want a commonplace love. In the same way that I love you, I want to be loved."

"Can you love me as no one ever loves down here, Prince?" Angélie asked, in the tone that can only depart from the heart. "I would not fear to measure my tenderness against yours."

"May God hear you, Dona Angélie Doria," said Coriolani, slowly

His gaze was burning Angélie. She turned her eyes away and said: "Tell me, Prince, how it pleases you to be loved."

"It would be easier," replied Fulvio, "To tell you how I love you. But this is not a conversation about love my adorable Angélie. I do not know how to talk about love, I only know love…."

A word pressed upon the young woman's lips.

"No, no," said Fulvio, gently, as if he had divined it. "Don't say that, Angélie. Those vulgar reproaches would ill befit your divine lips. I have loved, it's true; why deny it? Have I ever loved as much as I love you? Perhaps...the hour when the soul awakes produces those miracles... But what I can affirm is that I have never loved in the same fashion. You have given birth in me to respect; I might even say idolatry. It is with insistence, it is with reflection also, that I confide all my destiny to you. It is with an infinite pride that I nourish the hope of having you for the inseparable companion of my life. I do not promise you to be constant, Comtesse; even the thought of another love can no longer come to me; that would be an insult to you, and an outrage to me. I am yours; before God I swear it. There is nothing in my soul that is not yours, if you love me."

The final phrase killed Angélie's charming smile. Until the final phrase she had listened plunged in a kind of delight.

"Again!" she said, while her delicate brows furrowed involuntarily.

"I tell you this, Angélie," Fulvio continued, following the thought that dominated him at that moment. "All the obstacles heaped in my passage by envy or hatred have been set aside or broken. The name of Monteleone that belongs to me, but which seemed so far out of range, is at my mercy; I have only to reach out my hand to take it. I am at the pinnacle; I have triumphed; there is only one barrier between us and happiness, and that is you."

"Me?" protested the beautiful Doria.

"You, Angélie, who might not accept the conditions of my love."

"Are those conditions very unacceptable, then, signor?"

"Already your tone has changed," said Fulvio, in a melancholy fashion. "I see in your gaze nascent defiance and the revolt of pride. There is still time, signora; the act is not yet concluded..."

"Do you, then desire it to be broken, signor?" said the beautiful Doria, in tears.

"May God judge me!" replied Coriolani, "If the radiant hope that I have put in you is disappointed, I shall die."

She wiped her eyes and looked him in the face.

"Spare me this torture!" she pronounced, in an altered voice. "If you don't believe in me, put me to the proof."

"Signora," said Fulvio, "I have come for that."

And as she straightened up, offended, he went on in the beautiful and harmonious voice that was so familiar with the route to the heart: "You are as pure as the angels, Comtesse, I know that...but if, suddenly, some terrible revelation showed me your past in another light, I would not cease to love you."

A vivid redness colored Angélie's forehead and cheeks. Her anxious gaze lowered. She maintained silence. Momentarily, Fulvio seemed to hesitate, but only for a moment. His voice suddenly because curt and more incisive, as he went on: "What is the point of seeking roundabout ways. Comtesse? This conversation cannot be prolonged; we are both suffering..."

"That's true," Angélie stammered. "I'm suffering."

She withdrew her hand in order to put it to her heart.

"It's the cowardice of my conscience," said Fulvio, who stood up and whose gaze shone with all his pride. "This is what I want to know, Comtesse: is there anything in the world that could prevent you from loving me?"

She looked at him as if she were afraid of seeing madness in his eyes. Then she said: "I don't understand."

"It's necessary that you understand, however, Angélie, for everything depends on your response. You love me, I know; you've told me so. But would you love in me the unfortunate stripped of his prestige, the fallen man, the vanquished fighter? If you learned one day..."

"I believe...," Angélie interrupted herself, and resumed: "I believe that I would die then, Fulvio, but I wouldn't cease to love you."

"One doesn't die when one loves..."

"I am La Doria!" pronounced Angélie, slowly.

"Your pride is stronger than your love, isn't it?"

He had a chill in her heart, but she repeated: "I am La Doria." Then, with her yes full of tears: "Do I know what I would do, signor? In the name of Heaven, have pity on me. Explain yourself. Who are you? What have you done? I'm asking you for mercy. Speak!"

"I am Mario, Comte de Monteleone," replied the prince.

Joy shone in Angélie's gaze.

"But," he added, emphasizing each of his words in a tone that something provocative about it, "my past life does not go with my name. Comtesse Doria might reproach me later for having deceived her."

The young woman went pale again.

"You've been able to descend as far as shame!" she murmured.

"Shame?" repeated the prince. "That's a word, Comtesse...but don't interrupt me anymore; with one word, I can tell you everything. This morning Nina Dolci told you the story of a Calabrian bandit...."

"Il Porporato!" stammered Angélie.

"Il Porporato, Madame. That story struck you, I see..."

"Have you done as he did, signor?"

He took a step back and said, in a dull voice: "I am Il Porporato, Madame."

Angélie's beautiful head tipped on to the back of her armchair.

Fulvio waited. After a long silence, he said: "Angélie, I shall not plead my cause. I only tell you that, at this moment, you are my unique amour. Whatever happens, I swear on oath, that amour will be the last. You are the judge of supreme resort, and without appeal. A carriage with the arms of your house is waiting at the gate of the Palazzo that opens to the fields. No one saw you enter;

no one will see you leave. The hour for you to go to the Villa Floridiana has come. You are free."

A sob raised the breast of the beautiful Doria. Her eyes opened; her gaze fell on the portrait that was facing her. She had a kind of surge of horror. You might have thought that she was looking around for a refuge.

"No, no!" she cried, putting her hands over her eyelids "I don't want it! I don't want it!"

It was bewilderment. Her entire beautiful body was trembling with the shock of a mysterious fear. She stood up, and immediately tottered. Fulvio leapt forward to sustain her.

She threw her arms around his neck, saying: "I love you! I want to love you!"

There was something strange in that. Fulvio did not have the secret of that emotion.

"Swear to me," cried La Doria imperiously, her pride seeking shelter no matter where, "swear to me that you are Mario, Comte de Monteleone."

She had turned in such a way as not to see the portrait, but the image was before her eyes and her soul experienced an inexpressible distress. She was sinking, and I know not what irresistible magnetism as drawing her down. Her heart cried out the verity that was upsetting her: *Fulvio alone can defend you against this amour, which is a crime.*

Julian! Julian! Poor pure and holy soul! All of Julian's heart had been in the gaze that he had darted at her in the church of San Gennaro. When Fulvio was there with her, Fulvio, the amorous fascinator, she felt that passion, which she had fought in vain, becoming numb within her. She believed that she loved Fulvio, and perhaps she did. But with Fulvio absent, Fulvio lost forever, she no longer had any defense. Pious as she was, in the Italian fashion, horror took her at the thought that she might dispute a heart with God.

"I swear," Fulvio replied, meanwhile," that I am Mario, Comte de Monteleone."

"Then my brother and I have your heritage," said La Doria, swiftly.

"If you do not love me, Angélie," retorted Fulvio, simply, "I no longer need a heritage."

She straightened up, her gesture full of impetuosity and her gaze flashing.

"You announced just now that a carriage with the arms of my house is waiting for me at the palace gate. I want you to climb into it with me. I want to burn my boats and arrive at the court in your company."

"Do you think so, Comtesse?"

"I think so, signor. Will you recoil?"

He took her hand, which he pressed to his lips. Angélie inclined and put a kiss on his forehead. "I seal our betrothal!" she said, with a strange smile.

"May God render you, Madame," Fulvio said, in the fullness of his profound joy, "all the happiness that you will give me. You are mine henceforth, and woe betide anyone who tries to separate us."

He rang, and, tearing a page from his notepad, he wrote a few words in haste.

"To those who are waiting in the Apollo gallery," he said to the valet who presented himself, handing him the note.

Then he took Angélie's hand and drew her toward the carriage.

Thos who were waiting in the Apollo gallery were the Masters of the Silence: Amato Lorenzo, having become the banker Massimo Dolci; Policeni Corner, risen in rank under the name of the Cavalier Ercole Pisani; Marino Marchese, transformed into the superintendent of the royal police in exchange for the long new name Andrea Visconti-Armellino; and finally, the good great captain Luca Tristany, presently Colonel San-Severo.

They had been waiting there for a long time, and they were anxious. The note that the valet brought them on Prince Coriolani's behalf, which was in code, was thus conceived:

This evening, everything will be finished; you will be rich and free. Until further notice, stand down the ventas; we have no need of the alliance of the carbonari. Be alert and ready for anything. Sometimes, the most terrible part of the struggle is the hour of triumph.

There was no signature. Armellino, Pisani and old Massimo Dolci shook hands joyfully.

"*Corpo di Bacco!*" said the good Colonel San-Severo, "I'd like, all the same, to comprehend something of our own secrets."

"To our posts!" commanded old Massimo. "We're all going blindly, my good Tristany…but as long as the Master can see clearly, the game is good!"

IV. The Villa Floridiana

In the marvelous pleasure houses that surround Naples, and which are the pride of its countryside, perhaps the most delightful is the summer palace that the Prince of Torella had restored at the beginning of the century for his second wife, the beautiful Princess Duchess of Partanna and Floridia.[59] It is situated on the western slope of the Vomero, not far from that other terrestrial paradise, the villa of the Princes of Belvedere. The Chevalier Nicollini, a gracious architect, lavished all the resources of his delicate and slightly precious taste thereon. Ferdinand, King of Naples, had bought it in 1820, after the death of Duchess Floridia, in order to make a present of it to his daughter-in-law, the Princess of Salerno.

In 1823, the epoch in which our story is happening, the court of the Villa Floridiana was almost as numerous as that of Capodimonte or the Palazzo Reale, because of the splendid favor that the King accorded to his second son.

The magnificent gardens, distributed over the slope of the hill facing the cheerful hill of Chiaia, fanned out overlooking the beaches, the bay, the islands and, above the city, the menacing and redoubtable cone of Mount Vesuvius, from which the lava flowered that swallowed Pompeii.

It was four o'clock in the afternoon. For two long hours, in consequence, the assembly of the royal family summoned by Ferdinand in person should have been open; but the princesses, dispersed in the gardens, were still on the arms of their cavaliers. The King had not appeared.

The hero of that family council, Prince Fulvio Coriolani, was imitating the King; no one had seen him.

On the other hand, the courtiers, who wanted to know the result of that solemn council, were beginning to fill the green pathways, into which the oblique sunlight was only any longer sliding lukewarm rays. No one was unaware that it was a matter of Prince Coriolani. Everyone had divined that the principal point of the deliberation must bear on the marriage of the prince with Angélie Doria.

Among the great lords summoned, in fact was Comte Lorédan Doria, with his friend and cousin, the Marquis du Buffo, who was Angélie's vice-guardian. The council or assemble was to be composed of the King; his sons, the princes; his daughters and daughters-in-law, the princesses; the princes of the blood; Baron Anspach-Boccaromana, the Secretary of the King's Privy Chamber; three Secretaries of State, among whom was Signor Carlo Piccolomini; and five superior members of the Neapolitan nobility.

---

[59] Lucia Mugliaccio, Duchess de Floridia was actually the second wife of Ferdinand I, who donated it to her. The Prince of Torella was not involved in any way.

Everyone had been able to make the remark that the council, thus conceived, was exactly the same as the one that, three years before, had regulated the civil estate of Gaetano Biffi-Miranda, of the princes Biffi and Ducs Miranda, who had neither family papers nor palpable proofs of his birth. Gaetano Biffi-Miranda, Prince Biffi, one of the most intimate friends of Fulvio Coriolani, was among the five possessors of the order of nobility. Lorédan Doria was also among the number of voters. But no one was far from thinking that there was something else at stake, and that the deliberations of the august council would not only bear upon the marriage.

There was talk—vague, but nevertheless talk—of grave changes that might take place before long in the royal entourage. The events of the previous night at the ball at the Palazzo Doria had produced a profound sensation among the politicians of the Neapolitan capital. But above all, in the talk, the same question was in all mouths:

"Why isn't Coriolani here? Why hasn't the council been held at the appointed time?"

The groups disseminated, grave and busy.

At four o'clock, Lorédan Doria, pale and distraught, approached the circle surrounding the Princess of Salerno in the grand arbor. After having bowed respectfully to the King's daughter-in-law, he approached Nina Dolci and spoke to her in a low voice.

Nina replied aloud, with a dryness that did not escape anyone: "Is it given to me to guard the noble Angélie Doria?"

So saying, she exchange a glance with her mistress.

The rumor immediately ran around everywhere that Dona Angélie Doria had disappeared.

One singular thing is that the disappearance in question did not seem to disturb the royal persons, and on all sides, remarks were heard:

"The King is shut in his cabinet."

"The King is sad and worried."

"The King has refused his door to anyone...even His Royal Highness Francis de Bourbon!"

And if anyone chanced to ask: "Is the King alone?" some, supposedly the best-informed, replied, shaking their heads: "No, the King is not alone."

They people searched the crowd of courtiers in order to see who was absent; no one was lacking—at least, no one of importance. Who, then, could be with the King? A thousand questions overlapped, to which no one could provide answers.

The principal group of courtiers was posted in the main grove of orange trees, which faced the royal perron. From there one could see perfectly the windows of the cabinet where Ferdinand de Bourbon received his elite servants when he wanted to seek a little repose at the Vila Floridiana. The casements were all closed and the blinds carefully lowered. The pavilion had the air of an abandoned house.

At every moment newcomers came to swell the number of gentlemen assembled at that point; they interrogated, and were interrogated. Why was His Majesty's door forbidden?

Nothing was happening, meanwhile, in the gathering of the princesses, who were holding their court in the beautiful shade of the arbor. The Princess of Salerno had a charming gaiety. The belatedness of her royal father-in-law irritated her, but perhaps that was only because of the opera that it would be necessary to miss.

The princes were conversing to one side with some of their familiars. The heir to the throne had been heard to say, responding to an observation by the Count of Castro-Giovanni: "There's only one man capable of dominating the situation."

There are fiction writers in Naples, as everywhere; it is simply that the métier is a little more dangerous there than elsewhere.

"Signors, said the Marquis of Zanone, a young fool who was cheerfully squandering two estates he had in the Basilicata, approaching a group of courtiers, "the house of our respectable director of police is hung in black. I wagered that I'd see his face before his decease; that loses my a hundred double ounces!"

"Console yourself, Marquis," replied the camerlengo Casabianca, "the hangings are for the director's wife."

"An intelligent hunchback, it's said," added Brigadier Michel Madrona.

And everyone: "Is that the only news you have to tell us, Marquis Zanone?"

"My sack is full," replied the latter, "but since the worthy Johann Spurzheim isn't dead, I'll keep my mouth shut, my excellent friends."

"Do you think that we're going to repeat your nonsense, Zanone?" asked Madrona, laughing.

"I know," the Marquis replied, "that in such a venerable assembly, there can only be honest signors…but for some time, honest signors have had difficulty living. Truffles are dear and French wine has risen to extravagant prices. The dark passage that leads to the director's private study has its little secrets, my companions, and everyone knows that I'm prudence itself."

The entire circle burst out laughing at that unexpected declaration. The little Marquis paraded his gaze all around.

"Signors," he said, "if you'll promise me to guard appropriate discretion faithfully, I'll give you news to make your hair stand on end."

"We'll be as mute as sepulchers, Marquis. Speak! Speak!"

Zanone adopted a self-important air. "To begin at the beginning, dear signors," he continued, "Professor Zucco Cocomeo, sectary of the Academy of

Salerno, has predicted that there will be a terrible explosion of Vesuvius within days."[60]

"That's the will of God, Marquis. And?"

"The same professor, whom Europe envies us, remarks in the *Diaro di Salerno*, that shooting stars, so numerous in Paris in the months of August, abound, on the contrary, in January in the Neapolitan latitude. He concludes from that..."

"Marquis," someone interjected, "are you making fun of us?"

"God forbid, my illustrious friends. If scientific facts don't interest you, we can pass on to another order of ideas Last march, in Naples, three new ventas of carbonari were discovered in Naples The venta del Salute and the venta della Trinita Santa were, it's said, armed..."

The circle became agitated, gripped by a sudden anxiety.[61]

"Speak more quietly, Marquis," was said on all sides

"Permit me, in passing, my dear signors," mocked Zanone, "to congratulate you in the touching confidence that unites you with one another. You see me very moved. Since you don't like that subject of conversation, I will only add that those three ventas form less than the tenth part of those to be found in Naples. There are volcanoes other than Vesuvius..."

"Peace! Peace!" someone murmured.

Zanone saluted at a distance the Minister of State, Carlo Piccolomini, who was going past. The high functionary was alone, walking with his hands behind his back, pensively.

"Has he been replaced?" asked Zanone, when the Secretary of State had disappeared round a bend in the path.

"Not yet," someone replied.

"My dear signors, I believe you're mistaken."

All ears were pricked up attentively.

"Say what you know, Marquis," they cried.

"I don't know anything, but I suspect."

"The name of the new minister?"

"Fulvio Coriolani."

There was a long murmur of astonishment, but not of criticism.

"He's not a Neapolitan subject," observed Casabianca.

---

[60] In fact, there was no major eruption of Vesuvius in 1823, although there had been an eruption in October 1822.

[61] The Neapolitan aristocracy would, indeed have been troubled by this news. The Carbonari, very active in organizing opposition of Joachim Murat, had continued their revolutionary activities after Ferdinand's restoration, and their uprising in Naples in 1820 had forced the King to introduce a new constitution and a parliament. A revolution in Sardinia followed in 1821, prompting the Pope to excommunicate the members of the organization, but they remained a constant threat in Naples. The organization's units were known as venditi, or ventas.

"How do you know, signors? Everything about that noble prince is mysterious."

"Might it be him, Madrina put in, "who is with His Majesty at this moment?"

"As to that, no," riposted Zanone. "I can also inform you in that regard."

"Speak, Marquis, speak!"

"This time, Zanone was in no hurry. His audience was hooked. He used it to his advantage.

"My valet Antonio," he said, finally, "has seen the individual who is presently with His Majesty."

"And you recognized him?"

"On the contrary, signors, I did not recognize him...but if someone among you is cleverer than me, this is the description..."

The group had swollen; heads reached forward, avid and curious.

"This is the description," repeated Zanone. "A skeleton wrapped in shawls—they're my valet Antonio's own expressions—who descended from a sedan chair behind the palace."

There was a silence around the little Marquis. In his turn, he asked: "Do you recognize our man, signors, from my valet Antonio's description?"

No one replied.

"It is, however, unusual," Zanone went on, "and there can't be many gentlemen in Naples to whom such a description might apply. When the chair stopped out there, the bearers took that singular being in their arms, like a sick child. Antonio affirms that he saw emerging from those shawls, wrapped in the fashion of swaddling clothes, a veritable death's-head..."

Silence continued to reign in the group of courtiers. Is that to say that no one had divined? That is scarcely plausible. But there really were many people there who had not divined, and those who had did not want to appear to have done so.

We have said that the position of director Johann Spurzheim at court was most exceptional. Illness, if not some other motive, had kept him nailed to his apartment since the day after the one when the city had learned with astonishment the foreign and unknown name of the new magistrate charged with overseeing its security. Johann Spurzheim had never set foot in any royal reception; if, at certain times, he had gone to secret councils of the cabinet, only the ministers could say.

The rule was that one could only know him if one had crossed the threshold of his private study or his bedroom. Now, if, among the noble audience, few or many had had that dubious advantage, they were in no hurry to brag about it. To say: "I have seen him...I have seen that living skeleton in the darkness of the bizarre sentry-box in which he hides" would have been to inscribe the word "spy" on one's own forehead in legible characters. That is not done voluntarily, even in Naples.

"Perhaps it's a gnome," said the camerlengo Casabianca.

"A familiar spirit," said other voices, supportively.

That was a means of making a joke of it. Everyone clung on to it.

"In any case," said Brigadier Michel Madrina, "if he's a phantom, he's prolix in his communications, for the conversation is threatening not to finish, and the sun is already behind Mount Vesuvius."

"That's because…" commenced Marquis Zanone.

"That's because," interjected a grave and slow voice beside him, "The phantom, as you call him, signors, probably has many things to tell His Majesty."

No one had noticed that man. He was, however, at the center of the group, next to Marquis Zanone. He was almost a young man, but his costume, by virtue of its austerity, made a contrast with those of the other courtiers. His cold gaze sustained without effort the curiosity of those who surrounded him. People in the crowd were asking:

"Who is that cavalier?"

"Do you know him?"

"Oh, my dear doctor!" cried Marquis Zanone, who knew everybody. "I hadn't noticed you." He extended his hand swiftly, which the other touched with his fingertips.

"Doctor?" was repeated within the group.

"A Sicilian," murmured two or three voices. "Doctor Pier Falcone."

"Who is he?"

"A poor devil."

They were about to turn their backs when the little Marquis spoke, asking: "Is it true, learned doctor, that you've been appointed as one of the King's ordinary physicians?"

"It's true," replied Pier Falcone, laconically.

All gazes softened. The man who had called the doctor a poor devil cleaved through the crowd and came to offer his hand.

Platitudes were hard murmured on all sides:

"Very sincere compliments!"

"Very cordial felicitations!"

"For a long time, one hasn't had to rejoice in such a choice."

"And, dearest of all princes of science," added Zanone, "can you tell us the true name of the man we call the phantom?"

"His true name," said Pier Falcone, his expression darkening, "is the justice of God."

Such emphatic words are more effective in Italy than in France.

Anxious in advance, the crowd began to shiver.

"Phantom!" continued Pier Falcone, meanwhile, in his slow and muted voice, which could be heard distinctly throughout the circle because of the profound silence. "Phantom indeed; you have named him well. What is a phantom except the victim surging forth from the tomb and coming to seize the throat of the living murderer? What is a phantom except the death that stands up, which walks, which speaks, and which extends its fleshless finger to designate to the powerful of the world the criminal draped in his impunity? You have said it: it is a phantom avenger that is conversing at this moment with Ferdinand de Bourbon..."

He extended his hand toward the royal pavilion, whose closed windows had now taken on a sinister aspect for everyone.

"The King has been sad since this morning," he went on. "The King is anxious. You said that just now. I say: the King is sadder than you think, and more worried. The King was trembling with fever when he confided his pulse to me, in which the life of the Kingdom of Naples is beating. The King is stricken in the heart. Why is that? It is because the night has spoken...it is because the voice if the dead has made itself heard...it is because a cry has reached the ears of the King that had not emerged from a living breast..."

The courtiers looked at one another, but none of them asked a question.

"God waits!" Falcone suddenly said. "He is patient because he is eternal. The years pass. The earth has drunk blood, the deep sea rolls its waves over the cadaver; the earth and the sea, which are both mute... A cry goes up! Where does it come from? No one knows. But everyone listens. That cry is the voice of the divine conscience. God is not hurried. The hour has come. The archangel's sword is shining...."

"Oh, my dear doctor," said Marquis Zanone, while the orator drew breath, "What crime are you talking about, pray?"

"Let him speak! Let him speak!" was cried on all sides.

"A crime forgotten for a long time, signors," replied Pier Falcone. "Seven years...has a century more than seven years at the court? It is twenty times more than is needed, let us be just, to commit the memory of a dead man to forgetfulness."

His dark eyes had a mocking and bitter glint.

"Who has been dead for seven years?" he demanded, abruptly. "Murdered? You no longer know... not one of you! And yet I see old men and men in their prime in your ranks. But the memory brings nothing back, the memory of deaths. Will no one here reply to me?"

No one, in fact—but everyone was interrogating his memories.

"Well," said Pier Falcone, "the King is not like you; he has more memory. The King, who has less need of the living, remembers the dead better. The King is sad and worried, signors, because the voice that I mentioned to you just now has made itself heard, pronouncing two names at once, as always: the name of a victim and the name of a murderer..."

Falcone paused. You could have heard the sound of a fly's wings.

"The victim," Falcone went on, lowering is voice, "had an illustrious name...the most illustrious name there is in southern Italy. The victim was the King's dearest friend, the brother in arms of the Royal Prince."

"Monteleone!" said a single voice in the group of courtiers.

Everyone's memory awoke at the same time.

"Monteleone! Comte Mario Monteleone!" cried the doctor.

"The murderer! Is he murderer known?"

Pier Falcone did not reply, but a sinister smile creased his pale lips. He extended his arm toward various groups that were passing by.

A sudden and general movement began in the gardens of the Floridiana. To the name of Monteleone, another name, similarly pronounced by a hundred mouths, responded:

"Coriolani! Prince Fulvio Coriolani!"

V. The Explosion of a Mine

Prince Coriolani arrived at the royal villa in the company of Dona Angélie Doria. They arrived in Contessa Doria's carriage.

His entrance was an event. The heir to the crown, the princes and the princess, celebrated it. But in the numerous group composed of Marquis Zanone and his friends, minds were vividly struck. Certainly, he was not a vanquished individual, the brilliant signor for whom the court was assembled, and who was leading on his arm the noblest heiress in the Kingdom of Naples, in spite of her elder brother, Comte Lorédan Dora, the head of the family. But there was henceforth, for those who had heard the words of Pier Falcone, a mysterious threat suspended above his head. The crowd had pronounced his name at the moment when the name of Monteleone's murdered was being demanded. Falcone had remained silent, as he had judged it superfluous to speak after the crowd. Had not the crowd, in pronouncing that name, taken charge of making the response?

There was, moreover, a singular circumstance. When the courtiers, distracted momentarily by the movement taking place all around, turned back to Falcone in order to question him further, Falcone had disappeared. No one, not even the little Marquis, could say in what direction the new ordinary physician of His Majesty had lost himself in the trees.

But the astonishments were not at an end; in fact, the astonishments had only just begun.

"By San Gennaro!" Zanone suddenly exclaimed. "Am I dreaming? Now the illustrious Carlo Piccolomini is saluting those he had arrested yesterday!"

In the middle of the pathway, the Minister of State had, indeed, just found himself before Malatesta and Colonna, who were walking arm-in-arm.

Those young signors did not have the appearance of captives who had broken their chains violently. They were chatting and laughing.

"There's the major of the guards who's doing better!" said Madrina, wonderstruck. "He's chatting familiarly with Sampieri and Mareschalci..."

"Whom he seized by the collar last night" finished someone else.

What did that about-turn signify? For it was the exact truth. Wolfgang Baumgarten, major in the Swiss Guards, was supporting himself to the right and left on the arms of Sampieri and Mareschalci. Domenico Sampieri even had the expression of a victor who had just taken his revenge, and is joking.

But, in that regard, if you had seen the welcome given to Fulvio Coriolani in the circle of the princesses! Francis de Bourbon was holding one if his hands in his own, while the Comte de Castro-Giovanni was giving him the accolade.

In the meantime, Angélie Doria, placed between the Royal Princess and the Archduchess Princess of Salerno, was being heaped with attentions and caresses.

There was only one person in that august group whose face was not painted with joy. Dona Nina Dilci, the zingara, had just perceived Dr. Pier Falcone, who was slipping toward the King's apartments. She had tried to encounter Fulvio's gaze without succeeding.

Suddenly, the casements of the royal apartment opened noisily. The garden resounded with the complaisant clamors that, since the beginning of the world, no sovereign has ever lacked.

"Long live King Ferdinand!"

"Evviva il Salvatore di patria!"

"Evviva il Borbone! Evviva! Evviva!"

The King was on the balcony, accompanied by Comte Lorédan Doria and the principal ordinary physician, Doctor Wilhelm Bach."[62]

"Look," said the Princess of Salerno to Angélie. "His Majesty will have reckoned with your brother."

And Castro-Giovanni. Leaning toward Fulvio's ears, said: "His Majesty has just preached to Lorédan. We'll win all along the line."

A royal usher came to open both battens of the door to the royal pavilion. The King beckoned graciously to the princesses to invite them to mount the perron.

"His Majesty is smiling at you," people said to Fulvio.

It is necessary not to believe that the seed thrown by Falcone had not borne fruit. What had just been said in the group of courtiers gathered under the royal balcony as already running from mouth to mouth. Marquis Zanone, Casabianca and Madrina were excellent gazettes. But at the first repeated words of that emphatic and mysterious harangue, all those closely or distantly connected with the party of the princesses smiled scornfully.

No one was unaware of that. Everyone knew that something dramatic was going to happen today at the Villa Floridians. That solemnity was to lead to the rehabilitation of the great name of Monteleone, and doubtless the punishment of some guilty party, but how can one describe the scorn of all those well-informed people for those who were repeating vague and foolish rumors in which Prince Coriolani seemed to be placed on one side and the memory of Monteleone on the other, with the result that those blind fools seemed to think that a contest existed between Prince Coriolani and the memory of Monteleone?

The fiction writers and the impertinent curious confused everything, blurred everything. Emerging from their mouths, the truth had a carnival appearance.

"The *coup de théâtre* will be all the more striking!" the princesses said to one another. "Let them take their false route!"

They promised themselves the joy of a greater triumph.

---

[62] The author has presumably forgotten that he has already given this surname to the physician Daniel Bach.

Angélie and Nina found themselves next to one another momentarily.

"He loves me," said the young Comtesse in her friend's ear. "I'm sure of it. I'm very happy."

Nina looked at her. It was truly a triumphant beauty that Angélie had at that moment.

"And you?" murmured the zingara, whose voice had an involuntary hint of sadness. "Are you quite sure of loving him?"

"Silly!" replied Angélie.

Nina fixed her profound eyes upon her. "If all those who are here for his triumph united to bring him down," she continued, "would you still love him, Comtesse?"

Angélie's beautiful eyelids fluttered, and then lowered. But for the second time, and in a reproachful tone, she replied: "That's silly."

She passed on, drawn away by the Princess of Salerno, who took her by the hand. Nina's head inclined over her breast. She remained behind the other ladies accompanying the princess

I'm afraid! she said, in the depths of her soul.

At that moment, the usher cried from the top of the perron. "It is admissible to enter the King's house." That was the formula for announcing that the nobility was permitted to cross the threshold of the apartments where the King was.

The members of the royal family had not expected that. The princes and processes were seen to stop, astonished, in the vestibule.

In the gardens, however, the grateful crowd uttered long evvivas. Excited curiosity was about to be satisfied. It was the least one could do to wish the savior of the fatherland a long life.

Gentlemen and ladies flocked into the vestibule. Etiquette received more than one rude shock there.

Nina, cut off by the tumultuous flood, remained in the same place. Her gaze searched the distant avenues. She was expecting someone. She saw a squadron of light infantry coming through the gardens, posting sentinels at intervals.

The daylight was already declining. Five o'clock had sounded in the villa's clock.

"No further entry to the king's house is admissible!" pronounced the usher, lowering his cane behind the last to be introduced.

And that cry, passing from sentinel to sentinel, reached all the way to the gates if the garden: "No further entry to the king's house is admissible!"

An exclamation was stifled in the zingara's throat. She had just perceived at the very end of the main pathway those she was doubtless expecting: the old banker Massimo Dolci, her pretended uncle, and the superintendant of police, Armellino.

As she was about to advance toward them she saw the two sentries at the gate cross their carbines in front of the newcomers. The court banker and the second dignitary of the Neapolitan police!

Nina stopped. She went very pale. She ran into a dense thicket formed by magnolias and arborescent camellias. Almost immediately afterwards, a strangely modulated cry emerged from the thicket.

Massimo Dolci and Armellino, who were withdrawing, shuddered at that cry.

"That's Fiamma!" said Armellino.

Old Massimo said: "Let's separate, Corner. I'll go to the venta. Post men in the country, under the windows of the villa."

So saying, he climbed back into his carriage. The superintendent of police went around the villa and plunged into the surrounding woods.

Nina's ardent eyes were fixed on the casements of the royal pavilion.

"Johann Spurzheim is there!" she murmured. "I'd swear to it! This evening, there'll be a battle."

After a few minutes she emerged from the bushes, holding a bunch of flowers. She did not even try to bend the contingent of guards on the threshold of the main vestibule. The palace was her dwelling; she knew all the issues. She made a rapid tour of the royal pavilion and introduced herself by means of a door to the Princess of Salerno's apartments.

The corridors she traversed were deserted, but she soon stopped at a room where a veiled woman wearing mourning was sitting alone. At a glance she had recognized her companion on the ferry, the Comtesse.

"No one passes!" said a rude voice near the threshold. And the door was slammed.

That was a further detour that it was necessary to make. Nina went to another door and opened it. In that second room, seven or eight cavaliers were gathered. They were talking to one another excitedly. This time, Nina closed the door herself. She had recognized the gentlemen imprisoned the day before: Giulio Doria d'Agri, the Marquis de Malatesta, Sampieri, Vespuccio Doria. Mareschalci, Colonna, Ziani, Gravina, etc. They were talking to Carlo Piccolomini.

Even more convinced, the zingara said to herself: "Johann Spurzheim can't be far away."

Perhaps he was there, the terrible dying man who held all the threads of the tragedy in his hand, but he could not be seen. The spirit of evil is similarly everywhere and nowhere.

Nina went through all the rooms of the royal pavilion and did not discover Johann Spurzheim. When she finally reached the drawing rooms and gallery where the family assembly was taking place, her first glance was still to search for Johann Spurzheim. It was in vain. Johann Spurzheim, as invisible as the demon himself, was the soul of that council, but was not in attendance.

Unable to reach he platform where Ferdinand de Bourbon and his family were seated, Nina slipped into a boudoir whose door opened not far from the princesses and very close to Coriolani.

That boudoir overlooked the Vomero. The enchanted countryside adjacent to the villa of the Princes de Belvedere extended away from the window. It contained a harp and various instruments of accompaniment. The Princes of Salerno, one of the most distinguished virtuosos in Italy, often came there. The King loved to hear her play the dreamy fantasias that cradle the genius of Germany. There was a stone balcony outside the boudoir window.

That assembly certainly offered a solemn aspect. The royal family was complete. You could not have named a family illustrious in the Kingdom of Naples that did not have a representative there.

The King was sitting between his two sons. The armchair of the Minister of State remained empty at his feet. Lorédan Doria was placed behind His Majesty. The princesses surrounded Angélie, not far from the place where Prince Fulvio Coriolani was standing.

On Fulvio's face one could admire the noble and serene calm that was his beauty itself.

It was the King who was speaking, as in a family council. He announced what everyone expected, that the rehabilitation of the name of Monteleone was about to be pronounced, and that the great house in question had heirs. That was brief. The King's tone was curt and dry.

Fulvio was perhaps the only one who did not notice that detail.

"Comte de Monteleone," said the King, "approach."

Fulvio immediately advanced to the center of the stage. He thus found himself next to the empty armchair that awaited the new Minister of State.

The princesses exchanged glances, The King's favorite daughter-in-law even squeezed Angélie Doria's hand. They saw that as a presage.

Lorédan, cold and silent, as motionless as a statue, had not even turned his gaze toward Fulvio.

"Comte," said the King. "You have promised us proofs of your birth. We are awaiting those proofs."

"Silence!" said the ushers, for the crowd was agitated.

"Sire," said Fulvio, who had not yet spoken, "I have promised Your Majesty the birth certificate of Mario, Comte de Monteleone, the elder son of the one found dead in the Castello di Pizzo. Here it is. I also deposit at Your Majesty's feet the birth certificates of my brother and my sister, Giuliano and Celestina di Monteleone."

The King held out his hand. It was noticeable that he took the papers without looking at the new Comte de Monteleone.

"What more do you have?" he asked.

"The testament of my respected father," replied Fulvio.

Ferdinand de Bourbon had a cold smile, and his suspicious expression did not escape anyone.

"That's exact, Signor Comte." he said. "You promised us the testament of your dead father and the testimony of your living mother."

Fulvio bowed down to the floor and handed over the piece of paper that he had in his hand.

"That is half of my promise accomplished, Sire," he said.

Ferdinand de Bourbon's lips creased.

Nina saw all of that, placed as she was behind the princesses, ten or twelve spaces to the right of the throne. She was astonished by the calm, or rather, the bleak impassivity, on her Fulvio's features.

In the assembly, people were saying: "Carlo Piccolomini's resignation might not have been accepted."

A commencement of anxiety was beginning to take hold in the circle of the princesses; but Francis de Bourbon said to them: "Don't worry; I know the King, my father."

One fact that might have surprised the entourage of the beautiful Comtesse Angélie Doria was the malaise that she had been manifesting since the commencement of that scene. She was blushing and paling by turns. She seemed to be literally under torture.

Once, the cold gaze of her brother Lorédan fell upon her. She covered her face with her hands while she shivered from head to foot.

"Comte de Monteleone," said the King, meanwhile, "do you affirm that the testament deposited by you in my hands is truly that of your father?"

"Sire," replied Fulvio, "I affirm it on my honor."

The King had the paper passed to a man who had been standing for a few moments between the throne and Lorédan Doria's armchair.

That man headed for a door situated opposite Nina. Nina had recognized the man. *That's where Johann Spurzheim must be*, she thought.

Fulvio had also looked at the man, but without displaying the slightest emotion.

On seeing the King's gesture, the little Marquis Zanone had been unable to help saying to his companions: "It appears that Pier Falcone is truly in great favor.

Meanwhile, Pier Falcone had disappeared behind the door, which had closed again

"There remains the testimony of the living mother," the King pronounced, slowly.

"Sire," replied Fulvio, still maintaining the same respectful one, "it astonishes me that the Comtesse de Monteleone, my mother, is not yet in Your Majesty's presence."

The King replied, in a muted voice: "We are awaiting the Comtesse de Monteleone, your mother."

In the manner in which that last word was pronounced there was such an intention of bitterness that the Princess of Salerno turned swiftly to Francis de Bourbon.

The latter repeated: "I know the King, my father. Don't worry."

Fulvio had limited himself to bowing as a sign of thanks.

But at the moment when the King folded him arms over his breast, as if he were really waiting, the door through which Pier Falcone had just gone out opened. The Minister of State, Carlo Piccolomini appeared on the threshold, and introduced the Marquis de Malatesta, followed by his companions, prisoners the day before.

"What is it?" demanded the King.

Surprise was painted on all faces. The only calm individual in the entire assembly was Prince Fulvio Coriolani.

"Sire," said Carlo Piccolomini, "yesterday's affair was judged lightly, in the opinion of your council. These gentlemen offer to prove publicly the sincerity of their affirmations."

"What does this mean?" cried the Royal Prince from his place. "Are the accusations brought by these young fools on the agenda of his family assembly?"

A long silence followed that interjection by the heir to the throne. It was the King who broke it. "Prince," he replied, "in this assembly, as elsewhere, at no matter what time, the duty of the King is to watch over the threatened security of his throne. Let the gentlemen approach." And while the previous day's conspirators made their way through the crowd, the King added: "Signors, I believe I am surrounded here by faithful friends..."

A noisy acclamation interrupted him. He made a gesture of thanks and went on: "Signors, a vast conspiracy has been organized in our Estates against our person and our government...don't interrupt me! I believe in your devoted loyalty. This meeting, originally convened to glorify the memory of our cousin and faithful friend Mario de Monteleone, has another scope henceforth. Justice will be rendered to Monteleone. His legitimate heirs, if there are any, will recover their property and their rank...but it is necessary that justice be done. Before anyone leaves this palace, the traitors will be unveiled and punished."

Silence and stupor followed that declaration, made in a firm and loud voice. It was as if the princesses had heard a thunderclap. A void opened up around Prince Fulvio Coriolani. It was as if Prince Fulvio Coriolani were made of marble

At that moment, in the midst of that silence, a gentleman that the Princess of Salerno did not know had the audacity to touch her bare shoulder from behind.

"Highness," he whispered, "it is a matter of life and death. If this note does not reach its address, you will have to reproach yourself for a man's death."

The princess turned round. The unknown man as already lost in the nearby groups. There was a folded piece of paper on the princess's knee, addressed to Prince Fulvio Coriolani.

Women are always faithful and valiant in their sympathies. The princess, pale with emotion, stood up, crossed the space that separated her from Fulvio with a firm tread, and, pretending to offer him her hand, slipped the note to him.

The King frowned severely. The princess returned to her place, blushing.

This was one of the threads of the perfidious web woven around Fulvio Coriolani, and the Princess of Salerno, unknowingly, was making herself the accomplice of her favorite's enemies.

"Sire!" cried Piccolomini, "the compassion of a noble princess has just been abused before your very eyes. A note has been handed to the accused."

"The accused!" repeated a hundred contained voices.

Angélie Doria was as livid as a corpse. Fulvio's recent revelations loomed up in her memory like menacing phantoms.

Piccolomini had just, unwittingly or with premeditation, pronounced the truth of the situation. This was a tribunal, and Fulvio Coriolani was henceforth an accused. But such a prestige radiated round the man that everyone hesitated to believe it. There was an afterthought in everyone's mind that this might be a game, a proof, or what do I know? History is full of these quarrels between absolute monarchs and favorites. Those who hasten risk bruising their finger between the tree and the bark.

The accused, as he was called henceforth, turned his calm and disdainful gaze toward Carlo Piccolimini. The King, having his eyes fixed upon him at that moment, suddenly withdrew them, as if he were afraid of being drawn or shaken.

Fulvio was holding the note ostentatiously; he had not opened it. He put his hand on his heart and addressed a grateful and respectful bow to the Princess of Salerno. At the same time he saw Angélie and Nina Dolci: Angélie dejected, dying; Nina Dolci with her head held high, her eyes ardent, and so beautiful that her face seemed radiant.

The Marquis de Malatesta and his companions, numbering seven, were at the bar. They had an insolent air, according to custom, and Sampieri was heard to say to Major Baumgarten: "Today you aren't here for us."

The King pointed at the note handed to Fulvio.

Baumgarten advanced and saluted; he was a soldier. "Prince," he said, "it's to do my duty."

Fulvio immediately handed him the paper without even having unfolded it.

"One can put poison in a letter, Sire." he murmured. "Your Majesty's favor has made me many enemies."

A voice that came from the princesses' corner said loudly: "Courage! You aren't yet condemned."

The ushers demanded silence.

The Prince Royal and the Prince of Salerno were now behind the King.

He unfolded the note. His two sons leaned over his shoulder curiously. The note contained a line written in mysterious characters:

$$L^3NAM^2 I^2OI^2M^2 DI^2A^4CA^5: A^2A^5A^5I^2P!$$

The two Bourbon princes looked at it in astonishment. The King turned to them. "We have been audaciously tricked!" he said.

Then, choosing a piece of paper among those that were in front of him on the table, he held it out to his sons and said: "Translate!"

That paper was the key to the alphabet of the Silence, given to Johann Spurzheim by Manuele Giudicelli during their interview the previous night. After a few moments, the Prince of Salerno read the translation:

"You are lost. Flee!"

Francis de Bourbon made the observation: "Such advice, given in a place where flight is materially impossible, cannot come from the knights of the Silence, so clever and so prudent."

"Does it come from me?" asked the King, bitterly. Then he turned his back, growling: "You've all been warned. Have I not been bewitched myself? But I have open eyes now, thank God...and justice will be rendered."

He made a sign. Malatesta separated from his companions.

"Sire," he said, putting one knee down on the lowest step of the stage, "yesterday, I accused this man before Your Majesty of having stolen his name. I was speaking the truth, but I did not know how far his audacity extended. Between yesterday and today many things have happened. The first blow struck gave courage to the timid. In the depths of my prison, light came to me. What the instinct of my hatred made me suspect yesterday, today I know for certain. This man is the leader of the third carbonari, the rule of the Silence."

The murmur that rose up was one of astonishment, not of reprobation.

"Have you anything to respond?" the King asked, addressing Fulvio.

"Nothing yet, Sire," the latter replied.

Sampieri, in his turn, came to the foot of the stage. "We know," he said, why this man retains such an arrogant attitude in front of his judges. The ventas have been alerted and armed. This man is counting on a general revolt of the people of Naples, excited by the treacherous carbonari..."

A smile came to Fulvio's lips.

"If I wished...," he murmured. But he did not finish, and folded his arms over his breast.

"Continue!" ordered the King, addressing Malatesta and his companions.

It was Sampieri who responded. "Sire, yesterday, this man returned to you the noble and pure young woman adopted by your tenderness. For the needs of our honor, we ought to say why our hatred has assembled us against a single adventurer. Malatesta has spoken to you of his sister. I, Domenico Sampieri, was the fiancé of Biance Barberini.

"I, Pietro-Mario Colonna, was the fiancé of Dona Francesca Pisani."

"I, Andrea Pitti, had the amour of Preziosa Balbi."

"I, Vicente Mareschalci, had received the faith of Jeanne Palliante, of the Paleologue Princes."

"I, Vespucci Doria, loved Dona Isabella Doria d'Angri, and was loved by her."

The other two pronounced other names, and all seven extended their arms toward Fulvio, as straight and firm as a rock.

"That man, who is the devil on earth, abducted Bianca Barberini, Francesca Pisani, La Paleologue, La Doria d'Angri and La Balbi. That man is the brigand Porporato."

At that coup, a great cry went up. The princesses shivered, but beautiful eyes opened avidly!

The Princess of Salerno darted a glance at Angélie Doria; the latter was made of stone. Her eyes, wide and staring, no longer had any thought behind them.

The King's two sons had sat down behind His Majesty.

"Have you any response to make?" Ferdinand de Bourbon asked, for the second time.

"Nothing yet," pronounced Fulvio, distinctly.

"Continue!" commanded the King.

Marquis Zanone said to those surrounding him: "For a brigand caught in a trap, that Fulvio Coriolani seems very calm to me, my dear signors. I'll bet twenty old ounces that all this will finish well!"

"Malatesta and his company," someone replied, "already know the way to the prison."

"I shall pass on to proofs," continued Domenico Sampieri, who was the orator of the troop. "To the proofs of what we said yesterday: to wit, that this man penetrated the Castello-Vecchio yesterday visa the terraces of the neighboring houses, and caused his accomplice, Baron d'Altamonte, whose revelations he feared, to disappear. On the gloved hands of that man, two proofs exist."

Fulvio Coriolani shivered imperceptibly.

"Nina had the more violent reaction to that shock. She put her hands to her breathless breast.

The King's gaze was an order. Prince Fulvio removed his glove slowly.

"The ring of the Masters of the Silence!" cried Sampieri, as soon as the right hand was uncovered."

"My father's ring," replied Fulvio, without losing his haughty gravity. "The ring of the saint, Mario Monteleone, who was the master of the knights of charcoal and iron."

"That's true," said Francis de Bourbon in his father's ear. "We know that."

The King turned to his son and said to him: "You know nothing. Shut up." Then he added: "The other hand."

Fulvio took off his other glove. His left hand, as white and delicate as that of a young woman, had a recent scar, a burn. Malatesta and his companions uttered a cry of triumph.

The King already suspected that beforehand, for he adopted a more severe air.

"Where did you get that scar, signor?" he demanded.

"Sire, two poor children were dying...I'm not in the habit of boating about the good deeds that it is given to me by chance to accomplish from time to time."

That reply was made in a tone so frank, so decent and so tranquil that one might easily have believed that Prince Coriolani was involved in one of those frivolous and conversations in which the clever people of society assault grace and politeness.

But Domenico Sampieri cried; "This is the finger of God! The impostor saved involuntarily the lives of the two noble children whose heritage he wanted to steal."

Those of our readers who have followed this story attentively might perhaps be wondering what the purpose was of the emphatic harangue delivered in the garden of the Vila Floridiana. The lines that follow will respond to that question.

Pier Falcone had played the role of a pioneer opening the way. He had planted the footprint that gives plausibility to the boldest assertions. Thanks to him, Sampieri found people there ready to comprehend the implication. As soon as he made allusion to the heirs of Monteleone, the little Marquis Zanone and his listeners pricked up their ears like privileged individuals who were the first bearers of important news. They had talked, they were interested in advance in sustaining what they had said.

"Sire, Sampieri went on, in a grave voice, placing his foot on the first step of the stage, "it will, in fact, be given to your high justice to rehabilitate the heirs of the great Comte Monteleone, Comte Giuliano and Contessa Celestina, whose birth certificates are in your royal hands. And the rehabilitation will be all the more providential because those two children are attained by a terrible degree of misery and misfortune. The son and daughter of Monteleone, with no other protector than a poor vassal who even lacked necessities himself, lived in a mansard in the Folquieri house in the Strada di Mantua...

A touch of blood came to the cheeks of Lorédan Doria. His sister, the beautiful Comtesse Angélie, reopened her eyed partly, and uttered a long sigh.

"Last night," continued Domenico Sampieri, "believing themselves to have been abandoned by Manuele Giudicelli, their unique and supreme protector, whom they had not seen for three days, the two orphans resolved to end their lives. There is one sure and silent means of which imprudent science has recently informed the desperate: I mean asphyxia by carbon vapor. Julian and Céleste chose that door by which to exit the world...." Sampieri interrupted himself briefly. "The ways of Providence are strange! At the very hour when that man, the instrument of a criminal association, was scaling the Folquieri house in order to penetrate the prison of his accomplice, the two poor children, alone and discouraged, were lighting the fatal stove...the stove that left an imprint on your hand, Prince Coriolani! A few minutes later, the alarm having been given, the malefactor, pursued by the garrison of the Castello-Vecchio, was fleeing along the galleries. He found a poorly-closed window; he pushed it; it yielded...and the malefactor, violating that refuge in the interest of his salvation, caused air and life to penetrate with him. He escaped, but he resuscitated his victims. He ran away, but he had left behind him the traces of his passage. Human justice is henceforth on the track. Let him tremble: his hour has come!"

A nascent disdainful smile could be seen on the previously impassive face of Prince Fulvio Coriolani.

It would be difficult to specify the sentiments that were agitating the assembly at that moment. If a few sympathies for the accused survived in that crowd, they were hidden. The accused was abandoning himself; the accused was not defending himself. The circle around him had broadened, as always happens when lightning strikes a powerful man. The princesses were now maintaining a bleak silence; the King's two sons were doing the same.

Angélie Doria hid her head in the bosom of the Princess of Salerno, Nina Doria, standing straight, her eyes bright, her neck taut, seemed to be awaiting the explosion of some invisible mine. She was not alone under the empire of that mysterious expectation. The inertia of that lion was full of menace. Was he gathering his muscles to furnish a supreme and prodigious bound?"

The King made a sign. The door through which Malatesta and his companions had been introduced opened again.

Pier Falcone, who was next to Comte Lorédan Doria, leaned toward his ear. "Signor," he said, in a whisper, "watch carefully what is about to happen."

Lorédan turned, looked him up and down, and said: "I don't know you."

"What does the source of good advice matter, signor?" retorted Pier Falcone. "Look toward that little door, and afterwards look at the Comtesse your sister."

On the threshold of the door appeared, successively, Lieutenant Frazer of the Swiss Guard, an adolescent whom no one knew, and a woman in mourning whose face disappeared behind a thick veil.

Sampieri, Malatesta and their companions had retreated, leaving a large empty space.

Lieutenant Frazer advanced first. He declared that he recognized Prince Fulvio Coriolani for having stopped him the previous evening, clad in a seminarian's soutanelle, at the exterior door of the Folquieri house.

Prince Fulvio did not protest. But he suddenly shuddered. The usher had just announced: "Comte Giuliano de Monteleone."

There was a general movement of curiosity among the crowd, which drowned out a cry of anguish uttered by Angélie. Only two people heard that cry apart from the Princess of Salerno, who was holding the young woman in her arms: Nina Dolci and Comtesse Lorédan Doria. Nina had a smile of angry bitterness. Comte Lorédan half-rose to his feet.

Fulvio's gaze attached itself, mildly and calmly, to the young man who was advancing, pale-faced. Having arrived before him, Julian stopped and raised his eyes. His eyes expressed a grim hatred. He deposited at the King's feet the purse embroidered with pearls on which Prince Coriolani's name was legible.

Ferdinand de Bourbon asked: "Do you recognize this purse?"

"I recognize it, Sire," Fulvio replied.

"Does it belong to you?"

"Sire," replied Coriolani, "An august princess once made me a present of it in Your Majesty's presence."

"Sit down, Comte," ordered the King, addressing Julian.

Julian bowed, but instead of obeying, he made a tour of the stage and came to touch Lorédan Doria's shoulder with his finger. "You who are brave enough to abduct young women," he said, between his teeth, "what have you done with my sister?"

Lorédan looked at him, stupefied.

Pier Falcone was no longer there.

"We'll see one another again, Comte Doria," said Julian, with a somber expression. And he turned his back

The usher pronounced, in a resounding voice: "Dona Maria des Amalfi, dowager Comtesse de Monteleone!"

The veiled woman dressed in mourning advanced to the foot of the stage. The King raised himself up.

Maria des Amalfi threw her veil backwards. She looked at Fulvio. She made a movement as if to run toward him. He held out his arms, and everyone could see that tears came to his eyes.

At that moment, when all respirations stopped—for it was evident that a violent combat was taking place in that woman's soul—at the moment when the King, pale and profoundly moved, was holding his breath, when the entire court had risen with a spontaneous movement, expecting some mysterious occurrence, Falcone reappeared preceding two men who were carrying stretcher covered with a shroud. He came to set it down between the King and Maria des Amalfi. With an abrupt gesture, he lifted the shroud, thus uncovering the cadaver of an old man with a white beard.

At that blow, Fulvio started to tremble and became livid. A cry of horror escaped all throats, Julian, piercing the crowd, came to throw himself on the cadaver, moaning: "My father! My poor father Manuele!"

"I, Pier Falcone, physician to the King," pronounced the Sicilian, in a distinct and firm voice, "declare that I found the body of this poisoned man in the palace of Prince Fulvio Coriolani."

"It's true then!" stammered Maria des Amalfi, tottering. "All these terrible things are true, then?" Her gaze was suddenly burning. "I shall do my duty!" she said.

Then she added, extending her hand to point at Fulvio,

"That man is the murderer of Mario Monteleone."

That was her last effort. She fell, as if dead, while Julian, quitting Manuele's cadaver, launched himself toward her, crying: "Mother! Mother!"

VI. The Harp

Certain historic facts exist in which drama abounds so madly that the narrator has no other concern than to attenuate the glare. Such is, assuredly, the story of the Monteleones, which stirred all Italy in the last years of the reign of Ferdinand I, a drama of two stages, by way of the father and the children, a family epic, in which the incidents are crowded so numerously that those authentic events sometimes appear to be surpassing the limits of plausibility.

The end of the previous scene had been as rapid as thought. Everyone was standing up, including the King. Julian was hugging his inanimate mother to his heart. Fulvio, motionless, was looking at both of them. He had not spoken, but his physiognomy expressed the immense dolor that was gripping his soul. Falcone had thrown the veil over Manuel's body again.

When that moment of general stupor had passed, everyone could see that a change had taken place in the hall. A double rank of armed Swiss Guards surrounded the assembly. Six officers were in front of the stage, swords in hand. The denouement was evidently approaching. No one there thought he could not divine it. And yet, such was the prestige that had surrounded Fulvio Coriolani, and such was the fantastic glamour attached to the name of Il Porporato, that everyone vaguely expected some further surprise.

Fulvio Coriolani and Il Porporato, those two heroes of Neapolitan renown, were now confounded. They were one and the same man. What must the prodigious power of that man be?

People are accustomed to miracles when it is a matter of those demons of the mountains. They are only caught when they are dead. And this one was alive. This one was standing in front of the King. This one, pensive and somber, had not even accorded a glance to the bayonets that surrounded him. Had he in reserve one of those supreme resources that those sons of Hell never seem to lack? Was he about to shake the palace like Samson, the prisoner of the Philistines? Was he about to ignite the conflagration with a gesture, like the bandit Fra Diavolo? Hearts were beating rapidly, and it was not only the women who were afraid of the menacing impassivity of that man.

Baumgarten, the major of the Swiss Guards, was watching for the slightest sign that announced the will of the King. At a glance that Ferdinand de Bourbon darted at him, he made a gesture. The butts of carbines resounded loudly on the marble paving stones. The entire assembly shuddered. Fulvio seemed to emerge from a slumber.

He paraded his saddened eyes over the court that had still been begging for his smile a little while before. For the first time since the beginning of the session he turned toward the princesses. They lowered their heads or turned away. Fulvio seemed to be looking for someone among them.

The door to the boudoir where Nina Dolci had been standing previously was now closed. The space between Fulvio and the princesses was now entirely clear. He started walking slowly toward Angélie Doria. Lorédan quit his place behind the King and drew closer, but he did not seem to want to reach Fulvio rapidly. He even stopped a few paces away from him. As Fulvio advanced, Angélie changed color; her beautiful eyes became haggard and fixed. You would have thought that she had gone mad. When Fulvio was very close she uttered a feeble cry of distress.

Julian heard it. Julian released his mother, and bounded to his feet like a tiger. Quicker than lightning, he snatched Baumgarten's sword and launched himself toward Fulvio, who waited for him, his arms folded over his chest.

A cruel smile could be seen on Pier Falcone's lips. "That Johann is a man of genius," he murmured.

No one, not even Lorédan Doria—who did, however, make a movement—could have stopped Julian's impetuous surge. But the disheveled Angélie threw herself on her knees in front of him.

"Pity!" she said.

Fulvio's face cleared. He seemed suddenly to have grown. He was as arrogant and proud as in the days of his glory.

"Angélie Doria!" he murmured in her dear. "I love you; you are my strength and my life. You said that nothing in the world could prevent you from being mine. I doubted... Say one word and I will emerge victorious from this struggle!"

Angélie Doria did not look at him and did not reply. She extended her arms, bewildered and distraught, toward Julian, who was holding the sword aloft

"If you don't love me," murmured Fulvio, with tears in his voice, "why don't you want him to kill me?"

She turned round, her eyes crazed and her face distraught.

"Because it's necessary that he isn't a murderer like you," she said. "I love him."

Julian let himself fall to his knees. Prince Fulvio Coriolani put his head in his hands. He sobbed.

Lorédan Doria lifted Julian up by force. Their hateful gazes met.

"I've understood you, Signor Comte," said Julian, lowering the point of his sword, "I've just been born a gentleman."

Angélie, who had fainted, was in the arms of the princesses.

"Sire," said Fulvio Coriolani, returning toward the King—and everyone was able to admire the supreme dignity that he maintained at that dolorous moment, "I have just lost my last hope. I have sinned, I am punished. God is just. I am the son of Mario de Monteleone, the future will prove that; but I am an impostor in my conscience, since I did not know, until this morning, that Monteleone was my father.

"Sire, I did not kill that man"—he pointed at Manuele's body—"for that man was the witness for whom I was waiting.

"Sire, someone has poisoned the heart of that poor woman, my mother, who will spend the rest of her life weeping tears of blood.

"Sire, someone has put a sword in my brother's hand.

"God forbid that I render Your Majesty accomplice to such cowardly crimes. I am Il Porporato, Sire, but in listing them, my forehead has blushed with shame. The hand that committed them is revealed to me by their very atrocity.

"The day when I put on my finger the iron ring that was that of the saint Monteleone, I promised under oath that his death would be avenged. Today, the guilty party has denounced himself. I know him; I condemn him."

"Wretch!" said Ferdinand de Bourbon. "Dare you speak of condemnation!"

"When the hand of the law is upon me, is it not, Sire?" Fulvio Coriolani concluded, having recovered his tranquil smile momentarily. "I said to you once, in the very bosom of your capital, that you are the king of the day, but Il Porporato is the king of the night."[63]

"It's still daylight," said Pier Falcone, ironically

"It will be night!" pronounced a muffled voice in the assembly.

"Who spoke?" demanded he King,

That question had no response. Everyone, in the crowd of gentlemen, looked at his neighbor anxiously. Pier Falcone's piercing gaze tried to examine the groups.

"It's still daylight," repeated Fulvio, slowly. "They are precious hours that remain to you, Sire...for who knows what will happen in your city of Naples when darkness has replaced the light?"

"You're threatening your benefactor, bandit!" cried Francis de Bourbon, whose indignation was increased by having been the friend and protector of that man. "Sire, finish this...it is henceforth the affair of your Swiss Guards."

"And the executioner!" added Fulvio Coriolani.

"And the executioner," retorted the heir to the crown, harshly.

"Highness," said Fulvio, "you do indeed have the right to speak of benefits; it required, in order to change your heart, the infernal skill of Monteleone's murderer."

"It's you who is Monteleone's murderer!" cried the King's second son.

"But how do you know," Fulvio continued, placidly, "that your benefits have not been returned a hundredfold? Sire, and you, Highness, your protégé has been your protector. Without the bandit Porporato, Naples would be, at this moment, in the hands of the carbonari."

"Arrest that man!" ordered he King.

---

[63] The reader will probably remember, although the author presumably does not, that it was actually the King who said this to Fulvio, not vice versa.

"And if, in an hour, Prince Fulvio Coriolani is not in his palace," the latter went on, unhurriedly, "you will witness a fête, the memory of which will last for a long time."

Two Swiss Guards had advanced toward him, followed closely by Major Baumgarten.

"Do you not have a few faithful followers in this numerous assembly, powerful king of the night?" asked Francis de Bourbon, mockingly.

"Who knows?" replied Fulvio. He paraded his magnetic gaze over the crowd of noblemen, and then said: "Sire, there are so many carbonari here that I renounce counting them."

The assembly became tumultuously agitated. The two Swiss Guards laid their hands on Fulvio simultaneously. He thrust them away without any apparent effort and called Baumgarten by his name. "I surrender to you," he said.

The rejected Swiss Guards came back with naked swords. They found Lorédan Doria in front of them. The latter said to the King: "I am neither a carbonaro nor a bandit, Sire, but I need to talk to this man." Rapidly, he whispered to Fulvio. "I'm your friend…almost your bother. Do you want a refuge in one of my palaces or one of my castles?"

"You," murmured Fulvio, "are the last of the Romans. Thank you…I have no need of you. Only tell that child whom I love." His gaze designated Julian.

Before Lorédan could draw away, he took him in his arms and gave him the accolade. Almost immediately afterwards he was a prisoner in the middle of a squadron of Swiss Guards.

"Sire," he said, as he passed before the King, "night is falling. Guard me well!"

"Spare us the insolent bravado of that madman," commanded Ferdinand de Bourbon. "To the Castello-Vecchio! In secret! The high assizes! Those are my orders."

"I too am about to give my orders," replied the prisoner, whose smile became sardonic.

He put a finger to his mouth and compressed his lips, which produced he particular cry that we have heard already in the gardens of the Villa Floridiana, when Nina perceived Massimo Dolci and Armellino at the gate.

Fulvio cocked an ear attentively. The King, the princess and the assembly did the same, involuntarily. The sound of a harp immediately became audible in the neighboring boudoir. The harp was playing the song by Fioravanti: *Amici, alliegre, andiamo alla pena…*

"*Agere, non loqui,*" pronounced Coriolani, in the midst of the astonished silence that reigned in the hall.

The harp fell silent. Several gentlemen and Swiss Guards ran into the boudoir, without waiting for the sovereign's order, but the musician had disappeared. Those who leaned over the balcony to interrogate the countryside saw three riders, two men and a woman, galloping along the road that led to Naples.

VII. The King of the Night

Dusk was falling over Naples. The city was tranquil, at least in appearance. All the active, lively, busy people who return to the poor quarters after having excused the thousand fantastic industries that are the labor of Neapolitans, those idlers emeritus, were surely far from divining what was happening at that very moment in the royal enclosure of the Vila Floridiana. They had plenty to talk about in the events of the previous day. The disappearance of Baron d'Altamonte was supplying the material of all conversations.

There was a crowd in the Strada di Porto, the stock exchange of popular gossip. The improviser Mariotto and his colleagues were going to have a lot to relate!

Toward the middle of the afternoon, the servants and employees of the Great Britain Hotel, which had the honor of containing within its walls Peter-Paulus Brown of Cheapside, his groom Jack, his wife Penelope, and Melicerta, the latter's maidservant, had been able to remark the comings and goings of several people who seemed to be standing sentry in the street.

That was not unusual; the Great Britain Hotel, principally frequented by the English, is one of the best patronized in Naples. As we have already said, the English tourist is the property of the petty Neapolitan. People lay in wait for an English traveler in Naples as one lays in wait at the entrance of a church in Paris, if one is a seller of bouquets, a beggar, a lowerer of footplates, or whatever, for a baptism or a wedding.

At five o'clock, two men, one tall and one short, went into the office of the hotel and asked, with a sort of awkward timidity, whether one could see His Excellency. His Excellency, naturally, was Peter-Paulus.

Hotel staff are the legitimate enemy of thieves from outside, since they are thieves within; the hotel staff sent the two poor devils away rudely.

His Excellency was still in bed.

Our two poor devils bowed humbly and said: "We'll come back."

And they returned to an observation-post opposite the coaching entrance.

By chance the hotel staff had not lied. At that advanced hour, Peter-Paulus was still asleep, and Penelope too. Jack and Melicerta, the puritans, were imitating them scrupulously. For all four, the night had been stormy.

We know about the labors of Peter-Paulus and Penelope. Melicerta, after her first bowl of punch, bad asked for a bischof, which the third sommelier had helped her to drink. As for Jack, he had simply been brought back dead drunk.

It was Peter-Paulus who woke up first. He was still suffering from the after-effects of the girella. He rubbed his eyes and looked out of the window to see whether the casements of his neighbor in Cheapside were already open. At a single glance, so prompt was his intelligence, he realized that those were not the windows of a house in Cheapside.

He got up and went into the drawing room, which Penelope had just entered. Penelope was in the process of listening to distant footsteps that were resonating on the floor of the corridor. She believed that she recognized the sound of those footsteps. The happy emotion that agitated her had put two bright red patches over her cheekbones. She uttered a soft and harmoniously modulated cry at the sight of Colonel San-Severo, who was crossing the threshold of the main door.

The daylight was declining; nevertheless, Peter-Paulus recognized the colonel. He marched straight up to him and said, without transition, as was his habit: "I believe that you are a seducer. Jack! Being the pistol-box. I'm going to fight a duel against this gentleman."

Penelope launched herself between them and knelt down. "I forbid you to fight!" she cried, urgently. "It might put an end to my days!"

So saying, she shed a torrent of tears.

The colonel pushed the unfortunate woman away with one hand, and the jealous and irritated husband with the other. He was frowning deeply. One could see that an obsession was laboring his brain.

"Let's not recommence last night's follies, my good lady!" he said, rudely.

Penelope reared up like a snake.

"And you, fellow," added the colonel, and shaking Peter-Paulus by the arm, "Don't hope to play with us any longer. The diamond, or, by the body of Christ, we're going to play another game!"

The good Colonel San-Severo, formerly Luca Tristany, was a knight and master of the Silence, but his colleagues, lacking confidence in his genius, kept him slightly apart. His life was one long astonishment. He went forward blindfolded, never knowing in advance the terminus of the route. So, when he could divine a secret, it was a genuine conquest, and he hung on to it.

This was the case here. The Englishman Brown was the bearer of a diamond of enormous value, the Punjab. The colonel knew that. The association was occupied with something quite different today, but the colonel did not know that. He was here on his own account. He was being zealous. He had come to steal the diamond.

As Peter-Paulus fixed his wide bewildered eyes on him, he went on: "You're as cunning as a fox, we know that, and the lady plays her role as an English madwoman wonderfully, but you're dealing with a strong fellow. This is my final word: give me the diamond with a good grace, or come with me to prison!"

So saying, he unfolded an arrest warrant that his importunities had extracted from superintendent Armellino.

His plan had a certain merit of invention. If the famous Punjab had been in Peter-Paulus' hands, the good colonel would doubtless have had it.

It was not a matter, in fact, of a petty scene played timidly. The colonel had had himself accompanied by four police officers and there were two carriages downstairs.

While Penelope was sobbing and Peter-Paulus was attempting an impossible explanation, the colonel ordered Privato and his colleague to take hold of him. At the same time, he summoned the police officers.

"For the last time," he said, "do you refuse to give me the diamond?"

"I swear on oath," replied the associate of Marjoram, "that I do not have that diamond."

"I swear on oath too," cried the desolate Penelope.

And both of them added, in chorus: "Why did we come to this abominable country?"

"Do your duty," ordered the colonel.

As soon as the order was given, the apartment rented at great expense by the associate of Marjoram in the Great Britain Hotel was treated as a conquered country. The four police agents, aided by Privato and Beccafico himself, the brother of the Marchesa, searched all the items of furniture carefully.

They did not find the Punjab; but the colonel expected that.

"The seals!" he ordered.

Long strips of parchment were placed over the locks of the trunks. The baskets and night-bags were also closed with a seal bearing the arms of the royal house of Naples. Penelope and Peter-Paulus, plunged into a stupor, watched. The excess of common misfortune was approaching. They clasped one another by the hand and both repeated: "Why did we come to this country?"

But the peace was not of long duration.

"It was you!" said Penelope, suddenly withdrawing her hand. "You forced me to come to this country!"

"No, it was you!" retorted Peter-Paulus. "To cure your malady!"

"I say no: it was you!"

"I reply no: it was you!"

"Take it away," ordered the colonel.

The four or five parcels comprising Peter-Paulus' luggage were duly sealed. Aided by the hotel staff, whom the sight of the warrant had rendered as supple as gloves, the agents loaded everything on their shoulders and began to go downstairs.

Penelope started laughing in a provocative manner. "Tell them you're an English subject!" she cried.

"Your turn," said the colonel, when the luggage had been taken away. "On your way! You're going to leave before me so that I can make quite sure that you haven't hidden the object in some corner. You'll be searched in prison."

"Oh," moaned Penelope, wringing her hands. "I'd prefer to plunge a dagger into my own breast."

"On your way! On your way!" repeated the terrible San-Severo.

Peter-Paulus, Penelope, Melicerta and Jack were dragged downstairs. The hotel sommelier, with no regard for the great misfortune, had the effrontery to bring the bill to the associate of Marjoram.

He paid it, but in paying it he protested and said: "I'm an English subject. This country will suffer a bombardment because of me. Formally!"

The colonel pushed him into a carriage.

The hotel staff remained convinced that all that was done by order of the police. They had seen the documents, they knew the agents.

It was subsequent events that gave that adventure a mysterious and tragic character.

In the vicinity of Chiaia and around the royal palace no one knew yet what was happening in Naples that evening. The beach was deserted. The noble quarter only had its daily quota of strollers. Everything was profoundly calm. Two passers-by occasionally accosted one another asking for news. The name of Prince Coriolani, which recurred incessantly in those conversations, proved that the result of the royal assizes held at the Villa Floridana was beginning to spread, but curiosity, in those parts, liked nothing better than to wait for the next day.

However, an hour after night fall, the inhabitants of those noble dwellings were seen to descend, nervous and anxious, on to their terraces. The King had returned to the city. Instead of going to the palace, he had gone around Chiaramonte, and the doors of the Pizzo Falcone had closed on him. Everyone was able to observe the unusual deployment of military forces that accompanied him.

Scarcely a quarter of an hour had gone by when three squadrons of cavalleggeri descended at a great gallop from the Castel Sant'Elmo to the arsenal. At the same time, drumbeats were heard in the distance. When the drum fell silent, the wind brought indefinable and sinister sounds that rendered the popular emotion.

It was almost at that moment that the two carriages containing the Brown family of Cheapside and their luggage emerged from the Great Britain Hotel. The two carriages took the route that Peter-Paulus had followed on the evening of his arrival, in order to go and observe the mores of the Neapolitan capital incognito.

The colonel, enveloped in an ample cloak whose raised flap hid his face, had climbed up on one of the seats. The other carriage was driven by a tall fellow with a serious face whose large hat was pulled down over his eyes.

Peter-Paulus was not in the same carriage as his wife. We must attribute to that cause the fact that they were not arguing.

Having arrived in the vicinity of the Teatro del Fondo, they suddenly saw a strange and disorderly movement succeed the calm that had surrounded the thus far. Floods of people were turning the corner of the port and plunging into the neighboring streets. Cavalrymen were passing at a gallop, followed by running infantrymen.

A few cries, always that particular cry, the sort of mysterious appeal peculiar to the Companions of the Silence, were being exchanged here and there, without anyone knowing where they were coming from. Invisible hunting horns were transmitting from place to place the martial air by Fioravanti, *Amici, alliegre, andiamo alla pena*. Musket-fire, which seemed to be coming from the high city, resounded at intervals. The wind was bringing large clouds of smoke, explained by the clamor that sometimes emerged by night from back-streets: "Fire! Fire!" And somber, tightly-knit groups marching slowly past the houses, stopped under certain balconies in order to pronounce, in a lugubrious fashion:

"*Evviva la constituzione!*"

Most of the time, a man appeared on the balcony. Then the door opened and the man came to swell the group. When the group passed under a streetlamp, weapons were seen glinting. There was a crowd outside the post office. The people were surrounding a continent of Swiss Guards and trying to disarm them.

The two carriages stopped. The colonel got down from his seat.

"Get down, Gaspardo!" he said to the enormous fellow driving the other carriage. "We have other work to do now."

Peter-Paulus put his head out of the window and commenced "I beg you..."

"One more word and I'll blow your brains out," pronounced the good colonel, distinctly.

Peter-Paulus' head disappeared, as if by enchantment.

Penelope said to Melicerta. "That officer had certainly noticed me, though!"

"Bah! replied Melicerta. "He's hiding his game in front of your husband."

Penelope took her hand effusively.

Privato and Beccafico were next to the colonel. He charged each of them with one of the carriages, promising to break their bones if the two carriages did not arrive safely.

"Go up the Via Toledo at a gallop," he said, "Take the Via dei Tribunale, leave by the Porta Capuana, and at a gallop, always at a gallop, go all the way to Salerno."

"You can see," said Melicerte, "that we're not going to prison."

Penelope put her hands together. "I believe," she murmured, ecstatically, "that that officer is really going to abduct me!"

The carriages departed.

"*Alla pena!*" cried the colonel, hurling himself headlong into the center of the mob. "The rogues never tell me their affairs, but since we're dancing, let's get violins!"

He and Gaspardo the fisherman rushed two Swiss Guards whom they knocked down, and then they disappeared into the crowd, each carrying a captured musket.

"*Evviva la constituzione!*" cried the crowd.

At ten o'clock in the evening, cannon were growling in several places in Naples. People were saying that twenty thousand insurgents were under arms.

Barricades had been erected in the Strada di Porto and all the surrounding streets. It was like a citadel.

At eleven o'clock the sounds of warfare had ceased, but there was a great and sinister light in the sky, casting its coppery reflections over the mute city. Some immense conflagration was deducible. In fact, the ten times secular fortress, the Castello-Vecchio, was burning, along with the surrounding buildings.

It was a grandiose and terrible spectacle. The blaze had been ignited, one might say, on all sides at once. The flames were leaping in such prodigious abundance that it was impossible even to try to fight them.

In the profound shadow of the thick walls of the fortress, a black and motionless circle was visible; they were the guardians of the conflagration.

At eleven-thirty the hundred thousand spectators of that scene saw something so fantastic that we have hesitated to describe it.

The lightning-conductor of the Castello-Vecchio was still standing on the summit of the highest tower, which seemed to have been spared by the flames. Suddenly, a human being started climbing that strange greasy pole. He seemed very small and very black amid the violent glare that surrounded him. He was playing as he climbed; from time to time he executed *tours de force*. Having arrived at the extremity, he started turning around his frightful pivot, in the posture that gymnasts call the iron arm.

The crowd below cried "Bravo, saltarello! Bravo Cucuzone!"

A large number of gunshots departed from positions occupied by regular troops, but none carried.

Holding on to the lightning-conductor with one hand, Cucuzone used the other to unwind, slowly, a sort of interminable belt that was wrapped around his body. As it unrolled, the belt started fluttering in long pleats. Finally, he fixed it to the iron stem. At the first gust of wind that deployed it in its full extent, an immense standard was seen, illuminated as in broad daylight by the ruins of the blaze. It bore at its center a heart pieced by two blades: the escutcheon of the Comtes de Monteleone. Around the escutcheon ran the motto: *Agere, no loqui.*

Cucuzone descended again without encumbrance, and disappeared.

The southern part of the Castello-Vecchio collapsed soon afterwards, with a frightful din.

At that moment, Calabrian bagpipes, Abruzzian vezzi and hunting horns sounded the fanfare of the Silence on all sides. The black cordon surrounding the fortress massed. A tightly-knit column, at the head of which three Hercules were marching—Luca Tristany, Gaspardo the fisherman and Ruggieri the mariner—plunged like a shot from a catapult into the ranks of the Swiss Guards and pierced them.

In the center of the Strada di Porto, in front of the Fountain of the Three Virgins, a carriage stolen from the royal stables, draped in gold cloth, was stationed. Eight of the King's horses were drawing it.

A man clad in imperial purple and as handsome as a demigod appeared carried aloft in triumph. A hundred torches illuminated his march. He climbed into the royal carriage. A numerous troop of horsemen formed an escort. As he passed by, runners went forth acclaiming Prince Fulvio Coriolani. Then the thousand noises that filled the city diminished.

The fire reddened, and then paled, finding no further fuel within the thick stone walls. The light of torches still radiated for a long time in the darkness of the countryside in a south-easterly direction. After half an hour, none of them were visible any longer. All the clamors and fanfares had fallen silent. Nothing could be seen but the colossal smoke of the volcano, veiling the pale face of the waning moon with brown.

VIII. The Two Fishermen

The people who saw those events claim that Naples was, for one night, completely at the mercy of the third carbonari (the rule of the Silence). Perhaps it would only have required the will of one man to make a Revolution. The will was lacking. The armed ventas dispersed, leaving their dead on the battleground. The king of the night disdained the victory.

Ferdinand de Bourbon, the princes and the princesses spent twelve hours of anguish at the Pizzo Falcone. The order to make ready to sail had been given to a State frigate, in case of misfortune.

The Princess of Salerno, Bourbon's favorite, fell into disgrace for having pronounced the words that summarized the commencement of this chapter. She had said: "If Coriolani had wanted..."

She spent two years in exile on Capri.

The next day, Johann Spurzheim took the portfolio of Minister of State and the Presidency of the Council.

Three regiments departed in the direction of the mountains to put down the revolt. Doctor Pier Falcone accompanied them with a royal commission. It was not a pursuit but a war. Malatesta, Sampieri, Colonna, Vespuccio, Mareschalci, Gravina, Pitti and Ziani went with the expedition in the quality of volunteers.

It was the sixth day after the burning of the Castello-Vecchio. The sun was setting in the beautiful horizons of southern Italy, which we described several times at the beginning of this story. But there was no longer the profound calm, the smile of nature that we once admired at the moment when Athol, taking his leave of the coach-driver Battista Giubbetti, leapt from the road on to the rocks and from the rocks on to the golden sand of the beach.

The menacing sky had metallic tints, as always in those regions at the approach of earthquakes or volcanic eruptions. The sea had no more waves, but it suddenly swelled, gray with foam, and from time to time, nature seemed to utter a great and confused clamor. Whether that came from the air or the ground no one knew.

The atmosphere was heavy; appearances seemed to draw closer, as if the celestial vault, lowering at the zenith, tightening its horizontal circle, had compressed the perspective violently.

It was, however, beautiful, perhaps more beautiful. From the southern point of the bay of Sant'Eufemia one divined Sicily in a coppery cloud that seemed quite close, while the Aeolian islands, emphatic and firm, patched the bronze sea distinctly.

The gracious curve of the gulf stood out in light, marked by one dark spot at the place where the Brentola quit the valley of the Martorello to enter the strand, and the landscape was closed to the north-west by the black heights where the Castello di Pizzo was perched.[64]

Nothing could be seen inland because of the conformation of the coast except, to the north of Capo Vaticano, in the direction of Monteleone, the basilica of Corpo-Santo, somber and austere, surmounted by the ancient towers of the convent.

It might have been seven o'clock in the evening.

A rare thing in that place, two small warships were cruising in the gulf, both carrying the Neapolitan flag. One was a schooner-brig with a slender hull and a matinal appearance, the other a more specifically Ponantais vessel belonging to that family of Mediterranean ships, carrying a Latin sail. Feluccas have two masts, the *mestro* and the *trinchetto*. The larger ones carry a dozen cannon in a battery and thirty-two light carronades on the deck. In the Mediterranean their speed is superior to that of square-rigged vessels.

The brig and the felucca, tacking a league apart, often exchanged signals, not only with each other but with military posts established at intervals along the coast.

The status of the locale had obviously changed. There was active surveillance there, almost a state of war. Nevertheless, twelve or fifteen boats manned by fishermen, whose gray cabins could be seen stuck to the rock under the cliff, were coming and going at sea, occupied with their work.

One of those boats, stronger and better constructed than the others, left its sails in the wind in spite of the squalls in the north that were about to increase in strength as the night advanced. It was maintaining a distance of three leagues from the coast, tacking broadly in such a fashion as to monitor all the points of the cost successively.

Its crew was only composed of two men: one young cabin boy with an alert and charming face, and a bow-legged mariner with a Herculean body and a low forehead covered by a forest of thick black hair. The latter had a vast meerschaum pipe in his mouth.

He dropped the net, but only in a tokenistic fashion. When, by chance, they caught a tuna or a dorado, they threw the fish back into the sea. They were fake fishermen, and their net only served to deceive the warships whose telescopes were incessantly spying on the gulf.

The cabin boy had a frail and slim figure. His large dark eyes, surmounted by proud eyebrows, boldly traces, were interrogating the coast anxiously.

"To the net!" said the broad-shouldered mariner.

The cabin-boy made a weary gesture. "My good Ruggieri," he murmured, "it isn't courage I lack."

---

[64] In fact, the Castello di Pizzo was on the waterfront of the port, not on the crest of a hill.

"It's strength, signora, I know that," replied the sailor, in the abrupt tone employed by certain people to dissimulate their emotion. "Damn! You'd be better off in your boudoir, little one."

"You'd prefer another aide, wouldn't you, Ruggieri?"

"One more valiant, no," replied the mariner. "That's impossible...but one more robust. Listen: a mariner's equipment isn't as light as fans."

The cabin boy removed his multicolored bonnet to wipe his forehead, which was streaming with sweat. A mass of long black hair escaped from it and fell in beautiful curls over his shoulders,

"Quickly, signora!" cried the sailor. "To the net! To the net! That damned lieutenant over there is aiming his telescope at us as if he knew that there's a pretty woman here!"

An officer could indeed by made out on the deck of the felucca whose telescope was directed toward the sea.

"They say that sea air is good for you," the cabin boy replied, when the net was drawn in. "It seems to me that it's fire that I'm breathing...I'm out of breath."

The mariner passed his rough hand over his brow and drew it away bathed in sweat.

"That's because," he replied, looking at the horizon from the corner of his eye, "the sea isn't the same today, signora. There are demons in the air; I can sense is s well as you."

"The mistral?" asked the cabin boy.

The sailor shrugged his shoulders. "The mistral and I know one another," she muttered. "I'd give a dozen ounces for it to be the mistral. The mistral's old, it blows from the north-west like these infernal gusts, but it's continuous and raises waves..."

After a silence he continued: "The sirocco is as hot as this diabolical wind that is warming our cheeks, but it comes from the south-east and weighs upon the sail as if it were falling from the clouds. This one is lifting the sail; one might think that it were emerging from the water with every bubble of foam. This isn't the wind from the sky; it's the torment of misfortune that shakes our gulfs when the earth trembles and tears, when the volcanoes vomit lava. What were they saying about the volcano when you left Naples, signora?"

"Vesuvius has been smoking for more than a week," the cabin boy replied. "The day before yesterday it brightened, yesterday it began to throw our flames, but the lava hasn't yet overflowed."

"The lava will overflow."

"Tonight?"

"God alone knows...but before the week is out, Vesuvius will clear its gullet or split its sides. Shoulder to the wheel, blood of Christ! That accursed lieutenant is pointing a finger at us."

The officer had, in fact, just summoned one of his comrades, and was very evidently designating the boat with his extended arm.

The net was cast. The wind hardened. The edge of the sail dipped into the foam at every gust.

"What time do you have, signora?" asked Ruggieri "In my estimation, it must be past seven."

The cabin boy took an expensive and dainty woman's watch out of his fob pocket.

"Quarter past seven," he replied, "by the clock of Monte Oliveto!"

The mariner's gaze darkened. "Nothing yet!" he murmured. Then he added: "But this demonic wind might disperse the smoke. What if we won't perceive their signals?"

He gave a thrust to the tiller, changed the heading and clung to the wind, setting a course for Stromboli, whose blurred profiles were beginning to be confused in the distance by the evening twilight.

The boat headed rapidly out to sea, cleaving through the immense plain of foam. The wind seemed to drop as they drew away from the coast.

"I said so!" muttered the mariner. "These gusts are coming from the ground. It's the hurricane of misfortune!"

After a few minutes, the aspect of the coast changed. Our two mariners began to see the hills inland over the cliffs.

Ruggieri aimed his telescope successively at two points on the coast, one within Capo Vaticano, the other much further to the north, almost in the direction of Pizzo.

"San Gennaro!" he growled. "Half an hour late...and nothing! Nothing yet!"

A smile came to the feeble but bold and charming child the mariner addressed as "signora."

"God grant that he misses the rendezvous!" she murmured. It was an expression of hope, or better, a prayer.

"If the fire shows at the summit of Monte Pulcino," said Ruggieri, we have to head for Capo Vaticano; that will be easy; we'll be sheltered by the promontory. But if we see the smoke on the Colle delle Nari, that's a different matter. It'll necessary to head for Sant'Eufemia, beyond Pizzo. A headwind! Frightful coast! And time's passing."

He was pensive henceforth, that Ruggieri.

The daylight declined to the point that they could no longer make out the movement on the deck of the felucca; as for the brig, it was tacking so close to the shore that the cliff of the Martorello put it in shadow.

The cabin boy was sitting, exhausted, in the rear of the boat. He was dreaming. Suddenly, Ruggieri clapped his hands and uttered a great cry. The cabin boy, woken up with a start, raised his head. There were tears in his large eyes.

"Look, signora, look!" said Ruggieri, raising up his vigorous torso and inflating his chest.

To the left of the heights of Pizzo, in the open country, a thick column of smoke rose up: a red flame soon tinted its base.

The signora disguised as a cabin boy allowed a long sigh to escape. "The die is cast!" she murmured.

"The signal's at the Colle delle Neri," said the mariner. "The Devil's mixed up with it this evening; but we're not afraid of the Devil!"

In the blink of an eye, the boat came about and started to struggle against the wind, which put the sail in the foam.

It was an excellent pinnace of Sicilian construction, which ought to have been in tow behind some free brigantine. It hugged the wind, and although its progress almost caused it to take on too much water, its progress was scarcely retarded.

Ruggieri was at the tiller. The cabin boy bailed out the sea water.

The night was black; the sky was devoid of stars. Ruggieri was steering by the lights shining in the windows of the Pizzo. The fire lit on the Colle delle Nari had not been visible for some time, hidden as it was by the elevation of the shore.

The cabin boy suddenly felt someone grip his arm.

"Don't budge," said Ruggieri, in his ear. "Not a breath! It's a matter of life!"

The warning was not unnecessary, and it came just in time. A cry was, indeed, stifled in the breast of the signora.

Over the white and phosphorescent foam of the sea rose a black mass, which seemed enormous.

Between two gusts of wind, it was possible to hear the sound of voices and a song that as falling from the sky.

The voices belonged to officers who were chatting on the poop deck, the song to a mariner who was astride a yardarm directly above the heads of our pretended fishermen.

The black mass was the Neapolitan felucca.

The boat skimmed the flank of the large ship like an arrow, cut through its wake, and passed unnoticed.

A short while later it was dancing on the surf before a rocky coast half a mile beyond Pizzo. That was the rendezvous point.

To the right and the left, two small rocky points advanced into the sea, forming a microscopic cove, which smugglers often used as a shelter. That was in calm weather, for in the slightest storm, the sea was so terribly choppy that any disembarkation of merchandise would have been impossible.

Ruggieri tried to moor his anchor between the two rocks, but the teeth of the grapnel could not bite the bed of shingle in the required time. Ruggieri brought in his sail and tried to sustain himself with the oars. The cabin boy was now at the tiller.

A line of brighter foam announced the depths of the cove. Ruggieri hailed. That cry of a particular species, which we have already heard several times in Naples, was answered immediately, and two forms were detached from the black background of the rocks.

The sea was low and although the tide does not make itself felt on the Mediterranean coast, the difference between high and low water can change the landing conditions completely in certain inlets surrounded by reefs. Here, the lowering of the water left the rocky esplanade where the two unknown individuals were standing seven or eight feet above the boat, and he boat could scarcely advance more than two oars' lengths, under penalty of being broken into a thousand pieces.

Under the esplanade there was a steep ledge on which a chamois could not have set foot.

"Let's move quickly!" said an imperious voice on the rock. "Is Fiamma aboard?"

"Fiamma's waiting for you," replied the soft and sonorous voice of the cabin boy.

"Hello, Ruggieri," said someone up above, at the same time.

"Hello, Cucuzone," replied the mariner from below. Then he added: "Do you have rope?"

"Always."

"Put a stone on the end, for this wind will reject an anchor-cable…and be careful not to hit us."

"Can't Fiamma take shelter?" asked the first voice that had spoken.

"Don't think about me, Master," the young woman replied.

"I'll put her under the rear bench," said Ruggieri, "but hurry. I can't hold against the surf much longer."

On the kind of circular gallery that ran round the back of the cove, a proud and tall silhouette could be seen, under the folds of a cape that was flapping noisily in the wind. Another human form was agitating beneath; that was Cucuzone, occupied in knotting the end of his rope around a lump of rock.

A flash of lightning that rent the night, preceding a distant clap of thunder, suddenly illuminated the arrogant silhouette of the motionless man. We would have been able to recognize the sad but calm visage of the handsome Prince Fulvio Coriolani, the darling of the court of Naples.

IX. Ruggieri's Idea

Having tied the rope around a rock, Cucuzone advanced to the edge of the platform. He took his time, calculating the furious swaying of the boat, and threw his device in such a way that the stone fell into the water very close to the prow, within arm's reach of Ruggieri.

A first attempt failed, by the fault of the squall, a second because Ruggieri lost his balance. It is certain that the impact of the stone would have broken the boat, but it is also certain that no human power would have been able to throw a light rope in the teeth of that tempestuous wind.

Finally, at the third attempt, Ruggieri seized the rope and immediately fell with his breast against the gunwale. The boat nearly capsized and half-filled with water.

"Fortunately," said the mariner, "the chest and the pinnace are both sound!"

He felt the edge of the boat carefully, inside and out; then, bounding to his feet, he felt his ribs.

"No more damage to one than the other," he murmured, jovially. "San Gennaro! Cut to port, signora, cut with both hands! We're about to touch!"

He seized the gaffe and jabbed the rock at the moment when the boat was about to collide with one of the walls of the inlet.

When the danger was past he untied the stone and knotted the rope securely to the foot of the mast. Cucuzone had fixed the other end to a spur of rock.

"Go!" commanded Ruggieri. He picked up the oars and rowed vigorously to stretch the cable.

Cucuzone was the first to drop on to the vacillating deck, which every gust of wind rocked furiously. That was child's play for the saltarello. We must confess that he even executed, on the way, a few trapeze-turns on the taut rope.

Fulvio's passage was not as easy. Cucuzone, standing at the rear, was ready to dive into the water in case of a mishap. Fiamma, kneeling with her hands together, prayed ardently to God.

Fulvio remained suspended between the sky and the sea for a long minute. The wind shook the rope, which trembled like a thread, but Fulvio was young, nimble, skillful and fearless. He finally set foot on the boat.

Fiamma hung round his neck, weeping. They were still embracing when the barking of a dog became audible in the rocks.

"Detach the rope, Cucuzone!" Ruggieri commanded.

As the saltarello was having trouble untying the wet hemp, Ruggieri took a hatchet and cut the knot with a single blow.

"Down, everyone!" he cried. With one hand he knocked Fiamma down brutally; with the other he seized Prince Fulvio and dragged him down his own fall. He was just in time. The rocks lit up, sending back and forth the rolling echo of gunfire. A hail of bullets passed over the boat.

Ruggieri and Cucuzone took possession of the oars; by the second discharge the militiamen were out of range, firing at random.

"Trim the sail now," said the saltarello, "and let's rest."

Joining example to precept, he lay down full length in the bottom of the boat and began snoring like a saint. Fulvio and Fiamma sat down next to one another at the rear.

"Thank you, Fiamma, dear sister," said Fulvio. "What dangers you've braved to serve me!"

"I belong to you, Fulvio," replied the zingara, simply. "I have no will but yours. If she had loved you, I would have been glad to contemplate your happiness."

Fulvio let his head fall into his hands. "It's Julian de Monteleone that she loves, isn't it?" he asked.

His voice was as timid as a child's. Fiamma only replied with a nod of the head. There was a long silence between them.

"I knew that amour before Angélie herself," Fiamma said

"Angélie!" repeated the prince, as if he were savoring the sweet music of the name. "When I was triumphant, I didn't know how much I loved her..." He suddenly interrupted himself. "But why didn't you tell me?"

Fiamma put her beautiful hand over his mouth.

"I've told you incessantly," she murmured, "that there is only me to love you well! Our hearts flowered together. God has given you to me...outside of me, you will only find treasons and dolors..."

He was already distracted; she saw that. A deep sigh elevated her bosom.

Seven days! she thought, while a pleasure full of anguish squeezed her heart. *The oracle said seven days...and tomorrow is the seventh. I haven't had his life, God, give me his death!*

"Does he love her?" asked Fulvio, suddenly.

"Who?" said the zingara, woken with a start.

"My brother Julian," the Prince said. "Does he love Dona Angélie Doria?"

"Yes...and his love for her isn't perjured."

"In that case," Fulvio pronounced, slowly, in the tone of a judge passing sentence, "I want them to be happy."

He fell silent. The boat, leaning over, fled into the night. The coast was perceptible as a distant somber wall. From time to time, nocturnal signals indicated the position of the two warships. Cucuzone was snoring.

"Master," asked Ruggieri, who had taken the tiller again, "Where is it necessary to go now?"

"I don't know yet," Fulvio replied. Then, addressing the zingara, he added: "Speak."

"What do you want to know?" she asked. "Your heart will bleed."

"My heart is dead," the prince retorted, his voice dull and discouraged. "The dead no longer suffer. Speak. I've traveled twenty leagues through a hundred perils to have the news you're bringing me. I've abandoned my brothers, victorious but surrounded on all sides. I've deserted my battle post. Men call me brigand, the brigands will call me traitor. Speak, I tell you, speak!"

"I've seen Dona Angélie Doria," said Nina, in a low voice.

Fulvio shivered, and drew closer.

"If I had been saluted that day...that day when the King and his court were assembled at the Villa Floridiana...if I had been saluted with the name of Comte de Monteleone, would Angélie have betrayed me?"

"God knows!"

"Angélie had said to me, an hour before, her heart stirred, her voice trembling: 'I love you, and nothing can prevent me from loving you...' Was she deceiving me?"

The darkness hid the expression of disdain that was on Fiamma's face. "Perhaps she wasn't deceiving you," she murmured. "I've told you: Angélie Doria didn't know her own heart."

"You're not expressing your whole thought, Fiamma!"

"God forbid that I should hide anything from you, Fulvio. She's pious and fearful. She thought Julian was engaged in holy orders..."

"And she tried to love me, in order that that amour should have a shield. Is that it, my sister?"

The zingara remained silent.

Fulvio clutched his breast with both hands. "This air that surrounds us is leaden," he said. "I'm stifling."

When the wind stopped blowing, there was, indeed, a burning calm, so strange that the oppressed throat seemed to shrink.

They heard unexpected noises on the shore then. The invisible land was groaning loudly.

Fulvio asked: "Where did you see her?"

"In her prison." replied Fiamma.

"In her prison?" cried the Prince, quivering like a wounded lion. "Did I hear you correctly?"

There were tears in the zingara's voice when she said: "I beg you, Fulvio, don't ask me anymore. When you know, you'll want to go to her aid...and death is waiting for you out there."

"Ah!" said the Prince. "She has need of aid!" He turned toward Ruggieri and said, loudly: "To Naples, friends! We're going to Naples."

The muffled sobs of the zingara could be heard in the darkness.

Ruggieri changed course; for he had been allowing the boat to drift toward the Liparian islands for half an hour.

The two warships were now between the boat and the rocky inlet where the embarkation had been operated.

"Speak" said Fulvio, again, avidly this time. "I want to know everything. Tell me about my brother Julian, who is my executioner, but whom I love...tell me about my sister Céleste, toward whom my heart goes out...and my mother, the poor and saintly martyr. Tell me about Lorédan, my loyal enemy. I want to know, you hear!"

Fiamma collected herself momentarily; then she began.

"Angélie was at the Villa Floridiana; Céleste was waiting for you at your palace. She fainted on seeing the cadaver of old Manuele, murdered by that wretch Pier Falcone..."

"He's avenged," Fulvio put in. "I killed him with my own hand; may God give him peace. I would have liked to spare him."

"During the fusillade around the Castello-Vecchio in flames," the zingara continued, "Johann Spurzheim, named Prime Minister by the King, wasn't at his post; he was continuing his work. Do I need to tell you that he's been a traitor for a long time? You know that...you doubtless know why he's a traitor, and what implacable ambition had taken possession of that moribund?"

"I know everything," Fulvio interrupted.

"And what do you count on doing to that Johann Spurzheim, signor?"

"Our law wants his death...but he was condemned in advance for another crime. Speak, in the name of Heaven, Fimma, and don't stop!"

"Johann Spurzheim wasn't at his post. He was in haste to play his last cards, completing his victory in the game.

"Maria des Amalfi, the poor sweet woman, inert and already plunged back into the mental darkness into which Doctor Daniel's science had brought light, was taken to the house in the Piazza de Mercato. She was installed in the apartments of Barbe de Monteleone, who once did so much harm...

"Barbe's coffin had just taken the road to the cemetery when the workmen were attaching the draperies of the new wife..."

"What are you saying, Fiamma?" cried the stupefied Prince; he had been unable to divine that audacity.

"I'm saying what is," said the young woman. "Johann Spurzheim, the King, favorite, has obtained authorization from the King to marry Maria des Amalfi, who has gone mad again."

"But it's sufficient to tell the King..."

"That David Heimer was a Master of the Silence? The King knows that. The King believes that that faithful servant introduced himself into your midst in order to doom you. The King is now that man's slave...."

As if talking to himself, Fulvio murmured: "Doctor Daniel told me: 'Madness has the memory of madness...' If Maria des Amalfi has lost her reason again, she'll recognize her executioner."

"Well, isn't it an angelic devotion to marry a poor woman who, in her madness, mistakes you for a scoundrel and a monster? The King knows everything and the King has said: 'That Spurzheim is a saint...the marriage will take place!'"

Fulvio shivered in all his limbs.

"But that's horrible!" he said, between grated teeth.

"It's horrible," repeated the zingara, "and that's not all, Fulvio. David Heimer, that demon incarnate, can't stop on the road. He has the terrible logic of his criminal instincts; he's the genius of evil."

"What more is there?" demanded the prince, dejectedly.

"First of all, there's this consequence: Johann Spurzheim, in marrying Comtesse Maria des Amalfi, who, in her rare moments of lucidity, testifies a limitless gratitude to him, is taking the title of Comte de Monteleone, and becoming the natural guardian of the two children."

"Him!" cried Fulvio, whose clenched fists tightened. "Him! The impure scoundrel! The guardian of my brother and my sister."

"That's not all yet," said Fiamma.

The prince folded his arms over his breast.

"The title of Comte de Monteleone is only good for Johann," the zingara continued, "because it brings with it the immense fortune of that powerful house. Now, between that fortune and Johann, five existences loom up like an insurmountable obstacle."

"Five murders...," murmured Fulvio.

"You first, Prince, but you hardly count...the law is a weapon against you. Then Julian and his sister Céleste. Then Angélie and her brother, Comte Lorédan." She interrupted herself with a bitter laugh. "But who mentioned murders? Johann Spurzheim only resorts to the dagger or poison as a last resort. In any case, there is one of those four individuals who can become for him the hen that lays golden eggs. Doria has inherited from Monteleone; can Monteleone not inherit from Doria?"

"What do you mean?" said Fulvio, shuddering.

"What I mean, Prince is this: it's necessary that Julian dies; it's necessary that Angélie Doria disappears; it's necessary that Comte Lorédan is suppressed—but it's necessary that Céleste lives. Céleste is the unique and supreme heiress of the two most opulent families in Italy."

She stopped Fulvio, who tried to speak.

"Let me go on," she said. "I haven't finished. One doesn't attack princes like Julian or Lorédan with impunity. But two irritated young men who exterminate one another in a furious duel, without witnesses and without mercy...what do you think of that, Fulvio?"

"Explain."

"At the moment when the Castello-Vecchio was burning, Angélie Doria was abducted from the Vila Floridiana and Céleste Monteleone was abducted from the Palazzo Coriolani."

"By whom? Johann?"

"Who else? Except that, thanks to a skillfully managed intrigue, Angélie's abductor is called, so far as Lorédan is concerned, Julian de Monteleone, and so far as Julian de Monteleone is concerned, Céleste's abductor is named Lorédan Doria."

"And they fought to the death?"

"Johann Spurzheim is holding them prisoner. The court believes that he's protecting them. But tomorrow..."

"Enough," said Fulvio, curtly. "I understand.

He deposited a kiss on Fiamma's forehead and said "Thank you. You're my only friend."

Then he turned to Ruggieri. "It's necessary that we're in sight of Capo Campanella by daybreak," he pronounced, in an imperious tone. Before the mariner could reply, he went on: "Where is that man keeping Angélie and Céleste?"

"At Barbe Monteleone's villa between Castellamare and Resina.

"You heard, Ruggieri," said Fulvio. "It's there that we'll disembark!"

The mariner extended his cheek to the wind. "It's impossible, Master," he replied.

"What? Impossible? When I order it?"

"Master, the wind only obeys God."

Fulvio stamped his foot

Ruggieri continued, placidly: "With the weather we have and the boat we're in, it will take more than twenty-four hours to reach the gulf of Naples."

"By land," murmured Fiamma. "With good horses..."

"Instead of relays," Fulvio cut in, "We'd find light cavalry and men-at-arms all along the route. Let Ruggieri speak. I'm sure he has an idea. There's something you're not saying, isn't there, Ruggieri?"

"One never says everything," replied the broad-shouldered mariner, bobbing up and down on his bench; "there are the yeses...and then there are the buts. One can't make the wind fall...but suppose that the good God, instead of this nutshell beneath our feet, sends us a good felucca capable of running in the wind...a felucca like those cruising over there, full of beacons...."

"In that case, how long would it take you to double Capo Campanella?"

"Twelve hours."

"You'd prefer the felucca to the brig?"

"Of course! When it doesn't capsize, it goes against the wind like a racehorse." Ruggieri interrupted himself, resuming his indolent pose, which he had abandoned momentarily. "But to tell the truth, Master, we don't have the choice."

The prince raised his eyes toward the gulf.

"Yes we do, my lad," he replied, coldly. "There they both are, the brig to the right, the felucca to the left. Your choice is good. Brail your sail and pad your oars. We're going to take passage aboard the felucca."

X. All Sails Aloft!

Ruggieri did not take the trouble to hide his perfect contentment. While leaning on the tiller to set a course for the felucca, which was tacking indolently, he expressed his approval warmly. He was no longer the same man. Al his movements had a cheerful enthusiasm. In truth, he had not expected that windfall!

The windfall in question consisted of attacking a felucca of war, manned by a crew of sixty or eighty, within sight of a navy brig.

Having changed course, he delivered a joyful and amiable kick to the side of his friend Cucuzone, who sat up, grumbling.

"What's new?" asked the saltarello.

"A *tour de force*," replied Ruggieri.

Cucuzone rubbed his eyes, stretched himself, and demanded explanations. They were given by Admiral Ruggieri, to whom Fulvio had ceded command.

"To say that I hadn't given it a little thought," the worthy mariner commenced, "would be a lie. All evening it's been going through my head. I said to myself: 'If the master was today as I once knew him...but no one can know what's in his head nowadays. Anyway, no matter. He does what he wants, since he's the master.' Let me see...put your shirt over the right oar, grasshopper! I'll put my calzone over the one on the left...in view of the fact that I don't want to risk fluxions of the chest. Are we there?"

"It's done," said Cucuzone.

Fulvio added: "Tell us your plan, quickly. We can only get close to it near the rudder."

"The rudder won't enter into it, Highness...that's not how we'll take her. Look out to see a little. One couldn't see a straw floating in this infernal night in which the daylight seems to dissolve in the water...everywhere except the nor'nor'east, where the sky is giving a little light. It's not just now that I know this: at night, any light that comes from the horizon blocks the eye, in its field, of course. Ship your oar, grasshopper and float gently. You'll see how the trick will be worked."

The felucca had her prow turned toward the pale and faint light that we have just mentioned, which hindered the sight toward the north-north-west. The boat was exactly opposite—which is to say, to the south-south-east. Ruggieri maneuvered in such a fashion as to veer westwards in order to go around the warship

"I'd like to know what we have in the matter of arms," he said, already lowering his voice. "When I sit down for dinner, I always ask for the menu."

The prince and Cucuzone each had a two pairs of pistols; Ruggieri had a pair himself. In addition, all three had their knives, and there were two strong hatchets in the bottom of the bot.

Fimma wanted to have one of Fulvio's pistols.

Ruggieri shook his head. "Powder won't be any use tonight," he growled. "I'd give all our artillery for one more hatchet." He interrupted himself to order: "To the tiller, Highness, if you please. We need to pass to windward of the felucca, as far away as possible without getting to close to the brig, which doesn't seem to be asleep."

Fulvio seized the tiller.

"How are you going to take her, Ruggieri?" he asked.

The latter, who had not let go of his meerschaum pipe since the moment we encountered him in these parts, removed it from his mouth respectfully and placed it, like a precious object, in his bosom.

"Highness," he said, "it's a trial. I wouldn't like to attempt it with the French or the English, but our Neapolitan watchmen sleep standing up. There's a chance of success.

"Explain," ordered he prince.

Ruggieri obeyed, while continuing to row. His explanation did not take long. His two companions understood immediately. Any other woman in Fiamma's place would have cried madness. Fiamma placed her hand on Fulvio's shoulder and said: "I know that I'll die with you...if it's tonight so much the better!"

Those were the last words pronounced. They had just overtaken the felucca, which was swaying gently in the swell. Our adventurers were so close that they could hear the creaking of the wood in the mortises and the flapping of the flag that was whipping the horn.

When the swell lowered the gunwale our adventurers could dart a glance as far as he feet of the two masts. Around the mestre, where there was a beacon, half a dozen sailors were playing dice. At the rear, a few feet from the trinquet, two officers were chatting. There was only one man at the helm. There was only one watchman, to port, on the parapet. They could not see the rigging, where other sentinels might be posted. There were, therefore, without counting the unexpected, nine or ten visible enemies that they would have to combat in the first strike. It was necessary that the first strike should be decisive, and that there would not be a second.

The boat now seemed to be drawing away from its objective. It continued about two rifle-shots north-north-east of the felucca. After ten minutes, Ruggieri whispered. "Helm to starboard, Highness. Let's come about—it's time."

There was a movement aboard the felucca. A reef was taken in on the one sail that was still deployed. The wind was increasing in violence by the minute.

"Stop!" said Ruggieri. "Let her come."

Cucuzone stopped rowing with a manifest pleasure, and immediately resumed the nonchalant posture of which he was particularly fond. A kick from Admiral Ruggieri reminded him that idleness was not in season.

"Hold yourself ready!" he said to him. "Oar aloft. If we deviate ten palms to the right or left, we're dead."

Ruggieri was a true mariner. His calculation was rigorously exact. Merely by the action of the wind on the hull of the boat, it drifted slowly but surely toward the felucca. The King's mariners had gone down below.

"An inch to starboard, Highness," ordered Ruggieri. "And the rest of us, duck."

They all ducked down at the same time, with the result that no profile projected over the edge of the boat. Scarcely a hundred palms separated them from the prow of the felucca, which was heading straight for them, gracefully inclined, miraculously tight to the wind, when the officer of the watch put the loudhailer to his mouth.

"Prepare to come about," he commanded.

"Go!" ordered Ruggieri, at the same time.

At the very moment when the felucca came toward the wind under the action of its rudder, the boat, which had been subjected to a vigorous impulsion, presented itself sideways on to the prow of the felucca.

"What's that?" demanded the officer, who had felt the impact.

The debris of the pinnace, sliced in two, slid along the flanks of the big ship; but our four adventurers, knives between their teeth, were subtended like a human cluster of grapes from the windlass cables hanging down from the bowsprit, Fulvio holding Fiamma by the waist.

"There was no one in it," said the officer, gazing at the passing debris, "and I haven't heard a single cry,

A sailor leaning over the gunwale said: "it's some capsized boat. "Hey, watchman! If we'd encountered the Rocca Forcata instead of that nutshell, we'd now be with the tuna!"

Instead of responding, the watchman uttered a muffled, seemingly stifled gasp. He was distinctly seen to collapse along the deck.

At that moment, the captain, sticking his head through the main hatch, also asked: "What is it?"

He only just had time to throw himself down the steps. The heavy hatch, violently lifted, fell back with all its weight, noisily. Then there was a loud cry, imprecations and blasphemies.

Seven cadavers were on the deck: three with heads split to the shoulders, four with breasts opened by Calabrian knives. There was no one alive but the helmsman, who had fallen down, paralyzed by terror

The combat had not lasted a minute.

The two hatches were solidly secured in the blink of an eye with the aid of ropes. There was no more communication possible between the deck and the interior of the ship, except via the gunports.

It was the little cabin boy who, pistol in hand, was holding the helmsman in respect while the others worked.

As Ruggieri finished securing the large hatch, the sea suddenly lit up to port, the deck trembled, and a cannonball departed beneath his feet. The crew of the felucca were calling to the brig for help. The brig heard, for three beacons immediately lit up on the maintop.

Cucuzone started laughing.

"One would think that they're not content with us," he growled.

Then he approached the helmsman, turning a series of Chinese somersaults that would have won him numerous plaudits at the Largo della Carita.

Ruggieri had seized the loudhailer He leaned over the gunwale.

"There are thirty lads here of Il Porporato's flotilla. We have the powder to make your chaplet of caronnades sing. I'm Ruggieri! Beldemonio is with us. If you're good, nothing bad will happen to you. If you make any more noise, we'll put your boats into the sea, aim your caronnades straight down and smash your felucca like a nutshell. So, my children, be good!"

That paternal harangue was followed by a profound silence.

The brig had changed course and was approaching under its mainsail and its jib. That was all the sail it could carry in the torment. While moving, it was making signal after signal; but the felucca remained dark and mute henceforth.

The idea that there were thirty resolute and well-armed pirates on the deck above them, among who were those devils incarnate Beldemonio and Ruggieri, terrified the mariners trapped in the battery. They held council, sailors and officers, brought together by common distress; they were forced to agree that the pirates' threat was easy to realize. The caronnades, free and mounted in such a fashion as to be able to fire downwards, furnished the angle necessary to blast the ship apart. And God knew that Beldemonio, Ruggieri and their troop were not men to recoil from an extremity of that sort.

The silence was broken by a burst of laugher from Cucuzone. He had just jumped on to the shoulders of the trembling helmsman with a single bound.

"Hey, Ruggieri!" he cried. "Guess who we have here! It's Toniotto, the Tarentais, as cowardly as a chicken, but a good sailor. Three of us would never have been able to hoist the mainsail of the trinquet...here's reinforcements."

"The signora will have to take the helm," replied Ruggieri. "To work! That lumbering brig is traveling faster than I thought."

Cucuzone leapt down to the deck and gave Toniotto a shove, sending him sprawling at the feet of the prince

The great silhouette of the brig was now distinctly outlined in the night. Fulvio took out his watch.

"We still have an hour before moonrise," he said. "In an hour, we need to be out of sight."

"To the yardarm, Cucuzone!" commanded Ruggieri.

"Take the trouble to go aloft, Signor Toniotto," said the later respectfully doffing his cap.

Toniotto did not have to be begged. He was a sailor, but, as he was aloft as rapidly as the virtuous Cucuzone, it is necessary to say that fear had given him wings.

They each took one side the yardarm, or, rather, the immense antenna, and started to unfurl. The wind whipped the canvas into their faces, but Cucuzone had more than one talent. Thanks to his singular skill, they were able throw the unique sheet serving to maintain the Latin sails. Ruggieri and the prince, seizing the cable together, which lifted them up two or three times half a foot from the deck, succeeded in hauling in the sail. Then the felucca lurched so terribly that the tip of the antenna labored the foam. There was a loud cry of alarm in the battery, because water flooded in through the gunports.

"Block all!" commanded Fulvio, through the loudhailer.

The Neapolitan mariners obeyed. There was no hesitation. Ruggieri, bounding over the rigging, already had the tiller in hand. The hinges of the rudder screeched; the felucca reared up, supple and swift. A moment later she was cleaving the waves with the rapidity of a racehorse.

After an hour, bloody tints colored the south-east. There was a great cloud hovering like an enormous bird above the line of the horizon, leaving a narrow strip of sky free. The moon soon appeared in that empty space. It was the broken crescent of the final quarter, a partial disk of red-bronze that seems from a distance, at first, to be a gigantic conflagration, and then shrinks and pales as the crescent rises, so that the bronze buckler seems to turn gradually silver.

When the upper horn of the crescent pricked the cloud, the borders of the latter took on the tint of polished steel. The brig was lost in the distance; it required the telescope to make out its mainsail, which resembled the wing of a gull at the limit of vision. At the same time, the profile of the coast stood out in black.

"Belvedere!" murmured Fulvio, whose anxious eye was interrogating the shore. "The wind has got up, the tempest is driving us, we're making ten knots."

Cucuzone was asleep, lying curled up like a caterpillar. Ruggieri was smoking his meerschaum pipe at the helm. Toniotto was still on watch. When anything needed to be done, Cucuzone woke up, grumbling, and worked miracles.

Fulvio and Fiamma were sitting side by side. They were silent now. Once, Fulvio leaned over the zingara and kissed her forehead.

"I love you to the point of pitying you," she murmured.

They had passed Scalea; they moved out to sea opposite the gulf of Policastro in order to double Capo Palinuro. Soon, the Licosa lighthouse showed its light, alternately white and red.

It was a furious course. The felucca's timbers groaned to the utmost depths of her frame; and the calm of the four adventurers made a strange contrast with the storm wind.

There are many people in the region of Naples who still remember the night of the fourteenth of February 1823 and the one that followed, during which the great eruption of the volcano took place. The earth and the sea were in fever; the terrible convulsion that was in preparation was weighing upon them.

All was menace and suffering. Oxen torpid in the depths of the byre refused fodder; horses, those valiant creatures, wallowed in their litter, moaning. Wild birds took refuge even in the cities. Nature entire seemed to be gripped by a mysterious horror.

At first light, the felucca had all its sails aloft as it passed between the island of Capri and Capo Campanella. An hour later, as the sun rose, they dropped anchor between Castellamare and the Torre dell'Annunziata.

"Four of us are leaving," shouted Ruggieri, through the loudhailer. There are still twenty-six men on deck."

The captain of the felucca, his officers and his sailors remained silent. Henceforth, their most ardent desire was that the unfortunate adventure should not become known.

"In two hours," Ruggieri added, "it will all be over and you'll be free."

Cucuzone and Toniotto had put the launch to sea.

It has been remarked that torments that have for their origin some subterranean cataclysm often calm down during the day, to resume with more violence when the sun descends to the horizon. That is the progress of fever and almost all the maladies that attack the human machine.

The wind had dropped sensibly; the blue sea was choppy and was beginning to break up its white shroud of foam everywhere. The sky was clear, and, save for the alarming plume of smoke that Vesuvius was unfurling in great puffs, you might have thought it one of those mornings in March or September when the equinox brings abrupt alternatives of calm, and tempest.

It was in broad daylight, at eight o'clock in the morning, that our adventurers stepped ashore between the islet of Revigliano and the mouth of the little rivulet at Varno. A few coastguards were on the shore, trying to recognize the ship at anchor, where no human being was visible, for our adventurers had taken care to take poor Toniotto with them.

They immediately set off across open country, leaving the ruins of Pompeii to their left and marching in the direction of Angri.

At a bend in the Sarno, in a delightful oasis planted with fine trees, stood a villa of somber aspect, which seemed to have been built in the time of the Spanish domination. The windows of the external façade were all closed. Fiamma, who was marching in the lead, said: "That's it."

Fulvio extended his hand.

"You have your instructions," he said. "You two, Cucuzone and Ruggieri, you have yours. Leave right away for Naples, and come back quickly; I'll be waiting for you."

Immediately, he plunged into the trees surrounding the villa.

Fiamma followed him for a long time with a sad gaze. When she had lost sight of him she rejoined her two companions, who were climbing toward the little village of Angri. They found horses there and set off at a gallop for Naples.

Before entering the city they separated. Ruggieri and Cucuzone went down toward the port. Fiamma headed toward the Strada di Mantua, where the Folquieri house was.

XI. One of Mariotto's Stories

The previous evening, at about the time when our adventurers were slipping silently under the bowsprit of the felucca in order to attempt a maneuver that would render them master of a crew of sixty men, Naples had been in a state of muted agitation. That agitation was translated, as is customary in that noisy and talkative region, by a disorderly need for movement that gathers crowds, as soon as dusk falls, in places of popular assembly. People were flooding the vicinity of the port as if it were a public holiday. But it was not for joy—on the contrary. In this circumstance, Neapolitan joy took on a chagrined and anxious character.

It was in the permanent fairground of the Strada di Porto, above all, that the pulse of the city could be taken. The merchants were not selling much, and, unusually, not crying their merchandise very loudly. People seemed to have something else on their minds; the necessities of life were in abeyance.

In fact, the extraordinary heaviness of the atmosphere was not apt to sharpen the generally mediocre appetite of that idle and slack population. The wind, which was plunging into the streets, was hot; the warm earth was exhaling miasmas so penetrating that unfortunates had been seen falling down on the paving stones as if asphyxiated. Everyone sensed his vision troubled and his ears buzzing. Thus, it is said, in the Orient, are the inhabitants of condemned cities when plague is about to burst forth. Agitated people were seen accosting one another, exchanging a few brief words, and then quitting one another, as if each were in haste, searching the crowd for some undiscoverable object. Others wandered at random, languishing, paying no attention either to the jolts they received or the curses that buzzed in their ears.

At eight o'clock in the evening, all the cooking fires were extinct. No one was slipping on perfidious slices of watermelon, the debris of some joyful meal; no one had eaten any. One could scarcely hear, at long intervals, the cry usually so oft-repeated: "Co due tornesi, vive, magne et ti lave la faccia!"—you can eat drink and wash your face for four centimes. The only occupied individuals were the storytellers and improvisers, for there were no more printed pamphlets hawked with loud cries from the boundary markers; Signor Johann Spurzheim, the grand vizier of the King of Naples, had forbidden their sale on the public highway.

One can divine the vogue that the absence of competition gave to the improvisers. There was one on every boundary-marker and every doorstep; they were everywhere. Not only were none of the old ones lacking, but new ones were emerging continually. Many young unknown talents were making their debut on that memorable evening. That is because there was so much to say; news was coming thick and fast.

Vesuvius was smoking and blazing, but it was not a matter of Vesuvius. An earthquake was announced, but what do earthquakes matter? What interested everyone were the bizarre and dramatic events that had taken place in the last few days. Mysterious rumors were beginning to transpire. Everyone who thought that he knew something was burning to know more. They went from one improviser to another. Those who were reputed to be well-informed had hundreds of listeners. Mariotto, our Mariotto, the gracioso of the Neapolitan multitude, would certainly have had thousands, but Mariotto was not there. People searched for him; people called for him, but in vain. No one had seen him that day.

At the theater, we see it happen every year: when the great actors are absent, the petty talents climb on chairs and toot their horn, under the pretext of the proverb that in the kingdom of the blind the one-eyed man is a sovereign. The absence of the eloquent Mariotto left the field free for the host of his competitors. All the places were taken, including his own, the basin of the Fountain of the Three Virgins. It was Luigi the Syracusan who held that post of honor, and he was very proud of it.

"Holy Trinity, my friends!" he shouted, after finishing some story or other. "Could Mariotto have told it at greater length and better? He is as renowned as macaroni, you see; the macaroni of Sabione is the tastiest of all, and that is why it costs the most!"

Having perfidiously slipped in that jealous attack, Luigi continued the course of his success.

What was said that evening in the Strada di Porto had, moreover, a uniformly curious character. Even the slightest storytellers brought some interesting and new detail. A drama was being played out alongside that populace, and the populace knew it. It listened and looked, avidly seeking to grasp every scene of the momentous tragedy whose bloody and mysterious twists and turns were being accomplished invisibly. It really was a tragedy, because it had roles for the King, the princes and princesses and the ministers.

In the six days that had passed since the family assembly at the Vila Floridiana, the King had not quit the Pizzo Falcone, which was guarded on a war footing. For six days the King had refused to see the princes his sons, and the princesses. The Princess of Salerno was in exile in Capri.

Prodigious facts were recounted on that subject, which found credence in that multitude by virtue of their very absurdity.

It was said, for example, that on the night when the Castello-Vecchio had been set ablaze by the Companions of the Silence in order to liberate Il Porporato, the King, woken up by a fever, had found a dagger nailed to his night table. The dagger traversed a piece of paper bearing the Monteleone escutcheon: a heart pieced by two swords, with the motto *Agere, non loqui.*

"Which proves," added the improvisers, by way of explanation, "that Bourbon was, that night, in the power of the Companions of the Silence. It's as easy to pierce a breast as the wood of a night table."

There was also talk of the disappearance of the beautiful Comtesse Doria and the young woman from the Folquieri house who now bore the name of Monteleone. There was talk of the challenge exchanged between Lorédan Doria and the young saint, Comte Giuliano Monteleone.

There was something even more mysterious. For several weeks, an old woman nearly a hundred years old had been living in the Folquieri house. The people of the Strada di Mantua knew her well. She accepted alms and always murmured between her toothless gums: "I must speak to the King before I die."

The day after the day when Baron d'Altamonte had been murdered by his brothers, that old lady said to anyone who would listen: "I've seen all three of them. God protect them, the three children of the great Comte de Monteleone!"

The man that Johann Spurzheim had had appointed as a royal physician, Pier Falcone, had come to visit that old woman before departing for Abruzzo. The following night, the old woman had disappeared.

"Yes, my brothers," said the Syracusan, "there's a man who has a lot on his conscience! God forbid that I say anything against His Excellency Spurzheim, who is going to marry a madwoman out of the goodness of his heart, but Pier Falcone has done villainous work. You know the cadaver that was taken all the way to the King's chamber—the cadaver of the Calabrian Manuele Giudicelli? Well, Pier Falcone had been to see him at the Palazzo Coriolani under the pretext of replacing Prince Fulvio's physician."

"Fulvio!" people interrupted on all sides. "Prince Fulvio Coriolani! Where is he? What is he doing? Tell us about him!"

"Prince Fulvio Coriolani," Luigi commenced, self-importantly, "and the brigand Il Porporato are one and the same person."

Loud jeers went up.

"That's new!" cried someone.

"Is he making fun of us?"

"Down with Luigi! Where's Mariotto?"

The clamors suddenly changed into a formidable burst of laughter. Mariotto had just made his entrance. He had arrived behind Luigi, the usurper, following the edge of the basin very quietly, and had precipitated him unceremoniously into the fountain by tripping him up, as men of action put it.

"Bravo, Mariotto!"

Not content with having immersed his unfortunate rival, he watched him flounder and insulted him in his distress.

"Idler!" he cried, from the height of his reconquered throne. "Wretched stammerer, hawker of news that's been running around the streets for a hundred years, I'll teach you to profane Mariotto's place in order to recount your stories as old as the deluge!"

"Bravo, Mariotto!"

"Oh, you've discovered that Coriolani is the same as Il Porporato, my dove? What did you give to the fellow who whispered that to you? Don't come near me, you soulless scoundrel, or I'll fracture your skull with a kick!"

Luigi, covered in mud like a marine god, got up and came toward him with closed fists.

"To the girella, my true friends!" cried Mariotto, who was not without anxiety. "Avenge your good servant! Spin that rogue for me until he chokes! To the girella!"

"To the girella!" repeated a hundred voices.

Luigi tried to flee, but the thrust had been given. The unfortunate fellow was subjected to the impetuous movement of rotation that had thrown Peter-Paulus into the gutter in the Piazza del Spirito Santo a quarter of a league from his point of departure.

His cries soon ceased to be audible, drowned out by the unanimous clamor.

"Bravo, Mariotto!"

"Where have you come from, Mariotto?"

"Speak, speak, Mariotto!"

With a majestic gesture, the improviser in vogue imposed silence on the crowd surrounding him.

"Everyone follows his profession according to his conscience, isn't that so, my beloved?" he pronounced, in an emphatic tone. "There are demi-carlin rings and there are rings worth the price of a palace. It's the same, you see, with improvisers. Do you think I stand on my doorstep with my arms folded waiting for news?"

"No, no, Mariotto! Bravo! Bravo! The news you have, and quickly!"

"When have I ever lacked news. my friends and my protectors? You ask me where I've come from? I've come from far away, and I'll tell you things that the King probably doesn't know yet."

The crowd undulated. Mariotto knew so well how to make the mouths of his audience water. He paraded his suddenly saddened gaze around.

"There are good fellows missing here," he murmured, "who've been missing for a long time. Do you know where Mitelino is? Do you know where Farfalla is? Do you know where Ruzzola is? Three brave friends! And big Gaspardo the fisherman, who made silence when I spoke? Where they are, my doves, many others could go, for not all the Companions of the Silence have left Naples..."

He winked, and a little tremor ran through the crowd.

"I know everything," Mariotto went on, "but don't worry, I won't say anything. You're my clientele...it's you that enable my poor family to live. Come on, my cherubs, I'd be very sorry to tax worthy people like you. Give me a few carlins for my worthy wife's macaroni."

A good number of copper coins fell at his feet.

"It's me who'll talk to you about Il Porporato," he said, abruptly. "It's me who'll tell you what has become of Prince Fulvio Coriolani...and what has become of so many others...the dead and the living... A few more tournois, my benefactors!"

More coins arrived. Mario bent down counted them with a disdainful expression, and put them in his pocket muttering: "One more time..."

"So," he commenced, "you all saw, like me, and Englishman and an Englishwoman arrive on the *Pausilippe*, which is now ready to depart in the merchant port, awaiting the end of the torment."

"Yes, yes," was the reply, "we all saw them."

"That Englishman and that Englishwoman," the improviser continued, "were bringing the King a diamond worth millions of billions. Would you have suspected that? Would you have had the heart, if you had known that, to give such a rich man the girella? At any rate, the mountain rogues have taken him away with his wife and his two domestics."

"And the diamond?" a voice asked.

"And the diamond, Falimbello, poor in spirit, the diamond too, the diamond especially. You're going to ask me how I know that...but answer me first, do you know Stefano Marinone, corporal of the Buffalo regiment?"

"Certainly, certainly," came the reply from all parts.

"A good fellow, no? He was my cousin, via my poor wife, and we're in mourning, for Stefano is dead"

"Really? Dead how?"

"And if we weren't in mourning for Stefano, we'd be in mourning for Paolo Pescatore, my nephew, godfather of my last. Do you know Paolo Pescatore, soldier in the dragoons of the guard?"

"Yes, of course...is he dead too?"

"Him and a hundred others...and more than a thousand with them. Oh, my lambs, I tell you that I know more than the King!"

"But what do you know, Mariotto?"

"Poor Buffalo regiment! Poor dragoons! Those idlers who are babbling and howling all around on the boundary markers, could they tell you where and how Ferdinand de Bourbon—God preserve him!—has lost three thousand soldiers, all young and healthy?"

There was only one cry: "Three thousand soldiers! Has there been a battle, then?"

"Listen to me carefully, my preferred," said Mariotto, adopted a sentimental expression, "it isn't to drink Sicilian wine, oh no, or to put fried morsels in my mouth...you know me well I'm sober...but I have responsibilities. Oh, what responsibilities I have! Stefano has a wife; Paolo leaves two children. It's necessary to nourish them all, isn't it? If you want to hear me recount the most frightful story that has ever come to your ears, my protectors...the story of three thousand soldiers of the King put to death by a handful of bandits, it's necessary to give me a whole ducat, in order that the widow and the orphans have nourishment tomorrow."

Would you believe it? It wasn't difficult. Mariotto feared having asked too much, but the ducat was made up in the blink of an eye, so great was the passion to know in that crowd!

"God will return it to you a hundredfold, my favorites!" cried Mariotto, joyfully, stuffing the money in his pocket. "It's for a good cause! Ah, Fragola, you incorrigible pinchpenny, you haven't given anything! The girella isn't made for dogs, you old miser! But I'll begin, in order not to make my excellent patrons impatient.

"You know, don't you, that they're here and there, behind us and in front of us, everywhere—everywhere! Didn't you see, in the very place where we are, a week ago, the accursed saltarello Cucuzone, clinging by his feet to the holy image of the Virgin Mother, and cutting off my speech by whispering my ear their terrible password: *iron is strong and charcoal is black*?"

"How do you know their password, Mariotto?" interrupted an excessively curious auditor.

"Giovan, my only friend," replied the improviser, mildly, "if big Gaspardo were here, you'd be out on your ear. Isn't there anyone here to do a little police work? I know that, Giovan, as surely as I know that you're a spy paid every evening at the Largo di Mercato. I know that as I know your three or four rascally métiers. Watch your pockets, those of you who are around him!"

"How dare you!" cried the poor devil Giovan, who was a fellow as honest as one usually is in Naples.

"If you don't put him out," said Mariotto, "I won't say any more. His ugly face is chilling my enthusiasm."

Giovan was given the girella.

Mariotto went on: "That's well done, my Christians! Where was I? Oh yes, I was saying that those scoundrels the companions are everywhere. And I've known some"—he paused to wink mysteriously—"who were worth their price, all the same. Sansovina the sailor always had an open hand. Beccafico, Privato and many others were good lads...anyway, it's only the dead who don't come back

"So much that Signor Johann Spurzheim himself was one of them, you know that as well as I do. But Holy Trinity, that one was all good, all honor, for the service of the King. The proof is that he had affiliated His Majesty's own physician, the learned Doctor Pier Falcone, who would have risen very high, my true friends, if, unfortunately...but you'll see...."

"It was Doctor Pier Falcone who was Signor Spurzheim's right arm...but not for long. Signor Spurzheim often changes his right arm...

"But isn't it the case," Mariotto said, interrupting himself, "that people are saying now that the wife of the respectable minister, the illustrious Barbe Spurzheim, was poisoned? It was the learned Pier Falcone who cared for the good lady…and I've heard it reported that he stayed in the house in the Largo del Mercato on the night of her death from dusk until dawn. But that scarcely concerns us. The important thing is the Signor Johann, master of the Silence, knew all the secrets of the association. He knew the road to the mysterious palace built in the mountains by the Borgia pope, which is known as the Purple Castle. But are you listening to me, my comrades?"

That was certainly a superfluous question. Around Mariotto nothing could be seen but leaning heads and gaping mouths. The most avid curiosity was painted on every face.

"San Gennaro!" cried two or three voices. "We're eating your words, Mariotto."

"Good, my true fiends! That proves that you know what's good. The impossible thing, wasn't it, was for Signor Spurzheim to quit Naples, where his presence is so necessary, to go in pursuit of bandits? In any case, the worthy minister is only alive by the grace of God. He couldn't support such a long journey.

"He therefore took Pier Falcone into his study and revealed the secret of the mountain to him. There was a map drawn on a piece of paper, with explanations…and it was necessary, for the route to reach the Purple Castle is difficult! Pier Falcone took the plan, which said: *Take this road, turn here, then there…*in sum, what was necessary. And would you like to know why His Excellency Signor Spurzheim showed so much confidence in that Falcone? It was because Falcone had to avenge himself on Il Porporato, who had once taken his mistress…"

"But how does he know all this, that damned Mariotto?" cried a few overly impetuous admirers.

"Let him speak! Let him speak!" roared the crowd.

"Pier Falcone," the improviser went on, "had his vendetta to accomplish. He accepted in haste the mission to lead the King's soldiers in pursuit of the Companions of the Silence. He took with him Baron d'Altamonte's iron ring—the ring, a sign of mastery, that forces every companion to blind obedience.

"You saw the soldiers depart. They were joyful, believing that they were racing to an easy victory. It was almost an army: the entire Buffalo regiment, two battalions of men-at-arms, dragoons, light cavalry, what do I know? Nothing similar had been seen for years in this land at peace.

"For that's not all; at the same time, the military port sent a dozen ships to cruise along the southern coasts. All that for bandits? Isn't that a pity?

"But lend me all your attention, my devoted friends, for this is where the story becomes interesting.

"The troops traversed the ulterior principality in good order and separated into two corps in the vicinity of Sant'Angelo dei Lombardi. The Buffalo regiment, the dragoons and a battalion of men-at-arms went into the Basilicata; the rest—which is to say—a battalion of men-at-arms, light cavalry and a battalion of guard infantry, when into the nearer principality on the other side of the mountains. They wanted thus to circle the Sila, in which it appears that the marvelous Purple Castle is situated.

Pier Falcone was with the first corps. Marching with the second, in the quality of volunteers, were Malatesta, Sampieri, Mareschalci, Colonna and the others who had sworn death to our Fulvio Coriolani...

"When I say ours, that's an old habit, for we have nothing in common with bandits..."

There was a slight murmur in the crowd. Mariotto, winking and lowering his voice, went on: "He was the patron of poor people, my worthy comrades, I'll never deny it. For my part, and don't repeat this, I'd like the true princes to do as much. Everything was royal in him...his face, his bearing and his heart. Who ever saw Coriolani's hand closed? Gold fell upon us like rain from the window of his carriage. But in the end, may God curse him, the brigand, since Signor Spurzheim has made him an outlaw....

"The first corps arrived by night between Auletta and Brienza. Pier Falcone had the tents erected. They drank and rejoiced. The attack was decided for early the next morning. Pier Falcone was the true leader of the expedition. Under him came the lieutenant-colonel of the Buffalo regiment, Cavalier Bernoni and the major of the men-at-arms, Pietro Frascati.

At five o'clock in the morning, the Buffali and the Dragoons set forth into the mountains following the course of the Ghezzo stream. Falcone had his map in his hand. He guided the expedition at a sure and unhesitating pace, as if he had spent his life running those savage thickets.

"It's a desolate country, almost a desert. The flank of the mountain has large rips from which an odor of sulfur is exhaled. Many people believe that those fissures, from which clouds of smoke sometimes emerge, are the veritable mouths of Hell. Here and there, a few miserable herdsmen perched on the summits of rocks, watched the expedition pass by with astonishment. The buffali took prisoner all those they could reach, and asked them 'By what route does one climb to the Purple Castle?' They replied, with bewilderment: 'We aren't children, to believe in those old stories.'

"On the sides of the mountain where it's situated, no one knows the Purple Castle. There was a belief among the buffali, which was that the mysterious occupants of the Purple Castle had, by virtue of some magical grimoire, the power to render their retreat invisible.

"But that Falcone, my seraphim, is a man who doesn't believe in magic! He kept going, on and on, consulting his map and cutting resolutely through the most inaccessible gorges.

"Oh, believe me, that really was the road to the Devil's manse! As they went further the crests became higher, the peaks steeper, the rocks more menacing. There were no more herdsmen in the valleys, there weren't even any chamois-hunters on the peaks. They soon saw, between two waterfalls, the bed of the stream covered by thick ice. The temperature, so mild on departure, was extremely rigorous, and a few paces further on, the buffali would have been finding their way in the snow.

"I can see, my affectionate companions, I can clearly see that you'd like to ask me how I know all these details. Have I a wicked heart? Answer no, my friends, for I'll get you out of trouble. I haven't invented any of this. Oh no! That's good for the idlers with neither faith nor law that you listen to when I'm not here. I have seen, my children, I have seen with my own eyes, one of the unfortunates who escaped from that terrible enterprise..."

"Who? Who?" people asked, on all sides.

"Misalta, the man-at-arms, who is a distant cousin of my poor wife, via the Rospolis of Pompeii...Misalta, the unfortunate fellow that you all saw strutting throughout the streets a week ago. He only has one leg now...his right arm is broken...his poor head is no longer anything but a wound. And do you know why I wasn't at my post just now? It's because it's a long way from here to the military hospital at Portici. I had gone to obtain news of Misalta...news to bring to you, my benefactors."

There was a chill in the crowd. When Mariotto called his audience that, it was almost always the prelude to a further collection; but this time, it wasn't for himself that he was asking, the excellent fellow; it was for Misalta, the unfortunate soldier.

Half a piastre for such a great misfortune, was that too much to ask? He was given the demi-piastre.

"So, now we're at the top of the mountain. Oh, my friends," he went on, drawing new inspiration from that modest offering, "can you imagine that it was four o'clock in the afternoon, and that our friends had been climbing since daybreak? Before them extended a vast pine forest, whose treetops, powdered with snow, extended as far as the eye could see. To the right, there was a bottomless precipice; to the left, a peak, the last, about a mile distant, which the setting sun was causing to gleam like a colossal carbuncle.

"Pier Falcone—may God have his soul, for he's dead as I speak—stopped in that place and said: 'It's there.' Everyone looked around; there was the mountain, white with snow; there was no trace of any human endeavor.

"Cavalier Bernoni, the lieutenant-colonel of the Buffalo regiment, and Pietro Frascati, the major of the men-at-arms, asked Falcone: 'Where have you brought us?'

"'Within reach of the Purple Castle,' replied the diabolical physician.

"They looked; nothing could be seen but the white shroud of snow...no, I'm mistaken. Something could be seen, for a great cry of stupor escaped from all throats at the same time. What was it, then?

"On the summit of that peak, reddened by the setting sun, rising up like a gigantic pedestal, there was now a statue: a scarlet statue that would have seemed sculpted in bloody porphyry if the wind hadn't been unrolling the folds of his purple cloak.

"That man, if it was a man, was leaning, motionless, on the shiny barrel of a long rifle; he was standing straight and proud; those who were there had never seen such stature in the son of a woman. In the sun's rays, they could perceive the slightest details of his costume and his person. There wasn't a single thread in the cloth that covered him that wasn't red. The plume in his cap, which was as vermilion as a dazzling cactus-flower, hung down all the way to his shoulders. And from the height where he was, the proud king of the mountain, he seemed to be lowering a disdainful gaze on the impotent enemies who had just attempted to lay siege to his fortress.

"Cavalier Bernoni and Major Pietro Frascati—they're both dead, my brothers—pronounced in unison a name that was running from line to line, arriving at the last ranks of the soldiers.

"I'll wager, my companions, that you've all divined what name was pronounced by the colonel, by the major and by the two thousand soldiers who were marching after them..."

Mariotto paused.

The crowd agitated and unleashed a long murmur, from which four syllables escaped, repeated in low voices a thousand times:

"Porporato! Porporato!"

XII. The Danger of Telling Stories Too Well

That name resounded in the old popular street, where torches were lacking that night, full of menace and mystery. You would have thought it one of those terrible names that ancient people applied to their gods, which they too pronounced in low voices in the bosom of their nocturnal assemblies.

It was in an altered voice that the improviser continued.

"Was it really him, my brothers? The king of darkness, the lord of the unknown mountains? Was it really the handsome demon, as he calls himself? Was it really Porporato, always at war, always victorious? Yes, you've guessed it; it was him, or the spirit of revolt in person. Only he and the fallen archangel have that gaze, which numbs the heart. The soldiers shivered, the chiefs too. But Pier Falcone had a soul of bronze. Pier Falcone pointed his finger at him and said: 'Do you still ask where I have brought you? There is the damned brigand! He'll escape us!'

"At the same time—for those who aren't mountain men don't know how to measure distances, or perhaps that Pier Falcone had vertigo—he seized the rifle from the man-at-arms who was standing next to him. He aimed. He fired. The echoes sent the explosion back like aloud burst of laughter. The man in red took off his cap, with an ironic bow. The wind caught his blond hair, you would have thought it was made of flames! He extended his hand toward the soldiers, and then he disappeared.

"The great pines agitated on the neighboring slopes. Perhaps it was an illusion, but the soldiers thought they heard, to the right and left, in the gorges and the valleys, the proud echo of the fanfare that is the appeal of the companions of charcoal and iron: *Amici, allliegre, andiamo alla pena!*"

The sun was descending to the horizon. In the distance, night was overtaking the plain. The evening breeze suddenly raised swirls of snow everywhere. 'We can't camp here,' said the officers, seeing the discontentment of the soldiers increase.

"Misalto the man-at-arms told me, my friends, that Pier Falcone had the air of a fanatic. His eyes were burning amid the livid pallor of his face. 'Who mentioned camping here?' he said. 'This isn't a time for sleep, but for combat.'

"The word combat was repeated everywhere. Combat whom? Where were the enemies? And combat by what light? Black night was rising up like a great shroud. Oh, my favorites, there is more than one brave soldier who loses his courage in the darkness.

"Pier Falcone went on: 'We're going to lay siege to this infamous lair!' And as a murmur went up, the damned physician called the lieutenant-colonel and the major by their names. 'Signor Bernoni, and you, Signor Frascati,' he said to them, 'I require you, in the name of the King, to respect my supreme authority here!'

"He hadn't spoken in that tone before.

"Soldiers don't like being led by doctors. The murmur, timid until then, burst forth and became menacing. Falcone took a document from his bosom, which he unfolded. It was an order from the King, my friends, an order that put the entire expedition under the authority of the physician. That had been the pleasure of our respected Signor Johann Spurzheim, may God bless him!

"The officers were obliged to place themselves beside Falcone. When he commanded: 'Forward march!' the officers drew their swords.

"At the foot of the peak where Porporato had displayed his great silhouette, outlined against the sky, there was one of those fissures that I mentioned, my friends, telling you that they resembled the mouths of Hell. This one was wide enough at its base, which was supported on the rock, for two men to be able to introduce themselves into it abreast there. It was only a few paces from the edge of the forest of firs. Falcone pointed at the fissure with the end of his pistol, which he was holding in his hand. 'There's our route,' he said. 'In a path like that, it matters little whether it's night or day.'

"The soldiers gazed, bleak and discouraged. 'If you want them to march,' Frascati whispered in Falcone's ear, 'break out the barrels!'

"The valets of the Buffalo regiment were carrying a few barrels of gin and French brandy at the rear. But Falcone replied: 'Not yet! This is just the beginning.'

"It's necessary to admit, my friends, that he introduced himself first into the fissure, after having pushed back the boulders that seemed to be thrown there at hazard. The soldiers, poor sheep, followed him. Each of them, before entering that cavern, turned one last gaze toward the west, where the sun could no longer be seen but which still retained a few rosy tints. Each of them seemed to be bidding adieu to the daylight.

"The path was, however, much less dangerous than one might have expected. After a few paces the fissure widened sensibly and became a veritable grotto. One could march five or six abreast there. Underfoot, the ground was smooth and soft. The temperature changed as one advanced. The rigorous cold outside was succeeded by a pleasant warmth. Suppose a ray of daylight in that place, and it would have been, for our poor soldiers, a paradise; but the ray of daylight was lacking. There was the profound, absolute obscurity that is only found in the depths of the earth.

The soldiers went forward, holding on to one another by the coat-tails and allowing themselves to be guided blindly. Singularly enough, for they had expected to be climbing, they sensed the ground declining beneath their feet, rather rapidly. It was a slope at least as steep as that of the mountain itself, but in the opposite direction.

"After a quarter of an hour—and God knows, my preferred, how long that quarter of an hour seemed to our poor soldiers—they were able to hear a muted roaring around them. It was like the noise of a waterfall augmented by a thousand echoes. Those soldiers who were mountain men remembered that the stream of the Ghezzo suddenly emerges from the ground at the hermitage of Poggiolo. It launches itself, foaming, from a rocky vault, to which its own current forbid entry victoriously.

"Now, the Ghezzo torrent has its source in the snows of Mont Avello, one of the highest peaks in the Apennine chain. The people of the valley affirm that it travels more than ten leagues underground. That had to be the Ghezzo torrent. 'Halt!' ordered Pier Falcone.

"Everyone obeyed immediately, for, in that darkness, the sound of the water was a terrible menace. 'Light the torches!' ordered Falcone.

"The briquette was struck. Two torches were lit. They expected to see the torrent a few paces away, but sounds are deceptive underground. There was no torrent—or, rather, the torrent was flowing so far away that it couldn't be perceived.

"There was a large space, high-ceilinged, the rocky walls of which were oozing damp. Droplets of water were reflecting the light everywhere. The entire expedition was gathered there. Falcone had a roll call taken. No one was missing. Falcone's third command was: 'Break out the barrels!'

"You know, my friends, that it doesn't require a lot of eau-de-vie to enthuse us, we men of the south. With the pittance of a Swiss, cold, heavy and stupid, one could get half a dozen Neapolitans and Sicilians drunk. Two minutes after the cups had stated to circulate, songs could be heard under those vaults, gibes and bursts of laughter.

"Falcone climbed on to an empty barrel and said: 'Only a few paces now separate us from the greatest treasure there is in the world. All those who have entered here poor will emerge as rich as Croesus!'

"Someone cried *bravo*. Falcone added: 'Apart from everyone's share, there'll be bonuses. A thousand gold ounces for every bandit's head; ten thousand for every Master of the Silence; a hundred thousand for the head of the infamous Porporato!'

"The echoes of the cavern sent back the name of Porporato. And I know not what bizarre sound, which resembled the mocking laughter of the devils in Hell, was heard in the distance in the darkness. But our soldiers had French brandy in their heads. They cried: 'Hurrah!'

"Falcone seized a torch and made a tour of the chamber. To the right of the entrance there was a boulder whose weight must have been enormous, to judge by its size. Falcone seized it by one of its projections, and everyone was amazed to see the enormous stone rock slowly. As it rocked, it uncovered a hole, oval in form, into which one could only enter crawling. 'That's the way to the treasure!' shouted Pier Falcone.

507

"That cooled the enthusiasm of our soldiers somewhat, because it wasn't a good road. One might have thought, moreover, that the din of the cascades and invisible waterfalls was coming, most of all, from that tunnel. 'A hundred gold ounces to whoever goes first!' shouted Falcone.

"No one volunteered.

"Listen, carefully, my friends. The French are mad; they do these things, but we don't like to tempt God. 'Two hundred gold ounces!' Falcone promised

"And, as there were still no volunteers, he insulted our brave army. 'You're all cowards!' he said, foaming with rage. 'I don't carry a sword, but I have courage! If I go first, will you follow me?'

"'We'll follow you,' said those who had drunk the most.

"Holy Trinity, my brothers. He didn't hesitate, that enraged physician. He stuck his pistol in his belt, bit his open knife, and went into the hole head first. A buffalo followed him, then two, then three, then all of them. That strange procession lasted more than an hour, as true as we're Christians, my friends.

"When the last buffalo had gone into the hole, Lieutenant-Colonel Bernoni went into it in his turn; a chief ought not to abandon his soldiers. And everyone among those who were still in the grotto began to have a great hope, because no noise of a struggle came from the passage. Evidently, those who had taken that perilous road had arrived at their goal without a shot being fired

"It had been agreed between Falcone and the officers that they would wait a few minutes before launching the second detachment. They waited. Major Frascati, the men-at-arms and the dragoons were all ears. They held their breath in order to listen better. Nothing, except for the great vague murmur of the subterranean solitudes, among which growled the distant plaint of the invisible cascade.

"The few minutes had elapsed. But for all those who were there, chiefs and soldiers, that silence had something lugubrious about it. They would almost have preferred to hear the sound of a fusillade.

"Finally, Major Frascati, who was a brave man, as you know, my turtle-doves, gave the order to make ready. The dragoons were to pass through last. The major recommended his men to hold their bayonets between their teeth and their rifles in their right hands. A rifle doesn't prevent one from crawling—look at hunters. He examined his pistols, the worthy major; he bit his dagger, as Falcone had done, and put his head into the hole valiantly.

"In contrast to the path that the detachment had followed thus far, the hole had a shallow upward slope. The major hadn't disappeared completely when he was heard to murmur: 'This mud is slippery and fetid!'

"Those who had preceded him hadn't even complained about damp! The major went on, however, for two or three paces. Then he stopped, saying: 'It's suffocating! One would swear that it's the odor of blood!'

"He was seen to come back, backwards. As he stood up he took a deep breath of air, like a man almost suffocating. But no one had the leisure to notice that. A great cry, a cry of horror, emerged from all mouths at the same time: 'Blood! Blood! Blood!'

"The major was red from head to foot, red with blood. He had blood on his hands; he had blood on his face; his uniform was soaked in blood. Torches were brought, because the major had said as he came out: 'Look…that route is now a stream full of muddy water.'

"'Blood! Blood! Blood!' cried those who were following the torches, again.

"That muddy water was blood. Blood was flowing through the hole as wine from the press falls into the vat. The blood made a large pool around the rock. The blood of an entire regiment! That can make quite a pool, my friends…"

Mariotto paused and wiped his brow. He was very pale. There were not ten heads in his audience that were not bathed in sweat. Contained respirations produced an audible murmur as they were released.

"Well? Well?" a few voices began to say, on seeing that he was taking a long time to catch his breath. "What then, Mariotto, what then?"

"Where did the blood come from, Mariotto?"

"Who had killed the buffali?"

"And how…and where? And why hadn't they cried out?"

"And their rifles, Mariotto…why hadn't they made use of their rifles?"

Mariotto was still wiping his brow. He was emotional, the worthy fellow, sincerely emotional, but that did not prevent him from thinking about his petty commerce. He was wondering, silently, how much he could tax a curiosity so violently excited. It is not only a matter of being victorious, Plutarch has said, but also of knowing how to profit from the victory. Even though he had never read Plutarch, Mariotto was occupied in following his advice. He was seeking the best means of exploiting his success.

"Well, Mariotto, can you hear us?" commenced a few irritated voices.

"Are you going to leave us with our beaks in the water?"

"Have you become mute?"

Mariotto could hear perfectly, but he said to himself: *I believe that one can't shear a sheep more than once…and not without making them squeal a little. So it's necessary to shear them very closely and not to leave the slightest fleece on the beast.*

Neapolitan oaths were beginning to growl.

"Don't offend the Lord, my true friends," said Mariotto, finally, with unction. "Our poor soldiers would surely have regretted, as they died, having blasphemed as you've just done. Oh, my protectors, such catastrophes give one pause to reflect…"

"It's not a sermon that we're asking of you…"

"Listen to me, my benefactors. My hair is going gray…a poor woman is getting old too. What a misfortune it is that youth doesn't last longer!"

Feet were stamped, and there were imprecations.

"Oh, my good masters!" said Mariotto, straightening up, "since when am I in your employment? Do you take me for your valet? And if I'm your valet, my worthy signors, why am I going about the streets with holes in my calzoni? Why does my poor wife not even have a kerchief to put on her head? Why do my children have bare feet? Are we annoyed? That's all right! I'm weary, I tell you frankly, of working for ingrates. Those who sing and dance at the Teatro San Carlo are paid. The porters who carry bales, the horses that pull carriages, even the Bohemians who tell fortunes are paid, the men with money, the animals with nourishment. Is there only me, then, in this base world to follow my métier gratis?"

"But you've been paid, Mariotto, you scoundrel!" cried a hundred irritated voices.

"This evening you've already received two salaries instead of one, Mariotto, you rogue!"

"Insatiable miser!"

"Beggar!"

"Crook!"

"Bandit!"

Mariotto let the storm pass. We renounce describing the expression of supreme disdain with which he scanned his audience. When silence had been somewhat restored, he draped his blouse over his shoulders and threw back the mass of his graying hair. His eyes were shining like two ardent coals.

"Vile and degenerate race," he commenced, abruptly, "is it really me you're insulting, you troop of brainless men and mad old women? Is there a single one of you who is worthy to undo the strap of my sandals? You steal from me, however, all of you who call me bandit. You who call me beggar are imploring my alms constantly. When you've listened to me, so eloquent and skillful, you go and tell my stories in your trivial style. Isn't it a theft when lumpen geese take possession of the song of the swan? And isn't it mendicity, O Neapolitans to extract from a poor man his stories, which are poems, for a little small change that you measure out with so much parsimony? Go on, go on, I can see the day coming when I shall have to separate myself from you! I'll go to Florence, where fine language is esteemed. I'll go to Rome, where eloquence is in honor. And you'll never see me again, O Neapolitans. And I'll have shaken the dust of my sandals in quitting your inhospitable walls!"

He made as if to descend from the rim of the fountain.

Impossible! He was sustained at arm's length.

"Now, now!" people were saying on all sides. "Don't be foolish, Mariotto."

The crowd capitulated. Mariotto redoubled his arrogance, but while draping himself in his pride, he found a means of letting it slip that as well as the end of the story of Falcone and his unfortunate soldiers, he also knew that of the terrible death of Malatesta and his gentlemen accomplices.

In order to hear those dramatic stories and indemnify him for the outrage to which he had just been subjected, it required nothing less than a gold once.

Never in human memory had any improviser exaggerated his pretentions so foolishly. But the crowd had scented blood; the crowd was seeing red; the crowd turned out its indigent pockets and made up the gold once.

Mariotto pocketed it, and, already reconciled, continued.

"Yes, my benefactors, it remains for you to know the most interesting part, for the evening is advancing, and our Signor Spurzheim doesn't like loitering in the streets. I'll tell you everything: why the poor buffali didn't make a sound, why they didn't make use of their rifles—everything, in sum, I promise you. But first, let's go back to those who were around that red pool.

"The red pool was enlarging incessantly. One might have thought that the subterranean passage was rendering all the blood of the poor slaughtered buffali drop by drop.

"Soldiers and officers consulted one another with their gaze. Horror froze all hearts and all voices.

"Gradually, a confused and growing sound appeared to emerge from the subterranean passage. Was it the plaint of all those poor souls recently separated from their bodies? Chiefs and soldiers alike were seized by the same terror, but as they were preparing to flee, the mouth of the passage exploded like a cannon loaded with grapeshot. Bullets, buckshot and shrapnel started raining into the ranks of the men-at-arms and the dragoons. Major Frascati fell, his skull shattered. At the same time, a long cry of triumph emerged from the hole, followed by the accursed fanfare.

"Oh, my friends, what would you have done? Almost all the chiefs were dead. The men-at-arms and dragoons launched themselves into the route they had already traveled in order to get as far as that sinister place. They ran pell-mell all the way to the mouth of the fissure. Once outside, the stampede continued, at hazard, through the snow.

"The good Misalta was among them, and had no wound as yet. You should have heard him relate that, my beloved children; the tears would have come to your eyes—and it's me that is telling you that!

"And have no fear! I've promised you to go on to the end; I'll go, without asking any more of you.

"There they are, then, in the middle of the night, gone astray in the gorges of the Sila. You'll believe me when I tell you that they were no longer searching for the Purple Castle. They went forth, lost in the darkness, mistaking every spur of rock for an enemy, numb with cold, extenuated by hunger. Sometimes, in the depths of defiles, when they went past one of the gigantic fissures produced by earthquakes, they thought they could hear the sounds of orgies and drinking songs. The flanks of those mountains are alive.

"The entire night was spent in those terrors and fatigues. An hour before sunrise, they emerged from the snow, and that was a great consolation for them. They thought: 'We must be very close to our camp.'

"After a few steps, in fact, they perceived a camp by glimmer of first light. But it was not the one they had left the previous morning.

"There were sentinels in uniform who shouted 'Who goes there?' and fired immediately afterwards, falling back behind the tents. In a matter of seconds, everyone in the camp was on foot. Fortunately, the first rays of daylight put an end to the misapprehension; otherwise, there would have been a battle.

"It was the second detachment of our faithful troops; the one that had gone to the right of the Apennines.

"Our fugitives, instead of returning to their camp, had gone astray on the mountain; they had crossed the chain without knowing it, passing into the Basilicata in the nearer principality.

"It was then that they counted one another. At the separation, each of the two detachments had had about fifteen hundred men. Our fugitives were, by then, no more than two hundred. And God could enlighten us as to whether they wanted to renew that terrible assault.

"Among those who composed the second detachment, however, as I said, were Malatesta and his companions. They could not recoil; nor did they want to. They were all young debauchees, insolent, libertine and the rest, only stealing a little less than the bandits themselves. But they were gentlemen! They had the courage of those who had played with swords since infancy.

"Their troop, which was mostly composed of men-at-arms, dragoons and soldiers of the guard, were full of ardor. The Malatestas as they called the seven gentlemen, demanded to take the head of the column, and they set forth on the hunt as soon as the sun rose.

"This is how Misalta tells it, my dear brothers!

"Scarcely had they engaged in the gorge than they saw a peasant of sorts making as if to flee. Malatesta chased him and seized him.

"Do you know what our Misalta says? He says that that peasant was only there to get caught. Each of those bandits, you see, is wilier than a fox.

"The peasant was taken into the middle of the group formed by the officers and the gentlemen. He was asked if he knew the route to the Purple Castle. He stammered; he was troubled. He was threatened with having his fingernails torn out and the thumbscrews. 'Signor,' he cried, weeping, 'have pity on a poor man! The bandits would kill me if they knew that I'd delivered the secret of their retreat!'

"'So you now where their retreat is!' was cried on all sides.

"'Have I said that I knew, my good masters? Have compassion for a wretch. I know it, that's the pure truth, and I alone know it, for it required a great hazard for me to learn it. In the autumn, milords, I hunt chamois in order to nourish the little children who cry hunger in the cabin. One day I went astray in a country I didn't know. I arrived there before dawn and entire months went by before I found it again. It's like an interior valley surrounded by snowy summits. There's a stream bordered by beautiful trees on flower, because the nearby summits reflect the sun's rays into it, warmed up. One would think that spring never dies there. In the middle of the stream is an island...a paradise, my good lords on that island is a grotto whose entrance is hidden by red lotuses and creepers with odorous clusters of fruits....the grotto leads to caverns that are underneath the Purple Castle.'

"'You've been there?'

"'When one only has one's life to lose, milords, a poor life without hope, one is brave. I followed the road...I saw the grottoes, and from the orifice of the caverns I saw the valley where the Borgia castle stands, red, arrogant and terrible, like Il Porporato, its master.'

"The chiefs looked at him. Then Malatesta said: 'March in front of us and take us to that island.'

"The peasant immediately started climbing. He did everything he could to give the impression that he was going reluctantly. The chiefs said to one another: 'We have the ferocious beast!'

"The route was long. From time to time, the peasant took his bearings. Finally, he clapped his hands joyfully. He had led the troop to a plateau from which one could perceive, between two rocks resembling horns, the River Sele, which unrolled its silver ribbon in the distant plain. 'That's the Fronte-del-Diavolo!' he cried. 'Once we're there, the hardest part is done.'

The soldiers remembered having seen the bizarre escarpment known as the Fronte-del-Diavolo. The local people had affirmed that there was no means of reaching it. The peasant traversed the plateau at a run, went into a gorge where two men could not have passed abreast, and soon reached the first funnel, where the stream and the island were.

"The stream was more like a lake. That lake has no name. One supposes that it must be one of the sources of the Ghezzo torrent, which goes underground not far from there and traverses the mountain profoundly. It was necessary to cross the water at a ford.

"The peasant had been right to say that the island was a true paradise. As our men were admiring it, astonished to find that delightful retreat in that desolate country, the peasant cried: 'This is nothing compared with the second valley, where the Purple Castle stands!'

"Oh, my friends, the peasant was right about that.

"This is what happened on the island...but tell me, my brothers, before I continue, tell me, hand on heart, whether there is a man in Naples entire, in the provinces, in Europe, who can tell such stories? If there is one, one alone, show him to me!"

"There isn't one, Mariotto!" cried voices from all sides

"Bravo, Mariotto!"

"Don't make us languish, friend if you're a man of heart!"

It is necessary to confess that they had a little anxiety for the depths of their pockets. It was a bad sign when Mariotto interrupted himself. But the illustrious improviser had collected his receipts for the evening. He continued, gratis:

"On the island there was a holly thicket so dense that a roe deep wouldn't have been able to penetrate it. As the chiefs were astonished that the peasant had had the idea of going into it, he said to them: 'The storm is rumbling; let's see if there's another shelter in the vicinity.'

"At a certain place the branches had been cut in such a manner as to form a narrow and difficult passage. The chiefs and soldiers went into it one by one. In the middle of the clump, a round hole opened, surrounded by a granite rim. It was the orifice of a stairway, which had marble steps.

"As you have divined, my preferred, everyone went down. At the bottom of the stairway was a subterranean tunnel, broad and sandy, which sloped gradually upwards. According to all appearances, it had to pass under the waters of the lake.

The peasant walked hence forth between a man-at-arms and a dragoon. Each had a knife in hand. At the slightest alert, it was all over for the peasant. He did not seem to fear anything. He had said: 'As long as you give me a good recompense, for I'm a poor father of a family. I'll deliver them to you without suspicion. The route we're following leads to the very center of their fortress.'

"Our King's men thought they had already taken the city.

"But it's finally time, my dearest friends, to reply to all your questions. What had become of the poor buffali? What had killed them, if they were dead? How had they been massacred? In what place? Why hadn't they cried out? Why hadn't they made use of their rifles?

"Our King's men came out into a vast subterranean chamber filled with a muffled and continuous sound. One would have thought it the rumble of a waterfall. The air was cold and cut by damp currents. 'My good signors,' said the peasant, 'it's necessary to strike the briquette and light your pine branches. The route is difficult, the torrent has hollowed out precipices.'

"'Is there no danger in going up there by torchlight?' asked Malatesta.

"'Did you think,' said the peasant, 'that you would reach your goal without encountering perils?'

"Malatesta was ashamed. 'Light the torches!' he ordered.

"Five or six resinous pine branches were set alight simultaneously. It was very little for that enormous cavern. The darkness scarcely made them visible. They advanced. After a hundred paces, the wall they were following made an abrupt turn, and immediately, the vaults and the walls began to scintillate. It seemed that thousands of candelabra were suspended here and there. Every movement of the torches brought forth prodigious sprays of light from the cupola. It was given to them all to see a strange spectacle.

"The cavern was separated into two by a roaring torrent, invisible in its encased bed. The part where our King's men were was situated more than fifty feet below the other compartment. The rocky terrain rose up almost vertically on the other side to the torrent, and that slope, brightened by trickles of water that were oozing and flowing from all parts, resembled a wall of crystal.

"But that was only an object of fleeting astonishment. There was something else to see, something so horrible that everyone thought at first that they were dreaming. That tremulous light must be evoking phantoms!

"As they advanced, however, doubt ceased to be possible. A cry of anguish emerged from all throats simultaneously. More than eight hundred cadavers of the buffalo regiment were lying on the ground there. There was a pile, a veritable pile, at the entrance to a little subterranean passage facing the second cavern. That was the passage whose other extremity came out on the other side of the mountain, on the side of the Basilicata. Our King's men were only a few hundred feet from the place where the first expedition had stopped.

"Oh, my friends, have you guessed? The poor buffali, engaged in the narrow and slippery corridor, had arrived at the opening one by one. On each side of the opening was a sword, indefatigably sharpened. Those headless cadavers revealed why no cry had been heard, and why, in consequence, the first victim had not warned the second, why the misfortune of the second had not served to alert the third...

"Only the physician Pier Falcone had fallen under the dagger of the Silence. He wore the iron ring. He could only perish by the hand of a master. Porporato himself had stuck his knife in his heart...

"Our King's men were gazing at that field of carnage in stupor when a singular cry resounded under the vaults. An invisible choir began singing a mysterious air that you have heard so many times during our nights: *Amici, alliegre, andiamo alla pena!* Then there was a voice: 'To us, Cucuzone!'

The man-at-arms and the dragoon who were holding the pretended peasant fell, struck in the heart. Then the saltarello—for it was him—was seen bounding like a tiger above the heads. A rope was throw down from the upper cavern; the saltarello climbed up it with the skill and agility of a monkey. 'Fire!' cried Malatesta.

"It was not his soldiers who obeyed his command. A brilliant line appeared at the rim of the upper cavern. It consisted of hundreds of muskets that were lowered and aimed.

"Those who held the torches didn't have time to drop them in order to extinguish them. There was a terrible explosion, flowed by cries of agony. Then silence. The King's men tried to hide or run way. The majority formed a rampart with the cadavers.

"In the silence, a voice was heard: 'The council of charcoal and iron,' it said, 'has condemned to death Giulio Doria d'Angri, Marquis de Malatesta,

Domenico Sampieri, Vespuccio Doria, Vicente Pitti, Benedetto Mareschalci, Ziani, Colonna and Gravina. Let them die!'

'A great flame flew through the air. It was a firepot that came to fall in the center of the inferior cavern. Seven rifle shots rang out. Malatesta and his companions had ended their lives!"

It was eleven o'clock in the evening. The crowd that had previously filled the Strada di Porto had just dispersed. Silence and solitude already reigned in the streets. Mariotto the improviser was returning home. As he walked he counted his takings. Two or three times he thought he heard footsteps on the lava pavement behind him. He turned round and saw nothing. His route traversed the ruins of the Castello-Vecchio, recently burned. A plank had been set down in order to cross the northern ditch, which, hollowed out in the rock, was a veritable precipice. Before stepping on to that dangerous bridge, the prudent Mariotto looked behind him again. He thought he saw a shadow moving along the houses. As the shadow was distant, he said to himself: *I have time to pass over*.

As he reached the middle of the plank he suddenly felt it tilting. He made the sign of the cross as he uttered a cry of aguish. Behind him, a voice said: "Signor Johann Spurzheim has heard mention of you, Mariotto."

"Mercy!" cried the unfortunate fellow, who was already losing equilibrium.

"You tell too many good stories, Mariotto," the voice went on. "May God have mercy on your soul; I am doing what I have been ordered to do."

The plank tipped. A hoarse cry was heard from the bottom of the moat, and then the darkness remained mute.

XIII. Eavesdropping

Signor Johann Spurzheim was asleep in the alcove with which we are familiar. He had not yet quit his house in the Largo del Mercato to live in the palace of the Ministers of State, which was his official residence henceforth. He was comfortable there, in that old obscure house, in that remote quarter. He still had certain little affairs to settle, which did not require daylight.

He was asleep. By the glow of his night-light, very close to his deathly pale face, you would have been able to make out the black hairy head of a little English spaniel, exactly similar to the one that poor Barbe's last convulsion had strangled. There had been no change in the room. The armchair in which Barbe, and afterwards Pier Falcone, had been accustomed to sit was still at the foot of the bed. The cord communicating with the upper floor was similarly within reach of his hand. But neither Barbe nor Doctor Pier Falcone would ever sit down again in the armchair, and at the appeal of the little bell, neither Privato the unfortunate poet nor Beccafico the soft tenor came any longer.

If nothing changed in the material entourage of the worthy Signor Johann Spurzheim, the personnel of his friends and servants, by contrast, changed a great deal and frequently. He used them up rapidly.

Before Pier Falcone there had been many other confidants and many other favorites. After Pier Falcone, he counted on having many more. He had a hundred years of life in him, and his destiny was to bury everyone.

In fact, recent events had galvanized his weakness somewhat. For two days he had been able to get up and take a few steps in his room. There was better, and the particular disposition of his mind exaggerating the respite in his malady, Signor Johann Spurzheim was not far from regarding himself as one of the most robust and agile men in the Kingdom of the Two Sicilies.

All was going well. He had broken or driven away his enemies. The King only saw through his eyes. Within a courtier's memory, such ministerial power had not been seen in Naples.

One often pays the price in repose for such splendid victories. Once, that honest Johann, like all good consciences, at least slept tranquilly. Tonight, fever was agitating him: his thin limbs were wriggling under the bedclothes. He was talking in his dreams, and, by the vacillating glow of the night-light, which was about to go out, one could have seen droplets of sweat on his temples.

"Yes, Barbe, yes, my good and dear companion," he murmured, thinking that he could even deceive the dead, "it was that infamous Sicilian who did everything. Why did you grant him so much confidence? But he's been well punished, Barbe, my beloved wife. They've killed him out there. He won't poison anyone else."

Johann Spurzheim had a letter open on the night table. That letter contained a part of the details given by the poor improviser to his audience in the Strada di Porto. Johann knew, in consequence, everything that had happened in the mountains. He shuddered in his dream several times.

"Leave me alone, Barbe! Leave me alone!" he pronounced, in a fearful voice. Then, breathing forcefully: "That Maria that you detested, because she was beautiful, because she had taken your place and your happiness, it's to avenge you that I'm marrying her."

He fell silent. The vision had doubtless disappeared, for he was calmer. One might only have heard him murmuring, in a scarcely intelligible voice: "Seven days! The seven days have already passed!"

Then the dream changed. The agitation returned.

"I know! I know!" he said, in a hoarse tone. "They haven't all gone. I've searched for them, but they're hiding underground...they've threatened the King...they've threatened me...they're there...still! Still!"

Three hours after midnight chimed on the clock on the mantelpiece.

As if Johann Spurzheim's last words had evoked phantoms, the door that communicated with Barbe de Monteleone's study opened soundlessly. Two men emerged from the corridor carrying a voluminous object in their arms. The two men had faces veiled by pieces of black cloth. They stopped, and listened.

"He's asleep," said one of them. We would have been able to recognize that high-pitched voice. Signor Johann was right. They had not all gone!

The second unknown made a sign to the first to shut up. They deposited the object against the wall. It was a painting.

They searched the paneling with their eyes. The night-light was scarcely producing any illumination now.

"There's the nail!" said the one who had not yet spoken, however.

They immediately set to work again, seizing and rotating the picture in order to attach it to the wall. The indecisive glow of the night-light illuminated vaguely the pale and regular features of a woman's face. As soon as the painting was in place, the two men disappeared. One might have heard them sniggering in the corridor.

Johann was no longer talking. The dog had ducked under the bedclothes.

The lamp flickered. When it threw out the last bright ray that precedes the end, the austere face of Barbe Spurzheim seemed to emerge from the somber canvas.

At first light, Johann Spurzheim awoke. He rubbed his eyes, thinking that he was still dreaming. The portrait of his dead wife had quit the study in order to come into his bedroom. There was devilry in that.

But the daylight was increasing. Johann was brave in the daylight.

"They're there!" he murmured, as he had already done in his dream. "Still there! But I'm stronger than them, and I'll break them!"

As the light brightened, Johann distinguished a white strip underneath the portrait. He raised himself up in his elbow in order to see better. Gradually, he realized that the strip bore characters. Then the characters became legible. The white strip bore these words, written in the alphabet of the Silence:

$$II^2M^2O \ AA^5ENA^5A^4CL^2A^5I^3 \ RI^2 \ MI^2DOI^3I^2E^2I^2 \ ENA^5A^4!$$

Habituated as he was to spelling out those signs, Johann pronounced in a tremulous voice: "Today is the seventh day!"

Then he added secretly, while a frisson ran through his entire body: *So I only dreamed that it had passed!*

He agitated his bell-cord violently. The roof of his bed opened as before.

"What's new, Chiappolo?" he asked.

"Nothing, Excellency," replied the successor to our friend Beccafico.

At the same time, the tray descended, laden with correspondence. Johann opened the first letter that came to hand. It was written on mourning stationery. It only contained the words: *Today is the seventh day.*

"Oho!" he said rediscovering his sly smile. "Do the good folk think they can play with me? Wasted effort, my children, wasted effort! You can imitate poor Barbe's handwriting, but the dead don't write any more than they talk..."

He interrupted himself, and his bones creaked, so violent was the somersault he experienced. A voice had just murmured in his curtains:

"Today is the seventh day!"

"Is it you who spoke, Chiappolo, you rogue?" he cried.

"No, signor," came the voice from the floor above,

"And you didn't hear anything?"

"Nothing, signor."

Johann made an effort to pull himself together, but he had gooseflesh. His voice trembled when he said to his invisible interlocutor: "Send Signor Aurelio Caffarelli to me immediately."

The tray rose up again, and the trapdoor closed again.

It is not customary to introduce new characters in dramas so close to the denouement, but it is necessary for us to do as Signor Johann Spurzheim does, and replace the servants he loses.

Chiappolo had taken Beccafico's place. Aurelio Caffarelli was filling the functions of Doctor Pier Falcone. He came in after a few minutes.

He was a young man. Johann did not like old men. He was a gentleman. Johann had a liking for the nobility. He was tall, with a strong complexion, already ruined by debauchery. Johann needed people whose own vices could be put between their teeth like a bit.

Johann had chosen that man with particular care. The present task was rude and difficult. Among the bad lots of the Neapolitan nobility, Aurelio Caffarelli was perhaps the only one who suited Johan Spurzheim perfectly. There were two reasons for that. Firstly, Caffarelli, in spite of his ruination, had retained a certain pride. He remained a friend of the foremost members of the court. In the second place, Caffarelli was in love with Dona Angélie Doria—hopelessly, it is true, but hope that can be reborn at the right moment is one of the most powerful levers that intrigue can employ,

Johann was content with his Caffarelli. He regarded him as an umbrageous horse not yet completely tamed, but he thought himself too skillful a horseman to fear the bucking of that impetuous charger.

"Well, my dear Excellency," said Caffarelli, as he entered, in a detached tone, "How goes the health this morning?"

"Sit down, Aurelio," replied the Minister of State. "We have a lot of work to do. I'll inform you first of one thing: it's today that you'll recover you name or fortune...or never."

"My dear signor," replied the gentleman, sprawling nonchalantly in the armchair, "my fortune is in great need of recovery...all the more so as a lost two thousand ducats yesterday evening to the Tuscan ambassador...but I don't know that my name has ever been debased."

He crossed his legs, fixing his bold eyes on the Minister of State.

"Two thousand ducats, Aurelio, my child!" said the later. "And how will you pay that, I beg you?"

"I was counting on Your Excellency."

"On me? By what entitlement?"

Caffarelli lowered his eyes and almost blushed. The word he was about to pronounce, it was evident, wounded his mouth in advance.

He replied, however: "In the quality of a friend."

Johann smiled. "Holy Trinity!" he exclaimed. "That's an honor to which poor Johann Spurzheim is far from pretending. The amity of the noble Aurelio des Caffarelli, comte, vicomte, baron...without domains, it's true...but the proudest idler who has been beating the pavement of the Via Toledo for ten years."

Aurelio stood up, his lips pursed and his brows furrowed.

"Sit down," said Johann, severely. "If you take the attitude of a braggart with me, I doubt that we'll ever make anything of you, my poor fellow."

"By San Gennaro...!" the gentleman commenced.

Johann interrupted him. "Peace!" And, as Aurelio opened his mouth again: "Peace, I tell you! If you say one more word, you'll instantly become the Aurelio Caffarelli of last week, ruined, doomed, no longer even having what's necessary to sell his soul to the Devil."

"And if I shut up?" said the fallen nobleman, with a cynical smile.

"I'll intercede," replied Johann, his eyes fixed on the other's, "for the Devil to buy you at a good price."

Aurelio sat down. "Let's hear the price," he said.

Johann tried to sit up. As he moaned and became impatient, Caffarelli came to his aid with an ill grace, and arranged the pillow behind his back.

Instead of thanking him, Johann said: "You're not adroit, young man. I wouldn't want you for a valet de chambre. No ill humor, I beg you; I hold your future in my hand. I know you; there's something in you stronger than pride, and that's the desire to live...I mean to live well."

"When it pleases you to explain...," Aurelio commenced.

"You're right, this time!" snapped the Minister of State. "I explain myself when it pleases me and not otherwise." Then, instead of going on, he said: "Signor Caffarelli, are you familiar the story of Cardinal Richelieu, the minister of King Louis XIII of France?"

"Well enough."

"You're smiling! France is a great country...we're a very petty kingdom. But in sum, a king is a king, provided that he is the master of his domain, and, all proportions maintained, I, whom am speaking to you, am more powerful in Naples than the terrible Cardinal Richelieu was in Paris. Now, Cardinal Richelieu did not put on gloves to cut off the heads of gentlemen. That was his surest means. He had another: when the gentlemen did what he wanted, he recompensed them like the king he was.

"I have a whim to have you as a servant, Aurelio Caffarelli. I will use against you, at your choice, one of the two means employed by my illustrious colleague."

"Times have changed...," the gentleman wanted to say.

"Elsewhere, perhaps. In Naples, no."

"Well then, by San Gennaro, monsignor cardinal," cried the gentleman, brazenly, "since we were talking just now about pacts with the Devil, let's bargain and not get annoyed about it."

Johann held out his skeletal hand to him.

"Good," he said, "with his feline smile. You are, in sum, an intelligent fellow. I would have regretted having you punished. Listen to me carefully. You have a cousin who is an archdeacon at the cathedral. It's necessary that this very evening, I am the husband of Maria des Amalfi, Comtesse de Monteleone."

"But they say that she's mad," objected Caffarelli.

"They're right, but that obstacle ought not to stop us."

"However, civil law and religious law both forbid..."

"You're very strong on the law, Aurelio. Your cousin will have the first vacant miter."

"And me?"

"You'll have your former manor of Sorrento and the Villa Maffei."

"Good. Excellency you'll be married. Permit me, however, to make an observation, in your interest..."

"Don't concern yourself with my interest, Aurelio. Everything is foreseen, everything will proceed. Monteleone's widow is in my house...mad, as you say, and guarded by another madwoman. If you know the prodigy of politics and skill I've employed in this negotiation…but we'd don't have time to waste with unnecessary words…"

"Let me, however, signor, talk to you about the woman in the Folquieri house…the centenarian. The King is looking for her."

"When it is time," replied Johan Spurzheim, with a smile, "the King will find her."

Aurelio made a gesture translatable by the proverbial Biblical locution: *I wash my hands of it.*

The Minister of State went on: "Your manor of Sorrento and the Villa Maffei will not make you a great lord, Caffarelli."

"It's the wherewithal to gamble and win…"

"Or lose. I know a fortune with which you could gamble for a whole human life, always losing, without ever ruining oneself."

"A fine fortune, Excellency. There's only one similar in Naples, and that's my cousin Lorédan Doria's."

"I know a woman," the Minister of State continued, "for whom you would once have given no matter what fortune…even that of your cousin Lorédan Doria."

Caffarelli's eyes glittered, and then lowered, while a sudden pallor appeared on his face. "Let's not talk about that, signor," he murmured.

"What!" said Johann, in a compassionate tone. "Are you still amorous, friend Aurelio?"

"I beg you, let's not talk about that," the gentleman repeated, in an altered voice. At the same time, he stood up and traversed the room, heading for the window, which he opened.

The window overlooked the gardens. Facing him, there was a large plane tree. The inclined trunk approached so close to the window that one would have been able to touch it by extending a hand.

Johann followed Caffarelli with a fixed and mocking gaze.

Another one we hold, he thought.

Aurelio leaned out of the window; his forehead was shining. The garden was deserted.

Johann continued, aloud: "It's a strange thing, friend. The two most beautiful things in Naples, the fortune of the Dorias and Angélie's hand, are inseparable. One can't conquer one without the other. But I, whom am speaking, am powerful enough to give both to the man who serves me faithfully."

Caffarelli turned round swiftly. "On my soul," he pronounced, between clenched teeth, "I believe you don't know me very well, Excellency. With me, mockery is dangerous."

"Come back here, poor fool that you are," pronounced Johann placidly. "Why would I mock? I'm proposing a bargain in which we'd both gain…you more than me, but that's justice, since you're poorer than me. Respond seriously and frankly: would you like to be the husband of Angélie Doria?"

The gentleman, who had just sat down again, could not find words. His hands came together involuntarily; passion survived in the ravaged heart.

While Johann waited, the foliage of the large plane tree quivered suddenly. The Minister of State and his companion looked in the direction of the window.

"The wind...?" Johann commenced, his physiognomy suspicious and anxious.

"No," Caffarelli replied. "The ground is trembling today all around Vesuvius."

Johann was satisfied with that explanation, and his face became serene again. The foliage of the plane tree only quivered once.

"I believe I understand," the Minister of State went on, "that I just caused a string to vibrate in you. You're in love; I knew that before interrogating you. And it's that unfortunate amour, that hopeless amour, that has thrown you into the foolish life in which you've lost your wealth, while compromising your escutcheon..."

"Signor!"

"I'm speaking—shut up. Can't you listen to the truth when someone is bringing you both material and moral rehabilitation? You can be happy if you wish, Aurelio Caffarelli. I'll modify my question and ask: what would you do in order to buy the hand of Angélie Doria?"

"Anything," replied the gentleman, without hesitation.

"That's good. Then let's examine the facts. There is a mortal hatred between Lorédan Doria and the young man who is now called Comte Giuliano di Monteleone."

"Does he not have the right to bear that name?"

"That doesn't matter. He has to die today."

Aurelio shivered in his armchair.

"You have an interest in that," Johann went on, coldly. "Angélie Doria loves him. But he ought not to die alone; he needs a companion. That companion is Comte Lorédan."

"Lorédan?" repeated the gentleman, with an astonished repugnance.

"You have an interest in that," Johann repeated, in the same glacial tone. "Comte Doria will never accord you the hand of his sister. But don't go making phantoms for yourself, friend. I don't know why honest men like you immediately think of murder. It's a matter of a duel, only a matter of a duel. For six days, a barrier has been placed between those two champions, who are looking for one another. Today, that barrier will fall, that's all."

"But it's a misunderstanding that caused their hatred," said Caffarelli. "A word of explanation would make all that fall."

"It's precisely to prevent the explanation that I need you, friend," Johann replied.

A few dry leaves fell from the high branches of the plane tree. Johann only directed a distracted glance in that direction. The stormy wind that had died down toward the end of the night was beginning to get up again.

"Have you maintained relations with Lorédan Doria?" Johann asked.

"Relations at court, yes."

"And have you forged links with Julian de Monteleone?"

"Certainly...he's the star of the moment."

"A bright star," muttered the Minister of State. "A shooting star!" He raised himself up on his bed. "I engage you to redouble your attention now. I thought at first of facilitating the possibility of a duel between them, and I was counting on you for that...but the idea is worthless. Before putting oneself on guard on the terrain, a few words can be exchanged, and I don't want a single word to be exchanged."

"It seems difficult to me...," Aurelio tried to say.

Johann made a gesture of impatience. "Where would my superiority over you be," he murmured, "If I didn't know how to deliver coups that seem difficult to you? Lorédan believes that Julian has abducted Angélie, doesn't he?"

"That's the public rumor."

"Julian is convinced that Lorédan has abducted Céleste?"

"So it's said."

Johan sniggered.

"What is necessary, then, to set them in action?" he went on. "Let Lorédan know Angélie's retreat; denounce to Julian the place where Céleste is a prisoner. As Angélie's retreat and Céleste's are the same place..."

"By Heaven!" the gentleman interjected. "That's an infernal conception!"

Johann rubbed his hands, as if he had just been paid a flattering compliment.

"I can see you understand, friend," he said.

"I understand that if they encountered one another," Aurelio replied, "each of them would say: There's the kidnapper!'"

"*In flagrante delicto!*" Johann emphasized, joyfully.

"I understand," finished Caffarelli, "that if they had swords..."

"Ah!" cried the Minister of State. "That's the crux of the matter: it's necessary that they have swords."

For several seconds, something veritably strange had been happening facing the open window. The large plane tree was no longer quivering and no longer shedding dry leaves, but an object was sliding slowly along its trunk.

From outside, at a certain distance, you would have seen something like a gigantic caterpillar in human form, for it was scarcely probable that a man could climb on that smooth bark head-down. The caterpillar had its head down. From Johann's bedroom one could not perceive that colossal insect or monkey of an unknown species as yet, whose head remained slightly above the top of the casement. Having arrived there, it ceased descending. For a few seconds, it remained completely motionless. Then its head, which seemed stuck to the bark, only showing its bushy hair, was detached slowly.

The face of our good comrade Cucuzone, reddened by the violent position he was retaining, appeared among the streaming wisps of his hair. His eyes and ears were alert.

As we know, he professed the opinion that people exchanging confidences are never suspicious of the top of casements. Fortunate are those who possess the confidence of their métier!

The voices had risen; Cucuzone had been able to hear the latter part of the conversation that we have just transcribed. He stopped at the moment when Johann said: "It's necessary that they have swords."

Cucuzone maintained his position for about ten minutes. It was necessary to be Cucuzone to achieve that. In that interval of ten minutes he heard the final instructions given by the Minister of State to his new factotum.

Aurelio Caffarelli had first to go to the Palazzo Doria, and then the former Palazzo Coriolani, occupied by Julian de Monteleone. His mission was the same in each instance. He did not even have to envenom their hatred. Each of them was looking for his sister. It was simply a matter of saying to each of them: *Your sister is in such and such a place.*" It was then a matter of giving each of them a means of evading the surveillance of the King's private police, who, if forewarned, would try to prevent an encounter. It was a matter, finally, of doing it in such a way that Lorédan and Julian were both armed. Caffarelli took charge of obtaining that triple result.

Johann had simplified the situation in a few words: "As long as either of them is alive, there will be an insurmountable barrier between you and Angélie."

Aurelio left Johann's bedroom at ten o'clock in the morning, promising to return as soon as his task was accomplished. As the door closed on him, Johann had a kind of vision; he saw a dark mass slide down the tree with the rapidity of a falling stone. He stopped rubbing his hands. Then he started trembling in all his limbs, because he had just heard, in the garden, the cry of a particular species that has already struck our ears so many times.

Cucuzone traversed paths and bushes on his feet, on his hands and on his head, lending himself to gymnastics with a joyful heart. He was content, the worthy fellow, like a bloodhound that had fallen on a trail.

Having arrived at the garden wall, which went along the alley where Peter-Paulus Brown, English subject, had made his fantastic run a few days before, he braced himself and reached the top with a single leap; with another, he landed on the paving-stones of the street.

As her arrived in the Piazza del Mercato, he saw Aurelio Caffarelli on the threshold of the police house, searching with his eyes for a carriage. He made a sign. A broad-shouldered fellow who was occupying the seat of a cab and whose face was hidden by a broad-brimmed hat, immediately set his horses trotting. Two or three other carriages set off at the same time, but the coachman,

Cucuzone's friend, said to them placidly: "I want that cavalier. The first one that moves, I'll knock out."

His rivals stopped and drew back. Some said: "It's necessary not to tangle with that brute Ruggieri!"

Aurelio no longer had a choice. He climbed into the cab driven by Ruggieri. Cucuzone climbed on to the rear.

It was about three o'clock in the afternoon when the cab returned to the Piazza del Mercato. Aurelio Caffarelli got down from it in order to give Johann an account of his mission.

"At nightfall," he said, on reentering the bedroom where the Minister of State was waiting, "Lorédan Doria and Julian de Monteleone will encounter one another above the Camaldoli."

"Armed?"

"Armed," the gentleman replied.

"And measures have been taken for them both to stay there?"

Aurelio nodded silently.

"Good!" cried Johann. "I feel as strong as a Hercules today. I want to see that... yes, I want to see that."

He ordered the preparation of his Sedan chair, and could not help adding: "What progress my health is making! Will I not live for a century!"

While Signor Johann's chair was being made ready, the cab driven by Ruggieri set off at a gallop along the road to the Camaldoli.

Cucuzone had changed his place. Quitting the rear bench, he had installed himself on the cushions inside, where he was sleeping like a saint.

XIV. Two Madwomen

Johann Spurzheim had told his new confidant Aurelio Caffarelli the truth in speaking about Monteleone's widow and the centenarian of the Folquieri house; it was one madwoman who was guarding another. Old age, and perhaps remorse, had obscured Berta Giudicelli's intelligence a long time ago.

Maria des Amalfi had lost her reason again at the Villa Floridiana at the moment that the evidence forced her to bring down the murderer of Mario Monteleone, Prince Fulvio Coriolani, in spite of the fact that her heart went out to him involuntarily. Maria des Amalfi was mad. And since then, Signor Johann Spurzheim had not dared to confront her with his presence. He had faith in Doctor Daniel's principle that madness remembers madness.

He said to himself: *Now she'll recognize me as the man who came to disturb her sleep on the night of the thirteenth of October 1815, the man who made use of her as a mortal instrument to deliver the fatal blow to Comte Mario Monteleone!*

But that dread had not caused him to renounce his designs. In Naples, religious marriages have civil force. How long does it take to contract a marriage, when one is able to substitute for certain formalities and has a complaisant priest in hand? A few minutes. During those few minutes one can disguise one's face. Would not the witnesses to those sacrilegious acts, in any case, be gained in advance? No one had seen Maria des Amalfi since the scene in the Villa Floridiana; no one could say: "One such and such a day, at such and such an hour, she was mad." The act would create faith. The ambitious dream of that man, who had had everything against him, including his health, a death was about to realize.

He was on the point of winning that impossible game, engaged from such a low position, without any weapons other than his imperturbable perversity. A few more hours and that man, already the favorite of a King, would have made himself the heir of the noblest title in the land of Naples and two of the greatest fortunes there were in Italy.

For it is necessary not to forget that once Lorédan and Julian were dead, nothing stood in his way but Céleste and Angélie. Two young women! Two young women who were in his power.

There was one more obstacle: that was Aurelio Caffarelli, heaped with promises, but we know, via Pier Falcone, poor Barbe and others, what Johann did with instruments that had become unnecessary to him.

It is in Barbe de Monteleone's bedroom that we rediscover Maria des Amalfi and old Berta, her companion.

Signor Johann was sheltered from any vain scruple. He had put the murdered Monteleone's widow in the poisoned Barbe's bed.

As for old Berta, it is necessary to admit that it would have been very easy to make her disappear, but Berta did not know the name of Barbe Monteleone's accomplice. She had only ever had dealings with Barbe in the matter of the abduction of the children. It was Barbe who had given her instructions before the crime, and Barbe who had paid her afterwards. It would doubtless have required very little to put her on the track, but that very little could only be done by Monteleone's widow; now, Maria des Amalfi, when she had her reason, did not know anything; and Johann hid himself from her during her hours of madness.

Given the felonious character of Johann Spurzheim, however, it is certain that he would not have confronted that danger, slight as it was, without a reason. In any given circumstances, even supposing a sudden and unexpected reawakening of intelligence in Maria des Amalfi, old Berta, old Berta could serve as a scapegoat; she can take upon herself alone all the weight of past iniquities, and, in consequence, all the punishment. It was a reserve, or, if you wish, an open back door, for escape in case of a battle lost.

The two recluses had already been together for several days in the apartment of the late Barbe Spurzheim; they had recognized one another at first glance. Maria des Amalfi had been seized by horror and alarm at the sight of the woman who had been her tyrant for such a long time; on the contrary, the centenarian had experienced a sentiment of imbecilic joy. Her slave had been recovered. But, when the first moment had passed, she had become anxious. Since her departure from the Martorello, various events had struck her very vividly: firstly, her malady, and the order given to her by the priest to go and confess everything to the King; afterwards, the successive encounters with her three victims. She had seen, on the same night, the elder Monteleone, the second son, Julian, and Céleste, the idol of the father and the mother.

She was already no longer resolute in evil, as before. She had a vague remorse. As the same time, that extinct sentiment, the respect of a vassal for her lords, was reborn confusedly in the depths of her troubled conscience.

It is necessary for the reader not to misunderstand: all of that was indecisive, clouded and vacillating, like the impressions of early childhood; but it existed, in the limbo of that already dead intelligence. If the perversity survived, it was only out of habit.

Sometimes, you might have surprised her contemplating Maria des Amalfi while she slept. Something stirred in that human sepulcher. As there are no words made expressly for that supreme nullity, we are employing the words of ordinary language; we are saying: remorse, sentiment, respect, and we shall even add tenderness. But it is necessary to lower everything those words express to the intellectual and moral stature of the poor worn-out individual who had once been a woman, to the stature of Berta Giudicelli. They were the intermittent and smoky gleams of a lamp that is about to go out for lack of oil.

She had been given a spinning-wheel. She spun. While she spun, she sometimes sang, in a tremulous and broken voice, the old songs of the Calabrian region. Then, Maria des Amalfi, forgetting her fears, came to kneel beside her like a child. She listened, and then she wept.

Today, Maria des Amalfi was asleep, lying fully-dressed on her bed. Berta was spinning. It was four o'clock in the afternoon. Berta had already got up twice to go to the widow Monteleone and watch her sleeping. When she came back to sit down for the third time, she said: "I must go speak to the King!"

That was her refrain, and it was sufficient to put her conscience to sleep momentarily, as opium, disguise under the name of "Benin paste," calms the patient coughing of consumptives temporarily.

She took hold of the handle of her spinning wheel and started the rotation of her spindle.

"Oh," she said, without her petrified physiognomy expressing the slightest compassion, "That one has suffered a great deal. She was smiling and beautiful the day they put the crown of orange-blossom on her head. And no pride! She gave a friendly kiss to all the young women of the valley. That was a long time ago...a long time! And I too have suffered a great deal!"

The movement of her spinning wheel had a metronomic regularity. Suddenly, she stopped spinning. She rummaged in her pocket and took out a little box. In the box there was an object wrapped in paper. She unfolded the paper. Gold coins fell out on to her apron. They were the double ounces from the embroidered purse that Prince Fulvio Coriolani had left a few days before in the Folquieri house. She darted a sly glance toward the bed to see whether the noise might have woken her companion. Maria des Amalfi was still asleep: a feverish slumber, but profound. The old woman started to smile at the gold coins. She palpated them, one after another; she counted them; she caressed them. Gold: that was the demon that had doomed her; her, the poor old woman, who was about to die under the weight of the years, miserably, and having not yet slaked the puerile and terrible passion that damns two thirds of the human species! For several minutes, she remained as if absorbed in her contemplation, and then she said: "Barbe also gave me gold!"

Her wrinkles creased, and a darker cloud descended over her forehead.

"I must go speak to the King," she murmured.

The gold was warbling in the folds of her apron. She smiled at it again.

I've seen them all, she thought, distracted and amused by her treasure, *the mother, who is here... the elder son, who left these alms... the two young ones for whom it was destined. Did they know that he was their brother?*

At that moment, the widowed Comtesse de Monteleone stirred in her sleep.

"Fulvio...Fulvio!" she murmured.

There were tears in her voice. The old woman laughed stupidly, and muttered: "It's Mario she means. His name is Mario!"

Her hand touched the handle of her spinning-wheel, but she did not put it in motion.

"Mario!" she said, in a pensive tone. "Julian! Céleste! I remember all those names. Why have I forgotten things that are closer to us, and also the things most distant? I never think about my daughter, who died happy between her husband and her children. I always think of my daughter's daughter...Bianca! My last love! The remains of my heart!"

Her eyelids fluttered as if she still had a tear for that heart-rending memory.

"Bianca!" she went on. "Bianca..so beautiful, so young, so beloved, A great honor was given to her; she was her young master's nurse...Mario's nurse. The eldest of the Monteleones! And Barbe offered us money...money! Bianca didn't want it...Bianca my poor angel!"

She uttered a deep sigh before going on.

"But she started going out at night! At that age, it isn't money that tempts..." She interrupted herself with a savage energy. "Oh, if I knew him, the man who seduced her, who killed my Bianca!"

A little blood had risen to her cheeks; her eyes were burning amid her wrinkles. It was just a flash; all that disappeared.

"He hid himself, the tempter!" she murmured. "Bianca died without wanting to tell me his name...I was never able to avenge her."

That is the idea that survives everything else in Italian souls.

At that moment, Maria des Amalfi raised herself up on her elbow and uttered a loud cry. Then she leapt out if the bed, utterly disheveled.

"I've seen them!" she cried. "All three of them! All three of them...and I've seen the murderer who wants to kill them as he killed their father!"

She was under the impression of the nightmare that had enfevered her recent slumber. Her tottering footsteps took her toward the window. The window overlooked the courtyard where Johann Spurzheim's valets, in accordance with the orders transmitted by Aurelio Caffarelli, were preparing the Sedan chair. Maria des Amalfi continued, while walking: "He's there! He must be there! It's there that my dream showed him to me!"

Berta quit her spinning-wheel to go to her.

A terrible cry escaped the throat of the Comtesse, who put her hands over her eyes as if to flee a frightful vision.

"There he is! There he is!" she said.

Johann Spurzheim, sustained by two valets, was descending the perron of his house in order to reach his Sedan chair.

Old Berta put her eye to the window.

"I recognize that man!" she said, as if talking to herself

The Comtesse drew away in horror. "Ah!" she said, her voice like a death-rattler. "You recognize David Heimer!"

Berta repeated: "David Heimer!"

And, madwomen as they were, their gazes full of distraction met.

Berta pressed her forehead in two hands. "Where's my memory?" she murmured.

"Me, I remember! Me, I remember!" said the Comtesse. "It was that night. He came to my room and said to me: 'Would you like to avenge yourself on the man who has taken all your happiness?'" She interrupted herself with a heart-rending plaint: "My children! My poor children!"

"David Heimer!" repeated Berta, again. Then she added: "I saw him one evening talking to Bianca, my daughter's daughter!"

The Comtesse made an effort to pull herself away. She fell on the floor.

"Yes, yes…," she pronounced, between clenched teeth. "Bianca…Bianca Giudicelli…the infidel nurse…the child-stealer…David Heimer's mistress!"

The bent figure of the centenarian creaked as it suddenly straightened. Her eyes blazed. She only said one word: "Him!"

Then she seized the staff that had supported her during her long journey ad headed for the door.

"And me! And me!" cried the Comtesse, making an effort to get up. "He's going to kill them! He's going to kill my children! God told me so in a dream!"

Berta retraced her steps. She knelt down beside her mistress.

"Widow of Mario Monteleone," she pronounced, in a loud voice, "Support yourself on my arm. The strength I have isn't mine; it's Jesus, son of Mary, who is giving it to me. I shall defend you; I shall avenge you; I shall die!"

She extended one hand to the Comtesse; with the other, she put her rosary to her lips, saying: "I'm very old…but I am the punishment that walks. Where he is, I shall be!"

She drew Maria des Amalfi as far as the courtyard. There, Johann's valets tried to bar their passage. She took the box containing the gold coins—those dear gold coins—out of her pocket. She scattered them on the pavement.

"The King is waiting for me!" she said, with a singular authority. "My hours are counted henceforth. Woe betide anyone who puts himself between the King and me!"

XV. Speaking Arms

It was a striking spectacle made to inspire terror.

The sky, striped with wide bands of violent colors, presented one of those aspects that painters dare not render, fearing the imbecilic criticism of the vulgar, for the vulgar always say, on seeing something reproduced by the brush or the pen that they do not know: "That's a lie!"

The clouds, violet, green, orange and the color of blood, superimposed their symmetrical bands. On the horizon, there was fire. The sun was setting. Opposite the setting sun the giant loomed up who laid his heavy hand one day on Herculaneum and Pompeii, the buried towns: Vesuvius.

Vesuvius had its own atmosphere and its own meteorological conditions, which did not resemble the rest of the sky. It was a mass of opaque, heavy vapors, rolled up into twisted clouds, like those that emerge from the mouth of a cannon. The crests of those clouds were fringed with silver and crimson, depending on whether the light was coming from above or below. Streaks of lightning, in sparkling zigzags, were incessantly traversing that mass of darkness, the depths of which were thus illuminated bizarrely. But no sound of thunder could be heard.

The sound of thunder was confounded with the strange din of the mountain. There were immense murmurs, powerful voices growling, and seeming to envelop the city. The wind was no longer blowing. The earth was trembling, as if the boiling lava were there, beneath the feet of the spectators.

They were numerous, the spectators. The four hundred thousand inhabitants of Naples were there, dispersed on the slopes of hills or grouped on the terraces of houses. They were waiting, motionless and mute. They knew full well that the drama was only in its prologue. The lava had not yet overflowed.

They were there, the four hundred thousand spectators of Naples, and four hundred thousand others dispersed in the surrounding countryside, in the towns, in the islands, on the sea—everywhere—for the amphitheater around such tragedies is large. They were there, waiting for the lava. In the port, the yardarms of ships were bending under the weight of sailors. Everywhere, there was a supreme emotion and a devouring curiosity.

The volcanic glow became more intense as night fell. Strange radiances seemed to be passing through the smoke and projecting a blinding light over the slope of the mountain that faced Naples. The rest of the volcano stood out in silhouette.

There as one place above all that seemed to be radiant with its own almost supernatural light. It was there that the eruption was expected. All gazes went in that direction. It was the area comprised between the planes and mouths of 1794, in the southern part of the mountain, above the Camaldoli.

Strangely enough, no human creature was visible on the entre extent of the mountain, except in the place marked for the ultimate catastrophe. With telescopes, one could distinguish men who were moving out there. And as the mouths of the volcano reddened, the number of those men increased.

At the moment of the flux, the wind rose. The mass of smoke that was above the mouths began to oscillate. Stones and incandescent lumps were already being launched to great heights.

On all sides the words ran around: "The lava is about to overflow! The lava is about to overflow!"

Among the ships in the port there was one that was about to depart. That was the *Pausilippe*, out of Marseille. It was beginning its preparatory maneuvers, slowed down by the curiosity of the sailors. The deck of the *Pausilippe* was cluttered with passengers. Among them, two stood out by virtue of their fine clothing and the powerful telescopes that they were aiming at the volcano. We hope that the reader will be able to overcome his emotion on learning that those two passengers were Peter-Paulus Brown of Cheapside and his wife Penelope, both escaped safe and sound from the terrible dangers of their excursion to the mountains.

Certainly, it is not without profound regret that we pass over in silence the Odyssey of the two spouses in southern Italy. That would require several volumes, animated from the first line to the last, by the fine hilarity that the English do not have, but to which they generally give birth in others, similar in that to the unfortunate Pagliacci, a melancholy nature whose métier is always to make laughter.

Let it suffice for us to know that the brigands, after being convinced of their error on the subject of the famous diamond, the Punjab, had set Peter-Paulus, Penelope, Melicerta and Jack free, with their seventy-five packages.

Penelope's rancor against the officer, the huge Colonel San-Severo, was certainly betrayed by a few bitter remarks, but in sum, she was content with the majority of the brigands, who had shown themselves to be sufficiently shocking. She retained in her tender memory the names of five or six rogues who were bold with the ladies.

As for Peter-Paulus, he had seen things that left far behind the horrible story of the Cadaver. Until the end of his days, he would swing his nose and blow out his cheeks in recounting to the members of the Cotton and International Club his prodigious adventures in the caverns of southern Italy.

The other Brown—there are twenty-two thousand Browns in England—the true possessor of the Punjab diamond, succeeded in selling a copy to the King of Denmark. He kept the original at the disposal of his very gracious sovereign,

Queen Victoria,[65] in return for two hundred thousand pounds sterling. He is an alderman somewhere.

Before quitting that "detestable country," Peter-Paulus would certainly have liked to see the destruction of some important locale by the lava, but he bandied about his entitlement as an English subject in vain; the master of the *Pausilippe* lifted anchor with the tide.

Penelope went down to her cabin and opened her notebook. Her voyage was recounted her in these terms:

Kingdom of Naples. Southern provinces. Mountains. Forests, Caverns. I was noticed by several brigand captains. Their timidity. Various colors of hair. Ugliness of the women.

She wrote beneath:

Naples. Eruption of Vesuvius, volcano situated near that city. I observed it with my telescope from the deck of the ferry. A few male passengers noticed me. Female passengers ugly. Chinese shadows that move in the glow of the eruption.

The ferry had emerged from the harbor and was propelled by a good breeze. When Penelope went back on deck, Vesuvius was no more than a red dot on the horizon.

Peter-Paulus said to her: "I forbid you to say that we left this country before the end of the cataclysm…formally!"

For the first time in her life, Penelope shared her husband's opinion. Mel and Jack were summoned and bribed. In the reception room of Marjoram and Watergruel, there is now a painting by S. W. Thomas, esquire, representing Vesuvius in eruption. Close to the mouths are standing Peter-Paulus, in a black suit, Penelope, dressed in pink, Mel and Jack. They are striking. That canvas has made the reputation of Vesuvius in the environs of Cheapside.

The darkness was thickening. The volcano, an immense torch, incessantly brightening, was alone now in illuminating the landscape.

It is time for us to tell the reader who the human shadows were outlined in black on the luminous flank of the mountain which were exciting a curiosity as great as the eruption itself in the innumerable crowd of spectators.

Johann Spurzheim had been well served by his new lieutenant, Aurelio Caffarelli. The latter, a courtier, had presented himself successively at the Palazzo Doria and the Palazzo Coriolani, the dwelling of the young Comte Julian.

He had said to Lorédan: "Comte Julian has hidden your sister in a villa situated on the Portici road above the Camaldoli."

---

[65] As previously noted, he must have hung on to it for a long time, waiting for the monarch in question to inherit the throne.

He had repeated exactly the same sentence to Julian, changing the name of the kidnapper; it was Comte Lorédan who had abducted and sequestered Julian's sister.

We have not forgotten that Lorédan and Julian were being watched in their respective dwellings by the King's private police. It was necessary to remove that obstacle; it was also necessary for the two adversaries to be armed. Aurelio Caffarelli found a single an identical solution to the two problems He procured for Doria and for Monteleone, who both testified to him the gratitude that his zeal merited, the costumes of two officers of the guard. That was a passport to deceive the policemen, and it was also a pretext for the obligation to wear a sword.

The two Comtes succeeded in quitting their palaces at almost the same time. Lorédan emerged from the city via the Marinella, Julian by the Porto Capuana. They galloped for a quarter of an hour without encountering one another.

Julian dismounted first, because he had taken a short cut through the fields and gardens, nearer to the mouths. His frightened horse refused to go any further as soon as the wind carried the hot smoke of the volcano to its nostrils.

Lorédan was able to arrive on horseback all the way to behind the Camaldoli. There was not a soul in the neighboring fields, and all the houses situated on the southern slope of the mountain had been abandoned. Everything was, however, intact. The gardens were verdant; the houses, all opened, displayed their furniture.

The twilight was beginning to darken when Julian, who did not know the environs of Naples, started searching for a path through the deserted enclosures. The evident threat of the volcano forbade him to go to the left. To the right there were paths that formed a tangle as far as he eye could see. He was becoming embarrassed when god fortune allowed him to perceive an escort of sorts traversing the admirable clumps of lemon trees the surrounded the Villa Sant'Angela prior to the eruption of 1823.

The cortege was composed of a closed Sedan chair and four valets, who did not appear to be armed.

Julian called out and asked the way to arrive at the villa designated by Aurelio Caffarelli..

The porters ad the valets remained silent, but a voice emerged from the chair and said: "Bear right and follow that horseman who is going up ahead of you."

Julian set forth. The horseman in question was wearing the uniform of a lieutenant in the guards. Julian had doubtless forgotten that he was wearing an exactly similar costume himself.

As soon as he had gone the voice from the interior of the chair was heard again.

"Forward!" it ordered the porters. "Get as close as possible without emerging from the trees."

Those who had conversed, if only once, with Signor Johann Spurzheim, sheltered behind the walls of his famous confessional, would have had no hesitation in recognizing that voice.

At the sound of Julian's running footsteps, the horseman turned round.

By that time, night had fallen completely, but the volcano was terribly bright.

Julian and the rider uttered a great cry simultaneously.

"Wretch!" said Julian, who unsheathed his sword instinctively, as if he had done nothing else in his life.

Johann had judged him well.

Also drawing his sword, and smiling bitterly, Lorédan said: "You didn't expect to find me here."

They fell upon one another, swords in hand.

Lorédan, an accomplished horseman, was not unaware of any of the secrets of fencing. Julian, on the other hand, was a novice; but he was one of those novices that kill captains, with the heart and claws of a lion.

At the first impact he passed under Lorédan's sword and tipped him over with a blow of the guard, for the point had missed the body.

He allowed Lorédan to get to his feet.

In the clump of trees, Johann said to one of his pretended valets: "Remember, Signor Aurelio, that they must both stay there!

Lorédan got to his feet, still dazed. That alone was able to prolong a combat unequal in every respect. Doria put himself on guard and murmured: "Thank you, signor."

Then the blades clashed again.

Julian had retained all of his impetuosity. Lorédan was holding back. He parried and broke. Henceforth, there was a hesitation in him.

There were several causes for that. Firstly, there was his natural generosity; a single glance had revealed to him the inexperience of the young man who had come to give him his life. In the second place, by the increasing gleams that the crater was launching in sheaves, he had distinguished several shadows on the edge of the grove of lemon trees. One would have thought that they were men who had been posted there, and that was certainly strange, this evening, in that location.

Finally, on the slope that descended to the Portici road a few seconds before, he had seen a peasant cart harnessed to two oxen, which was advancing. The animals had their usual heavy and slow tread. From time to time they stopped, quivering, and their nostrils launched two cones of vapor, but it only required a thrust of the prod to start them moving again, because a board handing over their eyes prevented them from seeing the volcano.

On the cart there were two women: one of them, having reached the ultimate limits of age, was sitting, and holding her large staff like a scepter. The other, disheveled and very pale, was kneeling on the front of the cart and holding out her arms. It seemed that she was shouting.

That group, facing the luminous nucleus, was illuminated as in broad daylight.

There was a loud subterranean rumble. An immense sheaf of flame was launched from the mouth of the crater. In the distance, the hills, the sea and the islands emerged abruptly from the shadow.

Then, after the rain of fire, a black could of ash brought momentary darkness.

In the distance, the spectators of the prodigious conflagration made the sign of the cross and repeated: "The lava is overflowing! The lava is overflowing!"

The bells of the nearby monastery began sounding the knell. Everyone who believed in God had a prayer on the lips.

Johann Spurzheim said to Caffarelli: "It's take it or leave it. The moment has come: Angélie and fortune, or my vengeance, which is poverty and death."

Caffarelli's head was bowed.

Johann lifted the blind of his chair and held out an object that the thick shadow cast by the foliage of the lemon trees prevented from being seen distinctly. It had a form similar to a crutch.

Caffarelli took the object and wiped his forehead, which was covered with sweat.

Johann went on: "As soon as Julian de Monteleone falls under Doria's sword, aim at his heart...and you'll be a great lord."

Aurelio moved to the ultimate trunks of the grove. The combat continued.

The cart advanced. No one had heard the cries of the poor kneeling woman with the scattered hair. The frightful din of the volcano was increasing by the minute.

When the cloud of ash had dissipated, Johann and the men in the trees could see that Lorédan Doria's blood was flowing from two wounds. Anger gripped him. He began to close in on Monteleone, whose unskillful wrist was tiring.

But suddenly, the gazes of Johann and his companions were attracted by an unexpected spectacle.

A long streak of fire furrowed the south-western slope of the mountain in the direction of Torre-del-Mauro. By that new light sand brighter light a veritably fantastic cavalcade appeared.

At the head was riding, or rather devouring space, a man enveloped in a long red cloak, which was floating in the wind of his course. You might have thought him the fulgurant genius of those immense conflagrations. He was coming, flying, leaning over the neck of his horse, which seemed to be made of fire.

Behind him, other horsemen were following. The nearest of them was short in stature, and resembled a woman.

Johann's teeth clenched and chattered. "Fire, Aurelio! Fire!" he shouted—but his voice was lost in the din.

Julian broke off in his turn and drew nearer to the clump of trees where Aurelio was in ambush.

The cart suddenly stopped, and the oxen reared up. A frightful crack had torn the mountain. The mouth of the crater immediately vomited a mass of fire larger than the first.

In the surrounding area, the same cry emerged from tight hundred thousand mouths: "The lava! The lava!"

It was, in fact, the lava that was emerging.

For a minute, the cloud of ash that always follows each principal convulsion covered the scene like a thick veil. Everything disappeared: the combatants, the men in the lemon grove, the cart drawn by oxen and the cavalcade coming from Torre-del-Mauro.

Then a gust of wind chased the clouds away, and every detail of the drama became visible again, drowned in ardent light.

The cart was very close. The disheveled woman got down from it. She cried: "My son! My son!"

Julian de Monteleone, holding his sword with his arm bent, fell upon Lorédan, whose point was aimed at his heart.

Caffarelli took aim, supporting his rifle against the trunk of a tree in order to be sure of the shot.

It was the supreme moment.

Have you ever seen lightning strike? The rider in the purple cloak emerged from the clouds. His bloody spurs labored the flanks of his horse one more time, which bounded and then collapsed. The rider, seizing the saddle at the moment of the fall, by means of a bold vault, landed on his feet. He hurled himself forward at the moment when Julian and Lorédan were about to run one another through. The two swords penetrated his breast simultaneously

He did not fall.

The wind, in throwing his felt hat backwards, had revealed the noble face of Fulvio Coriolani.

"Mother," he said to the disheveled woman who was dragging herself along, gasping. "The Monteleone escutcheon was once put on my arm. I have it on my breast now. Do you recognize it?"

Julian and Lorédan had stepped back stupefied.

The two words remained planted in a saltire, funeral and speaking arms!

"My son! My son! My son!" pronounced Maria des Amalfi, three times.

Fulvio tottered.

It was Fiamma who supported him in her arms. Fiamma was the cavalier who has followed him closely along the route. Behind her came Cucuzone and Ruggieri, and then Céleste and Angélie, liberated.

The mariner and the saltarello had launched themselves into the clump of trees. Caffarelli's skull was fractured by a pistol shot.

Then Cucuzone and Ruggieri brought the litter in which Johann was lodged.

And the lava overflowed amid the prodigious conflagrations of the crater, from which a long and broad column of fire now emerged, seemingly supporting the vault of smoke tinted with bloody bronze.

The lava flowed, incandescent at first, toward the rim of the funnel, then red, then brown; it overflowed slowly, burning everything in its passage. As soon as the boiling flood touched the foot of a tree, the bark burst, the shriveled leaves writhed, and then the tree fell.

When the lava had passed, nothing remained standing.

In the distance, on the surrounding hills, on the terraces of the city, on the ships tossed by the sea—for the storm-wind had returned to the gulf—all the spectators said to one another: "What are they doing there, so close to death? They still have time to flee!"

From the nearest ridges, the man clad in purple could clearly be made out in that bright center. The others were now kneeling around him. The poor mother was still saying, her voice strangled by sobs: "My son! My son! My son!"

Lorédan was on his knees, Angélie too, her eyes lowered, her heart weak. Julian was the same, and Céleste, who was weeping.

The man in red, Il Porporato, had said: "Pray for me, mother, noble martyr! Pray for me, Lorédan, my friend of old, and you, Angélie, whom I loved so much! Pray for me, Céleste and Julian, my brother and my sister. I have sinned, but I am dying as a Monteleone ought to die."

Maria des Amalfi dragged herself as far as him. She embraced his knees.

Il Porporato bent down and placed a kiss on her forehead.

"I cannot put my arms around you, Mother," he said, "because my two hands are retaining my blood, which is my life.

Then, raising his head, he said: "Lorédan Doria, I accord you the hand of my sister; may she make you happy. Angélie Doria, I beg you to take for your husband my brother Julian. His voice trembled, but he was able to add: "May I see your hands enlaced before closing my eyes forever!"

They obeyed; the two couples were formed.

The poor mother murmured: "You can't die! You can't die!"

Il Porporato had a sad and proud smile.

"It's necessary that a Monteleone doesn't go to the scaffold, Mother," he replied. "The man whose life was a tempest ought to disappear in a clap of thunder. Lorédan, and you, Angélie, my brother and my sister will bring you a name that shame has not touched!"

"Live, Comte!" murmured Lorédan.

"Live, oh, live!" repeated Angélie.

Céleste and Julian were speechless.

Il Porporato turned his head toward the lava, which was coming. The hot wind could already be felt, and the ground was burning underfoot.

"We still have five minutes," he said. Then addressing Cucuzone and Ruggieri, who were holding Johann Spurzheim. "Let the wretch go!" he ordered.

They obeyed. Johann prostrated himself

"At the hour of death," said Il Porporato, whose inspired eyes were gazing at the heavens, "one hears the voice of the saints. My father, who is a saint in the eyes of God, is speaking to me...my father does not want to be avenged. Johann Spurzheim, it is the hand of the Almighty that will strike you!"

The living cadaver put his head in the dust, but there was a smile on his twisted lips.

"Nothing can be done against me! I'll bury them all!"

Porporato looked behind him again.

"All of you, flee!" he commanded, in an imperious voice.

"Leave you here, Comte!" Lorédan objected.

"Save my sister!" Il Porporato continued. "Julian, save my Angélie! Death is a minute away from you." Addressing his two faithful followers, Cucuzone and Ruggieri, he added: "See to my mother!"

"And me?" gasped Johann Spurzheim.

His voice choked in his throat.

The hand of God had not had to wait. Old Berta Giudicelli had slid out of the cart. She had crawled toward him. Her two hands had knotted around Johann Spurzheim's neck like a necklace. He stiffened in one final convulsion.

Old Berta collapsed beside him, pronouncing the name of Bianca, the daughter of her daughter.

The lava was a few feet away. One two remained: Il Porporato and Fiamma.

"Flee!" he said. "Flee! There's still time!"

She hugged him in her arms and put his charming head on her shoulder. Her face was radiant with joy and tranquil pride.

"You took your life away from me," she murmured, "but your death is mine. I'm happy."

Il Porporato applied his lips to her forehead, and said: "I love you."

The fugitives stopped on the crest of a hillock on the other side of the Portici road. The lava could not reach them henceforth.

They turned round.

They saw that tableau of death in a terrible and splendid frame, as radiant as an apotheosis.

Il Porporato and Fiamma were embracing one another with one hand; both were raising the other toward the sky.

They were so admirably young and beautiful, that the mind already saw them floating above the earth. They were smiling.

There was an aureole of fire around their wedded tresses. And all round them the volcano threw its rains of fire, like a glory.

The wave of lava passed. It made a puff of smoke above their submerged bodies.

PAUL FÉVAL

LES COMPAGNONS DU SILENCE 1

BIBLIOTHÈQUE
MARABOUT

géant

Afterword
An Exercice in Retroactive continuity

It is only in Chapter IX of Part I of *'Salem Steeet* (1867-68)—the third novel in the the *Black Coats* saga—that Paul Féval decided to tell his readers the backstory of that vast criminal conspiracy, retroactively connecting that series to no less than four of his earlier novels: *Les Mystères de Londres* (a.k.a. *Gentlemen of the Night*) (1843-44), *Bel Demonio* (a.k.a. *Beau Démon*) (1850), *The Companions of the Silence* (1857), and *John Devil* (1862). Until then, nothing had linked these works together, and it could be assumed that Féval had not yet decided to embark on a multi-generational saga to rival Balzac's.

Since Féval wrote the *Black Coats* over a twelve year span—from *The Parisian Jungle* in 1863 to *The Cadet Gang* in 1875—he introduced new story elements that sometimes contradicted earlier ones. As a result, while he remained generally consistent with respect to many of the basic facts, who did what to whom, etc., his chronology and the dates assigned to events occasionally conflicted from one book to another. It also left many questions unanswered.

How *The Companions of the Silence* fits within the revised chronology of the *Black Coats* is a particularly tangled knot to unravel. To understand that chonology better, we must start with *Bel Demonio*.[66]

Bel Demonio takes place in the Spoleto region of Southern Italy between 1625 and 1655. Ercole Vitelli murders his cousin, Francis Vitelli, who is the legitimate heir of the wealthy Monteleone family, under the eyes of Francis' son, Andrea. Fifteen years later, Andrea returns seeking revenge, posing as "Demonio," the leader of a ring of bandits. The novel seems to be a prototype for the more ambitious *The Companions of the Silence*. Andrea Vitelli is, therefore, the first "Demonio." Hia adopted daughter Regina (who is, in truth, Ecole's daughter), becomes in tirn "Bekl Demonio." This choice of an alias is thematically connected to other similar aliases used by Féval for other characters, such as *Fra Diavolo* (Brother Devil), *John Devil, Jean Diable*, and *Hans Teufel*.

The Companions of the Silence starts in Naples in 1801 and ends in 1823. In it, Mario Monteleone and the Countess Maria des Amalfi have three children: Fulvio Coriolani (b. 1801), who is mysteriously kidnapped soon after his birth, then Julian (b. 1805), then Céleste (b. 1807), who are also taken away by the same, mysterious enemy in 1808. Mario blames his cousin and rival, Giacomo Doria, for the disappearances. Meanwhile, his rightful liege and supporter, Ferdinand of Bourbon, is replaced by the former General Murat. In 1815, however,

---

[66] Also available from Black Coat Press, ISBN 978-1-61227-708-0.

Murat is overthrown. In November, he seeks and is granted refuge at Monteleone's, but is betrayed. Ferdinand has both Mario and Murat arrested and executed.[67] A secret society calling itself the Companions of the Silence arise to avenge Mario, but eventually turn to crime and become the prototype of the future Black Coats.

In 1823, a mysterious stranger walks into their midst, claiming to be the bandit leader Bel Demonio, now posing as the wealthy Prince Coriolani. In reality, this new Bel Demonio is Mario's eldest son, Fulvio Coriolani, bent on his own mission of vengeance. He takes over the Companions, defying the traps laid for him by the diabolical Chief of the Neapolitan Police, Johann Spurzheim, who is ultimately revealed to be the man who betrayed Mario, his former companion, Daniel Heimer.

In the first volume of the *Black Coats*, *The Parisian Jungle*, Féval introduced his recurring arch-villain, the secret master of the international criminal conspiracy known as the *Habits Noirs*, the *Veste Nere*, the *Gentlemen of the Night*, the *Rozenkreuz*, etc.—Colonel Bozzo-Corona. In it, Féval claimed that the Colonel was once the man known as Fra Diavolo,[68] Féval's Colonel Bozzo was born in Bastia, in 1722 (or 1739—his chronology is uncertain) and became the leader of a crime family called the "Brothers of La Merci," based in Sartene, connected to other families, such as the Reni of Sartene, the Coronas, the Gioja of Naples, etc. He eventually became the leader of the Black Coats known as *Il Padre d'Ogni* (the All-Father).

In *The Companions of the Treasure* (1870-72), it is revealed that the Colonel has three grandchildren: Fulvio Coriolani, who tried to kill his grandfather in

---

[67] In *The Companions of the Treasure* (Chap. III), the Colonel says that "he spent eleven days and eleven nights hidden in the Castle of Monteleone during the days of Murat." So Mario's death may have been the result of yet another of the Colonel's schemes to kill his sons before they can kill him.

[68] The real Fra Diavolo, Michele Bozzo (the name is also spelled "Pozzo" and "Pezza"), was born 7 April 1771 and died 11 November 1806. He was a famous Neapolitan guerrilla leader who resisted the French occupation of Naples, proving an "inspirational practitioner of popular insurrection." In 1806, the French offered Bozzo an enormous bribe if he would join them. When he refused, they tried him on charges of banditry, and sentenced him to death. They spurned an offer by Queen Maria Carolina to exchange 200 French prisoners for him, and on 9 November they hanged him in the Piazza del Mercato in Naples, ostensibly for banditry. His last words reportedly were "It pains me that I am condemned as a bandit and not a soldier." In *'Salem Street*, Féval claimed that he managed to escape that hanging. Bozzo also appeared in Alexandre Dumas' *The Last Cavalier* (not published until 2007) and in Washington Irving's *The Inn at Terracina*. He became the subject of an 1830 opera by Scribe, with music by Auber, adapted as *The Devil's Brother* (1933), starring Laurel and Hardy.

1839 but failed and was murdered in turn; Francesca (a.k.a. Fanchette, who was also assassinated with her husband, Count Corona, in 1842; and finally Julian, who appears to succeed in 1843.

We have seen that *The Companions of the Silence*, Mario Monteleone's children are Fulvio Coriolani, Céleste and Julian. The coincidence is rather strking. Could Mario Monteleone be the Colonel's illegimate son? If so, could the Vitellis of *Bel Demonio* be somehow related to Michele Bozzo, a.k.a. the Colonel of *The Black Coats*?[69]

But this still leaves us with two Coriolanis: the one who dies on the slopes of Mount Vesusius in 1823 at the end of *The Companions of the Silence*, and the one murdered by the Colonel in 1839.

It is up to us to untangle this knot.

(a) *Coriolani.* We are going to postulate that the Fulvio Coriolani who becomes the new Bel Demonio and dies on Mount Vesuvius is Mario's son, born in 1801. The other Coriolani, a few years older, is also the Colonel's grandson, but from Francesca Policeni, the Colonel's daughter introduced in *The Companions of the Treasure*.

(b) *Julian.* Are the Julians from *The Companions of the Silence* and *The Companions of the Treasure* one and the same? There is no reason they couldn't be, if indeed Mario is the Colonel's grandson. The Julian from *The Companions of the Treasure* who tries to assassinate the Colonel and goes on to impersonate him under the alias of "Cavalier Mora" claims to have been born six years after Coriolani, but that is only a two years discrepancy with what is stated *The Companions of the Silence*—not a significant one. We will note here that Julian's affair with a girl named Zorah produced an heir, Reynier, who also went on to impersonate the Colonel after his father's death in 1843.

(c) *Céleste.* We do not know what happened to Céleste after the conclusion of *The Companions of the Silence*.

(d) *Francesca* (a.k.a. *Fanchette*). Fanchette is said to have been born in 1820, so she cannot be Céleste, or even Mario's daughter, since he was already dead when she was conceived. Fanchette is the daughter of Francesca Policeni, identified as the Colonel's own daughter and therefore Mario's half-sister, since they are unlikely to have shared the same mother. Francesca was married to a member of the High Council of the Black Coats named Policeni. The identity of her mother is as unknown. Fanchette is married to a Comte Corona—they were both killed in 1842—and she has a brother named Orlando of which little is known.

In *The Cadet Gang*. Féval situated the founding event of the creation of the Black Coats in either 1803 or 1807, but the latter date is more credible. There, the twelve members of the High Council met with Michele Bozzo, a.k.a. Fra

---

[69] For more on this line of speculation, see our Afterword to the Black Coat Press edition of *Bel Demonio*.

Diavolo, a.k.a. the future Colonel, and his daughter, Francesca Policeni, to decide how to best deal with changing times. During the meeting, one of the members proposed splitting their fabulous treasure and disbanding—but he was found dead the next morning, his throat slit. Others wished to seek refuge in the Abruzze mountains, as they had done in the past, and wait for better days. But like a true Napoléon of Crime, the Colonel instead convinced them to leave him in charge of the treasure and spread throughout Europe to become an international organization, taking over other criminal underworlds like new Cortezes and Pizarros.

The Colonel also decided to move their headquarters to the Convent of La Merci in Sartene. Another meeting was held there, a month later; three other members asked again to split the treasure. They, too, were executed. In 1818, the Colonel relocated his headquarters to Paris, Rue Thérèse, and began to pose as an aging philanthropist.

In 1839, in Sartene, the Colonel thwarted a scheme by several members of the High Council to kill him and steal his treasure. He plotters, including his grandson, the other Coriolani, all perished under a rock slide triggered by the Marchef.

Jean-Marc Lofficier

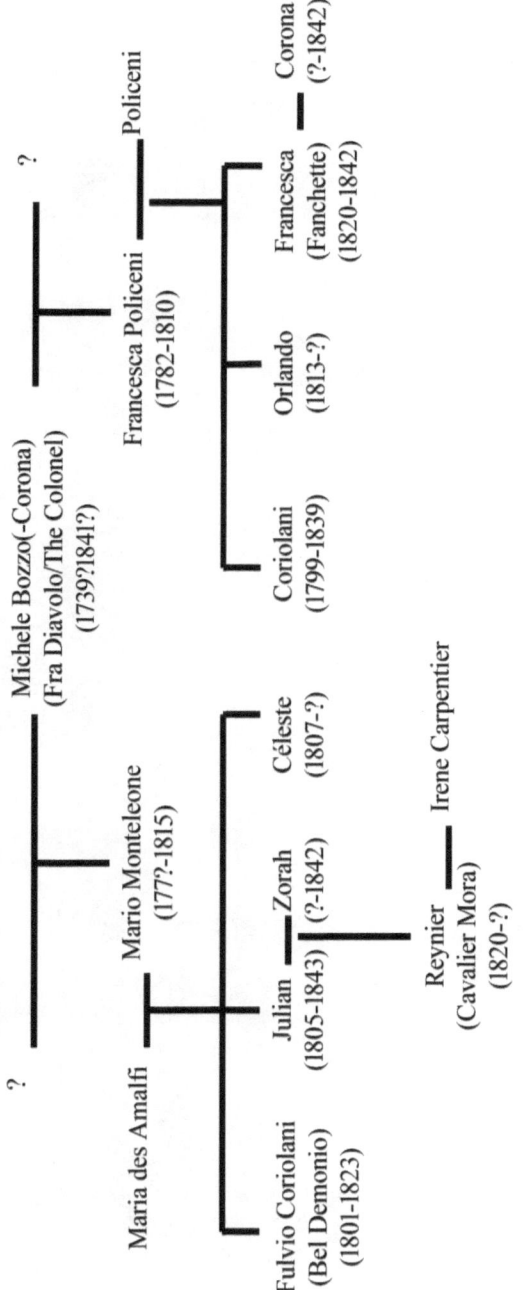

www.ingramcontent.com/pod-product-compliance
Lightning Source LLC
Chambersburg PA
CBHW030922020726
47498CB00001B/72